TOURT

THE QUEEN'S FAVOURITE, THE QUEEN'S REBEL,
THE QUEEN'S SPYMASTER

LAURA DOWERS

Copyright © 2018 by Laura Dowers

All rights reserved.

No part of this book may be reproduced in any form or by any electronic or mechanical means, including information storage and retrieval systems, without written permission from the author, except for the use of brief quotations in a book review.

ISBN-13: 978-1983865602

ISBN-10: 1983865605

VOLUME ONE

THE QUEEN'S FAVOURITE

'Droit et Loyal'

- THE DUDLEY FAMILY MOTTO

"I am now passing into another world and must leave you to your fortunes and to the Queen's graces, but beware of the gypsy, for he will be too hard for you all. You know not the beast so well as I do."

- THOMAS RADCLIFFE, EARL OF SUSSEX, ON HIS DEATHBED

"I am a Dudley in blood… and do acknowledge… that my chiefest honour is to be a Dudley, and truly am glad to have cause to set forth the nobility of that blood whereof I am descended."

- SIR PHILIP SIDNEY

PROLOGUE

SEPTEMBER 1588

She lay on her side on the canopied bed, legs drawn up to her chest. Every now and then, her spare, thin frame would shudder as another sob worked its way up from her chest to be belched out through her aching throat. The greying hair that was never shown to the wide world clung to her skull, bereft of its disguise of copper curls and jewels, which lay on the floor, thrown there after she had ripped it from her head in the first violence of her grief. The false hair had slid across the floorboards, its jewelled pins scattering, coming to rest beneath an oak coffer like some remnant of a beheading.

The sunlight dipped and darkened, marking the passing hours as it moved from one panelled wall to another. At last, the dazed, staring eyes blinked and moved to the paper that lay on the pillow beside her. Her long fingers reached for it, gripped it in her hand, the broken wax seal digging into her palm. She clutched it against her heart, wishing she could feel his touch upon it.

How could God do this to her? He had given her such a victory, a shining hour, and then blighted it by exacting a heavy payment. For defeating the armada, He had taken Robin. And left her alone. She screwed up her face as the pain came again. Could He have not taken someone less dear? Hatton, Walsingham? She could even bear the loss of Burghley if only she had Robin still.

She turned over and climbed shakily from the bed, still clutching the letter. She shuffled to her desk, stumbling on the folds of her skirts, and fell into the chair. Reaching for her quill, she wrote 'His Last Letter' upon the cream page, threw the pen aside and blew on the ink to dry it.

A simple letter had become a treasure, as precious to her as the jewels that lay in the casket by her bed. She opened its lid and placed the letter inside. As she did so, her fingers brushed against the metal frame of a miniature portrait. She withdrew it, berating herself for leaving it so long since she had looked at it last. Robert looked back at her, a younger Robert than the one who had departed less than a month before to take the waters at Buxton. He had been such a handsome man, she reflected with a wistful smile. A handsome boy too, even at eight years old. That was when they had first become acquainted, in the schoolroom they shared. He had been a friend to her from the first. He never stopped.

CHAPTER 1

GREENWICH PALACE, FEBRUARY 1542

Robert Dudley was bored. Bored with the lesson, bored with Master Cheke droning on about Seneca, Suetonius and other long dead Romans. Bored with sitting still for hour upon hour.

He sighed and ran his fingers through his dark hair. If only the rest of his classmates felt the same, perhaps there could be a mutiny. He knew he would be able to count on his brothers, Ambrose, Henry and Guildford. Ambrose sat beside him, his chin cradled in one hand while the other idly swept away wood shavings from where he had scratched his name into his desk with his penknife. Robert could hear Henry and Guildford playing cards beneath their desk behind him. But he knew the others wouldn't dare. Not Prince Edward nor Jane Grey sitting, all attention, at the front of the class. Not Jane's sisters, neither; the tall and pretty Catherine, nor the freak of the family, the hunch-backed dwarf Mary, at the back where no one paid her any mind.

But maybe Elizabeth would be with him? She was sitting in front of Robert, head bent, scribbling furiously. She too was paying little heed to Master Cheke, not because of boredom, but because she had learnt this lesson months before in private study and had now moved on to the Ancient Greeks.

'Master Robert!'

Robert jerked his attention back to his tutor. 'Yes, Master Cheke?' he said, his lips broadening into a grin.

Charming though his smile was, it had little effect upon the old scholar. Cheke sighed as he leant on a pile of books. 'Master Robert, I realize that study of the Classics holds little interest for such an energetic boy as yourself, but your parents have arranged for you to be educated with the children of His Majesty the King, and you would do well to follow their example and attend to your books instead of gazing around the room like a moonstruck calf. Do you comprehend me, sir?'

Robert bent his head in answer and dipped the tip of his quill into the inkpot, grinning as he heard Elizabeth snigger. Master Cheke, satisfied that Robert was behaving, turned his back and began to search through another pile of books heaped on a chest by the wall. Robert stole a look out of the window and saw that it had finally stopped raining. He leant forward and hissed at Elizabeth. When she turned her frowning face to him, he jerked his head towards the door. Her frown deepened disapprovingly and she shook her head. He glared at her, his black eyes insisting fiercely. She poked her tongue out at him and turned away. Robert eased his backside from the stool and groped around the desk. Ambrose opened bleary eyes to see what his brother was up to and watched in amusement as Robert grabbed Elizabeth's wrist, plucked the quill from between her fingers and tugged her from her stool. She grimaced but allowed herself to be led from the schoolroom. Ambrose's gaze wandered to Master Cheke, who was wholly unaware that his star pupil and the mischief-maker had absconded. He closed his eyes, wondering how long it would take the tutor to realise.

'I wanted to work,' Elizabeth protested feebly as Robert pulled her along the corridors of the palace.

'It was boring.'

'Let go of me,' she said, shaking her wrist free. 'Where are we going?'

'To the stables, of course.' Now that Elizabeth wasn't holding him up, he broke into a run. Elizabeth followed, hitching her skirts up to her bony knees.

'Wait for me,' she demanded as they dodged between servants, but his legs were longer and he reached the stable yard before her.

Curving his body around the door, Robert breathed in the aroma of straw and animal, too long absent from his nostrils. He moved along the stalls, murmuring greetings to the horses as they pressed their noses into his outstretched palm.

Horseshoes hanging from nails on the back of the door clattered, signalling Elizabeth's arrival. 'I told you to wait.'

He smiled, not looking up. 'They've missed me.'

'Stupid animals.' Elizabeth snatched an apple from a bulging sack leaning against the wall. She rubbed it against her bodice before snapping off a bite.

'*You'd* miss me if you didn't see me for a week.'

'Would not.'

'Would.'

'No, I wouldn't,' she insisted, stomping past him and flinging herself on a bale of hay.

He took the apple from her hand as she passed and held it to the mouth of Phoebe, his favourite horse, who began to munch contentedly. 'You're in a foul mood today,' he said. 'If you keep your face as sour as that, the wind will change and you'll stay that way.'

'Pig. Speak so to me again and...'

'You'll what?'

'I'll... I'll...'

'What will you do? Banish me to the Tower, cut off my—.' He suddenly realised what he was saying and spun round to face her.

Elizabeth's eyes had grown wide at his words and her hand flew to her mouth. 'Cut off your head,' she finished, her voice breaking.

He hurried to her side and put his arm around her shoulder.

'Katherine,' she whispered in explanation.

'I know,' he said. 'I shouldn't have said that. I'm such an ass.'

They both knew about Katherine Howard, the pretty girl who had caught the lustful eye of the King and married him, letting him believe that he was the first to enjoy her young body. To deceive a king, one who was vain and suspicious, was dangerous, but her charms were plentiful and she hoped that a lack of virginity in a bride could perhaps have been forgiven, that is if she ever dared to tell the King the truth. But she had grown complacent, so secure in the King's love for her that she began to take one of his gentlemen to her bed. She was young, after all, and wanted to hold a man's body that was slim and smooth, unlike the bloated mass of her husband. She and her lover had been discovered, and the King found he was not in a forgiving mood. Katherine's lover had already died for his crime. Katherine, it was said, practised for her own execution on a block delivered to her Tower prison.

'Why is my father doing this?' Elizabeth asked.

'You don't know?' Robert was surprised.

Elizabeth shook her head. 'I heard some of my women talking but they stopped when they saw me. How has Katherine offended my father, Robin?'

'I can't say, Bess. My father said I wasn't to mention it.'

'Oh, Rob, if you know, tell me, please.'

'All right, but you didn't hear it from me. She deceived the King with another man. She bedded Thomas Culpeper.'

'What does bedded mean?'

'Don't tell me you don't know?' he laughed. 'And you're supposed to be the clever one.'

'Don't laugh at me.' Her pale cheeks had flushed red.

'But if you don't know,' he said airily, 'I suppose I could tell you.'

'Tell me,' she insisted, drying her tears.

So, he told her what it meant, and laughed even harder when she clamped her hands over her ears and told him to shut up, to stop lying, that it wasn't true, her parents had never done such a disgusting thing.

'It is true.'

'I'm never going to do that.'

'You'll have to when you marry.'

'I'm not going to marry.'

'Of course you will.'

'Will not.'

'Will.'

'Will not.'

'There you are!'

They jumped at the shrill voice. Elizabeth's governess, Katherine Ashley, stood in the doorway, her hands on her hips, glowering at them.

'Kat,' Elizabeth said, 'how long have you been there?'

'Is it for *you* to question *me*, my lady?' Katherine retorted, holding up her skirts and stepping into the stable. 'My word, I could hear the two of you clear across the yard. Squabbling like brats from the docksides. Why aren't you in the schoolroom? I should have known *he* would have something to do with it. Do that again, my lad,' Katherine shook a finger at Robert as he rolled his eyes, 'and I'll have you up before your father before you can shake a stick.'

'He wouldn't care,' Robert muttered, kicking at the ground.

'What did he say?' Katherine demanded.

'Nothing, Kat,' Elizabeth said quickly. 'Come, let us go.' She jumped down from the hay bale and moving swiftly slid her hand into Katherine's. 'I'll see you tomorrow,' she promised Robert, pushing Katherine through the door.

'Fooling in the stable with a courtier's son,' he heard Katherine say as her charge led her away. 'Whatever would people say?'

His lips curled at her words. Young as he was, the Dudley family pride was strong in him. How dare she scorn him for being the son of a mere courtier? After all, what was her precious Elizabeth but a bastard daughter of the King? He at least was born on the right side of the blanket. And he wouldn't be just a courtier's son forever. No, his father would see to that. His father would become great and Robert great with him. Let Mistress Ashley look down her nose at him then.

He opened a stall door and lifted a saddle from its post. Phoebe whinnied and stamped, like him, impatient to be outside. 'There now, my lovely,' he said, kissing her neck and holding his cheek against the warm flesh. 'You know I can do it, don't you?'

CHAPTER 2

ELY PLACE, MAY 1545

The greyhound nudged its slim, silky body around Robert's legs. There wasn't much room on the window seat, so the dog used a long, trim thigh to rest its chin upon and thumped its tail in pleasure whenever fingers tickled behind its ears.

Robert was reading, the book tilted towards the window to make use of the setting sun. Its orange light bled through the window, picking up on strands of dark brown hair amongst the black and giving a golden glow to his tawny skin. His interest in the book was desultory and his gaze wandered towards the window, flickering over the hedges and flowers of the gardens and down to the river. The river was crammed with vessels; large boats carrying cargo, wherries ferrying their passengers, but it was a barge painted in blue and yellow, the family colours, that his eyes picked out and which he craned his neck to see.

Robert watched as the barge banged against the river steps and a figure climbed over the gunwale before it was even secured. He recognised the hurrying shape of his father and wondered what had brought him back from the court in such haste. Looking back to the boat, he saw a woman, who could only be his mother, taking the hand of the oarsman as he helped her on shore.

The dog lifted its head, ears pricked as the hall door banged. He thrust his wet nose against his master's hand as Robert's father called out. 'Be still, Rollo,' Robert said, closing his book.

The door opened and his father strode into the room. 'I've been calling you!'

Robert assumed his most innocent face and shrugged. 'I didn't hear you.'

'Didn't want to hear, more like,' John growled, flinging himself into a chair. 'Have you been idling in here all day?'

'No, Father, not *all* day.'

'You're in one of your facetious moods, I see.'

Robert smiled, looking up at the sound of swishing skirts dragging the rushes across the floor.

'Thank you for waiting, John,' Jane muttered as she entered, pushing a fat, white cat from a chair and sitting down. The cat immediately jumped onto her lap and submitted to her vigorous caresses.

John waved his arm at Robert. 'I wanted to find him.'

'I could have told you where he would be,' Jane said. 'Lying about with the dog.'

'Then it's about time he stopped laying around, don't you think, Jane?' He gave his wife a meaningful glance.'

'Tell him,' Jane agreed.

John looked at his son. He had been at home so little of late that it was quite a surprise to find how different Robert looked. In a few months, the chubbiness of extreme youth had fallen away. He had grown taller by several inches and his face bore the promise of handsomeness. 'Well, Rob, your mother and I have secured a position for you to serve the Prince in his household at Hunsdon. I hope you are pleased.'

'Rob?' Jane asked, holding out her hand.

'You're sending me away?' Robert said, a tremble in his voice.

'My darling, you knew you would have to leave sometime. After all, both Jack and Ambrose have been gone for a while now.'

'I know, Mother. I just thought maybe you would keep me with you.'

John let out a snort of exasperation. 'Do you have any idea how long we've been trying to arrange this appointment for you, Rob? And it's not something we have to consult you on. You will do as other children do and do as you are told.'

'I didn't say I wouldn't,' Robert retorted indignantly,

swinging his legs to the floor and standing up. 'What am I to do at Hunsdon?'

'Do? Do?' John cried. 'You'll do your duty.'

'Don't shout at him, John.' Jane waved Robert over, pushing the cat to the floor. Grabbing hold of his hand, she pulled him close. He fell to his knees and laid his head in her lap.

'Don't you dare cosset the boy,' John said.

'And don't *you* dare tell me how to treat my son.'

'*Our* son, Jane, *our* son. And I don't care how much he protests, he is going to Hunsdon.'

'Of course he will go,' Jane said, watching her husband as he crossed the room and took Robert's seat in the window. The dog jumped down and padded over to Robert. 'Once he realises how important it is to you.'

Robert lifted his head. 'Why is it so important?'

'The King is not well, Rob,' John said. 'So unwell, in fact, I cannot see him living much longer. Now that is not common knowledge and I don't want you repeating it to anyone. But the Prince will be the next king and the closer you are to him now, the closer I hope you will be in the near future.'

'When he is king?'

'Yes, when he is king. You can see what that will mean for our family?'

'I think so.'

'Good. So, we'll have no more tears.'

'I haven't cried,' Robert insisted, getting to his feet.

'No,' Jane said proudly, 'he hasn't.'

'All right, all right,' John held up his hands. 'Now, I want you to be on your way as soon as you can manage. A day or two, no more. And I expect you to make yourself useful to the Prince. I hope he will come to think of you as a friend.'

'In fact, Rob,' his mother said gravely as John left the room, 'your father insists on it.'

HUNSDON PALACE, HERTFORDSHIRE

'I've had enough for today,' Prince Edward declared. 'Barnaby, what say you to some target practice?'

Barnaby Fitzpatrick gave the tutor, William Buckley, a sympathetic half-smile and shrugged. 'If you please, Edward.'

'You don't mind, do you, Buckley?' Edward asked, already getting to his feet.

Buckley sighed, threw his quill into the inkstand and propped his legs up on the desk. 'It doesn't seem to matter whether I do or not, does it? Lesson over.'

The other boys in the schoolroom – Thomas Cobden, Henry Sidney and Christopher Kempe – chorused a hurrah and closed their own books with alacrity.

'Now, Buckley, don't sulk,' Edward chided.

'I'm not sulking, Your Grace,' Buckley said. 'Merely wondering how I am to explain your lack of education to your father's secretary when he demands a report.'

'That's easy. You can say I am progressing well and exceed all your expectations.'

The boys laughed and Buckley joined in, shaking his head. 'Go, you young ruffians, be gone.'

The sound of horses drew Thomas to the window. 'Hallo,' he said, 'is this the new boy?'

Edward joined him and pressed his nose to the glass. 'Yes, that's him. Rob Dudley. He used to study with me and my sister years ago. He and Elizabeth were always running off together. Our tutor, Master Cheke, would get quite annoyed.'

'I can sympathise,' Buckley muttered wryly.

'Are we going out to shoot or not?' Henry Sidney demanded impatiently, holding the door open.

'We're going out to shoot,' Edward declared, leading the way out of the room. 'Come on.'

The boys waved to Buckley and ran along the corridor and down the stairs, emerging in a huddle in the courtyard where Robert stood, wondering what he was supposed to do. He stood taller than the Prince and stared down at him for a moment before he remembered his manners and sank to his knee.

'Your Grace.'

'Robert Dudley,' Edward said, 'and I thought I had seen the back of you years ago.'

'I hope my presence will not be a burden to you, Your Grace.'

'Oh, let's have none of that,' Barnaby said, taking hold of Robert beneath his armpit and dragging him to his feet. He ignored the frown that appeared on the young prince's face, who appreciated the deference that his royalty provoked. 'Edward has enough of people bowing and scraping to him. We can excuse ourselves all that, can't we, Edward?'

Not wishing to seem a prig, Edward nodded. 'We're going to the butts, Robert.'

Robert wasn't sure if he was being invited to accompany them but was saved from making a fool of himself by Henry Sidney, who seeing his uncertainty, stepped forward and held out his hand.

'I'm Henry, Henry Sidney,' he said with a warm smile. 'How are you with a bow?'

Taking his hand and feeling a firm grip, Robert shrugged. 'I'm quite good.'

'*Quite* good? Are you being modest?'

'No. My mother says I don't know the meaning of the word.'

'Oh, that's nothing,' Thomas said, pushing past Edward, 'you should hear what my mother says about *me*.'

They laughed and Edward, who always liked to be the centre of attention, snapped, 'Are we going to the butts or are we planning to stand here all day?'

'We're going,' Barnaby said hurriedly, slipping his arm through Edward's and leading him towards the garden. The others followed.

'Don't mind him,' Henry said softly to Robert. 'He's very much his father's son, if you understand me. But then, you already know that. You studied with him.'

'About four years ago.'

'And you were friendly with his sister?'

'Yes, but I haven't seen much of her for a while. She lives at Hatfield and doesn't come to town much.'

'I should like to meet her. Edward thinks a lot of her, you know. Even if he does sometimes sound a little... oh, what's the word? Sanctimonious.'

They laughed, causing Edward to look around. 'Keep up, you two,' he ordered.

Henry raised his eyebrows at Robert and they quickened their pace.

CHAPTER 3

WHITEHALL PALACE, APRIL 1546

As the last of September's daylight faded, John Dudley studied the King.

Henry was certainly ill. His body, already corpulent, had seemed to swell like a bellows over the past month. The small eyes were bloodshot and yellowed, sunk into the flesh that rose in mounds of clammy pinkness, the contours of the bones long since buried.

Henry's fat, trembling hand laid down a knave of hearts. 'Can you match that, John?'

John scanned his cards. 'No, Your Majesty, I fear I cannot.'

'Ha ha, then pay up.'

John shoved four gold coins across the table to clink against the King's winning pile. He began to deal another hand.

'How does your son, John?' Henry asked. 'The one with the Prince.'

'Robert? I had a letter from him this morning. He is doing well. The Prince enjoys his company and Robert hopes he is of great service to him.'

'Ah, now,' Henry waggled a fat finger at him, 'service is a trait that runs in your family, John. Your boy serves my son, *you* serve *me* well, I might even say, very well.' The little mouth pursed and expelled a puff of sour breath. 'And your father... *your* father, John, served *my* father well.'

'So I understand, Your Majesty.' John felt the King's eyes upon him but he kept his own firmly upon the cards.

'I think much on the past, John. Too much, my Fool says, but I cannot seem to help it lately. I did a foolish thing, John, when I allowed your father to be executed.'

'A foolish thing, Your Majesty?'

'Yes, foolish. But I was persuaded to it by my Council. My father was a mean man, John. He loved money more than anything. And by using your father, *my* father extracted all the money he could from his subjects.' Henry reached for his goblet and raised it to his lips, feeling the hot wine spill over his slack lips and soak into his beard. 'I was persuaded,' he continued, 'it would show the love I had for my people to… to…,' he floundered for the right words.

'To offer my father up as a sacrifice?' John suggested, his voice brittle.

Henry frowned. 'You're still angry about it.'

'He *was* my father, Your Majesty.'

'But you must have been very young.'

'Old enough to remember his execution. Indeed, I wish I could forget it. The jeers, the shouts and the foul names my father was called. He tried to speak but the mob drowned out his words. And then came the kneeling, the wait while the axe was raised and then the bl…,' his voice broke and he willed himself to be strong, 'the blood.'

Henry's little eyes grew moist. He blinked and tears fell down his cheeks. 'I had hoped you would have forgiven me.'

John watched in amazement as Henry's massive body began to shudder with the violence of his sobs. John was unable to move, to offer comfort, torn between pleasure that the King should feel such remorse and yet horrified that he, John Dudley, had made the King feel so. Someone brushed past him. The crying had roused Will Somers who had been dozing in a corner of the room, and the loyal fool now took the King's hand and pumped it up and down playfully, trying to raise a laugh. He turned a scowling countenance to John and mouthed a question. John shook his head in bewilderment and moved to the King's other side, sinking to his knees, wincing as he felt his knee bones crack.

'Your Majesty, think no more on it. I do forgive you,' he lied.

'All is forgiven.' The little eyes opened and stared at him. John thought he could read gratitude in them. 'Indeed, Your Majesty, there is nothing to forgive. As you said, it was not of your doing. You were persuaded to it by others.'

'I was, I was.' Henry's hand clutched at John's. With a loud sniff, the tears began to subside and then ceased altogether. 'But look how you weary me,' Henry said, pushing John's hand away.

'Of course, Your Majesty,' John scrambled to his feet. 'It is late, I should let you get to your bed.'

John went to the door and called for the King's servants. As they fussed around the stumbling mountain of flesh, John made his goodnights and hurried back to his rooms.

'John?' a sleep-heavy voice mumbled from the bed as he entered and shut the door behind him.

'Yes, it's me.'

Jane sat up, blinking as John lit a candle. 'It must be late.'

'It is,' he said with a sigh.

'Is something wrong?'

He sank onto the bed and fell back across her legs. 'Christ's Wounds, Jane, what a night I've had. The King…'

'What?'

'He has such moods these days. There's no knowing what he will do.'

'Tell me,' she insisted, her fingers expertly massaging his skull.

He closed his eyes, enjoying her touch. 'I made him weep, Jane. He burst into tears right in front of me.'

Her nails dug into his skin. 'What in Heaven did you say to him?'

'Sheath your claws vixen, it wasn't my fault. He began talking about my father. Do you know Henry actually expected me to have forgiven him for cutting off my father's head?'

'I don't believe you.'

'It's true, I swear. And then that mood passed and he wanted to be rid of me.'

'Oh, John, are you in disgrace?'

'No, nothing like that,' he assured her, sitting up and untying his jerkin. 'I'm still his John, his good fellow, someone to while away the time with.'

'Then I thank God for that,' she said, sinking back into her pillow. 'Though I wish He would take that old monster to his bosom sooner rather than later.'

'Jane!' John barked, grabbing her wrist. 'Do not speak of the King in that way. I shall not tell you again.'

Jane shook her wrist free. She found her husband's unquestioning respect and admiration for sovereignty irritating. She watched him as he undressed. 'Anne Seymour was here earlier, snooping about. Whatever possessed Edward Seymour to marry that woman, I'll never know.'

'Aye, she's a shrew all right.'

'Still, there's no danger of her cuckolding him like his first wife. After all, who would want her?'

'Edward Seymour, obviously.'

'He must have ice in his veins.'

'Not ice. Ambition. And she is relentless, she drives him on.'

'Like I drive you?' Jane asked teasingly as John climbed into bed beside her.

'You don't drive me on, you hold me back.'

She pressed against him and rested her head on his chest, matching her breathing to his. 'Must we be friends with the Seymours really, John? I do dislike them so.'

'Nonsense, Edward's a good fellow. And if we're to rise further, Jane, he will be just the friend I need. As the Prince's uncle, Edward Seymour will be invaluable to him when he becomes king and, in turn, we will be invaluable to the King's uncle, you see?'

'I suppose so,' Jane nodded unhappily. 'I just wish his wife wasn't such an old cow.'

CHAPTER 4

HUNSDON PALACE, OCTOBER 1546

Robert's greyhound insisted on poking its sleek head through the window with the window's leather roll bunched around its neck like a bizarre headdress. It stood on the toes of Mary Dudley who had long since given up trying to hold the animal back.

'We're almost there, Rollo,' she said, joining him at the window and wrinkling her face at the chill October air.

'It's a pity Rob can't keep him,' Jack, the eldest son in the Dudley family, said through a yawn. 'He's been pining for him ever since Rob left.'

'I know, poor Rollo. Oh look, Jack, we're here.'

'Can you see Rob?'

'Yes, yes, there he is,' she cried, jumping down from the coach before it had even come to a stop.

Rollo was even faster than she. He bounded up to his master, nearly knocking him to the ground. Robert buried his face against the dog's neck and squeezed the small body.

'Don't we get a hello?' Jack joked, walking towards his brother with arms outstretched.

'Course you do,' Robert said, wrapping his arms around Jack's waist. 'Mary.' He pulled her towards him and kissed her chill cheek. 'You're freezing. Come inside.' He led them into the main hall where a large fire filled the room with heat. 'I've had food set out for you. You are hungry, aren't you?'

'Famished,' Mary admitted. 'We left so early we didn't have time to eat.'

'Well, help yourself.' Robert waved them to a table where small beer, bread and mutton were laid out.

Mary and Jack both tucked in. Rollo, who had been nudging Robert's hand with his nose, whined.

Robert snatched up a thick slice of the mutton and fed it to him. 'Has Mary been looking after you, old boy?'

'Of course I have,' Mary said. 'But he misses you, Rob. Can't you keep him here?'

'I don't know. I suppose I could ask.'

'What's it like here?' Jack asked, gulping down some beer.

'It's fine.'

'Just fine?'

'I miss home,' Robert confessed, 'but there's always something to do here and the other boys are good company.'

'And the Prince?'

Robert checked to make sure they were alone. 'He's a bit of a prig, truth to tell.'

'He always was.'

'Jack, hush,' Mary scolded.

'Well, he was, Mary.'

Robert continued. 'He studies a lot and expects us to as well. He always likes to win at whatever game we're playing and makes such a fuss if we sometimes refuse and win ourselves.'

'He *is* the Prince, Rob.'

'I know that, Jack, and I wouldn't dare say anything, except to you.'

'You didn't say this to Father when he was here, then?'

'Lord no, he'd have thrashed me,' Robert shuddered. 'Jack, when he came down last week, Father said he had been banished from court. Was that true?'

'It's true.'

'I thought he was joking. What happened?'

'It's quite ridiculous, really,' Mary giggled. 'He hit the Bishop of Winchester.'

'Hit him!'

'Struck him about the face,' Jack nodded. 'During a Council meeting. I don't know what Stephen Gardiner had said to him but it got Father worked up and he hit him. The King banished him from court.'

Mary stretched and opened her mouth in a wide, loud yawn just as Henry Sidney walked in. Her face reddened.

'Excuse me,' Henry said, making to leave.

'No, Henry, don't go,' Robert ordered, waving him over to the table. 'This is my brother, Jack, and my sister, Mary.'

'Pleased to meet you both.'

'Oh, and this is Rollo,' Robert said, bending down to kiss the dog between the eyes. 'My dog that I've told you about.'

'Oh yes, the fabulous Rollo,' Henry said.

'Fabulous?' Mary raised an eyebrow.

'Yes. Apparently, there has never been nor ever will be a dog quite like Rollo,' Henry said with mock seriousness, making Mary giggle again.

Robert threw a chunk of bread at him. 'Henry, try to amuse my sister without being vulgar while I talk to my brother.' Angling his body towards Jack, he asked in a low voice, 'Is Father really all right?'

'He's fine, Rob, really,' Jack assured him, dipping his bread in his ale. 'The King banished him more as a gesture than anything else. From what Father said the King had a hearty laugh when he heard about the slap. Said he wished he'd been there to see it.'

'So, Father's doing well?'

'It seems so. He and Edward Seymour are very thick. Mother doesn't like it because it means she has to put up with Seymour's wife, who is, to use Mother's phrase, a devil-whipped bitch. Father's almost constantly with the King, so there's really nothing to worry about. You just do what Father wants you to do here.'

'Oh, I can do that with my eyes closed. The Prince is a prig but he's manageable enough.'

'Yes, but you keep that kind of opinion to yourself, Rob, eh?'

'Yes, all right.' Robert sighed and slumped back in his chair. 'Now, Henry, what do you think? Should I ask if I can keep Rollo here?'

BANKSIDE

John Dudley pressed two pennies into the pit master's hand, one for himself, one for Edward Seymour, and climbed the few steps into the enclosure.

'Why we couldn't go straight back to court, I don't know,' Seymour said, leaning on the wooden barrier and gazing down into the ring of blood-stained sawdust.

'It won't hurt you to take a few hours rest,' John said. 'You're looking very worn, Edward.'

'Is it any wonder? Between the King and my wife...'

'Tell me everything I missed. How are we doing?'

'We're doing very well. I think I've persuaded the King to change his will.'

John's mouth dropped open in astonishment. 'You're not serious?'

'I'm perfectly serious. You see what you miss when you gallivant around the country?'

'I haven't been gallivanting, Edward, I was banished from the court. How is Gardiner, by the way? Recovered?'

'You only gave him a slap, John.'

'Ah, but it was a very hard slap, Edward. The poor man was almost crying.'

'Do you want to hear this or not?'

John grinned and nodded. 'I'm listening.'

Seymour looked about him uneasily. The cockpit gallery was filling up and the owners of the cocks had brought them into the enclosure. A hubbub filled the air. 'I'm not sure we should be having this conversation here.'

'Nobody's listening, Edward, they're far too interested in the cocks.'

'You can never be too sure.'

'Edward,' John snapped, 'just tell me.'

Seymour nudged himself closer. 'I've been dining with the King every day while you were away, trying to keep him amused. I know I'm not as good at that as you are, it's been hard work. But I think he's frightened.'

'Of what?'

'Of what will happen when he's no longer here. He fears for the Prince.'

A cheer erupted from the spectators as the cocks were set down to fight.

John leant forward, his gloved hands gripping the barrier. 'Not without reason.'

'The Catholics are a particular concern to him.'

'But the King's a Catholic.'

'He's a king first. And he wants his son to enjoy the same royal privileges he has enjoyed since he married the Boleyn bitch. He's worried that the Catholics will put the Pope back in power in England.'

'They would certainly try,' John agreed. 'And so, he's changing his will?'

'*Thinking* about changing his will,' Seymour corrected. 'So, that's what I need you to do. Add your voice to mine and together we should be able to change it.'

'Wait a moment, Edward, you talk of changing his will, when I don't even know what it contains. And now I think about it, how do *you* know?'

Seymour shrugged. 'Paget showed it to me.'

'Sir William Paget, the King's secretary?' John's voice rose in astonishment. 'But he's a Catholic.'

Seymour put a finger to his lips to quieten John. 'A Catholic that will bend with the prevailing wind. He sees the way things are, John, and he's anxious to side with us. He knows Gardiner is out of favour with the King. It was noted by all how short your banishment was.'

'And Paget showed you the will?'

'No, he didn't show me. It's locked away. He told me of its contents.'

'And they were?'

Seymour spoke close to John's ear. 'The will appoints a Council of Regency to govern for the Prince. Now, at the moment, it's a mixture. Catholics and Protestants in almost equal measure.'

'Am I on this Council?'

'Yes. As am I. Paget's there, of course, and Wriothesley. In fact, all those you would expect.'

'The Howards?'

'Unfortunately, yes.'

John grimaced. 'They are our biggest opponents, Edward.'

'I agree. If we really mean to remove Catholic opposition in this land we must first remove the Howards.'

One of the cocks drew blood and the spectators roared encouragement.

'You sound as if you have a plan.'

'No, John, no plans. Only a hope that the Howards will damage themselves.'

John's eyes narrowed. 'You mean Henry Howard.'

Seymour nodded. 'He's a reckless young man. In the last few years, he's displeased the King on more than one occasion. It shouldn't take much more to turn the King completely against him.'

'So, you're hoping he will make a serious mistake?'

'I am. We must keep our eyes and ears open.'

'Oh, they're open, Edward,' John assured him, licking his lips as wings flapped and blood spilt. 'They're always open.'

WHITEHALL PALACE

Anne Seymour pressed her ugly flat nose against the window pane. 'There's William Hampton again, disappearing into the bushes with that young girl from Frances Woolley's little group. I told his wife about his secret trysts but she didn't seem to care. And there's Knollys's boy walking that damned dog again, the one that bites my skirts whenever I pass. You said you would talk to him about the dog. Have you?'

Her husband, to whom the enquiry was directed, did not look up from his desk. 'Not yet, my dear.'

'Well, when are you going to?'

'When I have a moment.'

'You've had plenty of time.' She stepped away from the window and folded her arms. 'I shall have to speak to him about it myself, I see I shall.'

Seymour scratched his signature across a document. 'Perhaps that would be best, my love.'

Anne's dull eyes widened. 'Oh, I see.'

Recognising the signs of an impending tantrum, he added in a conciliatory tone, 'I am rather busy, Anne.'

Anne gave a snort of derision, gathered up her skirts and stomped past him, disappearing through a door into the small antechamber beyond. He was considering the possible benefits of following after her when the main door to his study was flung open and John Dudley strode into the room.

'What the devil—?' Seymour blustered.

John dropped into a chair before the desk. 'He's done it.'

'Done what? Who? What are you grinning like that for?'

John's eyes glinted in the early morning sunshine. Its unforgiving light caught too the grey hairs upon his head, the creases at the corners of his mouth and yet, Seymour thought with not a little resentment, how handsome he was. His own mirror only showed a man with tired eyes and sagging jowls.

'Henry Howard, Earl of Surrey, that reckless young man, has made the mistake we were hoping for, my friend.'

'How? What has he done?'

'He has had a portrait painted.'

Seymour's shoulders sagged. 'A portrait?'

John held up a halting finger. 'It is a portrait with dangerous content.'

'Well, stop being mysterious and tell me.'

The grin vanished from John's countenance; he became all seriousness. Moving the inkwell so he could lean on the desk, he began. 'Howard has had himself painted standing beneath an arch with statues on either side. At the feet of the statues are two shields, and here is where it gets interesting. There are symbols and devices upon them that should only be borne upon the arms of the Kings of England. No, wait,' he held up his hand as Seymour made to interrupt, 'let me finish. The earl himself leans upon a broken pillar. A broken pillar symbolising a broken house.' John sat back in the chair, watching and waiting for Edward's reaction.

'A broken house?' Seymour clicked his teeth. 'The House of Tudor?'

'Conceivably,' John said with a shrug. 'Couple that with the shields and what you have is treason.'

'Treason?'

John nodded. They sat in silence for a moment.

'Is it enough?' Seymour asked quietly.

'We'll make it enough.'

'How did you find out about this?'

'Through Paget. A friend of Henry Howard told Paget,

Paget told me. Henry Howard should choose his friends more carefully, eh?'

'But can we go to the King with this?'

'I think we can. But we must choose our moment carefully, the King's moods being what they are. My secretary is drawing up a statement even now.'

'Could we go to the King today?'

'Patience, Edward, let me choose the moment. I'll know when the time is right.' He rose and turned to go. Hesitating, he turned back to Seymour. 'This is it, Edward. Our chance to get rid of the Howards.'

Seymour gave the smallest of nods. 'I hope so, John.'

John left and Seymour sunk his chin into his hand. So deep in thought was he that he did not notice his wife emerge from the room behind him and gave a yelp of surprise when her hand clamped down on his shoulder.

'Edward.'

He looked up at her and read her expression. 'I know.'

'Can Henry Howard be such a fool?'

'Oh, that man is fool enough for anything, Anne.'

'And it will be enough to disgrace him? Is Dudley right?'

'He usually is.'

'So what will happen?'

'If the King reacts as we hope, Henry Howard should be arrested, tried and then…'

'And then what?' Anne demanded, her voice rising with impatience.

'There is only one sentence for treason, Anne.'

'Death!'

'Aye, death. For treason, it is hanging, drawing and quartering, but as the Earl is noble, the King would almost certainly commute it to a beheading.'

'So, we would be rid of one Howard. But what of the other? What of his father?'

Seymour shook his head. 'I don't know. The son will be tainted and perhaps we can spread that stain to the father. John said nothing about the father.'

'Edward,' Anne murmured, 'you don't think you're relying rather too heavily on John Dudley, do you?'

'No, I don't think so.' He paused and looked at her. 'Why, do you?'

Anne shrugged. 'I would just prefer it if you made some of the decisions. John Dudley has all the appearance of being the one in charge.'

'I hardly think so.'

'He restricts your access to the King,' Anne continued.

'The King enjoys his company more than mine.'

'So John Dudley claims. Has the King said so? You are brother-in-law to the King, Edward, uncle to his son. How can the King not value your company?'

Seymour fiddled with his quill and said nothing.

NOVEMBER 1546

As soon as dinner was over John rushed to Seymour's side, smacked him on the shoulder and whispered in his ear that it was time. Seymour spilt wine over his hose in his hurry to follow John and caught up with him in the corridor.

'Now?' he hissed.

'Now. I have just dined with the King and his mood is ripe for talk of treachery. Let's get the statement and take it to him.'

'You are sure, John?'

'You're not doubting me now, are you, Edward? Good God, man, where's your spine? Or has your wife beaten that out of you as well?'

'Watch your mouth, John.'

John grinned unapologetically. 'Wait,' he said, as they reached his chamber door. He ducked inside while Seymour waited impatiently in the corridor, stepping from one foot to the other in his agitation. John joined him a moment later, a rolled-up piece of paper in his hand.

'Got it,' he waved the paper at Seymour. 'Come on.'

Back they went to the Great Hall, past the idling courtiers and servants folding tables away, on through to the King's private apartments. The guards let them through without hindrance. The King sat by the window, one fat bandaged leg propped up on a footstool, a book in his hand.

'John,' he hallooed, taking off his spectacles, 'back so soon?'

'I fear so, Your Majesty,' John bowed.

Henry's forehead creased. 'You fear? Why so?'

John stepped forward and held out the roll of paper. 'I have here a statement that I fear will distress you greatly, Your Majesty. It is a deposition given by a reliable witness regarding the actions of the Earl of Surrey.'

Henry held out a hand for the paper. As he read, the fleshy neck and drooping cheeks flushed bright and the little, yellowed eyes bulged from their sockets. 'I'll have his head for this.'

John glanced at Seymour, who stepped forward and said, 'Shall I make out a warrant for his arrest, Your Majesty?'

Too hasty, you fool, John thought.

Henry looked up, his expression changing. 'You'd like that, wouldn't you, Brother Seymour? Get him out of the way, eh? I know you have no liking for the Howards.'

Seymour began to splutter a protest.

'With respect, Your Majesty,' John interjected, 'you yourself have no reason to love them. Twice have they hurt your generous heart with women of that family, and so rumour has it, would have tried to do so again.'

Both Seymour and Henry stared at him. 'What are you talking about, Dudley?' the King growled.

John looked down at his feet. 'It has been rumoured that the Earl of Surrey had entreated his sister to …,' he paused in disgust, 'to make herself pleasant to you.'

'Pleasant?' Henry snorted.

'In short, Your Majesty, to gain access to your most private person.'

Henry's colour rose once again. He struggled out of his chair. 'I will have his head,' he growled. 'To sully his own sister's honour, to impugn mine! Has there ever been such a rogue? Am I to be continually plagued by these Howards?'

'I beg you, sire, put an end to their malicious plots,' Seymour said. 'And but think, if they threaten *you* so, may they not threaten the sacred person of the Prince, your son?'

'Yes, yes,' Henry nodded vehemently, 'they would threaten him. The father too, then. Send them both to the Tower. Dudley, I trust you to see it done.'

John bowed. 'You can, Your Majesty.'

WHITEHALL PALACE, DECEMBER 1546

Prince Edward had been invited to court for Christmas and he and his companions looked forward to the change of scene and the entertainments they would be able to attend. But a few hours at court made them wish they had stayed at Hunsdon.

The arrest of the Howards had created a hushed, anxious atmosphere. People whispered that if the foremost peers of the realm could be arrested on a charge of treason for nothing more than having a portrait painted, then no one was safe. The King grew ever more irascible and unpredictable, and even the Prince came out from an interview with his father pale and shaking.

Everyone at court seemed to be living on nerves. Robert's parents had seemed preoccupied and paid him little attention. Worse, he had made himself a trouble to his father by attacking Edward Seymour.

Rollo had accompanied Robert to court, as he accompanied him everywhere now. Rollo was urinating in the corridor when Seymour passed by and he had kicked the dog. Rollo's yelp had alerted Robert and he had rushed out into the corridor and delivered a thump upon the back of his pet's attacker.

Seymour had boxed Robert's ear, sending him tumbling to the floor. Fortunately for Robert, his father had come along at that moment, frowned down at his sprawling son and had listened to Seymour's suggestion that the boy receive a severe whipping for daring to strike one of his betters. John had so far forborne from acting upon it, but Robert knew he was in disgrace for his father had hardly spoken to him and his mother had done nothing but find fault with him, cursing him for being a trouble to his father at such a time. Robert had wondered aloud why the time should be different from any other and his mother had shot him an impatient look.

'You have heard that Norfolk and his son have been taken to the Tower, Rob, or has that unimportant event passed you by?'

'I do know that,' he had protested sulkily.

'I'm very glad to hear it. Your father has been instrumental in bringing this about and he doesn't need distractions from you. Striking Edward Seymour! My God, Rob, what were you thinking?'

'He kicked Rollo.'

'I don't want to hear any more about it,' Jane had declared. 'And you stay away from your father if you don't want that whipping. He's got a lot on his mind.'

So, Robert had stayed out of the way. And yet another dinner in the Great Hall came around, where his father talked in whispers with Edward Seymour and his mother in earnest with the Queen. Robert leant against the wall and looked on.

'You look fed up,' Henry Sidney observed, smacking him on the shoulder by way of a hello. 'Hardly fun and games, is it? Look at Edward.' Henry jerked his chin towards the top table raised on a dais where the Prince sat alongside the King. 'He still looks scared to death. And oh my, look who's sitting next to him.'

Robert gave him an exasperated look. He was aware he talked of Elizabeth Tudor rather too often and the boys often ribbed him for it. Elizabeth sat next to her brother at the high table, eating very little, her pale brown eyes darting from one person to another.

'She's looking this way.'

'I can see that, Henry.'

'Why don't you go to her?'

'I can't just go up to her and start talking, you numbskull. She's with the King unless you hadn't noticed.'

'Go on,' Henry grinned. 'I dare you.'

'Don't be stupid.'

'You're scared.'

'I am not.'

'Prove it.'

Robert looked up at the dais, then back to Henry. 'All right. I will.' He made his way through the crowd and stepped tentatively up to the table, approaching it from the side, hoping that the King would not notice him.

'Robert!' Elizabeth hallooed loudly, making his cheeks redden as all eyes at the table turned towards him.

He bowed. 'My lady.'

'Come up here,' she commanded, pointing to the floor beside her. 'It's about time you came over,' Elizabeth chided, turning her pale, pointed face up to look at him.

'I would have liked to come sooner but I wasn't sure I should.'

'So, why have you come now?'

'Henry dared me.'

Elizabeth giggled. 'Well, I'm very grateful to Henry, whoever he is. How have you been, Robin?'

A chair was placed behind Robert by a servant and Elizabeth bid him sit. 'I've been very well, Bess. And you?'

'I sometimes get terrible headaches and then I'm in bed for days, but mostly I'm well. But Rob,' she said, lowering her voice, 'how do you think the King looks?'

Robert peered around her and cast a surreptitious glance at the King. The flabby cheeks shone with perspiration and the hand shook as it lifted a cup of wine to the pink lips. 'I don't know. A trifle hot, perhaps.'

'Don't lie to me,' she said earnestly.

'In truth, I do not think he is very well, Bess.'

'Nor do I.' She bit her lip, her pointy teeth turning the thin skin white. 'I'm worried, Rob. What if he were to die?'

'Then Edward would be king.'

'Edward, king! Look at him, Rob. Does he look like he can rule?'

'I don't mean now. When he's older.'

She looked down at her hands in her lap. 'I don't think Edward will be much older before he's... Oh, Rob, I'm frightened.'

He reached for her hand. 'I don't know what to say to you, Bess.'

'What shall I do when the King is gone?'

'I'm sure my father will look out for you, Bess.'

She gave a little laugh. 'You are so foolish, Rob. It will be my brother's uncle who will take matters into his own hands, you can be sure of that.'

'My father's very important, Elizabeth,' Robert drew himself up. 'And very close to the King. In fact, were it not for him, Henry Howard and his father wouldn't be imprisoned and what's more, he and Seymour are trying ...' he broke off, realising he was about to say too much.

'What?' She grabbed his wrist, her nails digging into his flesh. 'What do you know?'

'Nothing. Let me go, Bess, you're hurting me.'

She looked into his face for a long moment. 'What could you

know?' she sneered, looking much older than her thirteen years. She pushed his arm away. 'You can go now.'

Robert got to his feet, unsure whether to bow or not, so compromised with a deep nod of his head and hurried back to Henry.

'What's the matter?' Henry asked. 'Were you arguing?'

'No, of course not.'

'It looked like you were.'

'Well, we weren't. It's just that Elizabeth thinks she knows everything and she doesn't.'

'And you do?' Henry raised a sceptical eyebrow.

Robert snatched a goblet of wine from a passing servant. He drank the cup dry. 'I know a damn sight more than Elizabeth.'

CHAPTER 5

TOWER HILL, JANUARY 1547

Birds circled overhead, black bodies against the grey sky and dogs sniffed around the feet of the spectators, hoping for scraps of food. They lifted their legs and urinated against the upright wooden posts of the scaffold while the crowd swelled and the stench of unwashed bodies grew denser. They shouted and laughed in expectation of the morning's entertainment.

A crow swooped, perched on a wooden post and cawed loudly in John Dudley's ear. He winced and flapped his arm at the creature. It let out a cry of indignation, jabbed its beak at his face and retreated to a further post.

Seymour jiggled on the balls of his feet. 'Never mind the bird.'

'It's an ill omen,' John said.

'Of course, it's an ill omen. But for Henry Howard, not for us.'

'Must you be so damned cheerful?'

Seymour stared at him, his dark brown eyes hard. 'What's the matter with you? We both worked to see him here. It was your evidence that got him arrested. And now you baulk at this.' He gestured at the scaffold.

John shook his head, unable to explain that it brought back memories of his father. The cold clung to his bones and he tugged his cloak tighter about him.

Seymour studied his face for a moment longer, then looked

into the crowd that was parting to allow the guards through. 'Here he comes.'

Henry Howard was thinner, his skin greyer than at his trial, but his arrogance was still evident. He walked tall, head held high. Cries of 'God Bless You' mingled with 'Traitor'. As Howard drew near, he met both Seymour's and John's eye. He passed them without a word, and with heavy, thudding footsteps climbed the steep wooden stairs.

He shuffled through the straw laid down to soak up his blood. The executioner, his face obscured to hide his identity, knelt and asked for forgiveness. Howard gave it, along with a gold coin. A priest began to read from his Bible. The executioner thrust a blindfold before his victim's face. Howard gave it a disdainful look and shook his head. He turned and looked over the crowd. John saw his breath coming fast, turning to smoke in the cold January air.

'Good people, you come here to see me die, for I have been accused of treason. I tell you now, I have never been guilty of treason. I lay no blame for this injustice upon the King. He is the most kind and goodly prince beneath Heaven. The blame lies upon his advisors, those who spit venom upon their enemies and seek their removal for their own benefit and advancement. I confess I have been rash in my youth and caused much offence, but none so grievous that I deserve to be stood here. God knows my heart and will judge me fairly, as my enemies have not. Good people, I beg you, pray for me.'

Most of the crowd made the sign of the cross and a murmur of prayer bubbled up as Howard knelt and set his neck upon the curved block of wood. Howard's bloodshot eyes, bulging from their sockets with strain, locked on John's. 'May you suffer,' he hissed as the axe descended.

John shut his eyes, bile rising in his throat. When he opened them, dark red blood was trickling over the edges of the planks and the crowd was roaring. He leant towards Seymour. 'Let's go.'

He pushed his way through the crowd, glaring at anyone who seemed to offer resistance. It wasn't until they had left Tower Hill behind and entered into the twisting streets around the Tower that John slowed down and Seymour was able to catch up with him.

'Well, that's him gone,' Seymour panted, 'and his father's

turn will come. So, that just leaves Bishop Gardiner and Thomas Wriothesley for us to worry about.'

'Wriothesley's not a problem,' John said firmly, determined to get his mind back on work. 'Like Paget, he sees the way the wind's blowing.'

'Just Gardiner, then. We must be more vocal in our arguments against him when we speak with the King.'

'Agreed. We need to get Gardiner removed from the Council of Regency.'

Seymour touched his arm and they both came to a halt. 'Actually, John, I have something to tell you about that. I don't want to talk in the street. Come in here.' He led the way to a tavern, selecting a table by the corner, though John looked longingly towards the fire. 'Two cups of sack,' Seymour instructed the potboy who hurried away, anxious to please men of quality. Seymour waited until the wine was brought, then leant forward, gesturing John closer. 'William Paget has rewritten the King's will to exclude Gardiner and the other Catholics on the regency Council.'

John was stunned. 'On whose instructions?'

Seymour paused a moment before answering. 'Mine.'

'The King doesn't know you've done this?'

'No.'

'So, it's unsigned? What use is an unsigned will?' Seymour's face turned sulky and John shook his head. 'It's a dangerous thing you and Paget have done. Damn it, Edward, we've just had a man killed for treason. Do you want to end up on the scaffold, too? Why the devil didn't you tell me what you were doing?'

'I planned to. But it was during Christmas and you had your family about you—'

'We spoke every day, Edward. Don't say you couldn't have found a moment to tell me. If for no other reason than that I should have been consulted.'

Seymour raised his cup, knocking it against his lips painfully in his haste to avoid answering. He wasn't about to admit to John that he had listened to his wife who told him not to involve John. 'It's done now.'

'Yes, isn't it? And because of it, we better make sure we get the King to do what we want him to do, hadn't we?'

'Yes, John,' Seymour answered meekly.

'He said what?' Anne Seymour's reaction was exactly what her husband had expected it would be: incredulous, indignant, furious.

'He said I should have consulted him,' Seymour shrugged.

'Who does John Dudley think he is?'

'My superior, it seems.'

'And I expect you just sat there and said nothing, like always.'

'I suppose I did.'

She gave a snort of disgust, her skirts dragging the rushes around as she paced the floor. 'Why shouldn't you make a decision on your own? You don't answer to him. My God, I wish I had been there. I would have put him in his place. Did you tell him I told you not to involve him?'

'Of course, I didn't,' Seymour spat. 'I can just imagine what he would have said to that.'

'Oh yes, I know what the Dudleys think of me,' she said with a proud nod of her head. 'They think I rule you. Just because Jane Dudley is content to trot around after her husband, she thinks all women should do the same.'

There were moments when Seymour wished his wife *was* like Jane Dudley: demure, soft-spoken, yielding. 'The pity is,' he paused, rubbing his hand across his forehead where an ache had begun, 'I need him so much.'

Anne stopped her pacing. 'But do you really need him, Edward?'

'While the King is still alive, I'm afraid I do, Anne.'

'Well then, we have only to wait. When the King dies, you must seize your chance, and to hell with Dudley.'

WHITEHALL PALACE

Katherine Parr sank gratefully into the chair the page had brought for her and held a handkerchief to her sore eyes.

'Honestly, Kate,' Jane Dudley said, kneeling at her friend's side, 'I wouldn't dare say this to anyone else, but think what a relief it will be when he's gone.'

'Oh, Jane, how can you talk so?' Katherine said, blowing her nose. 'He is the King.'

Jane shrugged, turning her head as the floorboards moved beneath her knees. Thomas Cranmer was half-walking, half-running along the corridor, his loose, fleshy face unusually pink and moist. He came to a stop beside the women.

'My lady,' he said to Katherine, 'why are you out here?'

This question was answered by a fresh assault of tears. Jane rose and leaning close to Cranmer said quietly, 'The King didn't want her near him.'

'Oh, poor lady.'

'Have you been sent for?'

'I have,' he said, straightening the purple sash hanging around his neck. 'I received a message from Edward Seymour.'

'He's in there now,' she said, jerking her head towards the door.

'Tell me, Lady Dudley. The King. How unwell is he?'

'He was very bad a few hours ago, but we have heard nothing since. Seymour has allowed no one to enter.'

'Then I had best go in.' Cranmer stepped past her and tapped on the door.

Jane stood on tiptoe and, looking over his shoulder, tried to see into the chamber as the door opened, but Seymour, his dour face even more grim in the half light, quickly shut it again. Jane mouthed a curse.

'Jane,' Katherine grabbed at her. 'If Archbishop Cranmer has been sent for, then my husband must be very ill.'

'Kate,' Jane said, kneeling before her once again and looking earnestly into her face, 'the King *is* going to die. You know how ill he has been. It is only a matter of time.'

'But what will I do when he is gone?'

'Why, Kate,' Jane half-laughed, 'you rejoice.'

Katherine stared at her for a moment in horror, then raised her hand and laid a stinging blow upon Jane's cheek. 'How dare you? He is the King and I have loved him, though he has, I admit, given me little reason to. You will not speak so.'

'Oh, Your Majesty,' Jane protested, her eyes smarting. 'I didn't mean to upset you, only to relieve your suffering.'

'Oh, no, you meant what you said. You forget, Jane, how long I have known you. You're not like your husband. You always speak your mind.'

Katherine turned away from her and began snuffling into

her handkerchief. Jane rose once more, angry and hurt. She was tired of waiting and wished she had some news to send to John. With a glance at Katherine, she pressed her ear to the door but the wood was thick and she heard nothing. She almost kicked it in frustration.

Seymour took Cranmer by the arm and pulled him inside. 'Not long now,' he whispered, glancing towards the bed where the King lay, blankets domed over the huge body.

Cranmer peered at the King. The face seemed thinner, for the flabby cheeks had fallen away from the long-hidden bones and there were hollows in the cheeks where pink, plump flesh had been a week before. The King's eyes were closed and ragged breaths were drawn in through the small, thin lips.

Gathering up the skirts of his vestments, Cranmer knelt beside the bed. With great gentleness, he lifted the King's hand into his own. 'Your Majesty,' he said softly. 'Can you hear me?'

Henry's eyelids fluttered but remained shut and Cranmer knew that the end was indeed near. He closed his eyes and began to pray.

Seymour watched, his hand pressing against his jerkin, feeling for the key that was tucked inside, the key to the box that held the King's will. His heart beat faster at the thought of the coming hours, what he had to do, who he had to trust. He hated that he had had to involve others in his plans, but as he had told Anne, he couldn't execute the plan without Anthony Browne and William Paget, for Paget kept the chest containing the King's will and Browne as Master of the Horse had access to the stables. He wondered if the horses were ready. Browne had said they would be, but what if they weren't? No, he would trust Browne. The man had said the horses would be there, so they would be there. But it was the waiting… this damned waiting. And then there was Jane Dudley right outside the door. She mustn't get wind of what he was doing or she would go straight to her husband and then he would have John Dudley to deal with as well.

The King suddenly opened his eyes and drew a long, painful breath. The cold fingers gripped Cranmer's with a strength that made the bones crack. Biting back the pain, Cranmer leant closer so his face was inches from the King's.

'Your Majesty. The reform of the church. Am I to continue with it?'

The little mouth puckered, like a fish gasping for air. No sound came forth and the beady eyes looked into Cranmer's with fear.

'Am I to continue, Your Majesty?' Cranmer persisted. 'Say Yes and your soul will be saved.'

The head gave a feeble shake, not a negative but a gesture that meant speech was not possible to this once roaring man. The hand released, clutched and released Cranmer's once more. It fell back upon the blankets even as the head sunk deeper into the pillow. The eyes closed. The King was dead.

'He squeezed my hand,' Cranmer said breathlessly. 'He squeezed it. He meant Yes.' He turned, his eyes seeking Seymour's. 'He meant Yes.'

Seymour, his hands knuckle white across the foot of the bed, hissed, 'He's dead? You're sure?'

Cranmer held out an unsteady hand and placed it beneath the King's nose. After a moment, he looked up at Seymour. 'He is dead.'

Seymour let out the breath he had been holding. 'God bless his soul.'

'Amen. Should I get the Queen?' Cranmer asked.

'Not just yet, Cranmer,' he said, leaning over the bed and looking hard into Cranmer's face, 'can I trust you?'

Cranmer managed to look hurt and bewildered at the same time. 'My lord, I would have thought that an unnecessary question.'

'No man can be trusted entirely, not even a man of the cloth, Cranmer. Now, listen to me. I want this kingdom to continue the same way as you, in the Reformed faith. I cannot countenance a return to Rome. The Prince is just a young boy. If the wrong men get hold of him, who knows in what ways he will be influenced? You know what men are.'

'Indeed.'

'And I am the Prince's uncle, do not forget that. We are of the same blood. Who better to guide the new King?'

'Our sovereign lord is not even cold. Have you forgotten that so soon?'

Seymour smacked his hand on the bedpost. 'Confound me,

Archbishop, how can I forget it when I see him before me? I talk of the future. The King is dead, Cranmer. Long live the King.'

'It seems to me you act with unseemly haste, my lord,' Cranmer retorted, kneeling once more. 'Do what you must, it is not my concern.'

'But you will keep the death of the King to yourself? A few hours, Cranmer, that is all I need.'

'I am praying, my lord. I daresay I will be praying for hours for such a man as the King was.'

Seymour breathed a sigh of relief. 'I must leave for Hunsdon at once.'

'My lord,' Cranmer called over his shoulder as Seymour grabbed the handle of the door. 'Please be kind to the Prince.'

HUNSDON PALACE, HERTFORDSHIRE

Edward grunted in his sleep and kicked out at Robert again, raking toenails down his calf. Suppressing the urge to kick back, Robert turned over, yawning.

How he hated these nights when it was his turn to sleep with the Prince. He tugged at the blankets that Edward had pulled over to his side of the bed and wondered what time it was. Too early, he imagined and mentally cursed the moment when the sun would rise and bleed through the wooden shutters. He fancied he heard the thrum of horses' hooves, but that was nonsense. He punched a dent in the pillow and laid his head back down.

But then, there was a pounding reverberating through the walls. Someone was banging on the front door.

Robert sat bolt upright in bed, ears pricked. He heard a murmur of voices below and then the sound of someone running up the staircase, heavy footsteps tramping along the corridor, stopping just outside the door. A pause and then the latch lifted and the door swung open.

Robert tried to see into the darkness as someone said softly, 'Bring a light.' A candle was handed over and as the flame flared, Robert recognised the intruder.

Edward Seymour stepped into the room and held the candle high. 'Who are you?' he demanded.

'Robert Dudley. What's wrong?'

Seymour's gaze travelled beyond Robert to the boy who was propping himself up on his elbow.

'Who's there?' the Prince asked, his speech thick with sleep.

'It is your Uncle Edward,' Seymour answered, bringing the candle nearer his face.

'Uncle? What are you doing here?'

'You have to get up and dress, Edward,' Seymour said, grabbing the blankets and pulling them off of the two boys.

'But it's cold, Uncle,' Edward protested, reaching for the blankets.

Seymour held them fast. 'I must insist, Edward. You, Dudley, help the Prince to dress. I'll see to the other arrangements.' He spun around, flicking wax across the coverlet, and hurried from the room.

Robert climbed from the bed, grabbed his hose and hurriedly pulled them on. Sensing no movement from the bed, he turned his head. Edward sat unmoving, goosebumps pimpling his legs.

'Aren't you dressing, Edward?'

Edward shook his head. 'I don't understand.'

'Neither do I, but your uncle meant what he said. And if he comes back and you're still sitting there…'

'I'm not afraid of my uncle.'

Robert sat back down on the bed. 'I wonder why he's here. He didn't answer you when you asked, you know?'

'I don't care why. I'm not going anywhere.' Edward threw himself back on the bed.

'You must, Edward.' Seymour had returned. Crossing the floor in two strides, he grabbed the boy's thin arm and yanked him upright. 'I will tell you why later, when things are…,' he shrugged and shook his head, 'when they are better. Now, please, get dressed.'

Seymour waited in the corridor, leaning over the balustrade and watching the servants bustle in the hall below.

'Is the Prince ready?' he asked as Robert came out of the chamber.

'He's just coming.'

Edward appeared, pulling a heavy fur-lined cloak tighter about him and casting a surly glance in his uncle's direction.

'Ah, good,' Seymour tried to smile kindly. He placed a hand at the boy's back and steered him towards the stairs. 'Come along, Edward.'

'Rob,' someone hissed. Robert turned to see Thomas Cobden hurrying towards him. 'Rob, what's going on?'

'I don't know, but Edward Seymour is up to something. You should have seen how he was with the Prince.'

'He burst into our room and shouted at me and Henry to get up and start packing.'

'I know, I heard him. He hasn't even said where we're going.'

'I heard that other man,' Thomas nodded towards the hall where a tall man with a green feather plume in his hat bowed as the Prince and Seymour walked past, 'Browne, I think his name is, say Hatfield.'

Robert grabbed Thomas's arm. 'Hatfield? Are you sure he said that?'

'Yes, I heard him. Why? What's at Hatfield?'

Robert grinned and smacked him playfully on the arm. He skipped down the stairs, throwing the answer in a shout over his shoulder. 'Elizabeth!'

CHAPTER 6

HATFIELD PALACE, HERTFORDSHIRE

Winter had made the road to Hatfield crisp and hard and riding in the dead of night ensured the journey was not without peril. Many a horse stumbled and nearly threw its rider. It was a cold and miserable party that drew rein outside the red brick palace as the new day began to dawn.

A guard darted out from the entrance porch and pressed the tip of his halberd against the chest of Seymour's horse.

'Stand back, man,' Seymour ordered, his arm tightening around the Prince who he held in front of him on the saddle.

'Identify yourselves,' the guard insisted.

'I am Edward Seymour, Earl of Hertford, and I have here Prince Edward to see his sister, the Lady Elizabeth.'

The guard immediately lowered his weapon and called for the hall door to be opened. Seymour dismounted and pulled the Prince from the saddle. Cold and weary, the boy made no protest as Seymour propelled him inside the house. Boys began to appear from the stable yard, pulling on jackets and shaking straw from their hair. Robert thrust his reins into the hand of one boy and hurried after the Prince.

The Great Hall was rapidly filling up as Hatfield realised it had visitors. Yawning servants grumbled as they were hustled out into the cold to unpack the carts. Hot wine and food were called for and Robert found himself being divested of his cloak and gloves.

He looked around for Seymour and the Prince just in time to see a door to a small chamber closing upon them. He was wondering where he could find some ink and paper to write to his father when someone called his name. He looked around and saw Elizabeth standing on the stairs, clad only in her nightdress with a thin shawl around her shoulders. 'Bess,' he said.

'What's happening?' she asked, her red hair falling about her face. 'Why are you here?'

'Your brother's here. Edward Seymour brought him, I don't know why. Bess, can you get me some paper? I need to get word to my father.'

'What has your father got to do with this?'

'I need to tell him what Seymour's doing,' he said impatiently. 'Ink and paper, Bess, please.'

'Dudley!'

Robert turned. Seymour had come back into the hall, light from the inner chamber spilling onto the floor. His eyes flitted between Robert and Elizabeth. 'Do not detain the lady. Lady Elizabeth, would you kindly come in here?'

Unhesitatingly, she obeyed, pulling her shawl tighter as her bare feet slapped upon the brick floor. She slipped past Seymour and disappeared into the room. Robert heard the Prince call out her name. Seymour slowly closed the door behind him, his eyes never leaving Robert's.

The routine of the household had been disrupted by the new arrivals. Elizabeth's lessons had been cancelled and the servants wandered around, their duties mostly neglected as they gossiped. The Prince's company had been given rooms with extra beds crammed in to accommodate them all and they resumed their sleep, filling the silence with snores.

All but one, for Robert remained awake. Tiredness had completely deserted him, his mind buzzed with activity and his muscles twitched with a desire for movement. And a joy that after months of having nothing to report, he finally had something to tell his father.

He lifted the latch, opened the door and peered out. The corridor was empty. The house seemed quiet. With a deep breath, he stepped out into the hallway and tiptoed across the floorboards, which mercifully made no noise. He had found out where Elizabeth's rooms were from a pageboy whose eyes glinted at the coins Robert pressed into his palm and he made his way to them now. Reaching the door, he knocked softly. A few seconds passed, some murmurings from within, and then a voice hissed through a crack in the wood. 'Who is it?'

He recognised the voice. 'It's Robert Dudley, Mistress Ashley.'

'The Dudley boy, my lady,' he heard her say. A moment later, the door opened and Katherine Ashley jerked her head at him to enter.

Elizabeth stood by the bed. Her eyes bore the signs of weeping and her thin lips pursed and puckered.

'What's happened?' he asked.

She shook her head, unable to speak.

'It's the King, Master Dudley,' Katherine said quietly. 'He's dead.'

A sob burst from Elizabeth and she buried her face in her hands. Katherine hurried over and pulled her into an embrace. 'Look what you've done,' she scolded Robert. 'She had settled before you came.'

'It's not his fault.' Elizabeth pulled herself away and wiped her cheeks savagely. 'Robin,' she held out her hand to him.

He took it, feeling the wetness on her fingers. 'I can't believe it.'

Elizabeth slid her hand from his and climbed beneath the bedcovers, pulling them up to her chin. 'I wish it weren't true.'

'And Edward?'

'Edward's pissing himself,' she said with a hollow laugh, pulling at strands of hair that had stuck to her face. 'He's terrified that he's now King.'

'He *is* only nine years old, my lady,' Katherine said sternly.

'Yes, I know. Rob, you will look after him, won't you?'

'I'll do what I can.'

Her brow creased. 'You wanted paper earlier, didn't you? Kat, get him some.'

Katherine fetched paper, ink and a goose quill from a chest beneath the window and handed them to Robert. He hitched himself up on the bed and smoothed out the blankets to make a flat space. He pushed Elizabeth's feet away, leant forward on his elbows and dipped the quill in the ink.

'What are you writing?' Elizabeth asked, squinting at the page.

'I'm telling my father what Seymour has done. I don't know why he's done it, but I'm damn sure he's done it in secret.'

Elizabeth sniffed. 'I asked him why he brought my brother here and he said it was so we could be a comfort to each other.'

'And you believe that?'

'We *are* a comfort to each other,' she said indignantly. 'Edward needs me and I need him.'

'So, why are you not together now? Or did his tears not last as long as yours?'

Elizabeth swallowed, suddenly doubtful. 'Seymour said he would look after him.'

'I'm sure he will. Now,' Robert surveyed his letter, 'not my neatest hand but I don't think Father will scold me for that.'

Elizabeth kicked at him beneath the sheets for him to move as she nudged herself down the bed. 'What can your father do? Seymour has every right to be with Edward. He is his uncle.'

'My father likes to be kept informed.' Robert folded the letter and tucked it inside his doublet. He looked at her. 'Are you all right?'

She looked away and shrugged. 'I'll have to be, won't I?'

'She will be well enough,' Katherine said, smoothing Elizabeth's hair. 'Now come on, Master Dudley, time you were gone.'

'I'll see you later today,' he promised, jumping off the bed and heading for the door. 'I am sorry, Bess.'

She smiled thinly at him. 'I thought you weren't going to say anything kind to me.'

'Try to sleep,' he suggested.

'I'll try. Good night, Robin. Morning, I mean.'

The door closed upon him. As he turned away, his breath caught in his throat. Edward Seymour stood before him, so close Robert could taste his breath.

'What are you doing?'

'Visiting,' Robert answered quickly.

'And what have you to do with the Lady Elizabeth?'

'We're friends. She told me why you've brought us here.'

Seymour's eyes narrowed. His hand shot up and grabbed

Robert's jaw, his fingertips digging into the skin. 'Don't go behind my back, ferreting out information to send to your father. Always remember, I have the Prince's love. I haven't forgotten our last encounter, boy. First chance I get, I'll have you replaced.' He shoved Robert away. 'Now, get back to your room.'

Robert glared at Seymour, but his courage quailed beneath the anger in the man's eyes. He hurried back to his chamber. Falling against the closed door, he let out a shuddering breath. He squeezed his doublet, heard the crinkle of the letter he had stowed there and felt a tingle of satisfaction. If Seymour had wanted to frighten him into inaction, he had failed.

Robert manoeuvred his way back to his bed, careful not to nudge the protruding limbs of his roommates. He propped himself against a pillow and reached to open the shutter so that the light and the fresh morning air would keep him awake. While he waited for Hatfield to rouse itself again, he plotted a suitable revenge for Edward Seymour that only a boy of fourteen could dream up.

WHITEHALL PALACE

John Dudley barely glanced up from his desk as the door opened. 'How is the Queen?'

'Still crying. She's gone to her room for a lie down.' Jane yawned, peering through the leaded-glass window at the grey sky. 'What time is it?'

'God knows.'

She leant over his shoulders and pressed her cheek against his temple. 'Have you been to bed?'

'No.'

'Look at me.' He tilted his face to hers. 'You have black circles under your eyes, John.'

'So have you. You should go to bed.'

'Will you come?'

'Not yet.'

'I don't know what we think we can do,' Jane said, pulling off her headdress and tossing it into the bowl of a chair. 'All of us sitting up, waiting for the King to die.'

'What else should we do?' John growled, rubbing at his eyes.

'I don't know. But I suppose Cranmer will send word if there's any change.'

'Cranmer?' John looked at her. 'Why will Cranmer send word?'

'He's with the King.'

'Who else is with him?'

'I don't think anyone else is in there. Edward Seymour left hours ago.'

'Where did he go?'

'To his rooms, I suppose.'

'He didn't say?'

'Not a word, barely even looked at me.'

'It's strange that he would leave. How was his manner when he came out?'

'He was in a hurry, like always. What does it matter?'

John's skin prickled. 'Something's happening,' he murmured, buckling on his sword. 'See who that is,' he ordered as there came a knock on the door.

'A letter for Lord Dudley.' A young boy, his clothes speckled with mud, held out a sealed letter to Jane.

She took it and gave him a penny. 'It's from Robert,' she said, recognising the handwriting. 'For you.'

John snatched at the letter and tore it open. 'The devil,' he breathed.

'What's Rob done now?'

'He's kept me informed, Jane, which is more than you have done. Rob writes that Seymour's at Hatfield Palace. He's already been to Hunsdon and taken the Prince.' He crushed the letter, the wax seal cracking in his hand.

'So, now he has both the Prince and Lady Elizabeth under his control,' Jane said. 'I told you, you couldn't trust him.'

'You said Cranmer's in there,' John said suddenly. 'My God, Jane, the King must be dead.'

John rushed past his wife and ran to the Privy Chamber. He threw open the door, making Cranmer jump and scramble to his feet. 'My lord.'

'Archbishop,' John greeted him absently, his eyes looking past him to the King, lying silent and grey in the bed. 'How long?'

'The King died just before midnight.'

'But that was hours ago. Why has it been kept quiet?'

Cranmer raised an eyebrow. 'I wasn't aware it had. I haven't left this room. Edward Seymour asked me to stay with the King.'

'Seymour's left the court, Cranmer. He has custody of the Prince and is now with him and Elizabeth at Hatfield.'

'Well, he is the boy's uncle, my lord. Perhaps he thought the Prince would need comforting when he heard of his father's death.'

John barked a laugh. 'What kind of comfort could Seymour provide? Come now, we both know why he's done this. The Prince is too young to rule. Now, Seymour has him and Seymour does not like to share.'

'I assure you, my lord, I do not know his motive for leaving. But,' he paused and tapped a long finger against his lips, 'if, as you seem to suggest, Seymour aims to become Lord Protector, should we oppose him?'

'Protectorships have a poor history in this country, Archbishop. That's why the King stipulated that a Council of Regency should rule in the Prince's minority.'

'You allude to the Protectorship of Richard of Gloucester. I hardly think such a comparison is complimentary or apt. And you do surprise me, my lord. I had thought you were Edward Seymour's close friend. It does make me wonder why you are so aggrieved. Tell me, is it truly concern that the King's will may be disregarded or resentment that you seem to have been left out of Seymour's plans?'

'My God, what a courtier you have become, Cranmer,' John sneered. 'And I thought you were the only man at court with integrity.'

'You doubt my integrity, I think, because I speak uncomfortable truths.'

'I doubt you because I think Seymour's made you an offer, promised you something if you kept this quiet.'

Cranmer bridled. 'There were no offers and no promises, my lord. Now, you must excuse me.'

He turned his back on John and recommenced his prayers for the dead king. John had to bite down on his tongue to control the anger swelling up within him. It irked him that Cranmer was right. He had been left out of Seymour's plans, and he certainly didn't like it.

CHAPTER 7

WHITEHALL PALACE, FEBRUARY 1547

The executors of the King's will had been summoned to the Council chamber. Sir Anthony Denny, Sir Anthony Browne, Sir William Paget, Archbishop Cranmer, all took their places at the long table, each shifting along the benches as more of their colleagues arrived.

John Dudley breezed in. 'Good morning, gentlemen,' he greeted the company, taking a seat at the end of a bench. He looked around the table. 'Wriothesley not here?'

Cranmer glanced at him. 'Not yet, my lord.'

John nodded, noting the cool, dismissive tone. Cranmer evidently held a grudge from their previous meeting. 'And what of Edward Seymour? Any news from him?' He waited while Denny and Browne exchanged glances. *So, they're in with Seymour too*, he realised. He bit the inside of his cheek, a curb on his resentment.

'I,' Browne said with emphasis, 'have not had anything from him today.'

'I see,' John said. 'Ah, here comes Wriothesley.'

'Damn cold out there,' the Lord Chancellor declared as he strode in, the red tip of his long nose testament to the weather. 'There's ice on the river and the boatman took an eternity to row me back here.' He sank into his chair at the head of the table.

'Well, you're here now,' Cranmer said with a polite smile.

'Yes, I am. And as I've had a very tedious morning at the

House of Commons, I would like to get this business over with as few interruptions as possible. Now, I have informed the Commons of the death of King Henry and disclosed the contents of his will. The main point of which is that Prince Edward, his natural and legitimate son, succeed him to the throne. In regard to the Prince, he is being brought to London by his uncle, Edward Seymour, and they will arrive at the Tower…,' he looked around for information.

'Later this afternoon,' Denny supplied.

'Yes, so we had all better be there to welcome him.'

'To welcome the Prince or Seymour?' John wondered aloud.

Wriothesley shot him a quizzical look. 'The Prince, obviously.'

John gave him a playful smile and waved him to continue.

'While we are all here,' Wriothesley said, his brow creasing in irritation, 'we may as well discuss the fact that the Prince is in his minority and cannot rule alone. We must therefore consider a regency.'

'The Queen,' Cuthbert Tunstall, a small man with wide, watchful eyes suggested. 'She has acted as regent before.'

Wriothesley rolled his eyes. 'For a matter of mere months, Tunstall. The Prince is but nine years old, almost seven years away from his coming of age. We cannot trust the governance of the country to a woman for such a length of time. And fortunately, King Henry foresaw that he might die while the Prince was still a child and in his will he suggested a Council of Regency.'

There was silence for a long moment.

Then Cranmer spoke. 'From the way you phrase it, Sir Thomas, a suggestion, are we to assume that the King appreciated there might be problems with such a Council?'

Wriothesley pouted. 'He realised that it might be unmanageable.'

'So,' Browne said, 'if not the Queen as regent and possibly not a Council of Regency, then that leaves only a Protectorship.'

'I personally favour a Council of Regency,' Wriothesley said hurriedly.

'In my opinion,' Denny said, 'a Protector would serve the country much better.'

'I agree,' Browne said.

Cranmer inclined his head. 'I, too.'

'And,' Denny said, 'I think we need look no further for a Protector than Edward Seymour.'

Others voiced their approval. Wriothesley glowered. John bent his head to hide his consternation. Had Seymour primed all of the men around this table but he and Wriothesley?

'Oh, that reminds me.' William Paget held his finger in the air, insisting on their attention. 'As keeper of the King's will, I was quite naturally privy to its contents. King Henry had begun to make arrangements to bestow titles on several members here present in recognition of their services to him, which I'm sure Edward Seymour would feel duty bound to honour were he to assume the office of Protector. However, if a Council of Regency were to take over, those elevations might have to be re-considered as I think it would appear self-serving to bestow those titles on ourselves.'

'I suggest we take a vote,' Browne licked his lips greedily. 'What say you, gentlemen, to Seymour as Protector?'

A chorus of 'Aye' to which neither John nor Wriothesley contributed. With such a little word, King Henry's wishes had been ignored, set aside for a handful of titles.

'Well then,' Denny said, his long face broadening with a grin, 'if that's decided we had better make a start for the Tower.' He led the counsellors out.

'Well, what do you make of that, Dudley?'

John halted at the door. 'You don't seem happy, Thomas.'

Wriothesley lounged in his chair, left leg hooked over the arm, one elegant finger tapping against the table. 'The devil I don't.' He waved an arm at the departing counsellors. 'He's bought them.'

John sighed. 'It would seem so.'

'But it's obvious to me that Seymour didn't buy you. And you know that surprises me.'

John bridled. 'I can't be bought, Thomas.'

Wriothesley laughed, a high, girlish laugh that made John want to hit him. 'Every man can be bought, John. You just like to think you're more costly than most. But Seymour's done all this without involving you, hasn't he? And you two have been so close. So much for friendship, eh?'

'There's no such thing as friendship at court.'

'I suppose not. I notice you didn't vote just now.'

'There was no need. If I had said Nay, I would have been outvoted. If I had said Aye, I would merely have added my voice to the others.'

'You can stomach Seymour as Protector, then?'

'I don't see we have any choice. As you said, all the others are with Seymour. If we can't prevent it and we can gain by agreeing to his Protectorship...,' John shrugged, 'why not?'

Wriothesley grunted a grudging agreement.

'So, Thomas, are you coming to the Tower?'

With a great sigh, Wriothesley shoved away from the table and jerked his wiry frame erect. 'I suppose so, but you'll have to stop me from spitting in Seymour's eye.'

John laughed, patting him on the shoulder as he passed. *You'll have to wait your turn*, he thought.

CHAPTER 8

WHITEHALL PALACE, MAY 1547

'Do you mind if I sit here?' the pageboy asked, a wooden cup in one hand, a platter of meat in the other. 'I wouldn't normally ask, only the Pages Chamber is full.'

It was a liberty, Robert Dudley knew. Pages were not supposed to eat in the Great Hall, but most of the diners had departed and the servants were already taking down the trestle tables. Robert nodded and the boy clambered onto the bench and began to eat.

'You serve Edward Seymour?' Robert asked, pointing to the badge on the boy's breast. The boy nodded, his mouth full of food. 'What's it like?'

'It's all right,' the boy shrugged. 'He has a bad temper, though and his wife is worse. It's best to be invisible when she's around.'

Robert grinned understandingly. 'I've heard my father say that, too.'

'Who's your father?'

'John Dudley.'

The boy's eyes widened, impressed. 'Really? He was in the office earlier. My master was very upset.'

'Upset with my father? Why?'

'Well,' the boy wiped his mouth on his sleeve and leant towards him, 'it seems that Thomas Wriothesley has been placed under house arrest. Your father burst into my master's office demanding to know why.'

'Did Seymour tell him?'

'Something to do with the earl sending his clerks to do work he should have been doing himself.'

'That doesn't sound very terrible.'

'That's what your father said. My master swore at him and reminded him that he was the Lord Protector and warned him not to forget his place.'

Colour flooded Robert's cheeks. 'He said that to my father?'

The boy nodded.

'I don't understand,' Robert said, almost to himself. 'Thomas Wriothesley is Keeper of the Great Seal. How can Seymour expect to do without him? All official documents have to have the Great Seal on them.'

The boy shrugged, digging out slivers of meat from between his teeth with a fingernail. 'I don't know, but I was glad to get out of my master's way, I can tell you, the mood he was in after your father left. I feel sorry for the King having him for an uncle.'

'Was anything else said? After my father left, I mean?'

The boy frowned in thought. 'My master did instruct one of his secretaries to hurry through with the charges against Thomas Wriothesley. But then my master's brother turned up complaining again that he was being left out of things. My master began to turn purple so I sneaked out. I wasn't about to get caught up in their quarrels.'

'They're nasty, are they?'

'They've drawn swords against each other, you know?'

'Really?'

'I swear. They can't stand each other.'

'I never realised.'

'There's going to be trouble there, I warrant you.'

'Sounds like it.'

The boy licked his greasy fingers. 'I should get back. Thank you for letting me sit here.'

Alone again, Robert remained seated until the servants pointedly waited at the edge of the table. Robert took the hint and rose.

'Still eating, Robert?' his father remarked as he breezed past.

'Father.' Robert hurried to catch him up.

'You should be twice the size you are, the amount you eat,' John said, not slackening his pace. 'I expect most of the food bills for the household are down to you.'

'Father, I was just talking with one of Seymour's pages and he said you two had had a quarrel.'

John stopped so abruptly that Robert careered into him. 'Who is it you've been talking to? I won't have gossip, especially when it's about me. Tell me his name.'

'I don't know his name.'

'But you'll recognise him?'

'Father, surely he's not important? What he told me, I thought you would find of interest.'

John softened. 'What did he tell you, my little spy?'

'After you left, Seymour's brother, Thomas, turned up and they started arguing. The page said that it happens a lot, that they can't stand one another.'

'They're not very loving brothers, that's true.'

'They've drawn swords on each other.'

'Have they really?' John's eyebrow rose in surprise. 'Well, all right, so they quarrel. What of it?'

'I...,' Robert flung his arms wide despairingly. 'I thought it might be useful to know.'

John smiled and patted Robert's shoulder. 'It is useful. Thank you, Rob. Now, putting gossip aside, does the King talk about Seymour to you?'

'Sometimes. He's quite glad he has Seymour looking after things for him...'

'But?'

'But I don't think he likes him very much. He said his uncle is very grim and he much prefers his other uncle, Thomas, who makes him laugh.'

'I bet he does,' John said. 'Well, keep me informed, Rob.'

Robert nodded and began to walk away.

'And Rob?'

'Yes, Father?'

'You keep talking to pageboys. Yes, my boy?'

Robert grinned. 'Yes, Father.'

John had thought hard on what Robert had told him about the Seymour brothers. With Edward Seymour becoming more unreasonable by the day, John felt little reason to remain loyal to him. He was also worried; Wriothesley had been removed from office with barely a whimper. John could with very little effort envisage a time when he would become just as superfluous to Seymour's requirements, perhaps even a threat. Would he then be got rid of just as easily, with no word of protest from his fellow counsellors? John was determined that wouldn't happen. He peered around the corner. Further along the corridor two legs stuck out from a window embrasure. John walked towards them and contrived a trip.

'Jesus! Why the devil—,' Thomas Seymour roared as he jumped up to face whatever clumsy oaf had disturbed him. 'Oh, it's you.'

John tugged his doublet straight and grimaced. 'Those damn long legs of yours, Thomas.'

'You'll have to forgive me,' Thomas chuckled, 'I was somewhat distracted.' He gestured with his eyes to the woman curled up in the window seat, her cheeks flushed and dimpled.

She smiled shyly. 'I should be going,' she said, dropping her feet to the floor and smoothing her skirts. 'Excuse me.' She almost skipped away, her heels clicking against the floorboards.

'In the corridor, Thomas?'

'Oh, don't be so disapproving, you old dog,' Thomas said. 'A man must find his pleasure where he may. Anyway, sit down. Talk to me, now that you've scared my delightful little wanton away.'

'Very well. You can tell me why you weren't at the Council meeting today.'

Thomas's face clouded over. 'What Council meeting?'

'Oh,' John said innocently, 'I thought your brother would have told you of it. Obviously not.'

'Damn him,' Thomas snarled. 'He's determined to leave me out.'

'Tom,' John shook his head, 'would your brother do that? I'm sure he just forgot to mention it.'

'Oh no, he didn't just forget. You don't know him like I do, John. I know what he's doing. He wants the boy all to himself. But I'm his uncle too and I tell you, I will have something.'

'Well, if there's anything I can do, Tom, just ask. And *I'll* let you know when the Council is meeting again. I'm sure we can get some position for you.'

'Thank you,' Thomas said grudgingly. 'Well, I think I'll pay a visit to my nephew. See how he is.'

'I'm sure he'll be very pleased to see you. From what I hear, you're much his favourite uncle.'

'Really?' Thomas's face relaxed into an easy smile. 'Who told you that?'

John tapped his nose. 'A little bird, Tom.'

'Well, you'll let me know, about the next meeting?'

'Of course, I will.'

Thomas patted his arm gratefully and departed. John allowed himself a satisfied smile. He had a feeling causing trouble between the two brothers was going to be easier than he had anticipated.

Seymour fixed his expression into one of patience and waited for his brother to stop talking. He looked around the table, wondering which one of them had told Thomas about this meeting. Paget, Browne? No, they wouldn't have bothered. Cranmer? No, he looked more bored than usual. There was Parr, brother to the former queen, Katherine, who had once been in love with Thomas and might be still, for all Seymour knew. Maybe, but… no, John Dudley, of course! He was hiding it well, but Seymour could see the tiniest upturn of his lips beneath the thin moustache. Anne had been right. Dudley was causing trouble.

'And I say, my lords,' Thomas concluded, 'as the King's favourite uncle, and as my brother already has the Protectorship, I should have the Governorship of the King's Person.'

All heads turned towards Seymour. His insides churned with indignation and fury. It was ludicrous, there could be no worse person to govern the King than Thomas. What would Thomas teach him? How to gamble, how to swear, how to whore? In all these, Thomas was a true adept. Seymour didn't trust himself to speak. He rose, pushed back his chair and strode from the chamber, leaving the counsellors and Thomas to stare after him, open-mouthed.

'Thomas never ceases to amaze me,' John said, pouring himself wine from a jug on the windowsill.

'He is insufferable,' Seymour kicked at a log on the hearth, wishing it were Thomas. 'That he should do this to me.'

'He is an envious man, Edward, and, I think, will not be content until he has eclipsed you entirely.'

'Favourite uncle, he said? Where does he get this nonsense?'

'Oh, that's just Thomas's fancy. I'm sure the King does love him but no more than he loves you, never fear.'

'I don't fear that, John. I have nothing to fear from the King. I wish I knew how he found out about the meeting.' He looked sideways at John, who stared shamelessly back.

'You're going to have to give Thomas something to do.'

'I realise that. But what?'

'I do have a suggestion.'

'What?'

'He could have my position of Lord Admiral.'

'You'd give that up?'

'Yes. But, of course, I would expect some recompense for relinquishing the post.'

'What would you want?'

'Well,' John said, taking a seat, 'I do have a fancy for an earldom. Warwick would be most acceptable.'

'Then it's yours. Is that all you want?'

'That's all. Now,' John said and got to his feet, 'my wife expects me at home, so I shall bid you good night, Edward.'

'Good night, John.'

As he stared down into the flickering flames of the fire, Seymour had the uneasy feeling that he had missed something in his conversation with John.

John fell onto his bed and laughed aloud.

Jane rubbed her eyes and frowned at her husband. 'What are you laughing at?'

John rolled over onto his front. 'It's done, Jane.'

'What's done?'

'I've sown the seeds of discord between Edward and Thomas Seymour and received the earldom of Warwick as my reward.'

'I'm glad,' she said, settling back into her pillow and closing her eyes.

He nudged himself up the bed next to her, his boots becoming entangled in the bedclothes. 'Show me how glad you are,' he said, pulling at the laces on her nightgown.

She giggled and slapped his hand away. 'What made you think of setting those two against each other?'

'Rob. He found out they argue a great deal and he thought I could use that information.'

'He's already thinking like a courtier. He gets that from you.'

John pulled his boots off. 'He's ambitious. That's a good thing.'

'Gets above himself at times. Do you know, I heard him telling Guildford how one of the boys could be a king one day? He heard us talking about you asking for the Warwick earldom and he was telling the children about Warwick the Kingmaker and how that could be you.'

John smiled. 'Was he?'

'I beg you, don't encourage him too much, John.'

'Rob would make a fine king,' he protested. 'Although I suppose you would rather Guildford.'

'He has a better temper.'

'Only because you indulge him, you foolish woman,' he said, climbing into bed and holding out his right arm.

She moved into his embrace and began pulling playfully at the hairs on his chest. 'John, do you think it's wise to do what you're doing? Pitting the Seymour brothers against each other.'

'I'm just doing what I have to for the protection of our family. And anyway, I think the brothers would destroy each other before long without my interference.'

'Well, I suppose you know what you're about. Just be careful.'

He squeezed her gently. 'I always am, Jane, don't worry. I'm damned if I'll go the same way as Wriothesley. I'll have Seymour's head before he has mine, I promise you.'

CHAPTER 9

CHELSEA, MAY 1547

Thomas Seymour leant against the tree and wondered how much longer he would have to wait. The grass beneath his feet was wet, already seeping into his leather shoes, and the night had turned chill, so that he had to pull his cloak about him to keep warm.

Thomas heard a latch click open and then a voice in the darkness called softly, 'Tom, are you there?'

'I'm here.'

Katherine Parr emerged from the shadow of the doorway. She wore a dressing-gown over her nightdress and dark brown hair curtained her face. 'I've kept you waiting.'

'Shameful. You know how impatient I am for you.'

'I almost wrote to you and told you not to come. I'm sure this isn't right.'

'For Christ's sake, Kate, you were mine before King Henry ever looked in your direction, but he had you and I didn't. Was that fair? Was that right?'

'Don't be angry with me. I'm thinking of the children, Tom. Elizabeth and Edward. What will they say?'

'I'll find out,' Thomas shrugged carelessly. 'I'll go to Edward in the morning and ask him for permission to marry you.'

'But what if he says no?'

'Then I won't ask him. We'll marry and tell him after.'

'Do you think we could?'

He pulled her into an embrace. 'Yes, I do. What say you, Kate, will you take a risk?'

'Oh, Tom, I so want to be married to you.'

As she laid her head against his chest, his gaze raked over the façade of her splendid house that could, so soon, be his. Something caught his eye. He squinted into the darkness. It was Elizabeth, looking out from her window. Looking down at him. He had a small heartbeat of panic at what she must have seen, but then he relaxed. What did it matter if a twelve-year-old girl had seen his lovemaking?

He angled Katherine's head back and forced his lips onto hers almost cruelly. She moaned and pulled her mouth from his. As Katherine placed fervent kisses upon his neck, Thomas kept his eyes on the figure at the window. A shiver of excitement ran through him as Elizabeth continued to watch.

WHITEHALL PALACE

Robert's head ached. The sermon had been going on for hours, which was a long time to be sitting on a hard, wooden pew in a chilly chapel, forbidden to talk and only to listen. It was a relief when the sermon eventually came to an end and Robert, with the other companions, followed the King out of the chapel.

'It's not over yet,' Henry Sidney said to Robert with a sigh. 'We've now got to spend hours discussing the sermon that we've just spent hours listening to.'

'Don't remind me. My head's killing me and my arse is numb. I could do with some fresh air. What about sneaking off and having a ride?'

'We'd need an excuse.'

'I know. Think of one, will you? Hey, where did he come from?' Robert wondered as Thomas Seymour brushed hurriedly past him.

'Edward,' Thomas called, catching up with his nephew as he reached his chamber and clamping his arm around his shoulder. 'A fine sermon, don't you think?'

'Very fine, Uncle,' Edward said. 'I didn't see you in the chapel.'

'Oh, I was there. At the back,' Thomas lied. 'I've got something for you.' He delved inside his jerkin and pulled out a leather pouch. He threw it to Edward. 'There's ten pounds in there.'

Edward, always short of money, thanked him with blushing cheeks and turned away to put the money bag in a box by his bed.

'Not at all, my boy. Can't see you going short, can I?' Thomas stroked his beard thoughtfully. 'Actually, Edward, there is something I wanted to ask you. It's rather delicate.'

'Speak, Uncle.'

'Well, it's about your stepmother. She has a fancy to marry again and she's worried about what you might think. You know how women are, once they get an idea into their pretty heads. She thinks you might object to her taking a husband.'

Edward squatted to stroke his pet dog that had waddled into the room. 'My father's been gone such a short time.'

'I know, Edward, and your stepmother feels his absence keenly. But she is a woman who needs a man about her.'

'She's lonely?'

'I think so, yes.'

'Well, I don't want her to be unhappy. I'll ask Uncle Edward what he thinks.'

'No, don't do that,' Thomas said, too quickly. 'I mean, it's nothing to bother him with. Can't *you* make a decision without having to run to him?'

'Of course, I can.' Edward was indignant. 'Very well. Tell her she may marry.'

'Oh, my boy,' Thomas clapped his hands and laughed. 'I knew you would say that. But, to be honest, Edward, I've stretched the truth a little. You see, the truth is,' he paused and rubbed his beard again, 'your stepmother has already married.'

'Married? Without my permission?'

'Well, you've just given it, haven't you?'

'But—,' Edward protested feebly, 'but she didn't know I would.'

'Does it matter?'

'Well, who has she married?'

Thomas chuckled. 'Well... she's married *me*. There now, I knew you would be pleased. You're a good boy, Edward.'

Thomas departed, shouting a goodbye that resounded along

the corridor. Edward kicked at a stool, sending it spinning against the door and wishing it was his Uncle Tom.

CHELSEA, JULY

Thomas Seymour stormed into the hall and bellowed, 'Kate, where are you?'

Katherine appeared on the upstairs landing. 'Must you shout, Tom?'

He took the stairs two at a time, striding past her into the bedchamber. Unbuckling his sword belt, he threw it across the room. It landed with a clatter on the floor. Sprawling across the bed, he listened to Katherine's footsteps as she followed him into the room.

'What's he done now?' she asked quietly. 'He' didn't need to be named; she knew who would have upset her husband.

Thomas clasped his hands beneath his head and stared up at the tester. 'He won't let me have the jewels.'

'But they're the Queen of England's jewels,' she protested. 'They're mine.'

'But Brother Ned, Kate, says as you are no longer queen, you have no entitlement to them.'

She came to stand by the bed, her hand gripping the carved bedpost. 'We must appeal to the King.'

'I already have. He said the Protector knew best.'

'Edward said that, after all you've done for him?'

Thomas gave a careless shrug. 'I'm going to need more money, Kate. My young nephew's getting greedier by the day.'

'It's getting expensive, Tom,' she warned.

'I know, but the money isn't just for Edward. I need it to pay Fowler.'

'Who's Fowler?'

'One of the King's attendants. He's working for me now, passing on money to Edward. He also says very pleasant and encouraging things about me to him.'

'Not pleasant enough, it seems.'

'Fowler does what he can.' He looked at her through half-closed eyes. 'Come here.'

She smiled coyly. Hitching up her skirts, she climbed onto the bed. 'Husband,' she said, twirling her fingers in his beard, 'you are very serious today.'

'I'm tired.'

She slid her hand beneath his shirt. 'Too tired for this?'

His lips twitched in weary amusement as he looked at her, the shy yet passionate woman he had married. In the sunlight that streamed through the windows, her skin seemed dry and thin. The corners of her eyes and mouth had deep lines around them and he wondered why he had not noticed before how old Katherine had become. He placed her hand on his codpiece, an instruction.

As she began to untie the laces, there came the sound of running feet and Katherine realised they were no longer alone. 'Elizabeth,' she cried, pushing away from the bed and pressing her hands to her flaming cheeks.

'God damn you, girl,' Thomas roared, 'don't you know how to knock?' *How despicably like her brother she looks,* he thought, *the same superciliousness, the same arrogance.* Only the colour of her eyes was different. Edward's were blue and pale, like his dear sweet mother's. Elizabeth's were black, like the Boleyn whore, and they seemed to Thomas just as knowing. Could she really be only thirteen?

'You can't talk to me like that,' Elizabeth hissed, her fingers tightening around the book she had come to show her stepmother. 'I am the Princess Elizabeth.'

'You're the *Lady* Elizabeth,' he corrected with a snarl. 'No bastard can be a princess. And even bastards should learn some manners.'

Elizabeth hurled the book at him. It struck him on the chin and, suddenly, his anger which had been bubbling away all day, boiled over. He lunged forward and grabbed her arms. As she pounded futilely against his chest, he pulled her towards the bed.

'Tom, please,' Katharine said, 'she's only a child.'

'She's a witch. And she needs chastising.'

Elizabeth screamed as he forced her face down over his legs and clamped her wrists together with one large, powerful hand. With the other, he grabbed the hem of her skirts and yanked them up over her waist.

'Tom, no,' Katharine cried in alarm.

'By God's Death, stop kicking, you little devil.' He brought his hand down hard across Elizabeth's pale buttocks and she cried out in pain. The imprint of his hand showed red on the smooth white skin. The sight of it urged him on, smacking her again and again until his hand stung. He let go of her and Elizabeth slid to the ground. He shoved at her with his foot. 'Get out of my sight.'

Elizabeth, sobbing and pulling her skirts down, stumbled from the room.

Katherine turned on him, her face white with shock. 'Tom, how could you?'

'I will be master in my own house,' he panted. 'I won't have an insolent chit of a girl behaving like that.'

'She meant no harm—'

'Say nothing more,' he warned her, tearing off his jerkin and throwing it to the floor. He forced her back onto the bed and covered her body with his own. 'I will have obedience, Kate.'

On her knees in the hallway, Elizabeth tried to catch her breath, tugging strands of hair from her tear-dampened face. When she heard groans from the bedroom, she turned back to the open door, hoping they were cries of pain, that somehow, she had hurt him, but what she saw made her breath catch in her throat.

Katharine lay beneath Thomas, her eyes tightly closed, her body jolting with each thrust he made into her. He gasped and grunted, his face twisting grotesquely. She remembered a conversation from years before, when Robert Dudley had laughed at her ignorance and explained the carnal act to her. What he had described was an act of love, of mutual desire and pleasure. Surely, he couldn't have meant this!

CHAPTER 10

GREENWICH PALACE, DECEMBER 1548

Robert shuffled the pack of cards and yawned. It was tiresome having no company. Henry Sidney had been ill in bed with a head cold for two days, Barnaby Fitzpatrick had been shipped off to France on a diplomatic mission and the King was busy translating a Latin text into English. Or was it an English text into Latin? Robert couldn't remember.

He looked out of the window and saw John Fowler idly kicking gravel from the path onto the lawn. Robert unhooked the latch and leant out. 'John,' he halloed, 'nothing to do?' Fowler shook his head. 'Come in then, and play some cards.'

'What do you want to play?' Robert asked as Fowler took a chair on the other side of the table.

'Anything, I don't mind.'

Robert dealt the cards. 'You seem to be getting on well with the King lately. He must like your company.'

'I suppose so. Although it could be because of his uncle as well.'

'The Protector?'

'No,' Fowler shook his head. 'Thomas Seymour.'

'Oh, you're friendly with him, are you?'

'He places a great deal of trust in me, yes.'

'I've never seen you with him.'

'No, well, you wouldn't,' Fowler said uncomfortably. 'He likes to keep our friendship quiet.'

Robert grinned. 'Oh, yes?'

'Don't be filthy, Dudley, it's nothing like that. I act as intermediary between him and the King.'

'Doing what?'

'He gives me money to give to the King. You know how short the Protector keeps him.'

'Does the Protector knows you do this?'

'Good heavens, no.'

'But surely the King has mentioned it to him?'

'The King is most anxious that he doesn't find out because he is sure the Protector would put a stop to it. To tell the truth, Dudley, the King is growing mightily tired of the Protector.'

'You're very well informed, John,' Robert said admiringly. 'To have the confidence of the King *and* his uncle. Thomas Seymour must think very highly of you.'

Fowler preened. 'I flatter myself he does. He wouldn't entrust me with his plans else.'

Robert's heart quickened. 'And what plans are they?'

'To have the King all to himself.'

'How does he expect to do that?'

'He has a key to the Privy Chamber—' Fowler broke off abruptly. 'That is, I don't really know, Dudley. Whose play is it?'

Robert plucked a card from his hand and laid down a knave. 'Mine, I think.'

'So, he's got a key, has he?' John Dudley tapped his quill thoughtfully against his chin. 'What do you think he means to use it for, Rob?'

'I think,' Robert began tentatively, not wanting to sound foolish, 'that he plans to abduct the King.'

'I think you're right. I wonder if his wife, Katherine, dying in childbirth hasn't unhinged Tom's mind.'

'We could put more guards on the corridors to the Privy Chamber.'

'We could,' John nodded slowly, 'but I wonder if we should?'

'Why should we not?' Robert asked frowning.

'I'm just wondering whether it might not be better if we allowed dear Uncle Thomas to carry out his plan.'

'You're not serious, Father,' Robert said. 'We can't allow the King to be taken prisoner.'

'Well, I wasn't thinking of letting it get quite that far. Just allowing Thomas to make the attempt should be enough.'

'How can I help, Father?'

John considered for a moment. 'Anything he tries will be at night, I think, so he will try to take the King while he is abed. Did Fowler give you any idea how soon Thomas will try it?'

'No. He shut up when he realised what he was saying. I could try again—'

'No,' John held up his hand, 'say anything more and he may go running to Tom. We'll relax the guard on his rooms of a night, maybe even leave one of the doors open. Ah,' he jumped to his feet and exclaimed, 'I've got it! The King sleeps with his dog on the bed, doesn't he? And the little monster always barks at anyone who comes in the room, yes?'

'Always,' Robert confirmed.

'So, lock the dog outside the King's bedroom, just outside, mind, in the next room. Thomas will find it easy to get into the King's apartments and he'll get cocky. He'll get to just outside the bedchamber and then the dog will start barking and the whole corridor will be roused and we'll catch him red-handed.

'And that,' he patted Robert's face playfully, 'will be the end of Uncle Tom.'

JANUARY 1549

'Goodnight, Your Majesty.'

Robert bowed to the small, thin figure beneath the bedclothes. He looked about him, at Henry Sidney climbing into a pallet bed on the floor, at the dog sniffing around the edges of the room. He pulled the hangings together, enclosing the King in his bed. Waiting until Henry was settled, he moved to the dog and placing his foot behind its hind legs, gently nudged the animal towards the door. 'Goodnight,' he said softly, nodding to Henry that he could snuff out the candle.

He pulled the door shut behind him and locked it. The dog seemed unperturbed that he was away from his master but Robert knew that he would soon scratch at the door if he wasn't given somewhere soft to sleep, so he untied his cloak and threw it on the floor, bunching it up to make a bed for the dog. He whistled softly and the dog trotted towards him. Grasping the sturdy little body, he lifted it onto the makeshift bed. He waited to see the dog settle before moving out into the hallway where he locked the door, making sure the Yeoman Warders saw him do it. His room was a little way down the corridor. He made his way to it, laid down on the bed without undressing and waited.

Thomas had run across the gardens, almost slipping on the dewy grass, holding his sword against his hip to stop it jangling. Now, he was at the door, waiting for Fowler to let him into the palace. He wondered how long he had been standing there; cold was creeping up his legs and his nose was frozen. He also wondered if he could really go through with the night's business. *Good God, Tom*, he chided himself, *you're kidnapping a king.* But then that thought put a smile on his face, for the sheer audacity of the plan was something to be proud of.

He jumped as he heard the heavy bolt drawn back. A moment later, the door opened and Fowler stuck his head out of the black interior. His eyes widened as he saw Thomas.

'What?' Thomas asked with a roguish smile. 'Did you think I wouldn't come?'

Fowler gestured Thomas inside. As he closed the door, Thomas's strong hands gripped his arms and spun him around. Fowler smelt the wine on his breath as Thomas said, 'You're not going to let me down, are you?'

'No, my lord,' Fowler assured him, though there was a tremor in his voice.

'I'm glad to hear it. Now, come on.'

They soon reached the main corridor of the King's apartments and Thomas was surprised to see only one guard on duty. It made him stop and stare, so that Fowler nudged against him and asked an urgent, 'What's wrong?'

'Only one guard,' Thomas whispered through clenched teeth.

Fowler peered over his shoulder. 'So? That makes it easier, doesn't it?'

'I...,' Thomas hesitated, 'yes, I suppose it does.' Pushing the small feeling of unease to the back of his mind, Thomas strode towards the door. The guard turned his head but Thomas nodded at him and he looked away. Inserting his key into the lock, Thomas and Fowler stepped inside.

The darkness became total as the door closed behind them. Thomas's heart beat painfully in his chest and he heard the rushing of blood in his ears. Then there was another noise, loud and jarring. The dog had awoken and was barking furiously at the intruders. In the small room, the noise seemed to emanate from everywhere and Thomas stretched out his arms to find the source. His hand came into contact with something hairy and warm. Sharp teeth bit down, piercing the flesh of his hand. Blood burned as it broke free of the skin. Pain made him foolish. Thomas pulled out a pistol and shot blindly, the report deafening in the little room. The shot must have found its target for the animal gave an ear-splitting whine of pain and collapsed on its side, its little legs scrabbling at the air.

Thomas probed inside his purse, trying to find the next key. His bloodied fingers closed around it and he thrust it into the lock, cursing as he heard shouts from the corridor.

'My lord,' Fowler squealed, tugging at his cloak.

Thomas shrugged him off and he opened the inner door. A cry of alarm came from Fowler but he didn't look back. His eyes were on the bed, that enclosed box that held his prize. But before it stood a boy with his sword drawn, the tip pointing at him. It was all so absurd, he realised in a rush. How could he have hoped to succeed? He threw back his head and laughed, even as hands grabbed him and forced him to his knees.

'Is the King hurt?' someone shouted from the corridor.

'The King is unharmed,' Henry Sidney answered, his voice shaking with fear.

'What's that?'

'The King's spaniel,' a guard replied. 'It's been shot.'

A cry of anger and pain came from the bed. The curtains were torn apart and the young king stumbled out, tears streaming down his red cheeks. He flew past Thomas into the other room.

'Bring some light,' someone yelled. Almost immediately, a candle appeared. Other candles were held to the flickering flame and the darkness lifted.

'Who is it?' a new voice asked and Thomas's heart sank. *Please God, don't let it be him.*

'Thomas Seymour,' the guard said, entering the room.

Edward Seymour stumbled into the room and stared down at his brother.

'Yes, it's me,' Thomas snarled. 'God's Blood, but how this must please you, Ned.'

John Dudley strode in, Robert at his elbow. He looked at the scene before him and suppressed a smile. Fixing a frown upon his face, he took hold of Edward Seymour's elbow. 'My lord, what's happened?'

Seymour turned towards him, eyes wide and staring. He gestured at his brother.

'I see,' John said grimly. 'My lord, take yourself off. My son, Robert, will see to the King.'

'But Thomas?' Seymour managed to ask.

'He will be removed.'

'Yes, he can come with me.'

'My lord,' John said patiently, 'your brother must be put under arrest.'

Seymour raised frantic eyes to his. 'No,' he shook his head, 'he can't.'

'He must. You know he must.' Seymour continued to protest as John walked him out of the room. He gestured to the guard to take Thomas away.

Robert stepped back as his father passed. The King was curled on the floor, cradling the dead dog in his arms, its blood staining the front of his nightshirt. Robert knelt and put his arm around the boy's shoulder. 'Your Majesty,' he said softly, 'you had best come back to bed.'

'He... he killed him,' he sobbed.

'I know, Your Majesty.'

'Why did he have to kill him?'

'I don't know. It was a wicked thing to do.'

'I'll kill *him*.'

'Yes, Your Majesty.'

'I will, Rob, I mean it. I'll have his head cut off. I trusted him.'

'We have all been deceived in your uncle.' He pulled the boy to his feet. The nightshirt clung to the small body and Robert felt blood upon his own hands. 'We must wash you, Your Majesty.'

'My dog must be buried, Robert.'

'I'll see to it first thing in the morning. And if it will make you feel better, I have a bitch at home that whelped weeks ago. The pups are old enough to be separated from her now. I'll bring you one tomorrow. Shall you like that, Your Majesty?'

'Yes,' Edward sniffed. 'I would. Not that another dog could replace...'

Robert ushered him back to the bedchamber as the boy continued sobbing, and with the aid of Henry Sidney, stripped and washed him down. And if Henry wondered why Robert was fully dressed at such an hour, he made no mention of it.

CHAPTER 11

WHITEHALL PALACE, FEBRUARY 1549

Secretary William Cecil watched his master read the report he had just delivered. He almost felt sorry for him. It couldn't be easy reading of a brother's treachery.

'I can't—,' Seymour began, but the words caught in his throat. He swallowed hard. 'I can't believe my brother capable of all this.'

'It is quite incredible,' Cecil agreed.

'Kidnapping, piracy, counterfeiting, proposing marriage with the late king's daughters. Cecil, this can't all be true.'

'Your brother has confessed it, Your Grace.'

Seymour shook his head. Pointing to a section of the report, he asked, 'What is all this with the Lady Elizabeth?'

Cecil hesitated before answering. He liked Elizabeth. She was his idea of royalty: intelligent, charismatic and, most importantly, a Protestant. He was not eager to smear her character for he believed there was great promise in her, but there was no denying that she had endangered her reputation. It would be best for her if all the blame could be laid on Thomas Seymour.

'There is evidence that your brother behaved most inappropriately with her during his marriage to the late Queen Katherine. Apparently, he visited her in her bedchamber and played with her in bed. There is also an incident where he cut her dress to pieces while his wife held Elizabeth down. But I'm sure it was all just high spirits.'

'It says here she bore him a child.'

'That is only a rumour and one the Lady Elizabeth denies most vehemently. If you read further, she has demanded of Sir Robert Tyrwhit that a proclamation is made publicly clearing her name of the slander.'

'She demands?'

Cecil inclined his head in a sympathetic gesture. 'She does, Your Grace.'

Seymour shoved the report away and fell back into his chair. 'Thomas will be tried.'

'Indeed.'

'And found guilty.' Cecil did not reply. They both knew what a guilty verdict could mean for Thomas. 'The King will show mercy,' Seymour said decisively.

Cecil cleared his throat. 'It is my understanding, Your Grace, that the King is in no way kindly disposed towards his uncle.'

'He's angry, Cecil. Thomas killed his dog. It was a foolish thing to do.'

'It has been some little while since that incident, if I may say, and the King does not show any signs of forgiveness.'

'What do you know of it?' Seymour glared at him. 'Who have you been talking to?'

'No one, Your Grace,' Cecil lied smoothly. He had, in fact, been talking to John Dudley, who had been talking to his son Robert, who in his turn, had been talking with the King. Cecil's information was accurate. The King intended no mercy towards Uncle Thomas.

'I'll talk to him,' Seymour said. 'I don't doubt that Thomas will have to endure some little time in the Tower, but nothing more. And anyway, a spell in there will do him some good, knock some sense into him. Yes, I shall talk to the King.'

Cecil gave a tight smile and said nothing.

MARCH 1549

Seymour stood at his study window. Below him were the gardens, intricate, beautiful, but his eyes didn't see them. Instead, he saw himself and Thomas as young boys playing Hoodman Blind while their sister Jane looked on. There had been no rivalry then, no jealousy, and no ambition. What had happened to those children?

A shiver ran through him as he thought of that other child, his nephew, the King. He had talked with him, expecting mercy. Instead, he had discovered that Edward Tudor was every inch his father's son.

There came a knock at the door, and Seymour heard his name called. With dismay, he recognised the voice of John Dudley.

'Yes, what is it?'

John entered and closed the door behind him. 'I've just come from the Council chamber. We've been discussing the matter of Thomas Seymour and—'

'How dare you discuss anything without my being there?' Seymour turned on John.

'You were aware we were meeting,' John retorted. 'Business must continue, even if members choose to absent themselves.'

'I am the Lord Protector, Dudley. I am not a member of the Council but its head. Nothing is talked about without me.'

'We did think that perhaps it would be kinder not to involve you.'

'Kinder?' Seymour scoffed. 'I've never known the Privy Council to be kind.' He sat down at his desk and began sorting through his papers as if John wasn't there, as if he could will him away.

'I have the warrant here, Your Grace,' John persisted. 'Will you sign it now?'

'Warrant?'

'For Thomas's execution.'

Seymour gave a little, mirthless laugh. 'For God's sake, John. I know he has to be punished—'

'Punished?'

'—but aren't you taking this just a little bit too far?'

'I don't think so, no. Thomas Seymour has been tried and found guilty of thirty-three separate treasons. There is only one punishment.'

'He's the King's uncle, John. What would you have the King do?'

'What he must. Punish a traitor.'

'You would have the King execute his own uncle?'

'It is the sentence for a traitor.'

'I know that, damn you.'

John slapped the paper on the desk before Seymour. 'The warrant.'

'You expect me to take that to the King?'

'You have no choice.'

Seymour closed his eyes and sighed wearily. 'He's my brother, John.'

'It's unfortunate... but still.'

'I won't do it.'

'Edward—'

Seymour slammed his hand down on the desk. 'I will not condemn my own brother. You cannot ask it of me.'

'I'm not asking.'

'For Jesu's sake, have you no mercy?'

'Mercy?' John spat, blood rushing into his cheeks, his black eyes flashing. 'When I was nine years old, I watched my father's head cut off to the sound of the cheering mob, all so King Henry could enhance his popularity with his people. My father was no traitor, yet he was branded one and my family lived in ignominy for years. I've had to work hard and crawl my way back to favour, and you beg for mercy for your treacherous brother, who's not worth the shit he walks in. You waste your breath crying for mercy. Mine's all spent.' He wiped his mouth with the back of his hand. 'And isn't this sudden display of brotherly love rather out of place? I'll wager this is all just for show and truly all you feel is joy that you're finally going to be rid of him.'

With a roar, Seymour pushed against the desk. It turned on its side, papers and quills tumbling to the floor. John stumbled backwards, shocked, as Seymour landed a punch on his jaw and he dropped to the floor. Seymour kicked at him, weak, ineffectual kicks that John easily blocked. He grabbed at Seymour's ankle and pulled so that Seymour lost his balance and fell backwards against the wall. In an instant, John had jumped up and held Seymour by the throat. He drew back his arm, fingers curling into a fist. The fight went out of Seymour and he sagged beneath John's hold.

'I'll forgive you for that,' John panted, 'because I understand you're upset.' He released his grip and Seymour slumped to the floor. John snatched up the warrant. 'Now, will you sign this?' Edward turned his head to the wall. 'Then I'll go to the King. I doubt if he will have any qualms about signing it. You can explain yourself to him.'

'No, stop!' Edward grabbed at John's leg. 'I'll sign it, I'll sign it.' He scrabbled around on the floor, found a quill and jabbed it in a puddle of ink. John handed him the warrant and Seymour scratched his name on the bottom. 'I am the King's loyal servant,' he whimpered, trying to blow the ink dry. John snatched it from his hands.

'Good for you,' he sneered and stepped over Seymour's legs to the door. Seymour heard his footsteps heading towards the King's apartments. He reached out and pushed the door shut. Resting his forehead upon his knees, he wept for his brother.

CHAPTER 12

WHITEHALL PALACE, JUNE 1549

John Dudley yawned and wondered what the time was. It had been dark for several hours, so he reasoned it could be one or two in the morning. He rolled his head, wincing as bones cracked in his neck. He looked across enviously to William Paget who had fallen asleep hours before, his head resting on his arms.

It was a disturbing, worrying time for the Council. A recent law, the Enclosure Act, had caused outrage. Land that had always been free and open to the people and their animals to graze upon was now fenced in at the whim of the landowners who wanted to create deer parks and gardens. With their livelihoods under threat, the people revolted and began tearing down the hedges and fences, fighting to defend their rights and take back control of the common land. A successful uprising in Cornwall had soon encouraged others to act.

John rubbed his knuckles against his weary eyes. Opening them, William Cecil came blearily into focus. 'What news?' he asked of Cecil peremptorily.

Cecil took a seat next to him. 'I'm getting further reports of uprisings. In Essex, Hertfordshire, Oxfordshire, Suffolk... The list goes on, my lord.'

'Jesu,' John breathed. 'How far is this going to spread before the Protector decides to do something?'

'He's in his office issuing orders,' Cecil replied.

'Aye, and they'll contradict all the orders *we've* been issuing,

Cecil. God only knows what's going through Seymour's mind. First, he's against the Enclosure Act, then he's for it, then he's against it again. Is it any wonder the people think they're not breaking any laws when even the Protector can't make up his mind as to what's legal and what is not? My own parks have been attacked, Cecil. My pasture land ploughed up and sown with bloody oats.'

'I'm sorry to hear it.'

'I could bear it better if we had a plan to deal with these rebels. Even Paget,' John gestured at the snoring man, 'has told the Protector he's making bad decisions, but Seymour won't listen.'

'My master has certainly changed for the worse since the death of his brother.'

'He was never one to listen kindly to advice before. Now, he turns a deaf ear to even his closest friends.'

'Have *you* tried, my lord?'

John gave a short, hard laugh. 'He won't listen to my advice.'

The chamber doors suddenly burst open. Paget awoke with a snort. Seymour strode in.

'Dudley, you must go to Norfolk. A rebellion has broken out there and one of the damned landowners is leading it. Lord Northampton, who I sent there to maintain law and order, is in my office, quivering like a jelly because they chased him out. So I want *you* to go there and finish the job I sent *him* to do. I expect you to leave immediately.'

'I'll talk with Northampton first.' John pushed past Seymour, disappearing into the darkness of the corridor.

'Very well,' Seymour called after him. He looked at Paget, who jumped up from his seat. 'What the devil are you doing?'

'Nothing, Your Grace,' Paget protested.

'Well, you should be doing something, you lazy dolt.' With that, he turned on his heel and stormed back to his office.

Paget stared open-mouthed after his retreating figure. Cecil gave Paget a sympathetic smile and followed after his master.

STANFIELD HALL, NORFOLK, JULY 1549

Amy Robsart plucked one last flower to complete the daisy chain. Giggling to herself, she arranged it on the head of the boy asleep beside her on the grass. Yawning, she too lay down, making a pillow of her arms. She knew it was getting late and was expected home but it was very pleasant to be able to lie back and do nothing with the sun warm upon her face.

Ned snorted and woke up. Lifting his head, his pale blue eyes puffy and red-rimmed, he noted with some surprise, 'I fell asleep. What are you laughing at?'

'Nothing,' she lied.

Suspicion mounting, he raised his hand to his head and felt the floral crown. He threw it away with a snort of disgust. 'You let me lay there with that on my head?'

'Oh, don't be cross, Ned, there was nobody to see. Come, you're still sleepy. You can lay your head on me if you like.'

The offer placated him. He lowered himself to her lap and she began to run her fingers through his thin, fair hair.

'They'll be looking for me soon,' she said.

'They know you're with me.'

'But we have visitors this evening.'

'Who?'

'The Earl of Warwick and some of his officers.'

'The Earl of Warwick, John Dudley himself, eh? Aren't you honoured?'

She gave his face a harmless slap. 'My father *is* honoured.'

'They're coming because of Kett, I suppose?'

'I suppose so.'

Ned plucked a blade of grass and stuck the end in his mouth. 'Robert Kett and his men tore my father's fences down, you know?'

Amy frowned. 'I don't understand. Kett's a landowner like your father. Why would he join men who are against the landowners?'

'Father says Kett was never one of us. He has always been a nuisance.'

'Well, I think Robert Kett has a point. After all, what right do the landowners have to stop the people letting their animals graze where they always have?'

'Amy!' Ned knocked her hand away and sat up. 'You're talking against your own kind when you say such things. Your father and mine.'

'I'm only saying I don't think it's fair.'

'Well, keep your opinions to yourself. If the Earl of Warwick heard you—'

'Oh, he won't be paying me any mind. I've had instructions from Father. I'm to be obedient and quiet, and amusing too, if I can manage it. To tell the truth, Ned, I'm dreading meeting them. I'm such a stupid girl. What can I possibly say or do to amuse them?'

'You're not stupid, Amy.'

Amy smiled tenderly at him. 'You don't have to be kind, Ned. I know I'm not clever or accomplished. I can't read and I can barely write my own name. I can't compare with London girls, I'm sure.'

'I wouldn't want a London girl.'

'Oh, but you do want *me*?' she said coquettishly.

'You know I do, Amy.'

'I know nothing of the sort. It's been such a long time since you kissed me, I thought you no longer cared.'

'I didn't dare to. I thought you might not want me to kiss you again. I suppose I should have asked—'

'Why must you ask? Why can't you just kiss me, Ned?'

'Amy,' he said, shocked, 'you sound like a wanton.'

She glared at him. 'Passion, Ned, I want you to have a passion for me. So much so that you can't help yourself.'

'You want me to kiss you now?'

'God a'Mercy, yes.'

Ned licked his lips and looked about him, checking they were alone. He leaned closer to Amy and kissed her, his lips sliding clumsily over hers. She broke the kiss before him.

'I should go now,' she said, getting to her feet and smoothing down her skirts. She looked down at Ned, whose cheeks were reddening, aware that his kiss had not been a success. 'Why don't you come to the Hall tonight? You'll be support for me when I make a fool of myself.'

'Yes, all right. I need to go home and change though.'

'Yes, you must be smart before the Earl. But be as quick as you can, Ned.'

Amy watched him as he hurried away, reflecting that he was the boy she supposed she would marry one day. Her heart sank a little at the prospect. Ned was really very sweet and she knew he cared deeply for her but he fell so short of what she wanted.

Oh, Amy, she said to herself, *do you even know what you want?*

Amy tried to pull away. 'I must go.'

'Not yet,' Robert said, tightening his hold on her.

'It's too soon,' she protested feebly as he pressed kisses to her neck. 'I only met you tonight.'

'But, Amy, I could die tomorrow.'

'Oh, don't say that, I couldn't bear it.' *How was it possible to feel so much for a boy she had only just met*, she wondered?

Her fears for the evening had been quickly dispelled. The Earl of Warwick had been courteous and warm, not at all as she had expected. He had complimented her father on his pretty daughter and praised his house. And then his handsome sons had drawn her into conversation and it had been clever and amusing, so unlike the conversations she had with her family, with Ned.

Ned. How she wished she had not asked him to come. He had arrived late and behaved rudely, taking an instant dislike to Ambrose and Robert, though they had done nothing to deserve it. No, it was just Ned being ... well, Ned. He had stuck his fingers in dishes and sucked them clean; he had told vulgar jokes and been the only one to laugh at them. Amy wondered how she could ever have thought she could marry him.

She compared Ned to Robert, and Ned came out wanting. Ned was fair, lumpy and plain; Robert was dark, slim-limbed and handsome. Ned was dull and slow-witted; Robert was intelligent and quick.

So it was that midnight found them together in a dark corner of a stairwell with Amy wondering how she dared to make an assignation with a stranger, and Robert hardly able to believe his luck.

'It's true, I might die,' Robert realised, putting a dampener on his ardour. 'Father will offer pardons, but he doesn't believe Kett will surrender.' He slumped against the wall, still holding her hand.

'Are you frightened?' she asked.

'A bit. I've never been in battle before.'

'But you know how to fight?'

'Every man knows how to fight. It's what we're brought up to do. I just hope I don't disgrace my father.'

'You won't. I know you won't.'

He smiled then and pulled her towards him. 'Would you miss me? If I died?'

'I think I would die myself.'

He kissed her then, hard, and she pressed her body against his. She would have given herself to him, if he had asked. But instead, he said, 'I must get to bed. I wish I could stay with you, Amy, but I dare not be tired for tomorrow.'

'And I would not have you so,' she declared. 'Not if it puts you in danger.'

'Shall I see you in the morning? Will you see me off?'

'Oh, I will, I will. And Robert, my sweet Robert, you must come back to me. I couldn't bear it if you went back to London and never thought of me again.'

He gently kissed her forehead. 'I'll come back,' he promised.

The city of Norwich fell.

Robert Kett refused the offer of pardons and he and his men defended the city doggedly, but John Dudley and his army broke through their defences. Once inside the walls of the city, they encountered fierce resistance and it took two days and a night of ferocious fighting until the rebels were subdued.

There was no time to enjoy the victory. Examples had to be made of the men who had rebelled against their king. Robert saw a side of his father he had never seen before as a gallows was hastily erected in the marketplace and he had watched as forty-nine of the rebels were hanged, swallowing down vomit as their legs kicked in the air. At Norwich, Robert felt he had left his childhood behind.

Robert galloped across the fields, glad to be away from the camp and heading for Stanfield Hall. He pulled his horse up abruptly as he neared a large oak, as he saw Amy sitting beneath it.

She looked up, shading her eyes with her hand. 'Robert,' she cried, jumping up.

Without a word he dismounted, letting the reins trail on the ground. He embraced her, taking her breath away with his kiss.

'Is it over?' she asked when he released her.

He nodded, his face grim. 'It's done. The rebels are defeated.'

Her face fell. 'You're leaving, then.'

'In an hour or so.'

'You kept your promise to come back to me, though.'

'I always keep my promises.'

She stepped away from him, tears falling unchecked. 'I love you.'

'Amy—'

'No, don't tell me I don't. I know what I feel. I do love you. Won't you say it back? Couldn't you even pretend that you loved me, just a little?'

'I don't need to pretend. But I am going home, to London. I can't change that, Amy.'

'But would you marry me, if you could?'

He didn't hesitate. 'If I could, yes, of course.'

'You're already betrothed?'

'No.'

'Then why can't—'

'Amy, my father is an earl. Your father is only...,' he searched for a word that would not be too insulting, 'a gentleman. I'm expected to marry someone of my own station.'

'Am I so far beneath you?' she whimpered.

In truth, she was. She had little education, she could not read or write, nor ride nor sing. She lacked the gloss of sophistication that he was used to at court. She was in every way inferior and yet, he wanted her.

'I can ask my father about you,' he offered.

'You will?' she asked, her reddened eyes widening in hope.

'I will,' he promised.

ELY PLACE, SEPTEMBER 1549

John rubbed at his temples, trying to smooth away the pain. A day spent arguing in the Council chamber had left him tired and with a pounding head, so he had returned home, hoping to rest. But there was more work when he arrived home: letters from courtiers pressing their suits, others offering their services in the hope of some reward, and much to his annoyance, letters from the Protector's secretaries with more unnecessary instructions for him.

He reached for the wine his servant had left out for him. As the liquid trickled down his throat, he heard footsteps just outside his door. They didn't pass on but returned and repeated their measure. He listened for a moment, the noise grating on his fragile nerves.

'Christ's blood,' he roared, wincing as the shout jarred inside his skull, 'whoever that is, either go away or come in.'

The pacing stopped and a moment later, the door opened with a squeal. Robert's head appeared in the opening. 'It's only me, Father.'

'What do you want?'

Robert hesitated. 'It's nothing. It can wait.'

'You've already disturbed me. You may as well come in and tell me what you want.'

Robert stepped inside. 'Well, I'm not sure you will approve, Father, but I…,' he hesitated as the frown on John's forehead deepened, 'I have asked Amy Robsart to marry me and I ask your permission.'

John stared at him, taken aback. 'Who the devil is Amy—?' he began. 'Wait. You don't mean Sir John Robsart's daughter? From Norfolk?'

'Yes, Father, her.'

'You've got her with child?'

'No, Father, I have not,' Robert cried indignantly.

'Then, why do you want to throw yourself away on a squire's daughter?' John demanded. 'And anyway, what makes you think you can choose a wife for yourself? Your mother and I will choose who you are to marry, as we did for your brothers and sisters.'

Robert pursed his lips and nodded his head understandingly. 'I see. The answer's No, then?'

John's eyes widened. Must he suffer a thousand petty tyrannies by Edward Seymour at the court only to come home and endure insolence from his son? He jumped up from his chair and charged around the desk. His hand whipped across Robert's face.

'You dare talk to me like that again, boy, and I'll have you beaten for an hour. You understand me?'

Robert's eyes were watering from the blow. He turned his face away. 'Yes.'

'Yes, what?'

'Yes, Father.'

John returned to his chair, his hand stinging. 'What has this girl to recommend her, other than a pretty face?'

Robert swallowed, hoping his voice wouldn't quaver. 'She is an heiress, Father. She will inherit substantial lands in Norfolk. And I did think that as you have no lands in Norfolk at the moment, they might be of some use to you.'

John slowly rubbed his chin as he considered Robert's words. 'Well, you are right. I don't have any influence in that county. And the girl. I suppose you think you're in love with her?'

Robert nodded, his eyes still on the floor.

'Well,' John said, his voice losing some of its fury, 'as it happens, I don't have any marriage plans for you, and as you say, there would be advantages to the match. I'll write to Sir John in the morning.'

'You mean I can marry Amy?' Robert said, finally looking up.

'Yes, you can marry her,' John said, trying to avoid looking at his son's flaming cheek.

'Thank you. I apologise for my rudeness, Father.'

John gave a tight nod, dismissing him. As the door closed behind Robert, John slammed his hand down on the desk in anger at himself. Never before had he lost his temper with a child of his. It was his business at court, he knew, that was fraying his nerves, the behaviour of the Protector that was causing his headaches. He couldn't go on like this, taking his frustrations out on his family. Something would have to be done, and soon.

CHAPTER 13

ELY PLACE, OCTOBER 1549

'Really, John,' William Herbert made an attempt at a laugh, 'why all the secrecy?'

John had just ushered him into his study and was now checking the corridor to make sure there was no one lurking. He closed the door and turned to William.

'I'm sorry to involve you in this, William, but I need friends about me now.'

'Why, John, whatever's the matter?' William touched his arm in concern.

John barely noticed and strode past him. 'I've had enough. I can't allow this to go on.'

'Can't allow what? John, talk sense.'

John stood at the window and looked out across the garden. 'The Protector has to be brought down, William. He's gone too far. I put down a rebellion and how does he reward me? With scorn and indifference. And he mocks me. Lands that I had promised to a man who had greatly helped me, he deliberately gave to others. He made me look like a fool and a liar and for nothing but spite.'

'The Protector is acting unreasonably, I agree, John, and not just with you,' William said. 'But he is the King's uncle. His position is secure.'

John shook his head. 'No, not as secure as you might think. He's made a lot of enemies at court, not just me, and even the people have turned against him since he sent his brother to the scaffold. Even Paget, who as you know, has been his ally since before the death of King Henry, has been complaining about him and begging him to listen to the Council. I promise you, William, the Protector is standing on dangerous ground.'

'Well, you'll have my support, but how can it be done?'

'We'll have to be careful. We can't afford for it to look as if we're just trying to get rid of him to put ourselves in power. And, in truth, that's not what this is about. Seymour will ruin this country if we don't pull him down. I make no bones about it, William. This comes from me and men can either follow me or not. Now, Seymour's taken himself and the King to Hampton court. He's demanding the Council convene there. I shall not go. If he has any sense left in his head, he will realise what that means. Instead, I shall write to the other counsellors, telling them what I intend and if they're with me, they can meet here at Ely Place. We'll then send word to the Protector that he no longer has the backing of the Council and he should relinquish his post.'

'And if he doesn't?'

'Then we'll have to remove him forcibly. I don't want to do it like that, but if it's the only way...,' John shrugged.

'And then what?'

'Then the Council rules as one, as King Henry originally intended.'

'You seem to have it all planned out, John.'

John gave a mirthless laugh. 'William, it's the only way I work.'

Robert and Ambrose were up on the Minstrel's Gallery, watching as men and their masters entered the Great Hall.

'How many are there, do you think?' Robert asked.

'About fifty down there,' Ambrose replied, 'maybe three hundred outside.'

'That many?' Robert was impressed. 'And all at Father's request.'

'There you two are.' Their mother, Jane, entered, a little out of breath from the stairs. 'What are you doing up here?'

'Just watching,' Ambrose said, pointing at the hall below.

Jane joined them at the rail, standing between her sons. 'I hope your father knows what he's doing.'

'Of course he does,' Ambrose said, putting his arm around her shoulder. 'Just look at the support he has.'

She shook her head. 'It's dangerous, what they're planning.'

'You mustn't worry, Mother,' Robert said carelessly.

'Oh, it's all very well for you to say that, you haven't heard the latest news.'

'What news?' he asked.

A strained look came into her face. 'The Protector has taken the King to Hampton Court and issued a proclamation ordering the counsellors to bring their men to defend the King against your father. He's making out that your father is threatening the King's life.'

'But that's a lie,' Robert cried. 'Father would never do that.'

'I know that and so do you, but the people may not.' She pointed down at the men milling about below. 'Your father wants them to march on Hampton court and remove the Protector by force.' There were tears in her eyes as she spoke and Ambrose mouthed at Robert to keep quiet.

All three turned as the floorboards behind them creaked. John appeared at the top of the stairs. He took one look at his wife. 'Enough of that, Jane,' he said sternly. 'There's no call for tears. It seems we're not marching anywhere.'

'Why not?' she asked, wiping her cheeks.

'Some of the aldermen down there agree to muster men to defend London but not to remove the Protector. Without their support, we're going nowhere.'

'Then this could all be for nothing,' Jane burst out, 'and the Protector will have you arrested and sent to the Tower.'

John didn't look at her. 'We'll see,' he said quietly, moving to the rail and studying the scene below. A dog, brought by one of the counsellors, barked at one of the household dogs and began to strain at its leash. Angry shouts and strained laughter resounded around the hall.

John started. A man wearing the Protector's livery had just entered the hall. John called down to one of his men below to bring the man up to him. He waited, a cold chill running through him as his mind ran through the possibilities of what message the man had come to deliver. An order to be taken to the Tower perhaps, as Jane feared?

'My lord,' the man greeted John with a bow of his head.

'You have a message from the Protector?'

'Yes, my lord.' The messenger delved into a leather bag slung over his shoulder and pulled out a letter. He handed it to John.

John snatched it from him. He snapped open the seal and read quickly. 'The damned fool,' he laughed and brushed past the messenger. He ran out of the gallery, his footsteps banging on the wooden stairs and reappeared in the hall below.

'Listen to me,' he shouted and the room fell instantly silent. 'You good men of London, who are mindful of your duty and loyal to our king. Not fifteen minutes ago, you told me that you were not prepared to march against the Protector but only to defend this city should he attack it. Well, I have just received a letter from him and I feel sure that you will change your minds when you hear what he writes.' He paused, making sure he had their complete attention. 'He tells me that if we threaten and intend to kill him, then he will ensure that the King dies first.'

His audience gasped as one. The Protector would hold the King hostage!

'I tell you, I and my fellow counsellors never intended the Protector's death. We merely wanted him removed from office. He has claimed I threaten the King. That was and has never been my intention. This letter is proof that it is he who threatens the life of our beloved sovereign. So, now I ask you again. Will you help me remove this pernicious man?'

This was greeted by a loud shout of Aye and Robert heard his mother breathe a sigh of relief. She turned to look at him and shook her head in disbelief. 'Your father, Rob, has the luck of the devil.'

THE TOWER, OCTOBER 1549

John glanced down at the floor to a chunk of bread that had fallen from the table. 'You haven't eaten,' he said.

The man sitting on the stool by the fireplace turned his back to him. 'What do you care? Isn't it enough you have imprisoned me? Must you come to gloat?'

John sighed and rubbed his forehead. 'Edward—'

'You call me Lord Protector,' Seymour hissed.

'Your Protectorship has been rescinded.'

'You can't do that.'

'No, *I* couldn't. Not by myself. But the Council, acting as one, has ruled. That is how it should be.'

'Does the King know I am here?'

'He knows you are in custody, yes.'

'Ah, so he doesn't know I'm *here*. What other lies are you telling him, John?'

'No lies, Edward. The boy is not a fool, he cannot be ignorant of what you've been doing. You drag him off to Hampton Court—'

'For his safety.'

'For your own. I showed him your letter, Edward. You remember? The one where you promised to kill him if you were in danger.'

Seymour seemed to shrink into himself, pulling the blanket tighter about his shoulders. 'That was written rashly. I wasn't thinking properly. I didn't mean it.'

'That's a feeble defence. You didn't mean it? It's treason to even think of the King's death, let alone threaten to kill him yourself. Do you really think a 'sorry' will excuse you?'

Seymour didn't answer. John wandered around the small room, glancing idly at the graffiti cut into the stone walls by previous prisoners.

'Where's my wife?' Seymour asked quietly.

'At Somerset House.'

'Under guard?'

'We didn't think that was necessary.'

'So, what are you going to do with me? Put my head on the block like you did with my brother?'

'You signed his death warrant,' John reminded him.

Seymour nodded, his chin sinking deeper upon his chest. 'And I shall be damned for that. I have been damned for it.'

'This has all been of your own making.'

'And a little of yours, confess it, John.'

'You shouldn't have treated me so badly, Edward. You made enemies when you didn't need to.'

Seymour suddenly jumped up from the stool and hurtled

towards John, thrusting his face at him. John smelt his sour breath and noted the heavy, bloodshot eyes.

'You tell the King I'm here,' Seymour screamed, speckling John's face with spittle. 'I'm his uncle. You can't do this to me.'

John stepped back. The fury in Seymour's eyes was unsettling. He banged on the door to be let out and a guard swung it open. He stepped outside, watching while it was locked and barred. Seymour continued to scream his protests as John walked away.

WHITEHALL PALACE, NOVEMBER 1549

Robert ran up to his father in the corridor. 'I'm sorry, Father, I couldn't think of a way to stop her.'

'Stop who?' John demanded, not stopping. He hurried on through to the Presence Chamber and immediately had an answer.

Edward Seymour's wife, Anne, was on her knees before the King. John stopped dead. He glared at Robert who had hurried to catch up with him. 'How did she get in here?'

Robert shook his head in answer, mumbling another apology.

Just then, the King caught sight of John. 'Warwick, where is my uncle?'

John stepped up to the dais. 'Under arrest in the Tower, Your Majesty.'

The boy's small pointed face hardened. 'I was told he was ill. I thought he was being held at Somerset House.'

'He is ill, Your Majesty,' Anne said, her hands shaking, 'because of the threats to his life. The Council will kill him if you do not give him your pardon.'

'Godfather,' the King turned to Archbishop Cranmer, who was shifting uneasily from one foot to the other, 'is this true?'

'We feared for your life if he were to remain at liberty, Your Majesty.'

'But my uncle has never done me any harm,' Edward persisted.

'The lords of the Council had good reason to suspect his intentions—'

'No, I will not have it,' the boy stamped his foot. 'I want to see my uncle.'

John silenced a further protestation from Cranmer with a hard, brief stare. 'Of course, Your Majesty, if you wish it. We shall have him brought here so you may see him.'

'At once, my lord,' the King said, stepping down from the dais. John gestured for Robert to follow after the boy.

John turned to Anne Seymour and held out his hand. She looked at it scornfully, but then slid hers into it and struggled to her feet. 'I thank you,' she said, and John saw how much it cost her to say those words.

'I serve the King, my lady.'

'As does—,' she sniffed, 'as did my husband.'

'Indeed. Good day, Lady Anne.'

'Why did you agree for the King to see him?' Cranmer hissed in John's ear when she had gone.

John turned to him. 'Would you go against the King's wishes?'

'Not willingly, but the Protector *was* a threat and had to be removed. I would have thought you were the last person who would want the King and his uncle reconciled.'

'I didn't go through all this for personal gain, Cranmer,' John said heatedly. 'If I had, then I have failed, for Wriothesley has become closer to the King than I.'

'Yes,' Cranmer nodded, his face creasing into even more lines, 'I've been meaning to talk to you about that. Do you know Wriothesley's been corresponding with the Lady Mary?'

John did know, thanks to his spies, but he was ever one to keep information to himself. 'What has he been saying to her?'

'That he hopes and believes that soon she will be allowed to hear Mass again. And he's told the Spanish ambassador that the Pope will soon be restored as the head of the Church in England.'

'I would be very sorry if that were true.'

'And what of me?' Cranmer said, clutching his cross. 'If England returns to Rome, all my work will be undone. And my life, very like, forfeit.'

'Cranmer, you must stay calm,' John said. 'Let's just see what happens when the King meets his uncle.'

Cranmer walked away, muttering his unhappiness. John moved to a window seat to consider the changing situation. If the King would not believe his uncle to be guilty of treason, then it would be wise to appear to be a friend to Seymour. It would take a bit of deft manoeuvring on his part and Wriothesley was going to be a problem, John knew, but then when wasn't Wriothesley a problem? What John needed to do now was acquire friends. All right, he conceded with a wry smile to himself, perhaps friends was the wrong word. Allies then, he needed allies. He began making a mental list of his fellow counsellors, those who were likely to side with Wriothesley and those with him, and was pleased to find that the balance tipped in his favour.

CHAPTER 14

ELY PLACE, NOVEMBER 1549

Robert knocked and waited, his ear pressed against the door. He heard the murmurings of his father's voice and then the shouted 'Come in.'

'Yes, Rob, what is it?' John asked as Robert entered the room. William Paulet stood at his side.

'Could I have a word with you, Father?'

'Of course. William, would you mind leaving us for a few minutes.' It was a command, not a request, and Paulet demonstrated his irritation at having to make way for a boy with a very audible sigh.

'Well?' John asked when he had left.

'I've just been speaking with the King, Father,' Robert began. 'The meeting with his uncle this morning has unsettled him a little, I think.'

'I don't see why it should,' John said with a frown. 'The boy hardly said a word to him.'

'He said he couldn't think of anything to say. He's rather concerned at how his uncle is being treated at the Tower. He says he looked very much changed.'

'Well, he's thinner, certainly. Worry will do that to a man. But he's not been ill-treated, far from it.'

'I assured him he wasn't, Father, that you wouldn't allow that to happen. But he's no fool. Young he may be, but the King does understand what has happened.'

'Is he angry at *me*?'

'No, I don't think so. He admits that his uncle has behaved foolishly. He even said it would do him good to be shown his place. You know how close the Protector kept him—'

'Seymour threatened to take his life,' John cut in. 'Does he know that?'

'He doesn't believe his uncle would ever harm him.'

John sighed and rubbed his chin. 'Well, what does he want done with him?'

'I think he wants him to be set free.'

'But,' John floundered with his hands in the air, 'a process has begun. I don't believe this. Does he want him back as Protector?'

Robert shook his head. 'He hasn't said so, no. He understands that charges of treason have to be answered, but he doesn't want his uncle to be punished any more than he already has been.'

'He said that?'

'He implied it.'

'Well, then—'

'He sought me out, Father. He wanted to speak with me so I would speak to you.'

John nodded grimly. 'He certainly isn't a fool, is he?'

'No, Father.'

'Well, Wriothesley isn't going to like it. But still... I've had your mother become friendly with Seymour's wife, much to her displeasure because she thinks her an odious woman, just in case. So, that should serve me well, at least.'

'Can I tell the King anything?'

'You can give him my assurances that Edward Seymour is being treated fairly and I will do my utmost to have him back on the Council. But not as its head, Rob,' John pointed a finger at him. 'Make it clear to the King that his uncle no longer works alone. The Council of Regency, as his father decreed, will act in the King's name.'

Robert departed and Paulet came back in. 'What was that all about?' he asked.

John put his hand on his shoulder. 'Oh, William. It seems we're going to have to find a way to work with Seymour again.'

The door burst open and Wriothesley strode in. 'What the devil are you playing at, Dudley?'

John took a sip of wine before answering. 'Playing, Thomas?'

'I've just heard, from William Paulet, mind, not from you, that we're letting Seymour go free.'

'That is correct.'

'Would you care to explain why?'

'The King wishes it.'

'So?'

'I cannot gainsay the King, Thomas. He is prepared to show mercy and we can do nothing but obey.'

'I can see where this is leading,' Wriothesley nodded knowingly. 'Seymour reinstated—'

'No,' John cut him short, 'that will not happen.'

'But if the King—'

'The King understands. Seymour must answer the charges of treason laid against him. Providing he admits to them he will be released from the Tower and invited back onto the Council.'

'Back onto the Council,' Wriothesley spluttered. 'After what we had to do to remove him? And besides, I had a plan—'

John's eyes narrowed. 'You had what, Thomas?'

Wriothesley licked his lips. 'I had hopes that the country would be in better hands than Seymour's.'

'And it will be. Ours. Yours and mine.'

Wriothesley snorted a laugh. 'We disagree on so many things, Dudley.'

'Only on matters of religion,' John replied smoothly. 'Oh, don't look at me like that, Thomas. I know you cling to the Old Faith. That's no concern of mine. Of course, the King would prefer it if it were not so, but...,' he gestured with his hands. 'Tell me, the hopes you had. Anything in particular?'

Wriothesley stared into John's unblinking black eyes. 'No,' he lied. 'Nothing in particular. I'll go now. Good day, Dudley.'

John watched him leave with an amused smile. *Oh, Thomas,* he thought, *I know exactly what you had hoped for. A return to popery with Mary on the throne. Well, if I have anything to do with it, you're not even going to come close.*

ELY PLACE, JANUARY 1550

'You're the last to arrive, my lord,' Robert informed Wriothesley as he led him up the stairs to John's bedchamber.

'A damned inconvenience having to come here,' Wriothesley muttered. 'What exactly is wrong with your father?'

'A rheum in his head, my lord. He has been very ill.' Robert stopped and knocked.

William Paulet opened the door and said, 'Ah, there you are, Wriothesley.'

Wriothesley stepped through and Robert was about to leave when he saw John, propped up in the bed and swamped in blankets, discreetly gesture for him to enter. He closed the door behind him and moved to a shadowed corner of the crowded room.

John had summoned the entire Privy Council to Ely Place to hold their meeting there. He had been ill for a couple of weeks – Robert had told the truth – but it had become politic to prolong his illness. He wanted to be on home ground when the inevitable happened.

John knew Wriothesley believed he held John's future in his hands. Wriothesley had, along with William Paulet, interrogated Edward Seymour in the Tower. Vengeance mixed with envy had led Seymour to admit his treasons but he had told his accusers that John Dudley had been with him every step of the way. Whether this was true or not, Wriothesley didn't care to wonder. He saw an opportunity to get rid of Dudley, his chief rival and opponent on the Council. Unfortunately for Wriothesley, he had few friends, and William Paulet was not one of them. Paulet had informed John of everything Seymour and Wriothesley had said. So, John was ready for Wriothesley when he was about to accuse him of treason.

It happened rather sooner than John had expected. Arundel had just begun to speak of routine matters when Wriothesley silenced him with an, 'I must speak. You must listen to me.' All heads turned to Wriothesley, who swelled with importance under their scrutiny. 'Edward Seymour has confessed his treasons. Ordinarily, such a confession would mean death, but I'm told the King wishes Edward Seymour to be set free. Now, I have every respect for the King, but he is young and has a kind and generous heart. He does not see the evil in his uncle. And others close to him.'

His eyes met John's and a glimmer of complete understanding passed between them. John knew the moment to act had come.

'My lord,' he cried, throwing back the bedclothes and jumping from the bed, sliding a sword out from between the sheets and pointing it at Wriothesley. 'I believe you wish Edward Seymour dead, though the King would not have it so. *I* would not have it so. Anyone who threatens the life of Edward Seymour means to have mine also. You, sir, are a traitor.'

The colour faded from Wriothesley's face. He started towards John but suddenly, Robert appeared before him, his hand pressing firmly upon his chest.

'It's not true,' Wriothesley protested feebly.

'It is true, my lords,' Paulet said, moving to stand beside John. 'My lord Wriothesley planned to remove both Edward Seymour and John Dudley on charges of treason and establish himself as head of the Council.'

The counsellors muttered their astonishment, then loudly voiced their outrage. They appealed to John to act.

'Paulet,' John said, struggling to keep the triumph from his voice, 'Thomas Wriothesley must be placed under arrest. Escort him to Lincoln House and put him under guard. I shall inform the King of what has happened here.'

John threw his sword on the bed, his head suddenly swimming, his infirmity of the past few weeks catching up on him. 'Gentlemen,' he said, leaning against the bed for support, 'you must forgive me, but I cannot now continue. We will re-convene tomorrow. Our business can wait until then.'

The counsellors made their bewildered goodbyes, following the dumbstruck Wriothesley and Paulet from the room.

Robert helped John back into bed. 'You should rest, Father.'

'I will today, but I must get up tomorrow and go to the palace. I can't afford to absent myself any longer. I need to write a letter to the King about what's happened here. If I dictate, will you write?'

'Of course, Father. I'll just get some paper and ink.'

'Good boy,' John sighed, sinking into the pillars. 'Oh, and thank you, Rob.'

'What for?'

'For standing between me and Wriothesley. I truly think he would have struck me if you hadn't and in my poor state, I would have broken like glass.'

'You're welcome, Father,' Robert grinned. 'After all, I need you alive to make sure my marriage happens.'

'Oh, yes, your marriage, that reminds me. I've had a reply from Sir John. Naturally, he gives his consent and has proposed a dowry which I have accepted. So, you will get to marry your Amy and go and live in Norfolk.'

Robert faltered. 'Leave London?'

'I thought that was the whole point. You are to be my man in Norfolk. What's the matter?'

'Nothing, Father, but I will miss being at court.'

'Norfolk's not the other side of the world, Rob. I shall still need you here from time to time.'

'You promise?'

'I promise,' John said with mock solemnity. 'Now, get that ink and paper, will you?'

CHAPTER 15

ELY PLACE, JUNE 1550

Robert teased open the bed curtains an inch, wincing as a shaft of bright sunlight blasted across his eyes, confirming it was indeed morning. He let the curtains close, pressing his head deeper into the pillow.

It was his first morning as a married man. In the curve of his arm Amy moaned softly, her warm breath tickling the hairs on his chest. He thought back on the night just gone, when he and Amy had finally been left alone together, the awkwardness they discovered they shared, the heat of Amy's skin on his.

He wondered if his brother's marriage night had been anything like his. He doubted it. Jack had been married the day before Robert to Edward Seymour's daughter. Robert had tried to see the sense in such an alliance. He knew that his father had arranged it to try and bring the Seymour and Dudley families together, but in his opinion, the Seymours were not worth the effort. Robert had thanked God he had Amy, otherwise he would have had to marry the hard-faced Seymour cow.

Amy stirred and lifted her face to him. 'Good morning, my lord,' she purred.

'Good morning, wife.'
'Have you been awake long?'
'A little while. I've been thinking.'
'What about?'
'Just things. Yesterday.'

Amy shifted to lean on one elbow, wincing at a stab of pain from between her legs. 'Was I good yesterday? I mean, I didn't embarrass you in front of your family, did I?'

'Of course you didn't. Why would you think that?'

'Because I'm not used to such people, Robert. Just remembering yesterday makes my head whirl. Yesterday, I met the King!'

'It was good of him to attend. But I wish Father could have been there.'

'Is he very ill?'

'Mother says he's tired more than anything else. He works so hard.'

Amy yawned softly. 'I don't think your mother was very impressed with me.'

Robert said nothing. In truth, he was more than a little annoyed with his mother. Her disappointment in Amy had been obvious. She had loudly criticised Amy's clothes, exclaiming they were not good enough to be seen by the servants, let alone the King. Amy had been married in one of Mary's dresses, seamstresses working through the night to make the alterations necessary for Amy's plumper figure. Amy had accepted all this meekly, holding back the tears as Jane spoke about her to Mary as if she wasn't in the room.

'Mary was quite nice to me,' Amy continued, 'but Guildford hardly spoke to me.'

'I wish you wouldn't think on such things,' Robert said with a touch of impatience. 'My family have a lot on their minds at the moment.'

'I will be glad to get back to Norfolk.'

'What's wrong with London?'

'It's filthy and the people are rude.'

'I've lived here all my life and I've never found it so.'

'That's because you're used to it. I look at it with country eyes.'

'Well, we leave for Norfolk at the end of the week. Your father's preparing Syderstone Hall for us.'

'He didn't tell me that!' Amy cried delightedly.

'It was part of your dowry. Is it a good house?'

'Oh, Syderstone's lovely, Robert. Can't we go there straight away?'

'Of course we can't, you silly thing,' he said, laughing at the notion. 'I must conclude my duties at court and take leave of the King before I leave.'

Amy sighed and laid her head once more upon his chest, feeling his heart beat against her cheek. *Friday*, she thought. *Away from London and its stink, away from my formidable mother-in-law, living at Syderstone, where I can have Robert all to myself. I can't wait.*

SYDERSTONE HALL, NORFOLK

Robert quickly learnt to love Norfolk, as Amy had hoped he would. He found he did not even miss London as much as he feared, for there was much to do as lord of estates and tenancies. He would rise early and ride out on Salome, a beautiful chestnut mare, a wedding present from his parents.

Robert walked Salome back into the stable yard, throwing the reins to Dick, the stable lad. He slid his hand along her hot, moist neck, feeling the throb of her heart, and then, as he always did, pressed his face in the hollow behind her jaw and gave her a kiss. 'A good ride, my sweet,' he murmured. She snorted in pleasure. 'Look after her, Dick,' he called as he crossed the yard.

Robert entered the house through the kitchens, greeting the servants cheerfully and winking at two young maids, whose smiles dimpled their cheeks, and were roundly told off by a plump female superior as soon as he had passed through into the hallway. He smiled to himself as he heard their protestations.

'My lord,' his steward greeted him.

'Farrow, what have we got today?'

'Two complaints from tenants about the state of their roofs, a woman asking for your assistance in a matter of arbitration, and a letter from your brother.'

'It's about time Ambrose wrote. I'll read his letter first and then you can show them in. Where's your mistress?'

'I believe Mistress Dudley has not yet risen, my lord.'

'She's still in bed? God a'Mercy. Get her maid to get her up. I won't have her lying abed all day, it'll make her ill.'

'Yes, my lord. The letter is on your desk. And bread and beer are also laid out, as you ordered.'

'Thank you, Farrow.' He entered his study, wiping grime from the back of his neck with his handkerchief. He flopped into his chair and downed a cup of the beer in one gulp. He grabbed Ambrose's letter and broke the seal.

My dear brother,

Sorry for not having written to you sooner, but I've been busy. I don't know if you will have heard, living in that backwater you call home, but there has been a plot to kill Father. You will not believe it after all Father's kindness towards him, but it is all the work of Edward Seymour. You can imagine Jack's fury when he found out. I imagine his wife has suffered the rough edge of Jack's tongue because of it.

Now, before you dash off to London, Father is quite well and is no longer in any danger.

Edward Seymour is once again imprisoned in the Tower and I rather fancy the King will not be so forgiving this time. It is almost certain that Seymour was raising the people of London to attack and remove the Council so that he could rule once again as Protector. This, despite the King being quite the man these days and no longer a little boy to be governed. The King misses you, by the way, and wishes you continued good health. He relies on Father a great deal and trusts him completely. So, it won't surprise you when I tell you that Father is soon to be created Duke of Northumberland. We Dudleys do rise!

Father's gathering around him men he can trust. I'm sure he'll be sending for you soon.

I know you enjoy your sickening bucolic existence and are quite annoyingly healthy, breathing in the fresh air of Norfolk, but you must come. Father will need you, as will the King, I'm certain, when the time comes.

I don't know if Mary has written to you, but she has news as well. She is to marry your old friend, Henry Sidney, and though she pretends indifference, Mother says she is half in love with the clod already.

So, plenty of happenings here at court, enough to make you wish you'd never left, if I know my brother.

I hope to see you soon, dear Rob.

Your loving brother,
Ambrose Dudley

Robert refolded the letter, absently fingering the red wax seal. Ambrose was right. So much was happening and he had not been there when his father needed him.

The door opened and Amy, her eyes half-closed, shuffled in wearing only her nightgown. She eased herself onto his lap, curling her arms around his neck.

'Why did you make me rise so early?' she said in a soft, whiny voice, her face tilted to his so that he tasted the tang of her sour breath.

'It's not early, Amy. It must be at least nine.'

'That's early. Won't you kiss me?'

He gently pushed her from his lap and stood. 'Not now.'

'What's wrong?' she asked, a little stung by his rejection.

'Ambrose has written. I should be in London. My father needs me.'

'You're leaving?'

'Maybe.' He shook his head. 'Or maybe I should wait until Father sends for me. I don't know what to do for the best.'

'You should wait,' Amy said hurriedly.

'But wait for what? If I wait, I might be too late to be of any help. I think it far better I should be on hand.'

'Then I shall come to London with you.'

'I'll do better on my own.'

'Better?' Her bottom lip trembled.

'Amy, I'll be busy.'

'I won't get in the way.'

'You will. Oh, you won't mean to, but no, you must stay here. Now, I must get ready to leave.'

He strode from the room, shouting for Farrow. Amy fell into his chair, cursing John Dudley for taking Robert away from her.

GREENWICH PALACE

The court had changed. People now spoke in whispers and looked carefully about them as if wary of being overheard and when they looked at Robert, he saw respect in their eyes for the Duke of Northumberland's son.

He hurried to his father's rooms. 'Father.' He threw open the door and stopped short. John was sitting at his desk, his head resting on his hand. He had looked up at Robert's entrance and it was the change in his appearance that had struck Robert dumb. John had lost weight and there were dark smudges beneath his eyes.

'Do I look as bad as all that?' John asked with a half-laugh.

'You're ill?' Robert rushed to his father's side and knelt, taking his hand.

'I'm a trifle tired and I have a pain in my stomach that plagues me from time to time. But you mustn't worry.' He shook off Robert's hand. 'Go and sit down.'

Robert reluctantly obeyed. 'Ambrose wrote to me. Told me all the news.'

'Yes, I know. Seymour will be executed on the twenty-second.'

'That's just over a week away. Why the hurry?'

'Best to get it over with. Did you bring your wife with you?'

'No, I left her in Norfolk.'

John rifled through the papers on his desk. 'I want you to stay in London. Ah, here it is. I was going to send this on to you.' He threw a folded parchment with a heavy red seal to Robert. 'I've arranged with the King for you to take up the post of Master of the Buckhounds. That's your commission. You can send for Amy once we've found some rooms for you in the palace.'

'I will.' Robert said, quickly scanning his commission. 'I have a very good steward in Farrow. There's nothing he can't take care of for me. How is the King, Father?'

John yawned. 'Well enough. He was quite ill a month or two ago, but he seems to have got over it.'

'I meant about Seymour going to the block.'

'He signed the death warrant without any objection. He's his father's son, all right.'

'I should go and see him.' Robert rose. 'Where shall I be staying?'

'You can sleep with Ambrose for tonight. His rooms are further down this corridor. I'll get my secretary to find you some rooms for tomorrow. Come back after you've seen the King and we'll all dine together.'

'I'd like that, but I don't know how long I'll be. I'll probably have to wait to see him.'

'Not anymore,' John smirked and the tiredness seemed to diminish. 'Tell the guards who you are and you'll be let straight through. You're a Dudley, my son, and no door is closed to you now.'

King Edward was sitting on a cushion on the floor in his bedchamber, his back against the wall. Unusually, he was alone. He looked up as Robert entered and Robert saw that his eyes were swollen and red and his nose was running.

'Hello, Rob,' Edward said, attempting a smile.

'Your Majesty?' Robert knelt and placed a hand on his shoulder. 'What's wrong?'

Edward wiped his arm across his eyes. 'Don't tell your father. Please.'

'I won't. But why are you crying?'

'Uncle Edward. I'm sending him to the scaffold just like I did to Uncle Tom.' Edward began to cry again and Robert put his arm around him. Edward accepted the embrace almost gratefully. 'I killed my mother, too. She died giving birth to me. So, then I kill her brothers. Who's next? My sisters?' Edward pulled away with a sniff, searching in his doublet for a handkerchief. Robert gave him his. 'You mustn't think I'm not grateful to your father, Robert. I am. He does so much for me. I know your father would save my uncle if he could, but I know he has to be executed.'

'It's a terrible decision to have to make.'

Edward nodded and blew his nose. 'I've not been well, you know, Rob?'

'Father told me.'

'I'm better now, but I really was very ill. And I'm not even sixteen. What if I were to die? Who would succeed to the throne?'

'You're not going to die, Edward.'

'I'm not afraid of dying, Rob. If God wanted me, it would be an honour to be with him. But I do worry about England.'

'I suppose your sister Mary would become queen.'

'That's exactly what I fear. Archbishop Cranmer, your father and I, we've all worked so hard to bring this country to accept the New Learning. Mary would want to undo it all.'

'And return us to Rome,' Robert said grimly. 'So, assuming the worst were to happen – which I am confident will not – can anything be done to see that Mary doesn't inherit?'

'We're working towards that. We're seeing if she can be removed from the Act of Succession.'

'Leaving Elizabeth to succeed?'

Edward grimaced. 'She's another problem.'

'She's no Catholic, I know that,' Robert declared.

'But she is illegitimate. Her mother and my father were not married, so how can I leave my throne to her?'

'Well then, who does that leave?'

'My cousin, Lady Frances Brandon.' Edward made a face. 'She's a dreadful woman, and more importantly, she is not likely to have any more children. All she has are daughters.'

'And a king is better than a queen.'

'Of course. Women are not suited to sovereignty but there are too many females and not enough males in the Tudor tree.'

'A fact which your father struggled to correct.'

'And all he got was me,' Edward said sadly. 'Your father had a suggestion.'

'Which was?'

'To make Lady Frances's eldest daughter my successor.'

'Which one was that?' Robert tried to remember faces from the days in the royal schoolroom.

'Jane.'

'Oh yes, I remember Jane.' Jane Grey had been a small, thin girl with a pointed chin and freckles across her nose.

'I like Jane. She's clever and a Protestant, and if my successor must be a woman, then I would rather it was her. Hopefully, she will have sons when she marries.'

'Then I have a suggestion,' Robert said. 'Why don't you marry Jane?'

Edward coloured. 'Uncle Thomas suggested that once. But my health is not up to it and anyway, I feel Jane is too close in blood to me. Better she marry elsewhere, and soon.'

'Maybe you could suggest a husband for her?'

'Your father already has.'

'Really?'

'Yes. Your younger brother. What's his name?'

'You don't mean Guildford?' Robert spluttered.

Edward grinned. 'He's the only one left old enough to marry, I understand. You were foolish enough to wed a country girl and exile yourself to Norfolk, so that leaves only Guildford.'

'Do you mean to say that Guildford could one day be King of England?'

'Well, let's hope I'm here for some time yet.'

Robert nodded vigorously. 'For the sake of England, I sincerely hope so, Your Majesty.'

DURHAM HOUSE, MAY 1553

Guests had been arriving since ten o'clock, making themselves at home in the gardens of Durham House.

Robert hurried through the house, past the servants in the Great Hall laying the tables for the feast and up the stairs to Guildford's bedchamber, taking them two at a time. He gave a smart rat-tat-tat on the door and entered.

'Guildford, you lazy dog!' His youngest brother lay splayed out on his bed, his long legs hanging over the sides. He was half-dressed in silver hose and pumps, his torso bare, one arm thrown across his eyes. 'Father will whip your backside if you're late.'

'Plenty of time,' Guildford murmured.

'No, there isn't. The church bell has struck twelve and you're getting married at one.'

Guildford propped himself up on his elbows, his dark blonde hair falling over his forehead. 'Why the devil do I have to marry her?'

'You have to marry her because Henry's too young.' Robert snatched a shirt from the back of a chair and threw it into Guildford's lap. 'I don't know why you're complaining. Can't you see what Father's doing for you?'

'Yes, he's marrying me to a sour-faced girl.'

'Jane Grey is actually quite pretty.'

'She's always got her nose in a book.'

'Well, what if she has?'

Guildford sat up, put his feet on the floor and yawned. 'Because I can't see her being bonny and blithe in bed.'

'You never know, she might surprise you.'

'Don't build my hopes up.'

'Has it occurred to you, Gil, that she may not be overjoyed at the prospect of being married to you either?'

Guildford pulled on his shirt. 'Why? What's wrong with me?' he demanded. Robert lifted a sardonic eyebrow. Guildford stuck his tongue out and finished dressing. 'There,' he said, holding his arms out and turning around. 'How do I look?'

'Beautiful,' Robert mocked. 'Now, come on.'

They clattered down the stairs back into the hall, Guildford pulling at his collar as though it were strangling him. As they entered from one end, John and Jane's father, Henry Grey, the Duke of Suffolk, entered from the other.

'Ah, there he is,' John said cheerily to Henry Grey, but to Robert, the cheer felt forced. 'This is Guildford, Henry.'

Henry Grey looked Guildford up and down. 'He doesn't look like you, John. I thought all the Dudley boys were dark. He's got fair hair. Are you sure he's one of yours?'

'He has his mother's colouring. Are you ready, Guildford?'

'Yes, Father,' Guildford answered, struggling to keep the sulkiness from his voice.

'Good. I'm sorry to say that the King cannot attend today, but he sends his good wishes.'

'My daughter's waiting,' Henry said brusquely, edging back towards the door.

'Yes, let's to the chapel.' John gestured for Henry to lead, looking behind him to make sure Robert and Guildford followed.

'You see,' Robert said in Guildford's ear, 'your marriage has the blessing of the King.'

Guildford grimaced. 'Well, I only hope that if the King does die and Jane becomes queen, she makes me king.'

Robert grabbed his arm. 'For Christ's sake, Gil, hold your tongue. Never talk about the King dying. If anyone heard you—'

Guildford shook his arm free. 'To hell with you. I'll stand for Mother and Father telling me what I can and can't do, but I'll be damned if I have to take it from you.'

'Gil, I'm only—'

'I know what it is. You're jealous, aren't you? There's a chance I might be king one day and you're wishing it could be you.'

'That's ridiculous.'

'It's not ridiculous. If you hadn't been so insistent about marrying your stupid country girl, it would be you marrying Jane.'

Robert watched him hurry after their father. He had not dared admit it even to himself, but he *was* jealous. The King had seen it and now Guildford. Was he really so transparent?

GREENWICH PALACE, JUNE 1553

Robert knocked quietly on the door of the King's privy chamber. He heard footsteps on the other side and peered into the subdued light of the interior as it opened. 'Father?' he almost whispered.

'Come in,' John ordered.

The stench hit Robert immediately. A stink of vomit and shit and herbs, all mixing together to create a metallic tang that hit the back of the throat. And something else that Robert couldn't quite place. He looked towards the bed. The curtains were drawn.

Robert turned to his father. John looked old in the candlelight. 'How is he?'

'He's not at all well,' John said. 'I think... I don't think he has long.'

'Poor Edward. Is he in pain?'

'Terrible pain. The medicine the doctors give him,' John gestured towards two men sitting before the fire examining a bowl of the King's urine, 'make him feel worse than the illness. I've half a mind to tell them to stop, to let him die, but I dread the consequences. He can't sleep because of the pain. His mind wanders, but then he has moments of lucidity and he starts to worry.'

'What about?'

'He cannot rest easy in his mind for fear that he will leave the throne of England contested between two bastard sisters. He wants the matter settled.'

'I wish he would not think of Elizabeth so.'

'Is that all you can say?' John growled. 'After all, what is Elizabeth to you?'

'She's a friend,' Robert protested.

'She's not your concern.'

'No, Father.' A sudden cry arose. 'What's that noise?'

John led him to the window. 'Look down there.'

Robert peered through the glass. People had congregated outside the walls of the palace and were staring up at the window. 'What are they saying?'

'They want to see the King. There's a rumour going around London that Edward is already dead and the people want proof that he isn't.' John ran his hand over his face. 'God help me, but I would give anything for the King to be well again. I don't want to do what I must if he dies.'

'You mean Jane Grey. And Guildford?'

John nodded, but gestured for him to be quiet. 'Rob, I need you to show him to them.'

Robert looked down again at the crowd. 'How?'

John moved to the bed and carefully drew back one of the hangings. Robert caught his breath. The hair on Edward's head was thin and patchy, the skull covered with scabs. His fingernails had begun to fall out so that his hands were now blood-blistered claws clutching at the sheets. His legs were swollen but it was the skin that was the most shocking sight of all. The King was turning blue.

'Your Majesty,' John bent low so the boy could hear, 'Robert is here. Please forgive me, but we must show you to the people. They're waiting down below for a sight of you.'

The King's eyelids flickered open and he looked up at John. 'Do they think I'm dead, John?'

John smiled sadly. 'They're concerned about you.'

'I don't think I can walk to the window.'

'Robert will carry you.'

Edward tried to sit up, but he was too weak and fell back against the sweat-soiled pillow. Robert slid his arms beneath his body and lifted him, shocked by how little effort was required. The King was hardly more than a skeleton.

'Gently, gently,' John said.

Edward groaned with each step Robert took towards the window. John unhooked the latch and threw the window open. As the gentle summer air wafted in, contrasting with the foetid odour of the room, Robert understood what the smell was that he hadn't been able to place. The King's very flesh was rotting. Robert leaned forward, angling the boy so that his head was almost out of the window. The crowd cheered.

'Can you wave to them, Your Majesty?' John asked.

Edward tried to raise his arm, his face grimacing with pain. 'I can't,' he gasped, his head falling back against Robert's shoulder.

'It doesn't matter,' John said. 'It's enough.'

Robert returned the boy to the bed, glad not to have him in

his arms any longer, for the smell turned his stomach.

John laid the bedclothes back over Edward and with surprising gentleness stroked the King's face and bid the boy try to sleep. As he stepped back and drew the curtain, Robert saw tears in his eyes. John hurried towards the door and slipped out into the next room. Robert followed.

'How he suffers, Rob,' John said, wiping his eyes. 'It makes me wonder what God is about to let such a good servant to him suffer so. But I suppose he has his reasons. Anyway, we must proceed. The King wants his Device for the Succession making Jane Grey his successor made law. Tomorrow, I must convince the Council to ratify it and that will be no easy task, I tell you.'

'What if they will not?'

'Oh, they will,' John assured him vehemently. 'Even if I have to shout and threaten, they will do what that boy wants. I refuse to let him die in fear of what he leaves behind.'

John re-read the document before him, King Edward's Device for the Succession. John had indeed had to shout and threaten to get his fellow counsellors to sign it, stretching his patience and his temper to the limit.

He looked up as William Cecil, Seymour's former secretary, now his, lit a candle on his desk, for though it was only just past eight o'clock, the sky had darkened and a storm was threatening. 'This was hard won, Cecil, but it's law now.'

Cecil nodded and blew out the lighted spill.

John sat back in his chair and sighed. 'I get the impression you don't approve.'

'It's not my place—'

'What exactly do you object to?'

Cecil hesitated. 'If I may speak plainly, Your Grace, I fear the people will not like a change in the succession.'

'It is their king's decree.'

'The people may not view it as such.'

'What you mean is that they'll think it is all *my* doing.'

'Possibly, Your Grace.'

'It isn't, you know, Cecil. This,' John waved the document before him, 'came from the King. This is all his idea.'

'As you say, Your Grace,' Cecil moved away.

'But I'm being unrealistic, aren't I?' John murmured to himself. 'How can I expect the people to believe me when my own damn secretary doesn't?'

The door opened suddenly and Robert hurtled into the room. 'Father, he's dead.'

There was a pause as the news sank in, then John murmured, 'God keep him,' a look of resignation crossing his face. 'I knew it was useless, but I had hoped he would rally. This Device was signed just in time.' He got to his feet. 'Rob, I need you and Jack to escort the Lady Mary to London. I sent word to her that the King was ill and she should already be on her way, but I want you and Jack to make sure she comes straight here.'

'What about Guildford and Jane?' Robert asked.

'I'll deal with them.'

'And Elizabeth?'

John's eyes narrowed. 'I've told you before, she's not your concern. Anyway, she's sent word that she is ill and cannot move from Hatfield, but I'll send some men there, too. Rob, take some men from the Tower and get on your way.'

'I will, Father. By the way, Henry's with the King.' He meant Henry Sidney, his sister Mary's new husband and Robert's good friend. The King had died in Henry's arms.

'That's fine. I'll go and see him shortly,' John said, waving Robert to be gone. 'Now then, Cecil. Whether you like it or not, we have to issue a proclamation naming Jane Grey as Queen.'

HUNSDON PALACE, JULY 7 1553

The man had kept his hood up, despite Mary's insistence that she wanted to see who she was speaking with. His message had been brief and to the point. 'For your own safety, do not go to London. John Dudley will have you in the Tower.'

'What of my sister?' she cried.

'She too has been warned. She keeps to her house.'

'At least tell me who sent you,' Mary called after him as he mounted his horse.

He pulled his hood even further over his face. 'A friend.'

The rooms of Hunsdon echoed with their emptiness. Jack

Dudley checked all the rooms, the heels of his riding boots clipping on the flagstones. He returned to the Great Hall and something glinting on the floor caught his eye. He bent and picked up a gold coin almost hidden by the rushes. 'She left in a hurry.'

'Father did say she may be on her way to London,' Robert pointed out.

'There's only one way to London from here. We would have passed her on the road.'

'Where then?'

'Kenninghall, probably. It's the nearest place where she could expect to find allies.'

'Allies? Against us?'

'Well, someone has obviously warned her we were coming,' Jack said. 'Why else would she flee?'

'Who would have warned her?'

'Any number of people. There are plenty unhappy with what Father has planned. But anyway, it doesn't matter. She's gone.'

'What do we do now then?'

Jack headed for the door. 'I'm going back to London to let Father know what's happened. You carry on after her. Go on to Kenninghall, see if you can catch her up.'

'And if I do?'

'Not if, Rob. You must catch her, or I fear our family will be in danger.'

Mary Tudor was not to be found at Kenninghall. Robert rode on, growing desperate as he was told time and again at the houses where he made enquiries that he had missed her by only a few hours.

At the home of Lord Huddleston, Sawston Hall, Robert jumped down from his horse, weary, dusty and in a very bad temper. He banged unrelentingly on the front door.

'Open up,' he hissed impatiently, trying not to let his anxiety show to his men who watched and waited.

The door eventually opened to reveal a stocky, bearded man of about forty-five. He looked Robert up and down and raising an eyebrow demanded who he was.

'Lord Robert Dudley, son to the Duke of Northumberland. Get your master,' Robert barked.

'I can't do that. Lord Huddleston is not here. He's with the Lady Mary.'

Robert cursed and the man smirked. 'I'll wipe that smile off your poxy face, you whoreson,' Robert snarled, raising his whip.

The man grabbed Robert's wrist. 'No son of a traitor will ever strike me.' He shoved Robert away and Robert, who never in his life had been treated so, stared back at him in silent rage.

Then he found his tongue. 'Thompson,' he yelled over his shoulder. 'Fetch a torch. Brook, Tanner, Hope,' Robert pointed to three of the burliest men of his train. 'Get this fool out of my way.'

Lord Huddleston's servant was strong but unable to resist the tug of three men. He was pushed to the ground where Tanner promptly sat upon him. Thompson passed a flaming torch to Robert and he entered the hall. Tapestries adorned the walls of the main chamber and Robert moved to the nearest, touching the flame to the precious fabric. It took but a moment for the flame to spread and Robert felt the heat of the fire upon his face. He moved from room to room, repeating the action, until smoke began to choke him and he stepped back out into the fresh air.

'Release him,' Robert ordered his men, throwing the torch away and dusting himself down. 'I have left Lord Huddleston a message. I'm sure he'll understand it.'

The man made to lunge at Robert but Tanner and Brook stepped between them. Servants rushed out of the rear of the hall, the women screaming in terror, the men shouting for water.

Robert felt pleased with himself, but as he walked back to his horse, he looked at his men and read contempt for him on their faces. It put an abrupt end to his pleasure and he looked away, reluctant to acknowledge that perhaps he had been foolish. As he mounted his horse, one of the hall's windows burst outwards, scattering glass across the ground. The horses jumped and neighed unhappily.

'Away,' Robert ordered and spurred his horse back towards the road.

KINGS LYNN, NORFOLK

Robert rushed to meet his messenger. 'What news?'

Taylor jumped down from his horse. His face was stained

and bloodied, his clothes torn and dusty. 'Fearful news, my lord.'

'What's happened to you?'

Taylor gulped for air. 'I was attacked by followers of the Lady Mary. They saw my badge of Warwick on my arm and pulled me from my horse. Then they tore my badge from me and called me a wretch for serving such a vile traitor.'

'And you let them say that?'

Taylor was indignant. 'I said my master was none such.'

Robert shook his head in disgust. 'Have you any news of my father?'

'He has proclaimed the Lady Mary queen at Cambridge.'

Robert grabbed his arm. 'He has proclaimed her queen?'

'He has, but he's been taken to the Tower, your brothers with him. Jane Grey has been arrested as well.'

'Then it's over,' Robert said. 'This is what Jack feared. We're done for.'

'In that case, my lord, perhaps we should flee,' Taylor suggested hopefully.

'And abandon my family?'

'We can't help them, my lord. There's nothing to stay for.'

'We will stay,' Robert said, as much to himself as to Taylor.

'But they will come for us.'

'They will come for *me*,' Robert corrected and began to walk back to his tent.

'You're wrong, my lord,' Taylor hurried after him. 'We will all be taken, they will punish us.'

'You will not be taken, Taylor. You have my word.'

With sudden spirit, provoked by his recent misfortune, Taylor grabbed at Robert. 'What good is your word now?'

The frustration of the past few days bubbled up in Robert. He spun around and threw a punch at Taylor's jaw. Taylor fell to the ground, dazed.

'Leave if you want,' Robert snarled, nursing his knuckles, 'or stay. But do not dare to show your face to me again.'

He glowered at his men clustering around to watch the sport he was providing. He turned his back on them and entered his tent, and waited for Queen Mary's men to arrive.

CHAPTER 16

THE TOWER, AUGUST 1553

'They're bringing Rob in now,' Ambrose said from the window.

Jack joined him and looked down at his brother walking between two guards. 'He looks grim.'

'Well, wouldn't you?' Ambrose said. 'You know Rob. He's going to blame himself for all this.'

'So he should,' said a sulky voice from behind them. They turned to their brother, Guildford, lying on a truckle bed. 'Well, don't look at me like that. All he had to do was capture a silly old woman and he couldn't even manage that. Then he goes and burns a house down, as if that helped.'

'He made a mistake, Gil,' Jack said.

'One that's going to cost us our heads.'

'You don't know that,' Ambrose said. 'I think it was all lost as soon as Father had to leave London to march against Mary. Once he was gone, the Council didn't have to pretend to be loyal to him. And to think they are calling Father a traitor. The hypocrites.'

Ambrose and Jack turned back to the window as a door banged shut. They saw the two guards walk away.

'They've left Rob downstairs,' Jack said in surprise.

'Why would they leave him on his own?' Ambrose wondered.

Robert wondered the same thing. Was it to punish him further?

It was surprising, given the warmth of the day, how cold the stone chamber was, for little sunlight penetrated through the narrow slit windows. He sat down on the bed; it creaked and spread beneath his weight. He pulled his legs up to his chest and hugged them tight. While he had been in Norfolk, even when he had been brought before Mary and forced to his knees to do obeisance, it hadn't seemed possible that he was a prisoner. Entering the Tower had made it all too real. He felt cold, so cold. It was fear, he knew. Fear for himself, fear for his father. He thought of his mother and it hurt him to think how worried she would be. Then he thought of Amy, sitting at home in Norfolk, wondering what had become of him. He cried without knowing he did so, the tears drying and tightening his cheeks. He curled up on the bed. Exhausted, he soon slept.

He was alone for two days. On the third, his guard came in without his breakfast and told Robert to get up.

'Why? Are you taking me somewhere?' Robert asked, his fingers trembling as he hurried to pull on his boots.

'The Tower's filling up,' the guard said, unlocking a door in the wall. 'We're having to put prisoners together to make room. Come on.'

Robert grabbed his cloak, bundling it under his arm. 'You're putting me upstairs.'

'That's right. Up with your brothers. Won't that be nice for you?' the guard sneered, pushing him through the doorway.

'Don't you dare push me, you dog!' Robert growled.

His indignation amused the guard. 'Boy, haven't you worked it out yet? You're nothing, you're nobody. Soon, you'll be out on Tower Hill on the scaffold pissing yourself because your head is about to be cut off, after they've ripped your guts out first, mind. So, dog I may be, but I'm a dog that's going to be alive this time next year. Now, are you going to walk up those stairs there or do I have to throw you up?'

The door closed behind him. He blinked at the sudden brightness of the upper chamber. His brothers were sat around a small table in the centre of the room, playing at a game of cards.

'Rob?' Jack cried, coming towards him, his arms outstretched. Robert melted into his brother's arms, burrowing his face in his neck and breathing in his warm, comforting smell. Then it was Ambrose's turn to hold him. Guildford held back.

'Oh, Rob, it's good to see you.' Ambrose pulled him to one of the stools and pushed him down onto it.

Jack cradled his face and stared into his eyes. 'Are you all right? They haven't mistreated you?'

'I'm well enough.' Robert pulled his face away. 'Jack, I'm sorry.'

'Enough of that. It isn't your fault.'

'But if I had found Mary—'

'It wouldn't have made any difference,' Jack shook his head. 'Father lost the Council's support. They betrayed him. Mary being free was unfortunate, but it's not the only reason we've ended up here.'

'Father's here, too?'

'Over in the Garden Tower,' Ambrose said. 'Henry's with him.' Henry was their youngest brother.

Robert swallowed. 'What's going to happen to us?'

Jack glanced at Ambrose. 'We'll stand trial, and no doubt, will be found guilty.' He breathed deeply. 'After that—'

He didn't need to finish the sentence. They all knew what happened to traitors.

The door opened and the cot bed from the downstairs chamber flew through the air and clattered in a heap on the floor. 'Don't expect anything else,' the guard grunted. He pulled the door shut and locked it.

'Have they no respect for who we are?' Jack asked.

'Not any more, it seems,' Ambrose replied equably. He bent and tried to straighten the bed. 'Gil, shove along so we can get this in.'

Robert watched as his brothers rearranged their prison furniture. His eyes stung with tears. 'For us to come to this,' he said.

Ambrose straightened and looked at him. 'It is to be expected, Rob.'

'How can you say so? We are Dudleys, Ambrose.'

'We are traitors, Rob,' Ambrose countered, his voice rising. 'Don't you understand what we've done?'

'What have we done, tell me? We've tried to preserve

England as a Protestant country to save us from having a half-Spanish, Catholic woman as queen.'

'Rob's right, you know,' Guildford said, falling back onto his bed. 'After all, it was the King who wanted to change the succession—'

'Exactly,' Robert interrupted. 'Father was loyal to his king, carrying out his orders. How can he then be called traitor?'

'Edward had no right to change the succession,' Jack said wearily.

'No right?' Robert cried in exasperation. 'What does it mean to be king if one cannot create the law of the land?'

'This is not a land of tyrants, Rob,' Jack said, 'where a sovereign can act without the consent of the people.'

'He had consent, Jack. Parliament consented.'

'Only after Father bullied them.'

'If you've always thought that, Jack, why didn't you say so to Father?'

'I did my duty by Father, Rob.'

'As did I.'

'Hardly,' Guildford muttered.

Robert turned on him. 'What did you say?'

Guildford shrugged. 'I still say if you had caught up with Mary, we wouldn't be here.'

'You do blame me, then?'

'No, we don't,' Ambrose said, laying his hand on Robert's shoulder.

Robert twisted angrily out of his grasp. 'He does,' he spat, jabbing a finger at Guildford.

'What does Gil know?' Jack scoffed, glaring at Guildford to hold his tongue.

But Guildford was in no mood to be silenced.

'I know enough,' he said, scrambling to his feet. 'I know that if Father had succeeded, you would all have to bow your knee to me. And I tell you, I wouldn't stand for any of your insolence.'

'Bow our knees to you?' Robert sneered. 'I heard that your wife refused to crown you. Even she realised what a blockhead you are.'

Guildford stamped his foot. 'Oh, and I suppose you think you would make a better king?'

'Well, of course, I would,' Robert said. 'Can you be in any doubt?'

'Quiet, both of you.' Jack moved to stand between them and gave them each a shove backwards. 'You fools. Do you think Father would be pleased to see us at each other's throats?'

'Maybe he should have considered what his actions would lead to,' Guildford said.

'Father isn't to blame,' Robert insisted.

'How can you say that?' Guildford implored. 'No one who matters agrees with you. They're probably already building his scaffold.'

Robert swallowed, feeling sick. 'They... they wouldn't do that,' he stammered, staring at Guildford. Guildford turned away, unable to look him in the eye.

'Rob,' Jack said quietly, taking his hand, 'you must realise that it is likely.'

Robert snatched his cold hand away. 'No, Jack, they can't. Not to Father. Never.'

CHAPTER 17

THE TOWER

John Dudley pulled his cloak up to his chin and dug his fingers into his side in a futile attempt to press away the pain. It seemed almost constant now. Or did he imagine it? Had failure made it seem more real? He cursed Jane Grey for sending him out of London. That had been his undoing. Had he stayed, his fellow counsellors wouldn't have been able to stab him in the back. The stupid girl. He felt himself growing angry again and he knew it could do him no good, so he willed it away. After all, Dudley the Queenmaker! What a fool he had been to think he could have done it.

He looked up as his cell door was unlocked and Stephen Gardiner walked in.

Gardiner's countenance still bore the pallor that five years imprisonment in the Tower had given him. But it was moments such as this, looking down at the man who had been instrumental in keeping him a prisoner, when Gardiner swelled with satisfaction at the hand justice had dealt him.

John got to his feet and moved to stand before him. 'My wife, Gardiner. How is she?'

'The Queen bears her no malice and she is safe.'

'And my son, Henry. Where has he been taken?'

'To the Beauchamp Tower. He is with your other sons.'

'And are they well?'

'I don't know, nor do I care. I came only to tell you that your trial is set for three days hence. You will be found guilty. Both you and your sons.'

'And what will follow?' John asked cautiously.

Gardiner looked him in the eye. 'Death, of course.'

'For me, yes, I understand that. But not my sons, please. They don't deserve to be executed.'

'Indeed? Are they not as guilty as you?'

'They only did as they were told. They're just children, Stephen.'

'They're men.'

'They're my sons,' John said desperately. Gardiner looked at him with distaste. John composed himself. 'There must be something I can do. Let me see or write to the Queen. I will beg her to show mercy.'

Gardiner sneered. 'The Duke of Northumberland beg?'

'To save my sons, yes, I will beg.'

Gardiner considered. 'There is perhaps one way.'

'Tell me.'

'Admit that your religion is false. Admit the error you have made in following the Lutheran heresy and return to the True Faith. Admit this and your sons may be saved.'

John stared at him. 'It's not what I believe.'

'Then you won't do it?'

'It's no small thing you're asking of me.'

Gardiner turned to the door. 'Then I see no point in my remaining.'

'Stephen, wait,' John halted him. 'Will it really save them?'

'The Queen is not vengeful, Dudley,' Gardiner replied with a hint of regret. 'Your life is forfeit. But a public recantation of your faith will save your sons, I promise you.'

John had to believe he spoke the truth. 'Then I will do it. I only hope God will forgive me.'

Gardiner's lips twitched. 'You'll be able to ask him soon enough.'

TOWER HILL

This was the way his father, Edmund, had died. John had been there that day, so many years ago, on Tower Hill as a small boy, crushed between the bodies of the spectators. The sound of the cheers as his father's head was hacked off had stayed with him, haunted his dreams. Now, the cheers were for him, an eager mob shouting for *his* head to be hacked off. He was so tired, he could almost be glad his life was soon to be over, if it weren't for his family. He hadn't been allowed to see his wife or his daughters since his arrest and his last sight of his sons had been a torment to him.

It had been no more than an hour ago, when the Tower guards had hustled him from his cell to the chapel of St Peter ad Vincula and sitting in the pews had been his boys. He saw confusion on their faces, wondering what they had been brought there for. They had no notion that they were to witness their father's betrayal of their faith. He could still hear them calling out to him.

John moved to the block, shuffling through the sand and straw laid down to soak up his blood.

'Do you forgive me?' the executioner asked, his face made ghastly by the black mask worn to disguise his identity.

'Yes,' John answered wearily. *Yes*, he thought, *I forgive you, you're paid to do this. But I don't forgive them, those bastards who have made my life a lie and dishonoured me before my children. I will never forgive them, even if I burn in hell for it.*

Someone stepped up behind him and a white cloth was thrown over his eyes, making him flinch. A knot was hurriedly tied and John felt hands on his back, guiding him to the block. His trembling legs gave way and he fell onto his knees, gasping at the jolt of pain shooting through his spine. A few more minutes and bodily pain would be nothing to him. He leaned forward, feeling for the curve in the wood. As he lowered himself, the blindfold slipped and fell down around his neck. It made him shudder to look again upon the baying crowd with his head so near to the red-stained stump of wood. He sniffed in an attempt to hold back his tears, but it didn't work. *God damn you*, he chided himself, as they flowed so obviously down his hollow cheeks. His fingers fumbled at the knot, untying and repositioning it, this time tying it so tight it dug into his skull.

He thrust his neck into the hollow and shouted, wanting to be heard above the roar of the crowd, 'Jesus, into your care, deliver me.'

He spread his arms, the signal for the executioner to strike.

He felt the cold metal of the blade against the back of his neck as the executioner marked out his target, then a terrifying few seconds, an exquisite shock of pain and the world went black.

Jack, leaning against the fireplace, closed his eyes. He had just seen the cart carrying his father's body returning from Tower Hill. He had stood alone at the window. He alone had seen it and he didn't mention it now. 'It's done,' was all he said. Henry rushed to him, pressing his face against Jack's chest.

Guildford, his face white, swallowed. 'Is Father de—'

'Yes, Gil,' Ambrose cut him off sharply, then adding more kindly, 'yes.' He turned to look at Robert. Robert lay on his side on the bed, his back to the room. He was shaking. 'Oh, Rob,' Ambrose whispered, and moved to the bed. He reached out a hand and stroked the thick black hair.

Robert flinched beneath his touch. Jerking upright, he knocked Ambrose's hand away. 'I'll never forgive them,' he said, his black eyes fierce behind his tears. 'Not as long as I live.' His face suddenly crumpled. 'What am I going to do without him, Am?'

Ambrose looked across at Jack, hoping he had an answer, but Jack lowered his eyes. 'I don't know, Rob,' Ambrose said sadly.

'For Christ's sake, what's the matter with you?' Robert grabbed at him. 'Why aren't you angry?'

'I am angry,' Ambrose retorted, stung by the accusation. 'Do you think you're the only one who loved him?'

'Oh God, I wish they'd killed me with him.'

'Don't say that,' Jack scolded, giving Henry's head a savage caress. 'And don't believe what Father said in the chapel. He only did it to try and save us from the same fate. It hurt him to say what he did, but he did it for us. That's the kind of father he is... He was. And have you thought of Mother? How must she be feeling?'

'Oh God, Mother,' Robert looked up at Jack. 'Will she be all right?'

'I don't know,' Jack said. 'I worry about her. But at least she's at liberty and she's got Mary to look after her.'

'They didn't have to do this,' Robert said, punching the

mattress. 'They could have just kept him a prisoner. Why'd they have to kill him?' His sobs began afresh.

Ambrose pulled him close and held him tight.

'Because that's what the Catholics wanted,' he said bitterly. 'A human sacrifice to their religion, so they can say, 'Look, even the Duke of Northumberland admitted he was wrong and we are right.' They're heartless bastards, Rob. Every one of them.'

Jack nodded his agreement. 'The sooner that bitch Mary is dead and Elizabeth sits on the throne, the better.'

WHITEHALL PALACE, FEBRUARY 1554

Simon Renard, the Imperial ambassador, looked down at the woman sitting in the chair and felt sorry for his master, the King of Spain. This was the woman King Philip was going to marry and an older, uglier and less appealing woman than Mary Tudor Renard couldn't imagine.

'No. I can't do it.' Mary slapped her hand down on the pommel of her chair. 'They're innocents.'

Stephen Gardiner moved away from the window. 'Jane Grey and her husband were never that, Your Majesty. Madam,' he continued with a sigh at her expression, 'this rebellion of Wyatt's has shown how insecure your hold on power is.'

'I am loved,' she declared, rising from the chair and squaring up to him. 'My people supported me against Dudley.'

'Indeed, they did,' Gardiner agreed, bowing his head.

'And Wyatt claims to have only been protesting against my marriage to King Philip, not my right as queen.'

'What he claims and what he would have done once he had achieved power, Your Majesty, who can say?' Gardiner shrugged.

'I still don't see why it involves my cousin Jane and her husband.'

'Her father was free to join the rebellion,' Renard pointed out, reminding her of her former ill-judged mercy in not imprisoning him, too. 'And had Wyatt succeeded, the Duke of Suffolk would have put his daughter on the throne once more. While that girl lives, she is a constant danger to your security and while she lives and has a husband, she is a perfect candidate for a queen.'

'I agree with Senôr Renard, Your Majesty,' Gardiner said.

'The Grey girl is a threat to your throne and your life. You have shown great mercy in allowing her to live this long.'

'She is my cousin,' Mary protested.

Renard and Gardiner shared a look, Gardiner urging him to speak. 'Your Majesty, I do fear that my master, King Philip, will not feel secure in a country whose citizens are allowed to rise up against their sovereign without fear of punishment.'

'What do you mean?' Mary asked with a look of horror.

'I mean King Philip may not agree to your marriage, Your Majesty.'

'But he must. We are betrothed.'

'Alas, these arrangements are easily undone.'

'No, no, he must come here. My heart is given to him. He must, he must.'

'Then you must sacrifice your noble feelings towards your cousin, Your Majesty,' Renard said with as sympathetic an expression as his face could muster. 'Jane Grey must die.'

BEAUCHAMP TOWER

'Help me,' Guildford screamed, grabbing at the cloak Jack wore to keep out the cold.

Jack wrenched it from his hands. 'There's nothing we can do, Gil.'

'But you can't let them kill me. I didn't do anything. Why do I have to die?'

Ambrose stepped away from the door. 'They're coming,' he said.

The door opened. The Lieutenant of the Tower, Sir John Brydges, stood in the doorway, two halberdiers behind him. 'It is time,' he said, staring at Guildford.

'You can't do this,' Ambrose said. 'He's just a boy.'

'Stand aside, sir, if you please,' Brydges said. 'I have a warrant signed by the Queen.'

The brothers looked at each other, knowing they were helpless. Jack grabbed Guildford and pulled him into an embrace. 'Be brave,' he whispered. 'I love you.'

Ambrose was next. 'I love you,' was all he could say.

Henry pressed his face against Guildford's, their tears mingling. 'I'm so sorry.'

Robert stood stock still. It was unbelievable that another member of his family, someone whom he loved, was about to be taken from him. Guildford looked up at him, his face a mess of creases and redness. Robert stepped up to him and wiped his cheeks with his thumbs. Curving his hand around the back of his neck, the neck that would soon be a bloody stump, he pulled Guildford to him, biting down on his bottom lip to keep himself from screaming.

'I love you,' he hissed through gritted teeth, not trusting himself to say more, not knowing what else to say.

'It's not fair,' Guildford wept, his body shuddering.

'I know. It's not bloody fair,' Robert agreed, squeezing him tight.

'We have to go, sirs,' Brydges said.

He tugged Guildford out of Robert's embrace and before the brothers could protest further, had hurried him through into the passage and shut and locked the door. They heard Guildford's cries as he was taken down the stone stairs.

They moved to the window, waiting for him to appear. As he emerged, he looked over his shoulder, up at the window and gave a weak smile. They watched as the guards walked him across the cobbled yards, until they turned the corner by the White Tower and were lost to view.

•

CHAPTER 18

LIEUTENANT OF THE TOWER'S APARTMENTS, APRIL 1554

Time passed and no more guards came to take any of the brothers away for a rendezvous on Tower Hill. The Queen had married her Philip and was happy for perhaps the first time in her life. Whispers of her contentment filtered through to the brothers and they allowed themselves to hope that they would not die after all. The restrictions on them were relaxed, so much so that the Lieutenant of the Tower, Sir John Brydges, when he desired company, would invite the brothers to dine with him.

Sir John gestured to his servant to pour another drink for himself and his guests, Robert and Ambrose. Brydges was drunk, but Jack had warned Robert and Ambrose to add water to their wine, advising them it would not be wise to have muddled brains and loose tongues before a servant of the Queen.

'I am heartily sorry for your present conditions, dear sirs,' Brydges mumbled, setting down his cup. 'I don't care to see the sons of the Duke of Northumberland in such a place as this.'

'We don't care for it much ourselves,' Robert replied wryly.

Ambrose gave him a warning kick beneath the table. 'But we thank you for allowing us to dine with you, Sir John.'

'Not at all, not at all, my dear young man,' Brydges said, patting his hand affectionately. 'Though I may not be able to do this soon.'

'Oh, why not?' Robert asked.

'I shall have a new prisoner tomorrow.' Brydges leant forward and tapped his nose. 'A very important prisoner.'

'Who?'

'The Lady Elizabeth.'

Ambrose and Robert glanced at one another. 'You jest, Sir John,' Robert said.

'I assure you, no,' Brydges cried indignantly. 'I have received orders to expect her.' He pulled a letter from his doublet. 'Here.' He tossed it across the table to Robert.

'For conspiring with the enemy,' Robert read. 'The enemy being Thomas Wyatt, I suppose? How was she involved?'

'Oh, she received letters from Wyatt. Collaborated with him, I believe.'

Ambrose took the letter from Robert's fingers. 'Has that been proved? It doesn't say so here.'

'No, not proved, but suspected. Do you know the Lady Elizabeth?'

'Very well,' Robert nodded. 'And I hope I will be able to see her while she is here'

'Ah, there now, you hope in vain, Master Robert,' Brydges wagged a finger at him. 'I have orders she is to be close confined. No visitors.'

'We'll see,' Robert winked at him.

'No, no, no, on this I must stand firm,' Brydges insisted. 'It could mean my head if I do not.' He glanced at the window. 'It's dark out.'

'It's late,' Ambrose said, draining his cup. 'I suppose you had best be locking us up for the night, Sir John.'

The guards escorted them out into the open air, their nostrils filling with the scents of the flowers from Brydges's garden.

Robert threw his arm around Ambrose's neck and tugged him close. 'What do you make of that, Am?'

'Of what?' Ambrose yawned.

'Elizabeth, you idiot.'

'Put her from your mind, Rob. You heard Sir John. He won't let you see her.'

'Oh, but I have to,' Robert said earnestly. 'We can't both be in here and not see one another. Tell me, is it cruel of me, Am, to be pleased that she's coming?'

'Twice in as many weeks,' Robert said as they were shown into Brydges's apartments. 'Sir John must be lonely.'

'You're not complaining, are you?' Ambrose said. 'The dinner here is better than in our chamber.'

'No, I'm not complaining, but Henry and Jack were. It was their turn to dine with him.'

'Perhaps Sir John prefers our company.' Ambrose stared at the table. 'Look. The table is set for four.'

'Maybe his wife's joining us.'

'Possibly, but I get the impression she's not as sympathetic to us as her husband.'

'Then who?'

'Me.'

Robert whirled around at the voice. 'Elizabeth!' She was thinner than when he had seen her last and paler.

Elizabeth stepped towards him, holding out her hands. 'The very same. Why Robin, how you stare at me. Do you think I'm a ghost?'

'Certainly not,' he said with a laugh, taking her hands and kissing them. 'I'm surprised, that's all.'

'And Ambrose,' Elizabeth turned to him. 'How are you?'

'Very well, my lady. Sir John,' he called as Brydges walked in, 'what is this? You said to meet with this lady would be impossible.'

Brydges brushed past Elizabeth, frowning. 'Yes, well, the Lady Elizabeth can be very persuasive.'

'What he means to say,' Elizabeth said, 'is that I hounded him until he agreed to let me see you. Are you glad I did, Robin?'

'Beyond words.'

'You?' she mocked. 'Well, beyond words you may be, but I doubt if you are beyond dinner. I know you of old.'

They laughed and Robert led her to the table, guiding her to Brydges's accustomed seat. Brydges considered protesting but did not want to seem churlish and sat down next to Ambrose.

'I must say, my lady, you seem quite cheerful,' Ambrose observed.

'Do I?' Elizabeth said. 'It must be joy at seeing you two.

Imprisonment does not suit me. Yet, I must endure it, at least until my sister can decide whether to have my head or not.'

'Has she grounds for that, Bess?' Robert asked.

A flicker of annoyance crossed Elizabeth's face. 'No, not unless she can prove I knew of Thomas Wyatt's rebellion. And that she can never do, for I am not guilty.'

'So, you're locked up without trial?' Ambrose said. 'How can the Queen do that?'

'I am a threat,' Elizabeth shrugged. 'Mary has surrounded herself with Spaniards and she listens to their counsel and none other. To them, I am a heretic and a bastard, and am better out of the way. Do you know, they had me brought here in secret so the people wouldn't make any protest? I wonder if they even know I am here.'

'Lady,' Brydges warned, looking uncomfortable, 'I feel I must—'

'Oh, forgive me, Sir John,' Elizabeth laid her long fingers upon his arm, 'I know I must not speak against my dear sister. Come Robin, we'll change the subject. Let us eat and talk of happier times.'

Dinner became a long affair. Robert and Elizabeth talked, hardly pausing for breath, and Ambrose, who had not seen his brother so happy for such a long time, was content to chat with Brydges. They entertained themselves in a drinking game, downing cup after cup, until their heads drooped and they slept, cushioned upon their arms.

'It seems they have no head for wine,' Elizabeth joked, rubbing her arms. 'I feel a little cold, Robin. Let's sit by the fire.'

Robert tossed two cushions onto the floor beside the hearth. He held her hand as she lowered herself to the floor.

'Of course, I should hate you,' she said.

Robert plumped down next to her. 'Why should you?'

'For what your family did. For using Jane. For all of it.'

'Jane!' he scoffed. 'What did you ever care for Jane?'

'She was my cousin. And I did care for her, in my way. She didn't deserve her fate.'

'Nor did Guildford. Nor did my father, for that matter.'

Elizabeth shook her head. 'Really, Robin, after all that has passed, can you still be blind to his faults?'

'What do you know of his faults?' Robert snapped. 'You didn't know my father as I did.'

'I know he meant to take Mary's life, and he would have taken mine.'

'My father would never have—'

'Why then did he send for Mary and me to come to London?'

'Edward was dying. My father thought you would want to be with him.'

'I had received word that Edward was already dead. Forgive me, Rob, but your story does not cover the facts.'

'Who sent word to you?'

'I... I don't know,' she said, looking away. 'I received a note. It wasn't signed.'

'But who do you think it was?'

'Oh, Robin, I don't know.'

'Well, I can guess. I think I know who betrayed my father, and put ideas into your head to falsely accuse him. William Cecil. I've never trusted him.'

Elizabeth reached for his hand. 'Robin, dear friend, think. With Jane on the throne, and your father expecting Guildford to be made king, what need would he have for Mary and me?'

'He wouldn't have hurt you, Bess. He was doing what Edward wanted, what he set out in his will. You would have been safe. Mary forced his hand by marching on London. No, I tell you, the sender of those notes ruined everything. He put my father's head on the block as surely as Mary did.'

'Oh, Rob, will you never forget your father?'

He glared at her. 'Could you ever forget your mother?'

Elizabeth caught her breath, shocked by the question. No one ever spoke of her mother. 'I have one memory of her. A woman with black hair and black eyes, crying as she held me. I suppose that was just before she was arrested. There are times since I've been here that I think I am doomed to suffer the same fate as she.'

'Well, my father followed his. Maybe I will follow mine. There was a time when he had just been killed when I wished I could.'

Elizabeth looked at him then, with the firelight playing upon his face. Had he been that unhappy to have wished for death? She pitied him. How he must have loved his father. How different from herself! She had never truly loved her father; she had only been in awe of his magnificence.

'How dreary this conversation has become,' she said. 'Let's talk of something happier.'

'Tell me what to talk of, Bess. Soon, the sleeping Sir John will awake and we will be locked in our cells once again. Tomorrow will pass much as today has. What have we to look forward to?'

'It's selfish of me, I know, but I am glad to have you here for company. It makes me feel less alone.' She quickly kissed his cheek. 'Are you as frightened as I am, Robin?'

He returned her kiss. Her lips were cold. 'Just as frightened, Bess.'

'Some letters from your ladies.' Brydges handed them out.

'It's from Mother,' Jack said, as Henry stood to look over his shoulder.

Brydges made to leave but turned back to Robert. 'Oh, I thought you would like to know, Master Robert, the Lady Elizabeth has gone.'

Robert looked up from Amy's letter. 'Gone?'

'She was taken away last night. Gone to Woodstock, I'm told. Sir Henry Bedingfield has charge of her now. I can't say I'm sorry to see her go. One month of that young lady was enough to try the patience of a saint. No, you must not keep me, Master Robert, I have much to do today.' He pulled the door shut and locked it.

'Why didn't she warn me she was going?' Robert said, kicking at a stool. 'To just go off.'

'She hasn't just gone off,' Ambrose said. 'You heard Sir John, she was taken. She's still a prisoner.'

'Stinking bitch,' Robert cursed, screwing up his letter and throwing it into the fireplace.

'Elizabeth?' Ambrose asked in surprise.

Robert shook his head. 'Mary.'

'Well, I imagine Elizabeth is glad to be out of the Tower.'

'Oh, you imagine, do you?' Robert mocked. 'What of me? What about us?'

'She probably didn't give us another thought, Rob.'

'You think not?'

'Well, would you, if you hated this place as much as she did?'

'I *do* hate this place and with more reason. We've lost more than she has, Am.'

'Yes, I know,' Ambrose agreed. 'Yet, do not wish her back again, Rob. That would be unkind.'

'Well, I do,' Robert said, falling onto his bed. 'No, I don't. Oh God, Am, I fear I shall go mad in this place.

'We may see freedom yet, Rob,' Jack said, holding their mother's letter in front of his face. 'Read how Mother works for our release.'

'Yes, begging the Queen. Our mother, begging!'

'The Queen will take pity on her.'

'Pity!' Robert repeated, disgusted. 'Our mother going begging to a half-Spanish mule. My stomach turns at the thought of it.'

'Mother has found more friends amongst the Spanish at court than the English,' Jack snapped. 'So, stop your moaning and read Amy's letter that you have so thoughtlessly thrown away.'

OCTOBER 1554

Fever infected the Tower. Jack succumbed and Jane Dudley petitioned the Queen ever more vigorously to take pity on her sick son. The Queen, grown once again merciful, granted him his release and Jack was carried out of the Tower on a litter, mumbling in his delirium and drenched in sweat, unaware that he was leaving the dreaded fortress. The pure air of Kent was deemed best for him, and Mary, their sister, awaited his arrival at her house, Penshurst, with a mixture of joy and dread. Doctors were summoned, but their medicine could do nothing. Three days after his arrival at Penshurst, Jack died.

Ambrose, Robert and Henry, left in the Tower, received the news with surprising calm. They had known Jack was dangerously ill and recent experience had hardened them. They mourned his passing but could only wonder if they would suffer the same.

Jane Dudley soon followed her son. Worn out with cares, she died less than three months later. The very day of her death brought release for the three brothers. Queen Mary pardoned them. The brothers were free.

The news came too hard on the heels of misfortune to cheer them greatly, though they hurried from their prison, not once looking back. They made their way to Penshurst, where all the remaining family gathered. Reunions were tinged with sadness, embraces too desperate for happiness. Their mother's Will was read, and Robert heard with indignation how she did not want a grand funeral, preferring to be laid to rest privately and quietly. Robert would not allow it. He made all the funeral arrangements, having to borrow money to pay the coffin-maker and tradesmen. His mother would not be buried quietly, ignominiously. Her funeral was a lavish affair, as befitted the Duchess of Northumberland, widow of a once great general of England.

CHAPTER 19

HALES OWEN, NORFOLK, APRIL 1555

Amy Dudley lay in bed, looking at the man lying asleep beside her. Sunlight fell across his face, making his skin look almost golden. How handsome he was, and like this, asleep in their bed, Robert was entirely her own. It made her stomach lurch when she thought of how close she had come to losing him; first, when his father had been executed, then Guildford, and then when Jack had become ill. But Robert was strong and had survived, and she thanked God daily for it. He had changed, of course. He was thinner and there was a new wariness in his eyes. The joy had gone out of him, too. She must try to make him feel it again.

Smiling to herself, she slid her hand through the opening of his nightshirt, the hairs on his chest springy against her fingers. He moaned softly and turned his head towards her. His eyes flickered open. She smiled down at him. He closed his eyes and turned his head away. She cuddled up to him, her hand delving deeper inside his nightshirt.

'Amy,' he chided, pushing her hand away.

'Don't you love me?' she asked, her voice playful, but even beneath the fog of sleep, he sensed the hurt beneath her coquetry.

'I'm tired,' he said, relieved as he felt her fall back against the mattress.

'What shall we do today?' she asked after a minute's silence. Her voice was hard.

'I don't know.'

'You don't have plans?'

With a groan, he opened his eyes. 'I should go over the estate and see what needs to be done. Ambrose told me the estate manager, Anthony Forster, is very able, but I should still look it over. You should look into the household staff. See if there are any servants we can do without. Perhaps there are some tasks you can take over, Amy.'

'You want *me* to work?'

'Well, why not? We haven't any money, Amy, as well you know. If it wasn't for Ambrose giving us this house, we wouldn't even have anywhere to live.'

'Oh yes, remind me we're living on your brother's charity.'

'Why the devil do you say that?' Robert snapped, sitting up, suddenly wide awake. 'It's not charity, it's a financial arrangement. Ambrose has given us the house in exchange for paying off my mother's debts.'

'Which we can't afford to do.'

'Then I'll have to borrow more money, won't I? And it's better to have land than money, Amy. If the idea of work pains you so much, you can always go and live with your father.'

'You want to be rid of me, don't you?' Amy turned on him, her eyes filling with tears. 'Why don't you just say it?'

'Oh, for Christ's sake, Amy,' he said, throwing back the bedclothes. 'Don't start.'

'Where are you going?'

'Away from you,' he returned through gritted teeth, slamming the door behind him.

HATFIELD PALACE, MAY 1556

'So, how are you?' Elizabeth bit down on an almond biscuit, crumbs tumbling down her dress.

Robert watched her brush them away. 'Well enough.'

'That didn't sound convincing, Robin.' Robert didn't look up, but gave a half smile. 'I was sorry to hear about Jack and your mother.'

'Thank you.'

She leant forward and placed her hand beneath his chin, forcing him to look at her. 'What's wrong?'

Robert sighed, taking hold of her hand. 'I'm finding it... difficult, being free.'

'Surely you wouldn't rather be back in the Tower?'

'No,' he laughed, 'but the only worry I had in the Tower was staying alive. I've been released but there's nothing left for me. No estates, they've all been taken by your sister. I have no money, it's all gone to pay off debts. Ambrose had to give me a house to live in and the only horses I have are the ones that work on the land. If I want to go riding, I have to borrow a neighbour's horse.'

'Poor Rob. I hadn't realised things were as bad as that.'

'Well, they are. But never mind. They'll get better, I'm sure.' He smiled at her.

'How's your wife?' Elizabeth asked.

The smile fell from his face. 'She's fine.' Elizabeth looked at him. He noticed the query on her face and endeavoured to explain. 'It's me. I've changed and she's stayed the same.'

'You don't love her anymore?' If he noticed the hopefulness in her voice, he didn't show it.

'Not as I once did,' he admitted, 'but it's not her fault. I'm not the man she married. How could I be, after what I've been through?'

'Perhaps when you have children—'

'There aren't going to be any children,' he cut in angrily, throwing her hand away. 'We've been married for five years and not once has she been with child. She must be barren.'

'Then I'm sorry for you, Rob,' Elizabeth said sincerely. 'I think you would like to be a father.'

'Well, anyway,' he waved his hand in the air, signalling he wanted to change the subject, 'you're pleased to be back at Hatfield?'

'Immeasurably,' Elizabeth rolled her eyes. 'I wouldn't wish Sir Henry Bedingfield on anyone. My sister couldn't have chosen a better gaoler.'

'Do you hear any news from court?'

'I have my spies.'

'Indeed!' He made a face, impressed. 'And who would they be?'

'I'm not telling you,' she slapped playfully at him. She

became suddenly serious. 'Philip wants to war against the French.'

'A war? He'll be needing men, then?'

'Oh, look at you,' Elizabeth snorted in disgust. 'Why do men get so excited at the idea of war? And you would fight for the King of Spain?'

'I would fight for the Devil. I need to do something, Bess. I need money.'

'You could get yourself killed!'

'And what loss would that be?'

Elizabeth glared at him. 'Your wife would miss you. Your family would miss you. *I* would miss you.'

'Would you?' he pouted.

'Yes, God help me, I would.'

'Who should I write to? Oh, come on, Bess, tell me. Who should I write to, to offer my services?'

Elizabeth shrugged. 'To my sister's secretary, I suppose. But how are you going to equip yourself for war? That takes money, Robin, or hadn't you thought of that?'

'I'll have to borrow more, or sell some of the land around Hales Owen. I don't suppose you could...?'

'Me?' Elizabeth laughed. 'Next in line to the throne I may be, Robin, but I have no money of my own that isn't already spent twice over. My household costs a fortune to maintain. I should be asking *you* for a loan.'

'If I could, I would, you know that.'

'I know.' She leaned over and touched his knee. 'Money, I may not have, but I do have horses. Shall we go for a ride?'

Robert took her hand and kissed it. 'I was hoping you'd ask.'

HALES OWEN, FEBRUARY 1557

'And now you want to go to France?' Ambrose threw up his hands in exasperation. 'After what happened in London?'

Robert wanted to forget London. He had gone there, dragging Ambrose and Henry with him, needing to smell the stink of the city in his nostrils, desperate to feel part of something, if only for a short while. He had arranged to meet two brothers he had always thought of as friends. They turned out to be anything but. They had looked down their noses at him, reviled him for being a traitor and mocked his father. A fight followed, Ambrose having to pull Robert away. They had returned to their lodging house to find a stranger waiting for them. He answered none of their questions, merely informed them it would be better, safer, for them to leave London immediately. They had left the next morning.

'Forget London,' Robert said angrily.

'I thought you had learnt your lesson when we were warned to stay out of court affairs.' Ambrose shook his head wearily. 'We're not welcome.'

Amy poured Robert another cup of wine. 'Ambrose is right. Can't you be content with me here?'

Robert looked away with a deep sigh. 'No, I can't. Oh, for heaven's sake, Amy, be quiet,' he snapped as she began to whimper. He leant across the table, his hands held out to Ambrose. 'Come with me, Am. Henry and I are going to France whether you do or not, but I would so much like you to be with us.'

'You haven't dragged Henry into this?'

'I didn't have to drag him. He wants to go.'

'And what will going to war achieve? Tell me that.'

'Maybe we'll make our fortune. King Philip needs men, and if we serve him well, who knows what will be granted us?'

'*If* we come back,' Ambrose pointed out. 'We can't afford to equip any men, Rob, so we'd have to serve under someone.'

'I've already spoken with the Earl of Pembroke. We can serve under him. You'll remember, he was a good friend to Father.'

'Yes, he was.' Ambrose chewed on his bottom lip, thinking.

Robert grew impatient. 'Oh, say you'll come, Am.'

Ambrose glared at him. 'Well, of course I'll come. God knows what would become of you both if I let you go on your own.'

Robert laughed and clapped his hands. 'Oh, you won't regret it, Am. We will do so well, King Philip won't be able to ignore us.'

ST QUENTIN, FRANCE, SEPTEMBER 1557

The field stank.

Battered bodies spilt their life-blood into the mud of St Quentin. Robert held himself up by hanging over the side of a horse-cart and thanked God that he was still alive. A moment's rest was all he allowed himself. Pushing away from the cart, he stumbled over outstretched limbs, sinking ankle deep in the mud with each step. The mud had got everywhere, inside his boots, through rips in his shirts. His handsome face was grimed with it, merging with the blood of those he had fought.

Over the crackle and snap of fire, the moans of the dying and the shouts of the living, one voice rang out, hard and urgent, calling his name. He tried to find its origin, but black smoke blew into his eyes, blinding him. He stumbled forward, knuckling out from his eyes tiny pieces of ash and grit. Strong hands grabbed him and spun him around.

He blinked. 'Ambrose?' he croaked, his throat sore from the roar of battle cries. Ambrose was struggling for breath, his fingers digging painfully into Robert's flesh.

'Henry,' Ambrose gasped, his tears marking channels down his mud-streaked cheeks. 'Cannon shot. He's dead.'

Robert stared at him, his mouth hanging open. 'No,' he cried. 'No.'

'I've seen him. Lying by his horse, half his body gone.'

'You left him?'

'I wanted to find you.' Ambrose pulled Robert close. 'There was nothing I could do for him.'

Robert pushed away. 'Where is he?' he shouted, trying to hurry through the gripping mud. 'Where?'

Ambrose lurched after him. 'There's nothing you can do,' he protested, grabbing Robert by the arm and pulling him back, almost collapsing on top of him. 'He's dead.'

He repeated the two awful words until he felt Robert accept the truth of them and stopped struggling. The two brothers, half-lay, half-crouched in the mud, spent, struck down with grief, while around them England lost the war.

RICHMOND PALACE, SURREY, OCTOBER 1557

Queen Mary's eyes, set deep in her sallow, jowly face, squinted down at him. She sniffed pointedly at Robert's riding clothes, caked in mud and manure and stinking of sweat.

'You bring news from my husband?' she growled.

'I have, Your Majesty. Despatches from France.'

Mary stretched out her hand. 'Give them to me.'

Robert untied the leather roll and pulled out the documents. Mary held them close to her face as she read.

'I see you have lost your brother, Dudley.'

'Yes, Your Majesty.'

She offered no condolences. 'My husband is pleased with you. He professes you have been most valiant in France.'

'The King is generous to say so.'

'Indeed, he is.' Mary frowned, her mouth twisting as she looked down at him. 'More than you realise. My husband requests that your family be restored in blood.' Robert waited, not daring to breathe. He heard her rings tapping against the pommel of the chair. She sniffed once more, then said, 'Rise, Lord Robert.'

He took hold of the hem of her skirt and kissed it, taking a moment to breath in the dusty smell of the cloth and slow the blood pounding in his hears. He rose and bowed his head.

'I cannot adequately express my gratitude, Your Majesty.'

'Hear me, Lord Robert,' Mary said sternly. 'Though I do as my husband wishes, I do not forget that you are the son of the traitor Northumberland, whose actions caused me to take the life of that poor girl, Jane Grey. An innocent, who would never have thought of the crown had it not been thrust upon her by your father. I will not have you at my court.'

Robert kept his head down. 'I ask nothing further of Your Majesty. Your bounty has already been most generous. My only desire now is to return to the country.'

'A sensible desire, Lord Robert. You may go.'

He backed away from her, hearing the whispers of the courtiers as they discussed his new fortune. In a daze, he found himself back in the stable yard, laying a shaking hand against the brick wall. The Dudleys were back in the game. But what a price they had had to pay!

He walked towards the stalls. His horse was still resting, so he fell down in the straw and closed his eyes. It didn't bother him that the Queen didn't want him at court. He had no desire to serve Mary. No, he would go back home and wait for the next queen to come along.

CHAPTER 20

HATFIELD PALACE, NOVEMBER 17, 1558

Elizabeth waited beneath the oak tree. Cecil had sent her word that Mary was dying and to expect to be named queen before the day was out. It troubled her that she felt no sense of grief or loss for her sister. If the situation had been reversed, if it was Elizabeth that lay dying, Mary would weep for her.

She saw them coming. She smoothed her skirts and held herself erect. She was determined to look like a queen.

Sir Nicholas Throckmorton climbed down from his horse and fished inside his velvet purse for the ring that he had taken from Mary's stiff, cold finger, the ring that would symbolise the transference of sovereignty from the dead queen to the new one. He hurried towards her. He noticed her trembling lips, the eagerness in her eyes and knew he need waste no words of condolence. He fell to his knees and delivered his news that the Queen was dead. He handed her the ring.

'This is the Lord's doing,' Elizabeth said, trying hard not to smile. 'It is marvellous in our eyes.'

She sank to her knees before him, clapped her hands together and silently mouthed a prayer. Did she pray for her dead sister? Throckmorton doubted it.

'Come, my lord,' she said, holding out her hand for him to help her to her feet. 'Sir William Cecil is with you, I hope?'

'He follows not far behind, Your Majesty.' He heard her breath catch at the new title.

'Good. I shall need him. Escort me back to the house, my lord. There are plenty of letters to write.'

HALES OWEN

Amy looked up from her sewing as Robert stamped into the chamber and fell into a chair. His expression was thunderous. 'Robert, what's the matter?'

'That damn carthorse threw me.'

'You're hurt?'

'No,' he said, shrugging off her searching hands. 'What's that?' He pointed at a crumpled paper peeping out from the top of her bodice.

She pulled it out and tried to smooth out the creases. 'It just came for you.'

He snatched it from her and broke the seal. 'Oh, Amy,' he breathed, his face breaking into a grin, 'the best news. Mary has died. Elizabeth is Queen.'

'Oh, really?' Amy said, unimpressed. Robert disappeared up the stairs and she hurried after him. 'What are you doing?' she asked breathlessly, falling onto their bed.

'Elizabeth has sent for me.' He flung off his riding coat and washed hurriedly, slapping water under his armpits and down his back.

'Elizabeth wants you, so you go?'

'Yes, that's right.'

'And what about me?'

'What about you?'

'Can I come with you?'

'No,' he said, pulling on a clean shirt.

'Why not?'

'I can ride quicker on my own.'

'I suppose you think I'll be in the way?'

'Amy, please understand. This is what I've been waiting for.'

Amy looked away, determined to hold back her tears. 'When will you be back?' she asked quietly.

'Come here.' Robert held out his arms and Amy rushed to him. 'I'll return as soon as I can.'

'Promise?' she looked up at him with her large brown eyes.

'I promise.'

Robert had been made to wait, like all the others, in the Presence Chamber and he was growing bored. The room was filling up, courtiers jostling for space and more than once, Robert had been elbowed aside to make room. He was relieved when a page called out his name and instructed him to follow.

The page showed him into a much smaller room. Elizabeth was standing by the window, watching the new arrivals. She was dressed in a simple gown of black and white, her red hair brushed straight, falling like a curtain down her back. Robert took a step towards her.

'Good morning, Lord Robert.'

Robert turned. William Cecil stood behind a desk, its surface littered with papers. 'Cecil. What are you doing here?'

'I am Her Majesty's Secretary, Lord Robert.'

'Indeed,' Robert said. He turned pointedly away, striding towards Elizabeth and sinking to one knee. 'Your Majesty.'

Elizabeth held out her hand. 'Robin,' she purred, as he pressed his lips to it. 'How good it is to see you again. We have both had changes of fortune, haven't we?'

'Indeed, we have.'

'Oh, get up. I can't have my Master of Horse on his knees.'

Robert rose. 'Master of Horse?'

'Of course. Who else is more suited to the position?'

'No one,' he agreed.

'But I warn you, this won't be a sinecure. You'll probably have more work than you realise.'

'I'll be glad of it. I've had years of nothing to do.'

'Your first duty,' Cecil said, 'will be in arranging the transportation of Her Majesty and her household to London. May I ask if your wife accompanied you?'

'She stayed in the country.'

'Good. We haven't much room to accommodate too many spouses. Of course, once we are at court, arrangements could be made for her. Perhaps as one of the ladies of the Bedchamber?'

'No,' both Robert and Elizabeth said. Elizabeth turned away, her face reddening.

'My wife does not care for the town,' Robert explained. 'She would much rather stay in the country.'

Cecil raised his eyebrows, looking between Robert and Elizabeth. 'I see.'

'But I know my sister, Mary, would be pleased to serve you, Bes—,' Robert corrected himself, 'Your Majesty.'

'Mary! Of course,' Elizabeth said delightedly. 'Send to Lady Sidney, Cecil. She can be one of my ladies.'

Cecil made a note, gesturing towards the paperwork on his desk. Elizabeth understood.

'You must go now, Robin. I have so many other people to see.' She held out her hand once more for him to kiss.

She saw the disappointment in his face. He had hoped for more from her, more warmth perhaps, maybe an invitation to remain. But she wasn't a princess any longer. She was a queen and her duty must come first.

He took her hand, his fingers warming hers. 'I hope to see you later, Your Majesty.'

'Yes,' she answered, neither promising nor denying.

THE TOWER

Robert pushed open the heavy oak door to the chapel. It creaked on its hinges. He stepped inside, his footsteps echoing around the vaulted chamber. Passing the rows of wooden pews, he came to the altar. Flat stones served as grave markers for the executed, their names carved into the stone: Anne Boleyn, Catherine Howard, Edward Seymour, Jane Grey. Robert knelt and ran his fingers along the grooves of the last two names: John Dudley, Guildford Dudley.

'Robin?'

He started. 'Your Majesty. I didn't hear you come in.'

'Stay still,' Elizabeth said, walking swiftly towards him. She looked down at the gravestones, then across to him. 'You've been crying.'

'Have I?' He wiped his hand across his cheeks and was surprised to find them wet. 'So I have. You're unattended, madam.'

'My ladies are just outside. I saw you come in. Do you mind my being here?'

'Why should I mind?'

'I thought you might want to be alone.'

He gestured towards his face. 'Look what being alone does to me.'

She knelt down next to him and stroked his cheek. 'Poor Robin.' She nodded towards the stones. 'I wonder if they can see us now.'

He sniffed. 'They can.'

'You sound very sure.'

'I am sure.'

'My mother would be pleased, I think.' She smiled sadly. 'Would your father be pleased to see me on the throne?'

Robert stiffened. 'He would have served you, Bess, as he would any king or queen. I know what everyone thinks of my father. God knows they make no attempt to hide their opinions from me. But it was your brother who thought of changing the succession to Jane and Father was doing his duty by him. I don't deny there were certain advantages to our family in the change, but Father never would have thought of it himself. And when it came to it, he was reluctant to carry it out at all.'

'But you understand that people have a difficult time believing that, Robin?'

'Because they didn't know him, as I knew him. And Edward was right, Bess. Look what a state Mary brought this country to.'

'I know. When I think of those poor souls she sent to the flames in the name of her religion. Archbishop Cranmer—,' she shook her head. 'But I will change it, Rob, I promise you. And you will help me, won't you?'

'I give my life to you. It's yours to do with as you please.'

'And if I please to have you near me, always?'

'Then that is what I will do.'

'Your wife may not like that.'

'My wife can go to the devil.'

She laughed, pleased. 'Oh, come Rob, let us leave here. We've paid our respects to the dead. Besides, Cecil will send a search party to find me if I'm away much longer.' Robert made a face. 'Oh, I know what you think of him,' she said, as he helped her to her feet.

'With reason.'

'With nothing more than suspicion. But he is as dear to me as you and you will have to find a way of working with him.'

'Oh, I can work with the man, as long as you don't expect me to like him.'

'No, I won't expect that.' She squeezed his hand. 'And I must ask of you a favour. I want you to meet with John Dee. I know he's a friend of yours. I want him to divine the best day for my coronation. It must be propitious. I can't send Cecil on such an errand, he would disapprove greatly.'

'Leave it to me,' Robert said. 'I'll write to him at once.'

WHITEHALL PALACE, JANUARY 1559

The black crows were moulting and their fallen feathers were crunched underfoot as their owners half-skipped, half-danced to the edge of the stage. Their scarlet red robes flounced higher and crucifixes bounced against their chests to the sound of laughter.

Elizabeth, her chin upon her hand, glanced sideways at her Secretary. 'What's wrong, Cecil? Does it not amuse you?'

Cecil smiled politely. 'Yes, Your Majesty.'

'Now, don't pay me lip service. What is it you object to?'

Cecil cleared his throat. 'I applaud the anti-Catholic sentiment behind this entertainment, madam, but I question the wisdom in performing it, especially in front of the Imperial ambassador.'

They both looked towards King Philip's envoy, who looked anything but amused.

'Lord Robert devised it,' Elizabeth said carelessly.

'Ah,' Cecil nodded, as if that explained everything.

Elizabeth laughed. 'Oh, Cecil, we shall have to forgive him his daring. I like a man to be daring.'

'Daring, indeed, madam! But when daring becomes foolish or even reckless...'

The smile dropped from Elizabeth's face. 'I won't allow him to be reckless or foolish. I am his mistress, not he my master.'

Cecil looked her straight in the eye. 'I am very glad to hear it, madam.'

Elizabeth sank back in her chair, frowning as she looked about her. 'Where the devil is he, Cecil? I can't see him.'

'Who, Your Majesty?'

'Lord Robert.'

Cecil scanned the room. 'I can't see him either, madam.'

At that moment, Thomas Howard, Duke of Norfolk, walked past. 'Your Grace,' Elizabeth clicked her fingers at him.

Norfolk halted, a flicker of annoyance crossing his face. 'Yes, Your Majesty?'

'Norfolk, kindly go and find my Master of the Horse. Remind him his place is by me.'

Norfolk's jaw clenched. Good God, did this woman think he was no better than a servant? He was a duke, the highest noble in the land and here was the bastard brat of a notorious whore sending him to find her stable boy. His reply was curt. 'Yes, Your Majesty.'

Cecil lowered his eyes as Norfolk passed on, embarrassed for him, but Elizabeth seemed oblivious to the insult she had just given. He would have to find a gentle way of reminding her of the Duke's nobility.

The door to Robert's apartments was open. Norfolk strode inside.

Robert was standing at his desk, his shirt open at the neck, a smudge of ink scarring his nose. He was so engrossed in his work that he had not heard Norfolk come in.

'Dudley.'

Robert's head jerked up. 'Your Grace?' he made a bow, wondering what on earth Norfolk could want.

Norfolk moved to the desk. 'What is this?' he asked, gesturing at the paperwork.

'The route for the coronation.'

'Proving difficult?' Norfolk sounded as if the prospect pleased him.

'No,' Robert said defensively, 'but there is such a lot to do. And...,' he looked almost embarrassed, 'I want it to be perfect.'

'Perfect?' Norfolk laughed. 'I hear she had a necromancer decide the date for the coronation.'

'John Dee is not a necromancer, Your Grace. He is a scholar.'

'A scholar,' Norfolk looked disgusted. 'I tell you, it won't happen at all if my cousin can't find someone to crown her.'

Robert knew that many of the bishops, Catholics left over from her sister's reign, had refused outright to perform a coronation on a woman they believed to be doubly cursed, first as a bastard and second as a heretic. 'She'll find a bishop to do it.'

'She has less than two weeks. All this,' Norfolk gestured at the paperwork, 'may be for nothing.'

'She will find someone.'

Norfolk sniffed, bored. 'I hope you've put me in my rightful place in the procession.'

'Yes.'

'The first in line?'

'Yes.'

'Good. And make sure my horse has been purged by nine in the morning. I won't have it shitting all the way to the abbey.'

Robert sighed in annoyance. 'I do know what I'm doing.'

'Yes, I suppose you can be trusted with the horses, at least, though why my cousin gave you such a high position eludes me. She may have forgotten your recent history, but rest assured, I haven't. Once a traitor, always a traitor, in my opinion. She wants you, by the way.'

'What for?'

'I'm damned if I know. Perhaps her Fool has let her down and she needs someone to make her laugh.' He slouched out of the room, laughing at his own joke.

Had he been ten years younger, Robert would have struck the duke to the floor, despite his nobility, and to hell with the consequences. But if his sojourn in the Tower had taught him anything it was his place in the world. He was newly risen, and he would do nothing to jeopardise that. He shrugged on his doublet and closed the door behind him.

PALACE OF WESTMINSTER, JANUARY 15, 1559

Mary Sidney lifted the pearl-encrusted headband from Elizabeth's head, sensing her mistress's relief at its removal.

'Are you unwell, Your Majesty?'

Elizabeth rubbed at her temples, squeezing her eyes shut. 'Oh, Mary, my head feels like it is splitting in two. You wouldn't believe how heavy the crown and the ceremonial robes were.'

'And it's been such a long day,' Kat Ashley said, warming a nightgown before the fire. 'You must be tired, my sweet.'

'I am, Kat. Hurry with my— why, Robin!'

'Your Majesty,' Robert said, entering with Cecil close behind, 'I come to bid you goodnight, while Cecil comes with yet more paperwork for you.'

'The business of government is never at an end, Lord Robert,' Cecil replied tersely. 'Your Majesty, I have documents which require your signature.'

Elizabeth barely looked at him; her eyes were fixed on Robert. 'I think John Dee must be losing his powers, or else you passed on the wrong information, Lord Robert, for I tell you, today has not been at all propitious.'

Robert frowned. 'Pardon me, madam, but I had thought the day went very well.'

'Maybe it did for you, but you have not had to endure what I have this day. The oil Bishop Oglethorpe anointed me with was rancid. I've had it plastered all over my body and I have a terrible headache. It has been a very long day, Robin.'

'I'm sorry to hear you are not well, madam.'

Elizabeth grunted and sat down at her dressing table, signalling for Mary to brush her hair.

'Even more reason for you to get some rest,' Robert continued. 'Cecil, the paperwork can wait.'

Cecil bristled. 'It is for the Queen to dismiss me, my lord. I go at none other's say so.'

Robert rolled his eyes. 'Here,' he said, snatching up the nightgown and holding it out.

Elizabeth's lips twisted into a reluctant smirk. 'You really are too impertinent, Robin. Do you think I will undress before you?'

'I can but hope.'

She laughed out loud, her humour restored. 'Give it back to Kat, you monster, and be gone. Both of you go. I *am* very tired and government *will* wait until tomorrow, Cecil.'

Cecil hid his annoyance poorly, bidding Elizabeth goodnight with an audible sigh. Once in the corridor, he turned to Robert. 'I must confess your sense of humour escapes me, Lord Robert.'

Robert frowned at him. 'What are you talking about?'

'To talk with a queen about her state of undress or make insinuations of a, shall we say, familiar nature, is most improper.'

'Oh, nonsense,' Robert started off down the corridor, his long legs taking such lengthy strides that Cecil had to hurry to keep up. 'I was only joking.'

'Yes, I understand. But you must see how I could be mistaken in thinking you were in earnest?'

Robert came to a sudden stop. 'I don't care what *you* think. Elizabeth knew I didn't mean it.'

'You two are of a similar age, of course,' Cecil said. 'You understand the Queen better than I. But I would advise you to be careful, my lord.'

'For God's sake, careful of what?'

'Lord Robert, you are a married man, whose wife is, you'll forgive me, conveniently in the country. And the Queen is an unmarried young woman who cannot afford gossip to ruin any future marriage prospects.'

'I would do nothing to endanger the Queen's reputation.'

Cecil looked into his dark eyes. 'I trust *you* will not, my lord. Goodnight.'

CHAPTER 21

SYDERSTONE HALL, MARCH 1559

'ROBERT!'

Amy screamed with joy and rushed towards him.

I mustn't be impatient with her, he reminded himself as he slid down his horse's flank. *She hasn't seen me for months. It's only natural she's excited.*

Amy threw herself against him, nearly knocking him over. 'Oh, why have you stayed away so long, Robert?'

He gently pushed her away. 'I have duties at court now, Amy. I'm not free to come and go as I please.'

She stared up into his face. 'Are you tired? Are you working too hard?'

'Nothing of the sort. I'm very well. Now, tell me, how does my little wife fare?'

They walked into the house. Robert strode to the fire to warm his cold hands. She clung to his arm.

'To tell truth, my love, I am not very well. I have a pain, here.' She pointed to her left breast. 'And there is a lump.'

He frowned. 'Have you seen a physician?'

'No.'

'Why ever not?'

'Oh, I don't know. I hoped it would go away, and then, when it didn't, I grew frightened and now, I don't want to think about it.'

'Amy, you can't just ignore—'

'Oh, please don't be angry with me. Now that you're home, I'm sure I will feel better.'

Robert hesitated. *Best to tell her now*, he decided. 'Amy, I'm not home to stay.'

'What?' she said sharply.

'I have to leave no later than Saturday.'

'But that's only three days away.'

'I am Master of the Queen's Horse, Amy.'

'Well, then, I shall return to London with you.'

Robert shook his head. 'I can't take you with me. The Queen doesn't care for wives at court.'

'But your sister's at court. Is she not a wife?'

'Mary's a Lady of the Bedchamber, that's an entirely different thing. Even Cecil's wife has to stay at home.'

'But—'

'And I'll wager she doesn't complain to her husband for it, but accepts that it must be so.'

'Well, isn't Mistress Cecil a marvel, then!' Amy retorted scornfully.

'Amy!'

'I think you don't want me at court, that's what I think,' Amy said, her face screwing up in anger. 'You don't want me there, so you can whore with your women.'

'My women?' Robert laughed. 'I don't have any women. Good God, Amy, you're enough for any man.'

'Well, I see I must vex you very much, husband. Why you even bother to come home, I can't imagine.' She sat down and stared out of the window.

'I will send for the doctor to examine you,' Robert said quietly. 'Illness mustn't be ignored, Amy.'

'If you want,' she sniffed. 'Maybe you're hoping he'll tell you I haven't long to live. Then you'll be happy.'

He stepped up behind her and placed a kiss upon her flushed neck. 'You mustn't say such things, Amy. You know that isn't true.' She remained silent. 'Could you arrange for dinner for me? It's been a long, cold ride from London.'

'Dinner will be brought shortly,' she replied curtly. 'You had best go and change your clothes. You stink of horses.'

Only as he walked away from her did she trust herself to look at him. She hadn't meant to be so shrewish with him. She had wanted him to be pleased to be home. He would leave the sooner now, she knew it, eager to be away from her and her complaints. Oh, why had she not held her tongue? She could have worked upon him when they were in bed. He wouldn't have refused her anything then. The thought of their lovemaking reminded her of her earlier accusation. She didn't believe him when he said there were no other women. She had seen, too often, the wives of their neighbours making eyes at him and she had been proud that they should covet her husband. But then he had been at home, where he could not have disguised any infidelity. But at court he was free to do as he pleased, and she didn't doubt that he did.

A servant brought in a platter of beef and set it on the table. 'Oh, forgive me, my lady, I was told the master had returned. Shall I take this away?'

'Your master is but changing his clothes, Richard. He will be down for his dinner directly. And oh, he wants the doctor sent for.'

'Is he unwell, my lady?'

'The doctor's for me,' she said almost wearily. 'I don't think I'm very well.'

WHITEHALL PALACE

Elizabeth was so much easier to work with without Lord Robert Dudley around to distract her. It pleased Cecil to have her all to himself. He passed her another document and watched as she made her elaborate, beautiful signature.

'Next?' she asked as she passed it back.

'Your Master of the Horse has written, madam. He requests a further three days leave of absence from court. It seems his wife is unwell and wishes him to remain until she feels better.'

'What's the matter with his wife?' There was no trace of concern in her voice.

'He did not say in his letter, madam, but I have told him he may take the three days. I trust I was right to do so?'

'Yes, perfectly right.' Elizabeth seemed annoyed. 'His duty to his wife must come before his duty to me. What's next?'

Cecil passed a paper across the table. 'This is a list of names suggested by your Council as possible suitors for your hand, madam.'

Elizabeth read. 'Sir William Pickering, the Earl of Arundel, the Earl of Arran, King Eric of Sweden and ... King Philip of Spain.' She looked up at Cecil. 'He is my brother-in-law!'

'Dispensations for consanguinity can be obtained, madam,' Cecil replied, refusing to apologise for the inclusion of Philip's name.

She grunted doubtfully. 'Sir William Pickering, I already know. He is much older than me, Cecil.'

'But a very sensible man, Your Majesty.'

'These others, will any of them come to England so I may see them?'

Cecil tried hard not to appear shocked by her question. What was Elizabeth thinking? That her suitors would parade before her so that she could look them over to see if one took her fancy? Some of these men were princes, for heaven's sake. 'I don't believe that would be possible, madam. We could request likenesses if you wish to see their faces.'

'I have no intention of marrying a man I have not set eyes upon, Cecil. I do not want to start a marriage with that kind of disappointment.'

'There are other virtues besides a handsome face, madam. The nobility of princes—.' He broke off as he noticed Elizabeth scowl. 'I shall request likenesses.' He began shuffling once more through his documents.

'Enough,' Elizabeth said, slapping her hand on the desk. 'No more work. I'm getting a headache. I've been inside for too long.'

Cecil stifled a protest. 'Shall I send for your ladies, madam?'

'Yes, I will go riding.' She rose and moved to the window. 'I don't need Robert,' she told herself under her breath. 'I do not need him.'

APRIL 1559

Robert leaned over the pommel of his saddle and stroked Mirabelle's neck. 'I hope you've been looking after my horses, Samuel.'

'I have, my lord,' Samuel replied proudly. 'But they've missed you, that I will say.'

'I'm told the Queen is out riding.'

'Yes, my lord.'

'Which way did she ride out?'

'Towards the lake, my lord.'

'Who was with her?'

'Some of her ladies, the Lady Mary Sidney amongst them for certain. And Sir William Pickering.'

'Pickering?' Robert frowned. 'He hates horses.'

'The Queen commanded it, my lord,' Samuel grinned. 'He didn't look too happy about going.'

Robert nudged Mirabelle's sides and rode off towards the lake. Ten minutes later, he saw the Queen's party by a clump of trees and he cantered up to them.

Elizabeth was wearing a green riding habit which showed off her red hair. He was thinking how handsome she looked until that thought was shunted from his head by the stare that Elizabeth turned on him.

'Your Majesty,' he greeted her with an uncertain smile.

'Why, Lord Robert!' Elizabeth replied with affected good humour. 'How good of you to return to court.'

'My duty lies here, madam,' he answered.

Elizabeth brought her horse alongside his. 'I assume your wife is better now, as she has allowed you to leave her side?'

'She is more settled in her mind than she was.'

'Well, that is something. Perhaps now your duties as my Master of the Horse can be attended to.'

'I trust you have not been neglected in my absence, Your Majesty?'

'Not at all. Sir William Pickering has kept me most happily entertained.'

Sir William Pickering, keeping his seat with some difficulty, managed to project a proud smile at Robert.

'I'm glad,' Robert said, even as Elizabeth moved away. He had been wrong to stay away, he realised. Elizabeth thought he wasn't dedicated to his position. Maybe she was even considering giving the Horse to someone else. Damn Amy!

'Rob?'

He jerked in surprise as someone touched his arm. 'Oh, Mary, it's you.'

'I startled you.'

'I was thinking. Mary, has the Queen said anything about me while I've been away?'

Mary brushed a strand of hair away from her cheek. 'In private, she has spoken of you often. Too often, to my mind.'

Robert looked sharply at her. 'What do you mean by that?'

Mary hesitated. 'I think you should be careful, Rob.'

'Of Elizabeth? Is she displeased with me, Mary? Has my being away longer than planned angered her?'

'Oh, how can you be so blind? She cares for you, Rob.'

'Of course she cares for me—'

'More than a queen should care for a subject. More than a friend.'

Robert stared at her. 'You don't mean—'

'Yes, I do mean. She's in love with you, Rob. That's why she's so annoyed.'

'She's in love with me, so that's why she's angry with me?' Robert asked, thoroughly confused.

Mary groaned in exasperation. 'You've been spending time with Amy instead of her. She's jealous.' Robert said nothing, his mind busy. 'So, what was wrong with Amy?' Mary asked.

'Apart from the usual complaints, you mean? She has a pain in her left breast, and a lump. I sent for the physician.'

'And?'

'He said it could be a tumour.'

'She's in pain?'

'A little, yes.'

'Poor Amy. But should you not have brought her back with you?'

'I can't do that, Mary. Elizabeth won't have wives at court unless they're in service to her.'

'But, if she knows how ill Amy is—'

'Oh, talk sense, Mary. If, as you seem to think, Elizabeth loves me, she won't want my wife here, spying on us.'

'Spying on you?' Mary repeated incredulously. 'Robert, your behaviour with the Queen can be nothing other than honourable or her reputation will be ruined. She cannot marry you, so she must not love you. What do you think, that you can lie with her?'

'For Jesu's sake, keep your voice down,' he hissed at her. 'Spying was the wrong word. I didn't mean it.'

'I think you meant exactly that. My God, Rob, there are times when you disgust me. You don't care about Amy at all.'

She snapped her whip against her horse's rump and sped away after the Queen.

Robert barely noticed she had left him. Was she right? Could Elizabeth be in love with him? He searched his memory. That night in the Tower, when they had sat before Brydges's fire and shared their fears; the times since her accession when they had laughed together, gone riding together, danced. Her flushed cheeks as he held her during a dance, the holding of his hand just that moment longer than necessary as he helped her mount her horse. Other little intimacies too numerous to even catalogue. Good God, how could he have been so blind? Had he been so caught up in his new work, so eager to make a success of it, that he hadn't noticed the signs? Elizabeth, the Queen, was in love with him!

CHAPTER 22

WHITEHALL PALACE, OCTOBER 1559

Cecil clasped his hands behind his back and fixed his impatience behind an expression of polite attention. 'You wanted to see me, Your Grace.'

Norfolk was polishing a dagger, his full mouth pursing as he stroked the cloth along the blade. 'Yes, I did.' He set the dagger down and looked up, his brow creased in a frown. 'Tell me, Cecil, how long are you going to allow this to go on?'

Cecil stifled a breath of irritation. 'Forgive me, Your Grace, but allow what to go on?'

'The damned Gypsy.'

'Ah,' Cecil nodded, understanding. 'I believe you mean Lord Robert Dudley.' He had heard the nickname going around the court. He suspected that Norfolk had coined the term as a slur on Dudley's dark skin and also for the reputation of gypsies as pickers-up of anything they could get their hands on.

'Yes, I do mean Lord Robert Dudley. Did you see that display tonight?'

'The dancing, Your Grace?' Cecil was prevaricating, but he knew exactly what Norfolk was getting at. The Queen and Dudley had danced together practically all evening, their bodies moving closer with each measure.

'Dancing? Is that what you call it? They may as well have fucked right there on the floor.'

'Really, Your Grace,' Cecil admonished, his cheeks reddening.

Norfolk stood, his hands on his hips. 'Well, you may not care what everyone is saying, but I don't want this court made the laughing stock of Europe. He's her bloody stable boy, for Christ's sake.'

'Master of the Horse, Your Grace,' Cecil corrected with a wry smile.

'He's a Dudley,' Norfolk said, his voice growing louder with annoyance. 'When is she going to understand the kind of man he is?'

'And what kind would that be?'

'He's a traitor. He comes of tainted stock.'

'In truth, Your Grace, I am inclined to agree with you. The Queen does, in my opinion, act with little discretion in her relationship with Lord Robert. But,' he shrugged helplessly, 'I am at a loss to see what I can do about it.'

'Well, can't he be got rid of? Some way or the other?'

Norfolk had always been a brute. Cecil smiled politely. 'An assassination, Your Grace? He's hardly worth such an endeavour, surely?'

'I'd stick a dagger in him myself if I thought he was worth the trouble.'

Or worth the risk to your neck, Cecil thought. 'Perhaps the Queen will grow tired of him, Your Grace. He has but a handsome exterior to recommend him.'

'I agree, the man has no nobility, but what does that matter to this queen? She likes handsome men, doesn't she, Cecil? You remember Thomas Seymour?'

Cecil held up a warning hand. 'Your Grace, the Queen's involvement with him was never proven. She was but a child at the time.'

Norfolk leered unpleasantly. 'Oh, come now, Cecil, we both knew old Thomas. He couldn't walk past a woman without trying to get beneath her skirts.'

'Perhaps so, but I think it would be wise not to mention the late Lord Admiral, Your Grace, to the Queen or anyone else for that matter. He is a part of her history I believe she would not care to be reminded of.'

Norfolk pouted and fell back into his chair. He snatched up

the dagger once more. 'Well, then, let's hope she doesn't allow the Gypsy the same freedom as poor dead Thomas or it might be more than a maidenhead that is lost.'

MARCH 1560

Cecil had managed to avoid looking again at the letter. There it lay, on the furthest corner of his desk, occasionally getting covered by other paper during the course of the day, but always a sliver of white showed through to remind him that it was there.

But now he had no excuse. The work of the day was completed, his clerks had been sent away and the letter just had to be dealt with. He rubbed his chin, enjoying the rasping sensation as his fingers crushed his short beard. With a resigned sigh, he picked up the letter and re-read the words that had so disturbed him earlier.

'The Queen's behaviour with Lord Robert Dudley has become the scandal of the French court,' Sir Nicholas Throckmorton wrote in his usual abrupt manner. *'There is talk of Her Majesty visiting Lord Robert in his bedchamber, and he visits her while she undresses, and other such that I shrink to commit to paper. I myself cannot believe these rumours to be true, but the injury they do to Her Majesty's reputation is undeniable. Good sir, you have the Queen's trust. Cannot you persuade her to amend her favour towards Lord Robert, whose reputation here in France and the rest of Europe is near as black as his heart?'*

Nicholas was a good man, unwilling to believe the gossip, but he wasn't at court. The gossip was true. Was this what he had waited for? The girl, whose friendship and trust he had cultivated over many years, who had sought his advice, who had said that she knew him to be honourable and true! Was this the reason she had wanted the crown, so she could be free to sport with a married man of dubious reputation? Was this to be his reward? When he had struggled to find amongst her mutinous bishops one man who was prepared to crown her, and what persuading he had to do to get Bishop Oglethorpe to agree! When he was even now negotiating with the crowned heads of Europe to find suitable contenders for her hand. Would there be any takers for a queen who was behaving like any common bawd from the Southwark stews?

He refolded the letter, his fingernail rhythmically tapping the broken red seal. Norfolk had been right, he realised. Something would have to be done about the Gypsy.

CHAPTER 23

GREENWICH PALACE, MAY 1560

'She's like a hobgoblin sitting there.' Robert glanced over his shoulder and smiled at Kat Ashley, ensconced on a seat in the far corner of the box garden.

Elizabeth slapped his hand playfully. 'Don't be cruel. Kat's there for my protection.'

'From me?'

'Yes, from you. She thinks you have designs on my honour.' She gave a girlish laugh, but stopped when she realised Robert wasn't laughing too. 'What is it?'

He shrugged sulkily. 'Dishonour seems to follow me around.'

'How very melodramatic you sound.'

'You think I don't know what's being said about me? The Gypsy?' The look he gave Elizabeth dared her to deny she had heard it, too.

'It's only name-calling, Rob.'

'Well, it hurts, Bess. Especially when what's being said involves you. Oh, don't pretend you haven't heard the gossip. Why else the hobgoblin?'

'Gossip. That's all it is. You and I know the truth.'

'No, we don't. I don't know if you care for me.'

'Oh, Robin, how can you not know?' She reached out and stroked his cheek. 'Of course I care for you.'

'Yes, but how much?' he asked earnestly, grasping her hands and holding them to his chest.

She hesitated before answering. 'Rob, you are married.'

Robert let out a breath of exasperation. 'Oh, it's always 'Rob, you're married'. I damn well know I'm married. Do you think I could forget it?'

'I think you'd like to,' Elizabeth retorted. 'I know what you want.'

'What do I want?'

'You want to lie with me.'

'You can't blame me for that.'

'I do blame you. Why can't you be content with what we have?'

'*We* have nothing,' he spat through gritted teeth. 'I'm your Gypsy, the pampered pet you like to have following you around. I command no respect.'

'You're my Master of Horse.'

'Your stable boy as Norfolk puts it.' He took her hand and lowering his voice, he said, 'Bess, Amy is ill. She has a cancer in her breast. The physician says it's unlikely she will get better.'

'Rob—'

'No, let me finish. I sound callous, I know, as if I don't care for her. I do, I do care for her, Bess.'

'Care?' she scoffed. 'She's your wife, you're supposed to love her.'

'I can't say love, Bess, not any more. All that time apart when I was imprisoned, all that I lost then. It's difficult to explain. She couldn't understand what I had suffered. She wanted to pretend nothing had happened. She wouldn't let me talk about my family – I suppose she thought it might upset me. But it upset me more not being allowed to remember them, as if they meant nothing. If I even mentioned Father or my brothers, she would change the subject and start talking about other things, her clothes or her bloody embroidery. I hated her when she did that.'

'So, you're just waiting for her to die and then... what? You think you and I can marry?'

'Well... couldn't we?'

Elizabeth's heart beat faster. 'I... no... I don't know. You mustn't ask me.'

'Well, maybe I should just go back to Norfolk. Back home to Amy.'

'You can't leave. I won't let you.'

'Well, there's nothing for me to stay for, is there?' he shouted, not caring who heard.

'Rob!' she shushed, shaking her head at Kat who was in the process of rising. 'What do you want from me?'

'I want what Thomas Seymour got!'

Elizabeth stared at him, stunned. 'You believe that about me?'

He snapped off a leaf from the hedge and crushed it between his fingers. 'Everyone believes it.'

'It's not true. Robin, I tell you, it's not true. I never lay with him. I was but fourteen years old.'

'It's said you had a child by him.'

'I am still a maid.' She went to him and touched his arm. 'You do believe me, Rob?'

'You promise?'

'I swear it.'

He pulled her to him and kissed her forehead. 'Then I believe you.'

'I can't lie with you, Rob,' she said, almost apologetically. 'If I were to have a child—'

'It wouldn't matter if we were married.'

'I can't marry you, Rob. I'm a queen, I have to marry someone of noble birth.'

'Oh, I see. I'm not high enough for you.'

'No, forgive me, but you're not.'

'My father was a duke, Bess.'

'And he lost that title, Rob.'

'Then give *me* another one,' he suggested with a laugh.

She smoothed down her skirts. 'Not just yet. I show you too much favour as it is.'

Robert didn't press the matter. 'So, who are the prospective bridegrooms at the moment?'

'Much the same as they were,' Elizabeth said. 'Although, I think I have finally persuaded Cecil that I will not be considering Philip of Spain.'

'Where *is* Cecil? I haven't seen him for days.'

'In Scotland. The French Regent, Mary de Guise, has agreed to negotiate with us.'

'Oh, yes?' Robert said with little interest. Elizabeth smiled to herself. She placed her hand in his. 'Will it always be like this, Bess? You pushing me away?'

She brushed back a curl of hair from his forehead. 'No more questions.'

CHAPTER 24

WHITEHALL PALACE, JUNE 1560

No wonder the Romans never bothered with Scotland, Cecil thought as he shuffled wearily into his rooms. How could any civilised woman (and though she was a Catholic, he would concede that Mary de Guise was civilised) live and rule in such a place? The country was inhospitable and the people filthy savages.

And yet, he had reason to be proud of his time in Scotland, for had he not just negotiated a masterpiece of a treaty? The Auld Alliance, that centuries old agreement between France and Scotland to unite against a common enemy, was now broken thanks to Cecil, and the French ordered to withdraw their troops from Scotland.

He wanted to see the Queen to inform her of his success. He looked up as the door opened and his page returned with a jug of hot water. 'Set it down over there. Tell me boy, where is the Queen tonight?'

'She takes supper in her chambers, Master Cecil,' the boy replied.

'Why in her chambers? Is she not well?'

The boy smirked. 'Oh, she's well enough. But she has company there. Lord Robert Dudley dines with her most nights.'

'Take that insolent grin from your face, boy,' Cecil said sharply. 'Now, find me a clean shirt in that trunk and be quick about it.'

'Cecil,' Elizabeth halloed from the dinner table. 'Come in.'

'Your Majesty,' he bowed. 'Lord Robert.'

Robert grinned up at him, but did not rise from his seat beside Elizabeth. 'Cecil. How was Scotland?'

'Cold,' he answered tersely, 'but productive, I am pleased to say, Your Majesty.'

'Indeed?' Elizabeth raised an eyebrow. 'How so?'

Cecil swallowed uneasily. She sounded doubtful. Worse, she sounded scornful. 'The Auld Alliance is no more. A new treaty, the Treaty of Edinburgh, now takes its place.'

'It hasn't been signed though, has it?' Elizabeth said sharply, scrutinising a plate of sugared almonds that Robert waved beneath her nose. She selected one and looked up at Cecil enquiringly.

'Not yet, but it will be,' Cecil replied stiffly, realising with dismay she had already heard his news. *From who*, he wondered?

'This is the treaty that removes any claim Mary Stuart has to my throne?'

'Yes, madam.'

'Do you honestly think that woman will renounce her claim?'

'I do, yes.'

Elizabeth's eyes narrowed. 'I never took you for a fool, Cecil.'

Cecil could have sworn Dudley sniggered. 'Even if Mary Stuart doesn't sign, madam, and I am confident she will, there are other terms in the treaty that benefit your realm greatly. French troops are preparing to withdraw from Scotland even now. The Royal Arms of England have been removed from the royal flag of France. Mary Stuart can no longer lay claim to your throne.'

'That won't stop her. Still, I suppose you have done well enough, Cecil. What, Robin?' She bent towards Robert as he whispered in her ear. 'What of Calais?' Elizabeth suddenly asked. 'Do I get Calais back?'

Cecil glared at Robert. 'No, madam. Calais belongs, irretrievably, to the French.'

'And you dare to stand there and call it a victory?'

Cecil was taken aback. 'I claim no victory, madam, but I have toiled for your sake and I have, I believe at least, achieved a great deal.'

'Toiled—,' Elizabeth began incredulously.

'Yes, madam,' he interrupted her almost savagely. 'And had your head not been turned, you would now be agreeing with me.'

Elizabeth looked at Robert, who kept his eyes on the trembling Cecil. Cecil was angry and struggling to keep his temper under control.

'My head turned?' Elizabeth screeched. 'How dare you speak so to me?'

'Madam, if you will give me leave to speak with you alone.'

'No, I will not.'

'Then you break that promise you made me on the day of your accession, Your Majesty, when you said if I ever needed a private audience, you would grant it.'

'I will not hear you alone so you can malign my friends,' she stammered.

Cecil straightened. 'I have delivered my news, Your Majesty, and long for my bed. If you would be so good as to peruse this paper,' he said, holding out a list to her. 'It is an account of my personal expenses contracted during my business in Scotland.'

Elizabeth glanced at it. 'Do you think to dip your hand in the privy purse to pay your petty expenses?'

He felt the burn of humiliation upon his cheeks. 'I was in Scotland on official business, madam,' he protested.

She ignored him. 'Get the playing cards, Robin.'

'Of course, madam. Let me show Cecil out first.' Robert rose and took Cecil's arm.

Cecil shook him off. 'I know my way, sir,' he growled.

Robert smiled. 'Of course you do. I thought perhaps you needed help.'

'I need none from you.'

'You may find that you do soon enough,' he said, keeping his voice low. 'There may come a time, Cecil, when you will need all the help I am prepared to give you.'

'When, and if, that day ever comes, I will not stay around to ask for it.' He looked pointedly over Robert's shoulder. 'Goodnight, Your Majesty.'

Elizabeth gave a tight nod. 'Goodnight, Cecil. We will speak again in the morning when you're rested.'

He made her a bow, shorter than usual, and she knew she had hurt him.

'What an insolent fellow he is,' Robert said when Cecil had gone. He pulled open a drawer in a chest by the wall and retrieved a pack of cards.

'No more insolent than you,' she snapped. 'Why did you make me speak so to him?'

'I? What did I do?'

'You made me speak harshly when I had no cause.'

'Oh, his pride's just a little wounded, that's all,' Robert said, sitting and shuffling the cards. 'He'll be fine in the morning.'

'I did make him a promise.'

'So? He's only your secretary.'

'He's a good man.'

'Is he?'

'Oh, what do you know of it?' She grabbed up the cards and threw them at him. She rose and crossed to the window, staring out into the darkness.

'Bess?' Robert asked quietly. 'Forgive me.'

His voice was soft and her ears loved the sound of it. She turned and her anger melted as she looked upon him, his face half in shadow, the candlelight glinting in his eyes. It made her stomach flutter just to look upon him. 'I do. I fear I'll forgive you anything.'

He moved to her and took her hand in his. 'What sweet words, Bess,' he whispered, leaning in close, his breath hot upon her cheek.

'Sweet words,' she whispered back, 'sweet Robin.'

He heard the door close behind him. They were probably laughing at him now, her and Dudley. He could just picture them. Even the warders on either side of the door were exchanging glances. That one, the one with the crooked mouth, was smirking. Cecil glared at him.

'Look to your business,' he snapped and stormed off down the corridor.

'Master Cecil,' a heavily accented voice called out.

Cecil halted and turned. The Spanish ambassador, Bishop de Quadra, was hurrying after him. 'Bishop?'

'Master Secretary.' He peered into Cecil's face, noting his flushed skin. 'Are you unwell?'

'Not unwell, Bishop. Angry and disappointed.'

'Why so?'

Cecil took a deep breath. He was not used to sharing confidences, but why the hell not? 'I'll tell you why. I return from Scotland, having been away on the Queen's business, spending so much of my own money that I shall be in debt for years, only to find the Queen scorns all my efforts and bids me go so she can dally with Lord Robert Dudley.'

'Ah, Lord Robert,' De Quadra nodded, understanding completely. 'It is unfortunate that the Queen should have so ill regarded a man as Lord Robert so close to her. It does her reputation no good, no good at all. And he a married man.'

'Disgraceful, I agree. Though he may be a widower soon enough. Apparently, his wife has a malady in one of her breasts and is thought likely to die.'

'Indeed?' De Quadra raised both his eyebrows in interest.

'And,' Cecil hurried on, 'I have heard that his wife believes there are attempts to poison her.'

'By whom?'

'Who can say?' Cecil shrugged.

'The poor lady.'

'Of course, these are just rumours,' Cecil said. 'There may be nothing in them.'

'Well, yes, the court is a rumour mill,' De Quadra agreed unhappily. 'And yet, they must spring from somewhere.'

'Time will tell. But, sir, as you know the Queen and are a friend to her, I beg you, say nothing of this. I fear for her reputation.'

'You need beg nothing of me, Master Secretary,' De Quadra assured him, his brain already working on the wording of his next letter to his master, the King of Spain. 'If you will excuse me.'

Cecil willed his heart to slow as he watched De Quadra hurry away. He knew his words would be written down and repeated and was glad of it. Perhaps hearing the poison rumours would shock Elizabeth into ridding herself of Dudley. Better still, if Amy Dudley died, with all these rumours bruited abroad, Dudley himself would come under suspicion and then the Queen could not afford to have him near her. Oh yes, that would wipe the grin off that handsome face. Cecil allowed himself a little smile as he walked back to his rooms.

CUMNOR PLACE, SEPTEMBER 1560

Amy had heard them talking, whispering amongst themselves, thinking they couldn't be heard. Their filthy gossip had meant her mind had not had a moment of rest. She hadn't slept properly for months. She would wake in the middle of the night, stretch out a bare leg and feel only the cold mattress beside her and for a sleep-befuddled moment would wonder where her husband was. Then she would remember and there would be a drag at her heart.

It had been three months since she had last seen Robert. He had returned to Syderstone, full of concern for her, but he had seemed distracted, as if he was doing his duty but his mind, and perhaps his heart, was elsewhere. He had moved her to Cumnor Place so that she would be lodging with his friends. For her comfort, he had told her, and for his, of course, so he would know she was being looked after. She agreed without argument, even though the Odingsells bored her and irritated her with their kindnesses. Was it really for her comfort or for his? Every time she took a sip of wine or a mouthful of food, she wondered if the gossip was true and Robert was poisoning her. She found that she didn't care. She felt half dead anyway.

This morning the pain had been terrible. It had woken her from a troubled sleep, bringing tears to her eyes, the left side of her body aching unbearably. She had pushed herself upright, gasping and wincing, clutching her left breast as if touch alone could stop the pain.

Her maid, Pinto, had taken up residence on a truckle bed in her mistress's chamber for the last month, concerned at Amy's diminishing weight and pale, gaunt appearance. She had awoken early, as the first shafts of dawn's light penetrated the chamber, but had lain quite still, listening to the breathing of her mistress. At the first rustle of bedclothes, she had sprung up and rushed to the bedside.

Nothing could be done, of course, save giving Amy her medicine that would numb the pain. It would soon wear off, leaving her tired and irritable. As the pain faded and her eyes grew heavy, Amy complained about the noise from below. The servants were being too noisy; did they not know she was ill?

'Isn't there a fair today?' Amy had mumbled. Pinto had answered in the affirmative. 'Well, send them out to it. I want some peace.'

'They won't like going on a Sunday,' Pinto had said. 'Only the common folk go then.'

'I don't care. I want them gone.'

'What about Mistress Odingsell? I can't make her go.'

'She can do as she pleases. The servants *will* go. And you, too.'

'Me?'

Despite Pinto's protestations, Amy had been adamant. So, Pinto went to the fair, and made her complaints to the other servants, finding them more receptive than her mistress.

As the hours passed, Amy found she did not enjoy her solitude as much as she had anticipated. And the pain was returning. She fumbled through the medicine chest, cursing herself for not getting Pinto to make up her medicine before leaving. Well, she had seen Pinto make it often enough, she would do it herself. It tasted good, even if the consistency was rather thicker than usual. It didn't matter. If she had put too much in, it would last the longer.

Mistress Odingsell knocked on her door around noon and asked if Amy wanted to dine with her in her chamber. Not overly fond of the old woman but restless and wanting company, Amy agreed. She soon regretted it. Mistress Odingsell chattered and ate, chattered and ate until Amy grew sick of her fat, snapping mouth. She rose, saying she needed some fresh air and would walk in the garden. The old woman volunteered to accompany her if she would but wait until she had finished her dinner. Amy assured her that she would be fine on her own, especially as she knew her friend would want to take a nap after eating. She shuffled from the room before Mistress Odingsell could protest further.

She headed for the stairs. Her foot caught in her long skirt as she stepped onto the third tread. She kicked the heavy fabric away, annoyed at how fuddled her head seemed. Her need for fresh air had not been a fabrication. She needed it to blow the cobwebs away. She stepped down another tread. Again, her foot caught. She stumbled forward, coming down heavily on the next step, the impact juddering up through her spine. She cried out in pain.

And then she was falling... falling...

WHITEHALL PALACE

Tamworth stood at the foot of his master's bed and looked down at the sleeping man. 'My lord,' he said loudly. 'My lord, you must wake up.'

Robert turned his face into the pillow and mumbled for Tamworth to go away. But Tamworth persisted and eventually Robert opened sleep-encrusted eyes. 'What is it?'

'My lord, a man is here from Cumnor. He brings sad news.'

Robert was wide awake in an instant. He sat bolt upright and threw back the sheets. 'Is it my wife?'

'I'm afraid so, my lord.'

'Has she...?' he swallowed. 'Is she...?'

'Yes, my lord.'

Robert swung his legs to the floor and rose, crossing to the window and pressing his forehead against the glass. He closed his eyes. 'Was it peaceful?' he asked hopefully.

Tamworth hesitated. 'My lord, I think you should see the man who has come.'

Robert turned to him, wondering at his evasiveness. 'What is it?'

'The messenger can explain better.' Tamworth hurried to the outer chamber and returned with a short, red-faced man, dusty from the road. 'This is the man. Bowes.'

'You brought the news of my wife,' Robert said, pulling on a dressing gown.

'Yes, my lord,' Bowes said. 'Lady Dudley was found yesterday evening.'

'Found?' Robert thought it was an odd way to describe it.

Bowes looked sharply at Tamworth. Had he not told him? 'Yes, my lord. Lady Dudley was found at the bottom of the stairs. Her neck was broken.'

'What?' Robert gasped, taking a few shaky steps forward. 'But I thought her illness—'

'No, my lord,' Bowes shook his head. 'It was the fall that killed her.'

'But how did she come to fall?'

'No one can say. No one saw it happen. Only Mistress Odingsell was in the house and she was in her chamber.'

'But where were the servants?'

'Lady Dudley had sent them to the fair at Abingdon.'

'But my wife hated to be left on her own.'

'It's true, my lord. She even sent her maid away.'

Robert sat down on the bed. 'I don't understand it.' He put his head in his hands.

'My lord,' Tamworth said, 'I think perhaps you should dress now. You should see the Queen and tell her of this yourself before she hears of it from other quarters.'

Robert looked up and Tamworth saw that he had been crying. 'Yes, of course. Get out my black doublet and hose, Tam.'

'Yes, my lord.'

Elizabeth had not yet risen. Robert was told by a grim-faced Kat Ashley that it was unreasonable to ask to see the Queen at such an early hour.

'I must see her,' he said.

Kat looked at him. This wasn't the brash Robert Dudley she was used to. She noticed the tear tracks down his cheeks, the sniff of his nose. 'Is it important?'

Robert nodded.

'Wait here,' she said. She went back into the bedchamber and shook Elizabeth's shoulder gently. 'Your Majesty, Lord Robert needs to see you urgently.'

'Is something wrong?' Elizabeth asked, sitting up.

'I think so. He's been crying.'

Elizabeth hurried out of bed and Kat helped her on with her dressing gown. 'Let him come in,' Elizabeth said. 'Rob.' She went to him as he walked in and took hold of his hands. They were cold. 'What's happened?'

'Amy's dead.'

A pause. 'Oh my God,' Elizabeth said quietly. 'When?'

'Yesterday.'

'You'll be leaving, then.'

Robert's eyes widened. 'Yes, I'll be leaving,' he said incredulously.

'Why are you looking at me like that?' Elizabeth said angrily.

'Not 'sorry' or 'how are you'? Just, 'you'll be leaving then'.' He turned and headed for the door.

'You want me to say I'm sorry?' Elizabeth called after him. 'Are *you*?'

'How dare you ask me that?' he cried, forgetting in his anger and hurt that she was the Queen and he should not speak to her so. 'She was my wife. I didn't want her dead. And certainly not from falling down some damned stairs.'

'She fell? But I thought her cancer—'

'So did I,' Robert gave a strange little laugh.

Elizabeth fell silent, her mind busy. This news changed things. Perhaps she should have made an effort to be sympathetic, but her heart had been thumping so hard at the realisation that Robert was now free. He would want to marry her now and she would have no excuses left. But a death from a prolonged illness was one thing. Amy had died from a fall. She had heard the rumours and she knew people would be wondering. Did Robert Dudley's poor, long-suffering wife fall or had she been pushed?

'There will have to be an inquest,' she said.

Robert shrugged. 'I suppose so.'

'You can't stay at court.'

'I'll be leaving for Cumnor as soon as I am packed.'

'No, I mean,' Elizabeth sighed. 'I mean you won't be able to come back until the inquest is over and...'

'And what?' he asked.

'Rob, for heaven's sake. There have been rumours about you and I circulating around this court for a year. Rumours that Amy was being poisoned to get rid of her. And now, your wife dies, very conveniently, by falling down stairs.'

Robert looked at her aghast. 'You think I killed her.'

'No,' Elizabeth shook her head emphatically, 'I don't. But don't you think others will if it suits them?'

'It's monstrous.'

Elizabeth pointed to the door. 'You should go now.'

'You can't wait for me to be gone, can you? Why? In case I contaminate you?'

'I can't risk complicity,' she said slowly, hoping he would understand. 'Until it's proved that it was an accident, Rob. Until then, you must stay away from me.'

KEW, SURREY, SEPTEMBER 1560

Slouched in a chair by the window, his feet propped up on a stool, Robert turned the pages of a book idly. His shirt, stained with sweat, fell open to his navel and stubble showed dark upon his cheeks.

He tossed the book aside. It was no good trying to read, his mind kept wandering. He stood and stretched, groaning as he felt bones crack in his shoulders. He pushed the window open further and leant out upon the sill, breathing in the scent of the lavender bush below. He looked towards the gateway and was surprised to see a mule and a pony trotting along the gravel path.

He hastily tied his shirt and snatched up his doublet from the back of the chair. Thrusting his arms through the sleeves, he hurried outside, shooing away the servant who was heading for his guests. The gravel crunched beneath his feet. Masking his surprise at the identity of the rider, he took hold of the mule's bridle.

'Cecil, I wasn't expecting you.'

Cecil climbed down from his mount gratefully. 'Lord Robert. I trust my coming is not an unwelcome surprise.'

'Not at all,' Robert replied with sincerity. 'You will stay to dine with me, I hope?'

Cecil noted the quiet desperation in his eyes and was pleased. 'I thank you, yes. Can my page be attended to?'

'Of course. Boy, go around to the stables and ask for Gregson. Cecil, please come in.' Robert led Cecil back into the house. 'Forgive the mess,' he said, as he hurried to tidy up.

'That is a great deal of correspondence,' Cecil nodded at a pile of letters stacked precariously on a small table.

'Yes. Letters of condolence.'

'Of course.'

'Can I get you something to drink?'

'Beer.' Cecil took a seat. 'You must wonder why I'm here.'

'You have a message from the Queen?' Robert asked hopefully, handing him a cup of beer.

Cecil inclined his head sympathetically. 'I'm afraid not, Lord Robert. No, I come on my own account. To see how you are.'

Robert slumped in his chair, disappointed. 'I am as you see me,' he said gesturing at himself. 'In truth, I am not surprised the Queen sends no message. We parted badly.'

Cecil had heard of their last encounter. 'I'm sure there is no ill feeling on the Queen's part, my lord. Indeed, she is most distressed by this situation. Is there any news from Cumnor?'

'My steward, Anthony Blount, has spoken with all the servants in the house, including my wife's maid, Pinto. It seems Pinto made a comment which I find disturbing, to say the least.'

'Which was?'

'That she had often heard Amy pray to God for a release from her pain.'

Cecil nibbled his bottom lip, thinking. 'You think then that your wife may have taken her own life?'

'Not for a moment,' Robert shook his head vehemently. 'Amy was a good Christian and would not throw away the life that God gave her. Besides, if you wanted to kill yourself, would you trust Death to take you by throwing yourself down a flight of stairs? No, I can't believe it. I do think she fell.'

'A tragedy, my lord.'

'In more ways than one,' Robert murmured. 'I must thank you for coming to see me, Cecil. I had not expected such kindness, I confess.'

Cecil was almost moved. 'Think nothing of it, my lord. After all, we are both servants of the Queen.'

Mary Sidney exchanged a glance with her husband. He nodded his head in encouragement and they both looked back at Robert.

'How are you really, Rob?' Mary asked.

Robert, who had been pushing his food around his plate, looked up at her with tired eyes. 'Fine,' he said simply.

'You don't look fine,' she said. 'You look tired. And worried.'

Robert shrugged. 'Of course I look worried. The entire world thinks I'm a murderer.'

'Oh, please don't say that.'

Robert looked at her and laughed. 'Even Elizabeth has her doubts.'

'I'm sure she doesn't,' Mary said, stabbing another piece of meat with her knife.

'She sent me away, didn't she?'

'She explained why.'

'Oh yes, Elizabeth is very careful of her honour. It doesn't matter that I may have needed her support. These calumnies against me would not have dared to have been spoken if she had kept me with her.'

'Can we not go over this again?' Henry pleaded. 'Once the coroner has declared Amy's death an accident, you can go back to court. The Queen specifically instructed Mary to send her word of how you are. So, you see, she hasn't deserted you.'

Just then, the door opened and Sir Anthony Blount strode in with a huge smile upon his face.

Robert jumped up from his seat. 'What news?' he demanded.

'Accidental Death, my lord.' Blount said.

'Oh, God be praised,' Robert gasped as Mary threw herself against him. He clutched her tight and buried his face in her neck. Beneath her arms, his body shook with sobs.

Embarrassed, Henry led Blount outside. Mary pushed Robert back into his chair and she knelt at his feet.

'Rob,' she said, holding his hands, when they had gone. 'It's over now.'

'I know,' he nodded. 'I don't know why I'm crying.'

'It's grief and relief, you idiot. Now, Rob, look at me. It's over. Say it.'

'It's over.' He took her face between her hands and kissed her. 'Oh, Mary, what a time it's been.'

'I know. It can't have been easy.'

'Being suspected of murdering your wife?' He laughed sourly. 'No, it hasn't.' He pulled out a handkerchief from his doublet and wiped his eyes. 'Will Elizabeth send for me now, do you think?'

'Of course she will. There's no reason for her not to, is there? Maybe Cecil will come and get you.'

Robert snorted. 'Cecil! I'll wager this verdict will not please him.'

'He came to see you last week. You told me how kind you thought it was of him.'

'My brain wasn't working then, Mary. I was so lonely and distressed, I would have welcomed the Devil. He came to gloat. Elizabeth had got rid of me and he was back at her side. He's no friend to me.'

'Oh Rob, you see enemies where there are none.'

'Mary, how is it possible to have spent your entire life at court and still think good of people?'

'I do not know, Rob,' she said, her voice heavy with sarcasm. 'I cannot think where I get my good nature from.'

He laughed and pulled her towards him, embracing her so tightly she protested she couldn't breathe. Henry and Blount returned and the hours passed happily in their company. At eight o'clock that evening, a messenger arrived. He had a letter for Robert from the Queen, informing him his presence was required at court.

GREENWICH PALACE

Elizabeth thundered ahead of him, her horse kicking up great clods of earth. She headed for a clump of trees that provided cover from spying eyes and waited for him.

Robert slid down from his saddle and stood by Mirabelle. Elizabeth stood by her horse and they stared at each other for a long moment. Then Elizabeth's face crumpled and through her tears headed towards him, her arms wanting, needing to hold him. He let her press against him before he relented and cradled her in his arms.

'Oh, Robin, you can't imagine what I have had to endure while you were gone.'

'I think I can imagine it, Bess. I wasn't exactly enjoying myself exiled at Kew, you know.'

'I was all alone.'

'You had Cecil.'

She pulled away him from him. 'What is Cecil to me? A trusted counsellor, someone I can depend on. Not a... not a...,' she faltered.

'A what? A lover?' he suggested. 'Well, no more am I.'

'No, not in the physical sense,' she admitted as she wiped her cheeks. 'But what we have is so much more. True love, Robin, true and enduring.'

'True love is all very well, Bess, but I need more.'

Elizabeth made a gesture of despair. 'Why must you have more? I don't need it.'

'Because men are different.'

'Why can't you understand? If I were to have a child…'

'All the country would rejoice at that if we were married, Bess.'

'How can we marry with things as they are?' Elizabeth had quite recovered herself and her eyes were blotchy but dry. 'It may have escaped your notice, Robin, but you are hated the country over. I would be despised as well if I were to marry you. They may even turn against me.'

'Never. The people love you.'

'I wish I could be as sure as you. Perhaps in a few years' time, the situation would be different.'

Robert turned to Mirabelle and stroked her neck. 'Will it ever be different? You will always be queen and I will always be that traitor who isn't fit to kiss your feet.'

Elizabeth didn't disagree. 'The others will catch up soon. Help me mount my horse.'

He bent down and cupped his hands for her to put her foot into. He heaved her up into the saddle. 'Don't be angry with me,' she begged.

'What good would it do me?' Robert climbed back onto Mirabelle and nudged her sides, goading her to a gallop, leaving Elizabeth to follow.

CHAPTER 25

WHITEHALL PALACE, DECEMBER 1561

'It's not right, you know,' Mary said, shaking her head. 'Ambrose is the elder. He should be ennobled before you.'

Robert grinned at her. 'It's not my fault. It's the Queen's decision.'

'I haven't heard any protest from you.'

'Mary,' Ambrose scolded, slipping an arm around her waist. 'Don't fret so. My time will come. Quiet now, she's coming.'

Elizabeth strode into the room, her brow heavily creased and her mouth so pursed that her thin lips had turned almost white. She headed straight for the desk where the ennoblement documents were laid out, ready for her signature.

Robert wondered at her expression but now was not the time to ask questions. He sank to his knees before the table and looked up at her.

Elizabeth seemed to study his face for a long moment and Robert couldn't guess what she was thinking. She picked up the topmost document and squinted at it. 'Robert Dudley, to be raised to the peerage and given the title of...,' She stopped, tapping her finger rhythmically upon the wood.

Robert glanced at Mary and frowned. Mary gave the slightest shake of her head, not knowing what Elizabeth was thinking.

'No,' Elizabeth said, suddenly picking up a paperknife and

stabbing the centre of the document. She drew the knife down, tearing the paper in two.

Robert scrambled to his feet, barely registering the rising murmur of the watching courtiers' whispers. 'What... why?'

'I have my reasons,' Elizabeth replied coolly, quickly signing the other documents.

Robert was speechless. Why was she humiliating him so? As she finished and rose, moving around the desk, he grabbed at her arm.

Elizabeth shrugged him off angrily. 'You want reasons? Very well, here they are then. Your family have been traitors to the crown through three generations. You have been suspected of murder throughout my kingdom and Europe. Your arrogance and ambition threaten my throne—'

'I would never,' he declared. 'Elizabeth, why are you doing this?'

'I'm your queen, Lord Robert. Take care you never forget that.'

There was a sternness in her eyes he had not seen before. He released her and Elizabeth left the chamber, Cecil trotting after her.

Then he heard the laughter, the scoffs, the jeering and God's Death, how they hurt! But he was damned if he would lose control for them all to see. He raised his chin a little higher and walked back to his room.

But once inside, his control left him. He yanked off his cloak, throwing it on the floor. His fist hit the bed post, and he had to swallow down the sickening pain as the wood struck against bone.

There came an almost tentative knock on the door. For a moment, he actually thought it might be Elizabeth come to explain herself.

The door opened and Mary poked her head around. 'Rob?'

'Leave me alone, Mary.'

'No, I won't,' she said, entering and closing the door. 'Oh, Rob, that was so cruel.'

'I'm well enough.'

'Don't pretend with me. I know how much that hurt you.'

'How dare she!' he exploded. 'How dare she humiliate me like that?'

'Perhaps someone advised her to do it?' Mary suggested.

'Don't make excuses for her, Mary. She doesn't need anyone to tell her to be cruel. It comes quite naturally to her.'

'Well, don't think on it. Let her think you don't care.'

Robert laughed sourly. 'Turn my back on her if she comes calling, you mean? My, what an innocent you are! She's the Queen, Mary. Like it or not, I have to take her insults, her taunts, and thank her for them.'

'No, Rob, don't accept this insult. Let her know that she can't treat you so.'

'Our family's future rests entirely upon the Queen's good graces. To relinquish her favour would be to relinquish all my hopes.'

'Well, maybe that is true,' Mary agreed ruefully. 'But I don't have to like it. What are you looking for?'

Robert was rummaging through a trunk. 'My riding boots. I have to get out of the palace. Why don't you come with me?'

'I expect the Queen will notice my absence. I should get back.'

'She won't want a Dudley around her.'

'I'm a Sidney, Robert,' she replied, teasingly.

'You were a Dudley first, sister, never forget that. Oh, come riding with me, Mary, don't make me get down on my knees.'

'Very well, Rob, but you must defend me if the Queen demands to know where I've been.'

'I may very well need defending myself. Come on, let's leave before we're noticed.'

At that moment came a loud, peremptory knock. Robert's body sagged, as if he knew there would be no riding today.

'Come in,' he called.

A page entered and said, 'The Queen demands your presence, my lord.'

'You see, Mary. The Queen demands and I, as her minion, must obey. Come along with me, sister.' He grabbed her hand and dragged her along behind him, all the way back to the Presence Chamber.

Elizabeth turned as Robert and Mary entered, a sly smile playing upon her lips. 'Robin,' she purred, holding her hands out to him.

He, *dutiful as a dog*, he thought, went to her. 'Your Majesty,' he greeted her coldly.

'Now, Robin,' she said, adopting a mock scolding tone, 'your face is as sour as vinegar.'

'With reason, madam.'

'Oh, nonsense. Are you so easily overthrown?' she asked, laying her long fingers upon his cheek. The gesture was curiously sensual and intimate. Robert could hear no laughing now.

Henry Sidney, sensing an advantage, spoke up. 'So great a man is fit for a greater place, do you not agree, Your Majesty?'

'Indeed, Sir Henry? What greater place would you suggest?'

Henry gave a broad smile and shrugged as if the answer were obvious. 'At your side, Your Majesty, what other would suit?'

'You mean, none other would satisfy him.' Elizabeth gave a sideways glance at Robert. 'No, I will not marry a subject, for then men would come to ask for my husband's favour and not mine.'

'Your sister had no such fears with her husband, Your Majesty,' Henry pointed out.

'And remember how that turned out,' Elizabeth snapped. She turned to Robert. 'I will have here but one mistress and no master. Remember that, my lord.'

Robert nodded, his courtier's nod which hid the disappointment he felt. For he was beginning to believe that Elizabeth meant every word she said.

CHAPTER 26

MARCH 1562

Cecil waited until the other counsellors had filed out and the door had closed. Then he looked at Elizabeth and licked his dry lips thoughtfully.

'What is it?' Elizabeth asked, her eyes narrowing in curiosity.

'I wanted to speak to you in private about Mary Stuart.'

Elizabeth grunted. Her cousin was the last thing she wanted to talk about.

'Have you had any thoughts on who she should marry?' Cecil continued.

'Marry?' Elizabeth said. 'Cecil, she's only just been widowed. Her husband is hardly cold in his grave.'

'Nevertheless, madam, if Mary Stuart isn't considering her next husband, then her Guise uncles will be. I have received intelligence from Sir Nicholas Throckmorton. You are aware of the animosity between Mary Stuart and the Queen Mother, Catherine de Medici. It is believed that Catherine will not allow Mary to stay in France. If that should be the case and she doesn't marry soon, Scotland will be the only place Mary Stuart can go.'

'Well, it is her country, Cecil. Why should it concern me if she is there?'

'Madam, she is a Catholic.'

'But Scotland is mostly Protestant. Her half-brother, James, takes our money to keep it so.'

'Indeed, but he is a bastard and ineligible to rule. Of

course, he would hope that Mary would merely be the figurehead of Scotland, with himself in actual charge. But, I hear, she is strong-willed and may choose to be a queen in more than name. That would be a pity. James is an able man. If James were to lose his position of power, it could cause trouble for us.'

'She *is* a queen, Cecil. She has a right to rule.'

Cecil's face twitched. 'Indeed she does. But not all monarchs have the *ability* to rule. If I may say so, madam, Mary Stuart is not Elizabeth Tudor.'

Elizabeth's eyes softened. 'Have you turned flatterer, Cecil?' she asked with a smile.

'It is not flattery to speak the truth, madam. Bear in mind, Mary Stuart has a personal allegiance to France and a religious allegiance to Spain. And if she were to choose a husband not inclined towards friendship with England—'

'Yes, yes, I understand,' Elizabeth waved her hand at him impatiently. 'You want me to suggest a husband to her? Why would she pay attention to anything I say? She has already shown herself careless of my feelings. Does she not lay claim to my throne?'

'She does indeed maintain that position, madam, but has not the power or support to enforce it. But she may also have need of your goodwill. To get to Scotland, she will need to pass through English waters. You could withhold permission for her to do so, forcing her to take a different, perhaps more dangerous, passage.'

'Good idea,' Elizabeth said, impressed. 'If she intends to return to Scotland, I will withhold permission. She can go the long way around.'

'And a husband, madam?' Cecil prompted.

'You have someone in mind, Cecil?'

Cecil coughed nervously. 'I was thinking, just perhaps, of Lord Robert Dudley.'

Elizabeth stared at him. She couldn't speak. She was stunned. Had Cecil just suggested Robin marry Mary Stuart?

'Consider the advantages of such a match,' Cecil continued quietly. 'Lord Robert is a great friend to you and therefore to England. He is a Protestant. He is ambitious and such a match would raise him very high indeed. The only issue would be if...,' he paused and took a deep breath, 'if you could not bear to lose him.'

Elizabeth's mouth tightened. She smacked her hand down on the table angrily and rose, striding across to the window. Cecil got to his feet, tasting sweat on his upper lip, and waited. He could see the tension in her shoulders as she leant on the windowsill and stared out into the gardens.

She slowly turned to him. 'Robin would never agree.'

'If you ordered it, madam, how could he refuse?'

'There must be other possibilities. Is she not supposed to be beautiful?' Elizabeth sneered. 'There must be plenty of princes across Europe eager to wed her.'

'None that would be so advantageous to England, madam. And is Lord Robert not a handsome man?'

'The most handsome,' Elizabeth could not help but smile. 'Does Mary like handsome men, Cecil?'

'What woman doesn't?'

Elizabeth shot him a sharp look. 'I shall have to think about this, Cecil. Say nothing to anyone for the moment.'

'Of course not, madam. You will consider it then?'

'I've said I will, haven't I? But I will not be hurried into anything. Mary can marry no one until her mourning is over. There is plenty of time to consider husbands for my dear cousin.'

Cecil gathered up his papers and left the Council chamber, leaving Elizabeth alone.

It was an outrageous suggestion. How could she let that woman get her hands on Robin? She pictured Robert in Mary's bed, Mary enjoying him as she, Elizabeth, had never dared to do. Oh God, it hurt to imagine such things. But then, she admitted, there was security in the idea, for England and for her personally.

Oh Cecil, you clever man. In one stroke, you could secure Scotland as an ally for England, tame a dangerous Catholic queen and rid yourself of a nuisance rival.

Elizabeth had to admire Cecil for his ingenuity.

CHAPTER 27

HAMPTON COURT PALACE, APRIL 1562

'Oh, have pity on me, Rob, and sit down.' Elizabeth rubbed her eyes as there came another stab of pain. *God's Death, how they ached tonight!* And Robert would keep fidgeting.

'But Elizabeth,' he continued, heedless of her discomfort, 'they are Protestants. The Huguenots are being persecuted in France for their religion, a religion this country shares. If we do not answer the appeal of the Huguenots—'

'I don't care about the Huguenots. Let the French go hang themselves. Why are men always so eager to go to war?'

'We can't ignore them, Bess. If the Catholics were to gain the upper hand—'

'So, what then?'

'Then the balance of power in Europe would be heavily in favour of the Papists. And England could face a joint French and Spanish alliance.'

Robert was trying to frighten her into action, she knew, but Elizabeth was too tired to think.

'And if we aid them,' Robert continued, 'they have promised to cede to us the port of Newhaven. Think of it, Bess, a port in France once again. We haven't had one since Calais was lost.'

'I know, and how did we lose that?' Elizabeth said testily. 'By my sister, Mary, embroiling us in a foreign war, urged on her by men.'

'That was an ill-advised expedition. The gains this time would far outweigh the risks. And once we have Newhaven—'

'If we win.'

'Yes, if we win,' Robert conceded, 'and then we may even be able to reclaim Calais.'

'Cecil would prefer to act as intermediary between the Huguenots and Guises. Bring them to a reconciliation.'

'I imagine Cecil would. He is nothing if not cautious. But it would be wrong, Bess. Ask your Council.'

'Oh, is there any need?' Elizabeth asked, raising her eyebrows. 'I thought you had already been canvassing their opinions.'

He smiled, half-embarrassed at being caught out. 'Well, I wanted to ensure my argument had support.'

'You don't have *enough* support, Rob. I'm not deciding anything yet.'

He took her hand, meaning to try and persuade her with sweet words and kisses. Closer than he had been all evening, he saw now that she looked quite ill. Her cheeks and forehead were flushed and blotchy, her eyes bloodshot and sweat shined on her top lip.

'Bess, are you ill?'

'I'm tired. I want to go to bed and you keep me talking.'

'Well, then, let's get you to bed.'

'Oh, Rob, go away,' she said feebly.

'I will not.' He took hold of her arms and pulled her up from the chair. Even as he held her, Robert felt her strength fall away. She fell against him and he struggled to hold her upright.

'Guard,' he yelled over his shoulder. Two Yeoman Warders rushed in, their halberds lowered and pointing at Robert. 'The Queen has fainted,' he explained quickly. 'Help me get her to the bed.'

One of the guards dropped his halberd noisily on the floor and took hold of Elizabeth's legs. Between them, they managed to lay her on the bed.

Her ladies were beginning to come in from the antechamber, clustering around her prone body. Robert ordered one of them to fetch the Queen's doctor before he was shooed out of the room by Kat Ashley.

Robert ran a hand over his face. 'For God's sake, how long does it take to find out what's wrong with her?'

'Doctor Burcot is a fine physician,' Cecil said, distractedly tapping a quill against upon the Council table.

'He had better be.'

'There is an outbreak of smallpox in London. I understand two boys from the kitchens succumbed only yesterday.'

'Smallpox? Please God, not that.'

'I know. The disfigurement can be terrible. If the patient survives at all, that is.'

They glanced at each other, both considering the possibility of Elizabeth's death and the awful consequences.

Then Mary entered the room.

'What news?' Robert demanded, jumping up from his chair.

'Doctor Burcot says it's smallpox,' Mary said. 'The Queen woke shortly after you left, and when the doctor told her she had smallpox, she grew so angry, she shouted at him to get out. The Earl of Sussex had to drag him back.'

'I must see her.' Robert headed for the door.

'She's asleep again,' Mary grabbed his arm. 'And besides, you don't want to catch it.'

'I won't catch it, I don't catch anything. And I don't care if she's asleep. I want to be with her.'

Mary nodded wearily, seeing it would be pointless to argue further. 'Come with me then.'

Elizabeth lay in her bed, eyes closed, mouth hanging open, hair clinging to her sweat dampened forehead and neck.

Mary pulled a chair to the side of the bed and pointed Robert to it. He sat, finding Elizabeth's hand between the folds of the red flannel blanket she was wrapped in and pressed her clammy fingers around his.

'I'm here, Bess,' he whispered. 'I'm here.'

Elizabeth slipped in and out of consciousness for days. Robert stayed by her side. When eventually he was persuaded to retire to his room to sleep, Elizabeth, perversely, awoke. She thought she was dying. She had the Council brought into her bedchamber and once they were all assembled, declared to them that Robert

Dudley should be made Protector of the Realm in the event of her death. No one wanted to argue with a dying queen so they all murmured their agreement while giving each other uneasy looks. Dudley as Protector! Preposterous.

But then, Elizabeth had rallied. And when Robert heard what Elizabeth had said, he experienced strange and conflicting emotions. He felt great happiness that Elizabeth was recovering and yet strange disappointment that he would not get to be Protector, however remote that possibility had been.

Mary Sidney had no reason to rejoice, however. Elizabeth, by some miracle (or witchcraft, some murmured) had escaped the horrific disfigurement that smallpox could inflict, but Mary caught the disease. She too survived, but her face, which had once been so very pretty, was now painful to look upon, so altered and ugly had it become. She could not bear the embarrassed glances of people who didn't know where to look, nor their expressions of sympathy. She retired to her house at Penshurst.

CHAPTER 28

GREENWICH PALACE, OCTOBER 1562

Cecil rubbed his nose, leaving a smudge of ink upon its tip. 'Lord Robert has once again petitioned the Council to send men to Newhaven, Your Majesty.'

Elizabeth took up the paper upon which Robert had detailed the advantages and disadvantages of a campaign against the French in support of the Protestant Huguenots and which he had presented to the Council earlier that morning. Despite herself, she smiled at his assiduousness. 'He is proving a most energetic counsellor.'

'Indeed,' Cecil agreed regretfully.

Since Elizabeth had made Robert a counsellor, Cecil had not had a moment of uncontested control over the Privy Council. Robert and the Duke of Norfolk, who had been made a Privy Counsellor at the same time, were either too high in rank or too close to the Queen to be ignored.

'Shall I tell him the answer is once again No?'

Elizabeth smiled ruefully at him. 'I believe this time I must say Yes, Cecil.'

'Your Majesty?' Cecil asked, not quite believing he had heard correctly.

'I know you are of my mind that wars are costly businesses, but Lord Robert has been most persuasive.' She pointed to Robert's list. 'And thorough. Two ports in France would benefit England greatly and, in truth, I am inclined to help our Protestant cousins. And Robert is not the only one pressing me to act. My good Sir Nicholas in France urges me to it almost daily.'

'Yes, I'm aware he has written. Well, madam, if you are indeed resolved to act, then I shall begin with the preparations. But I do have one question. Who is to head the expedition? I know Lord Robert believes he should lead it, as the Huguenots have been appealing to him directly.'

Elizabeth nodded. 'Yes, well, Robert is going to have to be disappointed. I will not be sending *him*.'

'He will be *very* disappointed, madam,' Cecil said, trying not to smile.

'His brother can go instead. Now that I have ennobled Ambrose, it is proper that he should. And that way, the Dudley name will be represented.'

Cecil made a note. 'Ambrose Dudley, the Earl of Warwick, to head the army.'

'Is that all?' Elizabeth asked with a sigh. 'Lord Robert is waiting for me to ride.'

'Yes, that is all for the moment, madam. I shall let Lord Robert know of your decision.'

'No, I shall tell him myself,' Elizabeth said, getting to her feet and waving him to sit still. 'He will be petulant and argumentative, no doubt, and I, like a mother, must soothe and comfort him. That's not a role for you, Cecil.'

Cecil smiled gratefully.

'Rob, stop.'

Elizabeth reined in her horse and waited for him to come back to her.

'Tired already?' he asked, looking at her horse, not her.

'No, but I don't want you sulking all day. Walk on,' she nudged her horse's sides. 'I know you're disappointed but I really can't let you go. Ambrose will do well, I'm sure.'

'Of course he will.'

'Good. So, take that look off your face.'

Robert knew he was being childish and he made an effort to improve his temper. 'Sorry,' he mumbled.

'Well, I hope this will make you feel better. You remember Kenilworth?'

'Yes. It's a castle up in Warwickshire. It belonged to my father for a short while.'

'Well, now it's yours.' She gave him a sideways glance and was gratified to see a growing look of astonishment cross his face. 'I'm giving you Kenilworth.'

'Oh, Bess.'

'It will need a lot of work. I hear it's almost a ruin.'

'I don't care,' he said eagerly, 'I'll rebuild it.'

'It might be cheaper and easier to build new, you know. That's what Cecil's doing with his house.'

'No, not for me. I like to keep the history of a place.'

Elizabeth laughed. 'It's always history with you, Rob.'

He frowned at her. 'What do you mean?'

'Everything you do, every action you take, you're not thinking of now, what it means for this moment. You're thinking far ahead, years even. You're thinking of the legacy you'll leave behind. And I want you to have plenty of time to build that legacy. Which is why you're not going to France. You understand me?'

He met her eye. 'Yes, Bess, I understand.'

KENILWORTH CASTLE, WARWICKSHIRE, APRIL 1563

Robert jumped down from his horse and beheld Kenilworth. *His* Kenilworth. Elizabeth had not understated the matter when she said it was ruinous; some of the older structures had crumbled away and several chambers had lost their ceilings and were open to the air. But it was still impressive.

'Good day, my lord.' A large man with a shaggy beard waved a trowel at Robert from the bottom of a deep trench, touching his muddy fingers to his cap in deference.

'Turner. A fine day, is it not?'

'Aye, you picked the right day to come visiting, my lord. The sun hasn't shone this bright for many a day.'

'Has it slowed down the work?' Robert asked, wandering along the path. Turner climbed out of his ditch and hurried to catch his master up.

'A bit. But we have done quite a lot already.'

'Yes, it does seem to be progressing well,' Robert agreed, trying to stop his nose from wrinkling at the smell coming off of Turner. 'How soon before it will be habitable, do you think?'

'Oh,' Turner shook his head, 'you've got quite a wait for that, my lord. There's a fair amount of work to be done before you can think of settling.'

Robert gave him an apologetic smile. 'You'll have to forgive my impatience, Turner. My enthusiasm sometimes doesn't reconcile with common sense. The Queen will visit here when it's done, you know.'

'Well, in time, my lord, it will be fit for such a great lady, have no fear.'

Robert moved away, up the causeway which he was having turned into a tiltyard. Already the earth had been turned, the ramparts built, the weeds plucked out and the foundations of the viewing galleries at each end marked out with pegs. And there, to the right, would be the new stable block he had designed to house all the beautiful horses he was planning to buy, strong, graceful creatures from Ireland he knew Elizabeth wouldn't be able to resist.

'Robert!'

A female voice broke into his musings. He turned, one hand shielding his eyes from the sun to see a woman climbing down from a coach. She wore a dull grey dress and her head and shoulders were covered by a veil.

'Mary!' He waved back. He ran up to her and kissed her through the veil. 'Why didn't you tell me you were coming? I might have missed you.'

'I came to see the castle, not you.'

'Oh, so you're not pleased to see me,' he teased.

'Of course I am,' she said, taking his arm. 'I'm glad you're here.'

They walked back along the causeway. 'Well, what do you think?' he asked.

'I think it's going to take a lot of work. And money. Do you have enough?'

'I'll find it,' Robert shrugged. 'I can always find money.'

'I'm not sure the Queen was being generous giving you this. Couldn't she have found one that wasn't falling down?'

'It seems Elizabeth knows me better than you, sweet sister. I couldn't have hoped for anything better than Kenilworth.

There isn't anything better. Anyway, enough about me. How are you?'

'As well as I can be.'

'I wish you would come back to court. I miss you, and so does the Queen. I'm sure you exiling yourself at Penshurst makes her feel even more guilty.'

'So she should,' Mary retorted feelingly. 'Is it fair that I should bear all the scars of her disease and she emerges unscathed? Could she not have suffered just a little, too?'

'Don't be cruel, Mary.'

'Cruel?' she cried, throwing away his arm. 'Is it not cruel that my husband looks on me with disgust and not desire? And I can't blame him.'

'You are still his wife, Mary,' Robert said, grabbing her shoulders and bringing her to face him. 'He married you for yourself, not your face.' His fingers pulled gently at the veil. He meant to tear it from her head, to show her that she had nothing to fear from showing her cruel affliction to the world, but her pitiful, half-smothered scream halted him. Instead, he put his arms around her waist and pulled her to him. 'I won't do it, I promise.' He felt her relax and he released her. His eyes caught a movement back at the coach and his face broke into a grin. 'Is that who I think it is?'

Mary followed his gaze. 'It is. He jumped from the coach before I could stop him. I imagine he's been running around the castle, getting in everyone's way.'

'PHILIP!' Robert waved furiously.

The boy halted and looked around, startled, to find out who called his name. 'UNCLE ROB!' he yelled. He ran towards them and flung himself into his uncle's outstretched arms.

'Well, now I see who the favourite is in our family,' Mary laughed, as Robert propped his nephew on his hip

'It's been ages since I've seen you, Uncle,' the boy scolded.

'I quite agree. It's a great fault in your mother not to bring you to see me more often, Phil. You can't be nagging her enough.'

'Mother told me this was a castle.'

'It *is* a castle,' Robert replied indignantly.

'But it's all broken.'

'At the moment, Phil. But you see all the men hereabouts?

They're going to make this a dream castle and there will be no place like it in the whole of England. Shall it not look grand, Phil?' He tweaked the boy's nose and set him on his feet.

'The Queen will visit, of course?' Mary asked.

'Of course, and she shall enjoy her stay, by Christ, she shall, Mary. But enough of her.' Robert patted Philip on the shoulder, gave him a complicit wink and sprinted away, his spindly-legged nephew running after him.

CHAPTER 29

JULY 1563

Despite Robert's assurances, the French campaign to help the Huguenot Protestants was not a success. Ambrose tried but the Huguenots inexplicably turned on their English allies to join with their Catholic enemies. It seemed Englishmen setting foot on French soil was enough to unite the two factions and turn them both against the English.

Ambrose asked for more men, more weapons and money to fight the French forces, but Elizabeth would not send them. And then disease swept through Ambrose's army, weakening it still further. All Ambrose could do was seek a dignified surrender. He asked for permission from Elizabeth and she gave it, cursing Robert and Nicholas Throckmorton for persuading her to send men in the first place.

So Ambrose stood on the city walls of Newhaven, bargaining with the French below for terms of surrender. And a French musketeer, either bored or careless, shot him with a musket in the thigh. The surrender was made, and Ambrose and his army returned to England.

Robert rushed into the best bedroom in Master White's house, his face smeared with the dirt of the road. 'Ambrose. Dear Jesus, you look terrible.'

Ambrose tried to sit up, but he was too weak and sank back against the pillows. 'I can, at least, rely on you not to mince your words, Rob.'

Robert pressed his lips to his brother's hot forehead and sat down on the edge of the bed. 'Have you seen a doctor?'

'Yes, he left not half an hour ago, and Master White is looking after me very well. How is it you've come here?'

'Thomas Wood wrote to me, said you were ill. Is it just the fever or is it your leg as well?' Robert pulled back the bedclothes, wincing when he saw the bandage on Ambrose's thigh, his bright red blood staining the cloth.

'The fever is better than it was. My leg is very painful.'

'Trust you to get in the way of a musket ball.'

'I know. You should not get so close to me, Rob,' Ambrose said, giving him a gentle shove away. 'It would not do for you to catch my fever.'

'Oh, I never catch anything,' Robert waved away his concern and threw off his riding cloak.

'Still, you shouldn't have come.'

'Well, what could I do? I get a letter telling me my brother is gravely ill and it's a miracle that he's still alive. As if I could stay at court once I knew that. Well, now that I have seen you and you are not likely to die just yet, I think I should let you sleep. I will ask Master White to put me up here until you are better and can come back to court with me. No, no argument. Sleep, Am.' He stroked his fingers over his brother's already closing eyes.

'My lord.' Master White stood at the foot of the stairs as Robert descended, his hand outstretched, holding a letter. 'This has just arrived for you. I believe it is from the Queen,' he said reverentially.

'Thank you, Master White,' Robert said. 'It seems my brother will need to stay here for a while. May I too trespass upon your good nature and beg a bed for myself until he is able to move?'

'Certainly, my lord,' White said, his mind already calculating the extra expense he would incur for their provisioning. 'It would be an honour. I can arrange the chamber next to the Earl for you if that would serve.'

'It would serve admirably, Master White, I thank you. And don't worry about the cost.' Robert untied the purse at his waist and passed it to him. 'That should be enough for a few days at least.'

'Oh, my lord, it's not necessary,' White protested gratefully, clutching the money bag to his chest. 'Really.'

'Not another word,' Robert silenced him. 'Now, Master White, could I have somewhere private to read my letter?'

'Of course. Take my room, my lord. There is a comfortable chair and a jug of good wine you might wish to partake of.'

'I will gladly. I could also do with some food. It was a long ride here.' Robert smiled his charming smile and Master White scuttled off to order dinner for his guest.

Robert fell into the fireside chair and opened Elizabeth's letter. It was full of complaints. How dare Robert leave the court without permission? Ambrose had a fever, didn't he? Robert could catch it, become ill and then where would Elizabeth be? And what about her horses? Only at the close of the letter did Elizabeth think to ask how Ambrose fared.

Robert screwed up the letter and threw it in the grate.

CHAPTER 30

HAMPTON COURT PALACE, MAY 1564

Cecil leaned over Elizabeth's shoulder and spoke quietly in her ear. 'Madam, the question of Mary Stuart's marriage has risen once again.'

Elizabeth glared up at him. 'Why so?'

'It seems she is now actively looking for a husband.'

Elizabeth glanced across the room to where Robert was talking with Henry Sidney. She knew Cecil still thought Robert was the best candidate for Mary's hand. 'Sit,' Elizabeth instructed. 'Lord Robert would have to be ennobled before Mary would even consider him.'

'You had planned to do that anyway, madam,' Cecil said, taking a seat. 'Indeed, it is time he was.'

'Are you so eager to be rid of him that you would advance him so, Cecil?' she asked sharply.

'No, madam, but as you ennobled his brother, it is not unreasonable you would do so for one so close to your heart.'

'He is close to me, Cecil, but not so close that I am blind to all else. I see the advantages such a marriage would bring.' She paused. 'Write to Mary Stuart and propose Lord Robert.'

Cecil caught his breath. *A decision*, he thought, *a miracle*. 'I shall do so at once, madam,' he said and left before she changed her mind.

Elizabeth sighed and raising her hand, caught Robert's eye

and crooked her finger at him. She watched him excuse himself from Henry's company and make his way towards her.

'You wanted me, Your Majesty?' he asked.

'Come and sit by me, Robin,' she said, indicating the chair vacated by Cecil. 'I need to talk to you.'

'This sounds serious,' he said, settling himself down.

She took hold of his hand beneath the table and held it in her lap. 'I've told Cecil to write to Mary Stuart. He is going to propose you as a husband for her.'

The colour drained from Robert's face. 'What?' he gasped.

'Now, don't be angry. I have my reasons.'

'The devil you do,' he declared. Elizabeth shushed him to lower his voice. 'What have I done to deserve this?'

'It's an honour, my sweet. You would be married to a queen.' She added sharply, 'I thought that was what you wanted.'

He glared at her. 'You're the only queen I want to marry. I don't want to be packed off to Scotland. You may as well kill me now.'

'Scotland isn't that bad.'

'You'd know that, would you? You, who have travelled so very extensively?'

Elizabeth's mouth pursed. 'I'll forgive you your temper. I admit, it took me a while to get used to the idea. God's Teeth, Robin, I no more want to lose you to Mary Stuart than you want to go. But for my security and for England's, I need her to have a husband whom I can trust.'

'What makes you think she'll even have me? I have no rank. And worse, everyone knows I am your lover, don't they? Do you think she'll want your cast-off?'

'There's no need to be vulgar, Robin. And as for your rank, well, that can be easily remedied. I had planned to do it anyway,' she said, idly fingering a pearl on her dress.

'Do what?' he asked sulkily.

'Raise you to an earldom. I had thought Leicester would suit.'

Even that news could not lift Robert's spirits. 'Thank you,' he muttered. 'Did you say Cecil was writing to Scotland about me?'

'Yes.'

Robert shook his head understandingly. 'I see. He's outmanoeuvred me at last, hasn't he?'

'It *was* Cecil's idea,' Elizabeth admitted, adding slyly, 'I didn't think of it, wouldn't have thought of it, if it hadn't been for him.'

Robert stared out across the room, watching the dancers as they passed before him. 'Well, maybe it won't be as bad as I imagine. Mary Stuart is very beautiful, by all accounts, and comely. She'll keep my bed warm, if nothing else.'

'You can go now,' Elizabeth said coldly, throwing away his hand.

Robert rose and gave a slight, very slight, bow. 'I hasten to do your bidding, Your Majesty, in this as in everything. Good night.'

Elizabeth watched him leave with tears in her eyes.

ST JAMES PALACE, SEPTEMBER 1564

Cecil stifled a sigh. He had thought the Queen beyond this kind of display. But there she was, placing the heavy ermine-trimmed robes around Robert Dudley's shoulders and taking the opportunity to run her fingers along his neck and play with the short stubs of his dark brown hair. And there was Norfolk. He had seen the familiarity too and was fuming. Unlike Cecil, Norfolk could never keep his temper in check.

So, Robert Dudley was now Earl of Leicester and suitable for marriage with the Scottish queen. But Cecil had found out that Robert had written to Mary Stuart and told her he wasn't interested in becoming her husband. Cecil had wondered whether he should tell Elizabeth about it but he wasn't sure that the news wouldn't please her. She would, no doubt, interpret it as a reluctance to leave her. And now, seeing her act so familiarly, he wondered if she had ever really intended to let Robert go.

Women! Cecil thought in despair.

'What do you think of my new creation, Sir James?' Elizabeth asked.

Sir James Melville, the Scottish ambassador, looked over to where Robert chatted with Cecil and smiled. 'The Earl of Leicester well becomes his new position, Your Majesty.'

'He does,' Elizabeth agreed. 'Will your queen like him, do you think?'

'How could she not?'

'She would be foolish indeed if she did not,' Elizabeth remarked. Melville kept quiet. 'I must give you a present to give to my dear cousin Mary.'

Melville followed her around the bed. He watched as she lifted the lid of a silver casket, took out a piece of cloth and unwrapped it, handing a miniature of herself to Melville.

'A remarkable likeness,' he said. 'My queen will treasure it always.'

'I would like to have a picture of her in return.'

'Of course. And who else is in there?' he said, peering into the box.

Elizabeth liked his impudence. She showed him the other miniatures in her box. 'This is my late stepmother, Queen Catherine. This, my father. This, my sister. And this...,' she hesitated.

Melville took the picture from her hands. 'Ah, Lord Robert. Forgive me, I mean the Earl of Leicester. Perhaps I should take this to my Queen. She has not got a likeness of the Earl.'

Elizabeth snatched the miniature from his hand, placed it back in the box and slammed down the lid. 'When my cousin has the Earl of Leicester, I will have need of his portrait.'

Robert was playing with his new badge with its emblem of the bear and ragged staff.

'Can't you leave it alone?' Elizabeth teased.

'Give me something else to play with.'

She ignored the wink he gave her. 'Well, you'll be playing at tennis tomorrow. I've arranged for you and Norfolk to entertain the court with a match.'

'Can Norfolk even play?'

'He's actually very good.' Elizabeth leant forward and snatched the last almond biscuit from the plate as Robert reached for it. 'I hope you'll make it interesting.'

His eyes narrowed. 'What do you mean by interesting?'

'That's up to you.'

Robert frowned at her. 'I do believe, Bess, you want me to fight with him.'

'Don't be ridiculous. Why would I want my nobles fighting?'

'Because he's an idiot?' Robert suggested.

Elizabeth laughed. 'Robin, how dare you say such a thing about the noblest peer in the land?'

'Everyone thinks it.'

'Well, I will just say it would please me greatly if you were to win tomorrow. Norfolk doesn't care for me, which doesn't trouble me greatly, for I neither need nor desire his affection, but I do want his respect. So, I would quite like to see Norfolk suffer a public defeat at your hands. That would hurt his pride a very great deal, I think.'

'Bess,' Robert said admiringly, 'you are a wicked woman.'

So much for putting Norfolk in his place, Robert thought, as the ball bounced past him and Norfolk scored another point. It looked as if he was going to lose the match and it would be he who would look like a fool. He raised his arm to serve and sent the ball spinning across the net, heading directly for Norfolk. It punched into Norfolk's stomach, causing the duke to double over in pain.

'My apologies, Norfolk,' Robert called out, pleased to hear sniggers from the viewing gallery. 'Perhaps if you were quicker on your feet.'

That remark earned him a ripple of laughter from the spectators. Robert served again. Norfolk returned it with a vengeance, but Robert side-stepped it neatly. He lobbed the ball high. It hit the angled wall and bounced off. Norfolk was too slow and missed it. Another point to Robert and he began to cheer up. Norfolk's anger only increased and his frustration hampered his game. He lost point after point and Robert won the match easily.

'Congratulations, my lord,' Elizabeth called to Robert, 'and commiserations to you, Your Grace.' She unclasped a jewelled brooch from her bodice and threw it to Robert as a prize. He caught it and kissed it. 'God's Death, but you are both sweating like pigs.'

Robert grinned, leant over the railing and took her handkerchief from her lap. He wiped his forehead.

Norfolk's red face turned purple at his impudence. 'You knave,' he roared, quieting all the voices around. 'How dare you take such a liberty?'

Robert stared at him, open-mouthed. He could not believe

Norfolk was serious, but the duke was trembling all over with rage. Robert shook his head, laughing.

Norfolk lunged at Robert and grabbed his shirt. 'You bastard,' he hissed, spittle dabbling Robert's chin. 'I'll teach you.'

'Enough.' Elizabeth's voice rang out loud. 'How dare you presume so much, Norfolk?'

Norfolk lowered his arm. 'I was thinking of your honour, Your Majesty.'

'Indeed? Is my honour so fragile that it cannot stand some honest fellow's handling?'

'Honest fellow?' Norfolk scoffed, his bluster returning. 'Hardly a label I would credit a Dudley with.'

'Kiss my feet, you miserable dog,' Robert snarled and the two men squared up again, but Elizabeth had had enough. 'Will you brawl in my presence? Two of my nobles making such a spectacle of themselves! You, my lord,' she pointed at Norfolk, 'learn to contain your spleen or I will have you sent from court. And you, Lord Leicester, show due courtesy in future. ladies, away.'

Mary followed her brother back to his rooms. He had persuaded her to attend court for a few weeks, but he had not managed to persuade her to remove her veil.

'Honestly, Rob, you should be careful.'

He threw open the door to his bedchamber and strode inside. 'Careful?' he scoffed. 'I have nothing to worry about.'

'Not from the Queen. I mean, you should be careful of the duke. The Howards are a crafty lot, they always have been. Are you going to change?'

'In a minute,' he said, pouring himself a large cup of beer. He gulped it down, wiping his sleeve across his mouth. 'By Christ, I needed that.'

'Thirsty work?'

Both he and Mary turned. Elizabeth was in the doorway, smiling.

'Damned thirsty,' he replied. 'Are you coming in or are you planning to linger there?'

She stepped inside, one of her ladies, Lettice Devereux, the Countess of Essex, close at her heels. 'Lettice, you may go. Lady Sidney is here to attend me.'

Lettice glanced at Robert as she dropped a curtsey, gave him a quick flutter of her eyelashes and retreated, closing the door as she left. Elizabeth sat down on the bed.

'Mary was just saying I should be careful of the Howards.' Robert poured water from a jug into a large bowl. 'She doesn't like the duke.'

'Not many people do,' Elizabeth said. 'He's not an easy man to like.'

'He's a pompous ass,' Robert said, leaning against the cabinet.

Elizabeth looked him over, her gaze taking in his long legs, his chest where a thin long triangle of skin and dark curly hair peeped through his open shirt. She looked away as heat flooded up her neck.

Robert, recognising the signs of desire, looked at Mary and flicked his eyes at the door. Mary understood and frowned, but his eyes were insistent.

'Madam,' she said huffily, 'would you give me leave to fetch something from my room?'

'Of course, Mary,' Elizabeth answered quickly, a quiver in her voice.

Mary exited. Robert turned back to the bowl of water and pulled his shirt over his head. With his back to her, Elizabeth could look at him all she pleased; the smoothness of his skin, the curves of it as it stretched over bone and muscle. She watched as he splashed water on his face, over the back of his neck and chest. Water trickled down his spine. He turned, grabbed a linen cloth and slowly, deliberately, rubbed his chest dry. Elizabeth met his eye and a tremor ran through her.

Robert moved to the door and locked it, turning the key slowly, giving her a chance to protest. But Elizabeth said nothing.

She stood up to meet him, tilting her head back, ready for his kiss. His lips pushed against her, his tongue lapping at her teeth to open. She gave in and he thrust his tongue deep into her mouth. Her hands ran over his naked back, grabbing and scratching at the wonderful feel of his skin. Robert pushed her back onto the bed and made a grab at her skirts.

Her heart was pounding as she felt his hand on her thigh. Panic gripped at her stomach and she couldn't breathe.

Wrenching her mouth from his, she pushed him away and scrambled to the other side of the bed.

'Unlock the door,' she cried. 'UNLOCK IT.'

Robert hurried to the door and turned the key. 'Bess,' he asked quietly, 'what have I done?'

'It's not your fault.'

'I wouldn't hurt you.'

'I know. I just... I can't, Robin, I can't.'

She rose on shaky legs from the bed and smoothed down her skirts. She pressed her fingers to her lips, tentatively, as if they were bruised. 'You should get dressed. And then... then we will play a game of cards. I'll wait for you. In there.' She strode into the adjacent chamber, closing the door behind her.

'You took your time,' he heard her say and he realised Mary had returned. He pulled on a clean shirt and doublet. Taking a deep breath and fixing a smile upon his face, he joined the women.

CHAPTER 31

HAMPTON COURT PALACE, NOVEMBER 1564

Elizabeth was experimenting, trying to see if she could bear to live without Robert by her side. Thomas Heneage was handsome and very attentive. She liked him and his company did make a change. Yes, perhaps Heneage would do. For a while at least.

Heneage suggested a walk. Elizabeth agreed, taking his arm as he led her out into the gardens. She caught Robert's eye as they passed his card table, but she wasn't able to read the expression on his face.

'Your turn, Rob,' Henry Sidney prompted. 'Is something wrong?'

Robert selected a card and laid it down. 'No.'

Henry cast a look at the retreating queen and her companion. Her ladies trailed a discreet distance behind. 'Has the Queen upset you?'

'Why would she have upset me?'

'Well, she seems to be spending a great deal of time with Thomas Heneage.'

'She can spend time with whomever she likes,' Robert said carelessly, winning the game and taking his money. A ripple of laughter filtered through the window from the group outside. 'Heneage has taken her fancy, that's all. You know how she is, Hal. She's like a butterfly, flitting from one flower to the next. She gets bored and moves on to another.'

'The Queen's bored with you? I can't believe that.'

Robert shrugged.

'I'm surprised you're taking it so calmly. It can't mean good for you if you're no longer in favour.'

'What harm can it do me? I have my earldom, I have my estates and, if the plan holds, I'll soon have a royal wife as well.'

Henry's mouth dropped open. 'You mean you *are* going to marry—'

'Not Elizabeth. Mary Stuart. Maybe. Thomas Heneage is obviously my replacement.'

'The Queen would send you to Scotland?'

'That's why I was given my earldom, to make me more suitable for a queen.'

'You *want* to marry Mary Stuart?'

Robert leant back in his chair and blew out a puff of air. It was hot and he could feel his shirt sticking to his skin. 'The idea is growing on me. Especially now I see how Elizabeth treats me. She toys with me, Hal, and I am getting mightily tired of it.'

'So, seek a diversion. There must be plenty of willing women at court.'

'Oh, they're willing enough, but if Elizabeth found out, you know how possessive she is. Then again, now she has Heneage, she may not be watching me too closely.'

'Well, then. Let's pick one for you.'

'Henry,' Robert scolded, almost embarrassed as Henry twisted in his seat to peruse the company.

'I know,' he said. 'Lettice Devereux. Now, she, Rob, is a beauty.'

'A beauty with a husband.'

'Who is in Ireland, I believe, and none too sorry that he is there, I should say. What do you think of her?'

Robert glanced over Henry's shoulder, out of the window to where Lettice stood, looking bored and glancing longingly back to the chamber. He had noticed Lettice often, for her auburn hair, thicker and more lustrous than her cousin the Queen, made her stand out. She had perfect and soft, creamy skin, a comely figure and inviting eyes that often looked his way. They were doing so now. He met them with his own and inclined his head towards her. Lettice returned a surprised, happy smile.

Robert said, 'I think she will do very well.'

Robert hadn't planned to approach Lettice in the corridor but he had been on his way to the stables to inspect the horses when he bumped into her.

'Good morning, Lady Essex.' Robert made a deep bow, which she returned with a low curtsey, the fingers of her right hand playing with the low neck of her bodice. He noticed the round swell of her breasts beneath the green silk and felt the first stirring of lust. He sighed dramatically. 'What a very lucky man your husband is, Lady Essex.'

'To be serving in Ireland?'

'To be married to you.'

She gave a little laugh, smooth and low. 'Much good it does him, being so far away.'

'Do you mind so very much?'

'I find I can bear it well.'

'You're not lonely, then?' Robert moved closer.

She lowered her eyes. 'I sometimes yearn for company.'

'But you have the constant company of the Queen's ladies.'

Lettice shook her head. 'The company of women can become very tedious. I find the company of men more agreeable.'

She looked at him and he knew they need not play the game any longer. They both wanted the same thing.

'Dine with me, Lettice,' he said, lowering his voice.

'When?'

'Tonight.'

'I'd love to.'

'Lady Essex!' Elizabeth's strident voice made them both jump. 'What do you do here?' She strode up to them and glared.

'Nothing, Your Majesty,' Lettice said, her voice trembling.

'And you, my lord?'

'I was on my way to the stables,' Robert said, damned if he was going to show fear of Elizabeth.

'Indeed. Are my horses to be found in the corridors of my palace?'

Robert looked away, irritated by her sarcasm.

'The Earl of Leicester was kind enough to enquire of my health, Your Majesty,' Lettice said.

'Your health is no concern of his,' Elizabeth snorted derisively. 'And from the look of you two, I doubt very much that was his concern. Or is enquiring of your health a euphemism for intending to cuckold your husband, madam?'

Lettice let out a gasp of shock and surprise, her cheeks flushing red as the other ladies giggled.

'That remark is not worthy of you, Your Majesty,' Robert growled feelingly.

'Get out of my sight,' Elizabeth hissed, the tendons on her neck sticking out. 'Before my temper gets the better of me. By Christ, if my father were alive, he would have had your head for what you just said to me.'

'That being the case, perhaps you wish me to leave the court,' Robert suggested, his chin rising defiantly.

'Oh, no, sir. You have duties, do you not? And besides, it suits me to have you here. For when people see you trotting around court like the dog you are, they know I am here. And damn you, sir, you will be brought to heel.'

Elizabeth adjusted her bonnet and made her way across the lawn. She stood back a little as Robert drew the bow and watched as the arrow thudded into the edge of the butt. She clapped the poor shot to make her presence known.

Robert glanced over his shoulder. At first, the spectator appeared to be a dairy maid and he thought it impertinent of her to stop and watch him, let alone applaud. But then he looked a little harder beneath the flapping cloth cap.

'Elizabeth?'

She folded the fabric back. 'Yes, it's me.'

'What the devil are you doing dressed like that?'

'It was the only way I could escape the prying eyes of my ladies. Kat got the dress for me.' She held out the loose skirts and twirled round. 'Do you like it?'

He lied and said yes. In truth, the dowdy garb did little to flatter her thin, boyish body. Elizabeth needed the sparkle of jewels and fine fabrics to make her beautiful.

'Why did you need to escape?' he asked.

'I wanted to see you alone.'

'Oh, yes?'

'I wanted to say sorry.'

'Well, that can't be easy for you.'

Elizabeth held her tongue. 'Your aim's off,' she said, pointing to the butt.

'You called me a dog.'

'I know, I'm sorry. But you did provoke me.'

'By talking to Lettice Devereux?'

'She's a wanton.'

'She's your cousin. And did she deserve to be banished from court?'

'I don't want to talk about Lettice,' Elizabeth sighed. 'Robin, say you forgive me.'

'Get rid of Heneage and I'll forgive you.'

'I will,' she said gratefully.

'Very well, then,' he shrugged. 'After all, you can have him back when I'm in Scotland.'

'Yes, I suppose I can,' Elizabeth said quietly, handing him another arrow.

'I hear Lord Darnley wants to go to Scotland to look over his estates,' Robert said. 'Maybe he and I could travel up together. I'd be glad of the company.'

'Darnley's not going to Scotland.'

'Why not?'

'Darnley has a claim to my throne and Mary Stuart knows it.' Her voice grew hard. 'If she laid her greedy eyes on him, she would probably marry him to strengthen her own claim and annoy me. Mind you, I could wish her joy of him. Do you know, his mother thinks he's an angel? She has no idea of what he gets up to when he's out of her sight.'

'He's a great frequenter of the Southwark stews, I hear.'

'So Cecil tells me. His mother spoils and indulges him and he thinks himself the loveliest creature alive.'

'Well, if you won't let him go, I'll have to go on my own then.'

Elizabeth was silent for a long moment. Then she asked, 'Dine with me?'

'If you want me to.'

'I'll expect you.' She walked away. She was hoping he would say something, call her back, apologise for sulking, but Elizabeth made it back to the palace without Robert saying a word.

Elizabeth couldn't sleep. What Robert had said, about taking Heneage back when he was in Scotland, troubled her. As if Thomas Heneage could take his place! She had thought that perhaps he could, once. But the past week when she and Robert hadn't been talking had been unbearable. She couldn't live the rest of her life like that. No, Robert must not, could not go. She couldn't let Mary Stuart have him.

But what to do about Mary? Resolved on the matter of Robert, her mind began to clear. She knew Darnley's parents had ideas of marrying him to Mary Stuart, hence the sudden plan to inspect his Scottish estates. Did they think she was a fool? How she loathed Darnley; there was something about him that made her skin crawl. To think that he had Tudor blood!

No doubt Mary would think he was wonderful. Elizabeth felt almost sure of that. It was strange. Although they had never met, Elizabeth felt she understood her cousin, in spite of their differences. The thought of Mary being wedded to that poor excuse for a man! What a jolly dance Darnley would lead her. She pulled the covers up to her chin and closed her eyes. Seconds later, they snapped open. *Yes*, she thought with pleasure, *what a jolly dance*! Maybe Darnley should be allowed to go to Scotland after all.

GREENWICH PALACE, AUGUST 1565

They were listening to the boy singing. Robert reached for another grape and popped it in his mouth. With juice squirting over his tongue, he asked, 'So, when am I going to Scotland?'

Elizabeth slid him a sideways glance. 'You're not going. You know you're not going. Don't pretend to be ignorant.'

Robert smiled smugly. 'So, Mary Stuart has definitely married Lord Darnley.'

'Well and truly wed,' Elizabeth confirmed, biting down on a walnut. 'The stupid woman.'

'You really don't like her, do you?'

Elizabeth curled her lip. 'She rules with her heart, not her head. A woman like that is not fit to be a queen. And she wants my throne.'

'Might she not get it, with Darnley as her husband?'

'It's a risk, I know,' she acknowledged. 'But Cecil has heard that Darnley is already causing Mary problems and my hope is he will cause her more. She has had the sense not to make him king and he resents that. I suppose you take his part on that issue?'

Robert ignored her remark. 'Has Cecil heard anything about the little Italian, the Pope's spy – oh, sorry, the Queen's musician?'

Elizabeth laughed at his wit. 'He seems to be befriending Darnley.'

'Befriending? I know Darnley is game for anything, but is Rizzio a catamite?'

Elizabeth shrugged. 'He's a filthy little Italian, who can say what he gets up to?'

'They're very cunning, Italians.'

'They're not the only ones,' Elizabeth said pointedly. 'I thought you might tell me what you've been up to, Robin. With Norfolk, your new-found friend.'

Robert shifted uneasily. 'I don't know what you're talking about.'

'Oh, yes you do, you little toad. I know you and him and others on my Council are trying to get rid of Cecil. Don't deny it,' she held up a hand to halt his protestations, 'I know all about it.'

'Bess, I can explain—'

'I hope for your sake you can.'

'Norfolk approached me. He said it was because of Cecil's contriving that we had not married, that it was Cecil's idea to marry me to Mary Stuart and—'

'And you believed him?'

Robert gestured helplessly. 'He sounded plausible. Cecil has done me many an ill turn over the years. I know that to be true if nothing else. And I was angry with you at the time, all that business with Heneage and Lettice. I suppose I wasn't thinking properly. You can understand that?'

'I suppose I can. But what an idiot you must be to think I would ever give up Cecil. He is worth ten of you, all of you, and let me tell you, any mistakes he makes, I will forgive, as I would forgive them in you.'

'You mean—,' he reached for her hand and she didn't draw it away. 'You mean I'm not to be punished?'

'Oh, you're quite safe. It's Norfolk I blame. Oh, why am I plagued by such cousins?'

'Why don't you send him away? Back to the north, where he belongs?'

'Because he could cause more trouble for me there than here. No, I want him under my eye.'

'I'm sorry, Bess, truly. Tell me, does Cecil know about … about what we were planning?'

Elizabeth threw his hand away with a snort of contempt. 'Of course he does. Who do you think told *me*?'

CHAPTER 32

HAMPTON COURT PALACE, MARCH 1566

'Rob, Rob,' Elizabeth shook him roughly. 'Oh God, please wake up.'

Robert opened his eyes. 'Bess?'

She was leaning over him, strands of hair escaping from her nightcap and hanging down to tickle his face. The moonlight darkened the hollows of her face. 'I need you.'

'What time is it? What's the matter?'

She propped herself on the edge of his bed. 'I didn't know it would happen like this, I swear to God, I didn't.'

'Bess,' he took hold of her arm, 'tell me what's happened.'

'David Rizzio has been murdered. Cecil just told me.'

'But we knew that was going to happen. We saw a copy of the murder bond the Scottish lords signed.'

'I know, I know, but they killed him in front of *her*.'

'They did what?' Robert was aghast.

Elizabeth shifted on the bed to face him. 'They were having supper, Rizzio and Mary. The lords burst in on them and told Rizzio he was to die. Rizzio clung on to her skirts and begged Mary to help him, but they dragged him into the next room and stabbed him, again and again.'

'My God!'

'Mary must have heard his screams. They held her back. Those brutes took hold of their sovereign queen and used force against her.'

'Was her husband there?'

'Oh, he was there, the miserable wretch. He watched as Rizzio was killed and did nothing to protect her, not even when Ruthven held a pistol to her swollen belly and threatened to shoot. His wife and unborn child threatened and Darnley did nothing.'

'Is Mary hurt?'

She buried her face in her hands. 'I don't know. Bothwell helped her to get away. He had horses and they rode to ... somewhere..., I can't remember.'

'She's seven months gone with child,' Robert said in astonishment. 'To take to horse at such a time—'

'Could kill her and the child,' Elizabeth finished. 'Think how desperate she must have been.'

'So, she has Bothwell with her?'

Elizabeth gave a short, hard laugh. 'And Darnley.'

'Darnley?'

'She had to take him with her. She convinced him the lords meant to kill him next so he would help her escape. By Christ, if I had been her and had a dagger, I would have stabbed him for his treachery.'

'So, it seems Mary is safe for the moment, Bess. What upsets you so?'

She drew in a deep, shuddering breath. 'Is it my fault? Is it, Rob? I sent Darnley to her. I wanted him to cause trouble. Did I make this happen?'

'Bess, that's ridiculous, how could you have foreseen this? Darnley, of his own accord, made himself a friend to the Scottish lords. He may not have wielded a dagger himself but he signed their bond to murder the little Italian. All your Council knew of it and decided not to act. This is not your fault and I don't want to hear any more such nonsense that it is. You hear me?'

He wrapped his arms around her and she leant against his chest. 'Oh, none other can comfort me as you can,' she said. 'I thank God for you, Rob.'

'I'll always be here for you. But Bess — not that I mind, you understand — but I think it will do your reputation no good if you stay much longer in my chamber at this time of night.'

She laughed and gave a small nod. 'I'm sorry for waking you, Rob.'

'Don't be sorry. Come,' he gestured for her to move and he threw back the bedclothes, tugging his nightshirt down to cover his legs. 'I'll take you back to bed.'

He put his arm around Elizabeth's waist and led her back to the bedchamber, past the two ladies who had been searching the corridors, wondering where their mistress had got to in the middle of the night.

JUNE 1566

'How is she?' Cecil asked anxiously as Robert emerged from the Queen's chamber.

'Better, I think,' he sighed.

Cecil rubbed his forehead. 'I had no idea the news would distress her so, else I would not have told her in such a way.'

Elizabeth had been dancing in the Great Hall when Cecil had delivered the news that Mary Stuart had given birth to a son.

'Don't blame yourself. Elizabeth seemed merry enough.'

'Do you know what she meant by it? "I am of barren stock"?'

'It's obvious, isn't it? The Tudors were never good breeders, Cecil. Mary Stuart now has a son and heir and Elizabeth does not.'

'Maybe now she will look to remedy that,' Cecil said hopefully. 'With a suitable nobleman,' he added.

'Of course,' Robert replied sarcastically. 'Come, there's no point loitering outside her door, she will be abed soon enough. Do you care for a drink before turning in, Cecil?'

Cecil would not ordinarily be inclined to spend time with Robert but he wanted news of his concern for Elizabeth to get back to her. He followed Robert to his chamber and they settled before the fire, each with a cup of Rhenish wine in their hands.

'It's a wonder Mary didn't lose the baby really,' Robert mused. 'That long ride after Rizzio's murder. I suppose it is healthy?'

'The report from Sir Nicholas says the child is quite robust and, more importantly, Darnley has acknowledged it as his, which should put down the rumours about Rizzio being the father.'

'So, the boy is confirmed legitimate.'

'Indeed.' Cecil nibbled at his bottom lip. 'The Queen will be all right, won't she?'

'Cecil, Elizabeth will be fine. She has these sudden moods, you know, ever since Rizzio's murder.'

'Yes, I've noticed.'

'Talking of which, what has happened to the Scottish lords who killed him?'

'They've been imprisoned, all except Mary's half-brother, James Moray. He's on his way here because he is not safe from his sister in Scotland.'

'Is Mary Stuart safe on her throne?'

'It appears that she is.'

Robert rubbed his chin. 'I can't quite work out whether that's a good or bad turn of events for us.'

'Well, it means that Scotland does have a stable government once again, but it also means that it is ruled by a Catholic with affiliations to both France and Spain. Oh, if only Moray had been born on the right side of the blanket and he was King of Scotland.'

'What a lot of problems that would solve,' Robert agreed.

The Rhenish was making Cecil languid; he slouched in his chair. 'What is it, Leicester, that the Queen has against Mary Stuart? Do you know?'

'Other than the political reasons, you mean? In my honest opinion, Cecil, vanity and jealousy. Mary Stuart is reputed to be a great beauty, a great charmer of men. She is a rival to Elizabeth and Elizabeth has never liked competition.'

'Was she like that as a child?'

'She certainly liked to have her own way,' Robert laughed, 'but then, what royal child doesn't? I remember Edward could be almost uncontrollable at times, demanding this and that. Barnaby Fitzpatrick would often have to take a beating for Edward's behaviour. Elizabeth was a little different. She knew what liberties she could take and never went beyond them, but she always had to win, that I do remember.'

'And, of course, you let her.'

'Not always,' Robert replied with a grin. 'Well, she was a girl and, royal or not, I had my pride, too.'

'I've met Mary Stuart and she *was* very charming and quite lovely. She might be different now, of course, after what she's been through. She had a softer appearance than Elizabeth, I think. More womanly.'

'Elizabeth will be interested in your opinion,' Robert said, hiding his smile behind his cup.

Cecil sat bolt upright in the chair, holding his hand out to Robert. 'Oh, no, I didn't mean—'

'Cecil, I'm teasing,' Robert said, his eyes twinkling. 'She'd box my ears if I said that to her.' His face became serious. 'Is Darnley back in the conjugal bed?'

'I wonder,' Cecil shrugged. 'Is Mary Stuart a forgiving woman? I don't think so. Her great love for him seemed to die almost as soon as they had married. She had little time for him before the Rizzio murder and she stuck with him out of necessity. It is rumoured that Darnley has the pox.'

'That doesn't surprise me. I hear he was as great a frequenter of the Scottish brothels as he was of the English ones.'

'He certainly took no pains to conceal his visits.' Cecil looked down at his empty cup. 'There is another rumour bruited abroad. That of a relationship between Mary Stuart and the Earl of Bothwell.'

Robert's mouth fell open. 'Is it true?'

'It's a rumour. I can get it neither confirmed nor denied.'

'But if it is true?'

'Then the future may be very bleak indeed for Darnley.'

'You don't mean—'

'The Scottish are very fond of murdering people, Leicester, and they don't care if they're seen to be doing it.'

'You think Darnley's life could be in danger? But even if Darnley were out of the way, Mary would surely not marry Bothwell. He's a Protestant and only an earl.'

'You are only an earl,' Cecil pointed out, 'and yet you were considered suitable as a husband for her.'

'Don't remind me,' Robert muttered. 'But what then? I mean, if she were to marry Bothwell?'

'Who can say?' Cecil said. 'I think we're looking a little too far in the future to speak with any accuracy. Now,' he put down his empty cup and rose. 'I must get to my bed. You will, no doubt, see the Queen before I do tomorrow. You will convey to her my concern for her wellbeing?'

'Of course I will, Cecil. Get you to bed.'

'Thank you. Goodnight, Leicester.'

HAMPTON COURT PALACE, MAY 1568

'I think you must be a Master of the Dark Arts, Cecil,' Robert whispered in his ear, making him jump.

Cecil looked at him, shocked. 'What do you mean?'

'Well, don't you remember, you predicted this – why, it must have been nearly two years ago now. You predicted that Darnley would be in danger and, before long, Darnley is dead. Mary Stuart promptly marries Bothwell, who probably killed him, with or without her knowledge or instigation.'

'I merely prognosticated a chain of events based on experience, Leicester. I do not appreciate accusations of necromancy being hurled in my direction.'

'It was only a joke, Cecil,' Robert protested with a laugh. 'But you got it right, didn't you? If only you hadn't stopped there and foretold the rest.'

'I could not have predicted what followed,' Cecil assured him.

The Scottish lords had risen up against Mary and Bothwell and defeated them. Mary had been imprisoned at Lochleven Castle and Bothwell fled to Denmark. But then Mary Stuart managed to escape and she made her way to England, foolishly thinking that her English cousin would be sympathetic to her plight and help restore her to her throne.

'What a convenient memory that woman must have,' Robert mused. 'To have forgotten all the insults and trouble she has given Elizabeth over the years, and to think Elizabeth would too.'

Cecil grunted. 'Must you hover about my shoulder like a bad angel?'

'Prickly today, aren't we?'

'This situation makes things very difficult.'

'Why?'

'What are we to do with Mary Stuart?' Cecil gestured hopelessly. 'The Scottish don't want her back, which suits us very well.

Catherine de Medici won't have her in France. Spain may offer her a place to live in view of her Catholicism, but the truth is they don't want her, either.'

'We'll have to keep her,' Robert shrugged.

'I suppose we will but at a very great expense. And it's a dangerous situation to find ourselves in, Leicester. With Mary in England, it is a perfect opportunity for the English Catholics to try and put her on the throne. You know how they feel about our queen. I promise you, Elizabeth's life will not be safe as long as Mary is here.'

'Have you told the Queen this?'

'Yes, I have,' Cecil said, stiffening.

'And?'

'And she told me that if I was thinking of having Mary Stuart done away with, she would get one of her guards to run me through with their halberd.'

Robert burst out laughing. 'So, that's why you're so touchy. And were you?'

'Was I what?'

'Thinking of having Mary Stuart killed?'

'No, my lord, I was not.'

'Well, I don't care what's done with her, as long as I'm not expected to marry her again.'

'She's still married to Bothwell.'

'I'm glad to hear it. So, the Queen's in an ill temper, is she? Well, I've suddenly remembered I've got some work to do. If she asks, tell her I can't be found, will you, Cecil? There's a good fellow.'

Robert patted his shoulder and sauntered away. Elizabeth looked up and crooked her finger at Cecil.

Cecil took a deep breath and headed towards her.

CHAPTER 33

WHITEHALL PALACE, AUGUST 1571

Robert stroked the smooth white thigh laying over his own. It caused the owner to moan and turn over, presenting him with a full, rounded buttock. He smirked, raising his hand to give it a playful slap, but changed his mind. *Let her sleep*, he thought.

He yawned as there came a knock at the door. 'Wait,' he called, easing his legs to the floor. He retrieved his shirt from the floor and pulled it over his head where it barely covered his nakedness. 'Come in,' he said, pulling the bed hangings together.

Peters pretended not to notice the dress thrown over the chest at the foot of the bed. 'My lord, the Duke of Norfolk is in the antechamber. He wishes to speak with you.'

Robert groaned. 'What the devil does he want?'

'He didn't say, my lord. I did tell him you were not to be disturbed, but he insisted.'

'Very well.' Robert pulled on his hose and slipped his feet into shoes. 'But he shall have to take me as I am.' He followed Peters into the adjoining chamber, closing the door behind him. 'You wanted to see me, Your Grace?'

Norfolk looked Robert up and down, his lip curling at his disarray. 'Did I get you from your bed?'

'Just a short nap. The Queen didn't need me.'

'A nap? Really?' Norfolk raised a sceptical eyebrow. He sighed impatiently and glanced around the room, anywhere but at Robert and his naked legs. 'There is a rumour bruited about the court that I should marry Mary Stuart.'

'Yes, I've heard that rumour. But isn't she still married to Bothwell?'

'The Pope has already agreed that the marriage was forced upon her. An annulment could be easily arranged.'

'You sound as if you want to marry her.'

'If it would serve Her Majesty, I am prepared to marry the Stuart woman.'

'Well, I would wish you luck. Her husbands are not the most fortunate of men.'

Norfolk waved that concern aside. 'I am, of course, eminently suitable to marry with someone of her rank. I am the highest peer in England, I have royal blood in my veins—'

'And you are a Catholic,' Robert interrupted, bored with the pedigree, 'which should make you all the more agreeable to Mary Stuart.'

Norfolk's eyes narrowed. 'I am of the New Religion, Leicester—'

'No, you conform to it, Norfolk. You hide your true allegiance poorly.'

'I don't care what you think you know about me—'

'Oh, come now, you must care a little.'

Norfolk stepped up to Robert. 'Let me make one thing clear between us. We care not a jot for one another, and if it wouldn't mean my head on a block, I would gladly kill you where you stand. But the Queen has a misguided attachment to you and I admit that you have your uses. That is the only reason I am standing here now.'

'What do you want from me?' Robert asked.

'Nothing but your support for this marriage.'

'You want me to join forces with you again, after the fiasco of your Cecil intrigue?'

'We were foolish to think that the Queen would turn against Cecil,' Norfolk admitted. 'But she will see the sense in this.'

'Well, *I* don't see the sense in it.'

'For God's sake, Leicester, if I were her husband, I would tame Mary Stuart. There would be no need for the Queen to fear her. With England's help, Mary Stuart could be reinstated on her throne—'

'And you would get a crown.'

'Which is no more than you desire here in England.'

Robert considered. 'Do you think you could stomach Scotland, Norfolk? It's a savage country.'

'So is the north of England, Leicester. I manage that well enough.'

'Well, in that case then, you have my support.'

'I wonder...,' Norfolk began and paused, embarrassed. 'I wonder if you would speak with the Queen about it.'

'You want *me* to ask her?'

'I thought it might be better coming from you.'

Robert smiled, which annoyed Norfolk. 'Very well.'

'Good.' Norfolk shuffled his feet, unsure what to say or do next. Gratitude was called for, he knew, but he couldn't bring himself to thank Robert. 'I'll be going then.'

'You're welcome,' Robert called out as he left, causing Norfolk to nearly walk into the doorframe.

HAMPTON COURT PALACE, DECEMBER 1571

Elizabeth had declared it was too hot to move about and had instructed all the windows to be thrown open. Cushions had been strewn upon the floor and she and Robert lay there like bees drunk with pollen, too stupefied to move.

'Is that Norfolk hovering?' Elizabeth jerked her chin towards the opposite end of the corridor.

Robert glanced behind him. 'I'm rather afraid it is, Bess.'

Elizabeth groaned. 'Oh, what can he want? Go and find out, Rob, but don't bring him back with you. I don't think I can bear him today.'

Robert got to his feet and sauntered over to Norfolk. 'Can I help you, Your Grace?'

'Have you spoken to her yet?' Norfolk demanded.

'No, not yet.'

'Why the devil not?'

'I've been waiting for the right moment to approach her.'

'So, what's wrong with now?'

'All right, I'll talk to her now. But don't wait here. I'll let you know later.'

'I'll come to your rooms after six. Don't keep me waiting.' Norfolk strode off.

'Well, what did he want?' Elizabeth asked as he plumped back down on the cushion.

'He asked me a few weeks ago to speak with you on a delicate matter. Regarding Mary Stuart.'

Elizabeth looked away. 'Oh, yes?'

'He wants—'

'Since when have you and Norfolk been such good friends?'

'We're not,' Robert assured her.

'Then why are you doing his begging for him?'

'I'm not begging. Besides you don't know what I'm going to say yet.'

'I do know what you're going to say,' Elizabeth replied energetically. 'You must all think I'm stupid.'

Robert was startled. 'What am I going to say, Bess?'

'Norfolk wants to marry Mary Stuart. He wants you to find out if I'm agreeable to the idea.'

Robert stared at her, open-mouthed. 'I think you must be a witch, Bess.'

'Cecil keeps me fully informed,' Elizabeth said. 'Unlike some.'

'You think I should have told you this before?'

'Well, don't you?'

'It's only a question of marriage, Bess.'

'It's not just marriage,' she cried, her voice rising. 'God, what a fool you are! He's plotting rebellion, Robert, do you hear me? Rebellion. Marriage to Mary Stuart is only the first stage.'

'Bess, I didn't realise,' he protested.

'There seems to be much you don't realise.'

He swallowed and licked his dry lips. 'I'll tell him no then, shall I?'

'You'll tell him nothing, for the present.'

'Why not?'

'He expects me to say no, so he's making contingency plans. He's written to Mary, offering himself, and she's accepted him. They're not prepared to wait for my permission. What they are preparing for is to act. As uncrowned King of the North, he thinks he can raise an army to rise against me.'

'Bess, for God's sake, you must have him arrested.'

'Not yet,' she shook her head and reached for her fan.

'But if he's plotting against you—'

'We will wait. That's what I want and Cecil agrees with me. We wait.'

'I don't understand. Wait for what?'

'For Norfolk to incriminate himself. Which he will do, before long.'

'How can you be so sure?'

'Why, Robin,' she looked up at him, wide-eyed, 'it's a gift us witches have.'

EARL OF SOUTHAMPTON'S HOUSE, JANUARY 1572

'What is Elizabeth playing at?' Robert shoved Ambrose's letter across the table to Cecil. 'My brother tells me it is common knowledge the Northern earls are planning a rebellion, so why aren't they under arrest?'

'We want time to gather evidence against them.'

'Surely there is evidence enough!' Robert scoffed.

'We want more,' Cecil replied simply.

'What about Norfolk then?'

'Ah,' Cecil raised an eyebrow, 'there I have some news that will please you. The Queen has ordered his arrest.'

'But Norfolk has left the court,' Robert said, sitting up in agitation. 'I saw him leaving.'

'Don't concern yourself. He is being pursued and will be brought back to the Tower.'

'Thank God for that. Let's just make sure he stays there, where he can't cause us any more trouble.'

But Elizabeth released Norfolk. He behaved himself for a while, but he soon grew restless and began writing to the Scottish queen again. They picked up where they had left off, with talk of marriage and usurpation. Cecil knew about it from the start, of course. There wasn't a noble's house in England that did not house his spies. So, Norfolk was arrested and went back to the Tower. The Northern earls he had been plotting with heard of his arrest and decided to go ahead without him. Their rebellion failed, and they were punished.

Norfolk meanwhile begged the Queen to show him mercy. Elizabeth may have been prepared to forgive Norfolk, but there were men in her Privy Council who would not.

WHITEHALL PALACE, MAY 1572

Cecil winced as he shifted his swaddled foot on the stool. He looked across the bed. 'I didn't hear what the doctor said.'

Robert kept his eyes on Elizabeth, asleep in the bed. 'She's suffering from pains in the chest. He couldn't find any cause.'

'I wonder...,' Cecil scratched his temple, 'I wonder if it could be because of the Duke.'

Robert frowned at him. 'Norfolk?'

'Well, this latest treachery of his has struck at her hard, Leicester. She is ever inclined to be merciful, you know. She had expected the Duke to have learnt his lesson when she allowed him to leave the Tower. For him to betray her once again...,' Cecil shook his head.

'Why doesn't she just sign his death warrant and be done with him?'

'The Queen has not ordered an execution before, Leicester.'

Robert leant forward and gently took hold of Elizabeth's cold hand. 'Let Norfolk be the first, I say. If anxiety is the cause of this sickness, then she should execute him without further delay.'

'Have you spoken to her of the duke?'

'I've tried. She signed the warrant once and then tore it up.'

'Well,' Cecil sighed, 'he is her kin.'

'But she's not fond of him, so her hesitation can't be due to familial affection. It can't be a question of guilt. He's admitted his treason.'

'And the Commons do want his death. They petition me almost weekly to press the Queen to it.'

Elizabeth suddenly jerked, her feet kicking out beneath the blankets, and she cried out, her face screwing up as if in pain.

'Bess,' Robert said softly, reaching out to stroke her cheek. 'It's all right, I'm here.' She seemed soothed and turned on her side, drawing her legs up, becoming small like a child.

'I'm sure Norfolk plagues her dreams,' Cecil said, almost angrily. 'I wish she would act.'

'We'll have to work on her when she's better, Cecil.' Robert rubbed at his eyes. 'You know, you don't have to stay up, Cecil. I'll sit with her.'

'I'm quite comfortable, really.'

'But your gout must be painful.'

'It's better than it was. And I wouldn't be able to sleep if I went back to my rooms. I'm quite content sitting here.'

LEICESTER HOUSE, 1572

'Did you manage to get any sleep, Bess?' Robert asked, watching Elizabeth as she picked at a loose thread on a cushion she clutched to her chest.

She gave him a derisive look. 'How could I sleep?'

'Will you take some breakfast?' Robert asked, gesturing towards a table where bread and meats were laid out.

'I can't eat,' she cried, incredulous. 'The Duke of Norfolk, the highest peer in the land, my cousin, Robin, is even now walking out to his death on Tower Hill. At my command! I signed my name to his death warrant. His blood will be on my hands.'

'How many more times?' Robert slammed down his cup of beer. 'All your Council, the Commons, urged you to this. For your own safety, Bess.'

'I know, I know.' She sat down next to him. 'I wonder what he will say on the scaffold. Will he speak against me?'

'You'll get a report.'

'I'm not sure I want to know.'

'Then I won't let you see the report, Bess. Now, please, eat. You'll make yourself ill again.'

'Is there still time to stop it?'

'No,' he replied curtly and placed a plate of meat before her. She nibbled at a slice of beef until the Tower cannon fired and announced the death of the Duke.

As their thunder died away, Elizabeth began to shake. Robert hastily moved to her side and drew her to him.

'It's over,' he said softly into her hair. 'There will be no nightmares, I forbid it. And you will be safe, Bess. We will make you safe.'

CHAPTER 34

LEICESTER HOUSE, NOVEMBER 1572

Lady Douglass Sheffield sat stiffly upright as she heard Robert's voice in the hall. She pinched her cheeks, fearing they might be too pale just as the door opened and Robert walked in.

'Douglass,' he cried, holding his arms out. 'Why didn't you let me know you were coming tonight?'

'Sit down, Robert.' She patted the chair beside her. 'I have something to tell you.' Douglass took a few deep breaths and said, 'I'm with child, Robert.'

'You're...,' he gasped, his eyes widening. 'Good God.'

'It is quite natural, I assure you,' Douglass replied. 'The wonder is it hasn't happened sooner. And I need to know what your intentions are.'

'My intentions?'

Douglass's eyes filled with tears. 'Oh, Robert, are you going to make me beg?'

'Douglass,' he said, dropping to his knees and taking her hands, 'don't cry.'

'We must marry.' She slid her hands away and delved inside her bodice for a handkerchief.

Robert clambered back into the seat. 'Douglass, let's not be hasty—'

'I won't be known as the mother of your bastard, Robert.'

'Please understand, I have to be careful. You know how the Queen is.'

'I don't care about the Queen. She can't stop us marrying.'

'No, but she can make it damned unpleasant for us, Douglass. All I have I owe to her generosity. She could withdraw everything just like that.' He clicked his fingers to indicate the swiftness of Elizabeth's disapproval.

She grasped at his hands. 'Don't let me be your whore, Robert. I'll beg you, if that's what you want. Please, please, let us marry.'

Robert took his own handkerchief and wiped her eyes. 'Just give me a little time, Douglass. I have to go to Kenilworth in a few days to see how the building work is coming along. I'll be back in about a month and we'll sort it out then. Everything will be fine, I promise.'

WARWICK CASTLE, DECEMBER 1572

'I rode over to Kenilworth last week,' Ambrose said, pulling his fur cloak tighter about his shoulders. 'I couldn't believe the change in it.'

Robert stared into the fire. 'I'm going to see it tomorrow. It should be impressive, the amount of money it's costing me.'

'That sounds like regret.'

'No, not at all.' Robert ended the sentence with a sigh.

Ambrose narrowed his eyes. 'What's on your mind, Rob?'

Robert looked up. 'It's Douglass,' he said sulkily.

'The delectable Douglass?' Ambrose raised a surprised eyebrow. 'Whatever can she have done?'

'She's with child.'

'But Rob, that's wonderful. Why aren't you pleased?'

'How can I be pleased?'

'You've always wanted children.'

'It's difficult, Am.'

'Oh, you mean the Queen?' Ambrose nodded. 'Well, I admit it will be a trifle awkward for you, but surely she'll understand?'

'Oh, you think so? Be understanding, finding out that I've had a mistress for almost four years and that she is going to bear my child? Can you really believe Elizabeth won't mind?'

'I'm sure she'll be angry at first. But what does her anger matter when you have the prospect of an heir before you? And Douglass will make a fine wife.'

Robert grimaced.

'You don't still have hopes of marrying Elizabeth, do you? Oh, Rob, surely not?'

'She still might agree,' Robert said with a shrug.

'Rob, if Elizabeth was going to marry you, she would have done so years ago. You must marry Douglass.'

'Must I?'

'Of course you must. You don't want your child to be a bastard, do you? After all, who else do you have to leave all your worldly goods to?'

'I can leave what I have to anyone I choose, bastard or no. And bastards can be legitimised. Anyway, when Douglass and I began our relationship, I told her then she couldn't expect me to marry her. I kept nothing from her.'

Ambrose shook his head. 'I think you're a fool,' he said, his annoyance showing. 'You're free to wed whom you please. You have the prospect of an heir before you, yet you still hold out for a woman who has no intention, and to my mind, has never had any intention of marrying you.'

'And you don't, or won't, understand,' Robert retorted angrily. 'Everything I have, I owe to Elizabeth. What she has so freely given, she can take away. And then where would I be?'

'I do know that. What then of Douglass?'

'I don't want to hurt her, Am.' Robert rubbed his forehead. 'I have thought of a way out. What if I were to seem to marry her?'

'What do you mean "seem"?'

'I mean go through a ceremony but have no witness to it. That way, Douglass will be content believing herself married, but I can deny the marriage if Elizabeth ever does agree to marry me.'

'Rob!' Ambrose cried in horror.

'You think it despicable.'

'You know it is.'

'But I don't see I have any other option, Am. After all, I'm not saying I *will* disavow her. Just that I can if I need to.'

LEICESTER HOUSE, JANUARY 1573

Robert shook the rain from his cloak and handed it to his servant. 'Wine and cakes,' he ordered.

'At once, my lord,' the servant replied. 'Sir Henry and Lady Sidney have arrived. They are in their chamber.'

'Very well.' Robert, tired, climbed the stairs slowly. He knocked on the door and opened it. 'Hello, you two.'

Henry, stretched out full length on the bed, waved to him and lazily sat up. Mary, her ravaged face uncovered in the safety of her chamber, turned to him from the window and held out her arms. 'How dare you not be here when we arrive,' she scolded as they embraced.

'Forgive me, I've been in Esher.'

'And what were you doing in Esher?' Henry asked jauntily.

Robert hesitated, looking from one to the other. 'Has Ambrose not told you?' Both shook their heads. 'I've married Douglass. Sort of. Well, she's going to have a child.'

He accepted their cries of joy and congratulation tetchily.

'How is she?' Mary asked.

'She's well enough. I've sent her up to Warwick. She's going to stay with Ambrose until Kenilworth is ready and the baby is born.'

'But why have we heard nothing of this?' Henry asked. 'The court should be buzzing with this news.'

'The court knows nothing of this and that's the way I intend to keep it. The Queen must never find out.'

'But if you're married, she'll have to know. And what do you mean, sort of?'

Robert sighed impatiently. 'It's complicated, Mary. Oh, look, write to Ambrose, he'll explain. I'm sick of talking about it.'

'Forgive us for being pleased for you,' Mary replied haughtily, more than a little put out.

'Oh, don't be like that.' He put his arm around her waist. 'Are you going to court while you're in London?'

'Yes,' Henry said, 'we must pay our respects to the Queen.'

'Well, then for God's sake, don't mention any of this to Elizabeth. She mustn't know.'

'Don't worry,' Mary assured him, 'we won't.'

ON PROGRESS, SUMMER 1573

Robert hurried along the corridor. Clutched in his hand, a letter from Douglass he dared not read until he was back in his own room and alone. Courtiers importuned him as he went, hurrying alongside him even as he brushed them off. At last, he closed the door to his bedchamber behind him, moved to the window for the light and opened the letter.

Douglass's news was brief and to the point. She had given birth to a son and was calling him Robert. A cry of − joy, relief, disbelief − burst from him and he realised with happy astonishment his cheeks were wet. A son. He had a son. He was a father at last.

He wiped the tears away and read on. Both the child and Douglass were healthy and wishing he were with them. Robert thought it the most perfect letter he had ever received. He pulled out the chair to his desk and hurriedly wrote a reply, sending them both his very great love. Then he shook sand over the wet ink, folded and addressed it, sealed it, and left it for his secretary to send.

Then he gave his face one last wipe, clearing any trace of happiness from it, and began the walk back to Elizabeth.

CHAPTER 35

KENILWORTH CASTLE, SUMMER 1575

Henry Sidney helped his wife down from the carriage. 'He must have half the county here.'

Mary shielded her eyes against the sun. 'Robert never does anything by halves, you know. Well, Phil, it's been a while since you were here. What do you think of it?'

Philip Sidney climbed out after his mother, a tall, serious-looking young man. 'Uncle has certainly improved it.'

'Let's find him, shall we?' Henry led the way, past the people running to and fro, their ears ringing with the shout and clamour of voices. 'There he is. ROBERT!'

Robert turned around, a harassed expression on his face. He began to walk towards them, even as he continued to bark orders over his shoulder. 'Hello, Henry.' He kissed Mary through her veil. 'Phil.'

'Uncle.' Philip stepped forward and embraced him.

Robert held him tight for a moment. 'Oh, just what I needed.'

'Are things as bad as that?' Henry asked.

Robert nodded grimly. 'I've organised this sort of thing before, but never on this scale. And this has to be good. An extravaganza! Well,' he turned back to the castle and spread his arms wide, 'it's finished. What do you think?'

'It's wonderful, Rob,' Mary said.

'Fit for a queen, Uncle.'

Robert turned to him, grinning. 'You remember me saying that, Phil?'

'I remember everything you tell me, Uncle.'

'I'm very glad to hear it.' Robert turned as one of the workers called out to him. 'I'm sorry, I've still got so much to do. You know where your rooms are, don't you? Make yourselves comfortable and we'll meet for supper.'

'Is there anything I can help you with, Uncle?' Philip asked as Robert made to go.

'Actually, yes, Phil, I could do with some help. I have some players waiting for me. They should be in the hall. Could you go and see them, make sure they know what they're doing and run them through the play?'

'Of course, Uncle.'

They made off in different directions, making promises to meet later.

'You know, Mary,' Henry said ruefully as they began walking towards the castle, 'I sometimes wonder whose son Philip thinks he is.'

'What do you mean?'

'Well, his father's only a knight. His uncle's an earl.'

'Oh, Henry, you're not jealous?'

Henry looked away. 'Do you blame me? Rob's been given all this,' he gestured towards the castle, 'he has the Queen's favour, he has power and prestige. What do I have?'

Mary grabbed his arm, halting him. 'Now you listen to me. You have your knighthood and you're Lord Deputy of Ireland. And more importantly, you have me, you have your children. Rob may have power and prestige but he's not allowed to publicly own a wife, he's not free to acknowledge his own son. He has to take the taunts and insults of Elizabeth when she's in a temper, for it's not all billing and cooing in their relationship, I can tell you. So, I don't want to hear any more of how you're not good enough. Do you hear me, Henry Sidney?'

'I think the whole damned castle heard you,' he said with an embarrassed smile. 'And you're right. I have everything I could want. But I'm right too, you know.'

'About what?'

'You don't need this thing,' he gestured at her veil. 'Take it off. Please.'

'Don't make me, Hal,' she said, and he heard the tremor in her voice. 'I can't bear people to see me. They look at me for a moment and then they're too embarrassed to look any longer, so they look away. I'd rather they didn't see me in the first place. So, please don't make me take it off.'

Henry sighed. 'Very well, I won't. Come on, let's get to our bedchamber and have a lie down.'

'It's the middle of the afternoon, Hal,' she said, her voice curling with her smile.

'And we have nothing to do until supper,' he said, taking her hand.

Their horses trotted side by side as he brought her to the bridge of Kenilworth, just as the blue sky was beginning to darken. The castle rose out of the water, the reflections of a thousand torches glinting and rippling on the surface, the pennants on the battlements swelling with every breeze.

'It's beautiful, Robin,' Elizabeth congratulated him. She smiled down upon the people crowding around her, anxious to see a glimpse of their monarch. 'I want your people to see how high in my favour I hold you.'

'They're a good people,' Robert said, 'and loyal.'

'I'm very glad to hear it. I've learnt my lesson with the Duke of Norfolk. I don't intend to foster traitors in my country again.'

'No traitors here, madam, you have my word.'

'And I trust your word, Robin,' she said, reaching over to place her gloved hand upon his. 'Hallo! What's this?'

They brought their horses to a stop and Elizabeth peered over the side of the bridge. Fifteen feet below, a raft covered with green grass and flowers floated. Standing upon it, her naked feet crushing the flowers, was a young woman, clad in white silk, her golden hair, far too beautiful to be her own, streaming over her shoulders. Two children, cupid-like, with tendrils of green ivy wrapped around their legs and arms, knelt behind her, offering up bunches of wild flowers.

'I am the Lady of the Lake,' the woman said. 'Keeper of this sacred pool since the days of the great and glorious King Arthur, King of all the Britons. Never until now has England had such majesty. Never until now have I been able to entrust the keeping of this lake to anyone but our most gracious Queen.'

The Warwickshire accent was unmistakable and spoilt the mythic quality of the speech, but her words pleased Elizabeth and she smiled down at the woman. 'I thank you for your generous gift, but we had thought the lake had belonged to us already.'

Robert's jaw tightened. Couldn't Elizabeth accept a compliment gracefully, just for once?

'Very nice, Robin,' Elizabeth murmured.

A cannon discharged its shot. Robert touched Elizabeth's arm and pointed to a large ornate clock high on the tower he had named Caesar's. The hand moved slightly and then stopped. 'While you are here, Bess, no time will pass.'

'Old Father Time stands still. A happy thought.' She looked around her, at the fairyland Robert had created for her. 'If only.'

Days passed, all of them spent in pure enjoyment. Fireworks, dancing, hunting, masques, food, food and more food. Robert had prepared well and there were only words of praise for his accomplishments and murmurings of jealous admiration from the courtiers as the entertainments played themselves out.

One warm night, Elizabeth and Robert stood on the bridge by Mortimer's Tower, looking down at the dark, moonlit water where a mermaid glided through the water. Beside her, a dolphin, expertly crafted, floated and atop him, sat a masked Arion. When they were directly below Elizabeth, the mermaid thrashed her tail and Arion kicked his heels until the water foamed and tumbled. Up swam Triton, his long hair entangled with seaweed. He held a hand aloft.

'You winds, return unto your caves and silent there remain. You waters wild, suppress your waves and keep you calm and plain,' Triton shouted into the night, determined to play his part well. But Arion whipped his mask from his face and looked up at Elizabeth.

'I heed him not, my queen. Triton commands not me, for I'm not Arion but only honest Harry Goldingham.'

Robert scowled. The idiot had spoilt the whole scene. Was this what he had paid for?

But Elizabeth was amused. 'Well, honest Harry Goldingham, I would rather have you than Arion and I've enjoyed this more than all the other entertainments put together. Here.' She threw him a gold coin. 'A sovereign from your sovereign.' Honest Harry waved it above his head in triumph as he was dragged away by a sulky Triton.

Elizabeth moved off, laughing with her ladies.

'Is something wrong, Lord Robert?' Lettice Devereux's smooth, low voice curled into his ears.

'Not really,' he said, 'I was just thinking of how easily a fool can spoil my plans.'

'It wasn't spoilt. The Queen laughed.'

'Laughter wasn't the response I was after. I suppose it doesn't matter. So, Lettice! Are you enjoying yourself?'

'Well, you certainly put on a good show, my lord. But I cannot help feeling that there is more sport to be had indoors of a night.' She edged nearer so their sleeves touched.

Robert checked over his shoulder to make sure Elizabeth was not in earshot. 'How is your husband, Lady Essex?'

The green eyes looked slyly at him. 'He is well, and in Ireland, which is the best place for him.'

'You,' he said with an admiring grin, 'are a saucy wench.'

'As you would have discovered had you not abandoned me all those years ago.'

'Ah, yes, so I did. Tell me, were you very upset?'

'Devastated,' she mocked, laying an elegant hand upon her breast. 'To be wooed by the most handsome man at court and then forsaken as soon as the Queen clicked her fingers. And I can't believe that the Queen ever offered you more than I could. She has not the experience. At least, that is what she claims, our dear virgin queen.'

Robert said nothing.

'I believe you still wish to wed her,' Lettice said sharply, irritated by his silence.

'Only a fool would not want to.'

'But would you be marrying her for her crown or her body? Will you not answer me, my lord?' She moved closer, her mouth at Robert's ear. 'You will find my bed warmer than the Queen's, and free to visit whenever you wished.'

'And if I wished to visit tonight?' he asked quietly, turning at last to look at her.

Her lips curled as her heart beat faster. 'Then you would find my door unlocked, and I, alone in my chamber, waiting for you.'

'Leicester!' Elizabeth's voice, hard and angry, cut into their conversation.

Robert turned to her immediately. 'Yes, Your Majesty?'

'You're neglecting your duties as host, my lord.'

Robert moved to her. 'Forgive me. I had thought you were attended.'

'So I was but not by you.' Elizabeth's fierce eyes flashed at Lettice. 'You and I, sir, shall walk alone.'

She took his arm and they walked on through to the gardens, flaring torches on long poles casting shadows across the path.

'You have been most direct these past few days,' Elizabeth said as the scents of flowers filled their nostrils. 'Day after day, I am told I should marry. In masques, in poems, by people who jump out at me from behind trees. And who, am I told, should I marry? The answer, it seems, is you.'

'It's my greatest desire and no strange news to you, Bess.'

'No, indeed. But I'm afraid all your efforts have been in vain. For I do not mean to marry. Not you, not anyone.'

Robert came to a halt. 'I see.'

'I am sorry, Robin,' she said. 'When I think of the expense you've gone to—'

'Be sure, Bess,' he turned to her, his face grim. 'Be very sure. I'm going to ask you one last time. Marry me.'

He was in earnest, she realised. 'I am your queen. You are oath sworn to serve and love me.'

'I will always love you, Bess,' he said, bending his head to kiss her.

She pushed him away, angry. 'I can't marry you, Rob. I can't.'

'Why not?' he demanded.

'I have reasons you could not possibly understand. Now, you have your answer. Hate me if you wish.'

'I can't hate you, Bess, nor will I ever. You're my queen and my friend. But lover no more.' He sighed and looked back to the company. 'Shall we walk back? It's getting late.'

He pushed down the handle and opened the door. A solitary candle burned beside the bed. Lettice lay beneath the sheets, her hair fanned out over the pillow. Bare shoulders above the bed sheet, undulating over her breasts and hips. Robert stepped inside and turned the key in the lock.

She giggled as he began to pull the sheet away from her body. 'I was beginning to think you wouldn't come.'

He whipped the sheet away and drank in the sight of her. 'How could I resist such an invitation?'

Her toes prodded his codpiece. Robert grasped her ankle and pulled her further down the bed, spreading her legs and placing himself between them.

'Oh,' she moaned, curving her body towards him, 'thank the Lord for a proper man.'

'Your Majesty, the entertainments for today—'

'Are cancelled,' Elizabeth finished sharply.

His feeling of happiness faded quickly. *God's Death*, he thought, *here we go again.*

'Why, Your Majesty?'

'Get out,' she barked at her attendants. They retreated hurriedly, kicking against one another's feet in their haste. Robert watched them go and prepared himself for another quarrel.

'Where were you last night?'

'Why, Your Majesty?' Robert repeated.

'Answer me. Where were you?'

'I did not retire to my bed until late last night, Bess. At what time exactly do you mean?'

'Two o'clock this morning.'

'I do not rightly remember. Perhaps in my study.'

'Liar,' she hissed. Her hand thudded against the pommel of her chair and he watched her knuckles turn white as she gripped it. 'You were in some harlot's bed.'

He sighed heavily and ran his fingers through his hair. He was getting tired of this game. 'If you knew where I was, Bess, why ask me?'

Elizabeth jerked from her chair and slapped his cheek. Robert staggered back. The inside of his cheek had caught against his teeth and he tasted his own blood.

'Madam, you deny me your bed. Would you deny me comfort elsewhere?'

'Why do you need comfort, Robin? I do without. Why can't you?'

'It's not natural for a man to do without. To keep me from other women's beds you will need to send me to the Tower, madam, for I swear I was not made to live the life of a monk.'

The light of anger faded from Elizabeth's eyes. She fell against the chair, missed and tumbled to the floor. She fell on her face and sobbed into her arms. Robert was too angry to go to her.

'You will torment me to my death, Robin. I cannot bear the thought of you with other women.'

'Then don't think of it, Bess,' he said, none too gently.

'Who was she?'

'Does it matter? Besides, the less you know, Bess, the less it will torment you. How did you know I was not in my chamber last night?'

'I went to you. I wanted to talk to you. You weren't there. You were sweating in some bitch's bed. It hurt, Robin. I have cried all night long.'

'I'm sorry that you were upset, Bess. I didn't mean for you to find out.'

Elizabeth sat up and wiped her eyes with her fingers. Robert took a lace handkerchief from his sleeve and handed it to her.

'You're right, Robin. I don't want to know.' She pushed herself back into her chair, sniffing. 'As for the entertainments today, I'm sorry, but I'm not in the mood. Perhaps tomorrow. I have a headache. Leave me.'

Robert nodded and bowed out of the room. 'See to your mistress,' he instructed her ladies who clustered outside the door. 'Wait a moment,' he said, grabbing Lettice's arm.

'Gladly, my lord,' she said. 'Are you in disgrace again?'

'In disgrace and yet forgiven. She knows I wasn't in my own chamber last night.'

'Does she know whose you were in?' Lettice asked hurriedly.

'No, Lettice. Fear not, I didn't inform against you. It's better she knows nothing.'

'She shall not hear it from me,' Lettice promised. 'It's not to be the end though, is it, Robert?'

Robert pulled her to him and nuzzled her neck. 'I enjoyed you too much to forsake you again, sweetheart. I shall come...'

'Tonight?' she clutched at him. 'Come tonight.'

'Tonight,' he promised.

'Lettice,' Elizabeth's imperious voice called from the chamber. 'Cousin, is that you?'

Lettice shot a quick glance at Robert, then hurried to her mistress. 'Yes, Your Majesty,' he heard as he pressed his ear to the door.

'We will be leaving here in the next day or two,' Elizabeth said. 'I would like to stay at Chartley, cousin. You may leave at once to see to the arrangements.'

'Oh, but Your Majesty,' Lettice began to protest, 'Kenilworth is far more comfortable than my home can ever be.'

'If you don't want me there, cousin, just say so.'

The tone of Elizabeth's voice made Robert wince.

Lettice continued. 'No, Your Majesty, I just want you to be comfortable. I will leave at once to make all ready for you.' She backed out of the room and watched the door close upon her. 'She's sending me away. Do you think she knows?'

Robert shook his head. 'No, she would have said. She just wants to get away from here. Damn her, all the money I've spent.'

'I won't be able to see you tonight,' Lettice pouted, poking her finger inside his shirt and stroking his chest.

'No,' Robert agreed ruefully, 'but there'll be other nights.'

'Will you be coming to Chartley?'

'It depends. Elizabeth may not want me with her.'

Elizabeth did want Robert. At Chartley, she thought she would find some peace, but not solitude. One thing Elizabeth never wanted to be was alone.

'I came on ahead,' Robert explained to Lettice when he arrived at Chartley, 'to make sure everything was ready for her.'

'She's coming already?' Lettice asked despairingly. 'I thought she wouldn't be here until tomorrow at least. Just look at the place.'

'It's fine,' Robert said, looking around. 'Just have your servants throw fresh rushes down and all will be well.'

'Rushes? Oh, yes, rushes. I will tell them.'

'Not yet,' Robert put his arms around her waist and pulled her to him. 'You haven't said hello properly.'

'Robert,' she protested weakly, as his kisses trailed down her neck, 'my children might walk in.'

'Oh, I forgot your children. Your husband is a most fortunate man. He has you *and* four children to carry on his name.'

'I really believe you mean that,' Lettice said in surprise.

'Of course I mean it. What else did God put us on this earth for if not to have children?'

'Walter would agree with you,' Lettice said, settling herself onto a couch. 'Honour and family are all he thinks about.'

Robert smiled down at her. 'And you have other things on your mind?'

'Several other things. Oh, there are the children.'

Four youngsters tumbled into the room and stopped dead at the sight of Robert. 'Who are you?' the tallest demanded.

'Robert Devereux,' Lettice scolded, 'that is no way to address the Earl of Leicester.'

The young boy stared up at Robert. 'The Earl of Leicester?'

Robert nodded. 'That's my title. My name is Robert too.'

'What do you say?' Lettice said to the boy.

'I am most honoured to meet you, my lord,' the boy answered dutifully.

'Now, my darlings,' Lettice said, 'the Queen is coming to visit. She will be here shortly and I want you all to be on your best behaviour. Is that understood?' The children nodded. 'Very well. Now, all of you, go and play somewhere. I don't want you back in the house before six o'clock. There is a lot of work to be done and I don't want you underfoot. Now, go on. Go and play.'

'You were very strict with them, Lettice,' Robert said after they had gone. 'And what work have you to do? I told you all you have to do is lay down fresh rushes…'

Lettice twined her fingers into his and pulled him towards the stairs. 'Sometimes, Robert, I believe you are the stupidest man in England.'

CHAPTER 36

GREENWICH PALACE, FEBRUARY 1577

Douglass shifted her son on her hip as she strode along the alley. The child was getting heavy and she would gladly have put him down, but he couldn't walk as fast as she and she was determined not to be slowed down. She ignored the stares of those who passed her by; a small child was an uncommon sight at court. There were a few glimmers of recognition, but Douglass wasn't prepared to be waylaid by friendly greetings. She kept her eyes on the path before her and her feet moving fast. She was going to find Robert.

But she had no idea where Robert would be. The court was so large, it seemed ridiculous to try and find him, but Douglass suspected that where the Queen was, Robert would be too.

But then two ladies passed by and one said, 'That must be Lord Leicester's bastard' to the other and Douglass's courage left her. She hurried on, now hearing whispers all around her.

'Boy,' she stopped a young page. 'Where are the Earl of Leicester's rooms?'

The page directed her and she set her son on his feet and holding his hand, they walked slowly to Robert's apartments. She half-feared seeing a guard on the door, but there was none. She knocked and the door opened.

'Is your master here?' she asked of the servant who answered.

'No, my lady, he's at Council.'

'I'll wait,' she declared, stepping through the doorway. 'Perhaps you could take a note to him?'

Douglass's note told Robert she was waiting in his chambers to see him. She was prepared to wait however long it took, but Robert appeared within fifteen minutes.

'Douglass, what the devil are you doing here?' he erupted upon entering the room. Then he saw his son playing with his pack of cards on the floor by the bed and he picked up the little boy and held him close. 'Hello, Robbie,' he kissed the pink cheek. 'How does my little man?'

'He does well enough,' Douglass said. 'Which is more than can be said for his mother.'

'What's the matter?' Robert asked with a sigh.

'The matter is I haven't seen you for months.'

'I've been busy.'

'You're always busy.'

'I see you as often as I can, Douglass.' Little Robbie laid his head against his father's shoulder and closed his eyes. Robert pressed his cheek to the top of the little head, feeling his warmth. It was worth risking the Queen finding out just to have his son in his arms like this. He wouldn't admit it to Douglass, but she was right; it had been too long since he was with them.

'As I came here, a woman called our son Lord Leicester's bastard.'

'Douglass!'

'You see what people think? They *do* think I'm your whore, not your wife. Why, why can't you admit we're married, after all this time?'

'It's not the right time—'

'Oh, it's never the right time. It won't ever be the right time.' She fell onto a wooden bench and began to cry. Her tears had worked on Robert before but not this time.

'Stop crying,' he said sharply. 'That won't do any good.' He hitched himself up onto the bed. 'You should go home before anyone else sees you.'

'Home to Kenilworth, I suppose?'

'Leicester House. I'll come there tonight. You can stay for a week. But then you must go home, Douglass.'

'Why? Afraid I'll be in your way?' She turned to him, her tears drying.

Robert looked at her. 'What's got into you?'

'I'll tell you, shall I? Lettice Devereux.'

Robert started, jerking the slumbering boy awake, who began to cry. 'There, there,' he said soothingly. He looked back at Douglass. 'I don't know what you're talking about.'

'Don't pretend with me. I know she's your mistress. There's no point lying.'

'Very well,' he said, laying Robbie on the bed, 'so you know.'

'Is that all you can say? Don't you care that you're hurting me?'

'Of course I care,' he snarled. 'But I can't change what's done.'

'You can stop seeing her.' She saw the look on Robert's face. 'But you won't, will you? After all, you've killed her husband so you can see her more often.'

'What the devil are you saying? Killed Walter Devereux, I? Of course I didn't.'

'It's what's being said. Didn't you know?'

'I don't know where these rumours start but they're a pack of lies. He died of the flux. What good would it do me to have him killed?'

'So you can marry her. But, of course, you'd have to have me killed, too.'

Robert bit his tongue, not ready to disillusion her about their so-called marriage. 'Go to Leicester House, Douglass. I'll come there as soon as I can.'

He strode past her and left the room. Douglass curled up on the bed, curving herself around her now sleeping son and held him close. She'd lost Robert, she realised.

Perhaps, she thought, *I never really had him.*

CHAPTER 37

GREENWICH PALACE, APRIL 1578

'Oh, Christ's blood, is this nonsense to be resurrected?' Robert flung the letter he had been reading across the table to Francis Walsingham, the new Secretary of the Privy Council, whose thin lips curled up in distaste.

'It appears so, my lord.'

'I had thought it all dead and buried.'

'The Queen and Cecil believe it expedient to pursue the matter.'

'It amazes me that anyone can still believe the Queen will ever marry. This charade has been played out so many times before.' Robert sat down heavily and pointed at an empty chair. 'Is Cecil attending the Council today?'

'I fear not. He has sent word he is unwell again.'

'Hmmm. Ah Hatton, there you are.'

Christopher Hatton, the tall, elegant chancellor entered the Privy Chamber, munching on a crust of bread. 'Good morning, Leicester, Walsingham. What business today?'

'Have you heard about this?' Robert demanded, pointing at the offensive letter.

'About what?' Walsingham passed the paper to him. 'Oh, Alençon. Yes, unfortunately, the Queen has mentioned it to me.'

'No more than a mention?'

'No, not really. She wondered if he is really as ugly as everyone claims, that is all.'

'I wish *I* knew her thoughts on the subject,' Robert smacked the table irritably.

'She has not confided in you, then?'

Robert shook his head.

'Negotiations would be easier to carry out if we knew the Queen's mind,' Walsingham said. 'Does she wish to marry or no?'

'Walsingham, I tell you, this is a charade, like all the others,' Robert insisted.

'I hope it is, my lord,' Walsingham said sincerely. 'It would be a black day for England were a French Catholic sitting on the throne beside the Queen.'

Robert and Hatton exchanged a glance. Walsingham had been in Paris when the massacre that became known as St Bartholomew's Eve sent shockwaves of horror throughout Europe. French Catholics, whipped into a frenzy of religious hatred, pulled Protestant women and children from their homes and hacked them to death in the streets, while the corpses of the men were thrown into the Seine, their blood turning the river red. Walsingham had taken refuge, along with Philip Sidney, in the English embassy, but even from behind its walls he had still heard the screams. Any wonder then that he had no liking for Catholics, especially those that were French?

'This will be just for policy, Francis,' Robert said. Walsingham nodded a curt appreciation.

'Perhaps it would be better to ask the Queen,' Hatton suggested.

Robert laughed. 'You mean ask her outright if she means to marry the ugly dwarf?'

'Well, perhaps not couching it in such terms, but yes.'

'You may be right. Anyone know where she is?'

'I left her in the gardens,' Hatton said.

The other Council members trooped in as Robert left, and he gave them all a cursory greeting. The sunlight hurt his eyes as he entered the gardens. They were full of courtiers, the day too lovely to spend indoors. Several people plucked at his sleeve, requesting an audience with him at some convenient time. He told them all the same thing; that they should contact his secretary to arrange the meeting. It never annoyed him, these calls upon his person. Indeed, he feared the day when people did not ask him for help, to intercede for them. He cherished his closeness to the Queen. In Council, the other members looked to Robert to speak for them when they did not have the courage to persuade the Queen and sometimes feel the sharp edge of her tongue on their behalf.

He turned corner after corner before he came upon Elizabeth. She sat upon a wooden stool, three of her ladies upon the ground, each with a book in their hand.

'Your Majesty,' Robert bowed.

Elizabeth looked up and frowned. 'Yes, Robin?'

'The Duke of Alençon.'

'What of him?' she muttered, keeping her eyes upon her book.

'You are considering marriage with the Duke?'

'I am.'

'Seriously?'

Elizabeth looked up at him slyly. 'Maybe.'

'There is no need for such a marriage, Your Majesty.'

'No? Cecil seems to think so.'

'Cecil is wrong.'

'And I agree with him.'

'For God's sake, why?'

Elizabeth closed her book and looked up at him. 'You have been saying for months England should get involved in the Netherlands and protect those poor people from the Spaniards. My marriage with a prince of France would do that.'

'I proposed sending men and money to the Netherlands. I never countenanced you sacrificing yourself.'

'All I sacrifice is my virginity, and that is mine to do with as I please.'

'To which there are dangerous consequences, madam,' Robert said carefully. All three of the women at his feet glanced nervously up at him.

Elizabeth bit her lip angrily. 'Enough of this, Robin. This is for discussion in the Council chamber.'

'There was a time when I had your ear, madam.'

'And there was a time when I had your love,' she retorted, standing suddenly, her book falling to the ground.

'Your Majesty?'

'I said enough and I meant it, Robin. Now leave me.'

'Not until you explain,' Robert insisted.

'How dare you!' Elizabeth sneered. 'Must the Queen answer to her horse master? You will learn your place, my lord.'

'Have I not learnt my place well enough, madam?' Robert burst out angrily. 'Have I not been the recipient of your scorn more times than I can remember, endured your displeasure without complaint, denied myself—'

'Denied yourself?' Elizabeth repeated incredulously. 'I have never known you to deny yourself. Where do you think *you* are going?' she demanded of her ladies, who had tried to slip unobtrusively away. They about-turned abruptly and resumed their places. 'Denial would mean no fornication with Douglass Sheffield. Or my own damn cousin, Lettice.'

Robert was stunned. She knew about Douglass and Lettice! 'Madam,' he began to protest.

'Make no excuses.' She waved him silent. 'I know what men are.'

'Why then condemn me for it?'

'Because you try to stop any chance of happiness that may come my way while you enjoy yourself shamelessly.'

'You told me once, madam, that you would have no master. Has that changed?'

She raised her eyebrow contemptuously. 'I said that to *you*. I may not say it to a prince.'

'I am nothing to you, then?'

She hesitated, a mere moment. 'You are nothing to me. As I am to you.'

LEICESTER HOUSE

Robert went home, unable to remain at court after the quarrel. He went straight through to his private parlour and was surprised, and extremely pleased, to see Lettice there, sitting before the fire with a glass of wine in one hand and a plate of sweetmeats in the other.

'Lettice, why didn't you tell me you were coming here today? I only came home by chance.'

'Well, I would have sent for you,' she said, tugging at his arm to sit down next to her.

'Why? Is something wrong?'

'Not wrong exactly,' she shook her head, 'it's just that I have something to tell you. I'm pregnant again, Rob.' She laughed as Robert embraced and kissed her. 'You're pleased, then?'

'Of course I'm pleased. It's wonderful news.'

'Is it?' she frowned. 'I wonder. After last time. I lost that baby. Who is to say this time will be different?'

'It'll be fine this time.'

'You say that, but we are still in the same position we were before. I still have the same worry.'

'What worry?'

'That I may end up in the Tower. Or worse.'

'You won't.'

'If the Queen finds out…'

'There is no need to worry anymore, my love. Elizabeth already knows about us.'

Lettice stared at him. 'She knows? How do you know she knows?'

'*She* told me.'

'Oh my God, Robert,' she cried, grasping his hand.

'And she doesn't care.'

'Doesn't care? She *does* care, if I know my cousin.'

'Well, you're not in the Tower, are you? Nor am I, so she can't, can she?'

Lettice looked down at her hands, two fingers playing with her rings. 'Would she care if we were husband and wife?'

Robert rubbed his forehead thoughtfully. 'When is the child due?'

'October.'

'Let me think about it.'

'We haven't time,' Lettice protested.

'We have. A few months at least.'

'Oh, Robert,' Lettice pushed him away and moved to the fireplace. 'What are you still hoping for?'

'I… I don't know,' he admitted.

'Or is it Douglass? Do you want to pretend to be married to her still?'

'Douglass hasn't anything to do with us.'

'So, deny your marriage to her, Robert, and marry me. Answer me this. Do you ever believe the Queen will marry you? Yes or No.'

Robert was silent for a long moment. 'No,' he admitted finally.

'Then why should you not marry when and whom you please? I am to have your child. I shall pray for a boy and you shall have your heir.'

'I already have a son, Lettice.'

'Douglass's bastard.' Lettice said sharply. 'That's hardly the same thing.'

Robert looked at her. He loved her, he wanted to be married, and he wanted a son, *her* son. 'Very well, Lettice. We'll get married.'

'When?' she asked breathlessly.

'Soon.'

'And married with witnesses, Rob. I do not want you disavowing our marriage when you grow tired of me.'

'Oh, Lettice,' he said, drawing her into his arms, 'as if I could ever grow tired of you.'

Robert waited in the gardens. He paced up and down, ignoring the stone bench which would have given him some bodily ease. He had been easy and cool with Lettice, talking of ridding himself of Douglass, but now it came to it, he felt uneasy. *No, not uneasy*, he scolded himself, *ungallant, unkind, cruel*. He turned at the crunch of gravel.

Douglass was walking towards him, her arms outstretched.

He brushed her aside. 'Don't, Douglass. That's not why I'm here. Won't you sit down?'

'What's wrong?' she asked, and he heard the fear in her voice.

He turned aside. 'Lettice is pregnant,' he said, and heard her gasp. 'And she wants me to marry her.'

Douglass grabbed his shoulder and spun him around. 'I spit on your whore, do you hear me? I spit on her.'

'Douglass -'

'Let her have her bastard, give it your name if you want, but she won't have *you*. You belong to me.'

'I don't, Douglass,' he said angrily. 'We were never married, not properly. I am free to marry whom I please, and it pleases me to marry Lettice.'

Douglass stared at him, her mouth open. 'You're lying,' she breathed. 'Of course we're married. We went through a ceremony.'

'Not a legal one. I did it because you insisted on being married. You left me no option, Douglass, I had to act as I did.'

'You deceived me!'

'I did, and it was wrong of me.'

Her tears began to fall. 'Then you never loved me. It was all a lie.'

'Not all of it,' he sighed.

'But we have a son, Robert.'

'And he will be provided for.'

'He's a bastard,' she cried, sinking onto the bench. 'All these years, he's been a bastard and I never knew it. How can you do this to your own son?'

Oh, how her words hurt! His chest tightened and tears pricked at the back of his eyes, but he willed himself to be resolute. 'I shall give you seven hundred pounds a year, Douglass, for your welfare and our son's. It should be enough. I will even help you to find a husband, if you wish it. I couldn't bear the thought of you being lonely. Would you like me to do that, Douglass?'

Douglass rose from the bench and stared at him, her cheeks blotchy and her eyes puffy and red. 'I don't want you doing anything for me. I want you to rot, Robert Dudley. You and your whore.'

CHAPTER 38

WANSTEAD HOUSE, SEPTEMBER 1578

Robert decided to marry Lettice at his new house in Wanstead, close enough to London to get there and back to the court within a few hours, yet distant enough to be away from prying eyes. He took his friend, Lord North, with him to act as a witness. Lettice had insisted on witnesses. When he and North arrived at Wanstead House, they found the rest of the wedding party already there.

'Robert,' Lettice hallooed from her chair beside the hearth. She gestured at the man sitting opposite her. 'Father was worried you weren't going to come.'

Sir Francis Knollys frowned at his daughter. 'Not at all. Leicester, good morning.'

'Sir Francis,' Robert nodded, taking his hand. 'You know, seeing as we are about to be related, you should call me Robert.'

Knollys snorted, whether in agreement or not, Robert could not tell and decided not to pursue it. 'My love.' He moved towards Lettice, taking her hand in his and laying his lips to her fingers. 'How are you?'

'Fat and hungry,' Lettice smiled up at him. 'Lord North, how pleasant to see you again.'

North bowed, his eyes noting the swell of Lettice's stomach beneath her loose red gown. 'It's a very great pleasure to be invited, my lady.' He turned to greet Ambrose. 'A secret wedding. This is the most excitement I've had all year.'

Ambrose and Robert laughed, Sir Francis frowned. Lettice asked when dinner would be served and they all drank a toast to the wedding that would take place later that day.

'Husband,' Lettice smiled and held out her arms to him. He stretched full length on the bed and wrapped his arms around her, pressing his lips to hers. The deed was done and there was no going back. He was well and truly, lawfully, married. He pulled away from her.

'Rob, what's the matter?'

'Nothing.' He kicked off his shoes and untied his doublet and shirt. Lettice watched him with pleasure. A nightshirt hung over the back of a chair next to the bed and he began pulling it over his head.

'Robert, why ever are you putting that on?'

'It is best that we don't make love,' he explained. 'I don't want to endanger the child.'

'But it's our wedding night. Walter never let my being with child stop him, and it did no harm.'

'Nevertheless, Lettice. Not tonight. I have very weary brains for lovemaking.'

He climbed into the bed. She leaned into him, her slender fingers poking through an opening in his nightshirt and pulled gently at the greying hairs on his chest. 'It's not your brains I require, husband. You're not paying any attention, are you? Are you thinking of her?'

Robert did not need to ask who she meant; 'her' was always Elizabeth.

'Yes, Lettice, and before you shout at me, I must think of her. Everyone who knows of us keeps asking me the same thing: does she know? And they are all worried what will happen if she finds out. I must tell her of our marriage before someone else does.'

'That dried up old hag,' Lettice growled, pulling the bedcovers over her breasts. 'I trust this is not the effect she will always have upon you, making you unwilling in bed.' And with that, she turned on her side, yanking the covers over her shoulder and ending the conversation.

At length, her even breathing told Robert that she slept, and he felt guilty enough to curl up behind her, laying his arm over her waist, and clasping her hand in his, his chin on her shoulder. He felt supremely content, more so than he could ever remember feeling in his life before. He had a wife he loved who was already carrying his child and his influence and power at court stretched far and deep. But at the back of his mind, there was the knowledge that he owed almost all of that he prized most dear to Elizabeth, and he could lose it all so very easily.

WHITEHALL PALACE

'Ah, Leicester, you're returned,' Cecil said as he was helped into his chair by his page.

'How's the gout?' Robert asked, noting the bandage on Cecil's foot.

'Better than it was, which is all I can hope for.'

'Leicester,' Hatton halloed him cheerfully as he entered the chamber and clapped him on the shoulder. 'It's good to see you back. And you have some news, I hear.'

'Oh, God's Death,' Robert slapped his gloves upon the table, 'how do you know about it?'

'Leicester,' Hatton laughed, 'the whole court knows about it.'

'The Queen, too?'

'Everyone except the Queen. There isn't anyone brave enough to tell her.'

'Tell her what?' Cecil demanded.

'You don't know?' Hatton looked at him in surprise.

'I have been ill in my bed, Hatton,' Cecil said irritably. 'I have had very little news from the court and no gossip.'

'Don't you fret, Cecil, I have no doubt you shall find out soon enough,' Robert assured him grimly.

Cecil, annoyed, began slapping his documents about him on the table. 'Is Walsingham attending today?' he muttered.

'I saw him earlier. He said he would join us as soon as he is able,' Robert said. 'Now, tell me, has anything been decided about this damned Alençon affair?'

'Yes, you've missed quite a lot,' Hatton said. 'The little frog is sending his chief darling as he calls him, to woo on his behalf. A fellow named Simier.'

'And what do we know of him?'

'Only that he's a rogue. Murdered his brother when he caught him in bed with his wife.'

'Indeed? And what did he do to his wife?'

'No one seems to know.'

'Well, we can only hope his bad character will disgust the Queen,' Robert said.

Cecil looked up from his paperwork. 'You are still opposed to this marriage, Leicester?'

'I am, Cecil, and will remain so. Such a marriage is not fit for the country, nor the Queen.'

'The Queen does not agree.'

'Only because she listens to your advice. I wish I could persuade you of the danger such a marriage would mean.'

'But the negotiations are just for policy, aren't they, Cecil?' Hatton asked. 'The Queen does not really mean to marry this Frenchman, does she?'

'That, Hatton, only the Queen knows. But until she informs us otherwise, we must proceed with the negotiations as if the marriage was a decided affair.'

'When is this Simier arriving?' Robert asked.

'At the end of the week, if the Channel permits,' Hatton said.

Robert sighed and shook his head. 'Well then. We can do nothing until he arrives and declares their terms. So, what other business for us today?'

CHAPTER 39

LEICESTER HOUSE

'Rob, what's the matter?' Lettice asked him as they lay in bed.

'I've been thinking. Hatton told me that the whole court knows about our marriage. Elizabeth is bound to find out sooner or later and I think it would be better if it came from me.'

'Are you sure?' Lettice asked, propping herself on her elbow and staring down at him.

'You said it yourself, I am allowed to marry. And the Duke of Alençon's envoy arrives tomorrow and I want to get this out of the way before all this French marriage nonsense starts. Leave for Wanstead in the morning, Lettice. I will get Elizabeth to come here, away from the court.'

'Well, if you're sure,' Lettice said, settling back down. 'I just hope I will have a husband to come back to.'

Robert stared out of the window and looked down onto the river. It had been over two hours since he had sent the note to Elizabeth asking her to come to him. Surely Elizabeth would not ignore him? Surely, she would come?

His breath fogged a patch of window glass. He wiped it away with his sleeve and as the pane cleared, Elizabeth's barge came into view. One of his servants was waiting at the barge steps, his arm outstretched to help her from the barge, but Elizabeth hurried past, gathering up her skirts above her knees. She half-walked, half-ran up the path to the house.

Robert waited.

The door swung open, banging against the wall behind.

'Why aren't you in bed?' Elizabeth demanded. 'Are you ill?'

Robert stepped around her and closed the door. 'No, Bess, I'm not. I just needed to get you here quickly.'

'Then you've worried me for nothing.'

'Forgive me. It was the best stratagem I could devise.'

'And it has worked well in the past,' she frowned, taking a seat by the fire.

'For us both, Bess.'

'Well, what is it you want to say to me? If it is more about the Duke of Alençon, save it for the Council chamber.'

'No, Bess. It is not of your marriage I wish to speak of, but mine own.'

Elizabeth stared at him. 'Yours? You wish to marry?'

'I have married,' he said quietly.

'If this is some joke, Robin…'

'No joke, Bess. I have married Lettice.'

She turned her head towards him, her expression almost incredulous. 'You married that whore?'

'Elizabeth, please, do not speak of her like that.'

'That whore?' she repeated. 'For God's sake, why?'

'She is carrying my child.'

'A child,' Elizabeth whispered.

'Yes. I have always wanted children and this, well, this could be my last chance for an heir.'

'You already have a son with Douglass Sheffield.'

'I wasn't married to Douglass.'

'There was a ceremony.'

'But it wasn't valid. I paid a man to marry us but he wasn't a clergyman. You see, I wasn't sure I wanted to be married then. I was still hoping for you,' he smiled wanly, reaching for her hand, but she pulled it away.

'Why did you have to marry Lettice?' she wailed.

'God's Death, Bess, shall I tell you why? You told me there was no chance of our ever marrying and I believed you. Neither Ambrose nor I had a legitimate heir to carry on our Dudley name, and I am not about to let everything we have worked for and spilt our family's blood for vanish into the dust when we are gone. I want a son, and I married Lettice because I love her. And you know why? Because she is so like you. Except that she allowed me into her bed and you did not.'

'Is that it? Is that your reason? Is it me you think of when you two are rutting?'

'I told you once, I could not live like a monk. And why exactly are you angry? Because I am married, or because I am married to Lettice?'

'I don't know why I'm angry,' she cried, burying her face in her hands. 'I understand, Rob, I do, about you wanting a son. It's just that, that... I thought you loved *me*.'

'I do. I always have. That hasn't changed. But a man can only take so many refusals.'

'Robin, if we had bedded, would you have married her then?'

'I... I don't know, Bess. Why?'

'We will bed, if you disavow her,' Elizabeth said, looking up at him desperately. 'You can come into my bed as often as you like, if you do, and promise never to see her again.'

Robert was stunned. After all these years, after all those refusals, she was now submitting to him? For a moment, the thought of taking her to bed, of having her in his arms and burying himself in her, shut out all thought of wives and heirs. But the moment passed. He shook his head.

'I can't disavow her, Bess. The marriage was legal and we had many witnesses.'

She covered her mouth with her hand, stifling a sob. She felt her stomach lurch, sick and yet strangely relieved he had refused. 'I am alone,' she whimpered.

He knelt before her. 'No, you're not. I'm still here. I still love you.'

'How can you? When you say you love her?'

'I can't explain it, but I know I do love you still. And I hope you can forgive me.'

She looked at him, his handsome face so earnest. How she had dreamt of that face, dreamt about kissing it. How she had admired his body, felt her own heat just thinking of him. Now, she would not be able to do that, because in her thoughts he would be with Lettice, not her.

'I don't know,' she said. 'I can't believe you can love two women at the same time. At the moment, Rob, I hate you.'

'No, Bess, please...'

'I hate you,' she repeated, trying to make herself believe it. 'I hate you. I want to hate you.' She grabbed his head and kissed him fiercely. She pushed him back onto the floor and climbed on top of him. Her sharp teeth dug into his lips and he tasted blood. He pushed her away.

With a wrenching cry, Elizabeth stumbled to the window, pressing her burning forehead against the glass.

Robert lay where she had left him on the floor, catching his breath, his lips reddened with blood. He closed his eyes and waited.

Her head, her eyes, her throat, all were strained and aching. She focused her eyes on the boats on the river and waited for her heart to stop pounding. She could not look behind her, could not bring herself to look back at him. What must he think of her? Desperate, pathetic? To want him even when he no longer wanted her. She flinched when he spoke.

'What will you do?'

'I don't know,' she answered meekly.

'Will you send me to the Tower?'

Running her hand across her face, she said, 'I don't know.' She rose unsteadily from the window seat.

'Stay.'

'No.' She glanced at him, saw his bruised and bloodied lips and looked away, cringing with shame. She strode to the door. 'You will not return to court. At least, not until I give you leave.'

She clambered onto the barge, knocking past the hands extended in aid, and fell into the cushioned seat. For a long moment, she stared into space, an image of Robert declaring love for another woman imprinted on her lenses. She called out to the boatmen to start rowing and yanked at the hangings to shut herself in. The future lay before her, barren and bleak. Robert would leave her, more and more often, and she would be alone. Then Alençon walked into her mind, the prospective bridegroom she had thought to play with, make use of and then discard when his usefulness was spent. In him was a chance to not be alone.

Oh God, she prayed silently, *make me love him. I will need him now and I want to be married. And I so want to not be afraid of love any longer.*

GREENWICH PALACE, FEBRUARY 1579

Elizabeth eyed Jean de Simier surreptitiously as the players enacted their scene. He was concentrating hard, the bawdy humour of the English stage a mystery to him. Hatton had told her of Simier's history, of his savage revenge and murder of his unfaithful wife and his brother, and found she did not care. Hatton had hoped such a history would dissuade her from receiving Simier. Poor Hatton. He never understood her.

Simier must have felt her eyes upon him for he turned his head and his bold, dark eyes glinted at her. She smiled, a tight, one-sided smile, not giving too much. He was, after all, the servant of a foreigner, not one of her own.

But she liked him. Typically French, dark, all of him dark, lips that were too plump, too red to be attractive on a man, but his intelligence showed in his face. Elizabeth liked clever men. She enjoyed the conversations she could have with them, especially when they were peppered with phrases of love.

And God's Death, but Simier knew how to make love with words!

They were alone, taking supper in her private apartments.

'The Earl of Leicester-' he began.

She didn't want to ruin the evening with thoughts of Robert. 'What of him?' she answered shortly.

'He has a reputation.'

'For what?'

Simier waggled his head. 'For his admiration of Your Majesty.'

'Admiration?' she snorted. 'Is that what it is called now?'

He pouted. 'Perhaps admiration is not quite the word I meant. Forgive me. English does not come easily to me.'

She patted his hand. 'You speak it very well. But I know what you have heard and I can tell you it is not true.'

'Then there is no love between you. I see it is just duty that binds the Earl to you and nothing more.'

Elizabeth bit her lip. 'It is I who have misunderstood you, Simier. I thought you meant malicious gossip about our relationship.'

'My master will be greatly relieved. He was not looking forward to the prospect of sharing you with another.'

'My Monkey,' she said, addressing him with the nickname she had bestowed upon him, 'your master will have to share me with my entire kingdom.'

'Subjects he will love, as you do yourself, but rivals...' He laughed and shook his head.

'But Robin...,' Elizabeth said hastily, 'the Earl of Leicester is no rival, no danger to your master. Tell him that. The Earl cannot have me.'

Simier nodded understandingly. 'I understand. And that being so, I trust you will not allow the Earl to influence you against my master, who is a goodly prince and one who loves you dear.'

'I am not so easily swayed. You have reason to believe the Earl will speak against your master?'

'Your Majesty, I confess to no great talent with your language, though you flatter me I speak well. But I do know people.'

'And you always suspect the worst of them?'

'I fear it is in my nature to do so,' he grimaced playfully. 'But I feel it to be no bad thing. That way, I am never disappointed.'

Elizabeth threw back her head and laughed, then remembered that he might see the gaps between her teeth and quickly covered her mouth with her hand. 'The Earl will be back at court within a few days,' she said sourly. 'But I tell you, I know my own mind, Simier.'

'I am glad to hear it, Your Majesty. It would grieve me to have to comfort a disappointed master. He is hard to bear when he is melancholy.'

'Is it a humour he is prone to?'

'No, Your Majesty, no. Do not mistake me. He is of a most pleasant turn, amiable. But he has thought of nothing but you these many months and it would take much to remove you from his mind. Ah, such beautiful hands,' he said, taking her long fingers and pressing her knuckles to his womanly lips. It was an impertinent gesture for a servant to make and he knew it. He saw her eyes narrow and knew she was wondering whether to rebuke him or not. 'Such hands should not belong to a mortal.'

'They do not, sir. I am God's deputy on this earth. I am above you.'

'But madam, we all have feet of clay. And I am thankful for it. If you were not mortal, a woman not of flesh and bone, we poor fools would be blinded by your divine magnificence. As it is, we can look upon your beauty and wish ourselves princes.'

APRIL 1579

Leicester,' Hatton waved. 'How was Buxton?'

Robert hesitated. 'Oh, pleasant enough. The Queen told you …?'

'She said you had gone there for your health. I trust the waters helped?'

There was no hint of duplicity in his question. Robert's greatest fear, that the Queen had forsook him and would waste no time in informing everyone, had not come true. She had told no one.

'A little. But I fear this pain in my stomach will be with me for the rest of my days, Hatton.'

'No remedy, then,' Hatton said sympathetically. 'Will you dine?'

Robert nodded and gestured for Hatton to lead the way. As they walked through the corridors of the palace courtiers pressed their backs to the wall to clear the way for the great Earl of Leicester, and a look of relief passed over Robert's face. Nothing had changed.

'Have you met him yet?' Hatton asked, as they entered his small chamber where food was already laid out on a table.

'Who?'

'Have you not been listening to me? Simier, the Duke's envoy.'

'Oh, no, not yet, I've only just arrived,' Robert said, sitting and wrenching the leg off a chicken. 'Walsingham wrote to me of him but didn't commit too much to paper. Tell me, what is he like?'

Hatton made a face. 'Exactly like I thought he would be. But the Queen, God's Wounds, Leicester, the Queen thinks the world of him. She pets him, gives him presents. She's even given him a nickname. Her Monkey, she calls him.'

'Monkey?'

'Simier, simian,' Hatton explained. 'She has him to dine almost every night in her private chamber. I wish you had been here to distract her.'

'I don't think my presence would have done so.'

'Why? Has something happened between you and the Queen?'

'Why do you ask that?'

'Well, you left hurriedly, without a word, and the Queen has hardly mentioned you.'

'I am returned!'

'Ah, yes, but you have not seen the Queen yet, and here you are, dining with me. Usually the Queen is the first person you see and you would dine with her. This doesn't speak of high favour to me, Leicester. You will forgive me if I am prying?'

'You're right, Hatton,' Robert admitted. 'I'm not in favour at the moment, though I trust I will not remain so.'

'That is a thousand pities. May I know why?'

'You may, if I can trust you to keep it to yourself.'

'You can trust me.'

'Well, you know I've married. The Queen now knows it, too.'

Hatton whistled. 'And I thought you would end up in the Tower when she found out.'

'I thought it possible myself.'

'What made you confess it?'

'She would have found out sometime. Better it came from me.'

'And so, you're in disgrace. What did she do when you told her?'

'Suffice to say she wasn't pleased,' Robert said dismissively. 'Now, I have told you enough, Hatton, and you will repeat it to no one.'

'None shall hear it from me,' Hatton promised solemnly. 'Has your wife returned with you? When do I get to meet the new Countess of Leicester?'

'You don't. At least, not at court. Walsingham sent word that my presence was required but that I was to come alone. Decoded that means Lettice is forbidden to ever join me.'

'That will be hard for her to bear, I should think.'

'Extremely. Lettice is not used to being forbidden anything.'

'But perhaps it will make these marriage negotiations easier,' Hatton mused. 'If personal feelings between yourself and the Queen are at an end—'

'We still care for one another, Hatton,' Robert said sternly. 'Don't think otherwise.'

'I stand corrected, Leicester. I merely meant you cannot be accused of selfishness in regard to this marriage.'

'No, my reasons against this marriage will be purely political.'

'On the other hand,' Hatton said, 'it could make things difficult for us.'

'How so?'

'Well, it might make the Queen... eager.'

'I don't understand you, Hatton.'

'You haven't seen how she is with this Simier. I truly think he is capable of making her forget herself.'

'With him? A mere servant?'

'He is greatly in her favour. He has fair put me in the shade.'

'No, I can't believe it, Hatton,' Robert said. 'You're wrong.'

'I hope I am, Leicester. But if she feels she has lost you, one whom she considered as her very own, well, I fear you may have made her desperate.'

'Desperate enough to make a bad marriage?'

Hatton shrugged. 'See for yourself. The Queen is probably with him now.'

'I think I will. Excuse me, Hatton.'

Elizabeth's laugh cut off abruptly as Robert entered. He studied her face, looking for a clue of how he should be with her, but she merely stared back at him.

He bowed. 'Your Majesty.'

'You're returned, Robin,' she said coldly.

'As you instructed, madam.' Robert glanced at her companion. 'Good evening, sir.'

Jean de Simier half rose and made a slight bow.

Impertinent fellow, Robert thought, *am I not due more respect than that?* He looked at Elizabeth, but she had a sly smile upon her face. *I see*, Robert thought, *that's how she's playing it.*

'I merely came to make the acquaintance of the Duke's envoy and to let you know I had returned, madam. But as you have no obvious need of my company, I shall leave you to–'

'You will stay,' Elizabeth said sharply. 'I will decide if I have need of you or not, Robin.'

Robert smiled, wallowing in the dismay exhibited on Simier's face. 'Of course, madam. Whatever you wish.'

Elizabeth kept him for an hour, but then he said he should really check on his horses and he left for the stables. Robert tickled the nose of his favourite mare and she nuzzled his hand affectionately. He had missed the stables, missed the smell of them, of straw, horse sweat and warm manure. He talked and joked with the stable hands, gave medical instructions when he noticed sores on Arundel's bay, and watched the progress of the newest addition.

'So, what do you think?'

Robert jumped. 'Damn it, Hatton. How long have you been there?'

Hatton leaned against the stable door. 'Just got here,' he said, turning his foot to look at the sole. He muttered something and scraped his boot against the ground.

'What do I think of what?' Robert asked.

'The Monkey.'

'Oh, him. I think,' Robert paused, searching for the correct demeaning word, 'he's a typical Frenchman.'

'Ah, judgement enough.'

'He's dining with me tomorrow.'

'And are you going to warn him off or welcome him in?'

'Neither. I want to see what he's all about, that's all.'

'Huh, I could tell you that,' Hatton said sourly. 'He's the perfect courtier. Says all the right things, makes all the right gestures, never puts a foot wrong.'

'We'll see.'

'Shall I dine with you, too?'

'No, I don't think so. I may get him to talk more if we're alone.'

'I would not place a wager on that. Anyway, I can see you want to be alone. I shall leave you to your horses.'

'That was a fine dinner, my lord,' Simier said, dabbing a napkin against his mouth. 'You dine as well as the Queen.'

'Better,' Robert said, signalling to a servant to refill the wine cups. 'The Queen never has much of an appetite, and we have to finish when she does, so often we at court go hungry.'

'Well then, moderation does indeed have some virtue. The Queen is most slender.'

'She is virtuous in many ways.'

'Really?' Simier smirked.

'What do you mean by that, sir?' Robert asked, his face darkening.

'I have known virtuous women, my lord, and I have known whores. The Queen falls somewhere in between.'

'How dare you!' Robert was astonished at Simier's language. 'I shall tell the Queen of how you abuse her.'

'And I will tell her you lie, my lord. I am not one for pretences,' Simier said, picking through the debris on his plate. 'I know it is you who is most vocal against my master marrying the Queen. It is you who persuades your members in Parliament to protest against a French Catholic marrying the Queen. Why should I pretend with you?'

'I won't deny that I don't want this marriage and I have done all I can to prevent it and will continue to do so, Simier.'

'I expect nothing less from the Earl of Leicester.'

'As I am Earl of Leicester, how is it you dare to speak so of the Queen, to speak so disrespectfully of her?'

'I speak in the knowledge that you are not what you once were,' he shrugged. 'In truth, I so wanted to meet with the great Earl of Leicester, the Queen's notorious bedfellow. And what do I find? That you no more have access to the Queen's bed than I do. Perhaps even less.'

Robert was bursting with rage but he was determined not to let Simier see.

'There is something I would like from you,' Simier continued. 'Your support for this marriage.'

Robert barked an incredulous laugh. 'After all you've said? You believe I have no influence with the Queen.'

'Ah, but you still have influence in the country. And I admit, there may be some remnant of affection for you in the Queen's heart.'

'Why should I change my policy for you? What do I get?'

'The Queen does not find out about your marriage with Lettice Devereux.'

Robert drew his napkin to his face, hiding a smile behind the cloth. So that was why the Monkey was being so indiscreet with his words. He thought he had the upper hand.

'I see,' he said, pretending to consider. 'You must let me think on it, Simier.'

'Of course, my lord,' Simier said, popping a grape into his mouth. 'Now, I thank you for my dinner, but I promised the Queen I would attend her this evening. Bon nuit.'

MAY 1579

'Leicester, if this is your doing...' A purple-faced Sussex thrust himself at Robert as he entered the Council chamber, his spittle spraying Robert's doublet.

'Is what my doing?'

'Simier was shot at on the Queen's barge.'

'My lord Sussex,' Hatton interposed, 'there is no proof that Simier was a target.'

Sussex ignored him. 'The man responsible is one of your people, Leicester.'

'And you think I had something to do with it? Oh, this cannot be believed. Cecil,' Robert appealed, shoving Sussex out of his way, 'I know nothing of this.'

'Simier has himself accused you,' Cecil said.

'And the Queen?'

'The Queen does not seem overly concerned about the Monkey, Leicester,' Hatton said. 'Here, sit down.'

'No, I must speak with her.'

'She is with Simier as we speak, Leicester. I advise you to wait,' Cecil said. 'My lord Sussex, will you not take a seat?'

'Was anyone hurt?' Robert asked Hatton.

'A boatman was shot through the arm. The Queen behaved magnificently, Leicester. She tied a bandage for the man herself.'

'She is most brave,' Robert said, running his fingers through his hair distractedly. 'But why accuse me?'

'The man was wearing your livery,' Sussex spat.

'I'm not responsible for the actions of everyone in my service, Sussex.'

'Simier is no fool. He knows it is you who most often speaks against him. It would please you greatly to have him out of the way.'

'Yes, and I know I can rely on you to think the worst of me, Sussex. You are ready to believe I am the devil himself.'

'I know a rogue when I see one, Leicester.'

'And I a coward when *I* see one, Sussex. Meet me in the gardens and we shall settle this like men.'

They put their hands on their swords. Hatton and Walsingham stepped between them.

'What is all this?' Elizabeth stood in the open doorway, her hands on her hips, her face red with rage. 'Fighting in my Privy Council? Did I hear you challenge the Earl of Sussex to a duel, my lord Leicester? You know I have forbidden duelling and do not think you will not be punished for attempting one. Sussex, sit down before you hurt yourself, and you, sir,' she turned back to Robert, 'you explain yourself.'

'Your Majesty,' he began, 'I had nothing to with this attempt on the Duke's envoy, if indeed one has been made.'

'What reason had you to draw your sword on Sussex here?'

'He accused me.'

Elizabeth glared at Sussex. 'Is this true, my lord?'

'The man was wearing Leicester's livery,' he exclaimed.

'An accident, Sussex,' Elizabeth said coldly, 'as I have told Monsieur Simier, who accepts the explanation. If he can, then so can you.'

'But what of the man, madam?' Sussex blustered. 'What was he doing on the river with a loaded weapon near you? Can the Earl answer that?'

'Can you, Robin?'

'Of course I can't,' Robert replied angrily. 'I can't know the whereabouts of every man who wears my colours.'

'Sounds like a reasonable explanation to me, Sussex,' Elizabeth said.

'Madam, I cannot believe the French will let this lie,' he persisted. 'The man must be punished.'

'If I punish a man, who may very well be guiltless, how would my people react? They would be outraged, Sussex.'

'I understand your reluctance, madam. But what do you think the Duke of Alençon will think of such mercy?'

'Oh, let the Duke thinks what he likes,' Robert said. 'Who in God's name cares what a Frenchman thinks?'

'*I* care, Robin,' Elizabeth turned on him furiously. 'And keep a civil tongue in your head about the Duke. I have invited him here and I command you to be respectful.'

'If you wish it, madam, then I will be no other when he comes.' Robert bent his head in obedience.

'Then settle, you dogs,' Elizabeth sneered. 'Walsingham, keep these schoolboys under control or I shall dismiss you all.'

AUGUST 1579

The music had been playing for over four hours, and everyone, save the Queen and her partner, wished it would stop. Cecil's head sagged upon his chest, Hatton waved away offers of dance partners wearily, Walsingham read paperwork surreptitiously and Robert drank cup after cup of wine.

Robert belched loudly and wiped his mouth with the back of his hand. Pushing away from the table, he staggered over to the corner of the room where Walsingham sat with his secretary, William Davison, the two of them oblivious to the entertainment around them.

Walsingham looked up angrily as the table jolted against his leg. 'Take ca- , oh, Leicester. Davison, quick, get the Earl a chair.'

'Have mine, my lord,' Davison said, guiding Robert to his seat.

'What a farce this is,' Robert said, shaking his head.

'Are you well, my lord?' Walsingham asked carelessly, running his eye down a list of names Davison handed him.

'I am sick, Francis.'

'I am sorry to hear that, my lord.'

'Oh, for Christ's sake, leave that accursed paperwork and talk to me.'

With reluctance, Walsingham put down the document. 'What do you want to talk about, my lord?'

'Anything. That is if we can hear ourselves over this damned noise.'

'Indeed,' Walsingham nodded. 'The music has played overlong to my mind.'

'So has this scene.' Robert waved his arm at the dancers. 'This makes me sick.'

'The dance?'

'The dancers. Francis, do not play the fool with me. The Queen. When did she sign the Duke's passport so he could come here?'

Walsingham grimaced apologetically. 'When you were away, my lord.'

'Damn it, could you not have dissuaded her?'

'I made no attempt to, my lord. I know my limits in regard to Her Majesty.'

'Oh, look at them,' Robert scowled, as the Duke of Alençon leapt into the air. 'How ridiculous they look. He barely comes up to her shoulder.'

'Her Majesty seems pleased with him. See, they kiss.'

'How can she bear it? I thank God the people cannot see this.'

'But how long can his visit be kept a secret?' Walsingham wondered as Robert reached over and refilled his cup.

'When's he leaving?' Robert asked.

'He is here for about a fortnight.'

'Hell, we have to endure him that long?' Robert cried loudly. 'It will cost me a fortune.'

'The Queen will expect you to entertain him?'

'Do I not always entertain her guests, though it near ruin me?'

'You do, my lord,' Walsingham agreed, setting aright the jug Robert's elbow had just knocked over. 'Though you usually take pleasure in it.'

'Not this time. You are very quiet on the matter, Francis. What do you think of the Duke being here?'

'I think it a step towards disaster for England, my lord. I

would be grateful if you could allay my fears that the Queen means to marry.'

Robert sighed and shook his head. 'I can't. I hope she doesn't mean to marry, but I can't promise you she will not. Is there no more wine?'

'That was the last of it,' Walsingham said. 'We have a Council meeting early tomorrow, my lord. Perhaps it's as well the wine is gone.'

'Are you saying I am in my cups?'

'No, my lord. I am merely trying to spare you an unpleasant morning.'

'A broken head will only add to the unpleasantness,' Robert said. 'I understand you want me clear-headed, not brain sodden. Tell me, Francis, are you so used to people lying to you that you do not know how to speak clear yourself.'

'There is a distinction, my lord,' Walsingham said haughtily, 'between civility and dishonesty. I flatter myself I am exercising the former when we speak.'

'Oh, all right, all right. I am a little drunk, I confess. What is to be discussed at the Council meeting tomorrow?'

'The Queen desires our opinion on whether to wed or not.'

'She has had our opinions,' Robert cried exasperatedly. 'How many more times must she hear them before she will make up her own mind?'

'The indecision wearies me,' Walsingham agreed, his eyes looking longingly at his papers. 'Ah, at last the music stops.'

They looked towards the dancers, the Queen and her stunted partner. A few words were exchanged in French between them before the Duke took Elizabeth's hand and kissed her fingers, cradling her hand in his own as though it were a precious thing. A few more teasing words, a dozen meaningful glances and the evening's entertainment was at last at an end. The Queen rustled from the chamber, followed by her weary ladies. courtiers took their leave of each other gratefully and the crowd thinned.

'Well, now we can go to our beds,' Robert said, getting to his feet unsteadily. 'Our cold, lonely beds.'

'I sleep better alone,' Walsingham said.

'Do you? I prefer company.'

'It's a pity that the Queen will not relent and allow your wife to come to court.'

'It's a pity for me. Lettice complains continually. Perhaps when the child is born, she will not miss it so.'

'Her confinement must be near.'

'Next month. Well, till the morning, Francis.'

'Till the morning,' Walsingham said. 'Sleep well, my lord.'

SEPTEMBER 1579

Robert groaned as Sussex slammed his hand on the table. Could the man never make a quiet argument?

'The Queen desires the marriage-,' Sussex was saying.

'She has told you this?' Hatton asked in surprise.

'She has not actually said so. But her actions all point towards such a desire.'

'I do not think it wise to assume the Queen's desires, my lord,' Cecil said.

'Well, it is safe to assume our own, I suppose,' Sussex retorted. 'And I, for one, wish her to marry the Duke.'

'As do I,' Cecil nodded.

'I do not,' Hatton said fiercely.

'Nor I,' said Robert quietly, rubbing at his temple. 'Walsingham?'

Walsingham laid down his pen. 'I am against such a marriage.'

There was silence for a moment while the clerk's quill scratched and bowling balls clicked in the gardens outside.

'And if the Queen informs us that she wishes to marry?' Cecil asked.

'Then we will support her, of course,' Hatton said. 'But it is not just us. Parliament will have to decide and they will not give their approval. I know they will not.'

'That fortunately, is not our concern, Hatton,' Robert said with a smile. 'Let us tell the Queen that her Council is divided but we will support her in whatever decision she chooses to make.'

'And who is to deliver this report?' Cecil wondered. 'It's not what the Queen wants to hear and she will rail at whomever tells her so.'

'I shall tell her,' Walsingham said, getting to his feet. 'It's my duty as Secretary, and I am not likely to lose favour with Her Majesty for the news as some might.'

'She's in her chamber, Francis,' Robert said. 'We will wait here for you.'

Walsingham nodded and left.

'There goes a brave man,' Hatton said seriously. 'I would not wish myself in his shoes.'

'Nor I,' Robert agreed. 'I fear the Queen will not take this well.'

Robert's prediction was correct. Not ten minutes had passed before the Council door flew open and Elizabeth stormed into the room.

'Is that all you can say to me?' she demanded as they got to their feet. 'You will support me whatever I decide? That is not the advice I need to hear, gentlemen.'

'If you would just say whether or not you wished to marry, madam, then we could advise you,' Hatton said.

Elizabeth glared at him. 'How can I decide to marry if you will not advise me on it?'

'What Hatton means, madam,' Robert interjected, bored by her prevarication, 'is do you love the Duke and wish to be his wife? It's a simple question.'

'Do you dare to mock me?' she growled. 'You mock me, sir?'

'Indeed, madam, I do not.'

'Do I love him?' she cried incredulously. 'Love him? What does it matter if I do or not? I, sir, do not have the luxury of marrying whom I love. Policy governs *my* decision.'

'Then I shall counsel you on policy,' Robert said. 'It would not be good for England if you were to marry the Duke, madam.'

'In what way would it not be good, Leicester? Is an heir for England not a good thing? Is it not a good thing that the line of Tudor not die with me?'

'Then your reason for marrying would be the getting of an heir?'

'To have a child of mine own. Is it so unnatural?' she pleaded. 'You have wives, you have children, and yet you would deny me the comfort of family.'

Robert moved to her side and took her hand. She met his gaze with softened eyes. 'Madam, the time for that is past.'

Her eyes lost all their softness. She pushed him away. 'You rogue,' she rasped and rushed from the room, pushing past Walsingham who hovered in the doorway. Her sobs echoed along the corridor.

Walsingham stepped inside and closed the doors. 'I am glad it was you who said that,' he said wryly.

'Leicester, what possessed you?' Sussex asked. 'You as good as called her old.'

'What if I did? It's time some of us faced the truth. How old is the Duke? Seventeen, eighteen? And the Queen nearing six and forty. I tell you, Sussex, bed her with the Duke and we will lose her.'

'That is by no means certain.'

'It would be dangerous for her to bear a child now,' Robert persisted. 'Or does your ignorance prevent you from even realising that fact?'

'It seems to me that she wants to marry, despite her talk of policy,' Hatton said gloomily, falling into his chair.

'There is no other business today, gentlemen,' Walsingham announced, gathering up his papers.

'Do you really think she wants to marry?' Robert asked as he sat down next to Hatton, watching the others file out.

'I fear so, Leicester. I have heard from her ladies such things that... well, I shudder to believe them.'

'What have you heard?'

'That Simier had... Well, before the Duke arrived, the Queen permitted him great freedom with her person. And the Duke is visited by her in his bedchamber before he has risen. She stays and dallies with him. Alone.'

'I cannot believe it. She would not... No, I will not believe it.'

'I did tell you, Leicester, that your marriage may have made her desperate.'

'I should see her. Ask her to forgive me for what I said.'

'If she will see you,' Hatton said doubtfully, looking towards the door as there came a knock upon it.

'I must try. Come in,' Robert called.

A page entered. 'A message from the Queen, my lord. Her Majesty decrees that her counsellors are no longer required and will retire to their private homes.'

Robert and Hatton looked at one another in total surprise.

Lettice was in bed when Robert arrived at Leicester House. He told the servants they could retire and went up to her, opening the door quietly and peering round. Lettice lay back in the bed, the sheets stretched over her bulbous belly. He tiptoed in and began undressing.

'I'm awake, Rob,' she said.

'I didn't wake you, did I?'

'No, I was waiting for you.' She propped herself up on one elbow, her red hair falling over her shoulders. 'Well, what news?'

'No change.'

'You mean she still has not made up her mind?'

'No, and blames the Council for it.' He sat down on the end of the bed. 'Are you well? Your face is flushed.'

'No,' she said, pressing her fingertips to her forehead, 'I haven't felt well all day.'

'You should have sent word. I would have returned.'

'There was nothing you could do. I always feel like this when I am near my time. Don't fret so, Rob. Childbirth is something I am used to.'

He smiled and kissed her cheek. 'Well, you shall have me for company for the next few days, my love, whether you want me or not.'

'Why? Are you not needed at court?'

'Seems not. None of us are. Cecil, Walsingham, Hatton, myself, all of us are banished from the court because the Queen is annoyed with us.'

'Oh, she is being ridiculous. Get into bed and rub my back,' she ordered. 'How is she supposed to govern without you all?'

'She's frightened, Lettice.'

'Of what?'

'Of marriage. Of the wedding night, I think.'

'Someone should tell her to ignore the panic and enjoy the pleasure.'

'She's not like you, Lettice.'

'What do you mean by that?'

'The act of love is something to be feared for Elizabeth. Believe me, I know.'

Lettice turned to him, her interest aroused. 'And how do you know? Is our revered virgin queen no virgin?'

'Of the Queen's virginity, I can say only this. I, nor no man before me, ever took her maidenhead.'

'But you doubt her now? Why?'

'Hatton told me that Simier has been allowed certain liberties. Ones that I thought a mere servant, and a Frenchman at that, would never be allowed.'

'You don't mean to say…'

'But they are only rumours,' he insisted. 'And I prefer not to believe them. Elizabeth would not forget herself with such a man.'

'You hope?'

'I hope. But you're tired, Lettice. Put out the light.'

Someone was shaking him, but he didn't want to wake up. He was warm and happy, it was a bright, breezy summer day and he was playing. Winning, of course, until Guildford started crying and his mother said he was to let his brother win. Robert should have been cross, but he hadn't seen Gil for such a long time and Robert was happy to do anything to make him happy. A hand on his shoulder made him jump. He turned and there was his father, smiling at him. But then his father started talking. He looked as if he was shouting but Robert could barely hear him.

'Rob. Rob. ROBERT.'

He reluctantly pulled his eyelids apart. 'Wh… what?'

'The child,' Lettice panted, gripping his arm.

'It's coming?' Robert asked, suddenly wide awake.

Lettice groaned in answer. Within minutes, Robert had roused the household, lamps had been lit, doctor and midwife sent for and now all there was to do was wait.

Before the sun rose, Robert was holding his son.

CHAPTER 40

GREENWICH PALACE, OCTOBER 1579

Elizabeth and her counsellors waited in the Council chamber. Elizabeth spoke quietly and tiredly, patting Cecil's hand and shaking her head. He was ill again and in truth should have been in bed, but Elizabeth had summoned him and he was a dutiful servant.

The chamber door opened and Alençon rushed in, Simier and the French Ambassador, Fenelon, following more sedately behind. Alençon grabbed Elizabeth's hand which, to Robert's eye, she reluctantly offered and he pressed his thick misshapen lips to it.

'My lady,' he exclaimed in French, 'how cruel of you to keep me waiting for a glimpse of your face.'

Elizabeth smiled thinly and withdrew her hand. 'I would not willingly be cruel,' she answered in English, 'but my face is the better for seeing yours.'

Alençon began talking again in French. Elizabeth waved a reproving finger.

'My lord, English, if you please.' She indicated the Council members, though she knew they all understood the French language. Alençon looked contrite, bowed his head and took a seat alongside his countrymen.

'Let us to business,' Elizabeth said, looking pointedly at Walsingham, who seemed to be taking his time at starting the meeting.

Walsingham, who had been expecting the flattery and love play to go on a while longer, looked up in surprise and opened his mouth to speak.

'When are we to marry?' Alençon interrupted.

Elizabeth flicked a glance at him. 'Patience, my lord.'

'I am not a patient man.'

Elizabeth's lips tightened.

Robert saw his opportunity. 'My lord,' he said, leaning forward and placing his elbows on the table, steepling his fingers beneath his chin, 'there are further terms to be discussed before a date can be settled on.'

'I am not aware of further terms, Leicester,' Cecil said, frowning.

'No, I believe you were ill when it was discussed in Council,' Robert lied smoothly.

'When what was discussed?'

'A concession on the Duke's part.'

'A concession?' Alençon queried, looking between Robert and Simier. Simier's eyes narrowed as Robert continued.

'Indeed, for the many that England has already ceded.'

'Concessions have been made on both sides, my lord,' Fenelon pointed out in his best diplomatic voice.

'I agree, sir. But England has borne the brunt of the negotiations, and if you'll forgive me, we come off the worst for it. But let there be no lack of harmony between us. Our proposal is that since the late Queen Mary was so unfortunate as to lose Calais, we have had no port in France where we can trade and come and go in as we please. So, we propose that Calais be restored to English sovereignty.'

Robert sank back in his chair, enjoying the long moment of stunned silence as his words sunk in. Then the room seemed to explode with noise. The Duke rose to his feet, and began to exclaim in ridiculously fast French the outrage he felt at the Earl's words, while Fenelon appealed to Elizabeth to explain. Sussex harangued Robert for not having discussed this new tactic, while Simier sat, still and silent, his eyes locked in an understanding with Robert, whose own eyes dared him to act.

'Your Majesty,' Simier said in a low voice and, astonishingly, the room quietened. 'The Earl has made a most audacious proposal, and despite what he says, I do not think it a proposal discussed or agreed upon in Council. The Earl himself puts this forward to shatter any chance of making my master's happiness or your own.'

'That is a bold assertion, sir,' Robert declared. 'The Queen's happiness is more important to me than anything, second only to that of England, as the Queen would agree. If I thought she could find happiness in marriage to a prince of France, I would not oppose you.'

'So, you *do* oppose me?' Alençon demanded.

'I find you a most personable and charming man, my lord, a credit to France and an ornament to our court. But I would be no good Councillor if I did not advise the Queen what is best for her country as well as for her.'

'You deny that marriage would be good for Her Majesty?' Simier countered.

'Marriage between princes is a political contract. As I have said, the welfare of the country is the Queen's and my first concern.'

Simier slammed his hand on the table. 'You profess such concern for queen and country.'

'I am devoted to both, sir, and you will address me as 'my lord'.'

'Indeed, my lord,' Simier sneered. 'And how does your wife feel about being third in your consideration?'

'My wife is none of your concern.'

'But she may be of concern to Her Majesty, who has no knowledge of her, as you have seen it fit to keep her existence a secret.'

A silence fell upon the group. All eyes were upon Elizabeth. 'You will all leave,' she said finally. 'The Earl will remain.'

The company rose, the Duke reaching out to take her hand, but Elizabeth kept it resolutely by her side. Simier plucked at his sleeve and the Duke followed him out of the chamber.

'Bess,' Robert murmured.

'Must I be made a laughing stock, Robin?'

'You should have told them that you already knew about Lettice. Why didn't you?'

'And admit to them all that you didn't care for me?' She gave a hollow laugh. 'Well, they've known all along, I suppose.'

'You know that's not true,' he said, taking her hand. 'God strike me dead the day I stop loving you.'

She squeezed his hand. 'How can I face them?'

'You're the Queen, you can face anyone.' He reached up and smeared her tears across her cheeks. She nestled against his hand and smiled weakly.

'The pretence has turned sour now,' she said.

'What pretence?'

'I don't want to marry the Duke.'

'I'm so glad to hear you say that, Bess.'

'Even though you have the pleasure of being wed yourself?'

'I assure you, Bess, there are times when being a married man is anything but a pleasure.'

She stroked his face. 'You are a terrible liar, Rob.' She sniffed. 'They'll expect me to send you to the Tower.'

'Send me, then. If it will help you to face them.'

'I could never send you to that place, not again.' She smoothed her skirts and took a deep breath. 'You had best call Cecil in.'

Cecil entered, surprised to find Robert still in one piece.

'Oh, don't look so wary, Cecil,' Elizabeth said. 'I haven't murdered Leicester, nor do I intend to.'

'You see, Cecil,' Robert got to his feet, 'Simier thinks he has surprised the Queen. He has not. Her Majesty has known for some time that I am married.'

'Indeed,' Cecil raised an eyebrow. 'I was not aware.'

'I'm afraid I have an unpleasant job for you, Cecil,' Elizabeth said. 'You must tell the Duke there will be no marriage between us.'

'But—,' Cecil started.

She cut him off with a wave of her hand. 'I am resolute. There is to be no marriage. I have no doubt he will have to be bought off but I rely upon you to do it as cheaply as possible. Now, I dismiss you both. I am not to be disturbed for the rest of the day.'

The brush pulled gently at the Queen's thinning hair. She was melancholy tonight and unusually silent. No gay chatter, no laughter broke the quiet tension of the room. Her ladies looked at one another from beneath lowered lids and each trod carefully lest their footfalls rouse their mistress.

Someone knocked on the door. Elizabeth pointed to her wig with its tight red coils and jewels. With it fixed in place, she signalled for the door to be opened.

'Has he gone?' she asked as soon as Robert entered.

He nodded. 'I left the Duke of Alençon on a sandbank, madam.'

'Stranded?' she gasped. 'Oh, Rob, you didn't?'

'I did,' he assured her, taking a seat and helping himself to wine. 'And from what I hear, the Monkey is in high disgrace. One of my men overheard an almighty quarrel between him and the Duke.'

'Really?'

'Yes. My man doesn't understand French too well but he got the gist of it. Alençon seemed to think that Simier had let him down, that he shouldn't have said what he did and that he ruined everything.'

'Leave us,' Elizabeth waved away her ladies. They scurried from the room. 'The Duke was right. Were it not for Simier... I suppose I should be grateful to him.'

'A pox on gratitude. You owe him nothing.'

'I *am* glad they're gone. And do not flatter yourself it was done for you.'

'What?'

'That I ended it. I always said I never meant to marry. I was keeping my promise.'

'Hatton believed you wanted to marry the Duke,' Robert said.

'Oh, and you did not?'

'I knew better,' he shrugged.

'You presume to know me better, do you? Well, I tell you, little man, you know me not at all. What do you know of my heart?'

'Forgive me. I meant no... I merely meant—'

'Yes, merely. You would do well to remember your place, my lord.' She moved away to the fireplace, kicking at a log sticking out from the hearth with a slippered toe.

Robert searched his mind for something to say, wanting to ease the sudden tension between them.

'I have news, madam,' he ventured. Elizabeth turned her head slightly, still frowning. 'I have a son.'

'A boy,' she said dully. 'He is well?'

'Yes, bonny and lusty.'

'His name?'

'Robert.'

'You already have a son called Robert.'

'Yes, but this one is legitimate. The other was base born.'

'Oh,' she rolled her eyes, 'I remember your sister telling me about you.'

'What did Mary tell you?'

'Your obsession with the family name. How it must be continued.'

'I see nothing wrong with that,' Robert said defensively. 'My father thought the same.'

'As did mine,' Elizabeth agreed, 'but it is I who bear the scars for it. I wonder if he can see me now. Sovereign of such a country, with subjects a queen can be proud of. He would never have believed a woman could rule alone.'

'If ever a woman could, that woman would be the daughter of Henry the Eighth.'

'And of Anne Boleyn,' Elizabeth said quietly, looking down at her hands.

Robert's breath caught in his throat. Elizabeth had never before spoken of her mother to him.

'I killed my mother, you know,' she said. 'Had I been a son, she would have been safe. It's strange, but when I was a child, I thought my father was a god. He seemed one to me. People worshipped him, obeyed him and he had the power of life and death over them. And he exercised that power all too often.' She leant over to a side table and pulled a mirror towards her. She stared into it.

'No one ever told me when my mother died but I knew something was happening. All the servants, they all tiptoed around me, and everyone, everyone was whispering and casting furtive glances at me. My dear Kat, God bless her, told me as sweetly as she could. She said that my mother was in a better place but that I would not see her again, and I must not ask for her or say anything to anyone. I was but a child of three, but I understood she was dead. I asked Kat why my mother was gone.

As far as I knew, she had not been ill and I could not comprehend any other reason. I remember Kat hesitated. I suppose she was wondering what she could tell me. And then Kat told me my mother had offended the King and she had been punished. She would not tell me more. Only later, when Katherine Howard died, did she give me the full story, of what my mother had done. I believed her, believed that my mother *was* such a wanton, that she would fornicate with her own brother. If I didn't believe it, then my father was a murderer and my father couldn't be that. But the same thing happened to Katherine and I started to doubt.'

'After Katherine,' Robert said slowly, 'that was when you told me you would never marry.'

'Now you understand why I said it. I still cannot think ill of my father. Odd, isn't it? I know he had my mother murdered. And those crimes she was accused of would never have been brought against her if I had been the son my father craved. No one would dare to attack the mother of the heir to the throne. But the only child she had was a girl and I couldn't protect her.'

'You blame yourself? But Bess, it wasn't your fault. How could it be?' He reached out and squeezed her shoulder.

'You may not touch me,' she said, shrugging off his hand. 'I am pleased you have a son.'

'I could bring him to you, if you wish,' he offered.

'In time. Perhaps. When he is older.'

'My wife could bring him any time.'

Elizabeth's eyes narrowed. 'Robert, this is the last time I will tell you. As far as I am concerned, your wife does not exist.'

JULY 1584

Robert opened one bleary eye. 'What is it?' he mumbled into the pillow.

The head poking through the bed hangings smiled roguishly. 'The Queen wants to ride, my lord,' Johnson, his manservant, said. 'You had best rise.'

'Now?' Robert said incredulously.

'I am afraid so, my lord.'

Robert threw the bedclothes off and sat up. 'Get me my slippers. And take that grin off your face, you knave. How the devil does she do it?'

'Do what, my lord?'

'Stay up most of the night and still get up with the lark. Oh, who is that?'

Johnson opened the door. 'Sir Christopher,' he announced, holding the door open wider for the chancellor to enter.

'Leicester,' Hatton said loudly, 'are you still not dressed?'

'Should I be at this ungodly early hour?' Robert grumbled, moving behind the screen that enclosed his close-stool and emptying his bladder. 'What do you want, Hatton?'

'The Queen sent me to hurry you along. It's a good job I came.'

Robert grunted, shrugging off his nightshirt and grimacing at the sight of his rotund belly. 'Quick, give me my clothes.' He was almost dressed when there came another knock at the door.

'If that is someone else sent to hurry me...'

'Who are you?' Johnson demanded of the tall, ginger-haired lad standing in the doorway.

'Tom.'

'Tom who?'

But Robert recognised the voice. 'Tom, what are you doing here? Is something wrong?'

'The Countess sent me to fetch you, my lord. She begs you to return to her with all haste. Your son...'

Robert grabbed Tom's shoulders and swung him round to face him. 'Not dead?'

Tom blinked and swallowed uneasily. 'Not when I left. But he was very sick then, my lord.'

Johnson touched Robert gently on the arm and he flinched as if he had been struck. 'My lord,' Johnson said quietly, 'shall I pack?'

'No,' Robert's voice came out cracked. 'No time. We must leave at once.'

'Just your boots then, my lord,' Johnson said, leading him by the elbow towards a chair. Robert obeyed meekly, feeble hands, his own, tugging at the boots to pull them on. Johnson threw a riding cloak over his shoulder and tied it deftly under Robert's left armpit.

'Hatton,' Robert said, looking up at him blankly, 'will you tell the Queen—'

'Yes, yes,' Hatton waved him silent, 'don't worry, I shall tell her. You get to your son, my friend. I pray to God that all will be well.'

WANSTEAD HOUSE

Robert rode like the devil, Johnson and Tom struggling to keep up. When they reached Wanstead and the house was in sight, Robert closed his eyes. *Please God*, he prayed, *please do not let my son die.*

Robert flung open the front door and charged into the hall. 'Where is your mistress?' he demanded of a huddle of girls at the bottom of the stairs.

'In the nursery, my lord,' one answered timidly, pointing upstairs. They scurried out of his way as he sped past them. He paused on the top stair to catch his breath; he had caught sight of the nursery door, a weak light melting through the gap at the bottom. He continued on, his hand shaking as he reached for the handle.

Lettice sat beside the small bed that contained their son, the faint glow of the candles throwing into perfect relief the bear and ragged staff emblem carved on the wooden frame. She turned as Robert entered, her face oddly crumpled. Her hand flew to her mouth as their eyes met, muffling fresh sobs. She looked back to the bed, not wanting to waste a moment when she could be looking at her son. Robert's throat tightened as he approached his wife and child. Clutching at Lettice's shoulder for support, he felt her hand, cold and bony, grasp at his fingers.

The Noble Imp, their nickname for their little boy, so lovingly bestowed when he had run into their bedroom not three months before wearing the tiny suit of armour Robert had had made for him as a surprise, lay pale and unmoving, save for the slight rise and fall of his chest beneath the covers. His breathing was too shallow and his mouth, so sweetly cherubic, lay open, his lips pale and cracked. Someone, one of the doctors perhaps, stepped from the shadowy corners of the room and provided Robert with a chair. He sat down next to Lettice, held her hand, and with the other, took hold of his son's. He bent and kissed the small fingers.

Robert prayed every prayer he knew, promised anything. Lettice prayed beside him, all the servants in the house prayed, Hatton and Walsingham prayed, everyone at court friendly to Robert prayed.

But God was not listening.

At least, he wasn't listening to them. A jealous woman who had been told of the news thought a wicked thought. It was brief and she regretted it at once, but it had existed and it could not now be undone. If the boy died, she had thought, Robert would have no reason to stay with Lettice. As her father had once said, when a monarch prayed, God listened.

'Rob?' Mary stepped into the room. She saw her brother sitting by the fire, one hand against the side of his head, his dog, Boy, lying on the rug, his chin upon Robert's feet. She laid her hand upon his arm. Robert looked up, startled.

'Mary,' he said croakily and made to rise.

She stayed him with her hand and moved to the place vacated by Boy, who was pushing his wet nose into her hand. She knelt down and grasped Robert's hands, looking up earnestly into his face.

'You're not wearing your veil,' he smiled weakly, stroking her lumpy cheek.

'How are you?'

'I'm not sure, to be honest.'

'How's Lettice?'

'She cried herself to sleep.'

'Shouldn't you—'

'I'm not tired. I'm…,' he shrugged, 'I'm not anything.'

'I can't imagine how you must be feeling,' Mary rested her head against his hands and stared at the flickering flames. It was July and warm. 'Are you cold, Rob?' She looked back up at him. 'Oh, Rob.' Tears were streaming down his cheeks. She pulled him down to her, putting her arms about him, resting his head against her breast.

'Mary, I am cursed.'

'Cursed? What do you mean?'

'Everything I love dies.'

'Oh, Rob, that's ridiculous. You have Lettice. You have me and Ambrose. Now, sit back up in your chair.'

'Oh, my head hurts.' He smiled meekly. 'So, tell me, what do I do now?'

'Go back to work?' she suggested.

'What there is of it.'

'What do you mean?'

'Mary, I'm not what I once was. My influence is on the wane, the Queen doesn't care for me as she used to, my work abroad is being undone by my colleagues on the Council, and now, all hope of the Dudley name living on for centuries is gone.'

'You may have more children.'

He shook his head. 'Lettice is past bearing now. There won't be any more children. Ironic, isn't it? I have a healthy son, whom I have made a bastard, and Lettice had four healthy children by Walter Devereux to carry on his name. And yet, together, we couldn't make even one strong enough to carry on mine.'

'You will go back to court?'

'There is nothing there for me.'

'Robert,' Mary said sharply, 'you will be missed.'

'By whom exactly?'

'The Queen will miss you. Despite what you say. She wrote to me.'

'She sent a very sympathetic message. To *me*. Not to Lettice.'

Mary shook her head in disgust. 'She should have sent something to your wife.'

'No, not her. Even a mother's grief wouldn't soften that hard heart.'

'You sound so bitter against her.'

'I am. I have had to endure her scorn and public humiliation time without number. I tell you, if I don't go back to court, I shall not miss that.'

'But what else would you do? You tried your hand once at being a country gentleman and that nearly drove you mad.'

'I was younger then. And lustier. I did not have this belly when I was twenty.'

She rubbed at his stomach. 'Does it still pain you?'

'Now and again. It's nothing I can't endure. If I can endure losing my son….' He began to cry again.

Mary pulled a chair alongside her brother and once more laid his head against her breast.

WHITEHALL PALACE, AUGUST 1584

'Has Leicester returned yet?' Hatton asked, stopping Walsingham in the corridor.

'He's arriving this afternoon. I've just had a letter from him.'

'How does he sound?'

'Melancholy,' Walsingham said succinctly. 'And who can blame him?'

'Indeed.'

'And I curse the papists who put this together,' Walsingham held up a green book. 'A libel,' he explained. 'Against Leicester. A vile and malicious slander. Coming on the heels of the death of his son, I dread having to show it to him.'

'Must you, then?'

Walsingham sighed. 'I fear I must. It should be repudiated publicly. It will, no doubt, have a wide distribution by Catholic agents.'

'Can I read it?' Hatton asked eagerly.

Walsingham stiffened. He often found Sir Christopher Hatton's appetite for gossip distasteful. 'I have only this copy upon me at present.'

'Oh, well, I shall read it in Council, I'm sure.'

'Yes, well, if you will excuse me, Sir Christopher.'

'Of course. I shall see you soon.'

Walsingham continued on his way. He liked Hatton, who had not a vicious bone in his body, but Walsingham did not want the contents of the book spread before Robert had read it himself. He whiled away a few constructive hours with his secretaries who had intercepted at least half a dozen letters sent to the Spanish ambassador and were busily decoding their contents. The room grew dark and Walsingham reasoned that by now Robert would have arrived at court. He picked up the book and made for Robert's apartments.

'Am I disturbing you, my lord?'

Robert, dressed head to toe in black mourning, managed a smile in greeting. 'Not at all, Walsingham. Come in.'

'I thank you. Are you well? And your wife?'

'Well enough. Thank you for your letter, Francis. It was most kind.'

Walsingham nodded awkwardly. 'I should really have waited until you are settled.' He waved at the trunks being unpacked.

'Oh, no, not at all. This won't take long. It's just some mourning clothes. But you need me for something?' he asked, almost hopefully.

'Yes. This.' Walsingham proffered the book.

'What is it?' Robert asked, taking it and opening it to the flyleaf. *"The Copy of a Letter written by a Master of Art of Cambridge to his friend in London, concerning some talk passed of late between two worshipful and grave men about the present state, and some proceeding of the Earl of Leicester and his friends in England".*'

'A rather cumbersome title. I must warn you, my lord, it is not complimentary.'

'And it's about me?'

'Indeed.'

'I fill up a whole book?' Robert cried incredulously.

'The writer had a lot to say about you. I can give you the main points, if you wish, though I find them embarrassing to repeat.'

'Never mind the embarrassment,' Robert said, flicking through the pages as they both took a seat. 'Leave that till later,' he said to a servant, who was unpacking. 'Go and get your dinner.'

'The main points are,' Walsingham began when they were alone, 'that you have arranged the murder of the following: your first wife, your present wife's former husband, the husband of Douglass Sheffield, the Cardinal de Chatillon, Lady Lennox, Sir Nicholas Throckmorton and the attempted murder of Jean de Simier. Shall I continue?' he asked as he noticed Robert's shocked expression. Robert nodded, open-mouthed. 'That none of Her Majesty's gentlewomen are safe from your lust, that you are the sole reason why the Queen has never married—'

'Enough,' Robert snapped, his face as red as Walsingham's. 'I cannot believe it.'

'My lord, the people who write this filth do not know you.'

'Safe from my lust? I am probably one of the chastest men at court.'

'As I said, my lord, scurrilous filth.'

'It must be suppressed. How many copies do you think are in the country?'

Walsingham shook his head. 'It's difficult to say.'

'You are having the usual entry points watched?'

'Of course. But some copies are bound to get through. I can't stop them all.'

'Why am I so hated, Francis?'

Walsingham hesitated. 'It's not just you, my lord. All of us come under attack from time to time. Why, I had to suppress a similar pamphlet about Cecil only last month.'

'Was it as bad as this?'

'No,' Walsingham admitted, 'this is the worse I have seen.'

'Does the Queen know of this?'

'I have not yet informed her of it, but she will need to know if we are to issue a proclamation.'

'Let me read it first.'

Walsingham nodded. He looked at Robert for a moment. 'Have you seen the Queen yet?'

Robert snapped the book shut and met Walsingham's eye. 'No.'

'Oh. Do you not think you should?'

'I suppose so. Has she asked after me?'

'Only to ask if I had heard from you.'

Robert nodded, as if that was the answer he had expected. 'Will you dine with me?'

'I would like to, my lord, but I expect the Queen will want you to dine with her.' He got to his feet. 'Shall I see you in Council tomorrow?'

Robert sighed. 'Yes, Francis. Tomorrow.'

Walsingham left, and Robert began to read.

'How long have you been back at court?' Elizabeth demanded as Robert was shown into her chamber.

'A few hours.'

'Hours?' she stamped her foot petulantly. 'How dare you not present yourself sooner? I have to send someone for you—'

'Forgive me, madam,' Robert stopped her before she could really get started. He was in no mood for a display of her temper.

She glared at him, then noted the sombre blackness of his clothes and suppressed her irritation. 'What have you been doing?'

'Reading. Walsingham gave me a book.'

'Something special about it?'

'He thinks we need to suppress it. And I agree with him. If I may sit down?'

'What is it?' she said, also taking a seat.

'A libel about me.'

'Another?' Elizabeth rolled her eyes. 'Suppress it, like all the others.'

'It is rather more virulent than the others. I am used to being disliked but this goes past all bounds.'

Elizabeth's eyes narrowed. 'Does it say anything about me?'

'Only by association. It's me who comes in for the filth.'

'Well, let us eat. I shall see Walsingham about it later. Now, tell me how you are.'

'Well enough.'

'I *am* sorry.'

'I believe you,' he said, fidgeting with his doublet. 'But would it have hurt you to say as much to my wife?'

'I wrote,' she said testily.

'You wrote to *me*, and while I am grateful for the letter, it hurt me that even a mother's grief had not softened your heart towards Lettice.'

'She has my sympathy, Robin. That's enough.'

He nodded and cut a wing off a chicken. 'I see it will have to be.'

Elizabeth watched him eat. He still had an appetite, that was good. And the wine was disappearing fast enough. His belly was getting big, and she remembered Mary writing that it pained him sometimes. She wished he would talk to her, really talk, and not just pass barbed comments. She wanted him to talk of his son, tell her how he felt. But no doubt he kept that for his wife. Oh yes, Lettice had all the confidences, all his words. Well, Lettice would have to grieve alone. Robert was back at court. And he was staying.

CHAPTER 41

HAMPTON COURT PALACE, DECEMBER 1584

'Who is this fellow?' Robert gestured at the tall, handsome man with the country accent who was talking with the Queen.

'Walter Raleigh,' Hatton said.

'I know his name,' Robert said irritably. 'I mean, *who* is he? What is his background?'

'A Devon man, a respectable though poor family. I believe there is some family connection to Her Majesty's late mistress, Katherine Ashley. Perhaps that is why he is favoured by the Queen.'

'He's in favour because he's handsome and has a pleasing wit,' Robert said bitterly. 'It was ever so with her. Francis,' he reached out and touched Walsingham's arm as he passed. 'Have you got that information I asked for?'

'On the Netherlands? Yes.'

'Excellent,' Robert said. 'Hatton, please excuse me. Well, Francis, what can you tell me?'

Walsingham moved closer and lowered his voice. 'We should expect an embassy from the States, offering a crown.'

'They are willing to cede their sovereignty to us?' Robert asked in surprise.

'It seems so.'

'Will the Queen accept?'

Walsingham raised his eyebrows. 'She will not turn down a crown, surely?'

'She would,' Robert said, 'if it meant war with Spain. You know how she dislikes the very idea.'

'But it's a war we *should* be fighting,' Walsingham said passionately.

'You and I and a hundred other people in this court know that, but every time I broach the subject, she refuses to listen.'

'The Queen was ever wont to heed your words, my lord.'

'I know it,' Robert said grimly, 'but now, she has other things to occupy her.' He cocked his head in Raleigh's direction.

'He has found great favour with the Queen,' Walsingham agreed.

Robert's lips curled in distaste. 'Well, I'm not staying here to watch her fawn over him. I'm going home to Leicester House in the morning.'

'Then I shall bid you good day, my lord.'

'And you, Francis. Send me any further news you have.'

LEICESTER HOUSE

'Rob, what *is* the matter?'

He had been staring at his book for the last half hour, never once turning the page. 'Hmm? Oh, nothing, my sweet.'

'Very well,' Lettice said huffily, 'don't tell me.'

'It's Raleigh,' he said grumpily.

'Bess has taken a fancy to him, has she?' Lettice laughed. 'Well, I cannot say I am surprised. He is very handsome.'

'And when have you seen him to know that?' Robert demanded.

'I have passed him on the river, husband. Do not raise your voice to me because you are in a temper.'

'And is his pretty face reason enough to turn a blind eye to the plight of the Netherlanders?'

'If I remember rightly, your pretty face distracted her from policy in your time.'

'That's not true,' he said emphatically. 'She never neglected government. But this Raleigh.'

'Is he really that dangerous?'

'Dangerous? No, I don't think he is—'

'I meant,' Lettice interrupted impatiently, 'dangerous to our interests.'

'Possibly.'

'Then check him.'

'How?'

'By providing her with another distraction. One of your own choosing, who will serve your interests and not his. Give her my son.'

'Give her Essex?'

'Why not? He's as handsome as Raleigh, and as charming, I have no doubt. And it is your duty to advance him.'

'I know that,' he said irritably.

'Then why object?'

'I don't object to taking him to court. I am just doubtful of his reception. Lettice. He *is* your son.'

Lettice glared at him. 'He is also his father's son and she always claimed a fondness for Walter. Take him to her and see, but don't palm me off with feeble excuses, Robert. If she rejects him, then at least you will have tried. But if she does, she is a greater fool than I think her already.'

WHITEHALL PALACE

'Your Majesty, may I introduce my stepson, the Earl of Essex to you.'

Elizabeth squinted down at the young man and looked him over critically. She had known the she-wolf's cub would turn up at court one day and she had resolved not to favour him. But when she had made that decision, she had not expected him to be so handsome.

'Young Robert Devereux,' she said. 'Come nearer, my lord. Why, how like your father you are. Dear Walter.'

Robert rolled his eyes, causing Hatton to smile. She had never called Walter Devereux 'dear' when he had been alive. From the corner of his eye, he saw Raleigh stiffen as the Queen smiled on the new boy.

'You are most welcome to court, my lord,' Elizabeth said, evidently having made up her mind to be friendly.

The young man beamed, turned and grinned again at his stepfather. Robert nodded and smiled, surprised at how easy it had been.

'What did the Queen speak about with you?' Robert questioned when his stepson returned to his chambers after spending the afternoon with the Queen.

'Oh, many things,' came the answer, as the young Robert helped himself to some wine from the jug and propped his tall body in the window seat. 'I must confess, I had thought I would not care for her, after what Mother has told me.'

'You shouldn't heed everything your mother says about the Queen. She has cause to resent her. You do not. Now, I want you to listen, my boy. I've brought you to court because it is my duty to do so, but I'm not going to allow you to waste your time here. I shall be honest with you. I need you.'

'*You* need *me*, sir?' Essex shook his head. 'I can't believe that.'

'Believe it. The Queen does not like to be reminded of the passage of time. Entertain her, take her mind off such things. She likes young people about her. I remind her of growing old.'

'She doesn't seem old to me.'

Robert eyed him curiously. 'It's good you think so. It should make your flattery to her all the more convincing. Anyway, your role here is to take some of the attention away from that Raleigh fellow. You understand?'

Essex nodded. 'Completely.'

'Good. I'm relying on you, my boy.'

WHITEHALL PALACE, JULY 1585

'His Highness, William of Orange, has been shot dead in the Prinsenhof. By a Catholic.' Robert calmly folded the letter he had been reading from and resumed his seat at the Council table.

'Shot dead?' Sussex repeated incredulously. Robert nodded.

'The Catholics.' Walsingham shook his head as if he expected nothing less.

'This changes things,' Robert said, blinking away tears.

He was genuinely upset at the death of the sovereign of the Netherlands. He had met the Duke and they had formed an immediate friendship, maintained by family ties. Robert's nephew, Philip Sidney, had been acting as an unofficial ambassador for the Queen and a conduit of information and contact-making for Robert.

'I don't see how,' Cecil said.

'Of course it changes things,' Robert said. 'A Catholic has assassinated a Protestant leader, a long-standing ally of England, whose country is being overrun by Spaniards.'

Cecil waved his hand in an understanding gesture. 'Yes, yes, but we don't want to start a crusade over the death of one man.'

'I'm not speaking of a crusade,' Robert said impatiently. 'Too long have we sat back and watched, done nothing, while the King of Spain's forces conquer that which we should defend.'

'The Netherlands are not England's problem,' Cecil said.

'Then they should be. What are we without them?' Robert demanded, looking appealingly to his colleagues. 'Without them, who do we trade with? The Spanish have all the other trade routes and ports under their dominion.'

'That is not strictly true.' Cecil pulled out a letter from his sheaf of papers. 'Drake has sailed right through Spain's supposed rights of way and is coming back with a shipload of treasure. He anticipates there will be profit in the thousands for the Queen and those who invested in his venture,' he finished, looking pointedly at Robert.

'I, too, have had a letter from Drake, Cecil. He has managed to get through this time, I grant you, but King Philip's ambassador, Mendoza, is already insisting on punishment and restitution. Drake shall not do so well again. Besides, this is more than a mere financial argument.'

'I disagree,' Cecil snapped his folder shut, indicating he had said all he intended.

Robert raised his chin higher. 'Then I shall take this to the Queen.'

'I advise you not to trouble the Queen with this, Leicester.'

'I shall do as I think best, Cecil.'

'As you wish, my lord, but I doubt you will hear what you want.'

It was some hours before Robert was granted an audience with the Queen and it soon became obvious that Cecil had got to her first.

Elizabeth was at her desk reading when Robert entered. He glanced at the book over her shoulder. 'Ah, Spenser. He's one of my secretaries, you know. Good fellow. He gets on very well with my nephew, Philip.'

'That impudent pup,' Elizabeth snorted. 'I have not forgiven him for that letter he wrote to me, telling me I should not consider marriage with the Duke of Alençon.'

'Which he wrote for me.'

'Well, of course he wrote it for you. I am no fool, I know that,' she scolded. 'I will not have him back at court, so save your breath.'

'No, madam, that is not what I would say. In fact, he serves me better where he is.'

Elizabeth raised an eyebrow. 'And where is that?'

'At present, in the Netherlands. I received a letter from him today. Would you read it please?' He held out the letter to Elizabeth.

She turned her head away. 'I already know what it says *and* your opinion of what we ought to do about it.'

'I see,' Robert nodded, and refolded the letter slowly.

Her eyes narrowed. 'What do you see, Robin?'

'Cecil has prejudiced you against me.'

'Oh, don't be so melodramatic.' She looked up at him and grinned. 'Cecil tells me that Drake is returning laden with bounty.'

'Yes, your pirate is on his way.'

'My merchant adventurer, Robin,' Elizabeth smirked.

Robert settled into a chair. 'Bess, as you know, I have many friends in the Netherlands. With the Spanish running amuck, they're appealing to me to help them.'

'So Cecil told me. What form do they envisage this help taking?'

'They ask for an army. With me at its head.'

Elizabeth studied him for a moment. 'And how long has that idea been brewing, my cunning Rob?'

He smiled. 'For quite a while, I admit.'

'Then I will consider it,' Elizabeth said. 'For quite a while, I think.'

CHAPTER 42

SEPTEMBER 1585

Robert smiled at the two men sitting opposite, the deputation that Philip Sidney had promised were coming from the Netherlands. One of them spoke so little English he had barely said a word since he had arrived, while the other had been so flattered by Robert's greeting that it had made him appear a little self-important.

He smiled back at Robert. 'Our terms are these. Your sovereign provides aid to our poor country in arms and money. And in return, when the war is over and we have won, she will reign over our people.'

Cecil leant forward, peering at a piece of paper in his wrinkled hands. 'Just so I understand, sir. In exchange for men and money, the sovereignty of the States General will pass to Elizabeth, our queen?'

'That is correct.'

'That is quite an offer,' Robert said.

'We are in great need,' the envoy said earnestly.

'So it would appear,' Cecil said, his reluctance evident.

'We were led to believe,' the envoy said hastily, 'that our offer would be accepted.'

'And who led you to believe such a thing?' Cecil asked. The Dutchman glanced at Robert. Cecil caught the look. 'I am afraid the Earl of Leicester is not placed to provide you with assurances of any kind regarding Her Majesty.'

Robert felt the heat flood his cheeks. How dare Cecil humiliate him like this!

'Cecil,' he snapped, 'you mistake the situation. Her Majesty is quite aware of my involvement in the affairs of the States General. Understand, I speak for the Queen, and the Dutch need only confirmation from her regarding appeals.'

'Really, my lord?' Cecil raised a sceptical eyebrow. 'I spoke with the Queen this morning and she made no mention of such a bestowment of power.'

'You cannot blame me, Cecil, if Her Majesty does not keep you informed.' Robert laughed, sharing the joke with the Dutch envoy.

Cecil and Robert stared at one another for a long moment, then Cecil rolled up his papers and addressed the Netherlanders. 'This offer, gentlemen, *will* have to be discussed with the Queen before any decision can be made. I and my colleagues thank you for coming to see us. You will be shown the way out.' He gestured to a secretary. Cecil squinted at Walsingham. 'What is that you are writing?'

'A note to Her Majesty,' he said, still scribbling. 'Requesting her presence.'

'Surely this can wait?' Cecil said huffily.

'If you will forgive me, my lord,' Walsingham replied, 'I am Secretary of the Council and that is a decision for me to make.'

'I am here, gentlemen,' Elizabeth announced, flouncing into the room. 'What did the Netherlanders have to say?'

'As I mentioned to you last week,' Robert began, 'they offer you sovereignty of the Netherlands in return for aiding them against the Spanish invaders.'

'And as I told *you* last week, I will not accept.'

Cecil snorted quietly. Robert ignored him. 'I understood that you would consider their terms before making a final decision, madam.'

Elizabeth saw Cecil gloating and had no wish to embarrass Robert. 'Yes, I did, I remember now. Well, what are their terms?'

'Francis, that paper.' Walsingham handed it over. 'These are their terms.'

Elizabeth took the sheet he handed her and glanced down

the page. Her frown confirmed Robert's fears.

'No, I will not have it,' she said, tossing it aside.

'Madam—'

'I have done as you asked, Robin, I have read their terms and I am still not convinced. If I were to accept a crown from the Dutch, it would mean an open declaration of war on Spain, which may be what *you* want, Rob, but it's not what I want.'

'It's not a case of my personal wishes, madam,' Robert insisted. 'Francis, what do you say?'

'Aiding the Netherlanders is in all of our interests,' Walsingham said. 'If we do not become involved, the Spanish will take full control of the Netherlands and our wool trade will suffer, probably to the point where it will collapse altogether.'

'Oh, you exaggerate, Sir Francis,' Elizabeth said dismissively.

'No, he does not,' Robert said. 'Our trade *will* suffer, and if that is not reason enough, then it is our duty to aid the Netherlanders against the Catholic menace.'

'When Philip of Spain has done with the Dutch, he will turn his attention to England,' Walsingham said.

'Oh, his Enterprise of England?' Elizabeth said sceptically. 'He's been talking about that for years and nothing has ever come of it.'

'If the Netherlands were to fall, madam,' Walsingham continued, 'it would make the Enterprise far more likely.'

'I will not accept a crown,' Elizabeth said firmly. 'England is quite enough for me.'

'Then what of aid, madam?' Robert asked impatiently.

'I have agreed to aid them with men and money.'

'With whom at their head?' Walsingham asked.

Elizabeth glanced at Robert. 'Whom do you suggest, Sir Francis?'

Walsingham gestured towards Robert. 'The Earl is well known as sympathetic to the Netherlanders cause, madam. He is a known advocate of Protestantism and is one of the foremost peers of the realm.'

'And they know how close he is to me, so I am likely to favour him in any cause that concerns them,' Elizabeth finished.

'That was not what I was going to say,' Walsingham said tersely.

'That is what they are thinking though, isn't it, Rob?'

'I trust they are not, madam.'

'I hope not for their sake. You will not go. Someone else. Sir John Norreys maybe.'

Elizabeth jumped as Robert slammed his fist down on the table. 'They do not ask for John Norreys. They want *me*.'

Elizabeth glowered at him, her jaw tightening. 'Do not presume to raise your voice to me, sir. If I say you will not go, you will not go. I will hear no more about this. Sir Francis, you are to inform Sir John Norreys of my decision.'

She rose, ending the meeting, and left the chamber. Walsingham glanced at Robert and shook his head apologetically. Hatton wiped inky fingers on the tablecloth and said quietly, 'I did not think she would let you go, Lei – wait… Leicester, wait.'

Robert had thrown his chair back, ignoring the clatter as it fell over and thudded against the floor. He hurried after the Queen.

'Your Majesty,' he shouted as he turned a corner and spied her entourage further ahead. He quickened his pace as Elizabeth halted and turned. 'I must speak with you, Your Majesty.'

'I have said all I mean to, Robin.'

'You must hear me, madam.'

'Must?' she repeated, raising an eyebrow.

'I beg you.'

'Very well.' They walked to her chamber. 'I know what you would say,' she began. 'You can spare yourself the trouble.'

'Madam, I beg you, let me go.'

'I have already spoken on the matter.'

'I mean no disrespect but I fear you do not fully understand the matter. Let me explain, away from Cecil so he cannot influence you and I shall give you the clear, unvarnished truth.'

'That will be a first for you. Very well. On with your lecture, sir.'

'No lecture, Bess,' he said tiredly, taking a seat. He pointed towards her ladies. 'Must they stay?'

She smothered a little smile, and told them to leave. 'You never like my ladies around you, do you?'

'I'm not keen on giving Cecil's spies information. Anyway, whoever you send to the Netherlands will be there as your representative. Do you want a nobody to be your deputy? Who in the Netherlands has heard of Sir John Norreys?'

'He is an able soldier.'

'That I do not doubt, but he is a knight, I am an earl, thanks to your good graces. An earl who understands their plight and one who sympathises with it, and sees the potential damage to England, a country I love as much as you do.'

'That is quite a speech, Rob,' Elizabeth said, quietly impressed. 'You wish to leave my court?'

'I wish to be of service, Bess.'

'You *are* of service. Here.'

'I can serve you better there.'

'You would be away for months, perhaps years. I can't have you from me for such a long time.'

He leaned forward anxiously. 'The Netherlands are only a few days sailing away. I could return at a moment's notice.'

'And leave your men?' she asked sharply.

He smiled at Elizabeth being as contrary as ever. 'I would obey your orders.' He waited for an answer, but she just sat there, her chin upon her hand. 'For thirty years, I have served you faithfully and will do so until the day I die. But for those thirty years, you have had me tied to your skirts, as if I cannot be trusted away from you. You will have succeeded in unmanning me, Bess, if you do not send me on this mission.'

'I unman you?'

'I have not been on a battlefield since St Quentin,' he fell back exasperatedly. 'You refused to let me go to Le Havre and I obeyed you in that.'

'A good thing I did refuse, otherwise it might have been you who was shot and not your brother.'

'My point is I obeyed you in that, to my eternal shame.'

'There have been no other battles for you to fight in,' she said proudly.

'How can I persuade you?' he asked desperately. 'Tell me, how?'

'I will not be bullied,' she shouted, stamping her foot. 'Oh, I have had enough of this. If you so desperately wish to leave me, you can go.'

Robert fell to his knees. 'Oh, Bess, you will not regret it, I promise you. Just think of the benefits. I will serve *your* interests, none other, and I can anticipate your wishes, for I know you so well.'

'I shall hold you to that, Rob. Now, get up. But just one thing. Your wife stays in England. Do not argue with me on this, Rob. You can go to the Netherlands if you want, but you go alone. I won't have Lettice queening it over there.'

'Very well, Bess,' Robert agreed. If that was her one condition, he could live with it.

'Well, go. No doubt you will want to start making arrangements.' She waved him away. 'Send Essex to me. I could do with some entertainment.'

ELIZABETH'S BEDCHAMBER, NOVEMBER 1585

He was gone. Elizabeth lay in her bed, her favourite spaniel rolling against her legs, showing his belly, waiting for his accustomed caress. None came. The dog was forgotten for Robert was gone. Strange, she had not thought she would miss him so. She had other men now, younger and wittier, Raleigh, for example, and Essex. So, why, why should she miss him so?

He had been gone but three days. She leant over to the table beside the bed and fumbled in its drawer. Her fingers closed around the object she sought. A small oval frame. She smiled at its label: *My lord's portrait*. It was an old picture, of course, painted many years before. When had she last looked at this? Oh, yes, she remembered. It was when James Melville, Mary Stuart's ambassador, had come to court and she had just created Robert the Earl of Leicester. What had she said to Melville then? That when Mary Stuart had Robert she would need the picture, and she had snatched it from his hands. Why had she let him go to war? He could be hurt or killed. She knew she had been unkind, making him cold in the shade of her favour while she preferred his stepson and other handsome young men. But that was only because she was getting old and she did not want to be reminded of it every time she looked at him. And yes, she wanted to make him suffer, as she suffered. Her nights were tormented with thoughts of him and Lettice, and haunted by the ghost of the little boy she had wished dead. That was why she slept so little, demanded so many diversions. And now war, always men pushing her towards war. More deaths on her conscience, more danger for those she loved. Maybe she should recall him? But he would hate her for it, and then she would lose him completely.

God help me, she prayed, *tell me what to do.*

THE NETHERLANDS, DECEMBER 1585

The mighty cannons of the port of Flushing boomed and their thunder rolled across the sea, rumbling to the hull of the ship that carried the new Lieutenant General, Robert Dudley. A small boat carried him and his party to the dock where fireworks erupted high over their heads and the crowds hanging over railings cheered and banged their drums. Robert waved and smiled and wondered if this was how Elizabeth felt when she went out into the streets of London or on progress through the country. Was this what it felt like to be a king?

'Uncle,' Philip hallooed him from the dockside. 'It's good to see you.'

'And you, my boy,' Robert called, taking the hand of a sailor and setting foot on to firm land. 'I didn't expect such a reception.'

'Then you should have done, Uncle,' Philip said. 'The Netherlanders are a sorry people at present, but they have great hopes of you.'

Robert grimaced. 'I feel sure then that they will be disappointed.'

'Why?'

'I'll tell you later. Where do we go from here?'

'To your headquarters for the next two nights. Then you go to Middlebury, Rotterdam, Delft, other towns whose names I have forgotten, ending at the Hague. So, I warn you, Uncle, this will be a tiring fortnight for you. Pageants and entertainments—'

'No more than on one of the Queen's progresses, my boy. You must not worry about me.'

'Then I must defy my mother,' Philip laughed.

'Well, you can write to your mother and tell her not to worry about me, either. I'll be fine. I have you with me.'

'You have rather more than me. I understand on that fleet out there,' Philip pointed back to the dock where the English ships floated on the horizon, 'there are ten thousand horse and six thousand foot soldiers. Is that right?'

'Sounds right,' Robert nodded, 'and we shall need them.'

'And more besides, I should not wonder,' Philip agreed grimly.

'Well, don't hope for more men. The Queen has made it quite clear that she doesn't favour this operation and no doubt she will keep a tight rein on her purse strings.'

Philip moved closer to Robert and asked quietly, 'What are the terms of your commission from the Queen?'

Robert shrugged. 'To maintain defences.'

'Uncle,' Philip frowned, 'I have seen the terms of the Netherlanders commission to you. They expect you to perform offensive manoeuvres as well as defensive. I gave them a promise.'

'I know you did and I'm sorry. But it's not me, it's the Queen. What can I do?'

'But when the Netherlanders find out your limits?'

Robert patted his arm. 'We'll talk about it later, Phil. Just let me enjoy the moment.'

JANUARY 1586

'Uncle, let me call a physician,' Philip said, handing Robert a cup of hot wine.

'He would be able to do nothing,' Robert shook his head, wincing at another stab of pain in his stomach. 'It will be better in the morning.'

'I cannot stand by and see you in pain,' Philip persisted.

'Phil, I thank you for your concern but it must cease. The last fortnight has been something of a strain, that is all. Now, come and sit by me.'

'Well, now the pageantry is over, the real work can begin.'

'I have already started,' Robert said, handing Philip a rolled-up sheet of paper. 'That has been given to the commanders to be posted up all over the camp.'

Philip unrolled the paper and read aloud. 'Every man is to attend church services, no swearing or blaspheming, no whores or other camp followers, and under no circumstances are there to be violations of women.' He let out a low whistle. 'That is a tall order, Uncle.'

'I don't think so.'

'Women are considered spoils of war.'

'You think we should allow our army to rape women?'

Robert asked, aghast.

'Of course not, Uncle,' Philip assured him hastily. 'I can think of nothing more abhorrent than rape, any disregard for women. But you and I speak of our own station. Such strictures often do not apply to men baser than we. You and I are not the rabble that serve in this army. How can you expect to enforce such a law?'

'By the severest penalty. Any man found violating a woman will be taken and hung immediately. It says there,' he pointed with the tip of a quill to the broadsheet.

'Very well, Uncle,' Philip rolled the sheet back up and stuffed it into his doublet. 'I trust the proclamation will deter any man from testing your punishment.'

'I hope so,' Robert nodded, shifting uncomfortably in his seat. 'Phil, is there something you want to say to me? You seem to have an expectant air about you.'

Philip nodded. 'If we are only to defend the towns we already hold and make no overt gestures of war towards the Spanish, what are you going to do when the Netherlanders demand more?'

'I could tell them the truth, that the Queen hopes my presence here will make the Spanish pack up their guns and go home, but then, that would sound ridiculous, wouldn't it?'

'The Queen must be made to understand the situation here, Uncle. Is there no one you can send to her to explain?'

'Walsingham will do what he can for me,' Robert said. 'And I have been telling her for months.'

'I fear the Queen is ill using you, Uncle,' Philip said, patting Robert's hand. 'Does she know how unwell you are? Sending you here—'

'I asked for this command, Phil. I need it.'

'Even if it makes you ill, and it will do, Uncle, I can see it.'

'I can't expect you to understand,' Robert said kindly. 'You are a young man, and will, no doubt, do great things. My time is nearly up and what have I to show for it? Nothing. No son, *you* are my heir. No achievements, only a reputation for scandal. I need to achieve something before I die. You say nothing, Phil, I see, you know it's true.'

'I know you *think* it is true. But I assure you, Uncle, your family knows your worth, even if nobody else does.'

CHAPTER 43

THE NETHERLANDS, JANUARY 1586

'My New Year's gift to the Queen,' Robert said, holding up a necklace of pearls and jewels, a large central diamond flanked by enormous rubies. 'It cost a fortune. Do you think she will like it?'

Philip shrugged, raising an eyebrow at such extravagance. 'You know the Queen better than I, Uncle.'

'She *will* like it. Davison will take it back for me when he leaves tomorrow.'

'Talking of Davison, he's outside with a delegation from the Assembly. They want to see you.'

'But it's Sunday,' Robert protested.

'They know and don't care. Will you see them?'

'Oh, I suppose so, though don't let it go on too long. I want my dinner.'

Philip laughed and threw his arm around Robert's shoulders. 'I thought your wife insisted on you eating less, Uncle.'

'She can insist all she wants, Phil. *She* is not here.'

They strode out into the main hall to meet the delegation. Six men doffed their black caps and bowed. Then they offered him a crown.

Robert wasn't sure he had heard correctly at first, their accents managing to mangle some of their attempts at English pronunciation, but when he looked at Philip, who wore an undisguised expression of surprise and perplexity, he realised he must have heard correctly. They did not call it sovereignty, they termed it Supreme Governor of the United Provinces, but it amounted to the same thing.

Robert thanked them but told them, as any good subject would have done, that he could not accept without his queen's permission. They pressed him again. There was no time for prevarication, they insisted. Their States were divided without a leader. They wanted him to be their leader. Was it not a generous offer?

'God's Death,' Robert yelled as he strode back into his chamber.

'Uncle, what will you do?' Philip asked, grabbing the door and quickly closing it.

'I don't know,' Robert floundered. 'What are they thinking of, putting me in this position?'

'No doubt they thought it would please you.'

'Elizabeth refused their crown and now they as good as offer it to me.'

'You must write to the Queen,' Philip hurried to the table and sorted through paper until he found a clean sheet. He dipped a quill into the inkwell, scattering blobs of ink over the tablecloth. 'Shall I write, Uncle?'

Robert was not listening. He stood before the fire, gazing into the dancing flames. His mind was a whirl. Here on offer was what he had wanted all his life. He had briefly been brother to a king consort, son to a king in all but name, and had come close to marrying two queens. All that had escaped him. And now he was being offered the position of Supreme Governor. Well, all right, it was not King, but it was as good as. He wanted it, and God knew, he deserved it. Who but him had campaigned so vigorously for the Netherlanders cause? Who had lost favour, standing and health in the pursuit? Here, these people appreciated him, as he had never been appreciated in England.

Philip questioned him again.

'No, not the Queen. Cecil and Walsingham first.'

'What do you want me to write?'

'Tell them of the Netherlanders offer and how much they understand they are beholden to Her Majesty. Tell them that I am waiting to hear of the Queen's permission before accepting, but trust that her answer will not take too long, as I am importuned to accept with all haste due to the current deplorable situation here. How does that sound?'

'It sounds very good. I shall give it to Davison and he can take it back to England with him tomorrow.'

No word came from Elizabeth. The Netherlanders offer was made again and again. They grew impatient and irritated with the delay. Much longer and they would feel insulted, too. Robert did not know that bad weather had delayed Davison in reaching England, so Elizabeth didn't hear about the offer until weeks later. By that time, Robert felt he had to accept, but once accepted, he was not so sure he had done the right thing.

Sir Thomas Heneage arrived at Robert's headquarters, cap in one hand and a letter from the Queen in the other. He asked to see Robert immediately. Robert, whose brow had grown moist with the news of his arrival, had him shown into his private chamber, sure that he only brought news of condemnation with him.

'Sir Thomas,' Robert greeted him with a forced smile and took his hand. 'You had an easy journey?'

'I did, my lord. You must forgive me if I dispense with some of the pleasantries. I have a letter from the Queen.'

Robert swallowed uneasily as Heneage held out the letter with the Queen's seal emblazoned upon it. He took the letter and turned his back to read.

Heneage waited patiently while the Earl read. These two had once been rivals. Now, Heneage felt only sympathy for the man who suffered under the Queen's love.

Robert wiped his sweaty brow with his handkerchief. Elizabeth insisted that he renounce the title.

'My lord?' Heneage enquired.

'I suffer the Queen's displeasure,' he said, 'but no doubt you knew that already.'

'I did, my lord. But I can tell you, Cecil has worked on your behalf and has persuaded the Queen that a formal resignation of your title will not be necessary, just its relinquishment.'

'That was kind of him,' Robert said. 'I do feel the Queen's indignation at me could have been avoided, though.'

'In what way, my lord?'

'Davison,' Robert said. 'If he had told the Queen what I told him to say, she would have understood that I had no choice.'

'You feel Davison is to blame?'

'Well, am *I* to blame?' Robert replied indignantly. 'For myself, I would rather have not been put in such a position. I didn't ask for this title.'

No, but you did not refuse it either, thought Heneage, *and here you are, blaming a poor secretary.*

'My lord, perhaps you should write to the Queen herself, put your side to her. I am sure you will be able to placate her. You have her love.'

Robert was not so sure.

Robert did write, but it was some months before Elizabeth calmed down and stopped berating him in her letters. By April she was calling him her Sweet Robin once more. He could breathe freely again and return with a focused mind to the business of war.

Months passed and Robert was too busy to worry about Elizabeth. This great mission of his to help the Netherlanders chase the Spanish away was turning out to be the biggest disappointment of his life.

His army was suffering, diminishing daily as soldiers died or deserted. Their pay was not even reaching them but being diverted into the corrupt pockets of Robert's officers, and Elizabeth refused to send more. Robert began paying his remaining men out of his own dwindling coffers and it was a relief when he received a letter from Cecil recalling him to England.

There was a dilemma at court. A decision had to be made whether the troublesome Scottish queen, Mary Stuart, imprisoned but constantly plotting, should live or die. Elizabeth was being difficult, and only Robert, out of all her counsellors, knew how to handle her.

WHITEHALL PALACE, JANUARY 1587

'She has signed it.' Davison showed Robert, Walsingham and Cecil the warrant for the execution of Mary Stuart. 'But she said I was not to show it to the Council.'

Walsingham looked at Robert. 'Why sign it, then?'

Robert didn't answer but took the document from Davison.

'We can do nothing,' Cecil sighed. 'Leicester?'

Robert rubbed his chin. 'She wants Mary Stuart dead, I'm sure of it. She just doesn't want to be the one to give the order.'

'No one else can give it,' Walsingham said irritably. 'The order has to come from her.'

'She's worried about the precedent it will create if we execute an anointed queen,' Robert explained. 'She thinks if it could be done to Mary Stuart, then it could be done to her. And she's always been wary of executing her kin.'

'She's different from her father in that, at least,' Walsingham muttered. 'So, what are we going to do?'

'I say we send it on,' Robert said. Cecil and Walsingham looked at him in surprise. 'If we don't, this damn matter will never be resolved and Mary Stuart will continue to plague us with her plots to take the throne. Don't look at me like that. This is what you brought me back for, isn't it? To persuade the Queen to make a decision? Well, I've told her that she should execute the Scottish queen and, here, she has signed the warrant. What more do you want?'

'She expressly told me not to show it to you though, my lord.' Davison reminded him.

Robert, still believing that Davison had failed him with his handling of the sovereignty affair, looked up at him meanly. 'I think I have a deeper understanding of the Queen than a mere secretary, Davison. Leave this to us.' He was pleased to see Davison redden before he turned back to Walsingham and Cecil. 'Well, are you going to be cowardly or do as I say?'

Walsingham didn't mind being called names, but he agreed with Robert that they would never be free of Mary Stuart until her head was off. 'Send the warrant to Fotheringhay Castle,' he said. 'Have them perform the deed immediately.'

'Cecil?' Robert raised an eyebrow at him.

'Yes,' he said after a long pause, 'send it.'

'Thank God we've reached an agreement,' Robert said, handing the warrant back to Davison. 'Seal it and send it.'

'And if the Queen dislikes what we've done?' Walsingham asked when the door had closed upon Davison.

'Fortunately,' Robert said with a tired smile, 'I'll be back in the Netherlands by the time Mary Stuart's head is off, so whatever Elizabeth thinks of our decision, I won't be here to hear it.'

CHAPTER 44

THE NETHERLANDS, MARCH 1587

Robert returned to the Netherlands, and a siege. The Spanish inhabitants of the town, Zutphen, had barricaded themselves in against the Dutch and English forces.

'Uncle,' Philip cried, bursting into Robert's tent and waving a letter. 'General Parma has written to Marshal Verdugo. Our soldiers intercepted the messenger.' He paused to catch his breath. 'Parma intends to re-supply Zutphen. He is sending a convoy, guarded by only six hundred men.' Robert snatched the letter from Philip's hand. 'Six hundred, Uncle. We can take that supply train and end this siege. We have men enough, don't you think?'

'Yes, I think we do,' Robert agreed. 'Tomorrow morning then. Early.'

'An ambush, Uncle?' Philip grinned.

Robert smiled back, his first in days. 'An ambush, Phil.'

They woke the next morning to a thick fog and it pleased them, knowing that the fog would hide them. Then it lifted and Robert and Philip could see the supply train, but it was escorted not by six, but fifteen-hundred horsemen and at least three-thousand foot soldiers. The English position exposed, there was no time to retreat. They had no choice but to press on. Their attack had lost the element of surprise, but it was still quick enough for the

English cavalry to charge the Spanish and see them retreat beyond their own pikemen. But it was not enough, for no sooner did the English cavalry pass the pikes than they were driven back by musket fire.

'Leicester.' Norreys pulled his horse alongside Robert's and snatched at the mare's bridle. 'I could do with more men.'

'I can't spare any,' Robert shouted above the noise. 'You shall have to do the best you can with what you have.'

'If I must, I must. But you should be looking more cheerful, my lord. A mere handful of your men have driven the enemy back three times.'

'That should make me cheerful?' Robert scoffed. 'Yes, they have driven the enemy back three times, and three times have they returned. Get back to your men, Norreys. See if you can conjure a victory out of this debacle.'

Robert stood at the entrance to his tent, the flap batting against his arm, watching as the smoke and dirt of battle passed by him. 'How many men did we lose?' he asked as Norreys joined him.

'Twenty-two foot, no more than thirteen horse.'

'And the Spanish? How many did they lose?'

'Three hundred. Maybe more.'

'Well, that is something,' Robert said bitterly. 'For all your talk of victory earlier, the supply train still got through, the Spanish got their supplies.'

'My lord,' shouted a young boy, skidding to a halt before Robert, his short, dirty-blond hair sticking up in spikes where it was coated in dried mud. 'You are wanted in the surgeon's tent.'

Robert suddenly realised he had not seen Philip since that morning. He hurried to the surgeon's tent, his nostrils tightening at its smell of blood and shit from injured and dying men mingling with the noxious fumes of potions. It was dark inside, only a few lamps swinging from the poles holding up the roof. Beneath one of these stood a rickety table and upon it Philip lay, propped against a soldier who still wore his bloody and battered armour. Philip screamed as the surgeon's probe scraped against his bone, the cry ending in a whimper as he tried to stifle his cry.

Robert staggered forward, shocked and sickened by the sight. 'Phil, what—'

'God Almighty,' Philip cursed, the blasphemy sounding odd in his mouth. He screwed up his face as another bolt of pain seared through his body and he snorted, spittle flying from his mouth to sliver down his front.

'A bullet in the leg,' the surgeon explained, pointing at Philip's left thigh where the flesh was horribly torn. Bright red blood ran down to the table's surface, the skin at the edges of the wound black with thick, dark blood. White bone showed through the redness.

Robert stared at the wound. 'Where was your armour?'

'I didn't put it on. It slowed me down.'

'You foolish boy. Will it mend?' he asked the surgeon.

'I cannot say, my lord,' the surgeon said. 'Only time will tell.'

'You cannot say?' Robert repeated incredulously. 'You *will* say, damn you, or I shall run you through where you stand.' Robert pulled his sword from its scabbard and pointed it against the surgeon's chest.

'Uncle.' Philip's shaking hand pushed away the point of the sword. 'You do me no good by killing my doctor. He is a good man. He will do what he can.'

'He better,' Robert growled, sheathing his sword. 'This is my nephew,' he said to the surgeon, 'more, he is my heir and my son. You *will* take care of him.'

The surgeon nodded uneasily.

'Leave me, Uncle,' Philip tried to smile. 'You must be needed elsewhere. I think I could sleep for a while, if this fellow will only aid me by removing the bullet. Believe me, Uncle, I will be here when you come again.'

Philip's wound did not heal. Some two weeks passed and Philip appeared to be improving, but one morning he had lifted his bedclothes a little and the smell of putrefaction greeted his nostrils. Gangrene had set in, for which there was no cure, save for the amputation of the limb, but the surgeon shook his head and said it was too late even for that.

So, Philip, the hope of many, so beloved, so accomplished, died and with him, Robert's dreams of victory. He was sick of the Netherlands. He wanted to go home.

CHAPTER 45

HAMPTON COURT PALACE, OCTOBER 1587

Elizabeth tapped her foot impatiently while the ambassador before her twittered on. She had no idea what he was talking about, for she had stopped listening about ten minutes before, when Hatton had leant over her shoulder and whispered in her ear that Robert had arrived at the palace.

The ambassador finished his sentence and Elizabeth was suddenly aware that she was expected to make some reply.

She smiled gently. 'My good man, now is not the time for such a question.' *Whatever that question was*, she thought. 'We shall talk more another day.'

The ambassador opened his mouth, his brow creasing in confusion. This was not the response he had expected. But Hatton guessed which subject was occupying the Queen's mind and he expertly guided the poor man away from the Presence Chamber with an offer of dinner.

Hatton met Robert on the way out. 'Leicester, it's good to see you.'

'And you, Hatton. How is the Queen?'

Hatton bit his bottom lip and hung his head to one side, the ambassador at his heels, momentarily forgotten. 'Not so good. The death of Mary Stuart, it... well, it has not been easy, Leicester, that I can tell you.'

'I don't imagine it has, Hatton. I hear Walsingham and Cecil are banished from her presence for their part in it.'

'Yes. For Cecil's part, I think he is almost glad. The Queen sets a swift pace and he has difficulty keeping up these days. I know his wife praises the death of Mary Stuart for that reason alone.' Hatton grinned at him. 'The Queen is eager for your return. This fellow here,' he jerked a discreet thumb at the ambassador behind him, 'had no chance at all when I told her you were in the palace. She didn't listen to a word of his speech, poor man.'

Robert smiled gratefully. 'I am just as eager to see her. Good to see you, Hatton. Let's dine tomorrow.'

The warders opened the doors to the Presence Chamber, and as he entered, he felt dozens of courtiers' eyes fall upon him. He held himself upright, making a strong effort to ignore a new pain in his right leg as he placed his weight upon it. He paid no attention to the courtiers as he passed them, though he was aware they smiled and inclined their heads to him. He looked only at the woman who seemed years older than when he had left her six months before, the woman who never took her eyes off of him.

He stood before her, bent his left knee and suppressed a wince as his right banged against the floorboards. 'Your Majesty.'

'My Lord,' the thin voice croaked and he looked up sharply in concern. She smiled down at him, and he suddenly knew that everything was going to be all right, she was not going to hurl abuse at him for his failures, at least not in public. She held her hands out to him and stepped down from the dais, her skirts swishing on the wood. 'I am glad you are back,' she said, pulling him towards her and kissing his cheek.

'I am glad to be back, Bess,' he murmured against her ear.

She drew back, her eyes glinting with tears. 'Come with me, my lord,' and still holding his hand, drew him along behind her to her chamber. Her ladies moved to follow her but she shooed them away.

She turned the handle of her Privy Chamber door herself before her warders could do it for her and dragged Robert inside. Before he could utter a word, Elizabeth had thrown her arms around his neck and was crying, great shuddering tears. He held her tight until her tears gradually abated and she pushed him roughly away.

'I do not know why I should be pleased to see you, Rob,' she sniffed. 'You have done me many an ill turn.'

'Oh, Bess, please, don't let us begin like this. I know you have reason to be angry with me, I admit my faults. Is that not enough?'

'I needed you and you weren't here. They tricked me, all of them, those curs Cecil and Walsingham. They killed her, killed her without my consent. I didn't want her dead.'

'But Bess,' he soothed, taking her hand, 'she *is* dead and what is done cannot be undone. Why torment yourself?'

'Because it isn't over. There will be consequences, I know it. I have killed an anointed queen. What is to stop anyone else from doing the same to me?'

'You are well protected and well loved by your people.'

'Maybe that is true, but what of the Spanish? Philip has been waiting for years to attack England and now I have given him the perfect excuse by killing a fellow Catholic. God's Death, Rob, I have killed a saint.' She began to laugh, a high hysterical laugh that made Robert think of her mother, Anne Boleyn, who was said to have developed a hysteria while waiting for her execution. Without thinking, Robert slapped her cheek, hard.

'For your own good, Bess,' he whispered, his face close to hers. 'Now, I will not have this madness. Mary Stuart is dead. You driving yourself mad is no help, to you or your people. This must stop. I am here now.'

'Then stay here with me,' she pleaded, gesturing to her bed. 'Don't go home to Lettice tonight.'

He hesitated. 'What will everyone think if I stay?'

'To the devil with what everyone thinks,' Elizabeth snapped. 'At my time of life, why should I care for the tongues of gossips?'

'At your time of life, Bess? You are not old. You could dance those young scamps out there under the table every night.'

Elizabeth dismissed all her attendants and they supped till late, and Robert consumed a vast amount of wine and, for once, Elizabeth did not chide him for it. His head was nodding upon his breast when Elizabeth pulled him to her bed and laid him back on it. He was asleep as soon as his head touched the pillow. She pulled off his boots and threw them upon the floor. She stood for a moment looking down at him. This was Robert Dudley, Sweet Bonny Robin, lying bloated and red-faced upon her bed. She laughed to herself. Time was when Robert would have been anything but asleep at such a time.

But time had moved on. She felt herself growing old. She tried to hide the signs with heavy makeup and unnaturally red wigs, but these props could not change her inside. The death of Mary Stuart had heaped even more worries upon her, and she had felt alone, so very alone.

She allowed herself a satisfied smile. She was not alone now. Robert's first night back in England was spent with her, and the husband of Lettice was even now in Elizabeth's bed.

Robert began to snore and, like a mother, Elizabeth pulled the bedclothes over him, tucking them under his chin. For the first time she could remember, she undressed herself, her fingers clumsy with the unfamiliar lacings and hooks. Wearing nothing but her shift, she eased back a section of the bedclothes and curved her thin body around Robert's, covering herself again with the blankets. He moaned groggily as her leg rested upon his and he eased his arm under her body, arcing it around her waist. He did not wake up at all that night and the two of them slept late the following morning.

CHAPTER 46

WHITEHALL PALACE, MAY 1588

'We are sorry to say it, but we have a poor opinion of this Spanish Armada and fear some disaster,' Elizabeth said to the Council, reading from the letter she held. 'There, gentlemen. Even the Pope has no faith in the Spaniards. Why look you so, Walsingham? Do you doubt the words of your own spies?'

'No, madam,' Walsingham shook his head. 'I do not doubt that the Pope spoke those words, but I do fear he underestimates the power of Spain.'

'Ha,' Elizabeth snorted, pulling a plate of walnuts towards her. 'Drake has seen to the power of Spain. He has destroyed Spanish ships faster than Philip can build them.' She bit down and winced as a pain shot through her cheek. No one noticed and Elizabeth was faintly annoyed. All her counsellors were searching through the documents scattered across the table before them, trying to find some argument amongst the thousands of words to convince the Queen of the danger. 'Cecil and I will settle this matter with Spain. Peaceably.'

'You mean a treaty with Parma, madam?' Robert asked. 'The peace is a fraud, madam. Parma plays you for a fool.'

Elizabeth's eyes blazed. 'How dare you, I wil—'

'I dare, madam, because next to you, the thing I hold most dear is the safety of this country and its people.' It was a calculated answer, one that all present knew the Queen would not argue with.

'Do you dare to say I hold them any less dear?' Elizabeth said, 'I am trying to spare them from another war—'

'Walsingham,' Robert again interrupted her, holding out his hand, 'that letter from Lord Howard.'

Elizabeth watched tight-lipped as Walsingham sifted through his pile of papers, found the letter Robert wanted and handed it to him.

Robert held the paper at arm's length and read aloud. '*There was never, since England was England, such a stratagem and mask made to deceive England as this treaty of peace.* You see, madam? Even Admiral Knollys, your own cousin, knows this peace to be false.'

'Indeed?' Elizabeth tapped at her empty wine cup with her fingernail and Hatton poured more wine into it from a jug on the table. 'What else does the Admiral know?'

'Only what is known by us all, madam,' Walsingham answered. 'The Spanish are preparing a fleet for the invasion of England and may be on our shores at any time.'

'Such melodrama, my Moor,' Elizabeth sneered and Walsingham had to bite his lip. 'I will not tolerate such scaremongering. I want evidence of this armada before I set my people on a course of war. Bring me that evidence, and I may reconsider.'

'Enough, Rob.' Elizabeth took the wine cup from his hand. 'Any more and you shall be asleep and I want you awake. I want to talk to you about your stepson. He wants something to do.'

Robert belched. 'I thought he was busy keeping you amused?'

'Do you mind that?'

'Would it matter if I did?'

'Of course it would,' she said, leaning forward and stroking the swollen blue veins on the back of his hand. 'I wouldn't want you to think you are being replaced.'

'I'm teasing you, Bess. It's all right, I can see the attraction. He's a lively lad.'

Elizabeth grunted. 'Needs bringing down a peg or two.'

'Well, he gets that from his mother.'

Elizabeth gave his foot a gentle kick. 'Anyway, you are getting fat and overworked. I want you to give your stepson the Master of the Horse.'

'That would keep him close to you.'

'You *are* jealous.'

'Can you blame me?' he cried. 'And I've held the Master of the Horse since the beginning of your reign, Bess. I have made it what it is. You have the best horses of any monarch in Europe and now you want me to hand it over to a boy just out of his swaddling clothes.'

'He's hardly that,' Elizabeth giggled.

Robert was suddenly too tired to argue. 'Oh, give him the Horse, if that is what you want. What have you in store for me?'

'First, tell me what you really think of Spain and do not exaggerate the matter.'

'What I really think is what I said earlier,' he protested. 'The Spanish *are* planning to attack and at present, we will not be able to put up any kind of defence. It is as simple as that. And remember, you said yourself Philip of Spain now has the perfect excuse to invade.'

Elizabeth nodded unhappily. 'With Mary Stuart dead by my hands. She causes me more trouble dead than alive.'

'Mobilise the fleet, Bess. Walsingham and Drake can provide the evidence you demand. Parma deceives you with talk of peace. Philip *is* readying his fleet. The Spanish *are* coming.'

'I suppose I must believe you, as you all say the same thing. Except Cecil, of course.'

'Oh, Cecil is an old woman,' Robert said impatiently.

'What am I then, Rob?' Elizabeth raised an eyebrow.

'Cecil is a good man,' he replied hastily, sidestepping her question, 'but cautious, too much so. He has his eyes on his account books and the treasury. Of course, to prepare for invasion will take money and your treasury will shrink, perhaps desperately so. But if it is a case of an empty treasury or a Spanish-swollen England, I know what course I should take.'

Elizabeth considered for a few minutes. 'You always were most persuasive, Rob. Damn you.'

'Then you will—'

She nodded. 'I shall give the order for war, however much it goes against my conscience.'

'To hell with conscience. What have you to feel guilty about? It is Spain who are the aggressors, not us. And besides, your conscience will feel better when we are celebrating an English victory.'

TILBURY, ESSEX, JULY 1588

Tilbury was damnably cold and Robert wrapped his fur cloak tighter about his neck. Once Elizabeth had made up her mind to see off the Spanish, events progressed at a swift pace. Orders were sent to Dover and along the coast to prepare for an invasion, and Robert was despatched to Tilbury with orders to amass a land army in the event of an incursion into England via the Thames. Elizabeth had promised him an office to make up for the loss of the Master of the Horse and she had been as good as her word. Robert had command of the land army and the grand title of Lieutenant and Captain General of the Queen's Armies and Companies.

Robert had taken up his command with enthusiasm at first, but by the time he had set up camp, he had realised what a burdensome task he had ahead of him. It was like the Netherlands all over again. So much to do and few officers capable of executing his orders or willing. He had found some of his officers treating the whole thing as a joke, disobeying orders and sauntering off to the coast, where they had behaved like ruffian schoolboys, disdainful of Robert and his position.

For himself, Robert was often sent here and there, trying to raise up companies of men with patriotic speeches, or if those did not work, trying to generate self-interest with talk of rewards. The army was seriously understocked and a great deal of his time was spent trying to find supplies to feed the men.

It took time and much effort, but his army was eventually ready for a visit from the Queen.

Elizabeth arrived by a gloriously bedecked and canopied barge escorted by two thousand men. Her entrance was grand, but her land procession was to be intimate. She rode a white horse, herself dazzlingly arrayed in a gown of purest white, a steel corselet and bodice her only concession to the safety concerns of her counsellors. Robert walked on her right, his stepson, Essex, leading her horse on the left. The ranks of men parted as they approached and many dropped to their knees before this woman who appeared, goddess-like, in their midst.

She dropped down lightly from her horse into Robert's arms and he led her by the hand to a makeshift dais from which she was to address her subjects. Robert took up a position to the side and her words flew over his head to the men, who he noted, looked at their queen with awe. It was easy for a man like Robert, who had been almost daily in the presence of the Queen for thirty years, to forget that the ordinary people of England rarely had a chance of seeing their sovereign close up.

Elizabeth was remarkable. Her speech was full of rousing phrases and stirring words. She promised to stay and fight with them if necessary, to lay down her life for her subjects and her country, and they believed her. The cheering was overwhelming as she stepped down, her hand in Robert's and she smiled warmly at him, basking in her subjects' love. He led her towards the tent where a supper table awaited them and the officers.

'I bid you all, leave us.' Elizabeth said to the officers and they departed. 'So, Rob, how did I do?'

'You were glorious,' Robert said.

'I was, wasn't I?' Elizabeth laughed and clapped her hands. 'I still love to hear it.'

'You love to hear how wonderful you are?'

'The cheers of my people, you rogue,' she flicked her napkin at him. 'But I do love to hear how wonderful I am as well.'

Robert laughed, then wished he had not as it seemed to make the pain in his stomach worse.

Elizabeth's eyes narrowed. 'Rob, you are not well.'

'No, Bess,' he admitted, 'I am not. I will be glad when all this is over and I can go to Buxton.'

'The waters there will cure you?'

'They always have before.'

'You eat too much,' Elizabeth said, sinking back into the chair and fidgeting with a cushion.

'As you always tell me,' Robert agreed, wishing Elizabeth would dismiss him, for he was damnably weary and wanted nothing but his bed.

'You cannot stay too long at Buxton, though. I shall need you.'

'If you need me, I will not go.'

'Oh, you fool, of course you must go. But I want you back, sound in mind and body, you hear? You look tired, my love. Go to your bed.'

He smiled gratefully at her. 'Thank you, Bess. My stepson shall escort you to your lodging. Shall I see you in the morning?'

'Yes, Rob. Let us hope the morning will bring good news.'

The morning came, clear and bright, and with it, a muddied, horse-sweat stinking messenger from the coast with the news that the Spanish armada was defeated. Drums beat, fire beacons blazed, and there was wine and song aplenty throughout the camp at Tilbury. Money was always a concern with the Queen and Robert was instructed to break up his army and send his men home as soon as possible to avoid unnecessary expense. This done, he made his way to London.

He stayed only two days, enough time to celebrate and watch his stepson parade the remaining troops, but he was more than ready to make the journey to take the soothing waters at Buxton.

CHAPTER 47

Robert went home to Wanstead first. The journey had been beset by torrential rain and the road had turned to thick mud. He had pulled up the wooden windows of his coach against the foul weather and now sat huddled in the corner, wrapped in his thickest fur cloak and leaning his aching head against the side of the swaying, rattling coach.

'My lord.' His attendant, Richard Pepper, reached forward and gently shook Robert's knee. 'My lord, we have arrived.'

Robert opened a bleary eye. The coach door opened and Pepper stepped down, holding out a helping hand. Lettice waited for him at the door, looking bright and younger than her forty-six years. Robert supposed that was the effect of fornicating nightly with Christopher Blount, his Gentleman of the Horse. Robert knew he should care more, run the young scamp through with his sword. Ten, perhaps even five years ag,o he would have done, but not now. Now he didn't care, had not the energy to care, and in a perverse way, it even gave him a sense of relief. If Lettice was being serviced regularly by Blount, she would not pester him in bed.

'My dear,' he greeted her with a weak smile.

'Robert, you look ill. Are you sure this trip to Buxton is good for you?' She took him by the arm and led him into the hall. 'Perhaps you should just rest here?'

He walked away from her into the main chamber and sank

heavily into a cushioned chair. 'If you do not wish to accompany me, Lettice—'

'You are my husband, and I go where you go. If you allow me to, that is,' she added peevishly, settling herself into a chair opposite.

'I just thought you may have reason to want to stay here, that is all.'

'What reason could I have?' she asked sharply, wondering what he knew.

He sighed and said, 'We leave in the morning. I trust I can leave all the packing to you, my dear. You know what I want to take. I am going to bed.'

Lettice kicked the bedclothes back, for the night had turned very warm. 'I suppose you are writing to her.'

'Yes.' Robert sat at a table in the bay window. It was a light evening, and with the aid of a candle, he could just see well enough to write by. He dipped his quill in the ink and continued his letter to Elizabeth.

'You only left her three days ago.'

'She wants to know how I am, Lettice.'

Lettice sighed. She had grown tired of being jealous of the Queen. She still loved Robert, but since their son had died, a part of that love for him had died as well. She knew it was irrational, but some corner of her mind blamed him for their son's death. If Robert had spent more time with them and less with the Queen, maybe their boy would be alive. She shook away the thought, knowing that her eyes would fill with tears if she permitted herself to think of her dead son.

'Come to bed, Rob,' she called gently. 'Leave that damned letter to the morning.'

'I've finished anyway.' He threw down his quill and snuffed out the candle. He settled himself in the enormous bed gratefully and Lettice curled herself around him.

'Is that better?' she asked.

He grunted. 'Not really, Lettice, I feel like I'm wearing down.'

CORNBURY, OXFORDSHIRE

'Quick,' Lettice shouted to the gaping servants as she clambered from the coach. 'My husband needs to be taken to his bed at once. You,' she pointed at a young girl, 'go to the village. Order the physician to attend my husband at once. Tell him he is grievously ill.'

Robert cried out in pain as he stumbled to the front door of the lodge. Several pairs of hands gripped his arms and guided him towards the hall. A chair was placed beneath him and he fell into it, clutching at his burning stomach. He heard Lettice barking orders to the servants, then felt himself lifted into the air. Four men had taken hold of the chair and were carrying him up the stairs to his bedchamber.

He must have passed out, for he did not remember being put to bed, yet when he opened his eyes, he was flat on his back with the bedclothes pulled up to his chin. He licked his dry lips.

'Lettice?' he whispered, and from the window, a black shape moved to the side of the bed.

'I'm here,' she said gently, leaning over to stroke his brow.

'The pain—'

'I know, dearest. The doctor is here. He wants to give you something for the pain.'

'My lady,' the surgeon steered Lettice away from the bedside, 'there is nothing more I can do.'

'Nothing?'

'The earl is dying. It's only a matter of time.'

Lettice looked over the doctor's shoulder, at her husband who was in so much pain, dying before her very eyes. Even now, William Haynes, one of Robert's pages, leant over his master and attempted to place a cup of the doctor's medicine to his lips, but with what little energy Robert had, he swept William's hand aside. William came over to Lettice.

'My lady,' he said softly, 'he refuses the medicine. Perhaps you should try?'

Lettice suddenly gripped the doctor's wrist. 'There is something you could do. Your medicine. A larger dose, that would… that would—'

'My lady,' the doctor interrupted, horrified. 'I could not do that.'

'God rot you,' Lettice snarled. 'My husband is in agony and you yourself say that he is dying, that you can do no more for him. So, release him. Let him die, I beg you.'

'No, my lady. For the sake of my immortal soul, I cannot do as you ask.'

Robert slipped in and out of consciousness. When he was awake, he thought of Lettice. He knew she would survive without him. Knew it and was not upset. But then he thought of Elizabeth and was glad that at least someone would mourn him. How would she bear the loss of him? They had been together for more years than some people were married. They had had their arguments, their jealousies, and their separate betrayals. Yet, they had stayed together and loved. What was a marriage if it was not that?

He also thought of his family; not Lettice, not his stepfamily, but that family he had lost so many years before. Of his mother, of his brothers, but most especially, of his father. He had tried to live his life in a way that would have made his father proud but he knew he had failed. He had tried for a crown and Elizabeth and Amy's death had defeated him; he had tried to become a great soldier but pride had defeated him; he had tried to continue the Dudley line and death had defeated him. The room darkened still more and the voices grew fainter.

Robert Dudley closed his weary eyes and died.

CHAPTER 48

WHITEHALL PALACE

Cecil limped along the Long Gallery, wincing with each step, his gouty left foot a throbbing agony. As he passed the large windows, he looked out into the gardens of the palace and saw courtiers in an unusual state of happiness. He wished he was young enough to feel the same for he knew the jubilation could not last the month.

Or at least, he hoped not. He understood the need to celebrate; a little island had not only withstood but fought off the might of Spain and that didn't happen every day. But the expense! The costs had being going around his head all night and he wondered at the Queen's willingness to spend so much. But then, she was happy, and he was pleased to see her so.

He heard feet running up behind him and he turned stiffly.

'My lord.' One of his pages was holding out a letter to him. 'One of Lord Leicester's men just delivered this.'

Cecil took the letter and tried to ease his thumb under the sealed flap but he was hampered by his long walking stick. He gave the letter back to the boy and told him to break the seal on the letter. 'Read it, boy.'

The boy read the contents of the letter aloud and then looked up at his master.

Cecil's face had turned grey. He stared out of the window, watching the courtiers as they laughed. 'He gives with one hand, and takes with the other,' he muttered.

'Cecil,' Elizabeth halloed with a wide smile as the chamber doors opened. 'Sir Francis here was just telling me how the Irish are taking care of the Spaniards.'

Cecil gave a curt nod to the stocky Drake. 'Indeed, madam. You must tell me later, Sir Francis.'

Elizabeth grinned, curling herself into a chair. 'I don't mind hearing the story again.'

'I will hear it later,' Cecil said firmly. 'Sir Francis, would you mind leaving us?'

'Is something wrong, Cecil?' Elizabeth frowned when Drake had gone.

'Yes, madam, something is indeed wrong.' He paused, uncertain how to frame his next sentence. 'I have received news from the Countess of Leicester.'

'What news do I want to hear from that woman?'

'Madam,' he said with a deep sigh, 'the Earl of Leicester has died.'

Elizabeth stared at him. His heart quickened as her amber eyes widened and darkened to brown. Her throat with its sagging skin tightened.

She rose slowly, her hands gripping the pommels of the chair. 'Robin ... dead?'

'He died at Cornbury, on his way to take the waters at Buxton.'

'He wasn't well when he left,' she said falteringly. 'That's it,' she pointed a shaking finger at him. 'Your message got it wrong. He's not dead, he's ill. He will be well again.'

'Madam, there has been no mistake. The Countess herself has written this letter.

'You cannot trust that woman,' Elizabeth shrieked. 'She lies, she always lies. Look,' she said suddenly, passing through the open doorway that led to her bedchamber, 'look at this.' She snatched up a letter from a table by the window. She thrust it into his hand and he saw the image on the broken seal, the bear and ragged staff, the Earl of Leicester's emblem. 'He wrote to me not a week ago.'

'He died three days ago, madam. I do not lie to you.'

'He can't be,' she cried, shaking her head. 'He wouldn't leave me.'

'He would never have done so willingly.'

Elizabeth looked at him, her face contorting as her tears fell. He smiled sympathetically. Then she sprang at him. Her thin, bony hands pushed him backwards. He almost fell as she forced him from the room. She yanked the doors shut and he heard the key turning in the lock.

Then he heard a thud against the wood, a sliding sound, sobbing. He knocked lightly, pressing his ear to the door. 'Your Majesty?'

VOLUME TWO

THE QUEEN'S REBEL

"I was ever sorry that your lordship should fly with waxen wings, doubting Icarus's fortune."

- FRANCIS BACON

PROLOGUE

ASH WEDNESDAY, 1601

It was early at the Palace of Whitehall and the winter sun had only just begun to lighten the sky.

Servants had risen to perform their duties, but all courtiers were still in their beds. All except Robert Cecil. He had been awake for hours, listening to the steady breathing of his wife beside him. What sleep he had managed to get had been broken and inadequate. As his back began to ache from immobility, he grew worried that he would disturb his wife if he turned over to find a more comfortable position and so rose, thinking that as he was awake, he may as well go to work.

Cecil went to his office, savouring the slightly musty odour of parchment and herbs crushed beneath the rush matting and the smoky, woody smell of the fire his manservant was kindling in the grate. He opened the wooden window shutters himself, and when the fire had caught and was beginning to warm the room, dismissed his servant, refusing the man's suggestion that he bring food so that he could break his fast.

Cecil was not hungry, not this morning. He stood at the table that held pile after pile of state papers: reports from his agents, petitions for lands, requests for positions at court, and some that even asked for justice. He pulled out a file and opened it. He read a few sentences but their meaning did not register and he had forgotten them before he moved on to the next. The file was shut and thrown aside. In exasperation, he looked for something else in his office he could occupy himself with. His black eyes fell upon a small stack of items that had been delivered late the previous night by a Tower messenger. Two miniature portraits, a pair of leather gloves, a roll of parchment and a book, a book whose leather binding looked a little familiar.

Intrigued, Cecil opened it. He scanned the lines and recognised the story of Sir Gawain and the Green Knight. It was, he realised with surprise, his father's old copy of *Le Morte d'Arthur*. He carried the volume to his desk and sat, easing his misshapen shoulder into the padded rear cushion of the chair. Laying the book across his lap, he turned over the front cover. A memory came, immediate, without warning, making his eyes sting from the tears that pricked at their rims. He had forgotten what he had once written on the flyleaf: '*To Robert Devereux, Earl of Essex, from his loving friend, Robert Cecil.*'

He had been thirteen years old when he had written those words twenty-five years earlier. Had there ever been a time when he and Robert Devereux had been friends?

He re-read the inscription and the scene was suddenly, vividly, in his mind. He and Robert had been in his father's study at Burghley House on the Strand, he taking advantage of the old man's absence to show Robert some of the house's treasures. Robert had gravitated towards the room's collection of books that were kept on shelves in a recess. Cecil had stood at his father's desk, on the same spot he stood to watch his father work at his state papers.

Robert Devereux had only been at Burghley House a week, coming as a ward of court. His father, Walter Devereux, had died in Ireland, leaving his nine-year-old son the holder of the Essex earldom. Robert had been like all the other boys who came to the house to stay. Boys who laughed at Cecil's limp and pointed at the hump in his back, boys who rode horses and practised archery while Cecil stayed indoors and worked hard at his lessons, telling himself he enjoyed them because he could not join in with the others in their sport. He had dismissed Robert as just such another creature until the handsome boy had spoken of poetry and shyly shown some of his own scribblings to the stunted son of the house. The poetry had been poor, he remembered, but the gesture had been rich, and Cecil had felt warmth towards a fellow boy for what may have been the first time in his short life.

That day in his father's study, Cecil had obeyed an unfamiliar impulse and taken down the book from where it sat on the lowest shelf, believing Robert would enjoy it more than any other. He had shuffled back to the desk, dipped a quill into the inkpot and, dripping ink over the dark-brown oak desk, written the inscription. Drying the writing with a shower of sand from the shaker, he had closed the book and held it out to Robert.

Robert, his light brown eyes twinkling in the sunlight, had taken the book, read the inscription and thanked Cecil, declaring it to be a fine present.

It was also a costly one, as Cecil found out later that evening when his father returned from court and noticed the Devereux boy deep in study with the book in his lap. His father had taken Cecil aside and reminded him that the books on the shelves were not Cecil's to give away. But Lord Burghley, not being a mean man, had not embarrassed his best-loved son by making him ask for the book's return. Instead, Cecil had to pay for the book, which meant eight months without his allowance. It had been a memorable punishment, but the boy Cecil never regretted the present.

Cecil turned some of the book's pages at random. There, in the margins, was Robert's handwriting. It had not been done recently for the letters were almost clumsy, lacking the style of the adult. He had written words such as *wonderful*, *heroic*, *foolish* and Cecil thought how aptly they could be used to describe the man Robert Devereux had become.

He heard a click, loud in the quiet room, and looked up to see the latch on his office door lift and the door open.

Elizabeth Tudor stood in the doorway, dressed in a linen nightshift, a green silk dressing gown, and with a nightcap covering her thin, grey hair. It was only the second time Cecil had seen her look so unadorned, devoid of finery, devoid even of the white lead paint that he could now see hid several liver spots on her forehead and cheeks. The shock of her appearance passed and he realised he was still seated. He moved to rise, but she waved him to be still and stepped into the room.

'You are here early, Pygmy,' she said, shuffling past him to the window and pressing her forehead to the glass, sighing softly as it cooled her skin.

'I have much work, madam,' he pretended.

'You are always working. Such a busy little elf.' She turned and pointed to the book. 'But that does not look like work.'

Cecil laid his fingers almost protectively over the leather cover. 'No. It's Malory. *Le Morte d'Arthur*. It belongs to the earl.'

'His favourite book. Many nights he read to me...' She broke off and turned back to the window. 'What time is it?'

Cecil glanced at the clock on his desk, a gift from the Queen to his father, given some ten years earlier. 'It is not quite the hour. Madam, I must ask. Were you not minded to rescind the order?'

She looked at him over her shoulder, one plucked eyebrow arching. 'Would you have had me do that, Pygmy?'

He shrugged as if it were a matter of little importance. 'By law, he is rightfully condemned. I merely thought your fondness for the earl—'

'My fondness ended when he tried to depose me,' she snarled. 'Would you have me free such a traitor?'

'I would not have you free him, no,' he protested, getting to his feet, 'but why not imprisonment? Would that not be punishment enough?'

'Why, Pygmy, are you playing the advocate for your old adversary?'

He opened his mouth to answer, but church bells across London began to toll the eighth hour, the small clock echoing them with a more delicate chime. As the eighth bell died away, Elizabeth turned away from the window.

'You are too late, Pygmy. If you wanted Essex to live you should have appealed to me sooner. It would have been a pleasant surprise to discover you possessed a heart after all.'

She knocked a quick tattoo on the windowsill and left his office, closing the door behind her. Cecil sank slowly into his chair. He heard the rustle and drag of Elizabeth's dressing gown on the floorboards, the slap of her slippers as she made her way to the music room a few doors along the corridor. Moments later, he heard her playing a merry tune upon the virginals.

Cecil turned the book's pages back to his inscription, read the words once more, and held the book to his chest. He breathed in the smell of the paper and the leather, fancying he could detect the smell of Robert himself.

Elizabeth continued to play while Cecil wept.

CHAPTER 1

Elizabeth Tudor forced a wan smile onto her face as the young man sat opposite her at the table glanced up and shuffled the pack of cards.

It had been only a few days since she had unlocked her privy chamber door and allowed her ladies and counsellors in to tend her. She had not cared that her thin body was covered only by a soiled shift, her magnificent dress having been torn off, nor that her lustrous red wig had been discarded upon the floor. She had not cared, for Leicester was dead. Her dearest, truest friend was gone.

When she had first been given the news of the Earl of Leicester's death, she had locked herself in her rooms. She had cried, not quietly, not like a woman, but like an animal that had been mortally wounded, with savage sounds that forced their way up from the very core of her body. Her howls had scraped the sides of her throat, leaving it raw and capable only of mewling noises that came once her initial anguish had subsided.

For the first two days of her seclusion, she had not eaten, only drunk the wine she had found in a cabinet, not bothering to dilute it with water as was her normal practice. For once, she wanted to be drunk, to feel that sense of numbness, that insensibility to pain that alcohol offered.

On the third day, her stomach had begun to ache for lack of sustenance and her fingers had grabbed at the few walnuts that had been left over from a four-day-old meal. But they could not satisfy her long.

On the fourth day, having experienced enough of solitude, she had let the world back in.

Her ladies, hurrying in, had viewed with shock the chaos of her bedchamber: the books scattered upon the floor, her jewels, earrings and necklaces tossed aside, the stench of her piss and shit as it festered in the close stool. Her older female companions who understood better what she was feeling had fluttered around her, fussing without asking any questions, while the younger ladies held back, willing to concern themselves only with the tidying of the room, not the emotional crisis of an old woman.

Silent and distant, Elizabeth had let her ladies bathe and dress her. Silently, she listened to Lord Burghley and Sir Francis Walsingham express their condolences at the Earl of Leicester's death, while she secretly scorned them for their poorly hid relief at her reappearance. They were there even now, at the periphery of her vision, huddled together, anxiously looking out for any further signs of weakness from her. They need not have worried. Elizabeth had her mask back on.

So, here she was, dressed in one of her most glittering gowns, her face and bosom covered with a thin layer of white lead paste, her cheeks and lips smeared with red cochineal, her wrists daubed with civet perfume and her thinning ginger hair covered with a tightly curled red wig, playing cards as if Leicester had not died. Playing with Robert Devereux, his stepson, who she knew had been sent for to cheer her up. Robert was grieving too, for he had loved Leicester dearly. Elizabeth thought kindly of him for that.

Robert had dealt the cards and was looking at her expectantly. His brown eyes were kind, enquiring. He did not ask her if she were well. She would never be well again, and he, this boy of soft countenance and sweet charm, somehow realised that.

'I wish I could take the pain away,' he said, his hand reaching across the table to hers, not considering, or perhaps not caring, that it was not permitted for a subject to touch a sovereign uninvited.

'You ease it, my lord,' she replied, sliding her hand away to pick up her cards, 'which is all I can hope for.'

Robert spread his cards, fanlike, in his hand and began the game. 'My mother is broken-hearted.'

He mentions his mother ingenuously, she thought. *There is no inflection in his voice that points to a caution, the holding of a hidden meaning. He does not mention his mother, that she-wolf Lettice who stole Leicester from me, to wound, so I cannot be unkind to him.* 'Is she?' she murmured.

'I did wonder if I should be with her,' he continued, 'but then I realised she has my sisters for company, and of course, I could not leave you.'

To Elizabeth's ears, he actually sounded as if he meant what he said. *Does he? Can he? Is it possible?* 'You are very kind to think of me, my lord.'

'Please,' he said, leaning forward a little, 'will you not call me Robert? 'My lord' - it puts me at such a distance from you.'

She smiled, a true smile this time. 'Not Robert,' she said with a little shake of her head that set her pearl earrings jiggling, 'Robin.'

He frowned, his smooth, high forehead becoming marred by a single, deep crease. 'Did you not call the Earl of Leicester so?'

'I did,' she nodded sadly. 'He was my bonny sweet Robin. But it would please me to call *you* Robin. Do you object?'

'If it please you, madam, then, of course, I do not.'

Elizabeth nodded and laid down a card. No man could ever replace Leicester, but if any man could lessen the loss of him, she felt that perhaps Robert Devereux was that man.

Cecil opened the door of his father's private office and entered. Of all his father's offices in every of the Queen's palaces, it was this one at Whitehall with its small, diamond-leaded windows and panelled walls hidden behind piles of papers that he loved the most. He loved it for the feeling of comfort and security it gave him, folding around him like a fur cloak. He sat down in the special chair his father had brought in from home for him, custom-made so that his humped shoulder was cushioned as he sat.

'What is she doing?' Lord Burghley asked, not looking up from the papers he was working on.

'Writing poetry with the Earl of Essex, Father.'

Burghley pondered this for a long moment, tapping his quill against his lips. 'Good,' he decided eventually.

'Is it good?' Cecil wondered quietly, glancing at his father from beneath lowered lids.

'What harm can it do?'

'Well, that's the question, is it not?'

'My boy,' Burghley put down his quill and looked at his son, 'the Queen has her favourites. It took me a long time to accept it but accept it I did. I had to. For thirty years, her favourite was the Earl of Leicester. In the beginning, I felt him to be a problem, distracting the Queen from her duties and giving her ill advice, but it became obvious to me that the Queen would not countenance parting with him. I found I had to either work with Leicester or forsake the Queen. And I must admit Leicester did have his uses.'

'But the Earl of Leicester was of a similar age to the Queen. Essex is so much younger than she.'

'The Queen is missing her favourite, so she has found another to keep her company, that is all. Essex is a plaything, an amusement for her leisure hours. She has always had a need for handsome young men about her.'

'Which I am not,' Cecil said bitterly.

He knew he was not handsome, disfigured as he was with a hunched back and a shortened left leg that made him limp and could not help but envy his handsome peers who were. It seemed to him that people were ready to believe, forgive or excuse a great deal if a person had been blessed with a beautiful exterior. And it certainly did nothing for Cecil's self-esteem to be called Pygmy by Elizabeth. When Elizabeth had first called him so, even Burghley had been shocked and upset at so unkind a nickname, but he had tried to persuade his son that with Elizabeth a nickname was a mark of favour. Cecil knew that his father spoke true, but the name still hurt.

'What you are is better, my son. These handsome young men like the Earl of Essex are only good for entertaining and flattering the Queen. They cannot govern her kingdom for her, but *you* can, Robert. It is what I have trained you for all these years. When I'm gone—'

'Please, Father,' Cecil said, holding out his hand and closing his eyes, 'please do not talk of it.'

Burghley sighed and picked up the quill again. 'It will come, my boy, whether you allow me to speak of it or not. And when my time comes, you will be able to serve the Queen as I have done. She will have need of you then.'

'And what am I to do in the meantime? I cannot dance nor write poetry—'

'We will have to see. You will continue to help me with my work, I trust?'

'Of course, I will, Father.'

But, Cecil thought, *I would have liked it if I could have been made just a little bit handsome. Not to attract the Queen, but because... well, just because.*

As if he knew what his son was thinking, Burghley reached across the table and patted Cecil's small hand. 'Let the Queen have her young men, my boy. Your time will come.'

His wife was already in bed when Cecil returned to his rooms. Like many women of her generation, his wife was named Elizabeth after the Queen. In the short time they had been married, she had grown used to her husband's late hours and always left a candle burning by his bedside.

Cecil entered the bedchamber as quietly as he was able and began undressing, groaning softly as the action of taking off his shirt stretched the atrophied muscles in his shoulder.

A light sleeper, Elizabeth awoke. 'Husband?'

'Oh, did I wake you?'

'Yes,' Elizabeth yawned. 'Is your back hurting?'

'A little. It's been a long day.'

'Shall I rub it?'

Cecil shifted further up the bed and presented his bare back to her, unconcerned as he would have been with others that she would find the deformed shape of it unpleasant. Their marriage, like all alliances of their class, had been arranged, but Cecil could not have hoped to be conjoined with, in his eyes at least, a more perfect woman.

'Did you talk to your father?' Elizabeth asked as her fingers probed and rubbed his shoulder.

'I did,' he said, closing his eyes and wincing as her ministrations caused him both pleasure and pain. 'He said I should not worry about Essex.'

'You sound like you think he is wrong and you should worry. There, that's enough. Get into bed.' Elizabeth patted his pillows to plump them up.

Cecil leant back against them, a weariness creeping up on him. 'He doesn't see things the way I do. Father thinks that all I have to do is work hard and the Queen will reward me.'

'He has known her for a long time, Robert.'

'But he has a biased view of her. I am sure he still thinks of her as she was when she first became queen. But she is different now. I have seen the change in her. I remember her when I was a boy and Father let me come to court and watch him work. The Earl of Leicester was alive and everyone knew how close they were. She was, I am not sure… kinder, somehow.'

'She loved Leicester and maybe she was happier then. And with Essex, well, perhaps she feels she still has something of Leicester. I believe Essex and Leicester were very close, even though there was no blood tie.'

'Yes, I think they were. It surprises me though, that the Queen should welcome Essex as she does.'

'Because he is Lettice Devereux's son?'

'Elizabeth hates the woman for marrying Leicester and I know she is eager to do that lady all the ill she can. Why, as soon as Leicester died, she was calling in his debts so that the countess would have to pay them. Elizabeth may have been grief-stricken at Leicester's loss, but the Queen is never sentimental when it comes to money. So, you would naturally think that she would not wish to favour any of the Devereux children, would you not?'

'Perhaps she does so for Leicester's sake?'

'Perhaps,' Cecil said doubtfully. 'But I think she just likes the looks of Essex.'

'He is very handsome. So tall. He stands a full head above everyone else at court.'

'Does he indeed?' Cecil muttered. 'How very impressive.'

'Oh, husband,' Elizabeth scolded, slapping his arm lightly. 'What does he matter? I think your father is right to counsel you not to worry. You have no wish to be a favourite, do you? To be entirely dependent on the Queen? To have to write love letters to her? To be on hand at all hours of the day and night? To not be allowed to show interest in other women for fear the Queen will grow jealous?'

'Well, I already have my wife, and no other woman will look at me twice, so there is no fear of that.'

'Oh, shush. Why must you always think that I made such a bad bargain in our marriage? I love you, Robert, though you think you do not deserve it. I do not care that you are only a few inches taller than me or that your back is crooked. You have a fine mind and I know that you love me. It is enough. Had I made another marriage, who is to say that my husband would love me so well as you?'

'You would not have preferred the handsome Earl of Essex?' he asked playfully.

'No, I would not. I do not know him well, but I think he is not so pleasant as he appears.'

'He can be cruel,' Cecil said quietly, his mind travelling back to his youth. 'But then he can also be kind. In fact, he can be whatever he has in his mind to be. That is his attraction.'

'Do you know, I cannot work out whether you like him or not?'

'I admire him, and the truth is, I envy him, Elizabeth. He is loved by many, he has favour, he has beauty, he has talents. I could like him better were he not so proud. When we were young, he was always boasting about his family, how the Devereuxs could trace their ancestry back to the Conquest. "Mine is a proud and lofty heritage," he would say. "We Devereuxs are destined for great things. It is in my blood".'

Elizabeth laughed. 'He said that?'

'I swear he did,' Cecil laughed too. 'So you see, how can I possibly compete with his glorious destiny?'

CHAPTER 2

CHARTLEY, 1589

Sir Christopher Blount uncrossed his legs, careful not to tread on the skirts of Lettice Devereux sitting by his side. He looked sideways at her, wondering if she was going to speak, but her profile appeared resolutely silent. Her chin, somewhat marred by a bulge of sagging flesh, was thrust forward, her lips pursed, and her eyes fixed on her son as he stood by the window.

Christopher followed her gaze, wishing he knew what Robert was thinking. Anger, of course, and resentment, that was to be expected upon hearing such news, but what else? Christopher had known Robert since he was a young boy and had lost his father, Walter, to the flux in Ireland. Christopher had been in service to Leicester as his Gentleman of the Horse and had often taken Robert riding. He knew all too well of Robert's changeable moods that were almost impossible to predict and thought it best he remain silent, at least until it was clear what Robert's attitude to him was going to be.

Robert, dressed in travelling clothes, had arrived at Chartley, his country home in the county of Warwickshire, a quarter of an hour earlier, a little weary from the long journey from London, but otherwise looking fine and healthy. Lettice had greeted her son with a tight embrace and a smacking kiss that had left a patch of red cochineal on Robert's cheek. Christopher had followed at Lettice's heels into the entrance hall, and before Robert and he had had a chance to greet one another, Lettice had introduced him as her husband. Robert had stared at them both in astonishment, then stalked past them without a word into the room all three now occupied.

'Do you not think it unseemly, Mother?' Robert said at last, keeping his back to Christopher and Lettice. 'You have been but six months a widow.'

'Would you have me alone for the rest of my life?' Lettice retorted shrilly, grabbing Christopher's hand and holding it firmly in her lap.

Was it a gesture of defiance, Christopher wondered, *or was she worried I would bolt?*

Robert turned to face them. 'But you are not alone, Mother. You have Dorothy and Penelope and Walter. You have me.'

Lettice drew in a deep breath. 'Robert, my darling, as much as I love you, you cannot give me what a husband can.'

Christopher saw Robert's cheeks flush and felt the heat in his own, but he knew that if Lettice's cheeks flushed beneath her paint, it was through determination, not shame. He felt it was time he spoke. 'Do not criticise your mother, Rob, she is not the only one to blame. I know you think that I have betrayed our friendship and I am sorry for that.'

'And Leicester?' Robert demanded, coming towards him and almost knocking over a small octagonal table. 'Did you betray *him*?'

Before Christopher could reply, Lettice threw his hand away and rose. 'I loved your stepfather, Robert, but even you must have realised he was no husband to me by the end. I turned to Christopher for comfort.'

There, it was out, Christopher winced. *Did Lettice have to admit that we cuckolded Leicester?*

'Did Leicester know?' Robert asked, horrified.

Lettice's narrow shoulders shrugged. 'I think not. If he did, he never mentioned it. And remember, Robert, before you condemn me, that for all the time I knew him, I had to share Leicester with Elizabeth. I was never allowed to have him all to myself. Have you considered that?'

Robert raised his eyes to hers and Christopher saw that they had softened. 'You are right, Mother. I have no right to criticise you. Nor you, Chris. Forgive me.'

Lettice moved towards Robert and tugged his sleeve, an

instruction for him to lower his head to her to receive another kiss. 'Good. I do so hate to quarrel. Now, I shall leave you two boys to talk while I have a lie down. I am feeling tired. Be sure to eat something, Robert, not just drink. Christopher, my dearest, see that he does.'

Christopher assured her he would and Lettice withdrew, closing the oak door behind her. Christopher waited a moment until he heard her footsteps on the wooden stairs and then turned to Robert. 'Shall we have that drink first?' he asked mutinously.

Robert nodded, smiling at the conspiracy. 'We must toast your marriage. No,' he held up a hand as Christopher opened his mouth to speak, 'let us say no more on the matter. It is done and cannot be undone.'

Christopher handed him a cup of wine, realising by the last statement that could the marriage be undone, Robert would be happy to see it. 'Thank you, Rob, very generous of you.' He returned to his seat. 'It is happening again, of course.'

Robert took a seat opposite and stretched out his long legs towards the fire. 'What is?'

'Your mother having to share with the Queen. We hear you are greatly in favour.'

Robert smiled shyly. 'In truth I am, Chris. Elizabeth must have me near her, no matter what time of day or night. We talk, we write, we ride, we play games.'

'That does not sound very arduous. How wonderful. Tell me, what do you think of the Queen?'

'She is not unlike Mother,' Robert said and they both laughed. 'It can be quite disconcerting. They even have the same laugh.'

'Well, they are cousins. But I hope it is not all take take take on the Queen's part?'

Robert looked away, swirling the wine in his cup. 'I have the Master of the Horse.'

'You got that post from Leicester. What is Elizabeth doing for you? You must get something from her, Rob, else your attendance at court is all for naught.'

'I know, Chris, and I am sure something will come.'

'Then you must needs be patient? Is that how it is? You have many virtues, Rob, but let me tell you, patience is not one of them.'

'I am trying. I ask for this and that from Elizabeth, but I am not the only one petitioning her. There is Ralegh.'

'Still? I would have thought he would have disappeared on one of his voyages or swaggered back to Devon by now.'

Robert sighed and gestured hopelessly. 'He appears immovable. The Queen graces him with favour, yet I cannot understand why. After all, what is Ralegh? A lowly knight from some backwater in the West Country. Why should he enjoy sovereign favour the same as I?'

'Well, as for that, I am but a lowly knight myself, Rob,' Christopher reminded him, 'yet here I am, husband to a countess. I have risen.'

'Yes, my mother has certainly raised you,' Robert nodded, unaware of any offence he might cause, 'yet still you know your degree and pay me all due deference as your better. Ralegh is no respecter of rank. He seeks to rise, but what has he to recommend himself?'

Christopher shrugged. 'A handsome face, a ready wit, and a willingness to please. What else does he need?'

Robert grunted. 'Elizabeth has made him Captain of the Guard. He is always nearby. If I am in the chamber with her, then Ralegh is at the door. If the Queen and I walk in the gardens or ride in the Chase, Ralegh is there, not ten feet away. Remember when the Queen and I visited Warwick Castle? Dorothy was there too and when Elizabeth found out, she said she must stay in her room because she didn't want to have to look upon her, and just for marrying without her permission. My sister, Chris! I told Elizabeth that she was being cruel and she just laughed at me. I saw her look past me to Ralegh – he was standing by the door – and they both laughed. At me! I could not bear it.'

'You left, didn't you?'

'Of course, I left. I wasn't going to put up with such an insult, not just to my sister, but to me. And I certainly wasn't going to be made the butt of jests between Elizabeth and that bastard Ralegh.'

'You made your point though, Robert,' Christopher assured

him. 'After all, Elizabeth sent someone after you to fetch you back, didn't she? She obviously knew she had upset you.'

'Aye, brought back like a wayward child. I shouldn't have allowed myself to be treated in that way. And there was no rebuke to Ralegh. Elizabeth did nothing, though I insisted she punish him.'

'If she is that keen on him, you may then have to put up with the fellow.'

'I cannot bear to. The man is odious. I did think perhaps I should try to discredit him in some way.'

Christopher grunted and rubbed his temple. 'Be careful, Rob. That may take more practised hands than yours and such manoeuvring needs a subtler, more cunning nature than you possess. I would not want you to undo yourself.'

'Perhaps you are right. I have not the courtier's nature,' Robert said proudly. 'I should not concern myself with the Raleghs of this world. I must rise by my own merits, not by doing down another, an unworthy fellow. Let us talk of other, happier things. Mother gave her order and we have failed to obey, Chris. Let us eat.'

CHAPTER 3

HAMPTON COURT PALACE

Sir Walter Ralegh weaved his way around the box hedges of the palace gardens, nodding greetings to the men and women of his own station that he passed, bowing elegantly to those in rank above him. As he cleared the formal gardens with their beautiful roses and aromatic herb beds and painted figures of unicorns and other mythical creatures mounted on posts and entered into the wooded area, he looked about him to make sure that he was not observed.

'There you are, at last.' Bess Throckmorton pushed herself away from the tree she had been leaning against and waited for Ralegh to move nearer.

'My my, Bess, how very impatient you are,' he said, bending to kiss her lips.

Bess turned her head away, so that his lips brushed against her cheek. 'You know I will be missed if I am away too long.'

Less than an hour earlier, they had both been in the Queen's privy chambers, Bess in attendance on the Queen and Ralegh being given his instructions for the day as Captain of the Guard, receiving a list of who had an audience with the Queen so that they would be seen in the correct order. Ralegh had not looked in Bess's direction, had not greeted her or engaged in a pleasant exchange. It was not wise to pay attention to other ladies in the Queen's presence, though Bess would have been happy to receive even a fleeting glance from her lover. She had hastily scribbled a note while Ralegh talked to the Queen, then slid it into his hand under pretence of passing him a cup of beer. With consummate ease, he had placed the note inside his cuff, Elizabeth never realising that an assignation had been made.

'I can leave,' Ralegh said carelessly, 'if you think you ought to get back.'

Bess's throat constricted. How could he say such a thing unless he did not truly love her? She knew that there were plenty of women at court who would gladly submit to his caresses, but he had picked her out from all of them and she was not sure why. 'Do you not want to see me?'

'Of course, I do, my love, but not if you are going to nag me. There are far pleasanter things we could be talking about. Or doing.'

He leant in towards her and Bess felt herself melting as she breathed in the smell of his skin. She allowed herself to be kissed.

'There now, is that not better?' he said, nuzzling her neck.

She moaned, bending her body to his, only stopping when his hand began to lift her skirts. 'No, Walter, I must not.'

Ralegh let her skirts drop, disappointed but not displeased. She had said 'must not' when she could have said 'cannot' or 'will not'. There was hope yet. He sat down at the base of the tree, choosing a spot between its large, protruding roots. Bess settled alongside him and he lifted his arm to place around her shoulder.

'Walter, you will be careful, won't you?' she asked.

'Careful about what, you silly little thing?'

'The Earl of Essex. He means you ill.'

'I know he does, but I fear nothing from that quarter.'

'He has the Queen's favour.'

'As do I.'

Bess wanted to say that that was all very well, but as Essex had pointed out to anybody who would listen, he was an earl and Walter only a knight. Essex, by his very rank, was entitled to command the Queen's affection, and favour could be withdrawn as easily as it was bestowed. But she knew that such talk would only anger Walter and she did not want their tryst to be spoilt. 'It makes me furious to hear him talk of you,' she said instead, playing with a gold button on his doublet.

'What does the Queen say when he does so?'

'She rebukes him, but not strongly enough, if you ask me. I think you should criticise him when you are with the Queen.'

'And make me seem as petty as he?'

'Why not, my love?'

'I shall not do it, Bess, and do not entreat me to. Besides, I have better things to talk about when I am with Elizabeth. I am not going to waste my time talking of Essex when I could be furthering my own causes. I want her to fund expeditions to the New World, Bess. I need to convince her that they are worthwhile ventures. I cannot do that if all I do is complain about Essex.'

'Do you love her?' Bess asked.

Ralegh glanced down at her. 'Is this a trap? If I say I do love her, then you will ask whether I love you? If I say I do not love her, will you hurl abuse at me for being such a hypocritical wretch?'

'No,' Bess protested, 'I just wondered, that is all.'

'She is the Queen, Bess, so of course, I love her. She is an intelligent woman and I admire her for that. She is a survivor and I cannot help but think her great. When I consider what she has been through...' His voice trailed off as his mind considered the threats on Elizabeth's life, her questionable birthright, her dangerous adversaries and how she had outwitted them all in the end. 'She is a queen for a man to be proud of, that you cannot deny.'

'You would not say so if you were one of her ladies,' Bess replied sourly. 'What we have to endure! Boxings, tantrums, harsh words, and I know not what else.'

'She does not like women,' Ralegh laughed, patting her hand.

'You sound as if you understand her.'

'I do understand her for I have known other women like her. She does not like women because she sees them as rivals. Especially young women, like you.' He kissed her forehead. 'She is growing old, Bess, and the men who helped her in her youth are leaving her service to retire or else are dying. Look who she has to serve her these days, look who are all the old men's replacements.'

'You?' Bess teased.

'Yes, me, but I am the exception,' he said, only half in jest. 'Look at Essex. He aspires to a great office of state – I know he does, though he hasn't dared or thought to ask her yet – but would you honestly feel safe with the fate of the country in Essex's hands? And his friends, too. The Earl of Southampton, for instance. That young man only cares for himself. Cannot pass a mirror without examining his pretty face. And Cecil,' Ralegh drew a breath in through his teeth, 'that one. He has his eyes on the main chance. I doubt his own father knows what is going on in his mind, but it is not total subservience to the Queen, despite what old Burghley believes. I wouldn't be surprised if Cecil were already communicating with King James up in Scotland. Getting ready for when Elizabeth is gone.'

'Maybe so, but not all of the young men at court would make such ill servants for the Queen. If only she would allow them the chance to prove themselves.'

Ralegh was surprised and impressed by Bess's perspicacity and told her so, suggesting that Elizabeth should make her one of her counsellors for Bess would prove able in the post. Bess laughed and agreed with him, saying if she were a counsellor, she would speak of nothing but Ralegh, if only she could be sure that Elizabeth would not think her words suspicious. Ralegh became serious and holding her at arm's length, cautioned her against saying anything in his favour, telling her that unfortunately, it would be better for them both if they acted as if they did not know one another.

'But will it always be so, Walter?' Bess pouted. 'Will we never be able to meet unless in secret?'

Ralegh sighed. 'It does not please me, Bess, you know that. But until I have what I want from Elizabeth, it is necessary. I must write my poems to her, and yet in truth, it is no chore, for I enjoy the writing of them. And I must dance attendance on her. But know that it is only because I must, not because I will it, despite my fondness for her. Do you want to know what is in my heart?' he asked, running his finger down her cheek.

'I do, Walter,' she replied earnestly.

'Well, I shall speak truth, my love, and tell you that I hope one day we can marry.'

'Oh, Walter. Then there are no other women?'

Ralegh frowned. 'Of course, there are no other women, you silly goose. Why do you ask that?'

Bess looked away, feeling foolish. 'Because I do not know what you find to love in me. It cannot be my face for it is as plain as can be, I know that. So what?'

'For all of you,' Ralegh said. 'I am not so stupid a man as to love a woman purely for her face. Youth passes, Bess, and beauty fades. There has to be something more for a man and woman to be happy with one another. We have that, do we not?'

Bess nodded. 'But it is natural for a man to have mistresses and I would not blame you for it, though it would pain me greatly. Essex has mistresses, I know. Several of the Queen's ladies have been in his bed. Walter,' she sat up, an idea suddenly occurring to her, 'why do you not tell the Queen of his mistresses? That will put you in good favour with her.'

'And put several of your friends in danger of the Queen's wrath and cause harm to their reputations. Bess, do not be so unkind to your fellows and do not ask me to be a telltale. It is not gentlemanly.'

Bess sighed and stood, brushing dirt from her pale green skirts. 'I love you even more for that sentiment, Walter my dear, though I wager if Essex knew about us, he would not hesitate to do us harm. Now I must get back or else she will box my ears. Adieu.'

'Adieu, sweet Bess,' Ralegh said and blew her a kiss, watching her as she entered the gardens and disappeared from sight.

She was right. Essex would use everything he could against him. But Ralegh had seen Elizabeth's face when she had grown tired and could not maintain the pretence of being charmed and amused by Essex's words and changeable moods, and her manner had exhibited signs of irritability and frustration. It was entirely possible, he supposed, that Essex would do himself harm without any help from him.

Although small in comparison to some other houses — Burghley's Theobalds, Hatton's Holdenby, Bess Talbot's Hardwick Hall — Chartley was undeniably pretty. It sat amongst the green, almost endless fields of the Warwickshire countryside, a decorative moat encircling the house where willow trees dipped their branches in the water.

Penelope Rich, hearing of Robert's return to their family home, had begged leave of her husband to visit her brother. She and Robert now lay on their favourite spot on the whole estate, a shaded area close to the stone bridge that crossed the moat.

'Do you really not mind about our mother and Blount marrying?' Penelope asked, twining a strand of chestnut brown hair around her finger. 'I thought you would be furious.'

Robert waved a bumblebee away from his nose. 'I think Mother could have made a happier choice. Christopher is only a knight, after all, but no, I do not mind.'

Penelope giggled. 'He is half her age, though. Our mother,' she shook her head in admiration. 'I only hope I will still have men willing to marry me when I am as old as she.'

'Have you not enough admirers already, Pen? Sidney worshipped you, you know?'

Sir Philip Sidney had been Leicester's nephew and heir and one of Elizabeth's most accomplished courtiers: urbane, witty, highly literate, and loved by all, except those men who considered him a rival. Sidney had, despite their respective spouses, fallen in love with Penelope and she had been the inspiration behind some of his most beautiful poetry.

Robert knew that his sister's marriage was far from happy. Her husband, Lord Richard Rich, had a vicious, suspicious nature and kept Penelope on a very tight rein. She hated him but was powerless to change her situation. His other sister, Dorothy, Robert reflected, had been only slightly more fortunate in her marriage. She at least loved her husband, but her elopement had earned the disapproval of the Queen, and like their mother, was forbidden to go to court.

'I do not suppose you are allowed to have any admirers of your own, are you?' Penelope said, determined to change the subject. 'Not with Elizabeth's eagle eye on you.'

'She makes it difficult,' Robert admitted, 'but assignations can be managed as long as I am careful.'

'I think it's awful that you have to be careful. You are a young man and you should be allowed to love where you please. Just because she is a dried-up old maid, she refuses to let anyone else love. Elizabeth is a true tyrant.'

'Only if I allow her to be, Pen. I do not intend to let her rule me as she did Leicester. I loved him and it pains me to criticise him, but he should not have let a woman have such complete mastery over him.'

'Why did he allow it, then? He was no milksop. He argued with Mother often enough and often refused to let her have her own way. If a man can refuse Mother, he can refuse any woman.'

'I suppose Leicester felt he had to be careful. The Dudleys were not a distinguished family. Everything Leicester had he got from Elizabeth, so he had to do all he could to please her.'

'There must have been more to their relationship than that, Robert. I always felt Leicester cared deeply for Elizabeth.'

'He may have done.'

'But not you?' Penelope probed.

'No, not me,' Robert cried indignantly, propping himself up on his elbows. 'She is the Queen, Pen, not my paramour. Elizabeth cannot be treated the same as other women, I grant you, and I respect her as my queen, but I will not lose my head over her.'

She reached for him, her expression grave. 'Promise me, Rob.'

Robert laughed at her seriousness. 'I promise.'

CHAPTER 4

GREENWICH PALACE

The sun shone bright, warming the steel of Robert's armour. Sweat clamped his shirt to his body, the helmet flattened his auburn curls against his skull and his eyes, peering through the slits, were gritty from the sandy dust of the tiltyard floor. Robert's horse pawed the ground as they stood at the end of the tilt, perhaps feeling as he did, hot and impatient.

Robert held out his arm and his oak lance was placed in his hand. He gripped the pole, pressing his gauntlet up against the coned guard and anchoring the butt beneath his armpit. His muscles ached as they strained to hold the heavy weapon and he squeezed his arm tighter, afraid he would drop it and look like a fool.

The master of the tilt raised his warder to signal that the jousting knights should make ready, and Robert soothed his mount, guiding the mare up to the mark. The warder was dropped and Robert squeezed his heels against the mare's flanks, and then all he could hear was the reverberation of the animal's hooves, loud inside the steel helmet, bruising his skull. His opponent was coming up fast, the tip of his lance juddering with the rise and fall of the horse.

And then Robert felt a numbing thud against his left shoulder, which threw him backwards and made him tumble from the saddle. He hit the sandy floor with a crunch of metal that did nothing to cushion the fall. All was noise for a few, long seconds, and then he felt hands helping him to sit up. His helmet was pulled off, the riveted metal scraping the skin of his cheeks. Robert's vision blurred from the sudden harsh sunlight, then cleared, and he could see the spectator stands with their coloured awnings flapping in the breeze, their occupants staring down at him with concern. His eyes sought out Elizabeth and they found her, risen from her seat and leaning forward on the wooden barrier rail.

'Is he hurt?' she called and someone at his side asked him the same question.

Unsure how he felt, Robert tried to rise, but the weight of his armour was too great and he fell back on the ground. Strong hands grabbed him beneath his armpits and hauled him to his feet. Robert found he could stand unaided and heard his unknown helper call out, 'The earl is unhurt, Your Majesty.'

Assured of his condition, Robert saw Elizabeth straighten. 'Well done, sir,' she called, and Robert thought it odd for him, an earl, to be called sir when he realised she was not speaking to him but to his opponent, Sir Charles Blount.

Blount, a distant cousin of Robert's new stepfather, was a young man with dark hair, a thin moustache and a handsome face. Blount stepped up to the wooden rail and bowed, his armour clanking as his body bent. Robert watched Elizabeth throw something, something that glinted and caught the sunlight. Whatever it was she threw, Blount caught it deftly, closing his gauntlet possessively around his prize.

Robert drew near the rail, wanting to know what it was Elizabeth had thrown. Blount, seeing him approach, held the favour in his open palm for him to witness and Robert saw a chess piece, a golden queen. He looked up at Elizabeth, who returned his gaze with equanimity. He held out his hand, ready to catch the favour she would bestow on him, but nothing came falling through the air, and Robert withdrew his hand in embarrassment.

'I applaud you, Sir Charles,' Elizabeth said and Blount made a clumsy bow, dropping the gold chess piece and scrabbling in the dirt to retrieve it while the spectators giggled.

'Now I see that every fool must have a favour,' Robert said loudly and the rising chatter hushed.

The favour safely back in his gauntlet, Blount turned on him. 'I do not deserve such an insult, my lord.'

'Do you not, sir?' Robert said, squaring up to him. 'Yet I have said you are a fool and none here gainsays me.'

Blount raked his eyes over the stands. Robert and he had an audience, an audience who was waiting eagerly to hear his next words. 'I cannot let this pass. Honour demands—'

'Are you challenging me to a duel, sir?'

Blount paused only a moment. 'I am, my lord.'

'What's that?' the shrill voice of Elizabeth cut in. 'Did I hear talk of a duel?'

'Honour demands it, Your Majesty,' Blount called to her.

'To the devil with your honour, sir,' she sneered. 'I have forbidden my courtiers to indulge in duels and I make no exceptions. Ladies, away.'

The spectators rose as one, her ladies and her counsellors following Elizabeth from the tiltyard stands and onto the gravel path that led back to the palace. Fuming at his impotence against the insult, Blount moved away, savagely pulling his gauntlets from his sweating hands.

Robert cast a glance towards the palace and the party that was disappearing through its gates, well out of earshot. He hurried after Blount. 'Name the place.'

Blount halted and stared at him. 'The Queen has forbidden a duel.'

'The Queen need not know.'

'I... I...,' Blount stammered, wanting to say to Robert that he was as ready as he to prove his manhood, but that he was wary of the Queen's wrath, too.

'Come, man, what does a woman know of honour? Are you a man or are you not?'

'I am a man, my lord,' Blount returned the taunt with vigour. 'I'll meet you, whenever and wherever you please.'

Robert drew himself up, satisfied. 'Tomorrow morning at seven in Marylebone Park.'

Lord Burghley, standing in front of Elizabeth as she sat at her desk in her private chamber, winced as his gouty foot throbbed and he waited for the pain to ebb away before speaking.

'Madam, I have been informed that the Earl of Essex and Sir Charles Blount engaged in a duel this morning in Marylebone Park.'

Elizabeth looked up from her book, her amber eyes darkening. 'They did what?'

'They fought a duel—'

'I expressly commanded that they were not to do so. How dare they?'

'I have no doubt that it was at the earl's instigation rather than Blount's. Indeed, I have been told that Blount protested it was contrary to your orders, but the earl challenged him on his manhood.'

'By God's Death,' Elizabeth tutted and reached for her cup of watered wine. 'Oh, sit down, Burghley, I know you are suffering. The earl needs taking down and taught better manners, or he will never be ruled.'

'He is young, madam,' Burghley suggested, sinking into a chair one of Elizabeth's ladies promptly provided. 'I remember him when he was my ward of court. He was always willful. Perhaps this incident should be put down as a youthful indiscretion.'

Elizabeth tapped her long fingers rhythmically against the cover of her book and grunted, sliding a sideways glance at him. 'A wild stallion indeed. Am I to be plagued with reckless youths at my time of life, Burghley?'

Burghley nodded, raising his bushy white eyebrows. 'The court is a very different place from when Your Majesty first came to the throne.'

Elizabeth's lips crooked in a rueful smile. 'Were we ever that young, my lord?'

'Some of us still are, madam,' he replied, bowing his head towards her.

'Oh, you flatterer,' she reproved, enjoying the compliment.

'And perhaps the earl's injury will cool any further impetuosity.'

'His injury?' Elizabeth said sharply, her eyes opening wide in alarm. 'Robin was hurt?'

Burghley consulted a paper. 'Blount pierced him in the thigh, it seems. A great deal of blood ensued from the wound and required medical attention, but it poses no danger to his health. He will recover.'

Elizabeth slammed her book down on the desk. 'But the fool could have been seriously hurt, Burghley. What would I have done then? Does he never think of me? I shall send my doctor to him. I would have Robin well.'

'And is there to be any punishment, madam? For either the earl or Sir Charles?'

Elizabeth sighed and shook her head. 'No, no punishment for either of them. Blount is not to blame. Robin provoked and publicly humiliated him with that foolish remark. And yes, I know what you are thinking, that I should punish Essex, but he is headstrong, Burghley, and does not always think before acting. He is a young man and young men should act a little wild now and then, I think.'

She was right. Burghley did think that there should be punishment for the two men, even if it was only a token punishment to show that the Queen would not allow her subjects to disobey her without incurring retribution. He feared that such forbearance on her part would only encourage similar acts of disobedience and these young men around the court were already too sure of themselves for his liking. But he knew it would be pointless to argue with Elizabeth. He had seen that Robert was necessary to her, how she brightened and seemed to forget her cares when he was with her. To pursue a course of punishment would only anger her and make him seem vindictive.

So, Burghley squashed his feelings and merely sighed before saying, 'As you wish, madam.'

CHAPTER 5

A deep, lusty laugh boomed above the sound of chatter in the Presence Chamber of Whitehall Palace and everyone turned to look at the source, the stocky Devonian, Sir Francis Drake.

The room was crowded and Drake was short, so Robert had not noticed the hero of 1588, the man who had saved England, almost single-handedly so the ballad-makers claimed, from the Spanish Armada. Robert excused himself from the men and women who surrounded him, drawn by his fresh looks and charm, not to mention his closeness to the Queen, and cut through the crowd to Drake.

'Sir Francis, may I speak with you?'

Drake looked up at the tall stooping figure. His dark, suntanned brow creased as he tried to place his interlocutor. He was not often at court and was not familiar with all the young gallants. But the Queen's new favourite had been the subject of many a conversation and Robert was so unlike other men, being unusually tall, strikingly auburn-haired and who walked with an unusual forward stooping motion, that Drake was able to recognise him. 'My lord Essex, of course.' Drake's companions made way for Robert and Robert moved closer.

'I have heard a rumour you are forming a fleet to attack Lisbon.'

Drake's dark brown eyes twinkled. 'Have you, my lord?'

'Is it true?'

Drake cleared his throat, folded his arms across his chest and widened his stance. 'It is true. We thought we should give those Spanish dogs an English beating. We'll never have a better chance. Their armada no longer exists and we should attack before they have time to build another. We even have an excuse for attacking if we need one. The Portuguese want the Spanish invaders out of their country and Don Antonio, the poor usurped king, wants his throne back.'

'I wholeheartedly agree, Sir Francis. Can you find a place for me?'

'For you?'

'Yes, for me. I want to be included.' Robert noticed Drake's hesitation and was a little hurt. 'I am an able soldier, Sir Francis, I assure you. I have been in battle in the Netherlands with the late Earl of Leicester and Sir Philip Sidney. You must not think I would be a liability.'

'And I assure you, my lord, I was thinking no such thing.' Drake had in fact been thinking that Elizabeth would want her favourite close by her side, as she had with Leicester, rather than dashing off to war. 'No, indeed, you would be very welcome.'

'You will take me then?'

'With the Queen's permission, of course.'

'Why with the Queen's permission?' Robert asked irritably. 'Can you not just tell the Council I am required?'

'I can tell the Council that, my lord, but the Queen must approve you all the same, as she must approve every officer in the fleet.'

'Oh, I see,' Robert said, his chin sinking upon his chest.

Drake leant forward and tilted his head up to Robert. 'Don't despair, my lord. The Queen has not gainsaid any of my officers yet.'

Robert nodded glumly. 'If you'll forgive me, Sir Francis, there is none other so placed as I.'

'Ah,' Drake's shoulders jerked with a laugh. 'And I have always thought it an honour to be so favoured by Her Majesty.'

'It is an honour,' Robert agreed, 'but it has its drawbacks too, Sir Francis. If you could make it clear how valuable I would be as part of the fleet when you petition the council, it might help.'

'I shall do my best, my lord,' Drake assured him, thinking that he wasn't going to put himself out too greatly and risk a telling-off from the Queen just to have this eager young pup in his fleet.

Drake did petition the Council as he promised, but Elizabeth said Robert could not go and Drake let the matter drop.

Robert felt unable to let it drop quite so easily. He begged, he pleaded, he even argued and shouted, but Elizabeth was adamant. Robert was not to join the English fleet. He was not to risk his life in such a venture. He was not to try to gain a fortune by wresting it forcibly from the Spanish.

Robert did not listen. Elizabeth was not going to tell him what he could and could not do. He needed money and there was gold just waiting for him in Lisbon.

So, he made his plans secretly and drew friends into his plan, Sir Philip Butler and Sir Edward Wingfield, men who were, unlike him, not the favourites of the Queen and were, therefore, free to do as they pleased. They made arrangements on his behalf with Sir Roger Williams, captain of the *Swiftsure*, who was also a friend to Robert and had been since their days in the Netherlands campaign, and who was keen to help him escape from Elizabeth's clutches. Sir Roger would anchor the *Swiftsure* at Falmouth, a few miles away from the main English fleet at Plymouth, and wait for Robert to arrive in the early hours of the fifth of April. Robert would have slipped away from the court without any fanfare, without anyone even noticing he had gone.

This plan arranged, Robert sat down in his apartments to write dozens of letters, letters that would be delivered once he was safely away from the court.

One of his letters was to Elizabeth, explaining why he had disobeyed her, that he was sure she would forgive him, and assuring her of his undying love. He had gone to Lisbon to make her England safe and he promised he would bring back Spanish booty that would swell the coffers of Elizabeth's treasury for years.

The news of his departure soon spread, not just through the court, but through the city. Robert's departure was being talked about and being cheered in the alehouses of London. The young and handsome Earl of Essex had thumbed his nose at the Queen, so the talk went, and dashed off to sea to teach the hated

Spanish a lesson they would never forget. And the people loved him for it, loved his youth and his daring, were proud of his courage in defying the Queen and were proud to call him one of their own.

Elizabeth did not share their admiration. She had told Robert he was not to go to sea and he had defied her. She screamed at her Council, at their stupidity for letting Robert leave the court. She ordered Robert's grandfather, the elderly Sir Francis Knollys, into her presence and demanded that the poor old man ride after his wayward grandson and bring him back to court. And, she told him with an emphatic jab into his shoulder, if that disobedient Welsh cur, Sir Roger Williams, had not already hanged himself in shame for aiding Robert's escape, he was to be brought back in chains and thrown into the Tower where some suitably dank dungeon awaited him.

Poor Sir Francis spared his aged body nothing in riding after his grandson but when he arrived at Falmouth, the weather had turned and the small ship he set sail in to pursue Robert was tossed about by storms and forced back to port. Unhappily, he had to report to the Council that his prey had eluded him and he could do no more.

Robert, for his part, had begun to regret his action, for he and Williams on the *Swiftsure* had problems in finding the rest of the English fleet and sailed around hopelessly for more than a month before they had a sight of their sister ships. Robert climbed aboard Drake's ship expecting to be greeted with warmth and admiration. Instead, he had to endure a severe rebuke from Drake for putting him in such an awkward position. Drake showed him a letter from the Queen, which stated that when Lord Essex was found, he was to be told to sail straight back to England.

Robert opened his mouth to protest, but Drake halted him, telling him there was no need. As much as Drake wanted to obey his queen, the wind was against them and sailing back to England was not possible. The only way was forward, to attack the Spanish-held towns and ports in Portugal. Robert could hardly believe his luck. He had got away with it.

Another week passed and the coast of Portugal came into view. The English force clambered into their small boats and rowed towards the beach. One boat was lost, overturning in the tumultuous sea, but Robert kept his face forward, determined to be the first to land on foreign soil.

The Spanish saw them coming and the Spanish garrison at the castle of Peniche, just beyond the sand dunes on the beach, left their stronghold to see off the English invaders, leaving the town undefended. Robert, with the aid of Sir Roger Williams, outflanked the small party and forced the Spanish to flee. Robert and his men reached the town, took control and raised the flag of St George in victory.

But the main target of the whole expedition had been and still was Lisbon, sixty miles to the north. Sir John Norris took command of the land army and Robert insisted on going with him. They marched through the Portuguese countryside for seven days, the soldiers happily plundering every Catholic church of its gold as they went. But the early promise of the campaign soon dissipated as the army's supplies ran low and foraging parties often returned empty-handed.

And when the English army reached the gates of Lisbon, they found the Spanish occupiers disinclined to come out and fight. With nothing to do and no one to fight, a strategic withdrawal was suggested by the English captains, but Robert protested. He had not risked the displeasure of the Queen simply to turn tail and run away when things became awkward. If the Spanish would not fight voluntarily, then they must be made to.

He rode alone to the city, his pike lowered like a jousting lance, and thrust it into the wooden gates. He shouted up into the air, challenging any Spaniard inside the gates who would dare to question Elizabeth's honour to come out and fight him, man to man. Robert waited, but no one shouted back. He called again. Still silence. He rode back to the English camp, complaining to Norris that all Spaniards were cowards.

Meanwhile, Drake had sailed the fleet to Cascais and been delighted to encounter sixty Baltic trading ships full of valuable cargoes. These were quickly appropriated by Drake and his comrades. Drake had laid his hands on the fortune that Elizabeth would so delight in.

But Elizabeth had other things on her mind and still wanted Robert back. The army rejoined the fleet and another letter arrived demanding the return of the Earl of Essex and Robert felt he could not ignore the command. He boarded the *Swiftsure* one last time and landed back in England before the month of June was out.

As he rode back to London, Robert found his countrymen waving to him from the side of the roads and from out of their windows, cheering him and praising his name. He even heard ballads sung about his exploits in Portugal and read broadsheets that proclaimed him as the Shepherd of Albion's Arcadia. The people of England loved him. It didn't seem to matter that the adventure had failed to achieve its objectives. Many of the Spanish ports in Portugal were still in the enemy's keeping and Don Antonio, the usurped king, was still without his throne.

And it seemed that Elizabeth did not mind either, for when Robert came before her, there were a few sharp words from her, but there was also warmth in her looks. Elizabeth had her Robin back by her side, and she was content. All she needed to do was find a way to stop Robert seeking his fortune elsewhere.

Cecil re-read the paper his secretary had just handed him, sighed inwardly and dismissed the man.

'This is it,' he said, handing the paper to his father.

Burghley ran his eyes over the wording. 'The Queen is entitled to bestow monopolies on whomever she wishes, my boy.'

'I know, I know,' Cecil said, picking at a splinter in the wood of his father's desk.

'Then what is your objection?'

Cecil raised his eyes to the ceiling and shook his head. 'Why does it have to be to him? He has done nothing to deserve it.'

'If the Queen were to reward only those of her subjects who deserved a reward, she and we would be a great deal richer.' Burghley laughed at his own joke.

'This is a ten-year grant, Father,' Cecil persisted. 'Ten years of revenue from the import and export of sweet wines. It is a small fortune and the Queen has just given it to the Earl of Essex. For what? For playing cards with her, and dancing, and writing poetry.'

'Someone had to have the monopoly,' Burghley pointed out, 'and the earl needs money. A very great deal of it if he is to live as befits an earl. You know this, Robert. Why am I having to explain it to you?'

'Am I sounding petulant, Father?'

'A little, my boy. This is a lesson you should learn. Poor men with rich tastes should be given money to stop them from trying to acquire wealth through other means. An ambitious young man with a great deal of promise and no money with which to achieve it is a dangerous combination.'

Cecil pulled up a chair alongside his father and looked him in the eye. 'Did you suggest the Queen give Essex the sweet wine monopoly, Father?'

'Now you understand, Robert,' Burghley nodded, patting his son's hand. 'What has it cost us? Nothing. What do we gain by it? A great deal. Elizabeth is happy to give her favourite a means of income. She is grateful to us for allowing her to make the gift. And Essex is given the money he needs to wear fine clothes and travel around town in a coach, so that he is not finding other ways to make money, such as demanding gifts that are in the Queen's prerogative and that may soon come your way instead of his. Think of the future, Robert, always be thinking of the future.'

Burghley looked into his son's face, saw the doubtful look in his sharp eyes, and realised he had failed to convince him. 'I know you do not like the earl and I know why. Ah, you look at me like that, but I was not blind when Essex was my ward. I know you wanted him to be your friend and I know how hurt you were when he dropped you in favour of others. No, do not blush, not in front of me, there is no need. You are my son and I know what you are thinking and what you are feeling. What hurts you hurts me. But you are not a child anymore, Robert, and I do not want your thoughts and actions to be governed by the resentments of the child you were. Do you understand?'

'Yes, Father, I understand,' Cecil said reluctantly. 'And I know you are right.' He took a deep breath. 'So, the Earl of Essex is to be granted the monopoly on sweet wines for a ten-year period. I will take this to the Queen straight away and have her sign it.'

Burghley watched his son rise awkwardly from his chair, the paper in his hand, and limp out of the office. He felt the twinge of pain he always felt when contemplating his son's misfortune, but he also realised with another part of his brain that he still had much to teach him.

CHAPTER 6

HAMPTON COURT PALACE

Robert had enjoyed his morning. He had met his childhood friend, Henry Wriothesley, Earl of Southampton, in the palace's tennis courts and they had spent an enjoyable couple of hours hitting balls at one another, with the competitive spirit of the first hour relaxing into boyish humour in the second. Now, washed and wearing a fresh suit of clothes, he came out of his chamber and skipped down the adjacent stairs that led to the Queen's Privy Chamber. Two Yeoman Warders stood either side of the double doors, one of which stood partly open. As Robert drew nearer, he heard laughter. He recognised the Queen's voice and, with a stab of resentment, Sir Walter Ralegh's.

He looked through the gap in the door. Elizabeth and Ralegh were sitting upon cushions on the floor. Elizabeth sat upright, her stiff corset refusing to allow her to slouch and her orange skirts billowing around her, while Ralegh rested on one elbow like an ancient Roman, his long legs, encased in silver-threaded hose, stretched out and crossed at the ankles.

'Why, Robin,' Elizabeth said, noticing Robert standing in the doorway. 'What are you doing there?'

'I... I...,' Robert stammered, feeling like a child who had been caught spying on his parents. He pushed the door farther open. 'I heard... I wondered who you were with.'

'I am with my dear Walter,' Elizabeth said, smiling at Ralegh as she drew out the 'a' sound, a pun on his Devonshire country accent. 'He's been amusing me.'

'If you wanted amusement, madam, you need only have sent for me,' Robert said primly.

'I was on hand, my lord,' Ralegh said, pushing himself up to lean back on his hands. 'There was no need to bother you.'

Robert scratched his head and frowned. 'I am at a loss to conceive how a mere Captain of the Guard has anything to say to a queen that can be so very amusing.'

Ralegh's handsome face lost its geniality. 'Wit is not a quality only the nobility possess, my lord. In fact, I have known it to be wholly absent in some members of that rank.'

Robert felt the insult warm his cheeks. 'You mean me, sir?' he demanded, stepping into the room and moving towards the pair, only stopping when his boot nudged one of the embroidered cushions. He paid no attention to Elizabeth, who watched her two favourites with a thrill of satisfaction at their manly enmity. This was a scenario she had always enjoyed, two men fighting over her, and she encouraged such rivalry whenever possible, but always putting a stop to it before matters progressed too far.

'Why would you imagine I mean you, my lord?' Ralegh said, a smile curving his pink lips. 'Have you not wit?'

'More than a Devonshire peasant, I assure you, sir,' Robert countered, his hand curling around the hilt of his sword.

Elizabeth saw the movement and decided the encounter had played its course. 'Enough,' she said. She lifted her arms and both Ralegh and Robert bent to take her hands and help her to her feet, no easy task for her dress was heavy and cumbersome. 'Have you not had your fill of fighting, Robin? Your wound from your encounter with Sir Charles can have barely healed.'

Robert did not want to be reminded of losing a duel, especially not in front of Ralegh. He glared at Ralegh, who was still holding Elizabeth's hand.

'I insist you remove your hand from the Queen's person,' he said, pointing at the offending appendage.

Elizabeth's lips twitched in amusement. Robert could truly find an offence in the smallest of incidences. Ralegh made no move to comply, so she pulled her hand gently from his. 'There, Robin. Does that satisfy you?'

'It does not satisfy *me*, madam,' Ralegh protested in mock outrage.

Standing there in his habitually casual, self-assured manner made Elizabeth think of the differences between the two men and the opposite ways in which they responded to her. Robert sulked while Ralegh teased, and she knew it was the difference between a boy and man. But a man's character was already formed, and Ralegh, she had come to suspect, was not a man she could ever tame, though it irked her to admit it. But Robert, still so young in many ways, was made of wax, ready to be shaped into whatever she chose to make of him. She had power over him and the power pleased her.

'It was not to you that the question was addressed, sir,' Elizabeth rebuked Ralegh sharply, having made a decision to favour Robert.

Ralegh saw that Elizabeth was in a playful mood no longer and decided there was no profit or amusement in prolonging the encounter. He could make better use of his time elsewhere. 'Then I must ask your forgiveness, and if you wish it, take my leave.'

'Yes, you may go,' she said, her head already turning away from him.

Ralegh bowed, deeply to Elizabeth, less so to Robert, and left the room, signalling to the Yeoman Warder to close the door.

'You see how I do your bidding, Robin,' Elizabeth said, moving to a table by the window and selecting a sugared almond from a gold platter.

'I wish you would dismiss him altogether,' Robert said, pleased at his victory. 'He has no virtues that I can see.'

'Of course, he has virtues. I would not waste my time on him else. You do not believe me, I see. Shall I list them for you? Well then, he is a clever man, Robin, adventurous, courageous, charming—'

'Enough,' Robert protested, putting his hands over his ears. 'He may, indeed, be all these things, I know not, but you have nobles who have these virtues, too. Why give your company to one of such low degree?'

Elizabeth laughed. 'Because I am my father's daughter, Robin. He never put breeding before brains when it came to his servants and nor do I. I recognise virtue in all stations of Man.'

'Recognise it, use them, by all means, but do not keep them so close about you. Such a man sullies you by his presence.'

'Would you alone have access to your queen, Robin?'

'Of course. Why would I not want to keep the most beautiful queen in the world all to myself?'

It was a banal statement, lacking invention, but Elizabeth welcomed it all the same. 'You should have seen me in my youth,' she said, her eyes glistening in remembrance. 'I made a pretty maid then.'

Youth has its own beauty, so the statement may have been true, Robert could not say. All he knew was what his mother had told him of Elizabeth's early days as queen. That Elizabeth had managed to convince many a man she was beautiful by virtue of her sovereign station and the magnificence of her clothes and jewels. 'It was incredible how beautiful even a plain maid could look when she wore diamonds and emeralds,' Lettice had remarked in one of her more catty moments, Robert remembered, probably when Leicester had praised Elizabeth for some trifling reason.

Elizabeth, ignorant of his thoughts, picked up the plate of sugared almonds and invited Robert to stay and sit upon the cushions. The cushions that were, he noted irritably as he obeyed, still warm from Ralegh's arse.

'Gelly,' Robert shouted, striding into his apartments and throwing off his sword and baldric to land in a corner of the room.

Gelly Meyricke hurried through from the adjacent antechamber where he had been enjoying a quiet cup of beer with his feet up on a stool. Meyricke, a man whose Welsh heritage was everywhere exhibited in his person, in his short stature, his black hair and eyes, had been with Robert for many years, having served in the Devereux household for more than two decades. So long a service meant the Devereuxs were more like family to him than his own and Robert like a young brother. Meyricke cared deeply for his master and was concerned by the Robert he now encountered. 'Something the matter, my lord?'

Robert groaned and fell face down on his bed. 'What am I doing, Gelly?'

'At this very moment?'

'Here at court,' Robert punched the mattress and flipped himself over, disarranging the silk coverlet, one leg hanging over the side of the bed. 'What am I doing *here*?'

'Where else would you be?' Meyricke said, picking up the sword and baldric, wondering if this was the onset of one of Robert's notorious moods.

Throughout his life, Robert had been troubled with sudden changes in his temperament. For seemingly no reason, he would become melancholic, locking himself in his room and refusing all company. When his family asked what was wrong, he would truthfully be unable to answer, unable to identify the reason or the harsh word that had caused his sadness. And there were also the other times when Robert would laugh and be merry, almost to the point of hysteria. At such times, everything seemed possible to him, nothing was beyond his reach. The Devereux family had grown used to these changes of moods but were keen for no one else to find out about them. Indeed, part of Meyricke's job as Robert's manservant, as ordered by Robert's mother, was to keep an eye on him and even, if necessary, protect Robert from himself.

'What is it I do all day?' Robert asked, staring up at the canopy of the bed, his arms above his head. 'I play games. I win and lose money at cards. I see to the horses in the stables. I dance when music plays. I make the Queen smile.'

Meyricke moved to the side of the bed and leant over him. 'These are not insignificant things, my lord.'

'But are they work for a man, Gelly?' Robert demanded. 'Waiting on women?'

Meyricke held up a cautionary finger. 'I am not sure the Queen can be considered the same as other women, my lord.'

'Oh, do not be fooled about Elizabeth, Gelly. She *is* a woman. You have only to look beneath her skirts.' Robert sat up and hung both legs over the side of the bed. 'A man should perform deeds of honour. There are battles being fought in the world, you know, Gelly.'

'Not by England, there aren't.'

'No, indeed, not by England. The Spanish are overrunning Europe, enforcing their Papist creed and terrorising entire countries, but we,' Robert gestured at himself with both hands, 'stay in England and do nothing.'

'You want to go to war?'

'What else is a man fit for? If we men do not fight, we are no better than women. We may as well all wear petticoats and spin wool.'

'We have been to war before, my lord, if you remember, and not all that long ago, neither,' Meyricke remarked, reminding Robert that they had both served with Leicester in the Netherlands campaign against the Spanish. The campaign had been far less than successful, especially for Leicester who had been humiliated and disappointed while there, the former by Elizabeth when she had made him renounce a prestigious title the Netherlanders had bestowed upon him, and the latter by the later ingratitude of the Netherlanders themselves when the English army failed to achieve its objectives. The country was still trying to rid itself of its Spanish invaders.

'I remember, Gelly.'

'You will remember then a great deal of hardship. Men falling sick, men dying. Your friend, Sir Philip Sidney, among them.'

'I know. As if I could forget the death of Sidney. But I remember too, the riding into battle, the meeting of an enemy face to face. That feeling, Gelly, tell me you felt it too.'

'The thrill of battle?' Meyricke smiled and nodded. 'Oh yes, I felt it. Being a hair's breadth away from death, your heart beating so fast you fear it will burst out of your chest. A rapturous moment when you have nothing else in your mind but running your enemy through with your sword.'

'That's it,' Robert said excitedly, 'you do know what I mean.'

'I know,' Meyricke admitted, moving to the buffet and placing Robert's sword on its cradle. 'But I do not long for such a feeling again.'

'You are growing old, Gelly,' Robert scoffed. 'And I am sure I will be old before such an opportunity arises again.'

Meyricke, seeing that the conversation was going round in a circle and Robert growing more despondent, sought to change the subject. 'Come, my lord, your time here is well spent. You already have the license on sweet wines that brings you in a pretty penny. Your closeness to the Queen will provide more material rewards soon.'

'You speak only of coin,' Robert said sourly.

'Indeed, I do not. I see I must remind you of your stepfather.'

'Which one? I have a new stepfather now, Gelly.'

'The Earl of Leicester,' Meyricke continued doggedly, ignoring Robert's sarcasm. 'He was Master of the Horse, as you are now. He rose to become a Privy Counsellor and died the Lieutenant and Captain-General of the Queen's Armies and Companies, the highest title there is.'

Robert's eyes brightened. He rose and gripped Meyricke's shoulders with both hands. 'That's right, Gelly, he did. And what were the Dudleys? Mere parvenus. Why, Leicester's grandfather was nothing more than King Henry VII's tax collector. But you know I am a Devereux. I have more royal blood in my veins than the Queen herself. How high might *I* not rise?'

Meyricke glanced towards the door, relieved to see it was shut. He wished Robert would not say such things, or at least if he must say them, say them less loudly. If Robert had only given his words more serious thought, Meyricke reflected, he would have realised that the only title higher than the Lieutenant-General was King, and how could he aspire to such a position? Did he think he could marry the celebrated virgin queen? He put his hands over Robert's and removed them from his shoulders.

'Perhaps it would be best, my lord, if you were to keep those kinds of ideas to yourself.'

CHAPTER 7

Robert had heard Lady Frances Sidney was in London, visiting her father, Sir Francis Walsingham. Meyricke's mention of her husband, Philip, had reminded Robert of a promise he had made to the dying young man. As Sidney lay on the army cot bed in the cold surgeon's tent in the Netherlands, the smell of his gangrenous leg turning Robert's stomach as he sat at his side, he had reached for Robert's hand with his own clammy extremity and held it tight to his chest. Sidney's cracked lips had opened and asked Robert to look after his wife when he was dead. Robert had readily agreed, most willing to do all he could for a man he so admired. But the promise made, it was soon forgot, and Frances Sidney had seen her husband's deputy only once since he had returned from war. The realisation of his neglect made Robert ashamed and he determined to pay Sidney's widow a visit as a means of making amends. So, he had made the short journey from the court to Walsingham's house in Seething Lane and had been shown into a small chamber with a meagre fire and little comfortable furniture, so unlike his own abodes. He looked out of the diamond-leaded window while he waited.

Robert heard behind him the soft pad of footsteps on the rush matting, the rustle of silk, and turned. Lady Frances Sidney was dressed in a handsome mustard yellow damask dress that complimented her olive complexion, an inheritance from her sallow-skinned father, and a Venetian headdress that covered most of her dark brown hair. She was slimmer than when he had last seen her and he suddenly remembered she had been carrying Sidney's child when he died. *How could I have forgotten that?* he scolded himself.

'Lady Sidney.' He took her hand and pressed it to his lips. 'You must forgive me for not attending on you sooner.'

'I understand you are very busy, my lord,' Frances said, indicating a chair. 'There is no need to apologise.'

There was a moment's awkward silence between them. Now he was here, Robert had little idea of what he should say to this woman. He had only become a close friend to Sidney during the Netherlands campaign and had met Frances on only a few occasions before that when Sidney had brought her with him when he had visited his uncle Leicester.

'Your child?' was the subject Robert settled on. 'He… she?'

'She,' Francis confirmed with a smile, sensing his awkwardness. 'She is well, I thank you. I can see her father in her.'

They endured another silence while they both paid mental homage to Philip's memory.

'Will you be coming to court while you are in London, my lady?'

'On Friday. I must pay my respects to the Queen and I understand there is to be an entertainment.'

'Yes, a play by my late stepfather's company, Lord Leicester's Players. That is, they used to be called that. They're now under the patronage of Lord Strange, but they are still very good.'

'Indeed? I shall look forward to it then. I rarely see quality entertainment in the country.'

'Perhaps you would care to sup with me after the play?' Robert asked on impulse. Frances's colour deepened and Robert expected, almost hoped for, a refusal.

Instead, she raised her head and looked him in the eye. 'Thank you, I would like that. It is kind of you to think of me.'

'Not at all. It pleases me to be able to keep my word to your noble husband. I promised him I would look after you.'

Robert did not understand why the pleasure seemed to leave Frances's countenance. He could not know that she wished he had asked her to supper because he wanted to spend time with her, not out of duty to the husband who to all the world had seemed the perfect knight, but who in truth, had cared little for her.

Frances accepted another cup of wine from Gelly Meyricke and drank half of it down in one gulp. She had enjoyed the play, despite her disappointment at having to take a seat in the second row behind Robert and the Queen. She had been worried that Robert would be called upon to keep company with the Queen, but the German ambassador was in London and protocol demanded Elizabeth sup with him.

Frances had chosen her newest dress for the occasion, a green silk with gold thread embroidery and cut in the latest French fashion. She told herself that it was for no one's benefit but her own, that she had wanted to make a good impression at court, but as supper had begun she had had to acknowledge that it was not true.

To her dismay, Robert had not noticed her new dress. He had greeted her in the Presence Chamber before the play's commencement and they had talked of nothing, in particular, just pleasantries and a little court gossip. She, and perhaps Robert too, was very conscious of not only the Queen's penetrative stare but her father Walsingham's all-noticing eye. They had had only a few minutes together before Elizabeth had summoned Robert to her side and she had not relinquished him until the players had danced their final jig. During the short walk to his private apartments, Robert had seemed distracted and Frances had wondered if he was regretting his invitation, keeping him, as it did, from the Queen's presence. Through supper, she watched him eat without seeming to notice what he put into his mouth and noted with apprehension the quantity of wine he drank.

Her concern faded, though, as Robert relaxed, no doubt aided by the alcohol. He ceased to look at the door as if hoping or expecting a summons and Frances allowed herself to believe that he enjoyed her company after all. She even began to flirt with the handsome earl, a practice she had not been able to exercise since before her marriage. It made her feel desirable. Robert made her feel desirable. And she was grateful.

The expensive silk dress had been discarded, tossed in a crumpled puddle on the floor. Her skin was tight with dried sweat, her lips bruised and her throat dry. Frances turned over onto her side in the bed and ran a finger down Robert's spine, its tip bumping over each cartilage, coming to a stop only when it reached the base of his spine. A body so different from her husband's, the only other man she had known.

Frances knew that she would have to leave and resented it. She had not felt so content, so happy, for such a long time, but moments of pure pleasure could not last forever and she slipped from beneath the blankets to search for her shift. She crouched low and twisted her limbs as she searched because even though Robert had explored every inch of her body with an almost inconsiderate self-indulgence, she felt embarrassed now their passion was spent and did not want him to see her naked.

She struggled into her shift and dress, knowing that she would be unable to lace herself and wishing she had kept it on. *Just like a whore from the Southwark stews*, Frances mused. She winced at the thought, the full realisation of her actions filtering through to her just as the dawn leached in through the shutters and daubed the bedroom a sepia hue. She pulled on her stockings and slipped her small feet into her shoes. Her bodice flapped open, hanging upon her, and she had a moment of panic that someone in the palace corridors would see her in such a state of undress and know what she had been doing.

Frances moved towards the door and hesitated. She did not want to leave like a whore, creeping out in shame, nor did she want to think of the past few hours spent in Robert's bed as a sinful act. Wise it may not have been, but her heart refused to believe that it was wrong.

She tiptoed to the other side of the bed and bent over Robert, listening to his breathing. She kissed his cheek and his eyelids fluttered sleepily open.

He mumbled her name, but his head did not rise up from the pillow. Frances told him she was leaving and he nodded. Disappointed that he did no more, she left his room, pausing at the door to check the corridor before making her way quickly to her own chamber, situated next to her father's. Her maid, sleeping on a pallet pulled out from beneath the four-poster bed, awoke at her entrance, but thankfully said nothing as she helped her mistress undress once more and climb into her own bed, even though Frances could have sworn she saw the girl smile.

CHAPTER 8

Thomas Pope pulled the painted curtains of the Theatre's tiring house an inch apart and put his eye to the gap. The theatre was filling up; it was going to be a full house. Perhaps it was the draw of the new play, or maybe the talent of their leading man, Richard Burbage. Pope raised his eyes to the wooden galleries to see how many of the seats were taken. Plenty of ruffs and silk gowns, he noted happily. The company could truly claim to play to the quality. He looked back to the stage, where stools were being set down for the young noblemen who paid to sit on the raised platform to have a good view of the play, but more importantly, to be seen. William Sly called from the rear of the tiring house where he was climbing into his costume to ask how the house was and Thomas replied that it was busy and let the curtain fall. He started towards Sly to help him tie his ruff, but a ripple of applause drew him back to the gap in the curtain.

A group of three young men were making their way through the groundling pit, the crowd parting to create a narrow, uneven corridor to the stage. They were dressed magnificently, the rich colours and quality of their doublets and hose a striking contrast to the workaday garb of the commoners of London.

They reached the edge of the stage and unhesitatingly mounted the steps to the platform. The applause became augmented with cheers. Two of the young men acknowledged the acclaim with a raising of their hands before settling themselves onto the stools. The third turned to face the crowd, just as if he were one of the actors about to perform before them. His gaze travelled around, up and down the horseshoe of the theatre, his hand raised and his face shining with pleasure. He bathed in the people's adoration for a few glorious seconds longer, then joined his companions.

'What's happening out there?' Sly said, almost falling over as he pulled on a knee-length leather boot.

Pope turned to Sly, grinning. 'Guess who's arrived.'

'Who?'

'The Earl of Essex.'

It had been a long day for Elizabeth. She had risen at her usual hour of six, attended chapel, heard a sermon and then breakfasted. She had ridden out in the Chase, taking with her some of her younger ladies who did not object to being in the saddle, as well as a few of her courtiers. An exceptional horsewoman, she had never lost her love of riding, but she had had to reluctantly accept that her body could not endure its vigorous exercise as it once did. She was still in good shape, it could not be denied, but Elizabeth had entered her fifth decade and now her bones ached in cold and damp weather and an hour on horseback was all she could bear. Her dinner had been a simple, even meagre affair, and feeling weary, though not wishing to admit it, had declined to take part in the afternoon's dancing.

Cecil had appeared as the afternoon turned into evening, the usual stack of papers beneath his arm. In the early years of her reign, Elizabeth had attended assiduously to the business of governing, revelling in the power and yes, the problems that came with it, but as the years passed, she knew she could trust her counsellors and would let them get on with their work, so that now she only insisted on a daily report from her secretary.

Elizabeth had felt half-inclined to tell Cecil to go away, that business could wait until the following day, but decades of being a queen made even this small act of indolence unthinkable. She nodded to Cecil and led the way through to her private apartments so that they could attend to business.

Elizabeth signed the document and handed it back to Cecil who tucked it into his leather folder.

'And the last item, Your Majesty. A report from the Master of the Revels,' he said. 'Several new plays are being performed this week. *A Knack to Know a Knave*, *The Seven Deadly Sins*, and *Henry the Sixth*. The Master has passed them all fit for performance, nothing seditious in any of them, and suggests that *The Seven Deadly Sins* will please Your Majesty and recommends it for a court entertainment.' He paused to look at Elizabeth and, gauging her mood, decided it was safe to continue. 'He also writes that the playhouses are attracting some of your courtiers. The Earl of Southampton and the Earl of Essex, along with Lord Mounteagle, attended a performance of Master Kyd's *The Spanish Tragedy* at the Theatre on Wednesday, and the Master writes that the Earl of Essex was greeted with much acclaim by the playgoers.'

Elizabeth, whose body had begun to droop, jerked alert. Her bones ached, her eyes were heavy and she had been thinking only of her bed, but now she was wide awake. *Acclaim for Essex? Since when have any of my courtiers, my subjects, deserved acclaim for merely showing up at a play? That is my prerogative. I am Gloriana. My subjects cheer me.* 'So the people love Essex, do they? Why do they so?'

Cecil shrugged, a little surprised that her response had not been harsher. 'He is young, handsome, courageous. He is everything the people always love.'

'They see a hero, I suppose. He glitters, he shines,' Elizabeth laughed savagely. 'What is it Walter Ralegh wrote? "Say to the court it glows and shines like rotten wood".'

'A rather unfair simile, in my opinion,' Cecil murmured.

'No? I think it rather apt. These days, anyway. It was not always so. Time was my subjects knew their place.'

This is more like it, Cecil thought with glee, *here is the jealous queen.* 'Should I suggest to the earl that he refrain from visiting the theatre?'

'Upon what grounds, Pygmy?' she demanded sharply. 'I cannot forbid him from seeking out entertainment. He would simply do it all the more, like a petulant child. Leave him be. Do nothing, but instruct the Master of the Revels that I want to hear of it should any similar incident occur.'

CHAPTER 9

Frances Sidney was in her bedchamber at her home in the country when she should have been supervising the making of butter in the dairy. She had consulted her almanack, not just once but three times, just to be sure. The moon had come and gone again, but not so her menses. It had been two months since she had shared a bed with Robert Devereux and Frances knew her body. She had been pregnant twice before and she recognised the signs of being with child.

She was such a fool. She had not been some green girl, a coy virgin, unaware of what she was doing when she climbed into bed with Robert. She was a mature woman, a mother of two children and a respected widow. She was not a stupid woman either; she had known what would be the likely outcome of their encounter.

Frances sat on her bed and told herself to breathe deeply, else she was sure she would weep. She was so lost in her thoughts that she cried out when her bedchamber door opened, squealing on its hinges.

'Frances, what do you think of this clo—'

Her mother, Ursula, ceased abruptly and looked into her daughter's face, her maternal sense knowing something was wrong. 'What is the matter?'

Frances had feared, yet at the same time, wanted her mother

to ask the question, and now she burst out with, 'Oh, Mother,' and held out her arms.

Ursula immediately took a seat beside her daughter on the bed and put her arms around her. Frances cried against her mother's neck and Ursula patted her back, cooing soothingly, 'There now.'

When her sobs were spent, Frances unbent her body and relaxed her hold on her mother, sniffing to stop her nose running.

Ursula provided a linen handkerchief and told her daughter to wipe her eyes. 'Now, tell me what the matter is.'

'You will think me wicked,' Frances promised.

'No doubt, but I will hear it all the same.'

It took several moments but, at last, Frances confessed. 'I think I am with child, Mother.'

'Oh, Frances,' Ursula breathed, shutting her eyes, 'you foolish girl. Who was it?'

'I cannot tell you.'

'You will tell me, Frances,' Ursula declared, in no mood to brook any nonsense, 'or I will throw you out of doors.'

Frances knew it was a hollow threat, that her mother would not commit such an unnatural and brutal act, but it salved her conscience to be forced to tell the truth rather than volunteer it. 'The Earl of Essex, Mother. When I went to London.'

'Oh, Frances,' Ursula said again, 'of all the men at court, you had to choose the one closest to the Queen. And he! What was he thinking?' A thought suddenly occurred to her. 'He did not force you, did he?'

Frances shook her head. 'I cannot blame him.'

'Have you told him? Does he know?'

'No. How can I tell him?'

'How can you not, you silly girl?'

'Well, what good would it do?' Frances asked, wiping her nose. 'Surely, it would be best if I stayed here until the child is born and then I give it to one of the women on the estate to look after.'

Ursula was shocked. 'I will not have any grandchild of mine unacknowledged by this family, Frances. Give it to a woman on the estate, indeed. I am ashamed of you for thinking such a thing. No, we will write to the earl at once and say that he must wed you.'

Frances caught her breath, half-hopeful, half-fearful. 'But Mother, he is an earl. He will not want to marry me. And there's the Queen. She may not allow it.'

'You are the daughter of one of the Queen's most trusted counsellors, Frances, not a nobody. And quite frankly, as far as his and your status is concerned, if my daughter is good enough to be bedded, she is good enough to be wedded, by anyone. I do not care that he is an earl, he could be the tsar of Russia for all I care. And as for the Queen,' Ursula bit her lip, 'well, yes, that will be a problem, but we will have to think about that later.'

'And Father?'

'We shall go to London to tell him. I do not want to write to him of such a matter.'

'Would it not be best to wait and find out what Robert... what the earl says before telling Father?' Frances suggested, knowing that the news would greatly disappoint her father.

'He has a right to know, Frances. This is not the kind of secret we can, or should, keep.' Ursula disentangled herself from her daughter and rose. 'We were going to London next week in any case. We shall just bring our arrangements forward. We should be able to leave for London on Friday. Now, you write that letter to the earl and do not seal it. I want to read it first.'

Ursula strode out of the room in a determined manner. Frances, feeling much better now that her mother knew of her shameful condition, moved to her table by the window and began to write to her one-time lover.

Gelly Meyricke ducked his way through the crowd in the Great Hall at Hampton Court Palace, the press of so many bodies making him feel hot. He made his way to the raised platform at the end of the chamber where the Queen and the highest peers in the realm sat.

Robert, seated at Elizabeth's left hand, saw Gelly approaching and wondered what had brought him to the chamber. Whatever it was, it was important and from the look on Gelly's face unwelcome. Robert didn't want the Queen hearing anything he would rather keep quiet, so he excused himself to

Elizabeth and stepped down from the table. Gelly saw his master rise and halted to wait where he was.

'What is it, Gelly?' Robert asked.

'I am sorry to disturb you here, my lord, but this letter has just been delivered. The messenger said it was urgent. He came from Lady Frances Sidney.'

Robert took the letter from Gelly without a word, apprehensive of its contents. He felt he had acted dishonourably with Frances, seducing the widow of a man he had so admired, and he had written to her apologising for his conduct and asking for her forgiveness. Frances had replied, assuring him he had nothing to apologise for and trusting to his discretion. He had heard nothing more and had hoped to forget the incident altogether. He opened the letter and read the contents.

Gelly saw his master's expression darken and knew that the letter contained ill news. 'Something amiss, my lord?' he asked quietly, so as not to draw the attention of those nearby.

'Yes, Gelly, something amiss.' Robert refolded the letter and tucked it inside his doublet. He glanced back at Elizabeth. She was talking to Burghley, but her eyes were on Robert. He smiled bravely at her before turning back to Gelly. 'You cannot help me.'

'Are you certain?' Gelly probed, curious.

'It is not fitting that I speak of this matter to you,' Robert snapped, angered by the letter's contents and careless of who he took his anger out upon.

But Gelly was used to being reminded of his inferior status and his master's temper and was not upset by Robert's words. He said, 'The Earl of Southampton is approaching. Perhaps he can help.'

Robert looked around just as Henry Wriothesley slid his arm through Robert's. Robert dismissed Gelly with a sour nod.

'I sense something is wrong,' Henry, who had been watching Robert and was curious to know what was going on, said playfully. 'Will you tell me or must I guess?'

Robert drew Henry towards the side of the chamber, brushing against the magnificent tapestries that Henry the Eighth had commissioned from the tapestry weavers of Belgium fifty years earlier. Woven with gold and silver thread, they demonstrated the weavers' great skill and still had few rivals in

England, but the central fire of the hall had caused the tapestries to blacken in parts and they shone less brightly than they once had.

'Lady Frances Sidney has written to me,' Robert said. 'She is with child, Henry.'

Henry, who had been told of Robert's tryst with the widow, said simply, 'Yours?'

'She says so.'

'Have you reason to doubt her?'

'No,' Robert was vehement. 'Heavens, no, Henry. She is not every man's mistress.'

'I am only asking,' Henry said, putting out his hands in mollification.

'She is Sidney's widow. Do you think he would have married an unchaste woman?'

'No, of course not.' Henry thought it best not to add that for all of his married life, Sir Philip Sidney had hardly been a paragon of fidelity and had been less than loyal to his wife. 'Well, what will you do?'

'What can I do, Henry?' Robert asked hopelessly. 'She's bound to tell her father and then he will tell the Queen. Elizabeth will be furious. But I cannot, in all honour, abandon Frances. That would make me a blackguard.'

Henry drew delicate fingers across his smooth forehead and shrugged. 'But you will mar your fortunes if you displease the Queen, Rob. You know how she feels about her favourites marrying, especially without her consent, if that is what you are thinking.'

Robert sighed. 'Must I be in thrall to a woman? Why must I watch what I say and who I dally with? Damn, Henry, I am a Devereux, yet I am kept chained as any prisoner in Newgate.'

'The curse of our times, Robert. It is how we gallant young men must make our money,' Henry said with an exaggerated sigh, a trick he had picked up from the theatres he so liked to visit. 'If we had a war to fight, we would be able to make our fortune on the battlefield rather than at the court.'

'There's the Spanish, Henry. They are a bloodthirsty lot. They may threaten England again.'

'And hope too that the Queen will act? That is a fantasy, Robert. The Queen loathes war. And besides, she would never let you go. Look how she kept Leicester by her side for all those years.'

'I'll hide behind no woman's petticoats, Henry, queen or no.'

'I hear you, Robert, calm yourself.' Henry laid a hand on his friend's arm, wary of provoking his temper. 'Forget the prospect of battle. That is far off and we drift off course. The matter in hand is Lady Sidney.'

Robert said, 'I must marry her.' His tone was full of despair. He did not want to marry Frances Sidney; he had no love for her and no urgent desire for an heir. But he could not forget Philip. His conscience pricked and he knew he had no choice but to wed his dear friend's widow.

'But think, Rob. She is only the daughter and widow of knights. Hardly a fit wife for a Devereux.'

'Yet, she is a respectable woman, Henry.'

Henry pondered the virtue of pointing out that if Frances were a respectable woman, she would not be pregnant by a man who was not her husband, but he refrained. 'Marry her then, if you must.'

'I must because I have wronged her, do you not see that?'

Yes, I see and I agree,' Henry said, growing bored with the subject. 'Marry her, if it please you, but do not blame me for the Queen's wrath when she finds out.'

Sir Francis Walsingham returned home earlier than usual. The customary pain he felt in his stomach had been great during the day, making him cry out and double over in agony. His secretary, Thomas Phelippes, had pleaded with him to leave his work and retire to his bed, assuring him that England's security could wait until the morning. For once, Walsingham had allowed himself to be persuaded and he was looking forward to climbing into his bed, resting his aching head against the cool pillows and holding a cloth-covered hot stone to his tormenting side. He was to be disappointed.

Walsingham was surprised when his wife came into the hall while his servant was divesting him of his cloak and gloves, not having expected her until the following week. She said that she had brought Frances with her as if that was explanation enough for her premature visit, and asked him to follow her to her closet.

Ursula led the way, her heels clicking on the bare floorboards with a rat-tat-tat in her haste. They reached her closet and Ursula held the door open for him to enter.

Frances was standing by the small fireplace, staring down into the dancing flames. She looked up as her father entered, greeted him and made a curtsey. Walsingham noted that his daughter avoided his eyes, looking instead behind him at her mother, who also entered and closed the door. He felt his body stiffen in apprehension, knowing there was bad news coming, and the pain in his side intensified in a way he had not thought possible.

'Will one of you tell me what is wrong?' Walsingham said impatiently. 'Why have you come to London?'

'I have some news to tell you, Father,' Frances said after a terrible pause and at her mother's prompting. She took a deep breath. 'I am with child.'

Thank God, the news is not that she is ill, Walsingham thought, but his relief passed almost instantly. His daughter, his widowed daughter, was carrying a child! He had heard correctly, had he not? 'Your husband is dead, Frances.'

'Husband,' Ursula said quietly, placing a restraining hand on his arm.

He pulled it gently but firmly away. 'Tell me, am I wrong in that belief?'

'No, Father, you are not,' Frances admitted. 'The Earl of Essex is the father.'

'The Earl—', Walsingham's voice cracked and he put his hand to his mouth to clear his throat. 'The earl is the father of your child?'

'We wrote to him before we left for London, telling him of Frances's condition,' Ursula interjected. 'He would have received our letter by now.'

'And what do you expect him to do once he knows of our daughter's condition?' Walsingham wondered.

'Well, of course, we hope he will suggest marriage,' Ursula said, her tone unconvincing.

'And if he does not?'

'He is an honourable man, Father,' Frances said desperately.

'Is he, indeed?' Walsingham said, taking a seat. He leant forward, his elbows on his knees, an attempt to squash the pain that was making his upper lip perspire. 'I do not have the confidence in the earl that you seem to have. If he were honourable, he would not have seduced you, Frances.'

Frances could not admit to her father that she had been ripe for seduction and her cheeks flushed at the memory. 'Do you not think he will marry me, Father?' she asked quietly.

'How can I say, Frances?' Walsingham looked up at his daughter. 'This news has quite upset me.'

'I have disappointed you,' she said unhappily.

Walsingham looked away.

Ursula spoke. 'Go to your room, Frances. I must speak with your father.' When their daughter had gone, she said, 'You *are* disappointed in her, aren't you?'

'Of all the men she could choose, Ursula, why him?'

'I know. I said the same.'

'How could our daughter go from being the wife of a great man like Philip Sidney to being the mistress of Robert Devereux?'

'I know you do not think much of him—'

'With good cause, Ursula.'

'But he has the Queen's favour.'

'Which is another reason why I wish Frances had not… had not forgot herself.'

'But the earl is a favourite, like Leicester. The Queen forgave Leicester his marriage to Devereux's mother.'

'Essex is not Leicester, Ursula.'

'Frances must marry him, husband. She, and we will be shamed else. You must insist Essex marries her. In secret, if necessary.'

'Yes, I know. Of course, she must marry him. But I could have wished for a better son-in-law.'

'She…,' Ursula swallowed, 'the Queen will not punish Frances for marrying Essex, will she?'

Walsingham stared into the fire. 'I do not know, my dear,' he murmured.

CHAPTER 10

Elizabeth was grinding her teeth and it hurt. She had lost four on the left side of her mouth and those she still had were decaying. *But*, she thought, *if I do not clench my jaw or grind my teeth, I am going to scream, I am going to roar because it has happened again. A man has once again betrayed me!*

'They did not obtain my consent to marry,' she hissed.

'No, Your Majesty,' Walsingham admitted, keeping his eyes on the ground and wondering whether he dared to shift his weight onto his other foot. Movement had the potential to draw Elizabeth's wrath that was, mercifully, directed against Essex and not him at this moment. To his relief, Robert had agreed to marry Frances and the ceremony had been hastily arranged. Whether to tell Elizabeth of the marriage had cast a shadow over the celebrations, with Frances, Robert and Ursula wanting it to be kept a secret. But Walsingham knew that it could not remain so and decided that the best course would be to face the danger head on. He had hoped that Robert would accompany him to tell the Queen, but Robert had declined, finding that he had other matters to attend to elsewhere.

'Your daughter, Walsingham,' Elizabeth said accusingly.

'Circumstances, Your Majesty. This course of action would never have happened but for circumstances.'

'And what circumstances were they?'

Walsingham's dark face coloured. 'My daughter is with child by the earl.'

Elizabeth's throat constricted. Swiving. Always country matters. What was the matter with men that they were so ruled by their loins?

'I see,' she snarled, rising from her chair. Her ladies cowered, keeping their eyes low and pressing their backs against the walls. 'And where is the wretch?'

'Madam?'

'Essex,' she screamed, losing her control at last. 'Where is he?'

'He is at court, Your Majesty.' Walsingham looked around as if expecting, almost hoping, Robert would appear.

'Then you tell him to get himself from my court. I do not want that vile seducer anywhere within my walls. And as for his wife, you can look after her,' she spat at Walsingham. 'I won't have them living in the same house as one another. I'll teach them to go behind my back. They should think themselves fortunate I do not send them both to the Tower.'

It was the best offer Elizabeth was going to make, Walsingham knew. Better his daughter live with her family than languish in the Tower. He bowed, backing out of the room, and went in search of his new son-in-law.

'What a fool you are,' Lettice said, pinning her needle to her embroidery and moving to sit beside her son in front of the fire.

Robert had retired to Drayton Bassett, his mother's home in Staffordshire. When he had first arrived, he had been indignant, proud, haughty that Elizabeth should punish him for such an act as daring to marry, but as the days passed and no news came from the court, he lost his bluster and his old melancholy settled upon him. He had never liked to be mocked, not even in play, and he was fretting over how he was being talked about by his peers at court. *No doubt*, he thought ruefully, *they are calling me a fool as Mother has just done, and they are right. I am a fool. And what galls me most is the thought that that rogue Ralegh will be making the most out of my absence with Elizabeth.*

'Mother,' he said wearily, resting his aching head on his hand

and closing his eyes against the brightness of the day, 'it is done now. I am married. Help me make it better.'

'Why ask me?'

'Because you know Elizabeth. What must I do to win her favour again?'

Lettice sighed and pushed the embroidery stand aside. 'You forget how long it is since I saw her, my boy. God's Death, but I have not been at court for,' she raised her eyes to the ceiling as she searched her memory, 'twelve years or more. But I suppose she has not changed a great deal.' Her voice grew low as she reflected, 'Just grown older, as we all have.' She looked to her son. 'She is a vain old hag, Robert. Do what Leicester always did. Flatter her. Write her long letters of love.'

'I have just married another woman. She will not believe them.'

'Of course, she will,' Lettice could not keep the contempt out of her voice. 'She sincerely believes, and expects, every man at court to be in love with her.'

'I cannot tell such lies, Mother.'

Lettice slapped his hand, growing angry with him. 'Now, you listen to me, Robert. You do what you have to do.'

'I would rather stay here or go to Chartley.' The lie came defiantly. 'The court is no place for me.'

'How do you expect to make your fortune in the country, my darling? And what of your wife? You must write to the Council and be humble if you want Elizabeth to relent and allow you to have your wife at your side.'

'Oh, do not plague me with such questions,' Robert shook his hands at her in frustration. 'I cannot be thinking about Frances now. She can stay where she is, with her family.'

'Why, Robert! Do you not love her?' Lettice teased, a smile playing upon her lips. 'What is she like, this new wife of yours? She always seemed a very dull creature when she was married to Leicester's nephew.'

'She is pleasant enough, Mother.'

'You could have married better, my darling.'

'Perhaps,' Robert nodded in agreement, 'but there are advantages to this marriage that I had not considered before. I have elevated Frances from a lady to a countess and made Walsingham kin to me. He must therefore needs do what he can for me for his own family's good.'

'Silly boy. What can he do for you when you are banished from court?'

How Robert hated it when his mother was in the right. 'Oh, very well,' he said, moving to a desk and snatching up a quill, 'I will write to the Council, to Walsingham, and to Elizabeth, to anyone you want and abase myself. Will that satisfy you, Mother?'

Lettice raised her eyebrows, unappreciative of her son's resentful conformity to her suggestions. 'Do not concern yourself with satisfying *me*, Robert, when it is for your own good.'

Lettice returned to her embroidery stand and Robert wrote his letters to Elizabeth. He wrote words he did not mean, feelings he did not own. The words came to him far easier than he had imagined they would. Once begun, his declarations of love and loyalty, his pleas for forgiveness, flowed easily. He was almost able to convince himself that he meant every word.

Elizabeth's eyes opened stickily. She blinked, trying to focus. She pulled her arm from beneath the coverlet and pressed her fingers to the delicate skin beneath her myopic orbs. She felt wetness there and realised she had been crying in her sleep. She lay perfectly still on her side, listening to the sound of even breathing coming from the woman asleep on the pallet at the side of her bed, sleeping there for her safety and security.

The dream was already fading, even as she stared into the semi-darkness of her bedchamber, but she remembered how it had made her feel, why she had awoken with tears running down her face. Lonely. Unloved. Frightened. She had been experiencing dreams of this sad nature for some little while, but it was the first time one had carried over into reality.

Elizabeth was growing afraid of falling asleep, wary of the dark night and what it would torment her with. Her bed only held horrors and she wanted to avoid it as much as possible. She needed someone to sit up with her into the small hours, someone who would not complain that they were weary or become taciturn because they could not think of anything to say that would amuse her. She had had someone like that once.

Oh Leicester, she moaned into her pillow, *how I miss you, how I need you still.*

Thoughts of Leicester led inevitably to Robert, his replacement. He had betrayed her by marrying, it was true, but at least he had never claimed to love the woman. Robert had married Sidney's widow as an act of honour, as the unhappy consequence of fumbling beneath her skirts, and Elizabeth could not blame him for that. She knew how important honour was to him, had seen his eyes glisten when he read passages from books on chivalry and recalled the deeds of his ancestors. And, in truth, what real harm had been done? she asked herself. She had had letters from him professing regret that he had hurt her and assuring her of his unwavering love and devotion. She had no reason to doubt he was sincere. No, she decided, if Robert asked again to be allowed to return to her, she would let him. He would have to be punished, of course. He could not betray her and expect not to suffer a little, but there was no need to make the punishment too harsh.

Elizabeth slid her arm back beneath the coverlet as her skin grew cold, pulling the covers up to her chin, drawing her legs up to her stomach. She closed her eyes, prepared to risk sleep now that she had made a decision.

Walsingham came to her later the next morning with a letter from Robert that once more begged Elizabeth's forgiveness. Elizabeth read the letter, re-read it, held it to her breast and thanked God for it. She did not hesitate.

She looked up at Walsingham and, to his surprise, he found no malice in her eyes. He was even more surprised, but nevertheless pleased, to hear her say, 'Tell Essex he may return.'

CHAPTER 11

Robert hurried back to the palace at Whitehall as soon as he received word he would be welcome. He had been granted a private audience and felt Elizabeth's steely eyes upon him as her attendants filed out. He had to be humble, he reminded himself and so he had not just bowed, but knelt to Elizabeth, and she had kept him on his knees for at least three minutes by his reckoning.

'You may rise,' Elizabeth said at last, just as his knees were beginning to hurt.

He got to his feet. 'Thank you, Your Majesty. May I say—'

'How is married life?' she cut in. The words were solicitous but the tone in which they were delivered was decidedly not. Unsure how to answer, he hesitated. 'Do you find it amenable, sir?' Elizabeth persisted.

'I hardly find it anything at all, madam,' he returned, 'as I live as if I were not married. The lady, as I understand you know, remains with her mother in the country.'

'Do you miss her company?'

'I find I do very well without it, madam.' He gave Elizabeth his most charming smile and it worked its magic now. Her amber eyes widened and the thin-lipped mouth twitched. In pleasure? In amusement? Robert could not tell.

'And it pleases me to have you back at court, my lord. I have had so little company to offer me distraction.'

'Oh, you mean Sir Walter has not amused you? I find that odd. He always makes me laugh.'

'Now, Robin,' she said, deciding she would grace him with the old familiarity, 'do not say so. I will not have our reunion spoilt by jealousy.'

'As Your Majesty commands. Of what then shall we talk?'

'Of what you will, Robin.'

'Why then,' he said, emboldened by her warmth and wanting to press his advantage, 'may I speak of France?'

The coquettish smile fell from Elizabeth's face. She had expected love talk from Robert, not politics. 'France?'

'King Henri,' Robert explained. 'Has he not sought your assistance in his military endeavours against the Catholic League?'

The Catholic League was a society formed by Henry I, the Duke of Guise, in 1576, which sought to remove all trace of Protestantism from France. Many French nobles were Huguenots, defenders of the Protestant faith, and the Catholics in the country were concerned over the power they had. Henri, although the legitimate king of France, had been unable to enter its capital, Paris, because it was held by Catholics, and was forced to retreat into the southern part of the country. He had been appealing to all of Europe's Protestant leaders, but especially to Elizabeth, to help him take control of his realm.

'What if he has?' Elizabeth's voice had acquired a sharp edge. 'And how the devil do *you* know of it, anyway?'

'If he has,' Robert ignored her questions, judging it was not wise to admit that the French king, knowing him to be a champion of Protestantism, had written to Robert personally asking for him to plead with the Queen on his behalf, 'then I would dearly love to represent you in the field, Your Majesty.'

'What?' she scoffed. 'You go to war? Do not be absurd.'

'I am not being absurd.' Robert fell to his knees once more and looked up at her. 'See how earnest I am.'

'I do not care for your earnestness, Robin. Get up.'

'I will not, Bess,' Robert declared. 'I will stay on my knees until you give me leave to go to France.'

'Then you will be on your knees a long time, my lord.'

'At least allow me to speak to you on the matter, I beg you.'

It would not hurt to listen to what he has to say, Elizabeth thought, *and he does make a very attractive supplicant, kneeling there at my feet.*

But she had forgotten how persuasive he could be and, though she tried to resist him, Elizabeth found herself eventually agreeing to Robert going to France after he had petitioned her for two hours on his knees. Any qualms she felt at the prospect of his leaving were assuaged by the ardour with which he thanked her.

And, in fact, Robert had done her a service. He had reminded her that she need not be lonely without him, for he was not the only interesting young man at court, though he had been her most attentive and malleable. No, there was also Ralegh. With Robert to keep her company, Elizabeth had not thought of calling on Ralegh to stay up with her into the early hours. His attendance at court could be erratic. Though he held the position of Captain of the Guard, he often delegated his duty to others, convincing Elizabeth he needed to travel to some distant country on explorations, and she like a fool would let him go, inspired by his talk of strange encounters and riches. Well, that would change now. Ralegh would stay at court while Robert was away and keep her company.

And now Elizabeth thought harder, she found Ralegh sometimes easier to be with than Robert. Elizabeth understood Ralegh and Ralegh understood her. Perhaps it was because Ralegh was a decade or so older than Robert. Robert was such a boy and she enjoyed his enthusiasm and his youth, for it made her feel young again, but Ralegh was a pragmatist at heart, just like her. Elizabeth understood that Ralegh paid her the compliments she loved to receive because he wanted things from her. This, of course, was how the relationship between sovereign and subject worked. A subject swore allegiance to a sovereign, and in effect, allowed them to remain on their throne in exchange for material rewards.

And because they understood one another, Elizabeth knew she could bestow her attentions on others and not upset Ralegh too greatly. When she was bored with her other men, she could pick up with Ralegh where they left off, without there being rancour or bitterness on either side. Ralegh was also interesting, able to talk about life outside the court, about other people, about lives that she could not possibly know of or experience for herself. The conversations Elizabeth had with Ralegh were quite unlike those she had with any other. Robert, for all his charm, had an irritating tendency to talk only of himself. Ralegh had a thrilling intellect and sense of adventure that she could only admire and envy. He wrote poems as easily as he breathed, while other courtiers, Robert included, would struggle and agonise over every word. He talked of distant places and strange people, of getting on board a ship and sailing to lands that did not exist on any map but that he knew must exist. He talked of travelling to the New World and creating a new England, so that she, Elizabeth, would not just be a queen of one little island, but of a country whose undoubted wealth had not yet been tapped. Oh yes, Ralegh was a fine companion for her. And he, like all the others, did profess to love her, to adore her. For all she knew, he was speaking the truth.

I may not say that Walter is all mine, but he understands the game, she thought. *I will send for him and he can do his duty by me and keep me company while Robert goes to his wars. I never have to wake up crying again.*

'You would do far better to stay in England,' Henry Wriothesley said when Robert told him that he was going to France to help the French king regain his territory. 'Why go to France? You could become a statesman like your wife's father.'

'Oh, Henry, pens and paper are not for me,' Robert said dismissively. 'What glory is there in that?'

Henry shrugged, unlike Robert, not being particularly concerned with acquiring martial glory. He moved to Robert's desk and picked up the royal commission, rubbing his finger over the elaborate signature of the Queen. 'When do you leave?' he asked, watching Robert as he moved about the room, checking the flypages of books, choosing ones to take with him on his journey, discarding those he did not.

'Saturday, leaving from Dover. I will catch the noonday tide.'

'I think I shall come and see you off.'

'You could come with me, you know. Do you not fancy a spell of soldiering?'

Henry laughed and held out his hands. 'Thank you, Robert, but I am well enough here. My inclination at the moment is for the playhouse and the delightful whores I find in the taverns. If ever that changes, I will let you know.'

Robert laughed and playfully threw a shirt at him. 'You will get the pox and then where will you be?'

'Not dead on the end of a pike or with an arrow through my throat, which is where you may be heading.'

'Not I, Henry. I am not destined to die on the battlefield.'

Henry's expression changed to one of derision and told Robert that it was impossible to know what lay ahead for any of them.

'I do know,' Robert assured him, opening the cover of a book and taking out a folded parchment. He handed it to Henry and told him to take a look. 'Mother had my fortune foretold. You can see from that, glory awaits me, Henry, and you do not achieve glory by sitting at home and scrawling figures in account books.'

'Or playing the lover to an old woman,' Henry smirked, glancing over the esoteric diagrams and charts on the paper.

Robert glared at him, all mirth gone. 'Why do you say that?'

'Well,' Henry half-laughed, a little taken aback by Robert's angry expression, 'that is what you do, is it not? Flatter the old bird, tell her you love her?'

'I do only what others do,' Robert protested. 'The Queen likes to be spoken to of love. Tell me, who does not like to be admired and flattered? Elizabeth need not believe it. Maybe she does not.'

'I understand, Robert, really I do. It is a game, we all know that, and you play it well.'

'Then do not mock me for it, Henry.'

'You mistake me, I do not mock you. Forgive me, I am merely full of envy. The Queen will never look on me with such favour as she shows you. You are loved by the gods, Robert.'

Placated, Robert's grin returned. 'Of course, I am, Henry. I am a Devereux and I have a glorious destiny.'

CHAPTER 12

JULY 1591

Sir Henry Unton laid his gloved hands on the window embrasure and looked down into the courtyard of Burghley House, where one thousand men under the command of the Earl of Essex had gathered to be inspected by the Queen.

Unton had to admit that Robert had done well. He had heard that upon receiving his commission from the Queen, Robert had written to his stewards, instructing them to recruit every willing and able-bodied man on his estates for his campaign in France. And they had come, nay, they had flocked to the earl's banner as, Unton reflected, was often the way with young men desperate for a taste of battle. He could understand it. Elizabeth had, for the most part, brought peace to England, but while her people rejoiced at the benefits, particularly in trade, that peace brought, her nobles grew restless and frustrated by the lack of action. Were he still young, Unton would have felt the same way, too.

A few minutes later, Sir Thomas Leighton joined him at the window, Sir Henry Killigrew a step behind. Unton nodded a greeting and all three looked down on the courtyard as the Queen stepped out of her carriage, her gloved hand in Robert's.

'You have had your instructions?' Killigrew asked, giving Unton a sideways glance.

'Regarding the Earl of Essex?' Unton, his eyes still on the

couple below, raised his eyebrows understandingly. 'Indeed, I have.'

Leighton chuckled. 'Essex may be her favourite, but Elizabeth does not exactly place much trust in him, does she, Unton?'

'I think it a very wise precaution to send us as advisers to the earl. Essex has little military experience and we,' Unton looked at his companions, 'have plenty between the three of us.'

'Ah, but will he listen to us?' Leighton wondered.

'The Queen commands that he does,' Unton said, taking a folded paper from the purse that hung from his belt and handing it to Leighton.

Leighton read: *'The Queen commands Sir Henry Unton, Ambassador to the Court of King Henri IV, take especial care of the Earl of Essex and his actions in the French campaign. He is to disregard the difference in their respective stations and deal in the plainest manner with him.'*

He handed the paper back to Unton. 'I am very glad that it has been so set down. Will you show that to the earl?'

'I think not, Leighton,' Unton said, tucking it back in his purse. 'I doubt the earl would care to know that he is only in titular command of this campaign.'

A cheer drew the trio's attention back to the courtyard. The Queen had made her inspection and was now entering the house to take dinner with Burghley. They saw Robert eagerly relinquish her hand to stay behind with his troops and throw an arm around a young man who trailed at his heels.

'Is that the earl's brother?' Killigrew asked.

'Walter Devereux. Yes, that's him.'

'He looks very young.'

'Not all that young, but he does not come to court often. I heard he prefers the country. But Essex insisted he come on the campaign,' Unton said. 'I can only imagine the earl wants the Devereux name to be amply represented.'

They watched as Robert gave orders to his captains and the troops began to disperse.

'Well, gentlemen,' Killigrew said with a sigh, 'the earl will no doubt be impatient to sail and I still have matters to attend to. I will see you soon at Dover.'

A summer storm had blown up in Dieppe and the rain was

battering down on the canvas of his tent as it stood with all the others in the French field. Robert could have enjoyed its steady, soothingly soft rhythm were his mind not sorely troubled.

He had been so eager to leave England and fight in the French Protestant cause that he had not considered what his absence might mean. Elizabeth's favour was such a precarious thing as he had already found out. He had done what others had struggled to do before him, marry and retain the favour of the Queen, so he knew she regarded him highly. But he also knew Elizabeth was entertaining Ralegh with renewed vigour, and he suspected Sir Walter would attempt to put him out of favour, and the suspicion troubled him.

But his relationship with Elizabeth was not the only matter on Robert's mind. He needed action to ward off the depression he could feel lurking. It hovered at the edge of his thoughts; when he awoke, it was there to greet him, and when he climbed into his bed, it was the last creature to bid him good night.

And yet, action seemed determined to elude him. King Henri was on the move, marching onto Noyen, and despite Robert's repeated pleas to Elizabeth to be allowed to follow him, her permission had still not been granted. Robert's army had been forced to stay where it was, and Robert was beginning to wonder why Elizabeth had agreed for him to come to France if she were not prepared to let him do anything else. Robert had also written to King Henri, hoping that a request from a fellow sovereign might force Elizabeth's hand, but he had heard nothing from him either. Was it a foible of monarchs to withhold communication from their subjects and allies, he wondered?

Robert was irked too that he was under the thumb of an old man. Unton was a decent fellow, but damn it all, a mere knight. He had been ready to march onto Noyen, with or without the Queen's permission, but Unton had told him the uncomfortable truth of his commission that Robert must follow his advice. Robert had stared at Unton, almost unable to believe his words. Unton had authority over him? It hurt, it actually caused him physical pain to discover that Elizabeth had so little faith in him. She had humiliated him before Unton, and what galled him more was that he didn't know who else knew his queen did not trust him and that he held no real power in the campaign. Elizabeth was treating him like a boy, sending guardians out with him to war to make sure he didn't get into any trouble.

Robert poured himself another cup of wine from the jug and downed it in one gulp. He knew he was drinking too much, but it was the only thing that helped, the only thing that stopped him thinking and feeling things he should not and did not welcome.

Unton poked his head through the tent flap and asked if he could come in. Robert waved him to enter, swaying a little.

Unton frowned, wondering, then saw the wine cup and understood. 'I have something that will please you, my lord. Finally, a letter from King Henri.'

Robert snatched the letter Unton held out and broke the seal. His vision was a little blurry and he had to narrow his eyes to bring the words into focus. 'King Henri's captured Noyen. The town is his.'

'That is indeed wonderful news, my lord,' Unton said.

'He is inviting me to join him there.'

'Ah,' Unton stroked his beard thoughtfully, 'I am not sure that would be wise. The journey to Noyen would take you through enemy territory.'

'God's Death, Sir Henry, I cannot ignore an invitation from the King of France,' Robert said, appalled at the suggestion.

'No,' Unton agreed reluctantly, 'I do not suppose you can.'

Robert was determined. 'Make the arrangements. We leave in the morning.'

Despite Unton's concerns, Robert and his entourage made the journey to Noyen without encountering any opposition. With each mile covered, Robert's mood improved, glad to be finally doing what he had been sent to do. His pride was bolstered even further when a messenger rode up to his horse carrying the French standard and informed him that the King intended to leave his prize of Noyen in order to meet with Robert at a castle in the nearby town of Compiegne. *The king riding out to meet me*, Robert thought and shouted excitedly to Unton of the honour King Henri was doing him.

Unton, pleased for Robert, nevertheless advised his charge to wait. They had been riding for several hours and, in truth,

Unton could do with a rest, but Robert would not hear of it. King Henri was waiting and Robert would not brook any delay.

So, on they rode and Unton found himself cursing Robert as his bones begged for release from the saddle. A few more hours hard riding and they arrived in Compiègne. Not even stopping to wash or change his clothes, Robert presented himself in the castle's Great Chamber and was immediately conducted to the King, who was walking in the castle's pretty gardens.

Robert, as protocol demanded, knelt and bent his head before the French king, but Henri held out both his arms and welcomed the man who could, so everyone said, persuade the Queen of England to do anything. Robert, whose only experience of sovereignty had been Elizabeth, had been ready to flatter and praise King Henri as he had been used to doing with her, but was delighted to find that no such nonsense was necessary.

There was even familiarity and the sense of an almost brotherly bond between them as King Henri put his arm through Robert's and the pair walked in the gardens, talking in French of military matters. Robert enjoyed their conversation immensely. It was such a relief to not to have to speak of love and be able to talk instead of military strategies and battles won and lost.

This is how it should be between sovereign and subject, Robert thought as King Henri led him back to the castle where a feast had been prepared. *Not an endless round of tease and taunt, of insincerity and false emotions, but mutual respect between men. What a shame England has a queen and not a king. How much simpler things would be then.*

CHAPTER 13

The Council chamber was darkening and candles were being lit by pages as the counsellors settled down to business.

Burghley hemmed, his face crumpling in distaste as a gobbet of phlegm slid down his throat. 'Have we any news from the Earl of Essex?'

Cecil sighed, an involuntary reaction to any dealing with Robert, and showed his letter to the Council. 'The earl has written to the Council. King Henri has been successful in capturing the town of Noyen and is pressing on towards Rouen, his army enlarged by the forces of the Duke of Nevers and the Mareschal d'Aumat. If all goes well, writes the earl, once Rouen is taken, the whole of Normandy will surrender to the French king. And the earl assures us if and when this event takes place, the King will not forget what he owes to the Queen of England.'

'The Queen will not allow the French king to forget,' Walsingham said without a trace of humour. 'She wants English ports on the French coast again.'

'The earl does not mention any such intended remuneration in his letter.' Cecil continued, glancing up at Walsingham. 'The English force is now at Pont de l'Arch, but will move to Ravilly within the next few days.'

'But the French king does know what the Queen expects in exchange for our alliance, does he not?' Walsingham persisted.

'The Earl of Essex was instructed to make it clear to him, Sir Francis, but whether he has or not, I cannot say.'

'The question is,' Burghley cut in, 'should the army return to England if the French cause is so close to victory? The Queen is concerned by the cost of the army's maintenance.'

'The Queen is always concerned about money,' Walsingham said impatiently. 'I think it far more important that we remain in France to ensure the Catholic threat is completely eradicated.'

'We all know your hatred for the Catholics, Sir Francis,' Burghley said wryly, 'but our remit was to provide assistance to the French king and, I believe, that has been done. It is also the Queen's desire that the Earl of Essex be recalled to court.'

The counsellors seated around the table looked at one another, all privately thinking that the Queen missing her favourite was a poor reason for recalling Essex.

'But will Essex come, Father?' Cecil wondered. 'You know what he is like. He has defied the Queen's orders before.'

'That, fortunately, is not our concern,' Burghley said, taking the earl's letter from his son and filing it away in his folder. 'The Queen has written a letter instructing the earl to return and it is our duty to send it on. See to it.'

Unton entered the tent gingerly, ensuring the flap closed completely, not wanting to let any chill night air in. He moved to the far side of the tent and looked over Meyricke's shoulder, down to the cot bed where Robert lay. Robert's forehead was slick with sweat and his hair lay flat against his skull. His eyes were closed, his mouth open and his head moved fretfully from side to side.

'How is he?' Unton asked.

'He is still delirious, Sir Henry,' Meyricke answered quietly. 'The campaign must be preying heavily on his mind. He talks even though he is not awake and runs through the lists of the men and our armaments, of reaching towns and besieging them. But his mind seems fixated on the Queen and those he believes wish him ill.'

'The poor young man,' Unton said. 'God forbid this should spread to the army.'

'No, no, sir, do not fear that.' Meyricke led Unton away from the bed. 'This is not a camp fever. I trust you will not speak of this, but my master has suffered from such torments of the mind since his youth.'

'Indeed? What is the cause?'

'I cannot say. The doctors who have attended him supposed it to be a nervous affliction. Worrying, you see, sir, can make him ill.'

'I did not realise he was so sensitive to trouble.' Concerned though Unton was for Robert, he was also worried for the army that it should have so weak a leader. *Should I write to the Council of this nervous affliction?* he wondered, giving Meyricke's pleas for discretion no thought.

'Do you know if my master's brother has returned yet, sir?' Meyricke asked as he sorted through Robert's soiled clothing.

There had been constant skirmishes between the French and English allied forces and those of the enemy, the French Catholic League, and before he had fallen ill, Robert had sent his brother, Walter, out on a patrol into their territory of Ravilly. 'Only Master Walter can calm him better than I.'

'No, his party has not yet returned.'

'Do you think they have run into trouble?'

'How can I know?' Unton replied irritably. 'Of course, it is possible. We have been lucky so far that our losses have been so slight.'

Robert began to mumble, drawing Meyricke and Unton to his side.

'I hope for his sake his brother returns soon. Do what you can for him, Meyricke,' Unton said and left before Meyricke could point out that he had hardly left Robert's side for the past four days and needed no prompting from Sir Henry Unton to continue.

Robert's eyes opened and quickly shut again, for the light hurt and caused an intensely sharp pain at the back of his eyeballs. He waited for the pain to fade and then once more dared to open his eyelids, slowly this time. The pain was not so great and he kept his eyes open, waiting for his surroundings to come into focus. He experienced a moment's confusion at the walls that billowed and the shouts and strange noises from beyond them. Then he remembered where he was. His tent. Ravilly. France.

A head entered his field of vision. The mouth opened and said, 'My lord?'

Robert licked his lips, his tongue finding them rough and dry. 'Gelly?' he croaked.

The head smiled. 'Yes, my lord. Here, sit up and drink some water. You need it.'

Meyricke helped Robert to a sitting position, cradling his head and tipping a horn cup of water towards his lips. Robert sipped the water at first, then greedily. The cup was soon empty and Meyricke helped him to lie back down.

'Have I been ill?' Robert asked as Meyricke tidied the blankets.

'You have had a fever.'

'How long?'

'Five days.'

Robert groaned. 'The army?'

'Being taken care of, never fear.'

Robert allowed his eyes to close. A moment later, they snapped open again. 'Walter. I remember. I sent him on patrol. How long ago was that? Five days, you said. He must be back by now. Where is he, Gelly? Why is he not here?'

Meyricke's breath caught in his throat. 'I... I... I will get Sir Henry.'

Robert caught hold of his arm and held him fast. 'Where is Walter?'

Meyricke placed his hand over Robert's and squeezed. 'His party was ambushed. Your brother was shot. He is dead, my lord. The survivors brought his body back.'

Such terrible news. Robert had sent his only brother to his death while he had been lying useless on his bed, ill from a mere weakness of spirit. So much for a glorious destiny, he could not even protect his own brother. Robert's face crumpled, tears falling from the corners of his eyes to create damp spots on the pillow. Meyricke, afraid the fever would return, attempted to soothe his master, but Robert felt he did not deserve kindness and pushed him away. He turned on his side and cried into his pillow.

Terrible though his grief was, it provided a release, and

when all Robert's tears were spent, Meyricke could see that weeping had done his master good. He ordered meat and wine for Robert and made him eat, watching until more than half of the beef broth had gone and Robert said he could eat no more. The effort of eating and the effects of a full stomach that had shrunk over the past five days soon made Robert sleepy, and Meyricke laid another blanket atop the other and shaded the lantern so that the light would not disturb him. He felt that he too could afford to rest now that Robert was through the worst. He spread out on his cot bed, now bereft of blankets, and folded his arms across his chest to keep warm. As he did so, Meyricke heard the crinkle of paper and remembered the letter from the Queen that he had placed in his jerkin earlier.

'Damn,' he scolded himself, wishing he had remembered its existence before. Robert, he knew, would have been pleased to hear from the Queen.

Never mind, Meyricke told himself. He would give it to Robert in the morning. He strained to listen and satisfied that Robert was sleeping soundly, turned on his side and quickly fell asleep.

Meyricke gripped the back of the chair, his knuckles turning white in his anger. Damn the Queen. She was going to make Robert ill again.

Meyricke had given Robert Elizabeth's letter and he now watched in dismay as Robert's face changed. The brown eyes, a little sunken and purplish from his recent illness, hardened and his jaw tightened, a vein twitching in his cheek. Robert seemed to have become dizzy and Meyricke saw him stretch out a hand and grab the central pole of the tent to steady himself. Meyricke stepped towards him to help, but Robert insisted he was well and stopped his friend's and Unton's advance with an outstretched arm. He waited for his head to stop swimming, then held out the letter to Meyricke.

Meyricke read. No words of praise, none of concern, not even of friendship did Elizabeth write. She wrote instead words of criticism, of reproof, of disappointment.

'I wish I had never given you this letter,' Meyricke hissed and looked at Unton. 'The Queen does nothing but criticise my master, Sir Henry.'

Unton said nothing, trying to remember what he had written in his own letters to the Council. Had he been overly critical of the earl? Was the Queen's disfavour with Essex his fault?

'How can the Queen write such things, Sir Henry?' Robert wondered. 'Does she not know what I have suffered?'

'I assure you I wrote to the Council informing them of your illness and the situation here, my lord,' Unton replied indignantly.

'Then why, why does she berate me in such a manner? She calls me rash, negligent. And undutiful, Sir Henry, undutiful. Me! I, who have done nothing but in duty to her. She complains that I have not kept her informed. For heaven's sake, I am in command of an army. I have been ill. Does she not know all of what has happened? That I have lost my brother? Has no one told her all?' Robert demanded, suddenly doubtful. He searched his companions' faces for an answer. 'She cannot know, I am certain. *I* will write and tell her.'

He pulled out the chair from beneath the rickety table, and drawing a fresh sheet of paper towards him, dipped his pen in the inkpot and began to write.

'My lord,' Unton said, eager to return to army business and prevent any more accusatory questions, 'how are we to proceed? King Henri's man, Marshall Biron, wants us to help him capture Gournay, but the Privy Council—'

'We shall assist Marshall Biron, Sir Henry, never mind the Privy Council. It is what we came for. And we must do it at once, for the Queen commands that I return to England by the end of the month. And the Queen must not be gainsaid, must she?'

Unton winced at his sarcasm. 'No, indeed she must not, my lord.'

Capturing Gournay proved difficult. The town maintained their defences for an entire week, but their walls were unable to withstand a constant battery of cannon and two breaches were made by the French and English forces. At the sight of armed troops marching towards them, the townspeople realised the futility of continuing the fight and surrendered.

The action cheered Robert tremendously. Meyricke was pleased to see his master throw off his grief and his anger in the thrill of battle, and even more pleased to see Robert defy the Queen and refuse to return to England after all. In the explanatory letter he had written to Elizabeth, Robert claimed that it would be a dishonourable act to leave the French king after such a victory, but in truth, it was an act of defiance, a young man making a stand against a cantankerous and ungrateful old woman.

CHAPTER 14

Robert Carey, recently returned from the battlefields of France, stood at Burghley's left side at the end of the Council table. He was waiting, like the rest of the Privy Council. Each member seated at the table looked towards its head where Elizabeth sat, one hand holding a letter, while the other drummed its fingers on the wooden surface.

Burghley's milky eyes stared hard at her face, trying to make the blurred area of her eyes and mouth sharpen so he could tell what was about to happen. It was at times like this that he missed the Earl of Leicester. Leicester, who knew how to handle Elizabeth, who had been able to predict her mercurial moods, pacify her and make her see reason when she had had her tantrums and been blinded by rage.

'How dare he!' Elizabeth's voice was hard, controlled. 'How dare he send this letter!'

'Madam,' Burghley began but was silenced when Elizabeth grabbed her nearest neighbour's wine cup and threw it against the wall.

'You, Lord Burghley,' she jabbed a heavily ringed finger at him, 'you write to the Earl of Essex and you tell him that he is to return to England immediately or I will use him as an example of what can happen when a subject of mine loses my favour.' Elizabeth got up from her chair, causing all those present to rise as well. Her skirts whipped around their chair legs as she stalked the room. 'I should have expected this behaviour. He gets it from his mother, of course. She always was a disobedient bitch.'

'Your Majesty,' Carey blurted, visibly shaking as Elizabeth turned to him, 'I will, of course, deliver any letter you or this Council sends, but I know the earl will think he returns to England in disgrace and he will not be able to bear it. He will retire to the country, unable to show his face and he will diminish. His heart is already broken from the loss of his brother. The loss of your favour will surely kill him. But perhaps you require that satisfaction, Your Majesty. Indeed, I do not know.'

'CAREY!' Burghley cried, as loudly as his cracked octogenarian voice would allow.

'Calm yourself, Burghley,' Elizabeth said, her eyes locked upon Carey. Her gaze made his blood run cold. 'Well, Master Carey, you have courage, I allow you that. The earl certainly manages to inspire loyalty in his associates. Would I could say the same.'

'Madam, you have the most loyal of—,' Burghley began, but Elizabeth cut him off.

'In truth, I had forgot young Walter Devereux's death. Perhaps the earl is not himself and this is why he disobeys my command. I shall write to the earl in my own hand so he can understand how concerned I am over his conduct and how vital it is for his wellbeing that he obeys my command. I trust, Master Carey, that you will convey my feelings to your friend.'

Carey nodded, letting out the breath he had been holding.

'And know, too, Master Carey,' Elizabeth added before resuming her seat, 'that I will not tolerate such a disrespectful outburst from you twice.'

Elizabeth tapped her right foot against the ground impatiently as she waited, seated in her velvet-upholstered chair and shaded by her canopy of estate. She felt the anticipation in the Presence Chamber, knew her courtiers were all wondering and eager to see how the returning Earl of Essex would be received by the Queen who had so recently made known her displeasure with him.

A cheer and applause were heard in the chamber and the courtiers looked around to see who had committed such a daring act. Seeing no one responsible and realising that the sound was coming from outside, the courtiers, almost as one, raised their eyes to the windows. The people of London were cheering and clapping, the way they did when they saw the Queen. Except the Queen was here in the Presence Chamber. So, who were the people cheering?

A notion struck the courtiers as to who it might be and they returned their attention to Elizabeth, whose foot had stopped its tapping. The cheering died away and the courtiers, and Elizabeth, waited for the Earl of Essex, the only man in the country who enjoyed such public acclamation, to appear. When he did, positioned perfectly between the double doors of the Presence Chamber and flanked by liveried men on either side, Elizabeth had to admit that Robert looked every inch a hero.

He had some sense, she noted, not to solicit admiring looks from her courtiers as he processed towards her. Instead, he kept his face forward, his stride unfaltering, measured and unhurried. She knew that walk. She had walked it for more than thirty years.

Robert was before her now, his handsome face showing only the faintest signs of the past troubled months. It irritated her, the fact that he was young and handsome and popular with her people, even in her very presence.

'Your Majesty,' he bowed, elegantly, of course.

Elizabeth made a decision. She would show them all. 'My lord Essex. You are returned.'

'As you commanded, Your Majesty.'

'As I commanded several months ago, sir.'

'I could not leave your army without its commander, madam.'

'A convenient excuse, my lord, and not a credible one. Had you not three good knights upon whom you could rely? Were they not commissioned in this enterprise for that very purpose?' It pleased her to see his clear, unwrinkled brow crease. 'Did you think I would send out an untried cub alone to a battlefield? Did you flatter yourself I would place all my trust in such a rash youth as you have proved time and again to be?'

Robert's cheeks turned a gratifyingly deep red, and Elizabeth heard a whisper hiss around the chamber.

Robert shifted his feet, wanting to kick at Elizabeth's legs and truly hurt her, cause her as much pain as she was causing him. He drew his shoulders back. 'I see Your Majesty is determined to ruin me. If that is your will, I can do naught but yield to it, but I contend, madam, that I do not deserve such a welcome. And if you were to ask the people,' he pointed to the windows, 'the people out there, they would agree with me.'

'Unfortunately for you, sir, those people, *my subjects*, can do nothing for *you*. Your future, if you have one, lies in *my* favour.' She saw him swallow and his shoulders droop a little.

'I am your humble servant, Your Majesty,' he forced himself to utter.

Elizabeth rose and stepped down from the dais until her face was no more than a foot from his. 'Yes, my lord. I know you are.'

CHAPTER 15

HAMPTON COURT PALACE, 1591

Elizabeth had wanted to listen to music and practice her dance steps, so the dancing master had been called for. She enjoyed dancing, enjoyed the closeness it brought with a man, feeling his breath upon her cheeks and neck, his hands around her waist. She reflected that it was the only intimacy she was allowed to enjoy. She found her mind drifting towards memories of Leicester: his hand in hers, her head upon his shoulder. She would never feel such warmth again. She pushed the thoughts of him away for they were too painful. She hurried towards her chair and fell into it, waving her hands at her ladies that they should continue with the lesson.

First, Elizabeth Vernon moved into the centre of the room, her pretty face turning coy as the dancing master placed his hands around her slender waist. His fingers spread and pushed against the heavy fabric, and Elizabeth knew he was feeling the bumroll beneath her lady's skirts, knew too that Mistress Vernon enjoyed his chaste exploration. *What a little trollop*, Elizabeth thought, biting into a hazelnut. *Painting, already, I see. I did not paint when I was her age. I did not need to.*

'You! Enough!' she pointed at Mistress Vernon, waving her aside peremptorily to stand in the corner of the room. 'Bess, your turn.'

Another hazelnut was rolled around her mouth while Bess

Throckmorton, almost shyly, stepped up to the dancing master. *She is a good creature*, Elizabeth thought. *Not at all pretty, so no man is going to try and take her away from me.*

'Faster, dancing master, faster,' she instructed with a laugh.

The dancing master drew Bess in closer, putting the whole length of his arm around her waist and half-lifting her from the ground, whirling her around. He set Bess back on her feet and Bess held out her hands, her eyes on the floor. He took hold of them and spun her around again, according to Elizabeth's orders. At last, he stopped, but Bess continued to turn. She could not stop. Her vision was blurry, her head was spinning, and she felt vomit rise up her throat. And then the ground came up to meet her, and she felt her knees crack against the hard wooden floor.

'What is the matter?' Elizabeth called, rising from her chair and signalling Mistress Vernon to see to the fallen woman. She watched as Bess placed a hand against her forehead, then moved it to cover her mouth. 'Oh, for heaven's sake, unlace her. She is going to faint.'

Bess's stays were cut by Mistress Southwell, while for decency's sake, the dancing master was shown out. Mistress Vernon tugged the dress from Bess's body, who whimpered and tried to hold onto the masses of fabric. But Mistress Vernon was enjoying herself, taking delight in the little adventure, and Bess's dress was tossed aside.

'Get her up,' Elizabeth called, still from her chair. 'She needs to walk about. Open the window.'

Supported on either side, Bess was walked slowly around the room. She wanted to stick her head out of the window to breathe in the fresh air, but she was steered away from it. It was a relief to stand only in her shift, her body no longer tightly bound. She straightened to ease a crick in her back, and when that did not work, disengaged her arms and placed her hands on the small of her back, bending her body backwards, forgetting why her tight lacing had been so necessary.

Elizabeth's eyes widened and she started from her chair. A long, thin finger pointed at Bess's belly, which was round and pronounced beneath her shift. 'You little slut,' Elizabeth screeched, and Bess shrunk away, trying to hide her stomach.

'Your Majesty, please,' she begged, already crying.

'Your belly swells,' Elizabeth continued mercilessly, advancing on the cowering young woman. 'Fornication! Fornication! Who is he? Who is your seducer?'

'Madam, no.'

'Tell me. I command you.'

'He is my husband.'

Elizabeth stopped, her frown creasing. 'I have not given you permission to marry.'

'We married in secret, Your Majesty. We love one another. Forgive us.'

'Who?' Elizabeth demanded, fearing the answer. 'Who is he?'

Bess was snivelling and could not speak. Elizabeth moved towards her and raising her hand, brought it down upon Bess's head, slapping her again and again. The ladies in the room looked on, horrified. None spoke or moved to intervene. They knew better than to get involved when Elizabeth was in a rage.

'You will tell me who he is,' Elizabeth shouted, emphasising each word with a blow. When Bess crawled out of the way of her hands, Elizabeth lifted her skirts to aim a kick at her rump.

Bess cried out in pain. 'Sir Walter. Sir Walter is my husband. Please, please stop.'

Elizabeth did stop. She stopped in bewilderment. No, it was not possible. Walter Ralegh, this ugly girl's husband? But he was Elizabeth's lover, wasn't he? He wrote love poems to her, said he loved her, talked to her in private, made her laugh, made her dream. She looked down at Bess, at the girl's rumpled red face, tears and snot making it even uglier. How was it possible that Sir Walter, handsome Sir Walter, funny Sir Walter, intelligent Sir Walter, could love such a creature?

'Sir Walter Ralegh is your husband?' Elizabeth whispered, bending low.

'Yes, Your Majesty,' Bess sniffed. 'And the father of my child.'

'Call the guards,' Elizabeth instructed coldly, straightening, and Mistress Southwell hastened to obey. The Yeomen Warders promptly entered the Privy Chamber and Elizabeth addressed them directly. 'You will arrest Sir Walter Ralegh and Mistress Throckmorton immediately. They are to be taken to the Tower and kept there.'

One of the guards bent and placed his hand beneath Bess's arm, lifting her gently but firmly upright. Mistress Southwell put Bess's dress in her arms and stepped back. The guards led Bess out of the room and Mistress Vernon closed the door behind them. She and Mistress Southwell looked at one another, neither daring to speak.

Elizabeth, standing in the middle of the room, suddenly let out a loud sob, her body bending as she covered her head with her hands. No one moved. No one dared. Blindly, Elizabeth stumbled back towards her chair, grabbing the cushion and holding it to her chest, crushing it beneath her hands. Betrayed again. Was it all lies? Could no man swear he loved her and mean it? Her handsome Sir Walter had been lying to her all this time. He had loved another and given his beautiful body to be kissed and caressed by an ugly woman. But his body belonged to Elizabeth. She had admired its leanness, its strength. She had dreamt of touching it, feeling his skin beneath her fingers, pressing her cold lips to it and feeling his heat. But now she couldn't think of such things anymore, for they were now exposed as fantasies. Bess Throckmorton had undoubtedly enjoyed the reality of such desires, while she, Elizabeth, was only allowed to dream them. Another dream tarnished, ruined.

Well, they would pay. They would be put in the Tower and kept apart. Bess Throckmorton would have her brat in prison and Walter would never get to see either of them again.

Oh yes, I can be cruel, Elizabeth reminded herself. *Let all who betray me know just how damn cruel I can be.*

The news soon spread around the court. Sir Walter Ralegh, Elizabeth's darling, had got Mistress Throckmorton with child and they were both now imprisoned in the Tower. It was incredible, astonishing. It was worrying for all those young lovers who made assignations with one another and held each other close.

Robert was worried. Though he revelled in Ralegh's fall from favour and laughed about his imprisonment, he could not blame the man for acting as a man. He did wonder what on earth he saw in Bess Throckmorton. Robert had looked upon her and thought her very plain, not worth his attention. He had not guessed that she was Ralegh's paramour, not guessed that she was any man's paramour. Mistress Howard was another matter. There was a handsome woman and one that was ready to defy the Queen's commands regarding chastity. Robert had had Mistress Howard on several occasions. In his apartments, while Elizabeth entertained foreign visitors next door, in the gardens when night began to fall and all was shadow. Hell, he had even had her on the Queen's bed when he had paid a visit to the Privy Chamber and found Elizabeth away. And there was Mistress Southwell, another young woman who had caught his eye and who was currently sharing his bed at every opportunity. Robert pulled Henry Wriothesley aside after a game of cards with the Queen and spoke of his anxiety.

Henry, surprised that Robert should worry about mistresses when he had married without consent and still escaped Elizabeth's wrath, laughed and asked what Robert was proposing. To become a monk? To forswear all lusts of the flesh? What a dull life he would have, Henry told him.

Robert agreed, shaking his head. He had got away with a relationship with another woman once. He was not sure Elizabeth would forgive him a second time. What to do then?

Henry told him to just be discreet. Swear the ladies to secrecy and not to take any unnecessary risks. And besides, Henry pointed out, with Ralegh gone, who else did Elizabeth have to keep her entertained? Robert would be more necessary to Elizabeth than ever before, so even if he was found out, she couldn't afford to imprison him. And, Henry reminded him with a jab of his finger, Robert was an earl, not a lowly knight like Walter. She could hardly imprison one of her nobles without trial, no one would stand for it.

Robert nodded his head, choosing to see the sense in Henry's arguments. Yes, carry on as before, just be a little more careful. That is what he would do.

Cecil had heard the news of Ralegh's downfall with a similar pleasure. Ralegh had never been that much of a problem to him, for Elizabeth kept the man strictly on the periphery of government, but he had been an unnecessary nuisance when he inspired the Queen with talk of voyages to the New World and kept up a constant plea for funding, and it was better for Cecil that he was now out of the way.

Cecil laughed to himself. Perhaps there was some virtue in

being unattractive to the Queen, after all. Ralegh, another handsome man who had been the instrument of his own downfall. His mind turned to Robert.

One down, he told himself, *one to go*.

CHAPTER 16

LINCOLN'S INN

Anthony Bacon tugged the fur collar of his black cloak around his neck to keep himself warm, the biting wind blowing harshly through the narrow passages of the Inns of Court. Dodging other lawyers who were scurrying like black rats to their chambers, he half turned as he heard his name called, but it was too cold to stop walking.

'Anthony, stop, damn you.' His brother, Francis, ran up to him and grabbed hold of his shoulder. Thinner than his brother, he was similar in almost every other respect, down to the pointed black beard. 'I was calling.'

'Oh, was that you?' Anthony said, moving on again. 'Walk then. It is too cold to stand around.'

'I want to talk to you.'

'So I imagined. About what?'

'Our future, brother. I think it is time we accept that our uncle will not be of any help to us.'

'Francis, I have told you before we must continue to hope. Lord Burghley—'

'Lord Burghley may be our aunt's husband but he will forever put his own son before us.'

'But surely he will do something for us. If not a Privy Counsellor, then—'

'Then nothing, Anthony. Lord Burghley will not foster rivals for his son. He will keep us down if he can, I promise you.'

They reached Anthony's chambers and hurried inside. Keeping their cloaks on, they huddled around the brazier, holding their hands over the hot coals. 'What do you propose we do?'

'It's simple. We must ally ourselves with another.'

Anthony stroked his beard. 'You mean the Earl of Essex.'

'Who else would serve us better?'

'There is merit in the notion,' Anthony agreed. 'And I suppose it makes little sense to tie ourselves to an old man not long for this world.'

'Who will no doubt be replaced by his son when he dies,' Francis finished his thought. 'Lord Burghley is already grooming Cecil to take over, whether the Queen realises it or not. And our cousin Cecil will never be a friend to us.'

Warmer now, Anthony snatched up a jug of wine from the table and poured out two cups. He handed one to Francis. 'Essex *is* the coming man, he is the talk of all of London. And in truth, Francis, I have often thought our ideas and thinking are more suited to the earl's circle. The Cecils are cautious creatures, always wanting to preserve things the way they are. They will never countenance change.'

'I am glad you are of my mind,' Francis said, sipping his wine, 'and agree we should approach Essex. I hear you are to journey to Germany at the end of the week?'

'Yes. There are details of a trade treaty that require clarification. I will be away at least three weeks, maybe longer.'

'I don't think we can afford to wait. I think it best if I try for an appointment with the earl as soon as possible.'

'You can manage it alone?'

'Of course, I can manage it alone,' Francis snapped. 'You are my brother, Anthony, not my tutor.'

'Why, Francis, do not be such a shrew,' Anthony laughed and stroked his brother's cheek. 'I trust you not to make a mess of it. Here, have another cup of wine.' He raised his own in the air. 'Here's to better times and better fortune, brother.'

Francis's backside was growing numb. He had been sitting on the bench in the Great Hall at Essex House for more than an hour. Some of his companions on the bench had changed over the course of the hour, while others remained as static as he. He had expected to have to wait to see the earl, and he knew of some people who had waited weeks, even months, but unlike him, most of them had nothing to offer.

The person to his left attempted to strike up a conversation but Francis offered only monosyllabic answers and the man wandered off to find a more voluble person to pass the time with.

Francis looked around and saw the steward with whom he had first announced his request for an audience with the earl. He jumped up from the bench and hurried to him. 'It is most urgent that I see the earl,' he pleaded.

The steward, who was used to being harassed in this manner, halted, his annoyance evident. 'Master Bacon, you *are* on the list.'

'I have been on the list for the past eight days.'

'It is a very long list, sir. You are not the only one. As you can see,' he waved his arm in a wide arc that took in the room, 'many people want to see the earl.'

'Wait,' Francis said, laying his hand on the steward's arm as he made to walk away, 'I am not like all these others. I do not want him to do something for *me*. I want to do something for *him*.'

The steward met his eye for the first time. 'Make it worth my while and I will see what I can do.'

Francis delved his hand into the purse that hung from his belt and drew out four groats. He slid the coins into the steward's hand. 'I must see the earl today.'

The steward dropped the coins into his own purse, told Francis to wait and exited through a door in the corner of the room.

Francis resumed his seat on the bench and rested his sweating hands on his knees. He tried not to measure the passing time, but he found himself counting. Four minutes, five. *How long does it take*, he wondered, *to move me to the top of the bloody list?* His head jerked around as the corner door opened and the steward came out, scanning the room for Francis. Francis got to his feet and strode over to him.

'Come with me,' the steward said and headed back the way he had come, throwing one quick glance over his shoulder to make sure Francis was following. Along a short corridor and into a much smaller chamber, richly furnished with colourful tapestries and gold plate, a central desk and chair, and a chest heaped with a great pile of papers. At the desk sat Robert. The steward announced Francis, waited a moment to be dismissed and left.

'How much did you give him?' Robert asked.

'My lord?'

'My steward. I can always tell when he has been bribed.'

Francis did not know whether Robert was annoyed or simply curious and took two seconds to decide whether he should tell the truth or lie. He told the truth.

Robert raised his eyebrows, impressed. 'Then I appreciate how much you wanted to see me. He would have accepted less. And I would have got around to you, you know. I make sure I see everyone who wants to see me.'

'I am sure you do all your admirers that honour, my lord, but I did not want to delay being of service to you.'

'You are Sir Francis Bacon, yes?' Robert asked, consulting a paper. 'Your brother is Sir Anthony Bacon, currently abroad on Her Majesty's service, and you are cousins to the Cecils.'

'That is correct, my lord.'

'A notable connection, kinship with Lord Burghley.'

'Notable perhaps, but the connection does neither my brother nor myself any good.'

'Yet, you are clever,' Robert said, rising from behind his desk and sitting on its edge. 'No, make no denial. I can see it in your face. Does not Lord Burghley covet clever men?'

'Not if they could be considered rivals to his son's interests.'

'Ah, I see. So, you come to me?'

'Not as a second choice,' Francis said hastily.

'No? I am glad to hear it. The thought had occurred.'

Francis shuffled his feet. 'While my brother and I could seek to ally ourselves with the Cecils, the reason for doing so would be purely one of blood and natural affinity. But offering service to you, my lord, makes plain common sense and accords with our true inclinations.'

'Why so?' Robert frowned and folded his arms, his badge of Master of the Horse nestling amongst his lace cuffs.

'If you will forgive my familiarity, my lord, you are a peer of the realm, a scion of an ancient and distinguished family. You have the favour of the Queen. You are youthful, brave, handsome and the people love you. Lord Burghley can claim to have only one of these assets – the favour of the Queen. His son has none. And there is no virtue in allying oneself with an old man when the future belongs to the younger generation.'

'Indeed, Sir Francis,' Robert said, both impressed and flattered. He was used to being complimented, but not in so bold a manner. It pleased him to hear another speak of his attributes, even as it embarrassed him. 'What is it you believe you can do for me?'

'Innumerable services, my lord. Secretary, lawyer, confidante, intelligencer.'

'Intelligencer?' Robert sprang up, suddenly serious. 'You mean in the manner of Walsingham's agents?'

'I do, my lord. The late Master Walsingham cultivated a strong intelligence web that both I and my brother played some part in. On occasion, you understand, not with any great regularity. But our involvement meant we were able to cultivate our own contacts and sources of information. If you want to know secrets, my lord, my brother and I can find them out for you.'

'I will not deny, Sir Francis, I am in sore need of such service. I cannot be the man I wish to be without having access to such intelligence, here and abroad.'

'Then if may speak boldly, you need my brother and I. I have my sources here in England. My brother, Anthony, has considerable contacts abroad. If I may ask, my lord, do you already have a secretary?'

'A man who writes my letters, no more. The position is yours if you can make good on your boasts.'

'I can, my lord,' Francis assured him, thinking that Anthony would be proud of how he had handled the interview, 'and I thank you. It will be an honour to serve you.'

CHAPTER 17

GREENWICH PALACE

Cecil took the seat Elizabeth offered him in her Privy Chamber. He looked around the room, pleased that there were only two ladies present and they away in the far corner. The conversation he wanted to have with Elizabeth he wished to remain private and not be gossiped around the court. 'I have good news, Your Majesty.'

Elizabeth smiled back at him. 'I am very glad to hear it, Pygmy. From the Commons?'

Cecil nodded. 'Following the announcement of the renewed threat from Spain, this current threat being that they are considering the launch of another armada against England and are bribing disaffected Scottish nobles to join them in an attack against us, the Commons have agreed to double the subsidy granted to the Crown for the defence of the realm.'

Elizabeth laughed and clapped her hands. 'Excellent. I am glad they are so conformable to our wishes.'

'Indeed, madam. In fact,' he hesitated and tugged at his earlobe, 'I believe that we may be able to get a little more money out of Parliament.'

Elizabeth's eyes widened. 'More money?' she asked with interest.

Elizabeth always needed money, for the cost of maintaining her court and palaces was enormous and was the main reason why her ministers were not punished for accepting bribes, for while they were receiving money from other people, they were not demanding a salary from her.

'I believe so,' Cecil continued. 'If the House of Lords were to state to the Treasury that, despite the doubling of the subsidy, it is still not enough to defend the country against foreign threats, the Commons would be compelled, in their own interests, to increase the sum. I have the backing of the entire Privy Council in this matter, madam,' he added.

'Then pursue it, Pygmy,' Elizabeth said eagerly, waving him towards the door. 'There is always a need for more money for the Treasury. The defence of this country is my chief concern and I cannot defend it unless I am granted money. Make that clear to the Lords.'

'I will,' Cecil was happy to assure her and left to make his directions.

Unfortunately for Cecil, and for Elizabeth too, Robert sat in the House of Lords. He was present when the bill was read out in the chamber, and discussing it later with Francis Bacon, realised that Cecil was behind it. In truth, Robert did not care whether Elizabeth was given more money or not, for it would not be coming out of his household, but he was keen to thwart Cecil in any way he could. Francis suggested that as he was a member of the House of Commons he stand up and oppose the motion when Cecil rose to propose it, and Robert eagerly agreed. Block him, he told Francis, say whatever you must, but block the little Pygmy.

Elizabeth had never liked this part of being a queen, having to sit and listen while the members of Parliament made their speeches. She remembered the early years of her reign when she had been harangued by her Members of Parliament to marry. Already convinced that she would never marry yet unwilling to lose her advantage of being an eligible bride for all the bachelors in Europe, she had exercised her lifetime's experience of avoiding awkward questions and kept her subjects, and her fellow royalty, guessing. She had continued to provide her answerless answers to Parliament, provoking its members sorely and often delighting in the knowledge that she did so. Although Elizabeth was not like her father – she had not his surety of the demi-divinity of the sovereign, nor his lack of hesitation in removing heads – she often wished that she did not have to deal with Parliament, that she could just make laws and demand money from her subjects without having to get their agreement first.

Lord Keeper Pickering was making his address, telling his audience that even more money was needed by the Treasury to keep England safe from Spain and Scotland. The Commons had already shown their loyalty to the Crown with the approval of the double subsidy but the Treasury needed more.

Elizabeth knew that Cecil's plan of trying for more money was asking much of her people, perhaps too much, but she desperately wanted his scheme to succeed. Money, money, money. She always needed it and always seemed to lack it, no matter how many economies she made in her household. She scanned the assembly, squinting to try and make out the various expressions on the men present, but she could only make out those nearest to her. What were they all thinking?

'The Member for Middlesex,' Lord Keeper Pickering declared, relinquishing the floor.

Elizabeth leant towards her secretary to her left and murmured, 'Name?'

'Sir Francis Bacon, Your Majesty,' he promptly replied.

'Bacon?' *Oh yes*, she thought, *Essex's friend*. She straightened, her ears pricked to catch every word.

'Honoured gentlemen,' Bacon said, 'this proposal goes against all custom. It is not the place for the House of Lords to put forward a proposal for yet more subsidies, but the privilege and prerogative of this House. The privilege and prerogative of we members to make the offer of an enlarged subsidy for the benefit of Her Majesty and to take care of this nation, not for the Lords to demand one from us. Have we not given enough? Have not the people of England, gentle people who have had to sell their plate, farmers who have had to sell their pots to raise the money for the subsidy already agreed, have they not given enough? Spain has always threatened England and we have always survived, against tremendous odds. What true need then of yet more money? Is this not just a stratagem of the Privy Council to gather more money to themselves?'

Bacon's fellow members chorused their agreement, glad that one of them had had the courage to speak up, even in the very presence of the Queen. A few cast surreptitious glances at Elizabeth, wary of drawing her attention. What would she think of such flagrant disrespect and suspicion of her Council?

'This proposal for yet more money,' Bacon continued, 'should be rejected to preserve the integrity and inviolability of this House.' He sat down, tugging his cloak straight, pulling the fabric out from beneath his buttocks before he finally dared to look at the Queen.

As he knew she would be, her eyes, mere slits in the pale oval of her face, were fixed on him. He could almost feel her hate.

'You failed.' Elizabeth stood before him in the Council chamber. She was majestic, magnificent and frightening. She did not sit, nor did she invite Cecil to take his ease. She was in no mood to be kind.

Cecil took a deep breath, keeping his eyes firmly on the buckles of his shoes. 'Unfortunately so, Your Majesty.'

'So, my Treasury does not benefit from the extra money you promised me—'

'I made no promises, Your Majesty.'

'— and now the Commons believe my Council to be avaricious and grasping, and will begin to suspect any motion put forward by them in the future. This has not been a good day's work, Pygmy.'

'No, indeed.'

'And I have had to suffer the indignity of being refused by my Commons to my face. I was there, Pygmy, in the chamber, and those wretches insulted me.'

'Most regrettable, Your Majesty.'

'Regrettable, you call it,' Elizabeth sneered. 'I agree, it is regrettable. How could you allow it to happen?'

Cecil looked up at last. 'I fear, madam, that certain elements within the House of Lords acted against the Privy Council's intentions and incited the rebellion in the Commons.' He fell silent, waiting for Elizabeth to make the inevitable connection.

'Certain elements,' she echoed, moving to stand before him, her sour breath coating his skin. 'And I suppose you know who these certain elements are?'

Cecil said he did indeed have an idea and Elizabeth commanded her Pygmy to speak, that she would not have him keeping his idea to himself. He raised one eyebrow, trying to give the suggestion that he was loathe to speak. 'The Earl of—'

'Essex, was it?' Elizabeth cut in, her mouth forming a pout. 'Eh, Pygmy, was it him?'

Cecil nodded.

'Yes, well, it would be, wouldn't it? That Francis Bacon fellow is in his service, I believe. I thought he was a cousin of yours, Pygmy?'

Cecil confirmed that he was related to the Bacon brothers.

'So, why is he not on your side, eh?' she asked. 'Why is Bacon not speaking up for *you*?'

Cecil shrugged. 'I and my father have not thought Bacon and his brother suitable servants.'

'You don't like them. Why not? Is it because they are sodomites? I have heard that about them.'

'I really could not say, madam,' Cecil, his nose wrinkling at such a distasteful subject.

'Are you certain Essex has had a hand in this?' Elizabeth said, her expression turning doubtful and eyeing Cecil suspiciously. 'Essex knows how important the subsidy is to me. I do not think he would do anything that would be an act against me.'

Cecil wanted to say to Elizabeth that she was wrong, that Robert Devereux would do and say anything that furthered his own ends, but he suspected his words would be misconstrued and he would lose what little faith Elizabeth had in him. So, he kept silent.

Elizabeth looked at him for a long moment, then sighed. 'Well, never mind. We do still have the double subsidy. It will have to do. I trust in my Council to make the most of it. Can you do that, Pygmy?'

Cecil bridled at the insinuation. 'I will do my best, Your Majesty,' he said and backed out of the room at her dismissal.

And if nothing else, he thought as he walked back to his office, *this incident has taught me that the Earl of Essex has designs on playing politics against me. I shall not underestimate him again.*

Robert clinked his glass against Francis's and drank down the fine Burgundian wine. 'A victory, Francis,' he declared.

'For you and for the Commons, my lord,' Francis agreed, sipping his wine and taking a seat, pleased to have been invited to dine with the Devereux family at Essex House. Dinner was over and it had been a fine dinner, far better than he was accustomed to eating in his lawyer's room in Lincoln's Inn. He and Robert were now alone, sitting by the fire in Robert's private closet.

'Aye, we showed the little Pygmy, did we not, Francis?' Robert grinned, running his hand through his auburn curls. 'That was one in the eye for him.'

'The Cecils made a grave miscalculation,' Francis said, a touch smugly. 'They thought they could command the Commons. I am glad to say that they cannot.'

'What is more important, Francis,' Robert said, pointing his glass at him, 'is that they cannot command *me*. I know what they think of me. They think I am a boy, someone who knows nothing about politics and the running of a country.'

'They know different now, my lord,' Francis assured him. 'And if I may be so bold, I think you should continue to disillusion them.'

Robert licked his lips and frowned. 'What mean you, Francis?'

'Become a statesman,' Francis suggested with a small shrug. 'Indeed, what could be more natural?'

Robert tugged his earlobe. 'I already have a voice in Parliament, Francis.'

'But there you are one among many. If you were to become a Privy Counsellor, you would be one among a few.'

'A Privy Counsellor?' Robert sat up, a little of his wine splashing on his hose in his haste. 'I?'

'Why not? Are you not one of the foremost peers in the realm? Do you not have power and influence, both at court and in the country, as well as abroad? I can think of no better candidate for a Privy Counsellor. And it would certainly ensure that there is opposition to the policies of Lord Burghley and Robert Cecil. They would not have everything their own way. And since

Walsingham's death, you have no one well disposed to you in the Council.'

Robert rose and began pacing the room. Francis watched him, wondering if he had said too much, gone too far. His words might seem to Robert an impertinence, a lowly gentleman telling a noble how he should act, what he should do. But someone had to tell him, Francis reasoned, and he had learnt that Robert always wanted to be more than a mere courtier, that he needed to be more to satisfy the expectations he placed upon himself as a scion of the Devereux dynasty.

'You are right, Francis,' Robert said at last, wagging a finger at him. 'I should be on the Council. In fact, it is a disgrace that I am not already. Why have I not thought of this before? I mean, good Lord, what is Elizabeth thinking, keeping me from it? Am I not right, Francis?'

'You are, my lord,' Francis returned, inwardly a little amused by Robert's indignation, so strong yet so recently acquired.

'Then I must tell her to appoint me,' Robert decided, nodding his head emphatically.

Francis rose, a little diffidently. 'If I may be so forward, my lord, ask rather than tell. As you have said so often yourself, the Queen is a woman and women, in my experience, never take kindly to being told what to do. They are contrary and inclined to do the opposite out of spite.'

Robert smiled a crooked smile. 'In your experience, Francis? I thought your experience did not extend towards women.'

'Still, my lord,' Francis said, the smile stiffening on his face, 'the principle is the same. Ask, rather than tell.'

Francis found that a little of his resentment for the tactless slur on his manhood faded as Robert patted him on the shoulder and said he would take his advice.

They were in the gardens of Hampton Court Palace, for the day was warm and Elizabeth had wanted to feel the sun on her face. She had commanded the archery butts to be set up and ordered Robert to join her.

'You have something on your mind,' Elizabeth said as she aimed her arrow at the target some twenty yards away. She loosed the bowstring and, a moment later, the arrow thudded into the outer ring of the butt. 'Damn,' she hissed, stepping aside for Robert to take his shot. 'Well, have you not?'

'I have,' Robert said, stepping up to the mark and taking aim. His arrow hit one of the inner rings. 'May I speak of it?'

Elizabeth, with a show of impatience, said he may and gestured for him to take another shot.

'I was wondering, hoping rather, that you would consider me for some greater service than Master of the Horse.'

'What is wrong with Master of the Horse?' Elizabeth said sharply. 'Leicester held that position for over twenty years. It was only with the greatest reluctance that he gave it up to you.'

'And I do not mean to give it up, Bess,' Robert said. 'But Leicester was not just the Master of the Horse, was he?'

Elizabeth's breast heaved with a great sigh. 'You mean you want a seat on my Council?' She was surprised that it had taken Robert so long to get around to the subject.

'It's not too much to ask, is it?'

'My turn to shoot.' Elizabeth's skirts brushed him aside. She took aim again, too quickly, and her arrow thudded into the grass a yard short of the target. She was a poor loser and angrily thrust her bow at an attendant. 'I have had enough of shooting for today. Let us go in.' She began walking back towards the palace, striding ahead of Robert. 'Oh, do stop sulking, Robin. I have not said No, have I?'

'You have not said Yes, either.'

She took a few more steps and then halted. 'Being a Privy Counsellor carries a great deal of responsibility, dedication—'

'I know that, Bess.'

'Do you, Robin?' she queried, looking him square in the face. 'Do you?'

'Damn it, Bess, you have made Robert Cecil a Privy Counsellor. If you can make that hunchback a counsellor, why not me?'

'Is that all it means to you?' Elizabeth asked, playing with her pearl necklace. 'A chance to be even?'

'No, but—'

'Sir Robert Cecil has been made a Privy Counsellor because he has proved himself worthy. And I did it in deference to his father.'

'Oh well, that is it, is it not?' Robert flung his bow on the grass and started pacing up and down before her. 'I have not got a father to plead for me. I have to carve my own way—.' He stopped, his mind suddenly full of memories.

He had hardly known his father, it was true, for Walter Devereux had been away more on the Queen's business than he had been at home, but Robert had found a second father in the Earl of Leicester and had welcomed the warmth and security he had provided. When Leicester had died, Robert had truly mourned him, not just as a presence in his life but as a support, someone who had looked out for him and tried to advance his interests. Robert now lacked that kind of man in his life and unlike Cecil, who had a father, had to sail the stormy waters of court life alone.

'Have you finished?' Elizabeth asked with a loud sigh. 'I do not want to hear of your pitiful excuses. If we are reduced to haranguing one another with our personal losses, then I can beat your number ten times over. You hear me, young man?'

'Yes, madam,' Robert mumbled, his eyes travelling aimlessly over the palace windows.

Elizabeth softened, affected by the image he cast before her. And he was right, in his way. He was due a reward. Her hunched shoulders dropped, her jaw unclenched and her eyes lost their intensity. 'I do not mean to be harsh, Robin. You must think of me as a mother who chides her child only to improve him.' She reached her leather-gloved hand up to his cheek and gave the blushing skin a gentle caress. 'There now. Look at me, Robin. Look at me.' She felt a thrill of pleasure that was almost maternal as his dark eyes looked into hers. 'You can have a seat on my Privy Council. You are one of my nobles and it is only fitting.'

Robert's face brightened. He grabbed both of Elizabeth's hands and kissed them each several times. 'You are my most gracious queen,' he swore, making Elizabeth laugh and feel inclined to return to the butts.

Burghley held the parchment close to his face and read aloud. 'You do swear by Almighty God to be a true and faithful servant unto the Queen as a member of her Privy Council. You will not have knowledge or understand any manner of thing to be attempted, done or spoken against Her Majesty's person, honour, crown or dignity, but you will stop and withstand the same to the uttermost of your power, and reveal it to Her Majesty or to her Privy Council. You will in all things faithfully and truly declare your mind and opinion, according to your heart and conscience; and will keep secret all matters committed and revealed unto you, or that shall be treated of secretly in Council. And if any matter touch upon any fellow counsellor, you will keep it secret until Her Majesty or the Privy Council make publication of it. You will to your uttermost bear faith and allegiance to the Queen's Majesty. And generally in all things, you will do as a faithful and true servant to Her Majesty, so help you God.'

Robert, kneeling, raised his chin a little higher. 'I do swear it.'

There was a polite round of applause from the spectators in the Presence Chamber who had gathered to witness Robert's appointment. Elizabeth took the quill her secretary proffered and signed her name at the bottom of the parchment.

'The Earl of Essex may take his place at the Privy Council table,' she announced and gestured at the corridor visible through the door at the side of the room and the Privy Council chamber that lay beyond.

Robert forced down a smile as he knew it would be inappropriate, not to say childish, to display such pleasure at his appointment. He bowed to Elizabeth and followed Burghley out of the Presence Chamber, shortening his stride so as not overtake the old man or step on his long cloak. When they entered the Privy Council chamber, Robert felt strangely bereft, his pride no longer bolstered by an audience and disappointed that this was to be a private moment and not a public one, with just him and the other counsellors present.

'Just one more formality, my lord,' Burghley murmured, struggling to hide his unhappiness at Robert's admission to the Council. 'Your signature is required.'

Robert sat down at the table and a secretary placed a parchment beneath his hands. His eyes swept over the names of the Queen's Privy Counsellors and he felt a thrill of pride as a quill pen was handed to him and he signed his name on the official paper – *Robert, Essex*. Sand was shaken over the wet ink by a clerk and blown away.

It was done. Robert was officially a Privy Counsellor. He was a man of substance, of government. He was now one of a select few, men who made important decisions about the governance of the country and advised the Queen on foreign matters.

Burghley bowed his head and smiled down at the young man. 'Welcome to the Privy Council, Lord Robert.'

CHAPTER 18

WHITEHALL, 1593

Elizabeth winced as pain shot up her cheek and struck her temple. *Damn that tooth*, she thought. *I suppose I shall have to have it pulled as Burghley says I should.*

She glanced at Robert sitting further down the table and allowed herself a small smile at his serious and eager face. The boy wanting to prove himself a man. Elizabeth supposed that being a husband and father he had already proved himself a man, physically at least, but to her, those two states were proof of nothing more than lust. To Elizabeth, a man was a man when he demonstrated intelligence and knew when to exercise caution, but a man's chief attribute should be loyalty. She looked around the table, at the old men sitting there. Old men, yes, she knew that was what they were, but she also knew that she could rely on them. These new men at her court, the young men, they frightened her with their ideas and their energy, and their constant desire for change.

Even now, Robert was talking about the Spanish threat again. How he hated being at peace. She remembered Leicester when he was of a similar age as Robert. He had been just as keen to bloody his sword and the trouble she had had curbing his enthusiasm. Elizabeth felt too old to go through all that again, but she had the unpleasant feeling that with Robert she might have to.

Her gaze was drawn to Burghley, who was reaching for the

Bible that habitually lay in the centre of the table, dragging it towards himself with his crabbed fingers. He turned the pages quickly, knowing exactly what he was looking for. He twisted the book around to face Robert and jabbed a finger at a passage. He knew the passage by heart and declared, '*Bloody and deceitful men shall not live out half their days.*'

Elizabeth looked at Robert, who sighed and rolled his eyes. 'You are too cautious, old man.'

'My lord,' Cecil got to his feet, his chair scraping on the floorboards. 'I will not have you talk to my father in such a disrespectful way.'

Burghley patted his son's hand, a temporising gesture, but Cecil was too angry and continued to glare at Robert.

Robert held up his hands in a gesture of contrition. 'Forgive me, Lord Burghley, that was rude of me. But please, gentlemen, you know that the Spanish are making plans to attack us again. They are the very reason for the grant of the double subsidy to the Crown.'

'For defence,' Cecil said grumpily, resuming his seat, 'not attack.'

Robert ignored him. 'The Spanish failed the last time because God knew we were in the right, but the truth is we are woefully unprepared for another attack. The Spanish are making their plans and construing their plots—'

'You cannot possibly know that,' Cecil scoffed.

'I can know that,' Robert insisted. 'You and your father are not the only ones who have an intelligence network, Cecil.'

Ah, that has shut Cecil up, Elizabeth noted with interest. *So, Robert has his own spies, does he?* She watched Cecil look to his father, who shook his old white head and closed the Bible. Robert, who knew he had scored a point, was looking pleased with himself.

'I think that is enough for today, gentlemen,' Elizabeth said, noting that Burghley was looking tired. 'Essex, you will stay.' The counsellors filed out, leaving her and Robert alone. She chuckled. 'Why Robin, once again you look like a sulky schoolboy.'

'I am no schoolboy, Bess. I wish you would recognise that small fact. And am I now to be punished for speaking my mind?' Robert asked pertly. 'I thought I was allowed to do that. It is a perquisite of the Privy Council, is it not? Or perhaps you just want men who will say "Yes, Your Majesty" and "No, Your Majesty"? I hope so because that is who you have in your Privy Council. Pygmies, all of them.'

'Do not be insolent,' Elizabeth said, not as sternly as she knew she should. 'Cecil is right. You should have respect for your elders.'

'I cannot respect such a cautious policy in regard to the Spanish.'

'The Spanish have been our enemy since my accession,' Elizabeth said dismissively.

'Because they think we are weak, Bess. If we were to be the aggressors for a change, they would have to reconsider how dangerous we can be.'

'Enough, Robin. All you speak of is Spain this and Spain that. I have heard enough of Spain. I tire of Spain.'

Robert sighed and leant back in his chair. 'Must our conversations always be on your terms?'

'Should I allow *you* to dictate them, then?' Elizabeth asked, raising a thin eyebrow.

Robert leant forward and reached across the table for her hands. 'If you will not countenance war, then I would like to speak of another matter, if you would allow it.'

The warmth of his hands pleased Elizabeth and she bid him speak, if only to hear the sound of his voice, pleading with her.

'The post of attorney-general is vacant. I would like to propose Sir Francis Bacon.'

She had not expected this. This was no trivial matter, the appointment of a secretary or a new groom. This was a matter of the governance of the country. Did Robert really think she was so foolish as to make such appointments on a whim, simply because he asked? Elizabeth pulled her hands from beneath Robert's and put them in her lap. 'I am already considering Sir Edward Coke for the attorney-generalship.'

Robert waved that aside. 'Oh no, consider Bacon, Bess. He is a clever fellow. Quick-witted, knowledgeable—'

'He is a friend of yours.'

'He serves me well.'

'And would continue to do so as attorney-general.'

Robert was affronted. He was proposing a man who would serve her better than any other. He was thinking only of her and here she was, insinuating otherwise. 'Why do you say such things?'

'Sir Francis Bacon has spoken against me in Parliament. When I asked for more money to defend this country against the Spanish, that subsidy you spoke of just now, he blocked it with a cry that it was against parliamentary custom.'

'Ah yes,' Robert said, jabbing his finger against the table top, 'but when Cecil proposed that subsidy, Bess, he was asking for much more than normal, and Parliament knew it was unlikely that all of the money would go to England's defence. Bacon was simply protecting the interests of Parliament. All he did was speak his mind.'

'Speaking one's mind seems to be a common trait amongst young men nowadays.'

'Would you censure us for that, Bess? I know what is best for you and this country. If you love me, as you profess you do, then you will grant me this small favour.'

'Do not talk to me of love when you talk of matters of state. Burghley has a high opinion of Sir Edward Coke, and I trust *his* opinion in this matter.'

'Burghley does not propose Coke because he believes Coke has the talent for the position. He makes no recognition of Coke's talent. He proposes him because he has Coke in his power and he is a man who will do as he is told. And you cannot throw age at me as a reason because even if Coke were fifty years older than Bacon, he would still lack Bacon's wit and intelligence.'

'I see I must remind you that I am queen here, Robin.' Elizabeth rose and headed for the door.

'Will you at least consider Bacon for the attorney-generalship, Bess?' Robert called after her. 'For me?'

'No, Robin, I will not,' Elizabeth said and left, leaving him alone.

Robert slumped in his chair, angry with Elizabeth for denying him. He had promised Francis the attorney-general post would be his and now he would have to tell him he had failed. Yet again, Elizabeth had made him look like a fool and exposed his inadequacies.

Francis Bacon was waiting in Robert's apartments and bowed as Robert entered.

'Have you been waiting, Francis?' Robert said, untying his cloak, trying not to look him in the eye. He was embarrassed, ashamed of his failure. *What will Francis think of me?* he wondered unhappily.

'A short while, my lord. I was just wondering if there was any news on the post of the attorney-general?'

Robert poured himself a cup of wine before answering. 'I cannot get it for you, Francis. I am sorry.'

Francis frowned. 'But you said—'

'I know what I said,' Robert snapped testily. 'But the Queen is immovable. She has decided that the attorney-generalship will go to Sir Edward Coke.'

'I see,' Francis said, as calmly as he could, but the news was a blow. Robert had promised him that the attorney-generalship was as good as his and Francis had believed him. And why should he not? Robert was favoured by the Queen and had boasted that she would do anything he asked. Francis had trusted in his power and had even written to his brother to tell him of his imminent promotion. 'Then I shall not bother you any longer, my lord.'

'Wait, Francis. I will not let you go empty-handed.' Robert opened a small wooden box that stood on the buffet and took out a parchment. 'These are the deeds to Twickenham Park. The house and gardens are yours. It is a fair estate, worth two thousand pounds. Now, do not deny me this. I promised you a position and I have not been true to my word. You shall wound me if you refuse.'

Francis had no intention of refusing the gift, but took the parchment with a show of reluctance, thanked Robert and bid him good day. He made it to the corridor before his anger showed itself. He kicked the wall and cursed Robert for his false promises. He had needed that post, not an estate out in the damned country. Not that the house would not be an asset and it was generous of the earl, he admitted, but... Francis heard footsteps and turned to see his cousin, Cecil, walking towards him. *Damn,* he thought, *had he seen my little display of anger?*

'Cousin,' Cecil said, nodding a greeting and passing on by.

Francis hurried after him. 'Cousin Robert, may I have a word with you?'

'I cannot tarry, cousin.'

'I shan't detain you, but I was wondering if there was anything you could do for me?'

'Do for you?' Cecil repeated. 'I thought you were attached to the Earl of Essex.'

'Not attached, cousin. And we are family, after all.'

Cecil halted. 'Indeed we are, cousin, but I cannot help but think you chose to follow the Earl of Essex because you believed richer rewards lay in that direction.'

'Cousin—'

'I suggest you stay close to the earl, for he does indeed possess the favour of the Queen, and I am sure he can obtain for you all you desire. But Francis, a word of warning. The earl is, no doubt, a man of great charm and understanding, but I fear he would not look too kindly on one who would switch allegiance so easily. It would do you no good were he to hear of it. Good day to you.'

Francis watched his cousin limp away, annoyed with himself for his foolishness. By exposing his dissatisfaction with the earl, he had put himself in a dangerous place. His cousin would not help him, that much was clear, so it seemed Francis was tied to the Devereux star. He would need to make sure it did not fall.

CHAPTER 19

ESSEX HOUSE, 1594

'Shall we go to the playhouse tonight, Robert?' Henry Wriothesley asked, his feet up on a stool, a cup of wine in one hand and a book of poems in another. He was always ready to make himself at home in any of Robert's houses.

'If you wish it, Henry,' Robert replied distractedly, intent on the letter he was reading.

'Do you want to hear my poem?'

Robert declined, saying that he had other things on his mind, and Henry, surprised, demanded to know what they were, what all the paperwork was that Robert was sorting through. When Robert told him it was intelligence, Henry snorted and joked that he doubted it was Robert's own.

Robert smiled at the playful insult and told him that the intelligence came from Anthony Bacon, Francis' brother, who, Robert had discovered, had an astonishing network of contacts, as good as any network Walsingham had created as Elizabeth's spymaster. Henry protested that Robert could not know of such a matter, that as so much of Walsingham's business had been conducted in secret it was impossible to know how deep or how extensive his spy network had been. But Robert was insistent and not a little annoyed that Henry should think so little of him. He reminded Henry he was a Privy Counsellor and had access to state papers. Henry raised both eyebrows and said he thought it odd that Cecil would let Robert anywhere near such sensitive documents, causing Robert to retort proudly that Cecil could not legally stop him.

'And I do know Anthony's network is good,' Robert persisted. 'You will not believe me, will you? I'll prove it to you.' Robert held up the letter he had been reading. 'This is from Anthony Bacon. A man called Esteban Ferrara da Gama, a Portuguese, is corresponding with highly placed officials in Spain. This same da Gama is currently here in London and staying at the home of Doctor Roderigo Lopez.'

Henry, intrigued, moved his feet to the floor and sat up. 'Lopez? The Queen's doctor?'

'The very same. So, what does the Queen's doctor have in common with a Spanish intelligencer?'

'Tell me,' Henry demanded eagerly.

Robert coloured a little. 'Well, I do not know yet, but it is suspicious, would you not say?'

Disappointed that Robert did not have any firm evidence he could read, Henry flicked his hand at him. 'They may just be friends, Rob.'

'Well, yes, they may,' Robert admitted, 'but it is also conceivable that this da Gama is sending information to King Philip of Spain. Court gossip that Lopez tells him over dinner or during quiet fireside conversations.'

'Very well, Robert, suppose he is doing that. What of it? I suspect if you made enquiries, you'd discover that a quarter of the court receives a pension from Spain for the very same thing. I even heard tell of one courtier, years ago, who was approached by a Spanish agent to spy on the Queen. The courtier agreed, took the agent's money, and then told him that he just needed to get the Queen's permission first. Such arrangements are accepted. They are just another means that Elizabeth can get away with not paying her ministers.'

'You are not thinking, Henry,' Robert snapped. 'I agree, there is nothing in it if da Gama is just a spy, but what if Lopez is involved? Lopez is constantly at court. He attends many of the highest people in the country. He has even attended on me. Through Lopez, da Gama could hear so many secrets. And Lopez has access to the Queen. He gives her tonics for her health, ointments for cuts and other ailments. What is to stop da Gama from putting a poison in one of those?'

Henry nodded, succumbing to Robert's ideas. 'Very well, you are right, this da Gama appears to be a danger, but what will you do about it?'

'Not do, Henry. Done,' Robert grinned at him. 'I have already ordered da Gama's arrest.'

Robert had returned to Essex House. Anthony Bacon, back in England, had sent a message to the court with the news that da Gama had been arrested and placed in a room awaiting interrogation. Robert did not delay in instructing his bargemen to take him home. Robert wanted to interrogate the prisoner da Gama personally.

'In here, my lord.' Anthony led the way to a small room at the end of the corridor and Robert followed, his heart beating fast in anticipation of what he would find inside.

Da Gama was sitting at a table in the centre of the room. His black, bloodshot eyes widened in fear as Robert, Francis and Anthony entered. His whole body was rigid and he did not rise, just watched his visitors and swallowed uneasily as the door was shut behind them.

Anthony nodded at his brother, who sat down at the table, opened up his leather folder and placed an inkpot and pen upon the surface. He drew out some paper, dipped the pen in the ink and waited.

Now that he was here, Robert was unsure how to begin. But everyone was waiting on him. He had to speak.

'You are Ferrara da Gama of Portugal and you have been staying in Holborn at the home of Dr Roderigo Lopez,' Robert began. 'What is your exact relationship with Lopez?'

'We are friends,' de Gama said, his Portuguese accent strong.

'But you are in the pay of Spain?'

'I have business in Spain.'

'Does that business include passing intelligence to King Philip's ministers?'

'I do not understand.'

'You do not?' Robert glanced at Anthony. 'Yet I am told you understand English very well. And you seem to have very little difficulty in speaking it.'

Da Gama made no answer.

'Is Doctor Lopez also in the pay of Spain?' Robert continued.

'My friend has no business in Spain.'

'But he has a position here. A very good, a very elevated position. I find it hard to believe that Spain would make no effort to secure the services of one so close to the Queen of England. I find it very hard to believe that they would not employ you to persuade Dr Lopez to act in the interests of the King of Spain.'

Da Gama remained silent. The only sound was the scratching of Francis's pen as it recorded Robert's words.

'Senôr?' Robert asked loudly, insistently, worried that he was going to get nothing out of the interrogation, 'what have you been plotting?'

'I make no plot, my lord.'

'There is no point in lying, senôr. Why else would you be here, in the home of Doctor Lopez, if you did not want to get close to the English court? Have you tried to secure the allegiance of Lopez? He is a Jew. I am sure you could buy him for thirty pieces of silver.' Robert laughed and looked around at Francis and Anthony, who smiled loyally back.

'I make no plot. I am friend to Dr Lopez. No plot.'

Da Gama began to cry. Anthony stepped up to Robert and murmured that he was unlikely to get anything else out of him. Robert nodded an agreement. Francis collected his writing things and all three left the room, leaving da Gama still sobbing.

'My lord,' Anthony said, locking the door, 'I suggest we send an instruction to the ports of Rye, Southampton and Dover to intercept any letters from Portugal and have them sent on to Essex House for examination.'

'Yes, see to it, Anthony,' Robert agreed. 'We have the makings of a conspiracy here, I am sure of it. People may be in danger and I must do all I can to see no one comes to any harm.'

CHAPTER 20

Cecil trudged along the corridor towards Robert's apartments. He had been summoned and was irritated, but the summons was impossible to ignore or refuse. He knocked on the door and was greeted by Gelly Meyricke, who bade him enter.

'Ah Cecil, there you are,' Robert said, rising from his chair. 'You have kept me waiting.'

Cecil pursed his lips to bite back an uncivil retort. 'I had business that could not be delayed, my lord.'

'Well, you are here now.' Robert handed Cecil a paper. 'Read that. You will see that I did not ask you to attend on me for no trivial reason.'

Cecil read the paper quickly. 'You have proof that this da Gama is working for the Spanish?'

Robert had not given up on his idea of da Gama being guilty. He had given instructions that da Gama be interrogated again and again until he revealed his secrets. Kept confined, half-starved and terrified, da Gama had spoken at last. 'He has admitted it, Cecil. Francis Bacon is working on a full report of his confession. Da Gama has also admitted that he was engaged in a plot to assassinate Don Antonio.'

Don Antonio had once been the King of Portugal, but he was a bastard and King Philip of Spain had a legitimate claim to the Portuguese throne through his mother's bloodline. Don Antonio had been usurped from the Portuguese throne and forced into exile, persuading Elizabeth to give him a home in England while he worked to regain his kingdom. Elizabeth had agreed because if he were successful England would have a friend in Portugal. For eight years, Don Antonio had haunted the English court, but Elizabeth found him amusing and was, unusually, prepared to accept the cost of his keeping.

'Don Antonio's death would certainly be in the interests of the King of Spain,' Cecil agreed.

'Exactly so.' Robert snapped his fingers triumphantly.

'And you say da Gama has confessed this plot?' Cecil asked, wondering how on earth he could have missed such a plan.

'He has, and,' Robert paused to make Cecil look up at him, 'he has implicated Lopez.'

'Doctor Lopez? The Queen's physician?'

'Yes.'

'He has the trust of everyone at court. You yourself have employed Doctor Lopez, my lord.'

'Yes, I have, and what a damn fool I was to have done so.' Robert snatched the paper from Cecil. He had been examined by Doctor Lopez on several occasions during the previous year when his penis had developed some worrying lesions. Doctor Lopez had prodded and poked him, asked some impertinent questions, and charged Robert a fortune for ointment. The ointment had worked, Robert conceded, but the gossiping Jew had spread it around the court that Robert had suffered a disease of Venus. 'I have ordered the arrest of Dr Lopez and his home is being searched at this very moment.'

'My lord Essex,' Cecil folded the paper with vigour, wishing he could tear it up instead, 'why have you not informed the Council of any of this?'

Robert drew himself up. 'Why should I do so? *I* discovered this conspiracy, Cecil, I. Had I left it to you, the matter would have gone unnoticed and Don Antonio would have been unprotected.'

'That is a slander, my lord.'

'It is the truth.'

Cecil headed for the door. 'I and my father will also examine da Gama, but I cannot believe this plot to be true.'

'The evidence is being gathered, Cecil. Do feel free to interrogate the man yourself and you shall see.'

'Indeed I shall, my lord.' Cecil slammed his hand down on the door handle and left, forgetting to bow.

Burghley and Cecil were on the river, returning home after visiting da Gama at Essex House. Burghley settled heavily onto the cushioned seat of the family barge and tugged a fur blanket over his legs. 'So, my boy, what do you think?'

Cecil sat down next to him, clutching his folder of notes to his chest. 'It's a nonsense. Essex found no evidence of a plot in his search of Lopez's home and Lopez admits nothing. His account of his dealings with da Gama seems entirely plausible, do you not agree, Father?'

'I do. I feel sorely for Doctor Lopez that he has to suffer such treatment.'

'I do not like you being out on the river in this weather,' Cecil said, adjusting his father's blanket. 'I curse the earl for putting you through this.'

'It is not so much the matter itself but the reason why Essex has begun this action that concerns me.'

'He has done this to curry favour with the Queen,' Cecil said. 'To show how statesmanlike he is.'

'But that is not all. He wants to discredit *us*, my boy.' Burghley breathed deeply, prompting a coughing fit. When it subsided, he continued. 'I think it best that you go to the Queen and tell her of this affair before the earl does. Leave early for Hampton Court in the morning and be sure to mention to her that the earl did not share any of his intelligence information with the Council until he had already proceeded far in the matter. That should tarnish his image a little.'

Cecil settled back into the seat, hoping that his father was right.

The horse was sweating, flecks of white spittle spilling from its mouth, but still Robert pricked its sides and urged it on ever faster.

He reached the stable yard of Hampton Court and abandoned his horse to the ostlers. Hurrying into the palace, he ignored the stares of courtiers and servants who looked after the dishevelled earl in bewilderment. He had no time to waste making himself presentable. He had to get to the Queen.

Elizabeth was reading in her chamber when Robert burst in and demanded to speak with her. He closed the doors behind him, wanting no witnesses to the interview.

Elizabeth looked him over. Her nose wrinkled. 'Could you not have washed before presenting yourself?'

'There was no time. Has Cecil been here? Tell me.'

Elizabeth shut her book, closing her eyes in exasperation. 'Yes, Cecil has been to see me this morning.'

'What has he said to you?'

'Do you make demands of me, sir?'

'He defames me, Bess.'

'Does he, indeed?'

'You cannot believe a word that man says. He hates me.'

'Oh, do not be so melodramatic, Robin. Of course, Cecil does not hate you.'

'He does, I tell you. He seeks to undermine me at every turn.' He paused to catch his breath.

Elizabeth studied him. 'What is it you imagine Cecil has said to me, Robin? What secrets do you think he has told me?'

Robert heard the contempt in her voice and, knowing that he was already on dangerous ground, bit back the anger that had been fomenting inside him. 'I presume matters concerning Don Antonio?'

'You presume rightly, Robin,' Elizabeth nodded. 'He tells me that you believe you have uncovered a plot on Don Antonio's life. One that may involve my own doctor.'

'Yes, I have and—'

'And he also tells me that there is no evidence to support your claim.'

'That is a lie, Bess,' Robert said, unthinkingly pointing a finger at her. 'His associate has confessed his involvement.'

'I am satisfied with the opinion of Lord Burghley and Sir Robert Cecil.'

'They have blinded you to the truth, Bess.'

'ENOUGH,' Elizabeth roared, her patience suddenly exhausted. 'You are a fool, rushing into matters of which you have no experience and little judgement.'

'Bess!'

'You dare to accuse my personal physician of treason without any true evidence. Oh, and now I remember more. You do all this, make arrests, examine and accuse, without informing any of your colleagues on the Council about it.'

'I... I wanted to be sure,' Robert stammered, looking away.

'Oh no you didn't,' Elizabeth said, striding towards him and wagging her finger, 'you wanted all the glory. You wanted everyone to look at you and see how clever you are. Well, I will not have it, you hear? My court is no place for empty-headed braggarts. Not here in my court. Be gone from here. Get out of my sight.'

'You cannot mean it,' Robert begged. *Not again. Not banishment again.*

Elizabeth's eyes narrowed and she became very still. She had assumed her regal pose of aloofness, of untouchability, and even Robert, despite his anger, knew not to argue with it. 'I do mean it, my lord. I am quite sick of you. You will not come into my presence. I will not see you. Leave now.'

Robert arrived back at Essex House, his poor exhausted horse nearly collapsing beneath him. He ignored the worried calls of his servants, the questions they fired at him, the wary looks from the waiting petitioners.

He wanted to be alone. Elizabeth had humiliated him again, talked down to him as if he were a child. He was tired, dejected. He had pain in his temples and black spots were floating before his eyes. He strode quickly to his apartments, barked at his page to get out, then slammed the doors shut and locked himself inside.

Robert picked up the soiled napkin and wiped his forehead. His head felt tight, as though an iron band was wrapped around his skull, and he became dizzy when he moved. He recognised the symptoms and knew he was making himself ill. *No, I am not*, he corrected himself angrily. *Elizabeth and Cecil are making me ill with their accusations and unkindness. They would celebrate with a feast and dancing were I to die.*

I cannot be wrong about da Gama and Lopez, I cannot be wrong about their plot. Can I? Da Gama and Lopez had been plotting, da Gama confessed it. It has to be true.

Robert scanned Francis's record of the interrogations. There had to be something in the record that proved he wasn't the fool Elizabeth and Cecil thought him to be.

A sentence caught his eye. 'Lopez was in the presence of the Queen daily.'

Why mention the Queen? Robert wondered. *If the plan was to assassinate Don Antonio, why mention the Queen at all?*

His head fit to bursting, Robert began to frantically re-read all of the reports until he had found the answer to this question.

He unlocked the door and threw it open. He bellowed into the darkened corridor. 'Anthony!'

Burghley shuffled into the Council chamber and frowned down at his son who was sitting at the table. 'I was waiting for you in my rooms. You missed supper.'

'Forgive me,' Cecil said, rising and pulling out a chair for his father. 'This arrived an hour ago from Essex House.'

Burghley groaned. 'Oh no, not more nonsense. Read it to me.'

'I shall not bother you with most of it. There are just a few sentences we need concern ourselves with.' Cecil ran his finger down the page. 'Here. *"I have discovered a most dangerous and desperate treason. The focus of the conspiracy was not Don Antonio but Elizabeth. The executioner was to have been Dr Lopez. The manner, poison."*'

Burghley's rheumy eyes widened. 'Is he trying to make out that Dr Lopez was planning to assassinate the Queen?'

Cecil nodded. 'Essex has discovered this so-called conspiracy after spending two days locked in his room. Father, I have read the same reports that Essex has and there is nothing to support this new fantasy.'

'Yet, I sense there is something more you have to tell me, Robert.'

Cecil sighed. 'I have also had reports from the Master of the Revels. Marlowe's new play, *The Jew of Malta*, is proving to be very popular at the playhouse. There is a great deal of anti-Jewish feeling in the city, and I fear that when this new idea of Essex's spreads – and it will spread, he will make sure of that, it is just the sort of employment he will give to our Bacon cousins – there will be no good in us defending a Jew who, if it can be proved, has nefarious associations with Portugal and Spain. The earl has interrogated da Gama again, I suspect under threat of the rack, and he now claims that he was tasked with persuading Lopez to poison the Queen.'

'Men will say anything in such circumstances.'

'I know, Father, but the earl has chosen to believe it and I expect that our cousins are circulating the confessions around the city even as we speak.'

Burghley thumped the table in anger. 'That I should be troubled with such a creature as the Earl of Essex at my time of life.' He sighed. 'He has given us no choice. We will have to arrest Doctor Lopez.'

Cecil placed a paper beneath his father's nose and Burghley unhappily read the warrant that his son had already made out.

'An innocent man, my boy, I am sure of it.'

'I agree, Father.'

Burghley passed the warrant back to his son. 'Have it dispatched as soon as the Queen has signed this.'

'And if the Queen will not sign it?'

'Tell her she must,' Burghley grew emphatic. 'Even though we believe Doctor Lopez is innocent, the formalities must be observed.'

Elizabeth's throat was tight and a pulse throbbed painfully at her temple. Ever since this business had begun, ever since Essex had stuck his nose into business that did not concern him, she had been plagued with pains. She did not want to be present, did not want to hear what she knew Burghley and Cecil were about to tell her of Lopez's trial.

Burghley spoke first. 'Dr Lopez claimed he only confessed under torture, but I am afraid his words were ignored. He was sentenced to death. The spectators applauded, very enthusiastically, the report says. Our agents have already recovered ballads from the city that speak of Jewish villainy and the talk in the taverns is that the people of London are looking forward to the execution.'

'The ballads,' Elizabeth said sourly. 'Was anyone else mentioned?'

Burghley and Cecil exchanged a glance. 'The ballads,' Cecil said, 'praise the Earl of Essex for discovering the plot, for preventing your assassination, and for delivering justice on a murderous Jew.'

Elizabeth winced. A murderous Jew? Doctor Lopez? A man she had trusted with her very life, whom she had seen daily, who had talked with her, comforted her, proved himself to be nothing but her trusted servant. Oh, that cruel boy, Essex. What was it in his nature that made him so spiteful? She closed her eyes and rested her head on her hand. 'If only they truly knew him.'

'Your Majesty?' Cecil leant forward, struggling to hear.

'The people, Pygmy. All they see is a hero, a shining boy. They do not see him as we see him, do they?'

'I am sure the earl is greatly endowed with all the virtues,' Cecil said carefully, seeing his father out of the corner of his eye nod in agreement with his caution.

'That's generous of you, Pygmy,' Elizabeth said. 'So, even though we three know Doctor Lopez is guilty of nothing more than having a suspicious and cowardly companion, I must throw him to the dogs to satiate the earl's bloodlust. Very well, let it be done. I do not want to hear any more of this matter. I do not want to hear of the execution, the manner of it, how the people cheered. Nothing.'

'Understood, Your Majesty,' Cecil said.

Elizabeth rose slowly, suddenly feeling the weight of her dress with all its layers and jewels. 'And I suppose that as the Earl of Essex is so lauded throughout my capital, I had better welcome him back to court.'

'It would be wise, Your Majesty,' Burghley agreed. 'There is no sense in stirring up anger over the earl's treatment.'

Elizabeth nodded, pursing her lips. 'Write to Essex, Pygmy. Tell him he may return.'

CHAPTER 21

England was in trouble. The weather that had been so much in England's favour in 1588 and dashed the Spanish galleons against her coasts and rocks now drowned her fields. Crops rotted, people starved, disease spread, and rebellion threatened.

Young men at Elizabeth's court, many of them friends and acquaintances of the Earl of Essex, who had too much time on their hands and an excess of testosterone that could not be spent on foreign battlefields, was spent on bloody quarrels at home. All was now faction at Elizabeth's court.

Gloriana did not shine as brightly as she once did; Cynthia the silvery moon, as Ralegh had once called Elizabeth, was demanding too much of her followers and was on the wane. The virgin star of Elizabeth was being eclipsed and the celestial sphere that was moving into her orbit was young, it was dazzling, illuminating the lives of all it shone upon, who, because they were dazzled by its brightness, could not see its false fire. The new star was shining brighter and brighter, and Gloriana looked old and dull by comparison.

Lettice checked her appearance in the mirror on her dressing table and decided to apply a little more colour. 'I am telling you, Robert, this is your moment. The whole country is tired of Elizabeth. That book proved it.'

'Mother,' Robert said reproachfully, but unable to hide his pleasure at her words. He had returned to Drayton Bassett to visit his mother, confident after his success in the Lopez affair that he could afford to leave the court without his reputation being besmirched in his absence. As Francis Bacon told him, who would dare criticise the hero who had saved the life of the Queen?

'Do not 'Mother' me,' Lettice snapped. 'That book that was published was dedicated to you and all it spoke about was who was to succeed to the throne when Elizabeth dies. And the writer said that you would have the greatest say in the matter. Do you know what you should be doing?'

Robert sighed, tired of being told what to do, who to acquaint himself with, what to say, and waited for his mother to continue. He knew she would. She was indefatigable.

'You should be making yourself agreeable to King James. You should be writing to him—'

'Mother—'

'You should—'

'Mother!'

'What, my darling?'

'I am already writing to King James.'

'You are?' Lettice cooed. 'Oh, you clever boy. You should meet with him, too.'

Robert shook his head and told her that visiting the King of Scotland could be dangerous, for Elizabeth would not like it. She never liked to talk of the succession, was never willing to discuss who would come after her. Lettice pooh-poohed him, saying that as James Stuart was undoubtedly going to be England's king one day, it would be perfectly natural to pay him a visit. But Robert was convinced it was a bad idea and told her of a story he had heard from Francis Bacon. Bacon said Elizabeth had been heard comparing herself to King Richard II, the unfortunate English king, who had been usurped by one of his own cousins and murdered. Robert realised that by comparing herself to Richard, Elizabeth was implying that one of her own subjects could be another Bolingbroke. And Robert was the prime candidate.

Lettice's painted face lost its carefree expression. 'You do not mean that?'

Robert shrugged. 'It is what Francis said.'

'But, oh, my darling boy, if she has said that, then you could be in danger. She is such a suspicious old hag. If she thinks you are acting against her—'

'I will be careful, Mother,' Robert assured her. 'Francis Bacon looks after me in that regard.'

Lettice made a face. 'There is something very unpleasant about that man. Tell me, are the rumours about him being a sodomite true?'

Robert laughed and confirmed that the rumours were indeed true.

'He has not tried…' Lettice opened her eyes wider and nodded in his direction.

'No, Mother, certainly not.'

'So,' she smiled teasingly, 'if not Francis Bacon, who is keeping your bed warm these days? Not your wife, I know that.'

'I do perform my conjugal duty now and then.'

'I know that. The children do keep coming from her and she is such a little mouse I do not suppose she would cuckold you.'

'Mother, must you?'

But there are others?' Lettice persisted. 'Please tell me you are not wasting all your time and manhood on Elizabeth.'

Robert, taking and kissing her hands, assured his mother there were other women, plenty of them in fact, but that none were important to him.

Lettice was pleased to hear it and began talking of another subject that had been very much on her mind of late: her exile from court. She asked if he were still in favour with Elizabeth and Robert, surprised, assured her he was.

'Then why am I still not allowed at court?' she demanded shrilly. 'Do not look at me like that. Elizabeth has never allowed me to come to court ever since I married Leicester, and I am heartily sick of it. If you are so much in favour, you can persuade Elizabeth to receive me. Can you not?'

'I can try, Mother,' Robert promised half-heartedly. But it was true, he reflected. How dare Elizabeth continue to keep his mother in exile? What had his mother done but marry the man she loved? He would speak to Elizabeth and demand that she receive Lettice.

'How can she refuse you anything, my darling? Are you not Great England's Glory and the world's wide wonder?'

'You have been reading Spenser,' Robert said, blushing in recognition of the quotation.

'Of course, I have, we all have.'

'Do you think it's true, what he calls me?' Robert asked quietly, hardly daring to believe.

Lettice noticed the change in her son's mood and moved to sit by his side. 'It is true, my darling. You are the hope of the age. You should see and hear what I do. When I go out in my carriage, I am cheered just for giving birth to you. You are loved, Robert, and not just by your family and friends. I tell you, Elizabeth should fear you because you are everything she is not – young, courageous, noble – and, believe me, my darling, the country knows it.'

CHAPTER 22

Spain was continuing to be a thorn in England's side. The old sea dogs, Drake and Hawkins, had been almost constantly at sea since 1589, attempting to keep the seaways clear of Spanish ships and rob them of their treasures. Where this had worked in the past, the two men had been forced to discover that times had changed and they had not noticed. Gone were the heavy, cumbersome Spanish galleons that had proved so ineffectual in the Spanish armada of 1588, ships so large that they had not been able to turn quickly enough to see off the small English ships that darted in and out between them. But it seemed Spain had learnt her lesson. The ships they were now building were small frigates, ideally suited for sailing rings around any English ship. Emboldened by successes against Elizabeth's merchant adventurers, King Philip of Spain was preparing to launch another armada, one that would be faster, more manoeuvrable and ultimately more successful than any England had been threatened with yet.

Always aware of England's vulnerability, and kept informed by the Bacon brothers' spy network, Robert saw the danger from Spain. And he was not alone. Walter Ralegh, released from the Tower and trying to claw his way back into favour, warned of the dangers of not meeting the Spanish problem head on. Elizabeth would only approve small raids against the Spanish, but such endeavours, Ralegh warned, only taught the Spanish what to expect from the English and made them better prepared for the next battle. What was needed was one large, decisive action against the Spaniards. Robert voiced his support for such an action, not caring that he was siding with Ralegh. To Robert's surprise, Lord Burghley, long an advocate of not engaging in expensive military affairs, seconded him. Spain would have to be dealt with and soon, he said, adding that it would be far cheaper in the long run, a comment guaranteed to raise Elizabeth's interest. With Burghley's support, the Privy Council concluded that a major offensive should be launched against Spain. All they needed was Elizabeth to agree.

She did, at first. Elizabeth agreed to the putting together of a fleet of fifteen ships to be commanded by four commanders. These commanders were to be the Earl of Essex, Sir Walter Ralegh, the Lord Admiral Charles Howard and his brother, Lord Thomas Howard. But then news came that the Protestant King Henri of France had converted to Roman Catholicism in order to gain full control over his country and appease the Spanish. The Spanish were not convinced by this sudden conversion and decided to seize hold of Calais, the French port nearest to the England mainland.

King Henri appealed to Elizabeth for help to keep control and Elizabeth knew that England's trade would be severely hampered, even damaged, if Calais were to become controlled by Spain. So, the fleet that had been gathering to attack Cadiz, the largest and strongest Spanish port, was split in half, with Robert and the Lord Admiral tasked with ensuring the Spanish were not successful at Calais. But Elizabeth also wanted assurances from King Henri that once Calais was under his control, the English would still be allowed to trade from it. Robert continued to make preparations for Calais, but with no assurance coming from the French, Elizabeth cancelled the expedition. The Privy Council were astonished and dismayed at Elizabeth's decision, and even Burghley allowed his irritation with her to show. But Elizabeth was resolute. She was not going to spend money on a venture that would only benefit the French.

Robert began a journey back to court, furious with Elizabeth for changing her mind. Halfway back to London, he received another message from the Privy Council, stating that Elizabeth had decided to recommence with the expedition to Calais, for she had received news that the Spanish were not so secure in the port as she had been led to believe. Calais, it seemed, was still available for the taking. Overjoyed, Robert turned his horse around and headed back to the coast.

But Elizabeth's changes of mind had cost the English force dear. As Robert's fleet sailed across the Channel, there was no sound of gunfire coming from the French port that would signal battles being fought. The Spanish had made good ground and taken the port of Calais, wresting it from the French. Calais was now in Spanish hands and England had lost her only trading port in France. There was nothing left to fight for in Calais. It was best for Robert and the Lord Admiral to rejoin the fleet at Dover and attack Cadiz.

But when they arrived at Dover, they found chaos. No administrative system had been put in place and arms and men were arriving daily without any official to tell them where they should be put or who to report to. Robert proved himself an adept at administration, arranging men into companies and for supplies to be properly distributed. Which made it even more galling when he received a letter from Elizabeth complaining about his lack of action against the enemy. Robert railed and asked his fellows what more he could do? They all agreed with him. The Queen was being unreasonable. As if he needed more proof of this, Elizabeth suddenly recalled Robert to London, worried that an expedition to Cadiz would prove just as futile as the one to Calais.

Robert lost his temper. From Dover, he wrote to the Privy Council, pleading with them to make Elizabeth see reason. He did not know it, but the whole of the Council sympathised with him, for they too were exasperated by Elizabeth's frequent and irrational changes of mind. Against all his inclinations, Cecil presented an argument to the Queen of the absurdity of pulling out of the Cadiz expedition at such a late stage. Essex was poised, he argued, ready to do the Spanish a great hurt and all for love of her. And what of the money that had already been spent? he asked, appealing to her parsimony. Was that all to be wasted?

This question hit home and Elizabeth was at last persuaded to allow the fleet to set sail. Robert, wondering what the hell was happening in London, received a letter from Elizabeth that contained his commission to depart and attack Cadiz. She also wrote of her prayers that he, Robert, would return to her unharmed to the great joy of her heart.

Robert didn't give a damn about Elizabeth's heart. He was off to war.

CHAPTER 23

Robert had command of the *Due Repulse*, a ship newly built and still smelling of freshly cut timber and tar. Robert walked the deck proudly, pleased to be away from court, and especially pleased to be away from Elizabeth, whose prevarication and constant mind-changing had driven him and his fellow counsellors to the limits of their wits. Not only that, but Elizabeth had grown cloying, demanding his presence at all hours and laying her hands upon him at every opportunity as if to prove he belonged to her. He shuddered at the memory of those deathly white clawing hands. He endured her touch, as he had always done, but the scales had fallen from his eyes of late and she was no longer a magnificent royal creature, but simply an old woman who wore magnificent clothes and covered herself in white lead paste to hide her wrinkled and sagging skin.

A Council meeting, held that morning on the Lord Admiral's ship, the *Ark Royal*, had concluded that the Earl of Essex should lead the attack on the city of Cadiz. Robert had been exhilarated by the decision. What a glorious challenge! He had hurried back to the *Due Repulse* and given his orders. The wind had come up, the sails were full-bellied and the ship was heading for Cadiz with a plan to launch a surprise attack on the city.

It was near noon when the city came into view on the horizon. Robert's heart began to beat faster, the blood rushing in his ears indistinguishable from the water breaking against the ship's bows. This was what he had been born for: battle, not bowing.

The *Due Repulse* reached the nearest safe point and Robert ordered his men into the boats. Sitting proudly at the stern of the lead boat, Robert heard the clanging of the town's church bells, alerting the citizens to the attack that was approaching. The wind picked up. The wind that had aided their journey to the Spanish port now threatened the small English boats and barges. Each boat in the small flotilla began rocking from side to side, water spilling over the gunwales. Robert watched in horror as two of his boats capsized and the men, dressed in heavy steel armour, sunk quickly beneath the water. In less than a minute, fifteen men had been lost. Robert would remember their screams for the rest of his life.

Robert saw the Spanish troops mustering on the shore, taking up positions behind barrels, while their galleons bobbed on the sea some distance behind the English ships.

The thousand men in the English boats landed and, surprising the Spanish with their speed, overcame the soldiers and headed straight for the citadel. The citadel walls were already in a state of disrepair and Robert led a company of men through a breach in one of the stone walls, hacking down anyone who stood in his way and so on through to the centre of town. Skirmishes throughout the town were dealt with by men from the other ships and by the next morning, Cadiz was in English hands.

Knowing the frenzy and lust that soldiers were prone to in battle, Robert issued orders that the churches were not to be violated and that all the churchmen and women in the town were allowed to be evacuated to safety. But he also knew the city offered riches and he made no attempt to stop the English troops from plundering. It was their due, after all, as the spoils of war. The English soldiers pocketed a great deal of wealth, but they did not realise how much more of it was safe in the holds of the Spanish merchant ships that had been anchored in the bay. Unable to sail these ships past the English fleet, the Spanish fleet commander decided it were better the sea had his treasure rather than the English, and he ordered the ships to be torched. Twelve million ducats worth of cargo either went up in smoke or sank to the seabed.

Cadiz had been captured, but the fortune Elizabeth had been promised, and which had finally persuaded her to set her men upon the Spanish, was lying at the bottom of the sea, irretrievable. It was a blow, the four commanders knew, but Robert reminded them of the brave action they had just fought, and to reward the troops, knighted many of the officers and men. So, dear Gelly Meyricke became a knight thanks to Robert, as did Charles Blount, he of the golden chess piece, all former enmity forgotten. Robert had knighted men before, but he had forgotten, or chosen to ignore, Elizabeth's fury at his presumption in doing so. In Elizabeth's England, a man had to earn a knighthood through years of devoted service: to *her*, not to her nobles.

Meanwhile, the four commanders, troubled by the loss of the Spanish fortune, sought a remedy. There was a Spanish fleet sailing for Cadiz and this fleet carried more treasure than the one that had been lost. The best thing for the English, Robert insisted, would be to wait at Cadiz for the ships to turn up and then simply plunder them. He proposed the setting up of a permanent English base with himself as governor, but his co-commanders shook their heads. His commission from the Queen did not allow for such a position and they would not ratify it. Besides, the English army was growing thin as men deserted, their pockets filled with Spanish gold.

The question was, what to do with the men who were left? The other commanders suggested that they sail the fleet around the coast and raid a few more Spanish ports and grow rich that way. Overruled, Robert had no choice but to consent and gave orders that Cadiz was to be destroyed, making it useless as a port for the Spanish. Robert watched as the smoke rose over the town, and climbed into the last boat with a heavy heart, not at all certain that he had done the right thing in letting the other commanders tell him what to do.

Back at sea, matters were no better. The other commanders appeared to be sailing aimlessly around the Spanish coast, trying to find the Spanish treasure fleet. They passed Portugal, many of whose ports were in Spanish hands, and decided to raid the town of Faro in an attempt to line their pockets. But the inhabitants of Faro had heard of the English raiders and had taken themselves and their goods into the mountains so that there was nothing left for the English to plunder. Frustrated, the English set fire to the town and were pleased to watch it burn.

Once more on their ships, Robert tried to persuade the other commanders to sail to the Azores where the Spanish treasure fleet was certain to have landed, but the others were tired of fighting and refused and turned their ships homeward. They passed Lisbon on the way, and once again Robert appealed to Ralegh and the two Howards to attack the town, but he was shouted down. The commanders would have done better to listen to Robert. For, while they were arguing, the Spanish fleet had been only a few days' sail away, and had the army acted as Robert wished and hidden amongst the hills to lay in wait for the Spanish, they would have been able to rob the fleet of its valuable cargoes of gold and silver, worth twenty million ducats.

Another fortune had eluded English hands, simply because the four commanders had been bickering over whether to continue the fight or to head home. Elizabeth would not be pleased.

St Paul's was always busy, serving as a thoroughfare for people who wanted to buy and those who wanted to sell. Amongst the wares on offer were books, pamphlets, play scripts, pies, fish, meat and sex. A church may not have seemed the most suitable place for any of these trades but the Londoners did not seem to mind. The tradesmen shouted their wares, the punks bared their breasts and the preachers shouted over the noise. Some days they were listened to, some days they were not.

But everyone listened to the sermon on the day following the Earl of Essex's return to London, for the preacher in the pulpit was not talking of God or sins or hell; he was talking about greatness and giving thanks for the hero of Cadiz.

The Earl of Essex, the preacher said, had shown extraordinary military skill and unparalleled bravery in his command of the English forces, reminiscent of that other great English hero, Henry V. The congregation had agreed wholeheartedly with the sentiments being expressed and delivered a rapturous round of applause at the conclusion of the preacher's sermon. The applause echoed throughout the building and rumbled out of the doors, attracting the attention of those in the narrow London streets. It also attracted the attention of one of Burghley's men, who wrote a letter to inform the chief minister of the incident.

The letter was passed to Lord Burghley as a doctor unwrapped the bandage around his gouty foot. He put on his spectacles, but gave up trying to read it and instead, passed it to his son who was supervising the doctor's treatment. Cecil read it through to himself first, then aloud to his father, who at the conclusion, said simply, 'The Queen will not like that.'

Agreeing, Cecil resolved to make sure Elizabeth heard about it.

'There are to be no more sermons about the Earl of Essex or the attack on Cadiz. Is that understood?'

Burghley winced at the tone of Elizabeth's voice – cold, chilling even, the same tone she had spoken in when told of the Babington plot years earlier, when six of her subjects had plotted to assassinate her and put her cousin, Mary Stuart, on the throne in her place. Elizabeth had demanded that the six conspirators' executions be prolonged, so that they endured unimaginable agony, using all the skill of the executioner. The Queen could be cruel, Burghley had learnt that day. She could be very cruel indeed.

'No, Your Majesty,' his weary voice had answered. He wanted to leave, to go back to his rooms and lie down, to not have to bother anymore with the Earl of Essex, but he had to consider his son. For Cecil to rise, Essex had to fall. 'Especially in light of the report I have heard.'

Elizabeth's ears pricked and she gave him a sharp, questioning look.

He continued. 'That the plan for the campaign at Cadiz was not, in fact, of the earl's devising but Sir Walter Ralegh's. The Earl of Essex did have a plan of attack but it was a highly risky venture, reckless one might even say, and had he not been dissuaded from it by the other commanders, the outcome might have been different. Yes, very different indeed.'

He watched Elizabeth, her expression stony. She said nothing, merely turned her head away from him towards the window, raised an arm and waved her hand limply at him, telling him to go. He backed out of the room into the corridor.

'Did you tell her, Father?' Cecil's face was eager, his colour heightened.

'Yes, my boy. I told her.'

'What did she say?'

'Nothing,' he shrugged his bent shoulders and began walking.

'She said nothing?' Cecil, following after his father, was incredulous.

'What were you expecting?'

'I don't know. A rebuke, outrage.'

'My boy,' Burghley came to a grateful stop, for the pressure in his left foot was almost unbearable. 'The seed of distrust of Essex has been sown. It will take root and who knows what will grow. Be patient.'

Robert returned to London to cries of adulation and admiration, but if he had hoped for a warm welcome from Elizabeth, he was to be disappointed. He arrived at Whitehall Palace, and instead of being allowed through to Elizabeth's private apartments, was shown into the Presence Chamber where Elizabeth and the rest of the court awaited him.

He had ordered a new suit of clothing for his triumphant return and there was no missing Robert as he entered the chamber for he glittered with gold thread and jewels. He was surprised that no courtier stepped forward to greet him, that none offered their congratulations. No one even smiled at him.

Robert headed for the dais at the opposite end of the chamber where Elizabeth sat. As he drew nearer, he saw her unwelcoming expression and he felt sweat prickling on his top lip beneath his newly-grown beard.

'Your Majesty,' he bowed low.

'Lord Essex,' she replied coldly, 'you dare show yourself at my court?'

There was a hush and courtiers glanced at one another beneath lowered lids.

'Dare?' Robert queried. 'I do not understand. Our mission

was a success. Do you not hear the church bells? London rejoices in my triumph.'

'My people are ignorant of the true state of affairs,' Elizabeth sneered. 'Are you aware of how much your escapade has cost me? How much of my money has been wasted on a fruitless venture?'

'Hardly fruitless, Your Majesty,' Robert protested. 'Cadiz was taken.'

'What of it?' Elizabeth demanded. 'What good does that do me? The bulk of the Spanish fortune, which I was promised would be mine, lies at the bottom of the sea, and what wealth was brought back to these shores has been stolen from me at the dockside by your officers.'

'I am not to blame for their actions.'

'But you are to blame for bestowing knighthoods on such creatures, an act I expressly forbade you to do.'

'Those men deserved to be rewarded.'

'I choose my own knights, sir. I will not have them chosen for me by a rash, vainglorious youth.'

'I protest I am none such.'

'Indeed you are, sir.'

'Could you have done better than I?' he retorted, furious and indignant. 'Were you a man, you could go into battle yourself and see and experience the trials of command. Had you seen their courage, you would have knighted such men yourself.'

Elizabeth's eyes blazed. How dare he remind her that she was not a man? How dare he speak of her deficiency? Was he implying that she was unfit for rule? She did not trust herself to speak further, conscious of the hundreds of eyes that were upon her. She stepped down from the dais, and with a cruel cold stare at Robert, disappeared through the door that led to her private apartments.

A moment after Elizabeth's last lady had followed her, the silence in the room was broken and Robert found himself surrounded. He accepted gratefully their thanks and welcome, but his sensitive heart went out most to Henry Wriothesley, who took his arm and drew him aside.

'My dear fellow,' Henry said, embracing him, 'what a welcome.'

'She knows I speak the truth, Henry,' Robert said, his throat tight with impotent anger. 'How dare she treat me like this? How dare she subject me to such public humiliation?'

'She is a bitter old woman,' Henry said, lowering his voice, 'pay her no heed. Did you know that the Archbishop of Canterbury ordered a service of thanksgiving for your victory, and Elizabeth said it could only take place in London? The rest of the country has not been allowed to celebrate your achievement. She is frightened of you, Robert, and that is the truth. She knows that the people have grown tired of her and are just waiting for her to die.'

'Be careful, Henry,' Robert said, drawing his friend closer. 'You could lose your head for even thinking those words you just uttered.'

'Oh hell, I am sick of bending my knee to an old woman, Rob, and I tell you, I am not the only one.'

'Hush, Henry, hush.'

'You would not bid me be quiet if you only knew of her treachery towards you,' Henry said savagely.

'What do you mean? What treachery?'

'Burghley has retired. As soon as you left the country, she made Cecil her principal secretary. The hobgoblin clerk now holds one of the highest offices in the country and is very well placed to do you mischief.'

Robert shook his head in disbelief. 'She ignores and humiliates her nobles and raises a commoner to those offices which are rightfully ours, Henry.' He laughed without humour. 'But then, I should not be surprised. What is the Tudor stock, eh? Nothing but the offspring of a Welsh steward. And before you say it, Henry, I know my mother comes of the same stock, but my father was a Devereux. My ancestors came over with William the Conqueror.'

'Exactly my point,' Henry thumped Robert on the arm. 'With such an ancestry, what can you not do?'

CHAPTER 24

'I *am* going to write to him, Anthony,' Francis insisted.

Anthony snatched the pen out of his brother's hand. 'It is not your place to do this.'

'We are his advisers, Anthony. If we do nothing to curb his words and his actions, he may undo us all. Now, give me the pen.'

A moment passed while the brothers stared at one another, then reluctantly, Anthony gave the quill back and watched as Francis dipped it in the inkpot and began to write. 'What are you going to say?'

'I am going to tell him that he is a great nobleman, but that he has some qualities that anger the Queen.'

'You should name them so that he cannot be ignorant of what they are.'

'I will. Listen. He is unruly in his temper, he shows no obvious sign of the great intelligence he possesses, nor does he have the wealth to support his noble station. He has a martial spirit, which the Queen never admires. And most importantly, he has the affection of the people and courts it openly, which displeases the Queen even more.'

Anthony, still unconvinced at the rightness of the action, winced at the words. 'Francis, do you not think he will judge us impertinent?'

'If we do not check him—'

'Yes, yes,' Anthony waved him quiet, 'you are right. Continue.'

Francis wrote the letter and then passed it to his brother. Anthony read.

'Your lordship must hold his tongue and not complain so noisily nor so frequently of the wrongs committed by the Queen against your person. You should try to compliment the Queen as you once did, for your flattery has of late become insincere and inconsistent. Although contrary to your generous and open nature, your lordship must act as other courtiers do and mould your behaviour to please the Queen. As an example, you could announce an intention to visit your estate in Wales, a plan that would necessitate a prolonged absence from court, and then, if the Queen expressed displeasure at such an intention, cancel it, to prove that you conform yourself to her wishes. To this end, I can but only recommend you read *The Prince* and become a true disciple of Machiavelli.'

Anthony finished reading and nibbled on his bottom lip for a few moments, then nodded his agreement and told Francis to send the letter, quickly before he changed his mind.

Francis folded the letter, poured hot wax upon the fold and pressed his signet ring into it to form a seal.

'I fear we are wasting our time though,' Anthony said, running his fingers through his thinning hair. 'The earl is not capable of such subtlety and double-dealing.'

'I know,' Francis said, putting the letter aside and picking up another sheet of paper, 'but I am making a copy and it will at least show that we tried to restrain him. I do not want to be accused of treason at a trial if and when the earl decides to act.'

CHAPTER 25

Cecil was in his office at Whitehall Palace, reading the latest correspondence from his informants in Spain. The Spanish fleet had mobilised. King Philip, smarting from the English attack on Cadiz, had ordered his armada to set sail. Robert had once more been given command of the *Due Repulse* and, for some reason best known to himself, had announced that the Spanish had been sighted approaching the English coast, then that they were also making for Ireland, playing on the Queen's fear that the Spanish would use that country and the Catholic Irish to launch a two-pronged invasion on England.

Neither of these claims, Cecil's intelligencers reported, were remotely true. Nevertheless, as a precaution, Cecil had Elizabeth confirm Robert in his role as commander, but Elizabeth had insisted on telling Robert that he must stay around the English coast and not think of sailing off to Ireland on a wild goose chase, leaving England vulnerable to attack.

Robert, in Cecil's opinion, was better away from court than in it. He could do less damage at sea.

As it turned out, God still favoured the English, for He arranged for a storm, just like the one that destroyed the Spanish fleet in 1588, to blow up and the Spanish ships were forced to sail home.

Robert returned to court, only to be met with yet more complaints from Elizabeth, and to discover that in his absence, the Lord Admiral, Charles Howard of Effingham, had been raised to the earldom of Nottingham. Ostensibly, the elevation was in recognition of Howard's past service, but Robert in his present mood was unable to view it as anything other than a snub against himself. The news was made worse by the making of Howard the Lord Steward of Parliament. Such a position meant that Robert would have to walk behind Howard in any and all official processions.

This was too much to bear. Robert was furious and he let his anger show, continuously sulking and rebuking Elizabeth for her blatant efforts to undermine him. But Elizabeth refused to acknowledge her errors or insults, and Robert decided he had to get away, he had to leave court, for his own sanity, if nothing else.

He gave out that he was ill and retired to his house at Wanstead, locking himself in his bedchamber and refusing all company.

'Is he ill?' Elizabeth asked as she tried on another dress, her fourth that morning. Her ladies tried to hide their irritation at her indecisiveness. 'I heard that he is ill.'

Cecil, hidden behind a screen for decency's sake, scratched his nose and sniffed. 'Francis Bacon writes that the earl is ill, if locking himself up in his room and wrapping himself in blankets can be accounted an illness.'

'I pity him. Perhaps I have been a little harsh. I know the past few months cannot have been easy for him.'

Cecil suppressed a sigh. It had been pleasant in the earl's absence; there had been no outbursts of petulance, no ridiculous claims or demands made in the Privy Council meetings.

'I think I shall write to the earl,' Elizabeth was saying, 'and assure him of my affection.'

'If you think that wise.'

'You think it unwise, Pygmy?'

'Indeed, madam, I can think of nothing more restorative to the earl's health than your avowal of affection.'

Elizabeth pursed her lips, amused by Cecil's sarcastic rejoinder. 'It would be helpful though, would it not, Pygmy, to have the earl attending Council meetings once more? Especially in view of the French who are intent on paying us a visit.'

'It is true that the French king considers the earl a friend,' Cecil allowed carefully.

'And we would do well to present a united front to the ambassador. You know how keen the French are to make capital out of English divisions.'

'You are correct, as always, Your Majesty.'

'And indeed, I hear that Robert has been somewhat maligned. His conduct at Cadiz was not as foolhardy as I had been led to believe.'

Cecil looked at her quizzically. 'From whom have you received such information, Your Majesty? If I may ask?'

'You may ask, Pygmy. From Sir Francis Vere. He told me certain things and when I cross-examined that rogue Ralegh on the points, he was unable to answer to my satisfaction.'

'Indeed?'

'Indeed, Pygmy. So you see, Robert may have some justification in acting as he does.'

'His behaviour, if I may, does not befit a grown man but a child.'

'Oh,' Elizabeth wafted her handkerchief at him, 'let him have his sulks, Pygmy. What harm can it do? No, I am minded to have him back at court.'

'And if he will not come? The notion of the new earl of Nottingham having precedence over him seems to be a major point of contention with the earl.'

'Hmm.' Elizabeth tapped her finger on the table, pointing as she considered. 'Well, I can make Robin Earl Marshal of England. That way, Nottingham will have to walk behind Robert once again and poor Robin's wounded pride shall be salved. Make a note to that effect, Pygmy.'

Reluctantly, Cecil made a note, wondering why Elizabeth was being so considerate towards Essex. Was it some new stratagem, or was she simply being a woman?

Lettice smoothed her son's auburn curls, now flecked through with grey, and leant down to kiss his forehead. 'My clever boy,' she purred, squeezing him tighter.

'You see, Mother, this is power,' Robert said, his face glowing with pride. He held Elizabeth's letter under her nose, making her read it again. 'To gain such a title as Earl Marshal of England, and I had to do nothing, save retire to my house and refuse to attend court.'

'Yes, I know,' Lettice said musingly. 'Elizabeth must be growing soft in her old age. I doubt if even Leicester could have pulled off such a trick.'

'Do not call it a trick, Mother,' Robert scolded, carefully refolding the letter as though it were something sacred. 'It was a stratagem.'

'Whatever you say, my darling.'

'She needs me, you see, Mother,' Robert said assuredly. 'She has realised I am not just a plaything as Leicester was, someone to keep her amused. Leicester was never loved by the people. But the people do love me and Elizabeth dare not put me down for fear that the people will rise against her.'

CHAPTER 26

His father was in bed when Cecil arrived home at Burghley House. He handed his cloak and gloves to a servant and then made his halting way up the oak staircase. He knocked before entering his father's bedchamber in case the old man was asleep, but Burghley's croaky voice called for him to enter.

'How are you, Father?' Cecil asked, kissing his father's cheek.

Burghley pointed at his foot and informed Cecil that it was agony. Cecil cast a reproachful look at the swaddled foot, knowing that nothing could be done to ease the pain.

'What news today, my boy?'

Cecil sat down on the stool kept by the bed. 'I am to go to France to continue negotiations with King Henri. I wish I did not have to go, Father. I will be away some months and I hate to leave you.'

'Oh,' Burghley patted his son's cheek with a cold hand, 'you must not worry about me. It is an honour for you to be sent. A demonstration of Elizabeth's trust in you.'

'I know I should view it as such,' Cecil bowed his head, 'but much could happen in my absence. The Earl of Essex—'

'I wish you would not concern yourself with the earl, Robert.'

'I have to, Father, he has all the advantages I lack.'

'That is not true,' Burghley thumped the bedclothes with as much indignation as he could muster.

'It *is* true, Father. I know what I am. I can never fight in battle or woo the Queen. All I have are my wits to recommend me. Out of sight will be out of mind with the Queen, and you can guarantee that Essex will take advantage of my absence.'

'I think you credit that young man with too much intelligence, Robert. All you need to do is prepare the ground before you go.'

'How do I do that?'

'Make yourself a friend to the earl. Invite him to dine with you. Put him under obligations to you. Speak well of him to the Queen. He is always short of money. So, see that he gets some.'

'The Queen granted him the monopoly on the farm of sweet wines years ago. That brings him a tidy sum.'

'He has expensive tastes, my boy. The money he gets from the sweet wines is not enough. Those papers you left me this morning about imported goods. There are cargoes due shortly of cochineal and indigo. Let the earl buy them cheaply. That will make him a good profit.'

'Will he not wonder why I am suddenly such a good friend to him?' Cecil asked wryly.

'Tell him the truth. Let him know that you do not want him poisoning Elizabeth's mind against you and make him promise that he will not. I know that young man. I know how he thinks. He will not only feel grateful to you for letting him make money, he will also feel honour-bound to promise he will not act against you.'

Cecil shook his head. 'It will pain me to benefit him in any way.'

Burghley smiled. 'You do not have to like it, Robert, just to do it. Trust me, my boy.'

At Essex House, Lettice fingered her pearl earring and angled her head to see her reflection in one of the gold plates mounted on the cupboard. The image was a distortion, she knew, but she looked well enough to her eyes. She wondered how Elizabeth would look. It had been more than a decade since they had last been face to face and Elizabeth had already begun to paint then. Of course, Lettice painted, too. Elizabeth had made it fashionable to wear the white lead makeup over the skin and cover thinning grey hair with lustrous red wigs, but Lettice had the advantage of years, being several years younger than her cousin. She hoped she looked better than Elizabeth. That would be thumbing her nose at the bitter old crow.

'You look fine, Mother, stop worrying,' Robert said, coming into the chamber. He had finally persuaded Elizabeth to receive his mother back at court and this was to be their first meeting. He knew that Lettice was anxious and was determined to calm her.

'I'm not worrying,' Lettice protested, moving away from the plate. 'Do you have my gift?'

Robert dipped his hand into his purse and pulled out a velvet pouch. He passed it to her and Lettice checked the contents, an emerald that had made a huge hole in her finances. But Elizabeth liked expensive presents and Lettice deemed it a price worth paying to be allowed back at court.

'What time is it?'

'I heard the clock strike twelve,' Robert said.

'Then she should be here,' Lettice exclaimed. She hurried to the window, scanning the river for a sight of the royal barge. 'I can't see her.'

'She will be here,' Robert said, moving to his mother, placing his hands on her shoulders and kissing her cheek. 'She promised me.'

But when another hour had passed and Elizabeth did not arrive, even Robert had to admit that she had broken her promise. Lettice fumed and spat out curses against her while Robert quietly seethed. She had once again made a fool and liar of him, and not only him but his mother, too. He left Lettice consoling herself with a jug of his finest wine and took his barge back to Whitehall Palace. He demanded an audience with Elizabeth, who eyed him coolly as he spoke of his wrongs and her unkind treatment of him.

When he had run out of breath and self-pity, Elizabeth had stepped up to him, her face, the white paint cracked and flaking, mere inches from his. She had sighed, her breath, tainted by decay, wafted over him and his nostrils tightened in revulsion. She reminded him that she was queen and his mother little better than a whore, and if she chose to remain unreconciled with the woman who had seduced and deceived as good a man as the Earl of Leicester, then she was quite at liberty to do so.

Robert found himself unable to answer, stung, hurt, chastened by the hate directed towards his beloved mother. Elizabeth, victorious at silencing Robert, had smiled a crooked smile and joined the company in the next room who were settling to watch a play.

Robert had been left to consider the kind of life he was leading, in thrall to, as his mother had quite rightly called her and he could agree with her now, a bitter old hag.

CHAPTER 27

Henry helped himself to a cup of wine and put his feet up on the table. Francis Bacon looked at the booted feet with envy, admiring the soft leather and quality cut that only an earl could afford. They made him think of his own shoes, made for him by a second-rate cobbler and which rubbed both little toes every time he moved. *I am a martyr to blisters*, he thought.

'My only consolation,' Robert was saying from the window embrasure where he watched the wherries with their swinging lanterns on the river, 'is that Cecil achieved nothing in France. All the while he was there, King Henri was making a secret alliance with the Spanish.'

'Are we always to have the Spanish as enemies, do you think?' Henry asked, flicking his long hair back over his shoulder.

'If we pursue Cecil's inept policy of suing for peace, we are,' Robert muttered.

'But surely, the failure of the French alliance means that you can now pursue an anti-Spanish policy in Council, no?' Henry asked.

'I wish I could,' Robert shook his head. 'Burghley and Cecil are still advocating peace with Spain and the Queen listens to them because she does not want to spend money on war.'

'And I thought Burghley had retired,' Henry muttered into his cup.

'There is little money available for war, my lord,' Francis said, feeling the need to point out this small fact.

'Money can always be found, Francis,' Robert said. 'And, my God,' he said, his manner growing heated, 'I tell the Council, I do not know how often, that England should not even contemplate making a peace treaty with a Popish country, but do they listen? You cannot trust the word of a Papist, can you, Henry?'

'Certainly not,' Henry replied on cue with all the vehemence he could muster.

'I have to do something. I have to try to convince the Council and the Queen that we should not sue for peace with Spain.'

'I have an idea,' Henry said after a moment's thought. 'Write a letter.'

'To whom?' Robert asked sulkily, wondering how a letter could help him.

'Well, ostensibly to Francis's brother, but in reality, it will be made public. In it, you make a reasonable and well-judged argument both for and against peace, but come down on the side of the virtues of going to war with Spain. And then, of course, we get his brother to circulate it, anonymously. The power of the written word, Rob, it should not be underestimated.'

Robert glanced at Francis, who sat tight-lipped, his eyes fixed on his knees. 'What do you think, Francis?'

Not wanting to earn the scorn and derision of Wriothesley, who once he found a weakness in a person would continually work upon it, Francis agreed that it was worth considering but he carefully stopped short of saying it was a good idea. Robert may have asked for his opinion but Francis was becoming accustomed to his advice going unheeded.

'I will do what you say, Henry,' Robert said and began to pace the room. 'I shall be moderate, judicious, all the things Cecil thinks I am not. My arguments will be so damn persuasive that the Council will have to listen. I will beat that damn Pygmy yet.'

Elizabeth had decided to attend the Privy Council meeting, curious to see how matters were between her rash youth, *although*, she reflected, *he is not so young these days*, and her Pygmy. She had heard reports of their disagreements, their seeming reconciliations, even of Robert's sometimes disconcerting behaviour, and wanted to see for herself.

Now, Ireland was causing trouble. Encouraged by their fellow religionists in Spain, the Irish were denying their English masters and rebelling against them. Ireland needed a new English governor and the Privy Council were trying to reach a consensus as to who that should be.

It became apparent to Elizabeth during the course of the meeting that none of her subjects wanted to be Lord Deputy of Ireland. Perhaps it was not surprising. Ireland had defeated many English governors, Robert's father, Walter Devereux, included. But the post could not remain vacant and Elizabeth demanded names.

'Sir George Carew,' Robert offered.

Elizabeth glanced at Cecil. 'What think you of Carew, Pygmy?'

'I think not, madam,' Cecil said, too annoyed to elaborate his reason.

But Elizabeth knew his reason. She knew that Carew was a friend to Cecil and an enemy to Robert and that Robert thought the best place for such a man was a country as unpleasant as Ireland. She laughed. 'Oh, Robert, what a suggestion. Name another.'

Robert frowned at her. 'Why do you laugh, madam? I name Sir George Carew as the most suitable man for the post. I see no cause for merriment.'

'Do you not indeed?' Elizabeth said, her voice taking on a steely edge. He was defying her. Again.

'I cannot believe the earl is serious,' Cecil said, smiling at the Queen, sensing her anger.

'I am perfectly serious, Master Secretary,' Robert said through gritted teeth. 'And you had better take care how you mock me.'

'Be careful who you threaten, my lord,' Elizabeth said. 'Now, name another.'

'Sir George Carew,' Robert repeated doggedly.

'God's Death,' Elizabeth growled. She squeezed her eyes shut and clenched her fist. 'I will hear no more of your ridiculous chatter. Be quiet.'

'I will not be quiet,' Robert jumped up from his seat, his eyes blazing at her.

'You will be quiet, sir,' Elizabeth retorted, rising to match him, 'or you will suffer for it.'

As one, the counsellors rose, for it would not do to remain seated while the Queen stood. Robert opened his mouth to reply but he could think of nothing that would serve as a suitable rejoinder, nothing that would shut her up. He turned his back on her instead.

No one had ever turned their back on Elizabeth. It was unthinkable that anyone would dare show such disrespect. She stared at Robert's broad shoulders for a moment in astonishment before stretching out her arm and striking him savagely across the back of the head.

The blow stinging, Robert whirled around, his face red with rage. His right hand flew to the sword that hung on his left hip, and he had drawn it at least four inches from the scabbard before the Earl of Nottingham stepped between him and the Queen.

His hand stayed, Robert found his voice and it trembled with fury. 'I will not endure this insult. I would not have taken it from your father. I'll be damned if I'll take it from you.'

Robert pushed Nottingham out of his way and exited the Council chamber, leaving behind stunned counsellors and a shaken and silent Elizabeth.

Robert, to everyone's surprise, had not been arrested after the incident in the Council chamber, nor had he even been dismissed from the court, despite the counsellors' pleas for the earl to be publicly punished. Elizabeth had seemed shocked into inaction by Robert's assault, and had said nothing, done nothing, but retired to her private apartments and resumed her reading.

Robert had decided to remove himself from court, instructing Francis to spread the gossip that such discourtesy from the Queen and her ministers had made him unwell and he was retiring to his house in the country at Wanstead to recover. Lord Keeper Egerton, who had long been a friend to Robert, had followed him there.

'You've used this stratagem before, my lord,' Sir Thomas

Egerton said, warming his backside before the fire. 'You should be careful it does not grow stale.'

'I will not stay at court to be abused,' Robert said stubbornly, resting his chin on his hand and staring into the dancing flames.

'Self-imposed exile gives your enemies at court the opportunity to move against you without hindrance, do you not see that?' Egerton pleaded.

'I have had enough of court intrigue,' Robert snapped. 'I am no Machiavelli, Egerton, I am not cunning enough for court. Do you know, Francis Bacon sent me a letter telling me I need to act like a true courtier and be cunning and sly? I cannot, no, I will not do it.'

'The Queen herself wants you at court. She is not angry, I assure you, despite all.'

Robert turned on him. 'Why should *she* be angry? It was I who was insulted, Egerton. She struck me as if I were a child who had misbehaved.'

Egerton held up his hands. 'She is the Queen, my lord.'

'What of it?' Robert spat. 'Cannot princes err? And cannot subjects receive wrong? Is an earthly power or authority infinite? Pardon me, pardon me, my good lord, I can never subscribe to these principles.'

Egerton was aghast. 'My lord, it is treason you speak.'

'Treason? To speak the truth? I am no snivelling child, Egerton. I do not cower when the Queen snaps her fingers. I will return to court only when she apologises for her behaviour to me.'

'Well, what did the wretch say?'

It was morning, past nine o'clock, and Elizabeth was sitting up in her bed, still dressed in her night attire. She was not feeling well. She had a terrible headache that was causing black spots in her vision. She had still had her ladies make up her face, however. She was not prepared for any man to see her so naked.

Egerton returned to court, was aware that Cecil had spies in every noble's household and not wanting to be implicated in treason, gave Elizabeth a true account of his meeting with the earl: how he looked, how he acted, and what he said.

Cecil, standing at the other side of the bed, snorted. 'He

demands an apology from Her Majesty? Is the man right in the head?'

'In truth, Sir Robert,' Egerton said unhappily, 'I do not know. He is certainly changeable. In deep contemplation and melancholy one moment, choleric and enraged the next.'

'So, no change there, then,' Cecil muttered under his breath. He looked down at Elizabeth. 'An apology will not be necessary, Your Majesty. I have had a report this morning that the earl is already making preparations to return to court. He has heard of your favour towards Lord Grey and is determined to stop it. I believe he will be at the palace gates by the end of tomorrow.'

'Oh, how fortunate I do not need to apologise,' Elizabeth said with a tight smile, keeping her eyes closed.

'I was not suggesting that you did,' Cecil said, shuffling his feet.

'I know, Pygmy. It is just like Robin to cause trouble at such a time when your father is so ill. Does the wretch not know how greatly I am distressed by it?'

Cecil wanted to say that it was *his* father who was dying and he had every right and reason to be more distressed than Elizabeth, but he kept his feelings to himself. 'My father will be gratified by your concern, Your Majesty.'

'Indeed,' Elizabeth nodded. 'What is my headache and indisposition compared to his suffering? I shall rise from my sickbed and visit him today. I will not let my dear old servant think he is neglected by his queen.'

'And what of the earl, Your Majesty?' Egerton asked tentatively. 'Will you allow him to enter the court?'

Elizabeth sighed. 'I cannot have such discord within my Council. Yes, he may return to court. I will receive him. And neither of us will have to apologise to the other.'

The sun shone bright and warm through the window, but the hand Cecil held was already growing cold.

Lord Burghley was dead.

Cecil's mother, Mildred, and his wife, Elizabeth, were clustered around the old man's bed in Burghley House. Elizabeth, he blessed her kind heart, was crying. Mildred was stony-faced, not trusting herself to give way to her feelings. Cecil did not even realise he wept too and only became aware of it when the dried tear tracks tightened his cheeks.

He had lost a great love with his father's passing. His wife loved him, it was true, but his mother had only a regard for him as flesh of her flesh, bone of her bone. She had always loved his brother more. His father, though, had loved him deeply, felt his pain and resented his bodily misfortunes, perhaps more so than Cecil himself.

Cecil had an unpleasant suspicion that his own heart was hard, that without his father he would view the world as cold and unforgiving and treat all who were in it as such. He was what his father had made him in regard to his brain and his abilities, but his father had not been able to make him compassionate. The world regarded him as a freakish thing, so the world would have to be fashioned to dance to his tune.

Cecil stayed with his father, even when Mildred and Elizabeth had left to seek the warmth of their private apartments and the comfort of hot food and warm wine. Left alone, the force of his grief lessened and he was able to reflect. His father had never quite recovered from the shock of Robert's behaviour at that damned Council meeting when he had almost drawn his sword on the Queen. Burghley's last few weeks had been consumed with concern for Elizabeth and Cecil was convinced that it had hastened his father's death. Cecil knew that Robert was to blame.

CHAPTER 28

In the weeks that had passed, the Irish problem had not gone away. The Irish rebels, led by a man called Tyrone, massacred two thousand English soldiers. News of the Irish victory soon spread, and the rebels moved through Ulster and Leinster and reached the walls of Dublin. The English colonists, those who escaped the slaughter, watched as their homes were destroyed by the rebels and were forced to flee, desperate to reach one of the few remaining English strongholds in Ireland.

Tyrone had achieved almost all of what he desired through rebellion. To all intents and purposes, he had made himself king of all Ireland.

'Those poor people,' Elizabeth said when Cecil had finished giving her the news. 'What miseries they have suffered at the hands of those animals. And why has this been allowed to happen? Because my Council have refused to name a suitable governor to take charge of Ireland.'

The counsellors looked shamefacedly at one another. One spoke up. 'We would have been able to agree on an appointment were it not for the Earl of Essex, madam.'

Elizabeth grunted and looked around the table. 'Well, where is he? Why is Essex not here at this meeting? I know he is at court.'

'I believe the earl is ill,' Cecil said, adding, 'truthfully, this time.'

'Then send my doctor to him,' Elizabeth said, her tone peremptory. 'Tell him that as soon as he is well, he must attend the Council. We need to appoint a Lord Deputy for Ireland.'

Another of her counsellors spoke up. 'But the earl rejects all of the names proposed, Your Majesty. He claims none of them is able.'

Elizabeth gnawed at her bottom lip and then looked up at Cecil. 'Then who would be able in his lordship's eye?' she wondered. 'A man of proven military ability? A man who can command affection and loyalty?'

Cecil held her gaze. 'Someone very like the earl, in fact.'

'Just so,' she agreed, the corners of her thin lips turning up.

'However, I may be wrong to voice this,' Cecil said warily, 'but is it wise to give such an important command to the earl? He would, after all, have a considerable army at his disposal.'

'I am not sure I understand you, Pygmy,' Elizabeth countered. 'Are you suggesting the earl would betray me?'

Concerned he had misread Elizabeth, Cecil shook his head. 'No, Your Majesty. I am sure the earl can be trusted.'

'Then I shall appoint the Earl of Essex as Lord Deputy of Ireland. What say you, gentlemen?'

Her decision was met with a chorus of agreement and not a little relief. None of the counsellors had ever been comfortable when Essex was in their midst and it would be pleasant to have him out of the country so that their meetings could return to a semblance of normality.

Elizabeth decided she had spent long enough at the meeting. She rose and a secretary pulled her chair away to aid her exit. She touched Cecil on the shoulder. 'Do not worry, Cecil. He will have his hands full in Ireland and he will not have time to cause any trouble. That country has broken far better men than he. He will see his appointment as Lord Deputy as an honour, a confirmation of my faith in him. If he succeeds, he will be a hero. The people will champion him as the saviour of Ireland. The prospect of that is too great for him to refuse the post.'

'I wish I had your insight into his character, madam,' Cecil said.

She laughed. 'I have been looking into men's hearts for almost forty years, Pygmy. There is no mystery in them.'

It was a sombre dinner at Essex House. Robert had visited the court briefly upon Elizabeth's summons and had been told of his new commission. Stunned by the news, unsure whether it was good or bad, he had found himself thanking Elizabeth, making a few requests regarding the appointment, and leaving as quickly as he could.

'So, you are going to Ireland,' Henry said, wiping his fingers on the napkin laid over his left shoulder.

'Yes,' Robert nodded unhappily, pushing the remnants of his food around his plate with a knife. 'The Queen decreed it, the Council urged me to accept, and the people think I am the right man to go.'

'It is unfortunate. You will be away from court for a long time. Cecil will take advantage of that.'

'You do not need to tell me, Henry. But what can I do? If I refuse to go to Ireland, I disobey the Queen, and she may send me to the Tower. And I will be seen by everyone as a coward if I do not accept the post. And, in truth, I think it may be better to command an army in Ireland than have to do battle at court.'

Henry drained his cup. 'You look tired, Robert.'

'I am not sleeping well,' Robert admitted. 'Not just because of this business with Ireland. Elizabeth is demanding I clear all my debts to her. My debts amount to ten thousand pounds and more, Henry. Where the devil am I supposed to find the money to pay her all that? She knows I do not have it. And she has also refused to make you Master of the Horse as you bid me ask because of your marriage.'

'Curse her bones,' Henry spat. 'I had to marry Mistress Vernon, she carries my child.'

'Of course, you had to, but Elizabeth has no sense of honour. And I asked to have Charles Blount on my Council when I go to Ireland and she has refused that, too. She ties my hands before I even get to the hellish country.' Robert gulped down his wine. 'And there is more. Another book has been published with a dedication to me. This one actually compares me to Bolingbroke.'

'You should be flattered, Robert. I would be.'

'It makes my position so difficult. You know how sensitive Elizabeth is about the succession.'

'I have said it before, Robert,' Henry said. 'If the people are seeing you as another Bolingbroke, then Elizabeth has every reason to fear you.'

Robert threw his knife onto his plate and turned to Henry. 'Oh hell, come with me to Ireland, Henry. I feel I am going to need my friends about me.'

'Oh, I suppose I may as well. There is nothing for me here. Indeed, I think it might be a good idea to get some soldiering practice in.'

Robert's face brightened. 'You will not mind leaving your wife? The child?'

Henry had easily forgotten about his new responsibilities. Perhaps he should stay with his new wife? But stay and do what? Sit at her side and watch her grow fat? There was no reason for him to stay at court, not with Robert in England and the Queen scowling every time she looked his way. He shook his head, assured Robert that his wife and child would be well looked after, and said to sound the drums, for he was, like Robert, for Ireland.

CHAPTER 29

MARCH 1599

Robert had been wrong to worry about going to Ireland, he decided. It was an opportunity, not a punishment of sorts, and his reputation could only be strengthened by a military campaign. His popularity, it seemed, was growing ever stronger, if his departure was anything to go by. Prayers for his success and safety were said in all the churches, and as he and his friends who were joining him on the campaign made their way out of the city, the people of London thronged the streets to cheer him on his journey. For four miles his route was lined with well-wishers, their cheers only diminishing as the sky began to darken and rain began to fall. If Henry and Charles Blount, who rode by his side despite the fact that they had no official place on the campaign, for the Queen had not confirmed any of Robert's proposed appointments, considered the rain and hail to be an ill omen, they kept the thought to themselves.

The weather continued to be foul, so that by the time the party reached the disembarkation port at Beaumaris, their spirits were low, made worse by the stormy passage across the Irish sea that turned their stomachs and made them thank God when they stepped upon the solid earth of Ireland. Their stomachs settled and the weather more clement, Robert and his friends began to look forward once more to winning Ireland back for England. Robert was sworn into his office as Lord Deputy of Ireland, and soon he was being fêted and celebrated with feasts, pageants and jousts and Robert felt sure that his glorious destiny was soon to be realised.

But this feeling soon faded. His strategy for a land and sea attack was vetoed with the English officials who had spent many years in Ireland telling him it was not possible with the limited resources he had been provided with by the Council. It was also a poor idea, he was told, because there were rumours that Spain was preparing to launch another armada, and they might choose to attack from the Irish Sea. Then Robert received a letter from the Privy Council giving him his orders: he was to journey north and attack Ulster.

The leader of the rebels, Hugh O'Neill, Earl of Tyrone, was carrying out his own policy of stripping the land around the Pale of all its means of sustenance and travel so that the English forces found little food and no horses available to them. He was also encouraging formerly loyal nobles to the Queen to turn and join forces with him, so that soon, Robert and the English army were surrounded by enemies on all sides. It was hopeless, Robert decided, to carry on with the Council's policy of heading north. The only choice open to them was to go back the way they had come and try to secure the territory in the south.

When the Council received his letter, they were disappointed but Elizabeth was furious. Robert had had his instructions and was blatantly ignoring them. The more serious problem was not in the south of Ireland but the north, in fact, wherever Tyrone was. No one else in Ireland carried his authority or martial ability, and only by capturing Tyrone would the war turn in England's favour. What was Essex playing at? Elizabeth shouted at her Council as she paced behind their chairs, they keeping their heads down, not wanting to share in Essex's disfavour. But there was more. Even though Robert had been warned about dispensing knighthoods years before and had been expressly instructed that he was not to make any more knights on the Irish campaign, he was creating new knights by the dozen. Being a knight will no longer be thought of as an honour, Elizabeth snarled, if every raggle-taggle man in the army was made one.

Elizabeth had sat herself down at the Council table and bade Cecil take out his pen and commit to paper the words she spoke. So Cecil wrote that Robert must not create any new knights and that he must stop prevaricating, head north and attack O'Neill at once.

Robert tried to obey but the Irish rebels were too strong and had far more resources than he. Worse still, he fell ill and was confined to his bed for almost two weeks while his troops were either harried or killed by the stealthy attacks of the rebels, or were weakened by fever. The campaign dragged on and no gains were made. The spies the English lords in Ireland had cultivated were either returning useless information or disinformation, while the Irish spies in the English ranks were astonished at the free-talking English lords, who boasted and bragged openly of their strategies to subdue the enemy and who rushed to inform Tyrone so that he always seemed one step ahead of Robert.

But even Tyrone grew weary of fighting and, conscious of his own dwindling resources and not wanting to battle through winter, sought a means of bringing the fighting to an end, even a temporary one. Having heard of the unhappiness of the English Lord Deputy, he believed he would find the means quite easily.

The day was cold. Robert still felt ill, his body shivering not only from the cold but the fever he had contracted back in Dublin. He sat a little unsteadily on his horse, his legs encased in woollen hose, his chest swaddled with wool and a fur cloak around his shoulders, burying his face up to his cheekbones, which now stood out prominently on his pale and blotchy face. Henry Wriothesley had urged him not to get out of his cot bed, doubting his friend's ability to stand let alone sit his horse, but Robert was adamant. There had to be an end to the chaos and misery he found himself in, and the chief rebel, Hugh O'Neill, Earl of Tyrone, had offered him a way out.

'I think he is coming,' Henry said, astride his own horse alongside Robert.

Robert glanced at him, wincing at the pain in his neck muscles, to see where Henry was looking. He followed his gaze up to the ridge of the hill and saw a small party of horse against the grey sky, their pennants billowing in the wind.

'Robert, are you sure this is wise?' Henry asked. 'We don't know how many men are over that hill. This could be an ambush.'

'Tyrone's messenger says his master seeks the mercy of the Queen. He knows he cannot withstand our forces for much longer. He needs to make a peace.'

Henry sighed, wishing that Robert held a clearer picture of their situation. The truth was far from how Robert believed it to be. Robert's army had suffered setback after setback, their conventional warfare methods ineffective against the stealthy tactics used by the Irish rebels. Like Robert, the army had succumbed to the illnesses and diseases that beset the bog-ridden Irish country, and many had died from the flux or fever. Many had been ill and recovered but were still too weak to fight, while others, too many others, had deserted, no doubt fleeing back to the safety of England. Henry suspected that Robert was not truly unaware of how bad things were and was clutching at any straw that could save him. Henry wanted to get back to England too, but he was worried that by treating with Tyrone, they were engaging in a pact with the devil.

Henry and Robert watched as Tyrone came down the incline on his horse, leaving his escort behind. Robert gave Henry a look that seemed to say that he was right to trust Tyrone, else why would he risk a meeting alone? Henry nodded to concede the point and even managed a smile. They turned back to Tyrone, who was riding his horse into the ford, stopping in its midst where the water lapped at the belly of the mare.

'Stay here,' Robert said, and nudged his horse's sides, trotting to the ford and mirroring Tyrone's position.

Tyrone was a man in his late forties or early fifties, dark-haired and dark-eyed, and with a heavy black beard streaked with grey. His expression was cheerful and he greeted Robert heartily, almost familiarly. He noted Robert's gaunt appearance and saw confirmation of his spies' reports that the earl had been ill. His reports had also told of how dejected Robert had become and thought happily that the meeting would be easy.

'It is my honour to meet with the great Earl of Essex,' he said in good English but with a strong Irish accent.

'You do me too much honour, my lord,' Robert returned. 'I welcome the chance to resolve this matter.'

'Well now, I don't know about resolving,' Tyrone laughed. 'The problems of Ireland cannot be resolved in one merry meeting, my lord, but I hope that we can reach some agreement before the winter comes.'

'I too. What do you want to propose?'

So, he's going to leave it to me to decide, Tyrone thought and wondered at Elizabeth sending so poor a commander to fight her cause. *Well then, let's see what this man will agree to.*

'A truce,' he announced, 'to last for six weeks from today, and then six weeks after that, to give us both time to view the situation objectively.'

'I had thought you would rather fight,' Robert said, surprised.

Tyrone shook his head. 'I'm not a fine young man like yourself, my lord. I yearn for the comforts of home too much. And it pains me greatly to see Irishmen die because England cannot see that she would be better off leaving us alone.'

'The terms of the truce. You say for six weeks—'

'Renewable every six weeks, I said. And if either one of us feels like fighting, we need only give the other a sennight's notice and we can start bashing each other's brains out again.'

'And what else?'

'We've been quite successful in capturing our towns back from the English hands, I'm sure you'll agree, and as it took so much effort to get them, we'd like to keep them, if it's all the same to you. So, all our spoils of war are to stay in our hands. I'll also guarantee you and your army free passage to the English-held towns, and to the ports, for I hear you might be planning on returning to England.'

'How have you heard that?' Robert asked sharply, embarrassed by the insinuation.

'You have your means of information, my lord,' Tyrone winked, 'I have mine.'

Robert, dismayed to discover that he had Irish spies in his camp, looked down at the water that swirled around his horse's legs. But what did it matter? he decided. His battle here was over. He was sick, his men were deserting in droves, Elizabeth refused to send him reinforcements, nor the money or arms to equip the remaining troops properly. How could he fight a war without her support? The letters he received from her were full of nothing but criticisms, asking why he had not taken that town or this, why he remained where he was instead of leading assaults into the enemy territory. It was all very well for her, sitting there in safety and comfort in London. What did she know of battle, of trying to command an army? A truce, this truce that Tyrone was proposing, was the only way there could be some sort of peace in Ireland, the only way he could go home.

'I accept the truce,' Robert declared.

'That's grand of you,' Tyrone said, holding out his gloved hand to Robert. Robert took it, feeling the older man's strong grip almost crush his own weakened extremity. 'We must have it set down on paper, so you can see that it binds me.'

'I will not insist on that. I give you my word. I need no more than yours.'

'Well, that is a fine gesture, I must say, but I'd prefer it to be set down. I'll have it written immediately and send it to you.'

'I thank you and wish you good day.' Robert pulled on his reins and his horse turned smartly, eager to be out of the freezing water. It cantered up the hill back to Henry.

'Well?' Henry asked, one eye on Robert, the other on Tyrone riding back to his escort.

'I have agreed on a truce with Tyrone. Six weeks from now and renewable.'

'A truce, Robert?'

'Yes, Henry. It was the only thing to do. It means peace. For a time, at least.'

'What else does it mean?' Henry asked, unsure whether Robert had made the right decision.

'It means we can go home,' Robert replied. 'And I mean to.'

Robert was cold. The fur cloak could not keep him from trembling and his head was just one great throbbing pain. He listened as Henry read the letter from the Council, growing more despondent at every word. Elizabeth and the Council had heard of his truce with Tyrone and were outraged.

'It seems I can do nothing right, does it not, Henry?' Robert said when Henry had finished.

'The Queen and Council do not understand the situation here, Robert,' Henry replied wearily. He too was feeling ill and wished for nothing more than to be allowed to go to his bed. 'I thought perhaps you had been rash in agreeing to the truce, but upon reflection, I do not see what else you could have done. Your army is decimated by the flux and our supplies are almost spent. I tell you, this is Cecil's doing. He moves against you, defames you and misrepresents your every act to the Queen. I swear he is in the pay of Spain. If only he could be got rid of.'

'I will not stay here, Henry,' Robert said, pulling his fur cloak tighter. 'This country killed my father. I will not allow it to kill me. I shall return to England as I planned.'

'But the Queen forbids it, Robert.'

'Damn the Queen. Let her try and forbid it when I march into London with an army at my back. I will go, Henry.'

'What do you mean to do, Rob?'

'Talk to her. I can explain my actions if I can but see her, face to face. Surprise the Pygmy. Are you with me, Henry?'

'You know I am,' Henry assured him warmly, who had not enjoyed one moment of the campaign and was longing for the comforts of London and home. 'I wish I had never come to this bog hole. Let us march on London.'

CHAPTER 30

Elizabeth sank her aching feet into the gold bowl of warm, rose-scented water with a moan of pleasure. She adored her clothes with all their finery and delighted in the impression they made, but as she had grown older and her frame more frail, she found the weight of all the silk, gold and silver thread and jewels almost too much to bear. Ashamed as she was of her thin, grey hair, she was even glad to have the tight red wig removed from her head.

She leant against the back of the chair, resting her head and closing her eyes, aware of the tense silence amongst her ladies. She had shouted at them earlier for pricking her with pins as they removed her sleeves and they were being careful not to attract her attention.

There came a clatter from the adjoining room and Elizabeth lifted her head. She heard protestations from the guards, the sound of a scuffle, and then the doors were yanked rudely open. Elizabeth gasped at the intrusion, aware that she wore only her shift and nightcap.

'Bess,' the person in the doorway declared loudly, and with rising alarm, Elizabeth recognised the voice of Robert. He came nearer and at such close range, even her myopic eyes could read the shock of her appearance in his expression. Her blood rushed to the paper-thin skin of her cheeks, and she felt only a sudden and intense hatred for the man who had caught her looking so ordinary, so vulnerable.

'Robin,' she said, her voice trembling, 'what are you doing here?' She rose, stepping out of the bowl, her feet dripping water onto the floorboards.

'I had to come,' he said, recovering his equanimity quickly. 'I have to tell you the truth about Ireland.'

'What truth, Robin?' she said, signalling with her eyes for one of her ladies to fetch help.

'Cecil has been lying to you about me, Bess. The truce. I did what I thought best. You haven't been there. You don't know what I have suffered. Men dying by the dozen, deserting, and I know not what.'

'Oh, you poor man,' Elizabeth said, her bewildered mind trying to grasp what was happening. Cecil's words, spoken months before, about giving Robert an army came rushing back to her. *My God*, she thought, *has he come to depose me?* 'Did you come alone?' she asked, fearing the answer.

'I hurried on ahead. I had to get to you first, you see?'

'Ahead of who?'

'The army, Bess. I could not leave them in Ireland, could I? A commander does not desert his men, does he?'

So, he does have the army at his back, Elizabeth realised. *What is he planning? To march on the city, take it over? Kill me?* Her heart beat even faster.

'You must not worry now you are here, Robin. Look at the state of you, all muddy and wet. You need to wash and rest.'

Elizabeth almost cried out in relief as Cecil silently entered the room behind Robert, his clothes obviously thrown on in a hurry. He stared at Robert and Elizabeth knew he was thinking the same terrible thoughts as she. They exchanged a glance and Cecil understood that Elizabeth needed him to take charge of the situation.

'Good evening, my lord,' he said.

Robert jerked around and was dismayed to see Cecil. 'Bess,' he appealed. His long, perilous horse ride had taken all his strength and he, with great shame, felt tears course down his cheeks to soak his matted beard.

'It is all right, Robin,' she said, taking his arm to persuade him to rise. 'Cecil is concerned for you. See Cecil, does not the earl look tired?'

'Exceedingly so, Your Majesty. He must have had a hard journey.'

'Ladies,' Elizabeth called, 'have the earl taken to his apartments. See that he rests and has all he needs.'

Cecil and she stood side by side while Robert was led away. The guards closed her chamber doors, shamefaced because they had failed her, and Elizabeth said quietly, 'He has brought the army with him. I must be kind to him, Cecil. I must appear to listen. Reassure him of my affection.'

'Agreed, Your Majesty. We need to know his intentions.'

'I shall find them out,' she said vehemently.

'He has deserted his post, madam,' Cecil reminded her.

'I know he has,' she snapped. 'And when I have made sure that he does not come to depose me, he shall pay for it, I promise you.'

Robert was feeling better. He had fallen into his familiar and comfortable bed and sheer exhaustion had put him into a deep sleep. He had woken refreshed almost ten hours later, broken his fast and was eager for his meeting with Elizabeth. He was sure all he needed to do was explain and all would be well. He had said so to Henry and to those who travelled with him. If his companions had had any doubts, they had kept them to themselves.

Robert expected to have a private interview with Elizabeth, so was disconcerted to be told to present himself in the Presence Chamber. When he entered, he found Elizabeth sitting on the dais in the chair beneath her canopy of estate, erect, regal, so unlike the thin old woman he had encountered the night before. He found the change in her faintly amusing and had to stop himself from laughing. Was she trying to be magnificent still? He had seen her as she really was. She could not fool him any longer. He bowed and began by asking if their talk could not be held in private.

'I think it best we talk in public,' Elizabeth had answered coldly and her stern aspect knocked his confidence.

Before he could speak further, Elizabeth began questioning him. Why had he left his post? How did he explain his ineptitude at dealing with the Irish rebels? Why had he disobeyed her strict commands and bestowed knighthoods? One accusation followed another and Robert found himself stammering out answers, giving one reason and then contradicting it with another, blaming others for his misfortunes.

Elizabeth was unmoved and the events of the previous night still painful in her memory. 'I have heard enough of your excuses, my lord,' she said, her voice growing louder with each word. 'I never desire to see your face again.'

Robert was ushered, protesting, from the room and was taken to the Privy Council chamber. He was sat down at the end of the table while Cecil, Hunsdon, North, and his grandfather Knollys, sat at the other. Robert tried to appeal to his grandfather, but Knollys refused to meet his eye. So, he tried to explain what he had been through in Ireland. They did not understand, they did not even try to. Or refused to. They just took their damned notes and answered none of *his* questions.

Robert was returned to his chamber and told that he was not to leave it. The doors were closed upon him and Robert, with a sickening feeling, heard the key turn in the lock. To ensure he made no attempt to leave, two guards were posted outside Robert's door.

Alone in his room, Robert fell onto his bed and pummelled his pillows in frustration and despair. He had been tricked, by Elizabeth, by Cecil, by his friends who had spurred him on to this course of action. He had returned to England with an army at his heels. He had had an opportunity to make London his and only his sense of honour had stopped him. He had been a damned fool.

'Lord Keeper Egerton has removed the earl from the court and taken him to York House, Your Majesty,' Cecil informed Elizabeth a few days later.

'And what of his companions who returned with him from Ireland?' she asked. 'Southampton, Rutland and the others?'

'At liberty, madam. We have nothing to charge them with. They were never commissioned, so we cannot charge them with deserting their posts.'

'Are they not to be considered a danger then?'

'We think not. The earl is the figurehead. They are nothing without him.'

'I am glad to hear it.'

'The earl himself, Egerton reports, has fallen into a great melancholy, eating little, sleeping fitfully. And he appears to be afflicted with the flux. His friends have sued to visit him, but the earl says he will not see them unless they have your permission. So it seems he is becoming conformable, madam.'

'Well he has seemed so before, Pygmy,' Elizabeth said wryly. 'Let us wait and see.'

'Yes, madam,' Cecil said, happy that Elizabeth did not seem ready to forgive and forget just yet.

CHAPTER 31

'This cannot be an end to it,' Henry Wriothesley said to Lord Mountjoy, just as Julius Caesar was being warned to beware the ides of March on the stage of the Theatre.

'What option do we have?' Mountjoy retorted, his eyes on the play. 'Essex is under house arrest.'

'But look at the support he has, Mountjoy,' Henry persisted. 'Whenever men walk by York House, they cheer for Robert. And there are ballads being printed that laud his name and denounce Cecil as a Spanish agent. Essex is the people's champion and they are outraged at his treatment.'

'I have done what I can, Wriothesley. I have written to King James to assure him of Essex's fidelity. I wrote that in spite of what he may have heard, Essex has no designs on the English throne for himself and will support James's accession when Elizabeth dies.'

'Keep your voice down, man,' Henry hissed, looking about him uneasily. They were seated in the galleries rather than on the stage, pressed in on either side by fellow playgoers.

'Essex could always escape,' Mountjoy said, undeterred. 'Journey to France. King Henri would welcome him, I am sure.'

'We should put it to Robert,' Henry said, joining in the applause almost absentmindedly. 'Once he agrees to let us visit him, of course.'

'Ireland still needs a commander,' Cecil reminded Elizabeth.

They were in the music room and Elizabeth was playing on the virginals. She was very good, Cecil admitted, although he wished she would stop playing while he was talking to her.

'A commander who will obey commands this time, if you please, Pygmy.'

'Indeed, yes, madam. In fact, I do have a suggestion. Lord Mountjoy.'

'Mountjoy?' At last, Elizabeth stopped her playing, but only to frown at him. 'Are you mad? He is a friend to Essex.'

'Yes,' Cecil agreed, enjoying the look of surprise on Elizabeth's face, 'but he is also an able soldier. He already has experience of Ireland, he knows the situation there. And I do believe, removed from the earl's circle and influence, he will prove a most loyal commander.' *Divide and conquer,* Cecil thought. *It's a strategy that always triumphs.*

Elizabeth grunted and resumed her playing. 'If you say so, Pygmy. I trust your judgement.'

'Thank you, madam. Speaking of the earl's circle, I can inform you that the Earl of Southampton has visited the Earl of Essex and spoken with him at length about escaping to France. The earl replied that he would prefer to stay and risk his life in England than become a fugitive in France.'

'How noble of him,' Elizabeth snorted, not needing to ask Cecil how he obtained his information. She knew he had paid spies in every noble's household and had had good reason to be grateful for it.

'We must decide whether to take legal action against the earl or not. Public opinion is mounting in his favour. They think he is imprisoned unjustly in York House.'

'Proceed with the Star Chamber examination,' Elizabeth told him without hesitation. 'He will answer the charges against him and the people will know what he is guilty of.'

'And his punishment, madam?' Cecil asked, hardly daring to look at her. 'When he is found guilty?'

'I cannot be too severe, Pygmy,' Elizabeth said, her tone a little regretful. 'Not with the embassy from the Netherlands due. How would they react if I were to publicly disgrace a Protestant champion? One who has fought for them in their own country?'

'Very wise of you, madam, and I agree. What is his punishment to be then?'

Elizabeth rested her long fingers on the black and white keys. 'Exile. Let him retire to the country, never to come to court again.'

Cecil smiled behind her back. 'As you instruct, madam.'

CHAPTER 32

A year passed and still Robert languished in the country, moving from Chartley to Wanstead and back again to Essex House, in attempts to escape the ennui of banishment. His debts were mounting up and his money running desperately low. Away from the court, he had no access to funds. Again and again, he wrote to the Queen asking her to forgive his past indiscretions, assuring her he was sorry, that he knew he had acted badly, and asking to be allowed to return to court. Elizabeth ignored all his letters, for she knew the real reason behind them. The monopoly on sweet wines she had granted him ten years earlier, and which provided Robert with a handsome and regular income, was coming up for renewal. Without it, Robert's financial position would indeed be precarious.

Robert waited to hear about the monopoly, months of agitation and great concern. When the answer came, there was no consolation. Aware that the Commons were unhappy with her distribution of monopolies to court favourites, Elizabeth refused to renew his licence. In a stroke, Robert's chief source of income was gone.

His position as a man of influence and power had also melted away. No longer the favourite of the Queen, no one courted his good opinion or asked for him to act on their behalf. His reputation as a soldier had also been damaged, for his friend, Mountjoy, had accepted the post of Lord Deputy of Ireland and was ably suppressing the rebels, succeeding where Robert had failed.

Robert's desperate situation began to affect his mind. He railed at those about him, decrying his enemies, who, to his mind at least, had become legion. Lettice joined him in his exile at Wanstead House, worried over the decline in her son. Grown too old to have any fight left in her, she begged Robert to give up all thoughts of returning to court. Such a desire would only lead to disappointment, she told him, especially as Cecil was in command of so much power, but Lettice soon found that any mention of the hunchback Cecil only inflamed her son's anger and made him more distracted and his behaviour unsettling.

Cecil, Robert was convinced, was to blame for everything. If only Elizabeth could be made to see it.

'I am glad I can still count you as a friend, Henry,' Robert said, grabbing Wriothesley's hand with both of his own. 'I fear I have so few.'

'You must not think like that, Robert,' Henry said, concerned at the appearance of his old friend. Robert had lost a great deal of weight, his auburn hair was heavily shot through with grey and his skin was blotchy with small patches of dry, flaky skin. He was glad that Robert had, at last, agreed to see his friends, and so he and Sir Charles Danvers, a friend from the days of the Irish campaign, had paid Robert a visit. 'Cecil is not greatly liked at court and hated throughout the country. I am sure he is in league with the Spanish. He still counsels the Queen to make peace with them.'

'But what of King James?' Robert asked. 'Does he know of my situation?'

'I have kept in contact with him, never fear.'

Danvers poked Henry in the arm. 'Tell Robert what you told King James.'

'Very well, Danvers,' Henry said, shaking him off. 'I have written in my letters that Cecil is no friend to King James and that he is making overtures to the King of Spain because he wants to put his daughter on the throne after Elizabeth. I did say that you, Rob, know this to be true. I thought your name would carry more weight and I implied that King James needs to make himself your friend and not Cecil if he has hopes of the English throne. Was I right to do so?'

'Admirable, Henry, I commend you,' Roberts said, grasping him by the shoulders. 'I am convinced my future lies with King James. Elizabeth has abandoned me.'

'Mountjoy too,' Danvers said. 'We wrote to him, asking him to write to you a letter complaining of the way Cecil and his faction had taken control of the government, and that you are needed to set things right. We would then make sure the letter was read around court.'

'Anthony will help with that,' Robert said eagerly.

'Bacon?' Henry said doubtfully. 'I do not think we should involve him. He is loyal to the Queen. His brother, too.'

'Not to me?' Robert asked, aghast.

Henry shook his head. 'Not anymore. But it does not matter anyway. Mountjoy refused to write the letter. He says he is the Queen's servant, not yours.'

'The traitorous dog! After all, I've done for him.' Robert turned away, shaking his head unhappily.

Francis, Anthony, Mountjoy. All gone, all turned away from him and towards the Queen and Cecil. His worst fears had been confirmed. He had been deserted.

In the heated atmosphere of Essex House, isolated from the court and surrounded by resentful friends who whispered in his ear against the Queen and her ministers, Robert grew ever more convinced that Cecil was growing in influence and developing policies that were determined to ruin both Robert and the country.

Robert's friends, those who felt they had been overlooked by the Queen and disadvantaged by Cecil, were looking to him to help turn their fortunes around and place them at the centre of court and political life. Even King James had faith in Robert, for he had personally written a letter of encouragement and support that hung like a sacred relic in a black bag around Robert's neck.

Essex House was becoming a focal point for all the disaffected people in the country, with men coming from Wales and even Ireland to show their support for the earl or, at the very least, wanting to find shelter and food for a few nights.

Their true and various reasons for inhabiting the courtyard of Essex House were unimportant to Henry Wriothesley, who did not care whether they were true believers or simply men who had nothing better to do, but he did his best to convert them to the Essex way of thinking. He gave permission in Robert's name for a Puritan preacher to deliver a sermon criticising the pro-Spanish policies of Cecil and citing Calvinist doctrine that claimed men were entitled to depose a monarch who had failed to serve God and the country. The men grew rowdy, openly bearing arms and speaking treasonously against the Queen and her Council.

Reports of what was happening began to make their way to the Council and they caused great alarm. To try to calm the unrest at Essex House, the Council had the Lord Treasurer dispatch a letter to Robert, warning him in the friendliest language of the dangerous waters he was heading into. Robert read the letter with contempt, tossing it across to Henry to read for himself.

'They are just trying to delay the inevitable,' Henry said contemptuously. 'They can see how much support we have here and they are frightened. We need only rouse those men out there and we can take the court.'

Robert laughed. 'We will show that hunchback, will we not, Henry?'

'We certainly will, Robert.'

CHAPTER 33

Lettice had arrived at Essex House. She had been at her home in Drayton Bassett but the letters she received from both Robert and her husband who was with him had worried her. Their letters contained words that were blatantly treasonous, and she knew that Elizabeth's Council ensured they had spies in households they considered disloyal. What if Robert's and Christopher's letters had been intercepted? They could be arrested for simply writing such things. She had to stop them in whatever they doing. It was reckless, it was stupid, it was dangerous.

'Mother, you must stop this,' Robert emphasised his words with a gesture of finality. 'I have had enough of being ruled by a woman.'

'I am not a woman, I am your mother,' Lettice reminded him. 'Do you want to kill me, Robert? Because that is what you'll do if you carry on like this.'

'My dear,' Christopher leant towards his wife and took hold of her arm, 'do not agitate yourself.'

'And you,' Lettice shook his hand off, 'what do you think you are doing leading my boy into such danger?'

'I? I am leading no one, Lettice. Robert is perfectly able to make his own mind up about what he must do.'

'And what must he do, husband, eh? Tell me that?' Lettice demanded.

Christopher turned away, wincing at Lettice's mounting

shrillness. He raised his eyes to Robert and the two exchanged an exasperated glance.

'Mother,' Robert said, lowering his voice and hoping that Lettice would do the same, 'all I am doing is demanding my rights as a peer of this realm, as an earl and scion of one of the country's most ancient lineages. I am being denied all this and it is damaging me. I have no money. I have no power, cut off from the Queen.'

'But Christopher told me that Elizabeth will allow you to return to court,' Lettice cried, 'as long as you submit to her conditions.'

'Her conditions!' Robert cried, his eyes widening and bulging from their sockets. 'Her conditions are as crooked as her carcase.'

'Robert, hush,' Lettice entreated with a sideways glance at the two liveried servants who stood in the shadowy corners of the room.

'I will not hush, Mother. Have you not told me, time and time again, that Elizabeth is a bitter hag? Well, I did not believe you. I thought you were hurt by her treatment and spoke only in anger, but I have come to see over the last few years that you were right. I have been her companion, her friend. I have been her representative, her champion. I have gone into battle and risked my life, all in service to her, and how does she repay me? With complaints and accusations, with demands for money, by treating me like a child in front of lesser men, and this, this final insult, by banishing me from the court.'

'It is dangerous to talk so,' Lettice said, her face crumpling, almost in tears. 'Christopher, tell him.'

'No, Lettice, I will not,' Christopher said, emphasising his resolution with a slicing gesture. 'I have done your bidding in most things since we were wed, but not in this. Robert is right. This is no position for a man to be in.'

Lettice saw that it was useless. Even her husband was intent on putting the family in danger. 'What do you mean to do?' she asked wearily as she wiped her moist eyes with a silk handkerchief.

Another glance between Christopher and Robert. 'Do you truly wish to know, Mother?' Robert asked. 'Perhaps it would be better to remain ignorant.'

'No, you tell me,' Lettice glared at him. 'I want to know how reckless you plan to be.'

'Not reckless, I promise you.' Robert knelt in front of his mother and took her hands in his. 'The country is with me, Mother. You should see what happens when I go out into London. I am cheered, as you said you were, do you remember? You were cheered for being my mother. Well, *I* am cheered, Mother. You came through the courtyard, did you not? Well then, you must have seen how much support I have. The courtyard is full of men who believe I can bring them freedom from the crippling policies of Cecil and they urge me to act to remove him from power. I cannot ignore them, Mother, for their sakes. I must do something.'

'What are you going to do, Robert?' Lettice asked again.

'I have a small army out there, Mother,' Robert said with a half-smile. 'I, we, are going to march on the court and remove Cecil ourselves.'

'March on the court?' Lettice rasped. 'Are you mad?'

Robert did not care for the insinuation. He jerked away from her, seating himself on the floor, his back against a table, his legs drawn up and his hands grasping his head. 'It is not madness, Mother. Why can you not see the good I am trying to do? With Cecil gone, there will be no more supposed peace treaties with the Spanish. England will be allowed to be great, as she is destined to be.'

'And you, my darling? Do you have a role for yourself once Cecil is gone?'

'I will take up my rightful position, Mother,' Robert shrugged. 'I will replace Cecil as Elizabeth's chief minister and tell her how England should be ruled.'

'Tell her?' Lettice raised an eyebrow.

Robert paused. 'Advise her.'

'My darling,' Lettice held out her hand to Robert, but he did not take it. 'Do you suppose Elizabeth is going to let you remove her trusted minister and step into his shoes? Do you not think she will see you as a threat to her throne?'

'The throne is Elizabeth's, I know that,' Robert said, 'but I will be the power behind it.'

'You mean to marry her?'

'Of course not,' Robert spat, disgusted at the idea. 'I have a wife already, Mother.'

Lettice knew that wives could easily be got rid of, but said nothing about Frances. 'And if Elizabeth will not allow you to rule her?'

Robert scratched his chin, itchy beneath his beard, and stared at the tiled floor. 'She will have no choice.'

The theatre was empty, for no play was to be performed that afternoon. Only Richard Burbage and Augustine Philips were in the building, sorting through the company's properties to take an inventory.

'I do not like it,' Burbage said, slamming the lid on the chest that held the company's scripts. 'The Earl of Southampton, you say?'

'Special request,' Philips nodded, holding up a leather bag. He shook it and it jingled. 'We get the takings, plus an extra forty shillings.'

'But it is an old play. We haven't performed *Richard the Second* for years. I warn you, Augustine, we will not be able to remember all the lines.'

'I told the earl that and all he said was that he was sure we would manage. I've said we will do it now, Dick. I cannot go back on my word. Not with his money in my hand.'

'I don't like it,' Burbage said again. 'It's an odd thing to ask. He is a close friend of the Earl of Essex, you know. There is something behind this.'

'You are probably right, but I did not ask and I do not want to know. As far as we are concerned, we have had a request for a certain play from a noble patron and the fee is handsome. We are players, after all.'

'Well,' Burbage sighed, giving in. 'I'll dig out the scripts and bring them to The Mermaid.'

Philips deposited the leather pouch in a strongbox kept under the eaves and pocketed the key. 'I'll see you there.'

'And when was the play performed?' Cecil asked Lord Treasurer Buckhurst. He was working at Cecil House rather than the palace due to a severe head cold and he had summoned the Council to meet in his study. He planned to return to his bed when the meeting was over.

'Yesterday afternoon, Sir Robert. There was a sizeable audience, the majority of them friends of the Earl of Essex. Lord Mounteagle, Sir Gelly Meyricke, Sir Charles Blount.'

'I see.' Cecil looked around the room at his fellow counsellors. 'I do not believe that we can afford to ignore this incident, gentlemen. The play was deliberately chosen to illustrate to the people the deposition of a monarch. This, coupled with the reports we are getting regarding the activities at Essex House, and it is quite clear the Earl of Essex and his friends are planning a rebellion. Do you agree?'

His fellow counsellors voiced their agreement and it was decided that they would send a message to Robert, requesting his presence before them to give an account of himself and the activities at Essex House. Cecil gestured to his clerk to write the request and the letter was dispatched to Essex House before the hour was out. It seemed his bed would have to wait.

The messenger was sent away from Essex House, and so prevented from delivering the Privy Council's request. Cecil dispatched the Council's Secretary Herbert to insist that he be given admittance and brought before the earl. Secretary Herbert could not be ignored as a humble messenger could and was ushered into Robert's presence. But Robert was unimpressed by the Council's summons. Who did they think they were telling him to present himself and answer their questions? The time for that, when he would have slunk along to the court and submitted to the Council's questioning, was gone. He was the Earl of Essex. He had an army in Essex House. He had men ready to follow him into whatever he chose to lead them. Let the Council go hang themselves. Robert sat back down and told Herbert that it was out of the question for him to leave Essex House. Could Herbert not see that he was ill? And besides, he distrusted the Council's motives. Once outside the walls of Essex House, Robert said, he would not put it past the Council to have him murdered in the streets and blame it on a villain.

Astounded by Robert's words and unable to do more,

Herbert returned to the Council and gave a report of the meeting.

By this time, midnight was approaching and Cecil, blowing his nose noisily into a linen handkerchief, deemed it best to wait until the morning to act further. Robert feared for his life, Cecil scoffed. What, or who, in God's name did Robert think he was threatened by? Cecil went at last to his bed, his mind busy with wondering what Robert's next move would be.

Robert did not go to bed. He and his fellow conspirators stayed up making plans for the morrow, buoyed up with the promise Henry had wrung from the city's sheriff of one thousand men to aid his rebellion. No one questioned the veracity of this promise. The sheriff said he would provide men, so men would be provided. Did not all free-thinking men, men of vision, men who loved England, want to act against a government that was appeasing the Spanish?

Robert and his rebels were resolved to march on the Palace of Whitehall the following morning.

CHAPTER 34

FEBRUARY 1601

Whitehall Palace seemed almost deserted. Courtiers, whose only occupation was to stay at court and live off its bounty, sensed that something important was afoot and kept to their rooms. The palace guards had a more alert look about them than usual and they gripped their halberds tighter.

Cecil had advised Elizabeth to stay in her private apartments and she did not argue. This action of Robert's had been fermenting for months and in all that time she had been living on her nerves. But now the moment had come, she felt strangely calm. She may not have thought it possible five years earlier, but now she had complete faith in Cecil, in his planning and capabilities, and there was only the smallest concern that he would fail to put down the uprising.

It was what she wanted and had expected, so she had been surprised and angered by Cecil's desire to talk with the rebels to reach an amicable understanding. She and Cecil argued, Elizabeth shouting that she did not need to conciliate Essex. He had a duty, as her subject, to bend his knee and bow his neck to her. The rebels should be arrested and imprisoned. But Cecil had reminded Elizabeth of Robert's popularity and that harsh treatment would only rouse sympathy for him and damage her. She had reluctantly agreed that calm persuasion would be the best course.

Cecil had dispatched a deputation to Essex House to discover

Robert's exact intentions and to warn him of the danger he would find himself in if he attempted to carry out a rebellion. But Cecil's policy of persuasion failed. Robert claimed the deputation had been sent to kill him and his companions and drew the deputation inside the walls of Essex House and locked them up.

Robert had men enough to make his rebellion a true threat to Elizabeth, but as with so many of his ideas, the plot was uninformed, unplanned and lacking a strategy. The discontented men congregating in the courtyard of Essex House could not understand why their leaders did not march directly on the court, but Robert and his co-conspirators did not consider their confusion and gave no explanation that there were weapons in the city that they needed. Such men were followers and should be content to do as they were told.

Robert, Henry and Lord Mounteagle rode through the streets of London, shouting out their battle cry of 'For the Queen. A plot is laid for the life of Essex.' But the people were confused, bewildered at these knights and nobles on horseback, waving their swords in the air. They either closed their doors upon them or just stood and stared.

When Robert and his rebels entered the city, they found that a heavy chain had been drawn across the street at Ludgate to cut them off. Robert had not been prepared for opposition, believing what he had been told, that the people were behind him and would hold off the Queen's men. He began to panic. A severe pummelling began inside his head, making his vision swim. His body became drenched with sweat and made his skin itch. He could not bear it. There, in the middle of the street, he called out, 'I must change my shirt, my body burns.'

Henry and Mounteagle stared, amazed, at one another.

'Damn your shirt, Essex,' Mounteagle yelled.

But Robert was insistent, and to calm him, Henry pulled him inside a merchant's house and demanded a clean shirt from the astonished mistress. He waited with growing impatience and anxiety while Robert washed the sweat from his skin and pulled on the fresh garment. Mounteagle remained in the street, guarding the door, cursing Robert for such folly.

While Robert tarried with his wardrobe, Cecil had taken action. He sent out his brother to proclaim in the London streets that the Earl of Essex was a traitor to the Queen. The streets were emptying as merchants packed up their stalls and goods and sought safety behind their doors. Soon, all that were left were either followers of Essex or the Queen's men.

'I am called traitor,' Robert cried, his voice thick with emotion, with astonishment, bewilderment, indignation.

'They are the traitors,' Henry retorted, pressing his face to the window to see what was happening. 'Come, Robert. We have tarried here long enough. We must return to the streets. The citizens know not the truth, we must tell them. Come, Robert, come.'

Henry helped Robert buckle on his breastplate, and grabbing their swords, they rejoined Mounteagle.

'We must answer this lie,' Robert said. 'Go you, Mounteagle. Cry out that Sir Robert Cecil has sold us to the Spanish and—'

He was prevented from saying more for there came the sound of armed men, their boots ringing on the cobbles. All three men turned to see a troop of the Queen's soldiers, the Lord Mayor at their head, with his sword in his hand and pointing straight at Robert.

'My lord, you and your associates will throw down your swords and come with us.'

'We are not traitors, sir,' Robert declared.

'You are traitors, my lord, to wander the streets so armed. You have spoken treasons and I am charged to secure your surrender.'

'Robert,' Henry hissed, 'what shall we do?'

Robert's breath was coming fast. What was he to do? Surrender? No, he could not countenance it, surrender was for cowards. But what to do? And then it came to him. The deputation. Yes, that was it. He had hostages at Essex House. He must get back there. He whispered his plan to Henry and Mounteagle, and before the Lord Mayor could prevent them, they had run down Lombard Street, past St Paul's and come once again to Ludgate. *God's Death, I had forgot the chain*, Robert realised. His head was agony and he wanted to bang it against the wall in his torment.

But, mercy of mercies, he was not abandoned. In the narrow street, Robert was suddenly joined by friends, his stepfather, Sir Christopher Blount, amongst them, men who had been promised a fight and were determined to bloody their swords.

But the Queen's men did not just bear swords but pistols too, and they used them. The air became thick with smoke. Blount was shot in the cheek, and for good measure, knocked on the head by a queen's man. Another man was shot dead. Others were injured in their arms or legs.

Robert turned and ran back the way he had come, ducking down an alley to head for the river. He fell into a boat moored on the bank and Henry and Mounteagle jumped in behind. They grabbed the oars and rowed back as fast as they could to Essex House.

Yet more misery awaited them there. They found that the hostages had been released and had been free to return to court to tell their sorry tale. Within half an hour, Essex House was surrounded and Robert could not fool himself any longer. His rebellion had failed and only one place was being made ready for him – a prison cell.

But was it to end thus? Had he so mistaken his power? Was he not the man he had thought he was, the man his friends had assured him he was? Yet he could not deny the evidence of his own eyes. Even now, Henry was throwing all his papers on the fire - his letters from King James, his lists of arms, and details of the plot that he had been foolishly persuaded to make. The fire banked high, spilling out smoke into the chamber. With the Queen's men banging on the doors, Henry grabbed Robert and dragged him up the stairs to the roof.

'We are done for, Robert,' he said breathlessly, slipping and sliding on the leads. 'We must surrender.'

'Then what did you bring us up here for?' Robert cried despairingly.

'We cannot surrender until we have agreed on terms,' Henry said, peering over the side of the roof. 'They would take us and clap us in irons else. But we are no common men, Robert, and I will not be taken as such.'

'You have more heart than I,' Robert said, drawing Henry to him and holding him close. 'You are the lover of words. You must use them wisely now.'

So, Henry spoke for two hours until an agreement was reached. Dejected, exhausted, Robert and Henry descended and unlocked the doors of Essex House. Henry had negotiated that, though he and Robert were to be arrested, their wrists and ankles were to bear no shackles.

Elizabeth, waiting in her silent palace, had refused to retire to bed until she heard from Cecil's own mouth that the rebellion had been put down. At midnight, she crept beneath her bed covers, smiling into the darkness at the easy defeat of the Earl of Essex.

CHAPTER 35

The morning came brightly, bleeding through the cut-out diamonds and stars in the wooden shutters, proving to Elizabeth that Gloriana was not burned out yet. She basked in the sun's warmth, even as the dust motes floated around her. She even had a smile for Cecil as he came to bid her good morning.

They breakfasted together, Elizabeth enjoying the taste of her food for the first time in weeks. Before, with rebellion threatening, it had tasted like ash in her mouth, but now the bread and meats tasted sweet. They tasted of life.

Elizabeth had been put on trial by Robert. He had demanded of her people: 'Who do you want? An aged, cruel queen or a young, noble-hearted man?' And they had answered 'Elizabeth'. They had refused Robert the glory he craved. He was crushed, he was nothing. He was dust beneath her feet.

Curse the Pygmy, she thought as Cecil set his plate aside and picked up his ever-present folder of papers, *must he go on about the matter? Must he regale me with talk of men, of arms, and of surrenders? Must he spoil my joy with talk of how close I came to losing my throne?*

'So, London is secure?' she asked irritably.

Cecil resented her tone. Why should she snap at him so? Had he not saved her throne for her? 'We have brought in five hundred men from Middlesex to guard the centre of London and they are now stationed at Charing Cross. Three hundred from Essex are stationed in the east of London and three hundred more at Southwark. There are plenty of others throughout London as well. Your capital is entirely secure, madam.'

'And Essex's treason has been proclaimed?'

'Yes, and notices are being posted even now. The Privy Council is selecting lawyers to prepare for the rebels' trial and letters are being drafted to all the peers of your realm to come to London immediately to serve at the trial. Lastly, orders have been given to all the clergy to preach sermons denouncing the Earl of Essex.' Cecil glanced up at Elizabeth. 'Are the arrangements to your satisfaction, Your Majesty?'

Elizabeth slid her gaze towards him. 'They are, Pygmy. You have done well.'

'Thank you, Your Majesty. I am only sorry that it came to this pass.' Cecil meant it. He thought it was an ignominious ending for Robert, although he had had no desire to see his rebellion succeed, and Cecil's heart was heavy.

'I think I am partly to blame,' Elizabeth sighed, pushing her plate away. 'I should have seen the kind of man he was. He has his mother's blood, after all.' Her mouth turned down at the thought of Lettice. 'I am so very glad Leicester is not here to see it. His heart would have broken to see me treated thus.'

'Is it not likely he would never have allowed it to happen?' Cecil suggested, knowing that praise of Leicester was certain to please.

Elizabeth smiled and closed her eyes in memory of the man she had loved as no other. It was an answer.

'Will you wish to attend the trial, madam?' Cecil asked a few moments later when she did not speak.

His words brought her back to the present. 'No. I will hear your report. What? Why make you that face?'

Cecil fiddled with his knife. 'I did not think to attend, madam. I am not needed after all as a judge…' He left the sentence unfinished, feeling uncomfortable beneath Elizabeth's accusatory eyes.

'Do you not want to see him brought low, Pygmy? Is this not what you have wanted your entire life?'

'With respect, madam, no,' he said, indignantly. 'If things had been different—'. He broke off, his throat tightening. He looked down at his small delicate hands. 'When our paths first crossed, the earl and I, I was a queer, solitary thing, proud and disdainful of boys like him who could sport and laugh because they were perfect. No deformation touched them. And I had plenty of perfect creatures to compare myself to. My father's house was home to many of his wards of court. And then the earl arrived and though he too was perfect and so unlike me he was, on occasion, kind. I say on occasion. When it was just he and I. He changed when the others were there, became more like them, and I knew he resented the time he had spent with me. You will think me pitiful, madam, but I even tried to buy his friendship. I made him gifts of books, praised his wit. I even laughed with him when he mocked me. And then he was gone and I was left with the others.'

Cecil touched his cheeks, concerned that he had allowed some tears to fall, but they were thankfully dry.

'I missed him,' he shrugged and gave a little laugh. 'So you see, madam, despite all his insults, his dealings against me, I cannot rejoice in his downfall. There is something of the boy who thought Essex was wonderful in me yet.' He drew a deep breath. 'I do not want him to see me at the trial because I do not want him to think that I am gloating.'

He sniffed, expecting Elizabeth to speak. The speech he had just made had been difficult and he thought, expected, hoped, her words would be sympathetic.

'You are a fool, Pygmy,' Elizabeth said. 'Were your positions reversed, he would swing the axe himself.'

Cecil had lied to Elizabeth and he had lied to himself. He found that when the time came, he could not keep himself from attending Robert's trial. He needed to see Robert, needed to hear what he said with his own ears, not read it in a report. He entered Westminster Hall before the spectators had filed into the rear of the chamber before it was populated with nobles in their ermine clad red gowns and before the clerks and secretaries had set up their desks and before the accused had been brought in and made to sit inside a square box like any petty felon.

Cecil had hidden behind a curtain and listened as the treason charges against Robert and Henry Wriothesley, who were being tried together, were read out, as they were cross-examined, as they gave their excuses and pitiful lies. He listened as Henry Wriothesley showed himself to be both a coward and a liar, to deny all knowledge of Robert's plotting and even his own part in the rebellion. Cecil listened with a cold feeling as Francis Bacon stood to give evidence against his former master, but could not help but be impressed by his cousin's demeanour and statesman-like mind in the face of Robert's accusations of treachery. *Perhaps*, Cecil thought, *he had been wrong not to find a place for Francis.*

Through it all, Cecil remained silent. He was ashamed of Robert. This was not the boy he had once admired, nor was he the man who had promised so much. This Robert was a man who was far from seeing things as they truly were, who veered from bursts of confident talk to mumbling admissions of guilt. Was this wretched man the people's champion?

Cecil wished for it all to be over, that an end could be made of this farce of a trial whose judgement had already been made. But his breath caught in his throat when he heard Robert making an extraordinary accusation against him, Cecil.

'I was told that Master Secretary Cecil had said to a fellow counsellor that the Infanta of Spain's claim to the English throne was as good as any other,' Robert declared defiantly.

Cecil could not believe that Robert had spoken such an untruth. But God a'mercy, he was saying it again and louder this time. Each word was as a blow to Cecil and he could stand it no longer. He drew the curtain aside and, in the astonished silence that followed, limped towards Lord Treasurer Buckhurst, who was in charge of the proceedings. Not without causing himself some pain, Cecil fell to his knees.

'Forgive me, my lord Buckhurst, but I beg you to let me answer my accuser, who hurls a foul and false report at my head.'

Buckhurst waved him to proceed. Cecil rose and moved to stand before Robert, who looked him straight in the eye, unrepentant.

'My lord,' Cecil began, hearing his own voice quaver, 'I acknowledge that the difference between you and I is great. For wit, I give you the pre-eminence. You have it in abundance. For nobility too, I concede. I am not noble, yet I am a gentleman. I am no swordsman – there also you have the advantage. But I do have innocence, conscience, truth and honesty to defend me against the scandal and sting of slanderous tongues. Here, in this court, I stand an upright man and you as a miscreant. I protest before God, I have loved you and made much of your virtues, told Her Majesty that your virtues made you a fit servant for her, if she would but call you to the court again. And had not I seen your ambitions turn towards usurpation, I would have gone down on my knees to Her Majesty, would it have done you good. But you have a wolf's head in a sheep's coat. You are in appearance humble and religious, but in disposition ambitious and cunning. God be thanked, we now know you. And my lord, were it but your own self who betrayed the Queen, the fault would have been less. But you have drawn noble persons and gentlemen of birth and quality into your net of rebellion, and be assured, their bloods will cry vengeance against you.'

'Ah, Master Secretary,' Robert said, unimpressed by Cecil's scathing speech, 'I thank God for my humiliation, that you, in the ruff of all your bravery, have come here to make such a speech against me this day.'

'Indeed, my lord, and I now humbly thank God that you did not think me a fit companion for you, for if you had, you would have persuaded me to betray my queen as you have done others. But I challenge you to name the person who told you of my supposed preference for the Infanta of Spain. Name him if you dare. If you do not name him, we can only believe your claim to be a falsehood.'

'It is no falsehood,' Robert protested. 'I can easily name the man. He stands here beside me. Henry Wriothesley, Earl of Southampton. He knows I speak no untruth.'

Cecil and Robert both turned to look at Henry, who seemed to shrink beneath their gaze. His mouth opened, his breath came quickly. 'I... I cannot say.'

'Come, Henry,' Robert urged, his brow creasing in confusion. 'Speak the truth.'

'I do,' Henry protested, pulling his arm free from Robert's gripping hand. 'I cannot say I ever heard that Master Secretary Cecil spoke of the Infanta of Spain.'

'But Henry, you told me so.'

'I did not, my lord, and you cannot make me say I did.'

Robert stared at his friend, uncomprehending. What was the matter with Henry? Why would he not confirm his words? Had he been wrong? But he was sure Henry had said those very words.

'So,' Cecil said, 'your words are proved to be a falsehood after all, my lord.'

Robert fell back into his chair. He had nothing more to say. Even Henry, his closest friend, had betrayed him.

Cecil waited in the antechamber to the Queen's apartments. He clutched the transcript of the trial to his chest, wishing he could rip the papers to shreds and thereby pretend the last few weeks had never happened. *I wish you were with me, Father. I fear the Queen will have her revenge and Essex will die.* He wanted his father by his side because his father would tell him that such a judgement was just, that Essex deserved to die, and he would believe his father. His conscience would be salved.

The doors opened and one of Elizabeth's ladies gestured for him to enter.

Elizabeth was in bed, her nightcap tight on her head and her face free of any paint. It startled Cecil to find her so and he forgot to bow, failed to speak.

'Guilty, I presume?' she said, not looking up.

'Indeed, Your Majesty,' Cecil stammered. 'Both Essex and Southampton sentenced to death.'

'There were none of my nobles who were moved by Essex's words?'

'None. The verdict was unanimous.' *As we knew it would be*, Cecil thought. The guilty verdict had been decided before ever Robert and Henry set foot in Westminster Hall.

Elizabeth, at last, looked at Cecil. 'What is it you have there, Pygmy?'

'The transcript of the trial. I thought you might care to read it.'

Elizabeth paused, staring at the document, before telling Cecil he could leave it. Cecil placed it on the table by her bedside.

'What has happened to the world, Pygmy?' Elizabeth asked quietly.

'Majesty?'

'I have done nothing but serve this country of mine every

day I have sat on my throne. I have made so many sacrifices, Pygmy. I would not place England at the mercy of a foreign power, which meant that I could never marry a man of my own degree, and to marry a man of a lesser degree would have meant civil war. So, I remained a maid. Never to be a wife or a mother. I have signed the death warrants of those near to me in blood who coveted my crown and still it is not enough for me to sit safely on my throne. What have I done wrong that my subjects should treat me so?'

'You are loved, Your Majesty. The failure of the earl's rebellion proved this.'

'Does it? I think it proves nothing of the sort. He, the wretch, and his friends believed the people would join them in rebellion, and several thousands of my subjects did join them, your reports have told me that. So many discontents, Pygmy.'

Cecil sighed. 'The people are fickle, Your Majesty. Many of them have known no other sovereign but your gracious self. They believe their lives could be better than they are. They are mistaken.'

Elizabeth was silent, but nodded at the door, telling him that he could leave. Cecil bowed and left, glad to be out of her presence.

Elizabeth heard the door click shut behind Cecil and she watched her attendant snuff out the candles and settle onto her pallet at the foot of the bed.

Elizabeth tugged the bedcovers higher as her body grew cold. She felt wounded, as though Robert had stuck a blade in her side and her blood was trickling out. She had thought herself loved, adored, but she knew now that was not true. Cecil was right, her people were fickle. They always had been. She had seen their changing moods all her life, long before she became queen. How had she become blind to their nature?

But I am still Queen, and I will be Queen until I die. I have fought hard for my throne and no one is going to take it away from me.

CHAPTER 36

The Reverend Abdy Ashton perched himself on the end of the wooden table and looked over at Robert, standing by the small narrow window that looked out onto the cobbles of the Tower courtyard. 'Are you certain that you wish to see no one, my lord? Not even your wife or your mother?'

Robert shook his head.

'Your soul is heavy,' Ashton said, opening his Bible.

'I am to die, Reverend,' Robert said sadly, his voice breaking. He rested his head against the stone window jamb and closed his eyes. 'How do you expect my soul to be?'

'Indeed, my lord. You are going out of this world, but you do not know what it is to stand before your maker. Unburden your heart. Make confession of your sins.'

'Confess?' Robert turned to him and Ashton could not help but start at the pale skin and red eyes, the look of fever. 'Oh yes, I need to confess. They blamed me, Reverend, at the trial for it all, but it wasn't me, it was Henry. Henry Wriothesley. I thought he was my friend but he betrayed me. He stood by my side and denied that he had ever advised me to rouse the city. Denied that he had ever said Cecil was a true servant of Spain. Untrue, Reverend, untrue.'

'And the rebellion, my lord?' Ashton prompted. 'What were your true intentions?'

Robert sat down next to Ashton and Ashton smelt the stale

sweat on his unwashed body, proof that Robert had been neglecting himself as the Lieutenant of the Tower's reports to the Council had claimed.

'My intentions were not what they said,' Robert said, looking into Ashton's eye. 'I never wanted the throne for myself. I just wanted to free the Queen from Cecil.'

'But your popularity with the people, my lord. The hiring of the players to perform *Richard the Second*, a play which is concerned with the deposition of a king.'

'That was Henry's idea,' Robert said savagely, 'not mine.'

'But you were communicating with King James?'

'What of it?' Robert demanded. 'We all know the Queen cannot live forever. What harm was there in making myself known to the one who would succeed her? Many at court have done the same thing.'

'Can you name them?' Ashton licked his lips in anticipation.

Robert rattled off a list of names, not forgetting to include his stepfather and his sister, Penelope. So many names that Ashton knew he would not be able to remember them all and told Robert so.

Robert's eyes grew brighter. 'Bring me pen and paper and I will write their names down. They too must be punished as I. I want Elizabeth to know everything. I want her to know how ill-advised I was. I want to make a true confession, Reverend. I want my soul to be cleansed.'

'It will be, my lord,' Ashton said happily, laying out the small table with the writing tools. 'God loves a repentant sinner.'

It was late and a single candle burned in Cecil's study. Cecil was reading Robert's confession that Reverend Ashton had delivered up to him when a shadow fell over him. He looked up, startled.

'Has the wretch written to me?' Elizabeth asked.

Cecil got to his feet. 'No madam, he has not.'

Elizabeth wandered around his study, picking up books, pretending to read. 'I thought he would plead for his life.'

'I think he is resigned to death, madam. Reports from the Reverend Ashton and the Lieutenant of the Tower say he is in a very dejected state of mind. He does not sleep, he does not eat, but prays continually.'

'Then death will be a mercy, will it not?'

Cecil despised her for the callous remark. Would she not even show a hint of compassion, the smallest shred of feeling for the man who had once stayed by her side through the dark hours when her nightmares came, who had made her laugh and kept her mind off growing old?

'However, his mother has written to the Council. She begs for her son's life.'

'She wants him to go free?'

'She begs the same punishment for her son as Henry Wriothesley. Life imprisonment. She says she will be forever in your debt and praises your most gracious majesty.'

'Of course, she does,' Elizabeth nodded in satisfaction. She moved back towards the door. 'The She-Wolf turning hypocrite to save her cub.'

'What shall I tell her?'

'Tell her nothing, Pygmy. I am glad that she is upset. I want her to know what it is to suffer.'

'And you wrote to her?' Dorothy almost screamed at her mother.

Like Lettice and Penelope, Dorothy had travelled to London for the trial of her brother and was staying at Essex House.

Lettice sniffed and wiped her reddened nose. 'I have already told you, daughter, yes, I wrote to Elizabeth.'

'And?'

'And I begged her, you hear me, I begged her not to hurt Robert and Christopher. I pleaded with her to let them both stay in the Tower, like that bastard Wriothesley. And nothing. I received a letter from Cecil saying the Queen refused to listen.'

Dorothy fell onto the seat beside her mother. 'How can she? After all Robert has been to her. How can she let him die like this?'

Lettice began to cry again, rocking back and forth with her head in her hands. Dorothy looked across to Penelope who was sitting by the window, looking out at the rain. 'Pen, you must do something. I know he said you were involved in the plot, but you must do something.'

'Do you think I care that he tried to implicate me?' Penelope sighed. 'He's my brother, too, Dorothy, and we know that Robert has always said things he doesn't think about. He didn't mean it, I know that. And I have written. I wrote to the Council, the same as Mother. They gave me the same answer.'

A tear escaped from Dorothy's eye and she wiped it weakly away. 'Perhaps,' she said, 'perhaps Elizabeth means to make Robert think that she will go through with his execution, and then issue a reprieve. Pen? Do you think so?'

Penelope didn't think so. She had had experience of Elizabeth too and, like her mother, knew that Elizabeth could be cruel. But she met Dorothy's eye and gave a small smile. 'Maybe, Dorothy. I don't know. She loved him once. Maybe she still does. Maybe she'll realise she can't kill him.'

Lettice heard her daughters talking and refused to allow herself to hope. She was sorry for her husband, of course, but her heart was breaking because of her son.

Oh, how she hated Elizabeth. She thought she had hated her before but it had been nothing compared to how she felt now. Her son, her glorious, beautiful son was sentenced to die by Elizabeth's written command and there was nothing she could do to stop it. She had even thought of offering herself in Robert's place, wondering if her death would appease Elizabeth's wrath, but she knew her cousin too well. Elizabeth wanted her to suffer, she knew. Well, she *was* suffering, and it felt like she would die from the pain in her heart. She felt it everywhere, in her bones, in her head, in her stomach. She couldn't eat, she couldn't think, she couldn't do all the things she should be doing as mistress of a house. What did her house matter anyway? Her son was going to die. She knew that children died; she herself had lost a child in its infancy but that had been through illness. She had been able to cope with that, only blaming God for taking him away, and the pain had eased with the passing of time. But this, this was different. Robert wasn't ill, he was in the prime of his life, and that life was being deliberately ended. This was pain unlike any she had ever felt before. It was being powerless and knowing the exact moment when Robert was due to leave the world. To know that one minute before eight o'clock on the morning of Ash Wednesday he would be alive, but that at one minute past eight, his beautiful head would have been severed from his body and his blood would be dripping through the planks of a scaffold.

And her son would be no more.

CHAPTER 37

Robert was so very tired. He had not slept, for he had been told that he was to die in the morning and he felt that, despite his confession, his soul was still stained. So, he had spent the night on his knees in prayer, only the cold light of the moon for company.

There was no crowd around the scaffold, no one to cheer a traitor or cry, 'God bless you.' Just a few nobles present to witness his death.

He climbed the steps to the platform and bowed to the clergymen who stood grouped, ready to give him solace before his head was off. 'Oh God, be merciful unto me, the most wretched creature on the earth,' he murmured and moved to the centre, his black boots becoming covered with the sawdust that had been sprinkled over the wooden planks to soak up his blood.

Robert looked up at the grey sky above the White Tower. His mouth was dry and he had to swallow several times before he could speak.

'My Lords, and you my Christian brethren, who are to be witnesses of this my just punishment, I confess to the glory of God that I am a most wretched sinner, and that my sins are more in number than the hairs of my head; that I have bestowed my youth in pride, lust, vainglory, and many other sins, according to the fashion of this world, wherein I have offended most grievously my God. The good which I could have performed, I have not done, and the evil which I should not, I have done; for which I humbly beseech our Saviour Christ to plead for me. Especially for this my last sin, this great and bloody, infectious sin, whereby so many, for love of me, had ventured their lives and souls and have been drawn to offend God, their sovereign and the world. Jesus, forgive me, the most wretched of all. The Lord grant Her Majesty a long reign and bless her. I beseech the world to have a charitable opinion of me for my intention towards her Majesty, whose death, upon my word and salvation and before God, I protest I never meant. Yet, I am justly condemned and I desire all the world to forgive me, even as I do freely and from my heart forgive all the world. I beseech you all to join with me in prayer, so that my soul may be lifted up above all earthly things.'

Robert's fingers fumbled at his neck, trying to untie the cord of his black velvet cloak. He called for his manservant, Williams, to help him, then remembered that he was not at home at Essex House, Chartley or Wanstead, and would have to manage himself. His fingers began to obey him and he removed his cloak and ruff.

He knelt on the straw, his lips hardly moving as he recited the Lord's Prayer, and he was grateful to them when he heard the spectators praying, too. Only then did he remember his doublet and took that off too, revealing a scarlet waistcoat, the only point of colour in that drab scene. He turned to the executioner, his stomach lurching at the sight of the anonymous black mask hiding the man's face. He swallowed, trying to rid his throat of its lump.

'I forgive you. You are welcome to me, for you are the minister of justice.'

The block was only a few inches high. He laid on his front, feeling the sawdust prick his palms and fill his nostrils with a sweet, woody smell. He placed his neck in the cut-out curve, feeling the pressure against his Adam's apple. He was asked if he wanted a blindfold and he replied that he did not. One of the clergymen on the scaffold with him began reciting the fifty-first psalm. Robert listened intently, closing his eyes as the words 'cleanse me from my sin' floated in the air above him.

'Executioner,' Robert said, hearing his voice tremble, 'strike home. Come, Lord Jesus, receive my soul and into thy hands, I commend my spirit.'

The axe fell and Robert felt an intense, sharp pain in his shoulder. Such agony! He screamed. The second blow came, hitting him in the shoulder again and cutting off his scream. He could make no noise. His throat was too tight, the pain too great. The axe fell for the third time, hitting its mark at last, severing the neck and ending Robert's suffering.

The executioner, distraught beneath his black mask at his bungling, picked up Robert's head almost tenderly and held it aloft, feeling the trickle of hot blood down his forearm.

'God save the Queen.'

VOLUME THREE

THE QUEEN'S SPYMASTER

"He surpassed the queen's expectation and the Papists accused him as a cunning workman in complotting his business and alluring men into dangers, whilst he diligently searched out their hidden practices against religion, his prince and his country."

— WILLIAM CAMDEN

PROLOGUE

It is only just turned dark and there is a crescent moon hanging above the elms outside my window. It shines weakly through the casement and I have moved my desk to sit beneath the window, not only to make it easier to see during the hours of daylight but because I think this view will not be mine for much longer. That is to say, I do not think I will be here to see it for much longer. I think it a shame for I have been happy here, away from the court and all its distractions, its rivalries and pettiness. This place has truly been home to me and to my family. But the pain in my stomach and privates seldom leaves me now and I believe I know what that presages: I am soon for the dark. And this is why I write, to set down how I have lived, how I have served, what I have done and why I have done it. Others leave such accounts, why not I?

Ursula, my wife, has gone to bed and so I am at liberty to write this history of my life. She would scold me if she knew of it, for she tells me I am ill enough as it is without taking on extra work and, of course, she is right. But my reply to her would be if not now, when? I am running out of time. I feel my strength trickling away, like sand running down through an hourglass.

I look up from my page and see that the candle by my elbow contrasts with the encroaching darkness outside and it allows me to see my reflection in the diamond-leaded glass of the window. I seldom look into a mirror for to do so would be to succumb to vanity. I need no glass to wash my face or comb my short, thinning hair. So, it is a surprise to see my own eyes looking back at me.

Who is this man I see with his hooded, wrinkled eyes, his hollow cheeks and his hair receding and turning white at the temples? Is he truly what I have been called, a recreant, a heretic, a devil in a doublet? Or is he a man who has done what he had to do to protect his queen and his country and serve his God?

In view of these questions, you may think I write this account as some form of justification for my life's work. I assure you, it is not a justification. I have been constant in my faith and in my pursuit of those who seek to harm us, unrelenting in my work to rid England of the Catholics' malicious and dangerous influence and cleanse the country of their polluted religion. My work has been necessary, and I will not apologise for it or attempt to justify my actions, even if they have never been appreciated by her in whose service I performed them.

No, I must stop this, I must not be bitter, I must expect no earthly reward for I know I will be rewarded in heaven. That is what I believe. It is what I have always believed. I care not that I am disliked by those who do not know me, for indeed, *they do not know me*. To them, I am the persecutor of innocent souls and it is I who am the heretic. I delve into what traitors hope can be private and remain hidden, and I am scorned for finding them out. Such traitors call me vicious, diabolical, but I am far from being such. They may not want to believe me when I say I take no pleasure or joy in the execution of my work, and if they only ceased their treason, I would not need to do what I do. But because of traitors, I must do what needs to be done, and the times in which we live means I must needs work under cover of darkness, forced to be a keeper of secrets.

CHAPTER 1

So, to begin.

I will not weary the reader with a detailed account of my childhood. It shall suffice to note that I was born in the year 1531 at Foot's Cray, my family's home in Kent. My father was William Walsingham, a respectable and successful lawyer. My mother was Joyce Denny and sister to one of King Henry the Eighth's closest companions, Sir Anthony Denny, who was with the King at his death. I remember my mother was always so very proud of my Uncle Anthony for his loyalty and service to the Crown. *His* service was well rewarded by the King, who was able to recognise a good servant when he saw one. My mother was made a widow in 1534, my father dying suddenly, of what I was never told and I never enquired. I was but three years old when my father died, so I cannot claim to have known him. I do not remember him and only know what he looked like because of a portrait my mother always hung in whatever house she lived in. My father left my mother well provided for, despite having five daughters for whom she would have to find dowries when the time came for them to marry. As for my mother, she found herself another husband two years after my father died, a good man, Sir John Carey, and it is him I knew as a father. Yet, it was from my mother that I learnt to love the Protestant faith and believe it to be a pure and beautiful thing.

My childhood was as uneventful and contented as most childhoods are, I believe. Nothing disturbed the even rhythm of my days, even though I later realised the world had been tumultuous at that time in matters of faith, both large and small — King Henry making himself the Supreme Head of the Church in England, Elizabeth Barton, the Fair Maid of Kent, spewing her bile, threatening the King would not continue to reign if he did not return to Rome and acknowledge the supremacy of the Pope — as it would continue to be, off and on, throughout the coming years.

I first knew something of this worldly tumult when I was a student at Gray's Inn during 1552. Enrolling at Gray's Inn had seemed a natural progression, following on from my studies at King's College in Cambridge. My father had studied the law at Gray's Inn and rose to become Treasurer, but unlike him, I was by no means certain I actually wanted to be a lawyer. I simply knew that as a gentleman, I must needs study something and a working knowledge of the law would be an advantage, as it is common for property and land to be contested in the law courts. I wanted to be able to protect mine and my family's assets should they ever be contested.

Gray's Inn has not changed a great deal since my time. It is, in my opinion, one of the loveliest spots in London, where the noise and stink of the city does not creep. If you have not visited Gray's Inn, then you cannot appreciate how peaceful it can be. It sits on the edge of fields, and from my window, I could see the green grass and the grazing cows and sheep. It was like being in another world behind its walls, a place where I and my fellow students dined together in the main hall, studied great works in the library or retreated to our rooms or quiet corners when we wanted to be on our own.

I was ensconced in one such quiet corner, sitting in the garden on a stone bench with my back against the brick wall, when the world intruded into my life at Gray's Inn. The branches of a tree shadowed me as I read a book that my cousin, Thomas Walsingham, had recently sent me. It had been recommended to me for its opinions and insights, though many believed *The Prince* to be a despicable book, depicting those at the pinnacle of society as thoroughly unpleasant individuals. As someone who has been a witness to power for more than three decades, I can only say that in its pages I found truth, though I would not have recognised it then.

'Francis!'

I looked up, squinting against the sun at the dark figure before me. Richard Thorpe was also a student at Gray's Inn. He was a pleasant young man with dark brown hair and eyes and a stomach that grew bigger each term.

'Have you not heard the news?' he asked excitedly.

'What news?' I said.

'Come and see.'

Before I could utter another word, Richard grabbed my arm and dragged me into the hall, along the main corridor and out through the front door onto the street. Only then did he relinquish his grip, pointing across the street to the church and starting towards it, looking back over his shoulder to check I was following. A crowd had gathered around the church door, but Richard pushed his way boisterously through and in so doing, created a channel for me to pass freely along.

'Read that,' he said, pointing to the paper that had been nailed to the heavy wooden door.

I did as he told me, my ears registering Richard telling those nearest me to be quiet and cease their complaining that we had pushed in. The paper was a proclamation issued by the Council announcing that King Edward VI was amending the Act of Succession so that neither of his half-sisters was eligible to accede to the throne following his death.

The Act of Succession dated from 1534 and had gone through two alterations during King Henry's reign, bastardising first his elder daughter, then the younger, and then, finally, legitimising them both when it became clear that he was not going to beget a second son. This meant that after Edward, Mary would succeed to the throne and after her, Elizabeth, providing none of the siblings had children of their own. Edward's altering of the Act a third time meant that neither of his half-sisters was to succeed him, the throne going to Lady Jane Grey instead.

There had been rumours in the city for many months that

the young king was gravely ill and like to die. Many pitied the young man, but in truth, much of the talk surrounded not his illness but the steps John Dudley, the Duke of Northumberland, was taking to insinuate one of his own sons onto the throne.

Dudley had arranged the marriage of his youngest son, Guildford, to Jane, the eldest daughter of Thomas Grey, the Duke of Suffolk, whose wife, Frances, was the granddaughter of Mary Tudor, the much beloved youngest sister of the late King Henry. Jane Grey was the young king's cousin and a fervent Protestant, so to countenance her as a possible queen was not beyond reason, but everyone was raising eyebrows at Guildford Dudley. Who is he? they scoffed. Naught but the son of a notorious courtier, whose own father had been executed for treason. And yet, despite such a black history, John Dudley was known to have the King in his pocket.

I read on to discover why the King's sisters were now excluded from the succession. The reasons given were that the former was a Catholic and therefore not of the correct religion to wear the crown of England, whilst the latter's legitimacy was in question, for her mother, the infamous Anne Boleyn, had not been married in the eyes of the law, and some would say in the eyes of God, to King Henry. The first argument, to my mind, was unarguable; the second was possibly true but was it a good enough reason to disinherit Elizabeth? I could not say one way or the other. I did not have all the facts.

'Well?' Richard said as I finished reading. 'What do you think of that?'

We pushed our way back down the church steps. 'Astonishing,' I said, and I meant it. To have such power that the will of a great king could be so easily overturned. It was unconscionable.

'A bloody outrage, I call it,' Richard said, walking over to a shop from whose awning hung gloves and other leather goods. He picked up a thin belt and began examining it. 'John Dudley cannot do this.'

'The proclamation says it is the King's decision,' I said. 'Perhaps it is nothing to do with the Duke.'

'That's bollocks and you know it. Everyone knows it is the Duke who holds the power. The King just does as he's told.'

I took Richard's arm and led him away from the shop, out of

the hearing of anyone who was thinking of listening in. 'Do you not think this change may be good for us?'

'Us?'

'Protestants. Think, Richard. We've all heard of how devoted the Lady Jane is to our faith. If the King were not so ill, it is likely he would have chosen Jane for his wife, so it makes sense for him to choose her as his heir.'

Richard held up his hands, palms towards me. 'Wait, Francis, before you get carried away. Jane Grey is the King's cousin and there might have been an issue of consanguinity if he had wanted to marry her. The law—'

'Cousins marry all the time—'

'Yes, very well, Francis, on that point of law you are right, but it makes no difference now. Jane Grey is already Jane Dudley, married as she is to the Duke's son—'

'Marriages can be broken. We have seen that, Richard, with the last king. But even so, it does not matter to whom Jane is married in this case. The Duke, the entire Dudley family, are Protestants—'

'Ah,' Richard swiped at the air angrily, 'the Duke sways with whichever wind blows strongest.'

'So you believe, you cannot know.'

'But most terrible of all, Francis, and you as a student of law should know this, this Device for the Succession,' Richard said, giving the proclamation its proper name, 'to all intents and purposes overturns the Act of Succession instituted by King Henry.'

It was true. The Act of Succession was enshrined in law and this Device of King Edward's had not been passed by Parliament. It was therefore unlawful, despite bearing the King's signature.

'The Device may yet be passed by Parliament,' I said, almost hopefully.

'Aye, it may be. I wonder, though, if the King's sisters will accept this Device without a protest.' The church bell began to ring. 'Oh, curse it, I am expected home tonight. Forgive me, Francis, I must leave you.'

'Richard,' I plucked at his sleeve before he could go, 'you talk of the King's sisters. What do you think may happen because of this Device?'

Richard's jaw hardened. 'What always happens when there are more people wanting the throne than can sit on it. There will be a fight.'

He raised his hand in farewell and I watched him disappear into the bustle of the street. Slowly, pondering his words, I walked back to the Inn, where power plays only went so far as ensuring a junior fellow did not eat better food than a senior.

CHAPTER 2

King Edward died shortly after his Device was posted on church doors all over London. The gossip from the palace, told through the mouths of washerwomen and pages, was that the young king had been so sick that his very body had begun decaying, for the bedsheets he had lain upon had been soiled with sweat, blood and pus. There was even talk that the Duke of Northumberland had paid the doctors to keep the boy alive with potions until all the Privy Council had added their signatures to the Device. And it was only when all the counsellors had signed that the Duke allowed the King to die.

Unfortunately, I know that on this occasion, the gossip was true. I was not there in the palace, of course, but I learnt what went on during this period from William Cecil. He was then Secretary to the Duke and he witnessed virtually all of his master's machinations and even played a part in some of them. When later we worked together, and that work would take us late into the nights, he would tell me about his early career. I found it highly instructive.

Very soon after the King's death was made public, another paper appeared on church doors. This one announced that Lady Jane Grey, the wife of Guildford Dudley, was now queen.

I do not know when this young woman entered the Tower of London as queen for there was no procession to mark her arrival. She must have been brought there either in a discreet manner or by night when darkness covered her passage. I suppose that is an indication of how worried the Duke was that his coup (for what else can such a chain of events be called?) would be resisted or fought by the people.

But never mind the people; the Duke had plenty of others to worry about. Richard's last words to me were proven true.

Cecil told me that the Duke had sent messages to both of the King's sisters, instructing them to come to court to see their brother during his final days. I thought that sounded like the act of a considerate man until Cecil told me that by this time, the King was already dead.

'I did not like what the Duke was doing,' Cecil told me, staring into the fire as the flames licked at the logs in the grate. 'He was trying to subvert the law, disrupt the natural order of things.' He stabbed the arm of his chair with his forefinger. 'Everyone has their place in this world. Some can move up within their natural sphere but not outside it. The Lady Jane was not next in line to the throne.'

'But she was a Protestant,' I said, thinking it an important point to make.

Cecil slid his gaze towards me. 'That was of no consequence. Faith had nothing to do with the Duke's motives.'

'But it was thought that the Duke put Jane on the throne to stop the country being ruled by a Catholic, and a half-Spanish one at that.'

'Thought! Thought! By whom? Those out there?' he said contemptuously, waving his hand at the window. 'They know nothing of what goes on in the palaces.'

'Why did he do it then?' I asked.

'Because he knew Mary would have him in the Tower the moment she became queen. She knew he was no friend to her.'

'But it all went wrong.'

Cecil smiled smugly. 'Yes. I saw to that.'

'You?' I was incredulous.

'I was not about to let the Duke get away with overthrowing the line of succession. I sent Mary a message of my own.'

'You told her of his plans?'

'I merely told her she should not come to London.'

'That's all you told her?'

'Just that.'

'And Elizabeth?'

'Oh,' he laughed and shook his head, 'she didn't need warning. I tell you, Elizabeth has the keenest sense of survival.'

Indeed, I knew that Elizabeth had never left her home at Hatfield when her brother was dying, having given out that she was too ill to travel. Instead, she had waited, waited to see what would happen.

What had happened was that Mary had gone to Norfolk, rallied men to her banner and then made her way to London with an army at her back. The Duke had been forced to leave the court, ordered out to fight by the queen he had hoped would be his puppet, and rode out to meet Mary. Once he was gone, the Privy Council, seemingly regretting their earlier capitulation to the Duke, declared for Mary, and Jane and her husband were arrested and taken to the Tower.

And all this, Cecil had made possible with just a few words of warning, delivered to the right person at the right moment. I have learnt never to underestimate the power of knowledge, language and timing.

CHAPTER 3

The whole of London, it seemed, had come out to watch Mary Tudor enter the city in triumph. Ribbons and brightly coloured cloth were laid over upper-storey wooden rails to add vibrancy to the occasion and hawkers were taking every opportunity to sell their wares, some at hugely inflated prices, from pies and sweetmeats to small dolls of the new queen. The cheers were honest, the people, it seemed, happy to have a true daughter of Henry the Eighth on the throne, whatever her faith might be.

And I? Well, I did not cheer. I was not sure there was anything to cheer about. In truth, I had half-hoped that the Duke's plot would be successful because my faith prevented me from being pleased that a Catholic was now on the throne of England. The cleansing of England of the papist corruption, everything the Reformation had seemed to promise, would not now happen, it was impossible. A few of those who stood alongside me noticed that I did not join in with their happy cries and shouts and cast me sidelong, accusatory looks. An old woman in a mustard-coloured gown and red cap said, 'What's the matter with you? You look like you bit into a crab apple.' I started to reply, saying what I don't remember, but she wasn't interested in my answer for Mary had just turned the corner of the street and the woman and her companions began cheering in earnest.

Mary was seated in a chariot, resplendent in purple velvet and satin. The bold August sun made the gold embroidery of her skirts shimmer. Her clothes were the brightest thing about her. She herself was commonplace, the kind of woman you would pass in the street and not give another thought to. Mary was short, almost squat, and it was hard to believe that in her youth she had been thought of as fair. Her face was square, almost masculine, and her skin, which I understand had once had the fresh pinkness of her father's famed English complexion, had now yellowed. What most caught my attention, however, was the large, jewel-encrusted cross hanging around her neck and which she clutched in her hand, every now and then pressing it to her lips to bestow a kiss upon it. I understood. She used the cross as a symbol of her triumph in that procession. She believed God had given her back her throne, not that a series of mistakes had simply turned the wheel of Fortune in her favour.

Queen Mary's chariot passed on and some of the spectators rushed to follow it. Those who remained were the more fortunate, in my opinion, for they had a chance to see who followed the Queen and that was Elizabeth. Compared with Mary, Elizabeth was truly beautiful, the image of what a princess should be. She was slender, perhaps too much so upon reflection, for I remember her collar bones sticking out, but she was young and carried herself well. Her pale skin was accentuated by her red-gold hair, so very reminiscent of her father, which hung loosely down her back as befitted her maidenhood.

She was now one step nearer to the throne, so long as Mary remained unmarried and childless. Elizabeth was so very different to her half-sister. She was younger, of course, and that made a difference, but it was not just her appearance that made her so much more attractive than her sister. It was her delight in being in the procession. It was palpable. It made her shine. This was where she wanted to be, not stuck in a royal house, however grand, in the country where she was known only as King Henry's bastard daughter or King Edward's bastard sister. I have come to know Elizabeth very well and I know she lives for acclamation. It feeds her unfortunate vanity.

The procession moved slowly through the city, giving everyone who wanted to see the Queen and the most prominent members of her court a good opportunity. Through the streets of London, the cavalcade wound, making its sedate way to the Tower. Perhaps Lady Jane and John Dudley saw Queen Mary enter the Tower. Perhaps they reflected on how close they had come to having that power. They were only the first of many enemies that Mary was to incarcerate.

A mere ten days after she had paraded through London, Mary's fellow Catholics began to openly celebrate the Mass, even though the Act of Uniformity had made it an illegal practice. Those flouting the law were not prosecuted and Mary's ministers did nothing to apprehend transgressors. This did not fill me with much hope for the future.

I heard that Doctor Bourne, a canon, was going to preach at St Paul's Cross. He was quite well known and I knew he was a creature of the Queen's. I was interested in what he would have to say. Perhaps I could gauge some of the workings of the Queen's mind from his sermon. I joined the crowd already gathering at the Cross, greeted some people I recognised from my occasional visits to the Stranger churches, those set up by the foreigners forced to escape religious persecution in their own countries and which I sometimes chose to worship at, and waited for Doctor Bourne to appear. When he did so and climbed the stone steps, there were no cheers, no applause, only a few murmurs that lacked some civility. The majority of Londoners, even then, are Protestants and most of the crowd was consequently of that faith. Were the others like me, wondering what a Catholic preacher had to say?

Bourne talked of Rome and the Pope and how England had been made rotten by the Reformation. His words enraged many in the crowd and the previously merely uncivil murmurs became insults and shouts of protest. Bourne did his best to ignore them. He continued with his sermon, his voice growing louder in an attempt to drown out the jeers, but soon Bourne could no longer pretend the abuse was not happening.

And then something shiny glinted in the air, and as it neared Bourne, I realised what it was. Someone had thrown a dagger. Bourne was fortunate, for the dagger missed his shoulder by only a few inches, and in the brief silence of the crowd that followed, caused by shock or surprise, I know not which, I heard it clatter on the ground. And then there was a hubbub, a great deal of pushing and shoving, and I found myself thrust into the middle of the mob. My heart was beating faster as it became clear to me that the situation could turn very nasty.

But then something quite wonderful happened. Two men I recognised, John Bradford and John Rogers, beseeched those making the most violence to cease. 'Stop, stop,' they cried. 'For the love of God, stop. Hear him,' and they pointed at Bourne who was cowering behind two of the Queen's men-at-arms. 'Be true Christians and listen. These are only words he speaks and words cannot harm you. Do not harm your own souls by threatening violence upon a man who does you no harm.'

Their words worked for the crowd calmed and began once again to listen to Bourne, who had by now lost his courage. His voice trembled as he tried to continue and his sermon came to an abrupt, premature end. The crowd began to disperse and many there shook the hands of the two Johns, grateful for their timely intervention that had prevented violence. Unfortunately, there were those who were less grateful.

Later that same day, both of the Johns were arrested and, incredibly, charged with inciting the riots! They protested that everything they had done had been for the benefit of the Queen, that they had restored law and order, not attempted to disrupt it. But Stephen Gardiner, the Queen's chief minister who was one of those freed by her from the Tower at the end of her triumphal procession, would not listen. The Johns, he claimed, had been able to calm the would-be rioters, therefore, they must have been their leaders. Bradford was imprisoned in the Tower and Rogers kept under house arrest for nothing more than keeping the peace when the Queen's own men had been unable to do so. This did little for Mary's popularity which was already on the wane.

When we heard that, despite having been brought up in the Protestant faith, Elizabeth was attending Mass, there were disapproving murmurs about her, and not just amongst those with whom I studied or shared a church pew. Elizabeth had always presented herself as a Protestant — attending church, dressing in black and white to show her disdain for show; it was said that this was one of the reasons why the late King Edward had shown her so much love — and it was wondered aloud whether her faith was a flexible thing or even a sham if she could adopt the Mass so easily. However, these murmurs ceased when it became known, deliberately leaked some said by her servants, that she went most unwillingly to Mass and made such a show of physical discomfort that it was understood she did so to prevent discord and distrust between her and her sister. We chose to believe this.

And then there was the purging of the Privy Council. King Edward had had a Protestant and wholly competent Council but one of Mary's first acts was to remove six members of the clergy and replace them with Catholics, most notably Stephen Gardiner, who I mentioned earlier. Him, she appointed Lord Chancellor. Then there was Bishop Bonner, who had been imprisoned by Edward VI because of his refusal to act in matters of religion as the excellent Archbishop Cranmer wanted him to. Once out of his prison, Bonner set about his task of returning Catholicism to the land. In this, he was ruthless, and you will know of him by the nickname he was given, Bloody Bonner, for the number of Protestants he executed. Foreign Protestants were expelled from the country and the Queen and Council seized their lands and property so that these unfortunates were both penniless and homeless. With men such as these in power, what hope was there for us of the Protestant faith?

I do not mean to give the impression that every English Catholic was avaricious and unprincipled. To do so would be wrong and misleading of me. There was some, albeit too few, who believed in what was right and just and were willing to defy the authorities, the Council and the Queen, to uphold it. Mr Justice Hales was one such gentleman and his name spread swiftly around the town. Catholics would cite him as proof that they were not all bad. Justice Hales attempted to find those who were illegally celebrating Mass, for at this time, it was still a crime to do so. The Council heard of his intention and Stephen Gardiner summoned him to court to explain himself. I have read the transcript of their meeting.

'You must do as the Queen wishes,' Gardiner told him.

'I must do as the law decrees,' Hales countered. 'The Queen is subject to the law, too.'

Gardiner had Hales imprisoned. However, when news of his imprisonment became known, there was an outcry in the city and the Council, fearing a riot, was forced to release him. But Hales's ordeal must have caused some damage to his mind, for I later heard he ended his own life by sticking a dagger in his heart. The poor man. He must have been so very unhappy to commit such a sin.

This was England now.

The world seemed to settle down, for a time at least. No one was surprised when the Duke of Northumberland's head was struck off. He had committed treason, after all. At the Inn, my fellow students and I had all talked through the legality, or rather the illegality, of the Duke's intended coup and whether Lady Jane had actually committed treason herself when she accepted the crown. We decided that, in law, she had done so, but we, and many others in the city, thought she had had little choice in the matter. And Mary must have thought so too because she did not sign a death warrant for her young cousin, merely kept her prisoner, despite the urging by her counsellors to be rid of Jane too. We in the city thought Mary merciful.

But despite her protestations that she loved all her people, and despite our hopes that she would be tolerant of Protestants, Mary showed her true colours when it came to the punishment for the Duke of Northumberland.

When I first heard the story of Northumberland's last few days from one of his surviving sons, Robert, I thought it was merely how he had perceived the incident. Robert had been, after all, a young man devoted to a father whom he idealised, but I have seen the state papers written by Stephen Gardiner and know the truth.

Gardiner was sent by Mary to see the Duke in his cell in the Tower and make him an offer. The Duke had been tried for treason and sentenced to death, along with five of his sons who had aided him and had also been imprisoned in the Tower. There was going to be no reprieve, no mercy shown. The Duke was destined to die from the moment he was arrested. As the Duke sat dejected on a low stool in his gloomy cell, unshaven and unwashed, Gardiner told him his life was forfeit but that he could save the lives of his sons if he did just one small thing: renounce his Protestantism and declare Catholicism to be the only true faith and that to worship any other way was to be a heretic.

The Duke did it. He stood in the chapel of St Peter ad Vincula in the Tower, his sons watching nervously from the pews, and recanted his faith to save his sons. Mary and her ministers made a mockery of him and endangered his soul. I cannot say I blame him for doing what he did — God knows I would do anything, commit any treason, to save *my* daughter — but I have often wondered how easy a renunciation of his faith was for the Duke. I have never been asked to renounce my faith. I think I would struggle to do so.

The Duke did not have long to wonder whether he had done the right thing for he was executed the next day. The effect the Duke's recantation had on his son Robert, who was to become a close friend of mine in later years, was profound. It kindled within him a hatred of Catholics that for much of his early adult years was latent but which manifested so much more strongly later on.

A few months passed, and a rumour began to work around the taverns that Mary was to marry Prince Philip of Spain, a fellow Catholic.

I suppose it was inevitable that she would seek a husband who shared her faith. There had been talk of her marrying Reginald Pole and that was considered to be acceptable because he was at least an Englishman. But the English have never been fond of foreigners and we did not want a foreigner becoming our king. Some, though, were pleased at the prospect of Mary marrying, regardless of who to, and thereby having a king rather than a queen, for everyone knows it is not a natural thing for a country to be ruled by a woman. God knows I know that to be true. Often have I and my fellow counsellors wished we had a man to deal with rather than a woman.

But Mary had always demonstrated a fondness for her Spanish kin, and it had been her mother's dearest wish that her daughter should marry a prince of Spain. In her youth, Mary had been betrothed to Queen Katherine's nephew, Charles, but that betrothal had been broken, to the Queen's deep dissatisfaction, because King Henry had had other ideas that involved the betrothing of his little daughter to the French king's son.

Stephen Gardiner kept very extensive records of this period and not just official ones. Often, the official records of his time have been annotated with personal observations of his own, scribbled in the margins or even forming part of the official text. These annotations appear to have been written in his own hand. Perhaps he did not trust a secretary or clerk with his thoughts.

According to his papers, Mary became infatuated with Prince Philip after seeing his portrait. She would stare for hours at the painting of the prince, her hands clasped before her, and in this way, she fell in love. Her feelings, as Gardiner noted, were expertly fanned into love by the Imperial ambassador, Simon Renard. He pursued the idea of the marriage with vigour and even managed to persuade Mary that her feelings were reciprocated by the prince.

'Reading again, Francis?'

I was in the library at the Inn. I looked up to see Richard standing over me, blocking out the light that came through the stained-glass window.

'I am a student, Richard,' I pointed out, laying down my pen with which I had been making notes.

Richard held up a finger, inclined his head to one side and gestured for me to listen. 'Church bells,' he said after a moment.

'Yes, they've been ringing for over an hour.'

'And you know why?'

'I am not a hermit, Richard,' I said testily. 'The Queen is to marry.'

Richard sat down and frowned at me. 'That does not seem to worry you.'

'Should it?'

'Should it? Are you quite serious? *King* Philip of England?'

'The Queen has to marry someone.'

'But does that someone have to be him?'

'Why are you so opposed? Because he's Catholic?'

'Francis, why are you being so obtuse?'

Looking back on this, I now understand why Richard was getting so frustrated with me but then, I was young, concerned only with my studies and did not, could not, foresee the trouble that lay ahead.

'Do I really have to explain this to you?' Richard's shoulders sagged. 'We are already being persecuted for our faith. Once the

Spanish have a foothold in England, how long do you think it will be before we have the Inquisition here too?'

I thought persecution too strong a word and said so, but Richard was having none of my naiveté.

'You would not call it so, eh? Then you are a fool or... I know not what. I tell you, we are not safe, Francis, we are not safe. How many of our friends have already been taken and interrogated? Some of them we have never seen again. How long do you think it will be before the same happens to us?'

I will admit his words chilled my blood, but I protested. 'We have been careful,' I said, though my voice sounded thin and unconvincing even to me.

We *had* been careful. We obeyed the law in regard to church attendance and went unobtrusively to the Protestant churches when we had had enough of popery. I had even reduced the number of visits I made to the booksellers who sold the books the Council considered to be heretical.

'Maybe so, but there will come a time when being careful will not be enough,' Richard said, and I could tell that beneath his usual bluff joviality, he was truly frightened. 'It is not the fact that we attend our church, it is these.' He prodded the pile of books on my desk, the fruits of my most recent shopping trip to the booksellers in Paternoster Row behind St Paul's. The top two slid off the pile and knocked against my inkstand. 'We have been reading what we should not. John Day has left London, did you know?' he said after a long moment.

This was news I had not heard. John Day was well known in London, and indeed throughout the country, as a printer of Protestant texts. It was he who had brought John Foxe's celebrated *Book of Martyrs* to England. During King Edward's reign, he had been free, even encouraged, to print his texts but these were different days. I knew that other printers of books and pamphlets that did not meet with the approval of Mary's Privy Council had decided it was an apposite time to leave England. It seems Day had come to the same conclusion.

'He knew that they would come for him before too long. And, Francis,' Richard paused to make sure I was listening, 'John Day knows me and he knows you. If the authorities do catch up with him and he is taken and interrogated, even if they just show him the instruments to frighten him, he will tell what he knows. He will tell them about us and our friends and then it will be our turn to be taken to the Tower.'

Richard fell silent. His fingers tapped on the side of my desk. I looked up and met his eye. 'What should we do?'

He sighed. 'I don't know about we, but I know what I am going to do. I'm leaving England. This is not my home, not anymore, not while Catholics rule here. They will bring their hell to England and I am not ready to be consigned to that pit of flames for what I believe.'

'Must you leave England?' I asked. 'Maybe just leaving London will be enough.'

He shook his head. 'I think not. You see, to stay means to have to bow our knees in the Mass and take bread in our mouths and call it the body of Christ, to drink wine and say it is his blood. An abomination,' he hissed. 'Can you bring yourself to do that, Francis?'

I knew I could not, just as I knew there would be those who would bend their knee and their heads at Mass and pretend to be a Catholic. In fact, I daily breathe the same air as two who did exactly that, but I shall not name names in this history. They had their reasons for acting as they did and I will not judge them.

'Where will you go?' I asked.

'Germany, Switzerland,' Richard said. 'Italy, even.'

'Italy?' I almost laughed at the suggestion. 'You plan to leave England because of Catholics to go to a country where everyone is Catholic?'

A smile broke onto his face, making him look more like the carefree Richard I knew. 'I don't mean to Rome, you dolt. No, to Padua. There, they tolerate Protestants. More than tolerate actually, they welcome them. I will be safe there. It would be good for you, too, Francis. You could enrol at the university there. Finish your studies in peace.'

I said nothing and began stacking my fallen books into a pile. I could feel him looking at me.

'Think on it, Francis, please, I beseech you. Do not sit here and wait to be arrested.'

'I will think on it, Richard,' I promised, hoping that I would not need to, that the authorities would never come looking for me. 'When are you leaving?'

'Today. Now. I am going to my lodgings this very moment,

packing my trunk and making my way to Dover. There, I will book a passage to Calais and then... on to wherever feels right. Come with me, Francis.'

'Richard,' I shook my head at his impulsiveness, 'I cannot just up and leave. I have my family to consider. You know my cousins are with me.' I had lately become the guardian of my three young Denny cousins, Henry, Anthony and Charles, both of their parents having died. Whilst I was lodged at the Inn, I had set them up in a household a street away in Holborn where I could easily call on them and they on me. It was a heavy responsibility, this guardianship, but one that was my duty. 'They too are Protestants. Am I to leave them here to face... I know not what?'

'Forgive me, I had forgotten.' He smiled sorrowfully. 'That is one advantage of not having any kin. There is no one for me to worry about. Well,' he patted his knees and stood, 'I must go.'

I rose and held out my hand. 'God speed you, Richard, and I will think on what you've said. Who knows? Perhaps we shall meet again in Padua?'

He grasped my hand. 'I do hope so, Francis. Just do not leave it too long.'

CHAPTER 4

The idea of foreign travel was not unwelcome to me. I had been out of England before some years previously, journeying around the more congenial parts of the Continent. I had enjoyed my time abroad, finding the people there to be of greater interest, in some respects, than my fellow countrymen. Though I am an Englishman and would wish to be no other than I am, I have always found the English as a people to be rather insular, distrustful without foundation of our fellow man and superior in our opinions. Few of my associates back then would have believed it worthwhile to have a knowledge of the workings of trade in Holland, Germany or France, and fewer still that it would be useful to learn other tongues. But I believe time spent on education is never a waste, providing that the education gained is subsequently put to good use, which is why I was eager to learn French and Italian as well as my brain allowed. I believed then, and experience has proved I was right, that knowledge is valuable. One never knows when a little knowledge will come in useful.

Yet, despite my liking for foreign travel, I wanted to be in England at this time, at least, for as long as I could stomach the current state of affairs. It was well I stayed, for not long after Richard and I had our conversation, my stepfather became ill. I made plans to visit him at Foot's Cray but before I could return to my home, I received word from my mother that he had died.

I was at dinner with my fellow law students in the main hall when I received her letter. It was handed to me by a pageboy and I felt suddenly sick as I recognised the handwriting and the red seal on the back. I rose from the table, pulling the napkin from my shoulder and throwing it upon my trencher with a croaky, 'Excuse me'. I felt the eyes of my fellows on my back as I hurried from the hall and up to my small chamber. I sat on my bed, it creaking as I pulled my knees up to my chest like a child, and broke the seal.

'My dearest son,' my mother wrote, *'your dear stepfather died this morning. I know this will not come as a shock to you, as you knew he was ill, but it grieves me and no doubt you that he passed away before you were able to come home. Be easy in your mind. His passing was painless. Earlier, he had sunk into unconsciousness and I confess, it was a relief that he did so, for he had been unsettled in his mind and his talk was rambling. He is with God now and though I will miss him sorely, I know he is in a better place. Pray for him, Francis, though do not feel you need to hasten your intent now. There is no need to travel at night, and it will relieve my mind greatly to know that you do not do so, so full of villains are the roads from London to Kent. You will no doubt shake your head at your mother worrying so, but I cannot help it. I will make no funeral arrangements until you arrive, though I will be writing to the rest of the family to tell them of your stepfather's death. You need do nothing other than come here as soon, but as safely, as you can.*

'Your loving mother.'

I cried for my stepfather, holding my mother's letter to my chest, crushing it so that the seal broke and splintered on the floor. It had been many months, too many, since I had seen him, so involved in my studies had I been, and I felt such guilt for my neglect.

After a while, my tears dried to tighten my cheeks, and I rose from my bed. My trunk lid was open, waiting for me to pack, and I began this now, taking care with my few shirts so they did not crease, and counting out my money, putting some in the bottom of the trunk, the rest in my purse on my belt. I tried to work out how much I would need for my journey on the morrow. I would take my mother's advice and not travel at night, not just to please her for I myself had no desire to make an unnecessarily risky journey at night, so I would need a few pence for a bed in a tavern. I wished I had started for Foot's Cray sooner, though I knew it would have made no difference; my stepfather would still have died.

My journey into Kent was uneventful; I had no trouble with rogues. Had I hurried and travelled through the night and not stopped on the way, I would have reached home early the next morning. As it was, I rode up to Foot's Cray at around two in the afternoon. Our estate steward came out to meet me.

'Master Francis,' Peter said, raising his hand in greeting and taking hold of my horse's bridle.

I threw my leg over the saddle and dismounted. 'Good afternoon, Peter.'

'Sad occasion,' he said, stroking the horse's nose. 'Sorry about your father.'

'Thank you,' I said. I was very weary from the ride, but courtesy made me ask, 'And how are you, Peter, and your family?'

'We're well enough, thank you, Master Francis. Don't be standing around out here. You go in now and see to the mistress. I have just been in to see her. She's in the back parlour. Benjamin's just taken her something to try and tempt her to eat.'

'Has she not been eating, then?' I asked, struck by the way he had said his last words.

Peter waggled his head from side to side. 'Not as much as she should, if you ask me. She was by your father's side from the moment he fell ill. And, well, truth be told, she had a hard time of it, Master. Your father, he weren't right in his mind towards the end.'

'My lady mother wrote that he was rambling.'

'Aye, well, it were a bit more than that, but maybe I shouldn't say.'

'Tell me,' I said, snatching off my riding gloves and grabbing his arm.

He shifted uneasily. 'Your father, Master Francis, he said things he didn't mean to the mistress. Unkind things. She won't tell you, I daresay, but he criticised her over her prayers and accused her of wanting him to die without a priest to give him the last rites and so on because she hadn't summoned one to his bedside. But that weren't it, Master Francis. I just think your mother didn't want a priest there because it would prove your father was dying, that's all. She fetched the priest as soon as she realised it was so.'

I looked away. I was upset and angry at my stepfather for accusing my mother of such callousness. How had she borne it? Had she been hurt by his words?

As I wrote at the beginning, I got my faith from my mother, but both my father and my stepfather had stuck to the old ways of worship. My stepfather had never been strict in his beliefs and he never stopped my mother from teaching me Protestant ways, but he would sometimes find fault with us both for what he called our thin way of worshipping God. He liked the gaudiness of church wall paintings, the over-decorated altars, things that both my mother and I despised, but he agreed that priests were sometimes corrupt and unworthy of the reverence they received. In this respect, he was a halfway — halfway towards becoming a Protestant but halfway towards staying a Catholic. I knew, without having to ask my mother, that his funeral would be Catholic in form. I would not argue about it, that was his faith. He would be buried in the manner he would have wanted. But I would not pay a penny to have corrupt priests pray for my stepfather to leave Purgatory and make it to heaven. Purgatory is a Catholic fabrication, so my stepfather could not possibly be there.

I nodded a dismissal to Peter, who, even though it was not his place, took my horse to the stables, and entered the house in search of my mother. As I entered the hall, a strange sensation overwhelmed me. The smell, lavender and thyme crushed beneath the rush matting, beeswax rubbed into the refectory table to make it shine, told me I was home far more than the sight of the house had done.

I passed through the hall and as I neared the door that led to a short, narrow corridor at the end of which was the parlour, my eyes caught the portrait on the side wall. It was of my father, painted soon after I was born because, I was told, he was so proud to have at last produced a son after so many daughters that he decided to mark the event for posterity. His face, plump and smooth-skinned, told of his pride and I thought, with a lump in my throat, that it had been I who had made him look thus. The loss of my stepfather now mingled with the loss of the father

I had not known. I felt tears begin to prick at my lids and hurried past the painting, determined to be brave for my mother.

My mother was sitting beside the window in her parlour, gazing out towards the garden. She turned her head as I entered and her face broke into a sad smile. She held out her hands and I went to her, falling to my knees and placing my forehead against her legs. A moment later, I felt her hand smoothing my hair and I was glad to be home.

I have always found it surprising how life carries on following the death of close kin. One expects life to never be the same again, that their absence will create a huge void in one's daily life, but it is not so.

As a grown man studying and living in London, I had not seen a great deal of my stepfather over the last few years. Indeed, when I had been abroad, I had gone more than a twelvemonth without having him in my sight, but then I had always known that I would see him again. But now, there was no chance of that, not until I am dead and buried and we meet again in heaven. And yet, despite my regret and grief, there was so much to do that my days were quite full, especially as I was now the master proper of Foot's Cray. I had, in fact, come into the property when I turned twenty-one but had left it in the care of my mother and stepfather so that I could continue with my studies in London.

I could not remain in Kent, of course. My studies made that quite impossible, but I had responsibilities to those who lived and worked on my land, to inspect their living conditions and cast my eye over the estate books. My stepfather had been shrewd at business and the books and estate were both in good order. We were not rich by any means, but it was a relief to me to know that my mother would live a very comfortable life as his widow. And here my law training served me well, for I so managed matters that should my mother choose to marry again, she would retain all her assets. I did not want my mother to be a target for any lazy, would-be suitor who saw her as an opportunity for having an easy life by living on her money.

My stepfather's funeral also meant that I saw something of my other kin. My cousin, Thomas, lived very near Foot's Cray, only a few miles off at Scadbury. Several times, I rode over to see him, and we spent many happy hours together. He promised he would keep an eye on my mother, though, he joked, she rarely needed nor wanted looking after.

One visit especially has stayed in my memory. It was late in the afternoon when I arrived at Scadbury and the sky was darkening ominously, threatening rain. I had foolishly left home without providing for such an eventuality and hoped that my cousin would provide me shelter for the night, glad that I had told my mother where I would be so she would not worry. Even as I climbed down from my horse in Scadbury's stable yard, a spattering of rain speckled my shoulders and I did not waste any words on the stable boy who took the reins and led my horse into a vacant stall. I knew there was no need to present myself at the front of the house, being kin to Thomas and known to the servants, and made my way through the kitchen, giving a cursory greeting to those at work preparing supper, which smelt delicious. On the kitchen table, I saw roast tongue, brawn and rabbit, custard tarts, sweetmeats and salads. My stomach started growling noisily.

My cousin's steward, Anthony, was in the hall when I reached it, a clutch of papers in his hand. 'Master Walsingham! Forgive me, I did not hear you arrive. Henry!' he shouted, who promptly appeared and divested me of my cloak and gloves.

'I came through the kitchen,' I said. 'I hadn't anticipated rain, Anthony, and came unprepared. Do you think my cousin can give me a bed for the night?'

He hesitated and I wondered why. My question had been a courtesy only; my cousin would, of course, not turn me out, so why, I wondered, the hesitation?

Anthony collected himself and said, 'I'm sure he will, Master Walsingham, no fear there, but… he already has company.' He glanced towards the door at the end of the hall that led to Thomas's library.

'Shall I go in?' I suggested.

'Allow me to ask, Master Walsingham. Wait but one moment.' He gave me a sharp nod and darted off towards and through the door. He closed it after him, so I could not hear what he said. The next moment, the door opened and Thomas himself appeared. He gave me a smile that I felt was forced.

'Francis,' he said, holding out his hand and grabbing my shoulder, 'why did you not warn me you were coming?'

'Warn you?' I frowned. 'Must you be warned that I might visit? Would you arrange to be out if you knew?' I confess, I was a little stung by his manner and spoke shrewishly.

'No,' he protested, shaking his head, 'warn was the wrong word. I meant… I just… I did not expect you, that is all.'

'I can leave if it is not convenient,' I said, stepping away, but he lunged forward and pulled me back.

'Now, do not play the offended maiden, cousin Francis. My manner was brusque for a reason, but you are not unwelcome and,' he looked up as rain began to drum upon the hall's windows, 'you cannot go anywhere at present.'

'Master Walsingham requested that he be given a bed for the night,' Anthony interjected, looking sideways at his master.

'And he shall have one. See to it, Anthony. Now, Francis, come with me.'

Thomas led me to the library where a fire burned in the hearth. Warming his feet on the hearthstones was a thin man with blonde hair. He looked around as we entered.

'Luke,' Thomas said, 'this is my cousin, Francis Walsingham. Francis, this is Luke Greer. He is a friend of mine from when we were both at Cambridge. Before your time,' he added as he saw me wondering whether I should remember Greer.

Greer got up from his chair and held out his hand. I took it. 'Thomas has told me of you,' he said.

'Good things?' I asked warily.

'Oh, this and that,' he said and returned to his seat.

Thomas dragged a chair away from the wall and positioned it before the fire. He pointed me to it. I felt strangely unwelcome in the company of Greer; he did not seem to want me there. He was very serious, something I myself have been accused of often, but my seriousness, I like to think, has never been expressed in unfriendliness towards another who has done me no harm nor incivility.

I saw Thomas looking at me and he knew what I was thinking. 'Luke,' he said quietly to his friend, 'Francis is of our faith.'

So, they had been talking of faith. Had Greer been concerned I was a Catholic? Why would that worry him so?

Greer, who had been staring into the fire, cast a quick glance at Thomas, then at me, then back to the fire.

Thomas sighed and turned to me. 'You must forgive Luke, Francis. He has been sorely tried of late.'

'Do not apologise for me, Thomas,' Greer flared up suddenly. 'I need have no excuses made for my behaviour.'

'No, of course not,' Thomas said, and I noticed for the first time how strained he looked.

I wanted to help him, not be the cause of discord, so I said, 'I shall take supper in my room, Thomas, and leave you two to talk alone.'

I half rose but Thomas grabbed me and pushed me back into the chair. 'Certainly not,' and he cast an annoyed glance at Greer. 'I will not have my cousin feel that he must absent himself in my home because of the company I choose to keep.' It was a command to Greer, I think a command that he must make an effort to behave himself. 'There is no reason why you cannot partake of our conversation. I have no secrets from Francis, Luke.'

'You have secrets?' I said with an attempt at a laugh. In truth, I felt I would have preferred to be left free to retire to my chamber. Indeed, I was beginning to wish I had never ventured out of Foot's Cray.

'In these times, such as us must needs have secrets, cousin,' Thomas said, handing me a cup of wine he had poured out.

'Such as us?' I queried.

'He means Protestants,' Greer snapped.

'Oh, I see,' I said.

Greer looked hard at me. 'Do you?'

'Yes, I think so,' I said, determined not to be put down by this rude fellow. 'It is hard to be a Protestant in this country these days. The Queen promised toleration when she came to the throne, but her mercy is growing thin and every day more strictures are put upon us.'

'Indeed,' Greer said vehemently, 'and do you not think there will come a day when she will show no mercy at all and it will be recant or face the flames?'

I thought of Richard, how Greer's words matched his in sentiment.

'*I* think so, Francis,' Thomas said before I could answer,

looking at me from beneath lowered lids, 'especially now that the Queen is to marry Philip of Spain. And are we to allow that to happen?'

I frowned at him. '*Allow* it to happen? What do you think you can do to stop it?'

'There, you see,' Greer ejaculated, gesturing at me but talking to Thomas, 'that is what most people think, that there is nothing that can be done. I thank God not all of us are such cowards.'

'I am not a coward, sir,' I said, affronted by his words and the mean look he gave me. 'I merely asked what could be done?'

Neither Greer nor Thomas gave me an answer and my cousin steered our talk onto other subjects. The mood between us remained tense and soon after supper had been eaten I said I was ready for my bed. Thomas bid me sleep well. Greer said nothing.

Thomas prevented me from leaving early the next morning as had been my announced intention by arriving in my chamber as the sun rose and drawing my bed curtains to let its golden glow in. I tried to bury my face in my pillow, but he ripped its feathery softness away.

'I want to talk to you,' he declared unapologetically.

'Could it not have waited?' I groused.

'I show no mercy. You have given me a sleepless night, Francis, so I feel justified in waking you. I know you were angry with me when you came up here last night.'

'Not with you,' I said, sitting up and running my hand through my sticking-up hair.

Thomas sighed. 'Luke can be a little abrupt—'

'A little?'

'Many of his friends have been taken and he fears for himself. He is just very unhappy and scared.'

I was cruel in my youth. I cared not that Greer was unhappy, so said nothing.

Thomas was looking at me quizzically. 'Are you not going to ask what it was he was talking about?'

'Do you want me to ask?'

'I would value your thoughts, Francis. If it is not too early for you,' he added with a smile.

'Tell me,' I yawned.

'Luke wants to make a protest and he is not the only one. You have heard of Sir Thomas Wyatt? He lives at Allington Castle, a few miles away.'

'The poet's son?' I asked, my interest peaked. I had read a few of Wyatt's poems. My Uncle Anthony had passed on a few pages of his poems to my mother before Wyatt's arrest for consorting with the Boleyn woman, and she had kept them in a leather folio almost as if they were a sacred relic.

'That's him. Wyatt hates the idea of the Queen marrying Philip and he has rallied support to protest against it.'

'And what form does his protest take?'

'A martial one. What other course is there?'

'What kind of support does he have?' I asked, knowing that an armed protest was indeed the only action open.

Thomas, obviously happy that I had not ridiculed the protest, relaxed. 'Well, there is Sir Peter Carew of Devon, Sir James Croft—'

'Should I have heard of these men?'

'No reason you should, although you may have heard of Henry Grey.'

That name certainly got my attention, as Thomas had intended it to. 'The Duke of Suffolk?' I asked incredulously.

'It is not so remarkable, is it?' he retorted, amused. 'He joined with John Dudley to put his daughter on the throne.'

'But what can be his motive this time?'

'The same as Wyatt's, the same as Greer's...' He looked at me sideways. 'The same as mine.'

'Yours, Thomas?' I admonished. 'Why, how involved are you?'

'I have pledged my support. Men. Money.'

'Is that wise?'

'If it is wise for the others, why not for me? Come, Francis, someone must act to stop this marriage.'

'What do you want from me?' I asked, fearing I knew the answer already. 'More than my thoughts and approval, I think.'

'No, I do not want to embroil you in anything you do not wish to be involved in.'

I considered for a long moment. I was pleased there were people prepared to take action against the Spanish marriage and proud of Thomas for being a part of it. 'If I were to become a part of your protest — *if* I were — I could bring nothing to it. I have no men, save my tenants at Foot's Cray, and I would not ask them to become involved. I have no money to speak of that could furnish your men with arms—'

Thomas waved me silent. 'Very well. I appreciate your situation. Just come and listen, that's all I ask.'

'Listen to who?'

Thomas leant forward and patted my hand. 'Get up, say your prayers and then come down to eat. I'll tell you more over breakfast.'

Despite its nearness, I had never been to Allington Castle — I had never received an invitation — but I had heard of its beauty. Surrounded by a moat, the castle seemed to rise up out of it, its yellow-grey stone beautifully reflected in the water. It had been built two or three hundred years earlier and so was unlike the modern buildings that were only just starting to be built then but which are now in abundance all over the country. Someone was walking on the battlements as Thomas and I rode up the causeway, swans flapping their wings to get out of our way. I felt sure that any man would turn poet had he been brought up in such a place. When we reached the drawbridge, we found a large party making its way beneath the portcullis, they obviously having just arrived too. I saw Luke Greer amongst the party. He had not been at Scadbury for breakfast, so he must have either braved the weather the previous night or left early that morning. He and the rest of the party looked askance at us as we followed them into the courtyard.

'Perhaps this is not a good time to visit,' I said to Thomas, not wishing to intrude.

'Francis,' he laughed, running a critical eye over the party, 'they are here for the same reason we are.'

We both dismounted and waited for our horses to be taken by the stable boys.

'Thomas,' a young man hallooed, stepping away from the others and heading towards us, 'I am very glad to see you.'

This, I discovered, was Sir Thomas Wyatt. He had dark brown hair, cut short with wisps stroking the back of his neck and temples. A thin, curly beard framed his jaw, while his moustache was thin below a long, aquiline nose. *He looks earnest*, was my first impression of this daring young man.

'I would not wish to miss this, Sir Thomas,' my cousin assured him almost reverently.

Wyatt nodded his approval, then looked at me. 'Who is this with you?'

I had stayed back, waiting for Thomas to introduce me.

'My cousin, Francis Walsingham,' Thomas said, gesturing at me to step forward. 'I have spoken to you of him.'

'Of course,' Wyatt held out his hand. 'Master Walsingham. You are most welcome.'

I took his hand. 'Thank you, Sir Thomas.'

'Come in and I shall introduce you to everyone.'

Most of his guests had by now disappeared inside the castle. Wyatt clapped his hands delightedly and turned towards the porch. We followed him into the Great Hall. I found Wyatt's Great Hall surprisingly spare. The walls were decorated with portraits — I noticed one of his father alongside one of Anne Boleyn — as well as a few heraldic flags hangings from the timber roof rafters. A few uncomfortable-looking wooden chairs from a previous century were stationed along the walls, but the main item of furniture was the long refectory table at one side of the hall.

Wyatt made sure that everyone had a cup of wine and for those not fortunate enough to secure a chair of their own but were left to sit on the refectory table's benches, a cushion for his backside. The slight unease I had sensed upon our arrival continued until Wyatt moved amongst the party and introduced me as Thomas's cousin. Upon hearing of my kinship with Thomas, it seemed to me that the others relaxed, although I did wonder if Greer had been saying uncomplimentary things about me to them, for he still eyed me disdainfully. I began to understand the party's unease when I was told their names for they were the same Thomas had told me of that morning. The only man missing was Henry Grey, the Duke of Suffolk. Wyatt signalled to his steward who waited at the side of the hall and he gestured for the servants to bring in the food.

So, this was the company who were plotting to thwart the Spanish marriage. What had been talk only the night before and that morning was about to manifest before my eyes. It made me very nervous, excited, admittedly, but nervous. While the others selected meats for their plates, I kept my hands in my lap.

'Do you not have an appetite, Master Walsingham?' Wyatt asked, noting my empty plate.

All eyes turned to me. Before I had a chance to answer, Wyatt continued. 'Do you have an appetite for our intent if not for my food? I am sure that as you are here, your cousin has made you aware of our plans.'

I looked around the table and my eyes discovered that Sir James Croft, a powerful, well-built man with black hair and blue eyes, was smirking. Sir Peter Carew, thickset, long-bearded and ruddy-faced, was frowning. This planned protest was as much theirs as Wyatt's.

My cousin made to answer for me but Wyatt waved him quiet. 'Let him speak for himself, Thomas.'

I cleared my throat. 'My cousin has told me in only the broadest terms of what you intend, Sir Thomas. I know you are against the Spanish marriage, that your intent involves arms and of those men who have given you their support, most of whom are here, I see. Beyond that, nothing.'

Wyatt leant his elbows on the table and steepled his hands before him. 'That being so, before we divulge more, tell me whether you agree with us or no.'

'The Spanish marriage is not ideal,' I said carefully, 'but I think it is difficult to say what match would be. England has not had a queen regnant before. Mary's husband, whoever he may be, will take precedence; in fact, he will be the king and the highest authority in the land. Foreigner or Englishman, Queen Mary's choice for husband cannot hope to be popular with every man in the country.'

'If only King Edward had not died,' Carew lamented to the assembly, wiping his greasy fingers on his napkin.

'There's no sense in talking of ifs, Carew,' Croft shook his head at him.

'And there you have hit the nail on the head, Master Walsingham,' Wyatt said, ignoring their remarks. 'The problem we have is finding a suitable husband for the Queen.'

I agreed.

'Do you also agree that the worst candidate possible is Prince Philip of Spain?'

I hesitated just a moment before saying yes.

'Then you oppose the Spanish marriage, and as a firm believer in the Reformed faith,' he looked to my cousin for confirmation, 'and as an Englishman, you should do all you can to ensure it does not take place.'

I do not care for people telling me what I should think or do, and I liked it even less when I was younger. I had a mind to tell Wyatt that I was free, as an Englishman, to think how I pleased but I was conscious of my cousin's standing with these men and did not want to embarrass him or make him ashamed of me if I could help it. Also, I could not, in all honesty, say I disagreed with anything Wyatt had said. My only reservation was that I did not want to be a participant in his rebellion, for that was what it amounted to. Call me coward if you wish. I will not deny it.

'Your cousin understands this,' Wyatt continued when I did not answer.

'My cousin is free to understand what he will,' I said, not meeting his eye, 'as am I. Sir Thomas, I thank you for your hospitality and your confidence, but I feel no compulsion to act the rebel and take up arms against the Queen and her ministers, especially as I cannot think of a suitable alternative candidate for her husband.'

I looked sideways at my cousin seated alongside me, whose face was angled down towards the table, and I knew that I had disappointed and perhaps embarrassed him, despite my best efforts.

Sir Peter Carew drained his cup and poured himself another from the jug. 'Sounds to me like you want others to take all the risks while you reap the benefit.'

I expected my cousin to defend me against this accusation, but he did not raise his head nor his voice. Thomas did not demand that Carew retract his comment. He did nothing.

Wyatt spoke instead. 'Fortunately, Sir Peter, there are those prepared to take those risks. I am sorry you will not be joining us, Master Walsingham, but will you wish us luck in our venture?'

I shook the hand he held out to me. 'Of course, Sir Thomas.'

I had long left Kent and returned to Gray's Inn by the time Wyatt and the others made their protest. Thomas had taken me away from Allington Castle as soon as it became clear that I was not going to become involved. We had parted on the road, he to return to Scadbury, I to Foot's Cray. I apologised to him for not being what he had wanted me to be and he accepted my words grudgingly. Whether he felt no more than disappointment or full-blown anger kept under control, I could not tell. The coldness between us pained me but was not strong enough to change my mind. All I wanted was to return to my studies and let the world do as it would.

There was much talk around the Inn about the Queen and the Spanish marriage and it did indeed seem that Wyatt and his company had gauged the mood of the people, or at least Londoners, correctly. What I heard time and time again was that it was not right for the Queen to marry a Spaniard. It did seem that the proposed marriage had received a death blow when an MP stood up in Parliament and declared that he and his fellow members refused to pass the bill allowing it. Parliament had spoken, so the talk went, so there would be no marriage, and I was glad for my cousin's sake, for it meant he would not now need to put his life in danger

But astonishingly, and contrary to the law, the Queen refused to accept the judgement of Parliament and ordered her ministers to proceed with the marriage negotiations. I know now that even some of her own ministers were opposed to the marriage. I have read Stephen Gardiner's private memoranda that were enclosed with the state papers from that time between Spain and England and I know that even he did not want Philip of Spain to be King of England. This, I confess, astonished me for I had always thought that, because of his religion, such a marriage would be most welcome. But unlike her sister, Queen Mary cared not for the opinions of her ministers. She was in love with Philip and intended to marry him.

Looking back, I think I can understand why she was willing to defy Parliament. Throughout her life, Mary had been promised to one European prince after another as her father made one treaty only to break it and make a new treaty with a former enemy. Ever a betrothed and not once a bride. As queen, Mary finally had the chance to make her own choice and have the child my mistress Elizabeth claimed would have made her so happy. When she was made queen, Mary was already eight and thirty, perhaps only a year or two left her in which to bear a child. She had no time to consider other candidates for her hand.

But to return to the main matter. My fears for my cousin resurfaced when it was proclaimed that the marriage was going ahead. Proof of its progress came sooner than expected with the arrival of the Spanish delegation ahead of Prince Philip. I was crossing the street when they passed through London, having just paid a visit to my Denny cousins in Holborn to see how they fared, and I saw how the delegation was received. There were no cheers or wide eyes of curiosity; there were only glares of hostility and mutterings of abuse. Some children dressed only in filthy rags picked up the mud-ridden snow from the ground and pelted the Spanish with snowballs, so the delegation arrived at their lodgings soiled, humiliated and very angry.

The Council soon became aware of such treatment; this was not an isolated incident. They knew there was ill feeling in the country about the Spanish marriage. Indeed, I discovered from their papers that they had foreknowledge of the planned marriage protest. They had the names of several of those whom I had met at Allington Castle but believed Sir Peter Carew to be the leader of the plot. Somehow, Wyatt had escaped their notice, or mayhap they thought he was low down in the matter, a foot soldier, not an officer. Whatever reason they had for not immediately exposing the plot and putting an end to it, the Council did at least act and invite Carew to attend the court to provide an explanation of exactly what he was up to. But Carew knew what would be waiting for him if he did attend and he decided it would be better to decline their invitation and leave home for a while.

Understandably, my cousin Thomas did not keep me informed of the company's plan and I did not know then that Sir Thomas Wyatt had decided they needed someone more illustrious to be involved, someone who could be put forward as an alternative bridegroom. Perhaps my concerns that the plotters had not named any other who could become Mary's husband had not gone unheeded after all. To this end, Wyatt had chosen Edward Courtenay.

Edward Courtenay had been imprisoned in the Tower of London for most of his life. His father had been suspected of involvement in a Catholic plot to rise up against King Henry, who promptly had his head cut off. King Henry had become something of a tyrant by this time, so very different from the ideal of sovereignty he had been when he first became king, and even took his revenge on the father's family, imprisoning the wife and son, young Edward, of whom I write. Courtenay was freed upon Mary's accession and the Queen had looked with great favour upon the young man. But imprisonment at such a young age and for such a long time had fashioned a man who was wholly innocent of the way the world truly worked. Gardiner noted in his memoranda that Courtenay was a poor choice on the rebels' part. With Carew nowhere to be found, Gardiner having sent men to fetch him from his Cornwall home and bring him to London but failing to discover where he was, the Lord Chancellor decided to arrest and interrogate Courtenay. Gardiner was soon proved right in his assumption of the young man's unsuitability as a co-conspirator, and with very little pressure put upon him, at least according to the transcript of Gardiner's interrogation, Courtenay told all.

With Courtenay under arrest and Carew now unable to raise men and march on London, Wyatt and the remaining rebels decided they had to move quickly or not at all before the Council took steps to protect the Queen and put down the rebellion. But it was too soon, Courtenay's arrest having taken them by surprise, and their preparations for their protest were incomplete. Forced to act, Wyatt acted virtually alone. He and his men reached Southwark but found that the bridge was barred to them, forcing them to take an alternative route where the Queen's men were waiting. After a brief skirmish, Wyatt was taken and imprisoned in the Tower.

London is a noisy place, but the noise of the fighting was audible over the cries of the street traders, the animals penned up waiting to be slaughtered and the peal of church bells. I heard the skirmishing from my chamber in Gray's Inn. I stood by the window, craning my neck to see where the fighting was taking place. I was worried. Had Thomas been with Wyatt?

Was he too languishing in a Tower dungeon? In the days following the rebellion, I read every proclamation issued by the Council, hoping for news. My mother, whom I had told of Thomas's plans — I had not wanted to but she knew something had been amiss between him and me after my visit to Scadbury and Allington Castle and I had had to explain why — wrote to me, entreating me to return to Foot's Cray to be out of harm's way. She feared for me, for all of us, for if Thomas was questioned or even merely suspected of complicity, then it was likely all members of the Walsingham family would be under suspicion. My mother was wise enough not to put this in her letter, that she feared for my safety, merely that I was needed home to attend to an estate matter. My mother's advice was always worth listening to. I packed my books into my leather bag and returned to Foot's Cray.

'Are we safe?' my mother asked almost as soon as I stepped inside the front door of Foot's Cray. Her eyes were bright with weeping, her face drawn with worry.

'I do not know,' I said. 'Have you had any word from Thomas?'

'Nothing,' my mother shook her head sadly and drew me into the parlour. 'I rode over to Scadbury yesterday. He was not there and his steward could tell me nothing. I have been out of my mind with worry, Francis.'

I embraced her and her hands clutched at me. She lay her head against my chest and asked, 'Are you too part of this madness? Did he manage to persuade you into folly?'

'No, he did not, Mother. Thomas did not even try, he had already witnessed my refusal. He knows I thought the plan... foolhardy.'

'I thank God you had some sense,' she said, falling into her chair and adjusting the cushion behind her back to make her more comfortable. 'What made them think they could ever succeed? No one can ever stand up against the sovereign. Have the failed rebellions of King Henry's reign taught us nothing?'

They were a very anxious few days for me and my mother, waiting at Foot's Cray for any scrap of news that would let us know whether we were safe or no. News came at last in the form of Thomas himself. He galloped into Foot's Cray's courtyard and almost fell out of the saddle. He saw our faces at the window, roused by the horse's hoof beats, and hurried inside without preamble.

'Thomas,' my mother cried with relief, 'thank God you are safe.'

Thomas took her hand and kissed it. He assured her he was perfectly well, though, to my eyes, he looked very far from it.

'Francis,' he said, trying to catch his breath, 'what a mess.' He started to cough. My mother led him to a bench and poured out a cup of beer from the jug on the table. He gulped it down. 'It was a fiasco. Wyatt and his men were cut off before they even got near the Queen. I took a small party of men another way. We managed to elude the Queen's men, I don't know how, I suppose we were lucky. But I have been on the run ever since. I dare not go to Scadbury. I wasn't even sure whether I should come here. Or if I would be welcome.'

He took another gulp of beer, glancing up at me over its rim. He was embarrassed at how we had parted, I knew.

'Do not be foolish. Where else should you go if not to your kin?' my mother said, squeezing his arm, but I thought I detected a note of uncertainty in her words.

I think Thomas noted it too, for he said,' You are very kind, Aunt, but I endanger you by being here, I know that. I am not stopping, do not fear. I just wanted to let you know that I was well and to warn you.'

My mother stood abruptly, one hand reaching to the pommel of her chair to steady herself. When she spoke, her voice was sharp. 'Warn us of what? What is going to happen? Thomas!' She looked fearfully up at me. I took her hand and she grasped mine tightly.

'I know of nothing definite, Aunt,' Thomas said hastily, 'but Francis knows what I fear. The Council, they will be looking for others complicit in the plot. They have Wyatt. If they rack him, he will talk and he will give them names. He will not be able to help it.'

'You told me you were not involved, Francis,' my mother gasped.

'I was not,' I assured her.

'No, he was the sensible one,' Thomas grinned wryly. 'But they will know of me and they will learn of Francis. His name will have come up before as someone the Council will want to watch because of his activities in London.'

Mother looked at me, her eyes only asking if it was true. I nodded a confirmation.

Thomas touched my arm. 'Francis, you should leave England. Tomorrow. As soon as you can.'

'Go into exile?' my mother asked, aghast.

'For safety,' Thomas said. 'It is for the best, Aunt. Francis has been abroad before. You enjoyed it, did you not, coz? It should be no hardship to travel around Europe again.'

'Will I have to go, too?' Mother asked looking around at our house and I knew she was thinking whether she could bring herself to leave it.

'No,' Thomas shook his head, 'I do not think there is a need for that. You are out of things here, Aunt, and they have no reason to suspect you. But Francis, living in London and being a Protestant, his activities and sympathies… well, it is different for him. Francis, will you go? Please.'

I considered for a moment, but only for a moment. 'I think I had better. Mother, you understand?'

Mother had begun crying but she nodded through her tears. 'You will have to take your cousins with you. They are in your care and they have done what you have done in London, I doubt not. You cannot leave them here to face what you dare not.'

'And I will, not, Mother,' I said, kissing her forehead. 'I have made arrangements,' I looked at Thomas, 'just in case.'

'What arrangements?' she demanded.

'Passports, Mother. A few months ago, after Allington Castle, when I got back to London, I applied for passports for myself and the boys. Not for you, though, Mother. For two reasons, before you believe I did not think of you. The authorities would have wondered at a passport for you, raised suspicions when there was no cause. And secondly, because I did not think you would want to leave your home and come abroad. Was I wrong?'

My mother smiled and frowned at the same time, then lifted her hand and stroked my cheek. 'No, you were right, Francis. But then,' she turned to Thomas, 'you can all go together.'

'I fear me, no, Aunt,' Thomas shook his head. 'I must be on my way now. My plans are made and cannot be altered, and in truth, I think it best if we go our separate ways.' He stood up and pulled on his gloves.

'But surely you have time to rest awhile, to at least eat before you leave?' my mother protested.

But Thomas was already halfway out of the door. We followed at his heels. Our goodbyes were hurried, inadequate. We stood at the door and watched Thomas gallop away. My mother twined her arm in mine and pulled me back into the house. As she closed the door, she told me to go to my chamber and pack my trunk.

So, Wyatt's rebellion failed, as I believe all such risings are doomed to fail and history, I am sure, will prove me right. I cannot say whether I was glad the rebellion failed or dismayed. I was too intent on getting me and mine to a place of safety to consider my thoughts at any great length. What did perplex me at the time, though, was why so many of our faith supported Mary at the beginning of her reign and not John Dudley. I suppose that it was not just faith that united the country. They may have been Protestants, but they were also Englishmen who believed in the right of kings, or queens should England be so unfortunate as to have a woman occupy the throne. And then, of course, the Duke of Northumberland was deeply unpopular, especially in Norfolk where he had been ruthless in his putting down of the Kett rebellion when the people rose up to protest against the enclosure of common land. Another rebellion! Why do we never learn? How long has England been troubled by faction over the past few hundred years? It is only by good governance, and because of my own endeavours and intelligence, that Elizabeth's reign has been so peaceful.

CHAPTER 5

I took my Denny cousins to Basle. They were young and it was their first time out of England. The Continent can be a bewildering place, just as it can be wonderful. I knew that, although I was prepared to lose myself in whatever country felt welcoming to me, my young cousins would need the support, the familiarity, of a Protestant community. Such a community there was in Basle. I stayed with them for a month or two, but it was greatly on my mind that my law studies were incomplete, and I moved to Padua to enrol in the university there.

I did not know before I left England that the reason Padua was so welcoming to Protestants, despite being in Italy, was that it fell under the rule of Venice. And Venice was a place that obeyed no rule but its own. Its success can be wholly attributed to this attitude and why it is the preeminent trading centre of Europe.

And what of Padua? Was it everything Richard had promised me? Yes, unequivocally, yes. The university was, despite its age, thoroughly modern in outlook regarding the subjects studied there. These included philosophy, astronomy and medicine, as well as the law, which was the area I studied while there. I endured no censure, no restrictions on my liberty in the university, or indeed in Padua at large because of my faith. The university certainly lived up to its motto — *Universa universis patavina libertas*: Paduan Freedom is Universal for Everyone.

I found that studying in Italy was very different from studying in England. In England, the law is a practical thing, devoid of sentiment and entirely distinct from its past. In Italy, however, the law is almost a living, breathing creature, its roots firmly in its heritage, the ancient Romans from whence the Italian idea of law and justice came. It taught me much and would serve me well in the years to come. I tell you, those Englishmen who deride foreign learning as nonsense do not know of what they speak.

In Padua, I was brought into the orbit of Sir Thomas Wyatt's circle. There were many familiar faces in Padua or, at least, many family names I had heard of. One of these latter was Francis Russell, the Earl of Bedford, and even in self-imposed exile, he never forgot he was a true Englishman. He had been the conduit for the messages Wyatt sent to Elizabeth to apprise her of the protest, letters which my mistress claimed she either never received or else received but gave no answer to. The Earl, when I asked him, would never confirm the truth of her claims, but I have often wondered whether Elizabeth was as innocent as she professed. I suspect not. I believe it would fit with her nature if Elizabeth had received Wyatt's letters with a secret pleasure but was careful about how she responded. It would have been like her to voice neither pleasure nor condemnation for the proposed plot and to wait on events, to see how they played out without her involvement. Wyatt professed to Gardiner during interrogation, and maintained it even to the scaffold, that she was not part of the rebellion, but Wyatt was a gentleman and Elizabeth a creature of little honour.

But to return to the Earl. As I say, he never forgot his home and at his house both in Padua and later in Basle, he began assembling a party of other English exiles, thinking that perhaps he would one day be strong enough to mount a rebellion against Mary. It may sound foolish but perhaps not so much as you may think. He was in Venice for a time and his feelings and intentions were in direct accord with the powerful and influential Venetians, who were more fiercely anti-Spanish then than we were ourselves.

In Padua, the Earl became a good friend to me during these days of exile and indeed, for long after our return to England. I owe him much and have nothing but gratitude towards him for not forcing me to fall in with his plans to mount further rebellions. I am not nor ever was the stuff rebels are made of and he understood that. But I did what I could for him, taking messages where they needed to be taken, making contacts that might be of some value to him. And in this way, my real education began, the ability to work covertly, to look into men's eyes and know the workings of their minds and hearts, to develop means of subterfuge and the keeping of secrets. In short, to be the man I have been for decades now, what my queen, what my country, has needed me to be.

And yet, my studies completed, I felt compelled to leave Padua and return to Basle and my Denny cousins. Looking back, I can see that where we lived in Basle, the Protestant community formed a veritable little England. There were many of us who had felt too uncomfortable with what was happening at home, those who felt too strongly about their faith to bow their head and bend their knee to conform. Their consciences, like mine, were simply not that flexible.

So, you will believe me when I say, words cannot adequately describe the joy our community felt when we heard of the death of Mary Tudor in 1588. Her reign had been marked by blood and personal disappointments. Pregnancies turned out to be hollow bellies or cancerous tumours, and the husband she had been so eager to marry had left her as soon and as often as he could, allegedly disgusted by her physical appearance and resentful of her inability to provide him with a male heir that would secure Spanish power in England forever. Even before Mary's body was cold, her devoted courtiers were making the journey from London to Hatfield to bow before Elizabeth. And Elizabeth was more than ready to receive them.

We celebrated with a grand feast, all of us English exiles, at the Earl's home when we heard the news. Some of us had had letters from friends and family still in England, others heard the news from merchants travelling between England and the Continent. We all contributed to the feast, some bringing food, some drink, others musicians. I myself brought some of the great store of wine I had been building up, thinking it was as good a time as any to drink it. That evening, as the wine flowed and the music played and couples danced, we were all resolved to pack up and return to England with all speed. Over the next few days, despite the sore heads that our celebratory revels had caused, we made our plans, settled our business (those that had any) and sent letters to kin in England. The messages were all the same: *we are coming home.*

CHAPTER 6

Most of the men — bishops, nobles and gentlemen alike — who had served Mary Tudor joyfully resigned their posts upon the Queen's death, which left plenty of positions vacant for men such as myself, men of learning and ability who were of the Protestant faith. England had suddenly become a country of opportunity.

My friend, the Earl of Bedford, was one of the first to be rewarded for his loyalty to Elizabeth. He was made the Lord Lieutenant of Dorset, Devon and Cornwall and Lord Warden of the Stannaries and was now in a position to assist his friends... but I rush ahead too fast. There are other, painful, matters to relate.

I arrived back in England, tired, dirty but happy and optimistic. I wasted no time but made the journey home to Foot's Cray. As I rode my hired nag and neared my family home, unseen for almost five years, my heart swelled and I almost gave into sentiment entirely, sobbing like a child when the dear grey stones of the house came into view. England was a different country, I hoped, and I a very different man.

I had written to my mother that I was returning but had not been able to let her know when to expect me. Indeed, I had travelled faster than I anticipated, so I was not surprised that my arrival at Foot's Cray went unnoticed. I dismounted, not a little stiffly – I have never been a good horseman – and tried pushing open the front door. In the past, the door had rarely been barred or locked during the day, but it did not give to my pressure. I knocked and pressed my ear to the oak to listen for sounds of movement from the other side.

It seemed a very long time, but I suppose it was really only about a minute, before I heard the latch lift and the door opened. It was dark, gloomy inside and to me, it seemed as if Benjamin's face appeared out of nowhere, squinting at the sunlight. I was shocked by the change in him. Benjamin, our head house servant, had been in his middle age when I left England but now he looked like an old man close to the grave. Mother had written to me when, two years earlier, he had suffered a stroke and I reasoned that this was the cause of his ragged appearance. Surely, I thought, he should not still be working?

'Master Francis?' he frowned, and I wondered if his eyesight too was failing. 'Is that you?'

'Yes, Benjamin, it's me.'

He stumbled out of the porch and grabbed my hand with both of his own. 'It is so very good to see you, Master.'

'And you, Benjamin,' I said, gently pulling my hand free from his enthusiastic shaking. I gestured at my horse who was sticking her nose into a lavender bush beneath one of the windows. 'Can you get someone to see to the horse?'

'Of course, Master.' He ducked his head back inside the porch and I heard him shout. A moment later, a young lad hurtled out, almost running into me, and took hold of the reins. I did not know the boy; he must have been taken on since my departure. The horse reluctantly responded to his tugging and the boy led her around the side of the house. Benjamin gestured for me to follow him inside.

Benjamin began to bustle, ordering another young lad, again not one I recognised, to fetch a bowl of water so I could wash my face and hands.

'You hungry, Master?'

I told him that I had stopped to rest the horse, and my backside, a few hours earlier at a tavern and they had served a very tasty rabbit pie that had filled my stomach admirably so that I would wait until my mother dined to save the kitchen any trouble.

Benjamin looked down at the flagstones. 'Master Francis,' he said softly, 'the mistress, she don't eat much these days.'

His manner made my heart beat faster. I remembered the last time my mother's appetite had been poor; it was when my stepfather had died. It had taken weeks for her to start eating properly again. 'Is she unwell?'

'She hasn't been well for some months now, Master Francis. We think it's her heart. She gets a sort of fluttering here,' he pointed to the centre of his chest, 'and sometimes she has trouble catching her breath.'

'The doctor, what does the doctor say?'

Benjamin made a face and I recalled that he had a very low opinion of doctors, preferring to take the advice of Alice Greene, the local village's wise woman.

'The doctor, Master, he was called and he bled her, but that did her no good from all I could tell. He said she was not to eat mustard seeds or watercress because they would make her temper fierce. I ask you, Master Francis, when has your dear mother ever been fierce? She likes to rest and I do think that does her the most good. I reckon she'll be so pleased to see you home again.'

'Where is she?'

'She keeps to her chamber,' he jerked his head upwards to the floor above. 'She has the girl, Kate, with her to see she has all she needs, and for company, too.'

I was already halfway up the stairs before he finished speaking. I paused before my mother's chamber door, wondering with no little dread what I would find on the other side. The door creaked as I lifted the latch and pushed it open. The room was warm, stiflingly so, for the fire was banked up high. I felt sweat prickle on my forehead.

I closed the door quietly behind me. The girl seated by the side of my mother's bed turned her head towards me. I did not know her either. So many new people, so much had changed since I had left. This girl had to be the Kate of whom Benjamin had spoken. She looked from me to my mother and back to me. She stood, scooping up the sewing she had been working on. My mother was asleep, her head turned to the side, her mouth hanging open, her skin grey. She looked somehow unlike my mother. I felt the girl looking at me and I knew she was wondering who I was.

'I understand you are taking care of my mother,' I said.

'Yes, Master Francis,' she said, keeping her voice low. In a different situation, I would have been impressed by her quickness. 'Your lady mother will be pleased you have come home. She has been fretting.'

I wished she had not said so. My guilt at leaving my mother to face whatever the Council might choose to accuse her of, despite my initial belief that she would be beyond their suspicion, was hanging heavy upon me. I must admit, my studies and activities abroad had occupied too much of my time. I should have spared more thought for those I left behind.

'No one took the trouble to write to me and tell me she was ill.' My tone was very harsh, accusatory.

Kate started forward, shaking her head. 'She did not want to worry you.'

'I should have been told.'

My mother must have heard my voice through her slumber for she moaned and her eyes flickered open. I moved and knelt by her bedside and took her hand in mine, feeling the lightness of her bones, the coolness of her skin.

'Francis? Is that you?' she asked, her mouth curving into a feeble smile.

'Yes, it's me, Mother.'

'Here to stay?'

'Yes, here to stay.'

She squeezed my hand and promptly fell asleep again. Kate said that she slept most of the time now and that I should not be unduly worried. But I was. I had been fortunate so far in my life. I had not had to witness the slow death of those I loved. But now, I could escape it no longer. I was no physician but even I could see that there was no road back to health for my mother and the knowledge that I had had to be absent for the last few years of her life made me so very angry.

My mother clung on to life for almost another two months, during which time I watched her grow thinner until the bedcovers barely suggested they covered a body at all. And when the dreadful day came and she died, she was buried in the

Protestant manner, and I was glad for her sake as much as for my own.

One always wonders how life will continue when someone we love dies, believing that they will leave a space in our life, that we will be lost without them to guide and console us, but the truth is we carry on, we work, we toil, we forget, for moments at least. My mother had run Foot's Cray exceedingly well when she had been in good health but when her health had failed, the house and estate began to be neglected. I was glad of it, glad of the work that needed doing. It gave me a purpose, made me useful. Even so, it took only a few more months for Foot's Cray to be put back into proper order. But I was given no opportunity to rest for soon, there was different, more important, work for me to do.

I had turned my mother's parlour into a small office for myself, wanting somewhere I could be alone and could continue to work should I choose to. Benjamin was a good man, but he did like to talk and his chatter quickly wearied me. I would often retreat into my office of an evening for the solitude it gave me but also because it was warm. My years on the Continent had accustomed me to warmer weather than England often provides and I had still to reconcile myself with chilly mornings and evenings, even during the summer months.

My office was in the very middle of Foot's Cray, so I could not often hear sounds beyond its stone walls. It was a surprise therefore when one early evening in March 1559 as I sipped a small glass of Madeira and perused a copy of *The Decameron*, Benjamin, who had regained some of his wiry sprightliness in recent weeks, knocked on the door and proudly announced, 'The Earl of Bedford.'

I almost spilt my wine over my hose so hastily did I get to my feet. I bowed clumsily, cup in one hand, book in the other as the Earl strode in, looking even more hearty than he had when I left him in Basle.

'Rest easy, Francis,' Bedford said with a laugh. 'I know I am unexpected but not unwelcome, I hope.'

'Certainly not,' I assured him. 'Can I offer you something?'

'What is your wine like? Any good?'

'It is the same as we had in Basle. Incredibly, we did not drink it all that happy night.'

'Aye, that was a good night. And good wine,' he grinned.

I told Benjamin who was waiting at the door expectantly to bring up a jug of wine and some biscuits. I offered the Earl my chair, the one with the duck feather cushion that had been my mother's favourite, and he took it. I drew another chair from the wall and sat opposite.

'Were you passing by?' I asked, wondering if so, where he could be on his way to.

'No, I came to see you.'

'Me?' I said in surprise.

'It is not so unbelievable, surely? I have a position for you, Francis, which I hope you will accept. Do not worry, it will not interfere too greatly with your current role of country gentleman.'

He looked about him with a comically raised eyebrow and downward turn of the corners of his mouth to express his amusement at what he perceived as my rustication. He was always wont to mock me and I took this as I always took his gentle taunts, with good grace.

'What is the position?' I asked, very much interested.

'The Member of Parliament for Tintagel. The post is vacant and I have taken the liberty of recommending to William Cecil that you be put up for the seat. He is Elizabeth's chief minister now, you know? Well, what say you?'

A seat in Parliament. It was what I had wanted, what I had hoped for one day. And yet, ingrate that I was, a part of me was disappointed at where the seat was. Tintagel!

'I thank you, my lord,' I said, 'but the West Country. Am I a good choice for a seat as remote as that? I have never been to that part of England.'

Benjamin came in with a jug of wine, two cups and biscuits on a tray. I pointed him to the table at the Earl's elbow and he set the tray down.

'It's all right, Benjamin, I'll see to it,' I said as his hand curled around the jug handle. He bowed his head and left us alone. I rose and poured out the wine.

'I know what you're thinking, Francis,' Bedford said, taking the cup I handed him. 'Aye, Tintagel is a long way from Foot's

Cray, but you don't have to go there, you know, it isn't necessary.'

'It isn't?'

'No. Good God, I know some members who could not tell where their seats are if you asked them to point to them on a map.' He laughed at his own joke. 'No, the fact is the West Country is... well, to say lawless might be exaggerating the matter but it is not all that far from the truth. And the Council wants men they can trust representing that part of the country to put it in some sort of order.'

'And I qualify as a trustworthy man?' I said, resuming my seat.

Bedford sniffed the wine and took a mouthful. He raised his eyebrows and nodded. 'As good as I remember it.'

'Am I?' I asked, eager, I suppose, to hear him say it.

'Trustworthy? Well, of course, you are. You've proved your loyalty to your faith and your new queen. You left England because you could not stomach what Queen Mary was doing to your fellow man and returned as soon as you heard Elizabeth had acceded to the throne. You have wit and learning and an ability to think for yourself. I could not have recommended a better candidate. William Cecil agreed with me. So, the seat is yours if you will but take it. Will you think about it?'

I did not need to think about it. I said yes at once and thanked him. Bedford dipped a biscuit into his wine and I heard the crunch as he bit into it.

'Of course, there is something else you should do, you know?'

'And what is that, my lord?'

'Get a wife.' He leant forward and patted my knee. 'It is high time you were married, Francis. A man cannot be content forever as a bachelor. And besides, you will need a wife to take care of the house when you are at work. It is all very well you taking care of your estate for these few months, and I am sure you have an excellent steward, but there's no better person than a wife to look after your best interests for you. Get you married, Francis, get you married.'

I smiled, a little self-consciously, because in truth I had been considering marriage for the past week or two. The Earl, who I fear knew me better than I knew myself, laughed.

'You sly dog,' he said, poking me with the toe of his boot,

'you have already been a-wooing, haven't you?'

I shook my head, my mouth full of wine. It did indeed taste good but wine is better sipped, not gulped. 'I have not been wooing anyone. Not yet.'

'But you have a lady in mind?'

'There is a widow,' I admitted. 'A lady I see in church.'

'Name?'

'Anne Carleille.'

'Husband long dead?'

'A few years.'

'Children?'

'One boy of seven years, I believe.'

'Godly?'

'Devout.'

'Rich?'

'I believe her husband left her well provided for.'

Bedford gestured for me to refill his cup. 'She sounds just the thing. Do not delay. Go a-wooing, Francis, before you are too old to know the joys of having a woman in your bed.'

I was not thinking of marrying for the reason the Earl spoke of. The pleasures of the flesh... God gives us such pleasure as a gift, not to be squandered in idle lust, but as a means to beget children, our legacy to the world. But the Earl was right. I did need a helpmeet to run my home and look after my personal interests. Why not choose a young woman, you may ask, one that is unknown to man and can be moulded to suit me? Why choose a woman who has already buried one husband and has a child living? Well, young women may suit some men, I suppose, indeed, I have seen it many times, but such are not and have never been for me. Young women can be skittish creatures, greensick with love and expecting every day to be a day of earthly delights, endearments and gifts from their husband. That is all very well when one has the time and the temperament for such trifles, not when one is busy. And besides, there is a more practical reason to consider. With a maid, a man never knows if she can breed. A widow with a child has proved herself to be fertile. A man need not take his chance with such a wife.

And what of my choice? Anne Carleille was as I described

her to the Earl, but I did not tell him, nor did he enquire, of her comeliness.

I had first seen Anne Bourne, as she then was when I was going up to Cambridge in my youth and she was soon to wed Alexander Carleille. I saw her in church, sitting in her family pew across the aisle from my family's. I suppose she was pretty. She had brown hair that hung down her back as befitted a maiden and a round face with cheeks that always seemed delicately pink. I had gone to Cambridge and did not make her acquaintance again until I returned home. Upon seeing her once more when I returned from exile on the Continent, I found that her cheeks were still rosy though her face seemed less round, the plumpness of her youth a memory only, and her waist had thickened, all the marks of the woman rather than the girl.

I had enquired into her history, probing Benjamin's once, and I hoped, still retentive memory as to her faith and current finances. Her faith was proudly Protestant. I did not judge her harshly for remaining in England during Queen Mary's reign of terror. Many people did, of course, stay. Her finances were in good health, as I told the Earl. She had property left to her by her late husband, which would, of course, become mine when we wed. I had no immediate need of her estate but the property was of some worth and land always holds its value.

I wrote to Mistress Carleille the day after the Earl's visit to request a meeting. I had not intended to be so precipitous in my courting, but the Earl's news and remarks pricked me on. I did not say why I wanted to meet with her, thinking it not seemly to put a marriage proposal into a letter. Her reply did not come back immediately; indeed, I had to wait until late the following day for her permission to visit her.

I took care when dressing for my meeting with her. I understood my usual choice of attire to be sober, tasteful not gaudy, but the Earl had frequently told me in Basle that my sense in regard to dress was sombre, not sober. Indeed, he had once given me a present of silver buttons, the work of a very talented Italian goldsmith, to brighten me up he had said, and they had lain in a drawer, still wrapped in linen, ever since my return to England. I dug them out and handed them to Marjorie, my late mother's seamstress, to sew onto my finest doublet, it being made of black washed silk. They did look very fine, I admit, and I believed would help me make a favourable impression upon Mistress Carleille.

I ordered my horse ready, and when she was saddled, set off for my appointment. It was a beautiful morning, a little chilly, yes, but I knew the sun would rise and burn the mist away. I was more than a little anxious; I had never gone a-wooing before. I was not unknown to woman, of course, my student days had initiated me in that particular rite, and there had been an Italian lady in Padua with whom I became friendly. But wooing with the intent of wedding? This was going to be a new experience. For the entirety of that short ride, my mind was busy trying to work out how I should behave with the lady. Should I pretend a love I did not yet feel, claim to have suffered sleepless nights and lack of appetite because of my longing? Or should I be forthright and declare at once my intentions and dearest wish? I was not sufficiently acquainted with Mistress Carleille to know which approach would work best. I also suspected that if I declared love for the widow, I would not be able to maintain the pretence, that I would eventually be discovered in my dissembling. In the end, I decided a business-like approach would suit me best and not demean me in the lady's eyes.

I soon reached Mistress Carleille's home, it being only a short distance away. I had ridden past the house on countless occasions and was familiar with the grey stone exterior, but I had not, as far as I could remember, ever been inside. I was punctual to the hour of my appointment and a groom was waiting by the front porch. I dismounted and handed him my reins. As he led my horse away, a servant appeared from inside the porch and bid me enter.

I was shown into the Great Hall, which though not as large as Foot's Cray, was not wholly unworthy of the name. My eyes caught a rather fine tapestry hanging at the far end where the family would eat at the high table, and which could not have been bought for less than one hundred pounds I reckoned, but I could not linger on its fineness for beneath it, looking almost regal, sat Mistress Carleille. So, it seemed I was to be received in state. I believe I almost smiled.

I made my bow and spoke. 'Good morning, Mistress Carleille.'

'Good day to you, Master Walsingham.'

Her voice was high, though not unpleasant. Did I detect a trace of amusement in her few words? Or was I being fanciful, my nervousness making me so?

'I thank you for allowing me to visit.'

'You are most welcome. Will you take some wine?'

I needed a drink, certainly. 'Thank you,' I nodded.

She gestured to the maid standing by the window to pour me a cup of wine from the jug on the sideboard. Another maid placed a three-legged table and stool at her mistress's elbow.

'Please, sit,' Mistress Carleille bid me.

I tucked my gloves into my belt and sat down on the stool. How to begin? Should I make conversation, talk of small things? Or should I just get on with it? As it happened, Mistress Carleille made this decision for me.

'And the reason for your visit?' She stared at me, wide-eyed.

My throat had gone suddenly dry. I tried to speak but the noise that came out could not be called speech. I reached for my cup of wine and took a mouthful.

'Perhaps you have guessed it, Mistress Carleille,' I said, swallowing the liquid down and hoping that she would say yes, she had guessed, give me her answer straight away and spare me the awkward interview, but she just looked at me. I had to continue. 'I find I am in need of a wife now I am, as you know, solely responsible for Foot's Cray and its tenants.' This all came out in a rush.

'Your mother did a most admirable job of running the house in your absence,' she said, her voice lingering on the last word.

'I wish my absence had not been necessary,' I countered. I do not know why but of late I had taken to justifying my exile on the Continent to my neighbours. Often, there were no reproaches, no resentment that I had gone when they had stayed, but I had become sensitive to the idea that they felt I had done wrong. Not without reason, as Mistress Carleille's next words proved.

'*Was* it necessary?'

I looked at her sharply then. Her eyes were guileless yet inquisitorial. It was a question, a sincere enquiry, not, I felt sure, a reproach.

'Necessary to me, yes. My conscience would not permit me to stay, to have to conform.'

This was true, of course, so I felt no need to elaborate further and say that it had been for reasons of safety too. There was no need to speak of my associations with Wyatt and my cousin Thomas, who had, incidentally, returned to England from Geneva around the same time as me.

'Some of us did not have the luxury of choice,' she said almost coldly.

I knew her then to indeed be a good Protestant; her words and manner proved it.

'Yes,' I admitted, 'I was more fortunate than most. It must have been extremely difficult for you.'

'It was most difficult,' she said vehemently, making her gold and ruby earrings shake.

We were getting off the point. I did not want to enter into a theological or political discussion with her. That was not the purpose of my visit.

'As I say, Mistress Carleille, I have come to ask whether you would consider marriage with me.'

Seconds passed as she studied my face. 'The idea is not disagreeable to me,' she said after a long moment. 'I confess, I do not find widowhood amenable. And, of course, there is my son. I must consider his future. What provision would you make for him?'

It was a direct question but a not unreasonable one and I had my answer prepared.

'He would be entitled to a portion of my estate, according to law, as my stepson. Any children we have will inherit the majority of my estate and its revenues. I would seek to place your son in a profession suitable to his talents, whatever they proved to be. The details would all be set out for your approval in the marriage contract.'

She nodded, thinking this over. 'Would you retain this house?'

'In truth, Mistress Carleille, I had not thought that far ahead. It would depend on my future prospects.'

'And they are? You are a lawyer, I understand.'

'I have an education in the law, but I have never practised. I have been offered a seat in Parliament for a West Country constituency, which I have accepted, and I have hopes that, in time, a more local seat will be mine. The Earl of Bedford is working on my behalf.'

I thought a little namedropping would do me no harm and I was proved right. Her eyes widened visibly at the mention of the Earl.

'Then I agree, Master Walsingham,' she said with a decided nod. 'You can have the marriage contract drawn up and assuming it is agreeable, the banns read.'

'I thank you, Mistress Carleille. You have made me the most happy of men,' I finished, feeling such a sentiment was due.

She blushed at that. 'Would you like to meet my son?'

I said I would be pleased to and she sent the maid to call him from the schoolroom. When he arrived, with his tutor in tow, I could not help but notice the resemblance to his mother and it made him a very pretty boy. He bowed politely, correctly, and it pleased me that he had been educated in good manners. I asked him about his studies and he rattled off the usual curriculum, only growing animated when he spoke of his history lessons. I probed deeper and discovered he had a good enough learning of the ancient Roman writers. I found I liked him a great deal and asked if he thought he would find me an agreeable father.

I confess it was the wrong question to put to him. He gave a look of perplexity at his mother who rose from her seat and put her arm around his shoulder to cradle him. She explained the situation in soft terms as only a mother can do to her child. His eyes bubbled with tears and Mistress Carleille gave me a look that told me the boy had loved his dead father much. I do think she should have prepared the boy, told him she was thinking of marrying again, but the damage was done and could not be undone. Mistress Carleille told the tutor to remove the boy and she watched him leave with sorrowful eyes. She turned to me.

'He will become accustomed to the idea.'

I considered saying that he would have to become accustomed to the idea but held my tongue. It was, after all, no matter for a child to dictate.

'I should take my leave,' I said, pulling my gloves from my belt and occupying myself for the moment with fitting them to my fingers. 'I shall send my steward to meet with yours and go over your estate accounts if you will allow. When all that has been reviewed, I shall have the contract drawn up and give instructions for the banns to be read.'

I looked up at her. She was looking back at me and from her

expression, I saw that I had managed to hurt her and I was sorry. My manner had been too abrupt. Or was she still thinking of her son, concerned that he was against her remarrying?

'I am sure that Christopher and I will get along well enough, and I promise, I will do all I can for him,' I said to placate her.

Her face softened. I had said the right thing. 'Shall I call on you tomorrow?' I asked. I was not sure if I was supposed to dance attendance on her now that we were betrothed.

'If you wish,' she said with the smallest of sighs.

'If you'd rather just wait for the contract,' I said hurriedly. This was going all wrong. I took a deep breath. 'Forgive me, Mistress Carleille, I am being wholly inept. You are the first woman I have asked to marry me and I have no idea how to go about it.'

There was a moment's silence while we looked at one another and then she burst out laughing.

'Oh, my word,' she said, covering her mouth with her fingers.

'Am I that ridiculous?' I said, conscious of the presence of the maid, who I felt sure was laughing at me too.

Mistress Carleille came forward and laid her hand on my arm. 'Not at all, Francis.' She said my name as if trying it out to see how it sounded. 'I am surprised at your honesty. And flattered that I am your first choice.'

'My only choice.'

'Come tomorrow. In the afternoon. We may go for a walk if the weather is good.'

'I will come tomorrow, Mistress Carleille, and be glad to.'

She walked me to the door and we talked of small matters while waiting for my horse to be brought round. That done, I kissed her hand, mounted my horse and rode back to Foot's Cray.

And that was how I became a married man. I visited Anne, as I should call her now, the next day and not quite every day but nearly so. I came to be very fond of her the more I learnt of her in the brief weeks of our courtship. And yes, Christopher and I became much better acquainted, so much so that I did come to think of him as my true son and he came to look upon me as his father.

Anne had begun sending some of her most prized and personal possessions, including the tapestry I had admired, to Foot's Cray in the weeks before our wedding, so that when she entered my house as my wife she said it already felt like home.

She settled quickly, adeptly, finding favour with all of my servants, especially Benjamin, who said it felt almost as if my mother had returned in spirit to have a woman in the place again. And Anne proved an excellent bookkeeper, keeping the estate's accounts as neat as any trained clerk. She said her first husband had instructed her in bookkeeping, following on from her father's more rudimentary teaching of mathematics. Anne proved useful in other ways too, for as I soon discovered, she was extremely well-connected within merchant circles and within London political milieus too, her father having served for a time as Lord Mayor. One night as we lay in bed, both lying on our sides facing one another, I realising how young she looked in the candlelight and feeling tender towards her, she told me how her husband had supported the Duke of Northumberland when he attempted to put Lady Jane Grey on the throne. I had had no idea.

'How did he fare when the Duke fell?' I asked.

Her eyes flickered and looked away to examine the embroidery work of the pillowcase. 'It was a frightening time, Francis. My father feared for his life, he feared for us all. We had no way of knowing how Queen Mary's vengeance would fall. But he did all he could to prove his loyalty to Queen Mary. I think perhaps he was too small a person for her ministers to be bothered about.'

Was this why she had stayed in England when others like me had fled? Had this been why she had asked if my leaving had been necessary that first meeting when I had asked her to marry me?

Anne had great hopes of having another child and her disappointment when each month passed and her menses came upon her was made manifest in irritability with me. Though she never said so, I do think she believed me to be at fault for her failure to conceive. Indeed, the thought had occurred to me also. Her fecundity had been proved with a healthy son, after all. Perhaps the fault was mine. Unfortunately, we were not to be blessed in this way.

I did sell Anne's former home about a year after our marriage as it was proving to be an unnecessary drain on my resources. Although I had not previously had any intention of so doing, I also sold Foot's Cray. My work as MP and my duties locally was becoming greater and my domestic status needed to rise to be commensurate with it. Foot's Cray was simply not grand enough. So, I leased a manor house in Hertfordshire named Parkbury.

It was while we were living at Parkbury that I became a Justice of the Peace and discovered what it was like to directly serve the crown, albeit from a distance. Anne enjoyed our new status and our new responsibilities, for it meant we began mixing with the highest gentry in Parkbury and were able to wear damasks and satins.

Poor Anne. She was able to enjoy this status for such a short time. She became ill, coughing up blood, her skin strangely rosy yet her body wasting. She took to our bed, insisting that I have another made up in an adjoining room so that she would not disturb me. I protested at this but she was insistent. Within a few months, she was nothing but a bag of bones and as she lay unmoving in what had been the bed we shared for so brief a time, she reminded me of how my mother had looked and I knew she would not be with me long. At the end, her greatest concern was for Christopher, entreating me to do my best for him. I promised her I would do all I could, as was my duty, and indeed, my own desire.

Anne had asked that she be buried alongside her first husband and when the time came, I did as she requested. I missed her, missed her presence about the house, her companionship, her adeptness with the finances and yes, I confess, I missed the warmth of her in our bed. I had found it very pleasant to be married. It seemed to suit me so much more than my bachelorhood had done. As much as I missed her, I found I did not want to remain a widower. I wanted to be a husband again.

And in the spring of 1566, I met the woman who would become my second wife. Her name was Ursula Worsley.

CHAPTER 7

I heard about the death of Ursula's husband, Sir Richard Worsley, through William Cecil. I have mentioned him before in this account, but you would have heard of William Cecil anyway. He has been by Elizabeth's side ever since her accession. Indeed, from before that time, because he looked after some of her lands and legal matters while he was the secretary to the Duke of Northumberland, and after, when he served Queen Mary's Council. By this time, he was Elizabeth's head of the Council, its Principle Secretary, and the most powerful man in the land.

Cecil was a near neighbour at Parkbury when he wasn't at court, and ever since dear Anne died, he had been keeping an eye out for a suitable wife for me. At the time, I thought he was merely showing a friendly concern for my best interests. Later, I wondered at his true motive. I am still not sure.

Ursula Worsley, he believed, was eminently suitable. Her husband had been the Captain of the Isle of Wight and they had lived in Appuldurcombe in a fine house as befitted his station. When Worsley died, he also left Ursula in possession of good land and property in Lincolnshire. Land and property — there are no better assets. Ursula had good connections, too, for one of her uncles was a Gentleman of the Privy Chamber, one of only a few who have access to the Queen. Such a connection might prove extremely valuable to me in time.

As far as looks went, well, I must be truthful here, Ursula was never as pretty as Anne had been. Her nose is rather long and bony and overhangs her mouth somewhat. Her lips though, are rather fine, being of a pretty, rose-like hue. Her eyes, like mine, are very dark and they give one the feeling of being bored into. Do not be concerned that I will hurt her feelings. Ursula would be the first to admit that she is not beautiful, but what she lacks in beauty, she more than makes up for in brains and common sense.

Ursula, however, was not easily won. She was the daughter of a knight and had been the wife of a knight, too. I was merely a gentleman with training in the law. Had it not been for Cecil's backing, I have often wondered whether we would ever have wed. As it was, our marriage was brokered on a sound financial basis. It took almost eighteen months of letters between Ursula and myself and to her brothers to agree the marriage contract. I travelled to the Isle of Wight twice to meet her at her request. She has told me since that she was not displeased with my person, nor was I with her. But Ursula, it seemed, had had some notion not to marry again; my friends and her family convinced her that it was best that she did. And so, she was persuaded to marry me. I considered myself then to be a most fortunate man and she has never given me any reason to think otherwise.

I was already responsible for my stepson, Christopher, and marriage with Ursula would mean that I would become the guardian of her two sons by Sir Richard. Their names were John and George, and they were both a few years younger than Christopher, but the age difference was not so great and I was pleased that they would be able to share the same tutor in the schoolroom.

One day at Parkbury, I received a letter from Cecil asking if I could visit him at his home. I had been intending to visit my tenants that day but a summons from Cecil, however politely worded, was not something to be put off or ignored and I ordered my horse saddled.

When I arrived at his house, I was shown into Cecil's study. I had been granted access to his study on previous occasions and never been failed to be astonished by the number of papers he had collected. *If this is his office at home*, I thought, *what must his office at court be like?* I came to realise that Cecil never stopped working; wherever he was, he was always on the Queen's service.

And the Queen's service kept him busy. As I entered the study, another man exited, dodging me adroitly, his head down so I did not see his face. I wondered at his discourtesy, but now know that he was probably one of those agents who served Cecil best by being anonymous.

Cecil was seated at his desk when his page announced me. 'Ah, Francis, you are here. Good. Come in. Sit.' He looked back down at his desk and waved his quill at me. 'Allow me to just finish this.'

The page pointed me to the chair before the desk and left, closing the door quietly behind him. I sat and waited, watching Cecil as he scribbled and then signed his name. He dropped the quill in a pot and looked at me.

'You are well?'

'Yes,' I said, 'thank you.'

'Good. Now, I asked you here because I've had a letter from Lady Worsley's brother-in-law regarding the terms of your marriage contract.'

'*You* have had a letter?' I asked, a little annoyed. 'Why did he not write to me? And of what? I thought all the terms had been agreed.'

'He knows we are acquainted,' Cecil said, closing his eyes as if I was being tedious, 'and he wrote of other matters too, unrelated to you. Do not take offence, Francis, where none is intended.'

I resolved to take his advice. It was good advice, I have always remembered it. 'What did he say?' I replied more equably.

He leant forward, arms on the desk. 'Let me ask you, are you very attached to your house at Parkbury?'

'He wants my house?'

'Yes, he does.'

'It is a fine house.'

'You would be reluctant to relinquish it?'

I thought for a moment. It occurred to me that it was unlikely there would be no recompense for handing my property over to my future brother-in-law, and I trusted Cecil to ensure that such a bargain would not be detrimental to my interest.

'It is but a house, Sir William,' I said with a nonchalant shrug.

Cecil nodded. 'Of course, you will have the house at Appledurcombe to live in when you are married. I believe it is very fine.' He looked at me for confirmation. I nodded and he continued. 'And I understand Lady Ursula has expressed a fondness for the place. Any objection you make to moving to the Isle of Wight may prove a difficulty.'

I understood what he was saying, that the marriage might not happen if I did not agree to give up Parkbury and move permanently to the Isle of Wight.

'In truth, Sir William, one place is as good as another to me,' I replied.

'Good. The Isle of Wight is remote, I suppose, but I do hope that you will find it agreeable.'

'*You* hope? Why so?' I asked, curious.

The side of Cecil's mouth curved up into a small smile. He folded his hands, one over the other. 'You have talents, Francis. You speak several languages, which is something not many Englishmen can do. You have a large number of contacts throughout the Continent, and you have tact and diplomacy. Do not think I mean to flatter you. I do not pay compliments. These are all traits that can be of use to Her Majesty, and to me.'

His meaning was beginning to become clear to me. I let him continue.

'I have a belief. And that belief is that we can never afford to become complacent, never allow ourselves to believe that we, England, are safe. We may be an island with tempestuous seas to protect us, but our enemies are clever and determined to harm us. The Queen needs good men, men that can be trusted, who are clever and resourceful, who will do what needs to be done, not just what she thinks she wants.' His voice had grown forceful and he took a breath to stop himself, careful of showing too much emotion. 'Good men in important locations. That is what is needed.'

I understood. 'The Isle of Wight is important?'

'Strategic,' he nodded. 'The island guards Portsmouth and Southampton, protecting our shores from enemy attack. And there is Carisbrooke Castle. Have you seen it? No? A redoubtable stronghold, a prison if need be, a convenient place to keep persons of interest.'

He raised an eyebrow, indicating that I should understand him. I did.

'You will be of use to me on the island, Francis.'

'He can have Parkbury,' I said, trying to control my excitement. This was what I had been waiting for, recognition of my talents and an opportunity to serve. 'I am happy to move to Wight.'

'Good,' Cecil said, satisfied. 'And, of course, you still have your property in London for when state affairs bring you here. So, I shall write to Lady Worsley's brother and say he can amend the marriage contract to include the transfer of the deeds for Parkbury. I see no reason why you cannot be wed very soon.' He smiled and picked up his quill. 'Very good to see you, Francis.'

I rose, tugging my cuffs down from my sleeves. 'Thank you, Sir William.' I bowed my head, opened the door and walked out, looking forward to moving to the Isle of Wight.

CHAPTER 8

We were very happy, my new family and I, on the Isle of Wight. Ursula made an admirable companion, an exemplary wife, and I found her two boys delightful. They got along well with Christopher. My work was interesting and satisfying. God was being good to me.

And then he stopped being so good.

It was one morning in summer of 1566. Ursula and I had risen late and were breakfasting in her parlour. We had retired late the night before for we had been entertaining some of the local gentry, and my wine must have been very good because they showed a merry disinclination to leave at a sensible hour and allow us to go to our bed.

Ursula was yawning behind her hand when Anthony, her steward from before our marriage, entered with some letters that had arrived. He handed them to me and reminded me that I was engaged to dine with Sir Nicholas Throckmorton, a neighbour of ours and a colleague of Cecil's, and that he had also given the instructions for the servants to dry out the gunpowder stored in the gatehouse.

I had been surprised to discover that our house at Appuldurcombe was used as a storehouse for munitions. Ursula shrugged when I asked her about it and said that her husband, Sir Richard Worsley, had thought their home the best place for such a dangerous material, otherwise who knew who could get their hands on it. Ursula was accustomed to writing to Cecil, they being on very friendly terms, and had evidently mentioned my surprise to him, for I had received a letter from Cecil explaining the necessity for the custom and trusting that I would have no objection. What could I say to that?

The problem with gunpowder is that, even if it is stored correctly, and I ensured that it always was, it can become damp in this cold climate of ours and it is necessary to dry the powder out. The summer is the best time to do this and I had told Anthony the day before to see to the matter.

Anthony departed, and Ursula and I ate in companionable silence for about ten minutes when the quiet was shattered by the loudest thunder I had ever heard. That is how it sounded, like a burst of thunder, but even as I thought it, I knew it was not possible. There were no clouds on that beautiful summer day.

I rushed to the window. I felt and heard Ursula at my back, her voice loud and screechy, asking what the noise had been. I pressed my face to the glass and saw black smoke rising from where I knew the gatehouse was.

'What is it? What's happened?' she asked desperately.

She tried to grab my arm as I ran around the table, desperate to get to the door. I wrenched it open and hurried out into the hall. There, it was all commotion. Servants had hurried out of the kitchen and other rooms, shouting questions at each other and receiving no answers. We all made our way outside, almost tripping each other up in our haste. I saw Anthony a few yards ahead of me and I hurried to catch him up.

'The powder,' he said breathlessly, spotting me over his shoulder but not slowing.

'I know,' I said.

We ran down the path, our steps slowed by broken stone and timber, debris that littered our way. Pungent black smoke began to smart my eyes. And then I nearly puked as I realised we were scrambling over body parts. Charred, blackened.

I stumbled and fell, my face hit the dried earth and I tasted the coppery tang of my own blood. I lifted my head to see Anthony running on to the gatehouse, dipping his head beneath the door jamb that was one of the few parts still standing.

I pushed myself up onto my hands, drawing my legs up to

stand upright – no one stopped to help me – and then I heard Anthony cry, 'Oh God, no, no,' and I knew, my throat tightening, that the very worst had happened. The gatehouse was where my stepsons, George and John, were studying with their tutor. I remember thanking God that Christopher was not at home that day.

Back on my feet, I rushed through the doorway. Anthony was kneeling on the floor, something small and blackened across his thigh, his right hand reaching out towards a bundle on the floor. His head turned as I entered and I saw tears streaming down his cheek.

'Master,' he sobbed, 'the boys.'

There was a scream and somebody stumbled against me. I put up my arms in reflex and I found Ursula in them, her scream becoming a wail. Anthony huddled over to cover the body – it was George, I recognised the shoe on the leg that hadn't been blown off – and I mentally thanked him for the gesture designed to spare Ursula the sight of her son's mangled carcass.

'Take her out,' he instructed me hoarsely, and I hooked my hands beneath her armpits and dragged her away out onto the grass, onto the path, her kicking, resisting legs sending the gravel flying.

I do not know how we got through that day. It is a blur, a haze of shouting and smoke and bodies covered with either sheets or sacks, whichever was to hand. A headcount was taken. Our boys were killed along with their tutor and three servants. Others were injured with minor burns and cuts. All of these were unsteady on their feet for days, their balance thrown off because they had a ringing in their ears, the shock, I suppose, of the violence of the explosion.

Ursula cried and cried outside the wreck of the gatehouse, her body fighting every attempt I made to remove her from the scene. Then, she could cry no more and her exhausted body slackened and fought me no longer. I gave orders for her maid to take her back to the house and put her to bed.

I confess I was of little use that day, too stunned and shaken to help. Fortunately, Anthony took charge, ordering the servants to tend to the wounded, shoring up the ruined gatehouse to make the structure safe and laying out the bodies, what was left of them, on the table in the Great Hall. How did it happen? I wanted to know, but all that could be gleaned from those servants who had survived the blast was that one moment they had been spreading out the powder on the gatehouse floor and the next there had been the explosion. There must have been a spark, something that ignited the powder. Perhaps a metal implement had been used to rake the powder instead of a wooden one. I could not discover the cause. And anyway, what did it matter? Our boys were dead. There was no bringing them back.

After this terrible accident and quite understandably, Ursula lost her fondness for the house at Appuldurcombe. Grief affects each of us differently. For myself, I have always found work to be the greatest solace, for it forces you to concentrate on something other than that which has been lost. Ursula had her own occupations in the running and management of the household, but such duties do become routine, and after a time, come to manage themselves. As a consequence, Ursula found herself starting to brood.

'This house is too full of memories,' she said to me as we lay in bed one night, my arms around her waist and her head on my shoulder, her face angled back towards mine. The accident had brought us closer together so that we were no longer mere partners in a mutually beneficial alliance. We were lovers now in every true sense of the word, finding comfort in one another. There was a plea in her voice, unspoken but audible.

'You want to leave,' I said, more of a statement than a question.

'Can we?'

She knew as well as I how important my being on the island was to my career.

'Perhaps,' I said noncommittally, but in truth, I was thinking that it would be best to leave the Isle of Wight. As important as Cecil had made me feel by pushing for me to take up residence on the island, I had come to feel that Wight was too out of the way, too far from London, to be of much use to me for long. If I didn't watch out, I was worried I would be forgotten, I would simply be the Queen's man on the Isle of Wight. I did not want that to happen. I wanted to be the Queen's man at her elbow. I did write to Cecil, ostensibly to tell him of the dreadful accident and of how Ursula had come to feel about the house and the island, but mostly to sow the seed that the Isle of Wight was not the place for me for much longer.

I received a letter back, not immediately, indeed, it took so long I wondered if he had received mine. He commiserated with me and Ursula for our loss, expressed his regrets that service to the Queen, namely the storing of the gunpowder, had been the cause of such a tragic event, but then assured me that he knew it would not cause me to slacken in my duty to Elizabeth, that I would continue to keep good care of her island.

I understood. Cecil was not ready for me to leave the Isle of Wight. I showed his letter to Ursula, who read his words and then sniffed. It was her only response. She gave the letter back to me and carried on with her household duties.

Fortunately, as the months passed, I realised that my career was not stagnating as I had feared, but moving on.

I had become the Member of Parliament for Lyme Regis, taking over the seat from Sir Nicholas Throckmorton, who had become my very good friend, and giving up that of Tintagel. Parliament work meant I had, from time to time, to travel to London. I was loathe to rely on the kindness of family and friends to provide a roof over my head on such occasions or stay in an inn or boarding house, so I had been keeping an eye out for a London property that would suit. I quickly found one in the parish of St Giles Cripplegate, not large but sufficient for my needs, and Ursula's if she chose to accompany me.

Meanwhile, at home on the Isle of Wight, I was continuing to fulfil my unofficial duty to Cecil. My connections, mostly acquired there through Ursula, knew of my association with the Queen's first minister and so were keen to help me keep him informed about foreign visitors and the news they brought over from the Continent. In truth, at this point, I knew not how valuable was the information I passed on to Cecil, for he never told me of any consequences or actions he took following my letters, but neither did he complain that I was not telling him enough nor asked for fuller information, so I assumed I was doing all he expected of me. In fact, the only time I knew my intelligence made a difference was when I had to act on behalf of Sir Nicholas Throckmorton.

Nicholas had fallen ill with a stomach complaint and was confined to his bed. He had, several years previously, served as the English ambassador in France. While there, Nicholas had become and continued to be sympathetic with the Huguenots, the French Protestants. The Huguenots were in a difficult situation, living and openly practising their faith in a staunchly Catholic country.

The Huguenots were fighting against their persecution that was being carried out ruthlessly by the French king but needed aid to do so effectively. As a fellow Protestant, they sought the help of the Queen. They had sent an emissary, one Robert Stewart, to plead their cause and to impart, so they claimed, important information to Cecil. Stewart had sailed to England and made his way directly to Nicholas, the person his Huguenot masters had told him to contact. But Nicholas was in no position to take Stewart to London and so he dictated a letter to his secretary to be sent on to me. Nicholas wondered if I would do him a favour. Would I get in touch with Cecil and arrange a meeting with Stewart? This was the sort of work I wanted to be involved in and I hastened to grant his request. I dashed off a letter to Cecil, gave it to my best rider and bid him make haste. He certainly did. In only two days, I received a reply from Cecil. It was not lengthy. It simply said, 'Bring him to London immediately.'

I wrote back to Nicholas telling him of Cecil's reply and he sent Stewart to my house. From Stewart, I learnt that he had already approached Cecil about an interview, but that Cecil had replied that Elizabeth had no desire to see Stewart and so the interview had been denied.

'Because she does not like my religion,' was the reply I got from Stewart when I asked him why he thought he had been refused.

'What is your religion?' I queried, taken aback. Was he a Catholic?

'The same as yours,' he shrugged, allaying my concerns.

'Then... why?'

'I am a true believer and the Queen... well, she only plays at it.'

I nodded understandingly, yet obviously, Cecil had persuaded Elizabeth that it would be as well to see Stewart, hence the summons to London. Stewart and I both went to church and prayed that our journey would be safe. I had risen when my prayers were over after five minutes, surprised to find that Stewart's eyes were still tightly closed, his hands still clasped and his mouth moving silently. I took a seat in the front pew and waited. Another five, perhaps ten minutes passed before Stewart rose and said he was done and that we could now go. He was a true believer, I could see that, ardent, devoted, and simply too Protestant for Elizabeth's taste, as I was myself to discover.

Stewart and I travelled to London and I conducted him to Cecil. I had hoped to be allowed to stay for the interview, but Cecil thanked me for my accompanying Stewart and told me I could return home at my earliest convenience. I do not know if the information Stewart provided was as urgent as he and Nicholas seemed to believe, but I had at least been useful and my involvement, however minor, in this matter had whetted my appetite for more of its kind. I knew I needed to be more than a watchman on a remote outpost.

As it turned out, I soon got the opportunity to be more than just the watchman for the south of England. This was primarily because of Mary Stuart.

This woman had been forced to return to her native country in 1561 after being sent to safety in France by her mother, Marie de Guise, when she was little more than a babe. The young Mary Stuart took readily to life in France and as a consequence, was brought up as a French girl. When of age, she married Francis, the eldest son of the King and his queen, Catherine de Medici. The King dying, Francis succeeded to the throne and Mary Stuart became Queen of France. Then Francis died and Mary became a dowager queen and of no further use to the French royal family. Never having liked her, Mary's mother-in-law, the Medici woman of notorious memory, refused to provide a home for Mary any longer and had only waited long enough to be sure that Mary was not carrying the heir to the French kingdom to send her packing. The possibility of Mary carrying Francis's heir was remote. We had received intelligence that suggested Mary's marriage had never been consummated for

Francis had been deformed in his genitalia and was incapable of emissions.

Mary Stuart was a Catholic, but that was not her only fault. She believed that Elizabeth was a bastard and a heretic and consequently she, Mary, with legitimate Tudor blood in her veins, had the greater right to the English throne. She had even gone so far as to quarter her arms with the arms of England while Queen of France, an audacious act that had thrown Elizabeth into a rage.

That woman! Oh, that woman! What dreadful deeds have been committed for her. And she, so unrepentant, so happy that so many men died in her name. A perfidious woman. When I think of the torment and anguish she caused Elizabeth who was ever gentle towards her against my better advice, I cannot but wonder at human nature.

So, Mary Stuart found herself back in Scotland, whose people did not want a Catholic for a queen as most of the country was fiercely Protestant, save for a few Highlanders who clung to the old faith. And, to no one's surprise, Mary began causing problems for us, and herself, as soon as she could.

It was also at this time that I became a father for the first time. Ursula and I, we had a daughter, who, Ursula insisted, be named after me. Our little Frances was a delight from the moment she was born, despite the fact that Ursula cried constantly for days after her birth. When I asked her why she wept so, she said she did not know. When I asked what I could do to make her feel better, she said to give her time. So I did and stayed out of her way as much as was possible and kept our daughter from her, for Ursula did not seem to want to have her babe in her sights. Therefore, it was I who kissed our daughter goodnight and ensured the wet nurse was clean and dutiful. Ursula did eventually stop crying as she had promised and I think I came to understand the cause when she told me she was glad we had had a girl. She was pleased that Frances had not been a boy because she would have felt as if her dead sons had somehow been replaced, and of course, that brought memories of her boys fresh to her mind. For my part, perhaps because I had my stepson, Christopher, I did not care that I did not yet have a son of my own. Some men I have known, men from the nobility mostly, become obsessed with siring sons, wanting their line to continue, to have their family name pass on, King Henry being the best example of this, to his great tragedy. I suppose it is important for those who have names of note, but for such as I, it is simply not that important.

Frances's arrival made it even more crucial to me that I further my career. I worked very hard, so hard in fact that I grew tired from late hours and early mornings, ended up not bothering to eat regular meals nor take exercise. It pains me to admit it but this fatigue resulted in me missing things, important things, and I made mistakes, for example, sometimes informing Cecil of plots and intrigues that existed only in the minds of lunatics to tallying up figures incorrectly in the estate's account books which then took hours to unravel.

I did not make mistakes all the time, though, I am pleased to say. I was correct when I wrote to Cecil to warn him that there was a plot afoot to kill the Queen by means of sending her a gift of a dress impregnated with poison. I was correct when I warned him that two men, one French, one Italian, and both sympathetic with Mary Stuart's belief in her right to rule England, were meeting secretly in London to devise a plot to assassinate Elizabeth and put Mary on the throne. I even dared to make a suggestion following this discovery, that Cecil start making innkeepers and tavern keepers make records of foreigners who took rooms with them so that we would know just who was in England and where they were. This, I told him, would make it much easier to find such miscreants should we need to do so. He told me he thought it a good idea.

But I also received bad information, not recognising it for what it was. One such mistake, I wince to remember it, was information I received that there was a plot afoot to land soldiers from Marseille in the north of England to perpetrate some devilish Catholic plot. I should have known, I should have realised it was ridiculous. The information I received was too vague, no details given, names of those involved unknown. It was nonsense and I had proudly put it all in a letter to Cecil. He wrote back to me more than a week later, and though he did not berate me for wasting his valuable time with unfounded news about plots, I sensed he was thinking it nonetheless.

Still, this mistake taught me a valuable lesson: never believe anything without sufficient evidence. I resolved that, in the future, if I had information whose provenance seemed doubtful, I would pass it on to Cecil and his clerks to be on the safe side, but always include the caveat that such information had not been verified to be accurate. Cecil, therefore, could do with it what he will.

I was determined never to be made a fool of again.

CHAPTER 9

Soon after Frances was born, Ursula and I left the island and moved to London to settle in our house in St Giles Cripplegate. Ursula's aversion to Appledurcombe and the Isle of Wight had receded somewhat with the passage of time, but she was still keen to live in London, for the time being at least. I do know that with my career progressing in the manner it was, she was hoping she would get to visit the court and even be received by the Queen. I told her that she should not hope for this, that I was only associated with Cecil on an unofficial basis and that I was not a paid servant of the Queen. Ursula smiled and patted my cheek. 'It is only a matter of time, my dear,' she said. I remember hoping she was right.

We stayed for a month or two in our Cripplegate abode but Ursula came to feel that the house was not good enough for our improving social status, and through her friends, of which she had many in London, she heard of a house that would suit us better. It was called The Papey and had once been a hospital for poor priests. Poor priests, indeed! I never once met a priest who was poor. Anyway, The Papey was very well placed; it was within easy reach of several of the royal palaces should Cecil ever call on me to come to court. Do not think this was mere fancy, mere wishful thinking, on my part. Cecil did, in fact, call me to court in February 1568.

On the day appointed, I took a wherry to the Palace of

Whitehall. The day was chilly and it felt even more so on the water. My wherryman was old by common standards and he had to fight hard against the current to keep a straight course. So hard, in fact, that it took quite a while for us to reach the palace's river steps, plenty of time for me to ponder on what Cecil wanted to see me about and whether I should ask him whether he had a more official position in mind for me. Ursula had been pressing me to ask Cecil outright, saying that I had pussyfooted around him for far too long and that if I didn't ask, she would. I must say, I was inclined to agree with her, though I did not want her interfering. The way I saw it, I deserved a position under Cecil, an official one. I did not want to be just one of his come-and-go agents any longer.

I gave my name and with whom I was meeting to one of the liveried guards on the palace gates, pushing through the men and women who habitually clustered at such entrances, their hands out for any trifle a person cared to place into their palms. The guard allowed me through, ordering the gate to be opened a few feet, and I walked up the flagged path into the courtyard, stepping around others who, like me, were not members of the nobility but people of my class and even lower. A court must have its nobles, of course, but these were the people who kept the palaces working.

Once in the Great Hall, I had to explain who I was and why I was there again to a steward, who gestured for a page to come over. Once instructed, the page led me out of the hall through a warren of corridors, up and down stairs until we reached a door, which he told me to go through. I did so and found myself in a small antechamber. A clerk I recognised as being one of Cecil's men looked up from his desk, spectacles perched on the end of his long nose and tied back behind his ears.

'Good morning, Master Walsingham,' he said.

'Good morning. I have an appointment with Master Secretary Cecil.'

'Yes, he is ready for you.' The clerk came around his desk and extended his arm towards a door at the side of the room. He knocked and inclined his head to the door to hear the answering, 'Come in.' He pushed down the handle and went into Cecil's office. I followed.

'Master Walsingham here to see you, sir,' he announced to Cecil, who, as usual, was at his desk.

'Yes. Francis, come in and sit down.' Cecil held up a wine cup, gesturing to ask if I wanted any. I shook my head. 'It is good to have you in London. Is your wife pleased to be here? I expect she is.'

'She enjoys the increase of company. And the shopping,' I added with a smile, remembering the costly bill a goldsmith had presented to me that morning.

'All women do,' Cecil agreed ruefully, coming around the desk. He pulled up a chair next to the one I sat upon and sat down, his knee brushing against mine. 'I will get straight to the point. A merchant, an Italian, Signor Roberto Ridolfi, is in London. By the very nature of his business he moves around the Continent a great deal and so knows a great many happenings abroad. I need to know if he knows anything about Mary Stuart's involvement in her late husband's death.'

To say I was stunned by his last sentence would be to understate the matter. Mary Stuart had married Lord Henry Darnley soon after her arrival in Scotland to take up her throne. What she saw in him no one could fathom for he was vain and idle, and promised to make a bad husband, so the world said of him. But Mary Stuart would have her way and they married. She swiftly found out what a bad choice she had made, though, for Darnley was soon frequenting the Scottish whorehouses to satisfy his appetites and had become pox-ridden as a result. His disease manifested in a horrible disfiguration of the face, with boils and pustules erupting upon his previously perfect skin. This, after he had plotted with the Scottish lords against his own wife, who was pregnant with his child at the time, to remove her close companion, David Rizzio. Rizzio was an Italian, ostensibly serving as Mary's musician but we all knew that he was a creature of the Guises, Mary's devilish family on her mother's side. The Scottish lords resented the influence this little Italian had over their queen and conspired with the jealous Darnley to have him murdered. This they did before Mary Stuart's very eyes. Darnley, coward that he was, suddenly became convinced that the lords would finish him off too and so changed allegiance to side with his wife and help her escape to safety, in this case, to the home of the Earl of Bothwell. Mary had become enamoured of Bothwell and, so rumour had it, became his mistress, so that her husband became very inconvenient indeed to Bothwell, who was as ambitious as he was cunning and had plans to marry Mary. And so, Darnley too was to be got out of the way. This is how they do things in Scotland.

By the time of my interview with Cecil, the whole world had heard about the murder of Darnley in Scotland, how the house he was staying in at Kirk O'Field was blown up with gunpowder and he, attempting to escape, strangled in its grounds. It was not absolutely known who had murdered him, but rumours had been rife that Mary Stuart herself had been complicit. Until this point, I had given her the benefit of the doubt and thought they were just that, rumours, but here was Cecil giving voice to them and implicitly acknowledging the truth. My surprise must have shown on my face because Cecil gave the smallest of laughs and said, 'Yes, we believe she may have ordered Lord Darnley's assassination.'

'Her own husband?' I stammered.

Cecil frowned. 'You think it impossible? That a woman could want her husband dead?'

When he put it like that, I had to admit the possibility was not beyond reason. A woman, as we all know, was responsible for tempting Adam with forbidden knowledge and their subsequent expulsion from Eden, and woman is the cause of so much tragedy in this world. I have often reflected that Mary Stuart was very like Eve. Did she not seduce many men to her will and cause them to die horrific deaths, all in the pursuit of a cause that had no basis in fact? Had she not been found out by her Scottish subjects, discovered to be a scarlet woman, a whore, and chased out of her own country, forced to abandon her throne? She had been foolish enough to think that she could throw herself on Elizabeth's mercy and expect help to take back her country. More fool her. Once Elizabeth had Mary in her clutches, she was not going to let her go and Mary was now kept very closely guarded. And still, despite all that she had been through, Mary believed she had a right to the English throne that was better, more legitimate, than her cousin's. I never believed this to be true. Elizabeth is the daughter of Henry VIII by his true and lawful queen, Anne Boleyn, regardless of that lady's sad fate. If Mary Tudor had a right to rule despite being judged a bastard by law, then Elizabeth had, and has, an equal right.

But I am moving away from my narrative. Cecil needed proof that Mary Stuart had been complicit in the murder of Henry Darnley and he wanted me to obtain that proof from Ridolfi if he had it.

'Your house is secure, private?' Cecil asked.

'It is.'

'And you have no objection to questioning a man there?'

'None whatsoever,' I assured him.

'It should not be too difficult,' he said, leaning back in his chair. 'Ridolfi sometimes provides me with information, but it is necessary to ask the right questions with him. He does not offer information so much as it must be drawn out of him.'

'Is he an agent of yours, then?'

'I hesitate to call him that. He works for himself always and only feeds me information if it does him any good. I have nothing on him to enforce his cooperation and he knows that he need not be obliging if he does not wish to be so. But on this matter, well, it would be helpful to know what is being bruited abroad. I do not have the time to question him myself and, to tell truth, I would like to put some distance between myself and him.'

I asked him why he thought that was necessary, curious about their relationship.

Cecil sighed. 'He does not fear me. He talks to me as if we were friends, which we most certainly are not. A new face, yours,' he gestured to me, 'may give the spur to his sides and induce him to reveal information of interest.'

'I understand,' I said, not entirely sure that I did.

'Also, I have my hands full with another, related matter. Mary Stuart's half-brother, the Earl of Moray, is convinced he has letters written in Mary's hand discussing Darnley's murder with the Earl of Bothwell.'

'Indeed?' I said, wanting to know more but Cecil did not want to divulge anything further.

'I know you will have questions, Francis, but you must forgive me, I do not have the time to answer them. My clerk will give you a little more information on your way out.' He dismissed me.

I returned to the small antechamber, my head full of the

conversation I had just had and thinking how best to accommodate Ridolfi in my home.

'Master Secretary said you would give me more information about Signor Ridolfi?' I said to the clerk.

'Yes, please, come and sit.' I took the chair he pointed at. He opened a leather folio that had been lying on the edge of his desk. 'Signor Ridolfi is involved, to what extent we do not know, with a plot to depose Queen Elizabeth and put Mary Stuart on the English throne. He has supporters on the Continent and in this country, including the Duke of Norfolk.'

My surprise must have shown on my face.

'Yes,' the clerk smiled smugly, 'the Duke of Norfolk. Shocking, is it not? The Queen's own cousin.'

'Has he been arrested?'

'No, at least, not yet. It is thought better to let this plan play out a little longer. We know where he is, though. We can take him any time we want.'

'What is the Duke's role in this... this plot?' I asked, a little jealous of the way he referred to 'we' so often. This clerk, it seemed to me, was more useful to Cecil than me.

'He is to marry Mary Stuart.'

'That would legitimise further Mary's claim to the English throne,' I said my thought aloud.

'Indeed, it would. Although,' he laughed, 'if I were the Duke, I would be worried. Mary Stuart's husbands do not seem to enjoy a quiet or long life.'

I managed a small smile. The clerk meant it as a jest, but his words were indeed true. Francis had died young, Darnley had been murdered and Bothwell had rotted in a Danish dungeon. It would give any man pause.

'And what bearing does this have on Ridolfi?' I asked.

'Master Secretary is concerned that he is working for many individuals, all of whom may have different agendas, different objectives. Put simply, we do not know how far, if at all, we can trust Ridolfi. Indeed, we have reason to believe that he orchestrated this entire plot and that he personally enjoined the Duke to be a party to it, to what end we do not know. Your questioning should focus on that aspect, if I may be so bold as to tell you how to work, Master Walsingham, as well as what he knows about Darnley's murder.'

I nodded to suggest that he might be so bold. I asked him if that was all and he said it was. I rose to go.

'If I may be even bolder, sir,' he said, 'be careful with Signor Ridolfi. He is a slippery character.'

'Slippery?'

'As an eel.'

'Thank you for the warning,' I said, and pushing down the door handle, made my way out, taking several wrong turns down identical corridors until I found the right one out of the palace and back to The Papey.

What can I say about Roberto Ridolfi?

He was a clever man, and it shames me to admit it, more than a match for me at that time, inexperienced as I was. I remember his eyes more than anything else about him. They glinted darkly, like they had the devil behind them. Perhaps they did because I never knew what he was thinking. At the time, I believed his thoughts matched his words, but… I don't know. I failed in my task. I could never be sure where Ridolfi's loyalty lay, nor who he was really working for and reported so to Cecil. To this day, I do not know.

When Ridolfi arrived at The Papey, accompanied by men dressed in the livery of the Mayor of London, I had only just told my wife she was to expect a house guest. Ursula began to protest that the house was not in a suitable state to receive guests — we were having some work done to the staircase as the newel posts had become rotten and needed replacing, and repair work was also being carried out on the panelling in the hall, which meant that there was dust, debris and workmen all over the place — but I patted the air in what I hoped was a pacific gesture and reassured her that Ridolfi was not that kind of guest.

'Well, what kind of guest is he, then?' she demanded, hands curled on her hips in a pose I knew only too well.

Ursula was not unaware of the work I performed for Cecil but I had never gone into any details about it. How was I to tell Ursula that our guest was one of those men who walked in the shadows, whose every utterance was a move in deception? Ridolfi was the type of man I have been surrounded by for much of my life, but I neither like nor admire them for the work they perform. I view them as a necessary evil. And I did not want my wife to become more acquainted with him than was necessary.

Ridolfi bowed magnificently when he was deposited upon my threshold, a gesture I was forced to return. His glinty eyes raked over me and Ursula at my side, and then beyond to the hall and stairs. I found myself feeling as Ursula did, at a disadvantage because of the state of the place. He was sizing us up, I realised, working out what kind of hosts he was to have, what kind of creature he should be. Like all intelligencers, Ridolfi was adaptable. He could mix with tapsters and bawdy house madams and seem like one of them, or display exemplary dining manners at a gentleman's table. I had wondered why such a man, if he was guilty of plotting Elizabeth's deposition and of stirring up the English nobility, was being given what amounted to kid glove treatment by Cecil. Why was he not being questioned at the Tower, for instance? A night's racking of my brains had led me to conclude that Ridolfi was simply too influential in the banking and merchant community to risk offending. His money contacts with whom the crown had a precarious and, dare I say it, subservient relationship, might suffer if Ridolfi was mistreated. So, I reasoned, I had to tread carefully.

'I must thank you for your gracious offer of accommodation,' he said in a thick Italian accent, as though he had a choice in where he was put up.

'Not at all,' I said, thinking I may as well keep up such a pretence. 'This is my wife, Lady Ursula.'

Ursula curtsied and I could tell by her face that she did not like the look of our house guest. 'Good evening to you, sir. Your room is being prepared. If you would care to take some refreshment...' she gestured towards the parlour.

'Thank you. The London roads, they are rather dusty.' He gave a little cough to demonstrate how dry his throat was.

I didn't want him to get too comfortable, so I spoke. 'When you have had a drink and a rest, Signor Ridolfi, we shall talk. Anthony, my steward, will bring you to my study.'

I left them then, nodding to Ursula who scowled at me. I went to my study and began noting down a list of questions I needed to ask my new Italian acquaintance.

'Was Mary Stuart complicit in Lord Darnley's murder?' I asked once I had shut the door and sat down at my desk.

Ridolfi picked at his nails. 'Why am I not meeting with Master Secretary Cecil?'

I sniffed. 'Master Secretary Cecil is busy with other matters.'

'Ah, so I am not important enough, is that how it is?'

'That's how it is,' I said testily. 'Now, of Mary Stuart's complicity. What do you know?'

Ridolfi sighed. 'Nothing.'

'Nothing?'

'Nothing.'

'But you are very well informed of all matters relating to Mary Stuart,' I persisted. 'Were you in receipt of letters regarding the matter? Your contacts, did they talk to you of it?'

'Gossip, Master Walsingham, mere gossip. I heard some rumours that Darnley was to be got rid of—'

'By whom?'

'No names, sir. Talk.'

I kept asking him about the murder and Mary's supposed knowledge of it, but try as I might, I could not get Ridolfi to say anything of value. I knew Cecil would be disappointed at this failure, but Ridolfi either had nothing to tell or was resolute in keeping what he did know to himself.

I had to move on.

'Tell me what you know about the Duke of Norfolk,' I said, my quill tip poised over a blank sheet of paper.

Ridolfi took a sip of wine — my finest, brought over from Italy — looking at me over the top of the cup's rim. He dabbed at his lips with a linen cloth. 'I know only what everyone in our line of business knows, Master Walsingham. That the Duke of Norfolk is in discussions with the Scottish queen about a marriage between them. They have corresponded at some length, I understand. It is not an unreasonable alliance,' he shrugged. 'Mary is in need of a husband—'

'In need?' I queried, wondering at his choice of words.

He smiled. 'Mary Stuart is a woman who likes to have a man by her side. And in her bed,' he winked. 'Unlike your queen, sir.'

'Indeed,' I said, making a note.

'If you stop to consider,' Ridolfi continued,' the match is good. The Duke is cousin to your queen and English. Is that not what Elizabeth wants? Mary brought under control — no, how do you say — brought to heel? An English husband, well, would that not stop the French or the Spanish offering aid to her?' He looked at me, eyebrows raised.

'The Duke is also Protestant,' I said, keeping my eyes on my notes.

Ridolfi laughed. 'As you say.'

'What do you mean by that?'

Ridolfi took another sip of wine. 'I mean nothing, Master Walsingham, nothing at all.'

I let that enquiry drop, fool that I was. I discovered later through talking with Cecil that Norfolk was suspected of having Catholic sympathies; in fact, more than sympathies, that he was Catholic and only conformed outwardly to the Protestant faith. That was what Ridolfi was smirking about. I should have pressed him further.

'What else?' I said, moving on. He hesitated, probably wondering what I knew and his best course of action. 'Come, signor,' I said, 'you have said this much. Tis but a little step to say more. Your plans are broken, but you can do yourself some good. Speak again.'

'Do you think I am a fool, sir?' Ridolfi asked and I suddenly realised that he was not afraid or wary of me at all. On the contrary, he seemed to be enjoying this. I struggled to find an answer. Ridolfi continued. 'I know you know of my part in the rebellion in your country's north. I served Mary well, got the good opinion of King Philip, and had your Englishmen managed things better, you would be serving a different mistress now, would you not, Master Walsingham?'

The Northern Rebellion. It was that of which Ridolfi was speaking, a plot in which forty northern lords, Norfolk included, conspired to capture Elizabeth and put Mary on the throne, emboldened to do so by the Bull the Pope had issued a year earlier in which he claimed that it was no crime, nor no sin, to kill Elizabeth. This was not just a political war we were fighting, it was a holy one. The plot had been discovered and Norfolk had even been imprisoned for his part in it before Elizabeth had shown mercy and released him. You would have thought that incarceration in the Tower would have been enough to dissuade the Duke from becoming involved in any other plot, but no, the man was evidently a fool, blinded by ambition.

'The rebellion was a failure, signor,' I reminded him with not a little pleasure. 'It seems with all the support you claim to be able to muster, Elizabeth is destined to keep a hold on her throne.'

'As long as she has men like you around her, eh?' he grinned. 'But I tell you, as long as the lady continues in her present plight—'

'The lady, as you insist on calling her, is not in any distress at all.' I felt compelled to interrupt him here. 'She is housed most comfortably and attended by many servants, all at my queen's expense and out of the goodness of my queen's heart.'

Ridolfi snorted, spraying some of my wine across the tablecloth. 'Now, now, Master Walsingham, do not claim so. Have you actually met your queen of whom you speak so assuredly?'

I had not yet. I said nothing. He was baiting me.

'Your queen does not provide a sanctuary for Mary Stuart. She provides a prison. Oh, a very comfortable prison, I agree, but a prison nonetheless. Can you blame the woman for wanting to escape?'

'I blame Mary Stuart for her continual plotting against the Queen and this country,' I said vehemently. 'She has no right to consider herself the rightful queen and she causes nothing but problems. My queen should have her head off and be done with her mischief.'

'Such violence, Master Walsingham,' Ridolfi said, his face assuming a horrified expression and I knew he was mocking me. My dislike for him increased. 'And you, a gentleman.'

I had given too much away. This was not how it was supposed to be.

'What part have you played in this scheme regarding the marriage?' I asked, determined to regain the upper hand and have something to tell Cecil.

'Oh, I? I am of little consequence, sir. Naught but a humble merchant trying to make a little money.'

There was nothing humble about Ridolfi. 'Your role, signor?' I pressed.

Ridolfi shrugged. 'I carry letters, when there are letters to be carried.'

'For whom?'

'For whoever is the most generous with their money,' he laughed. 'I am a businessman, Master Walsingham, I appreciate the value of money.'

'Do you ever pass money on?'

'Between whom?'

'Between significant parties,' I said impatiently. 'Between the Stuart woman and the King of Spain, for example. Or vice versa.'

He shrugged again. 'Sometimes. How else can the woman reward her servants or buy clothes for her delectable body? Your queen provides only a little to sustain her cousin. Mary must make up the shortfall by other means.'

'You say this money is only for her maintenance?'

'I do.'

'Not to pay for men and arms?'

'To what end, sir?'

'To gather an army to rise up, free the Scottish queen and depose Elizabeth?'

Ridolfi's eyes opened wide. 'Such an imagination you have, Master Walsingham. I had not considered that the money I convey to the Scottish queen would be put to such purposes, nor I imagine do the men that send it. Englishmen must be available to be bought very cheaply if so. Are Englishmen particularly dissatisfied with the way things are, do you think, sir?'

We carried on in this vein for some time, but I could not shake Ridolfi's composure nor get him to admit any more complicity than that he had already confessed. I sent a message to Cecil of my findings and he wrote back that I was to leave it for a week or two, then to examine Ridolfi again. During that time, Ridolfi was to be treated as an honoured guest, much to Ursula's chagrin, and he, well, he lapped it up. My wine store diminished considerably because of his self-alleged connoisseurship and my food expenses tripled. I examined him once more three weeks after our first interview but discovered nothing further. I informed Cecil and the letter that came back was terse and barren of thanks. I was to allow Ridolfi to leave my house and return to lodgings of his own. I was embarrassed at my lack of success in the matter but must confess to being very glad to see the back of my unwanted house guest.

I later found out from the Earl of Leicester that Cecil and the Queen had entertained hopes of my turning Ridolfi, that is of making him entirely our man rather than anybody's, particular the plot's conspirators. Cecil told me nothing of this at the time. Had he said so, I would probably have altered my approach and the result may have been very different. I always got the impression that Cecil believed I had blundered in my handling of the matter. I believe Cecil blundered in not confiding in me.

CHAPTER 10

Towards the end of 1570, I was called to court and finally met the Queen. I had seen Elizabeth from a distance, of course, when I had stood in the Presence Chamber and admired her from afar, but this time, I was a mere two or three feet from her. She was taller than I had thought her to be, far taller than any other woman I had met, and this meant that we were almost eye to eye. Her face was thin and long, her skin pale, her lips narrow. Her eyes were her best feature, darker than should be expected for one of her complexion. They have the habit of seeming to bore into your skull.

I was at court for a reason, of course, not just to help make the court bustle for the Christmas festivities. Ursula had accompanied me for the matter was of great interest to her. I had an official appointment at last. I was to be made ambassador to the French court. It was a great honour, of course, to serve the Queen in such a function, but I could not help feeling it was an appointment I would rather not have had. Such a position meant moving to Paris, having to find suitable lodgings, for the position did not come with a house, and I would no doubt be charged an exorbitant rent by the French landlords who were ever ready to take advantage of foreigners, especially an Englishman. My financial state was not such that I could take up a post without feeling something of a pinch, and I pointed this out to Cecil when he first told me of the position. He obviously conveyed my concern to the Queen, because I was told she had graciously agreed to increase the ambassador's official daily allowance. This little victory having been won, I felt I could not make any further excuses lest I be put down as troublesome and never considered again for any other royal post.

I also had to suffer Ursula's complaints when I told of her my new position. She had enjoyed living in London and did not relish the prospect of moving to France. 'We will be surrounded by Catholics,' she said.

Indeed, that was a reality that weighed heavily upon me, especially when I received a letter from the current incumbent. Sir Henry Norris wrote to apprise me of what I should expect as ambassador. His letter made very weary reading. He had had a very bad time of it, he wrote. Like me, Sir Henry was a staunch Protestant and had openly supported the Huguenots in their Protestant faith. This had made him deeply unpopular with the French king and his formidable mother, Catherine de Medici. As a consequence, poor Sir Henry had been slighted whenever he attended court. His requests for audiences were often ignored or cancelled at short notice so that he seldom had any good news or made any progress in English affairs that he could put in his reports to Cecil and Elizabeth. What concerned me most though was the fact that he had been forced to attend the Catholic Mass. A refusal, he wrote, would have had him expelled as ambassador, making him of no further use in France and no doubt, ostracised for failure in England. The Mass had been a torment to him, having to listen to the Latin mumblings of a French Catholic priest, to swallow down the bread that was supposed to represent the body of Christ and to drink his blood. My stomach turned at the very thought of it. Would I be forced to attend also, I wondered? Could I, in all conscience, do so? Or would I be compelled by my conscience to refuse and so risk expulsion and the displeasure of Cecil and Elizabeth?

And then, as I have already said, there was the expense. The reason Sir Henry was quitting his post was that he simply could not afford to carry on any longer. The allowance for the ambassadorship was pitifully small. Out of it, Sir Henry had had to pay not only for his lodgings and its maintenance, including horses and their stabling, but he also had to bear the cost of employment of all the secretaries, clerks and pages an ambassador needed to have at his disposal. In addition, Sir Henry added, it was necessary to set money aside with which to bribe servants and pay informants. I had heard, and have discovered for myself, that Elizabeth inherited the notorious parsimony of her grandfather, Henry VII, and is ever loath to pay her servants what they deserve, indeed, the very capital they need to carry out their duties. Sir Henry found that money was draining out of his own pocket at an alarming rate, so much so that he feared he would be a very beggar indeed if he did not return to England a man free of such royal service.

All this was going through my mind as I stood before Elizabeth in the Council chamber at Whitehall Palace and received my commission as ambassador. I could only hope that my post would be of short duration.

CHAPTER 11

Ursula, our daughter Frances and I walked down the gangplank onto the quay, our small retinue of servants burdened with our trunks following behind. I had written ahead to Sir Henry's head steward, who was staying on in this capacity to serve me, of our arrival date, instructing him to meet us at the quay with transport, and sure enough, he was there, a ruddy-faced, portly man who waved his arm at us above the crowd.

'Master Walsingham?' he queried as our entourage approached.

I nodded, thrusting my hand out from between the folds of my cloak, which I had found to be not nearly warm enough against the chill of the sea air. 'You are—'

'Richard Metcalfe,' he said. He greeted Ursula and smiled down at Frances, who had not enjoyed the sea journey. She had been sick twice over the side of the boat and once all over Ursula, and the smell of vomit still clung to their clothing. She was now hanging off Ursula's skirts, putting her face against the folds and crying quietly. 'Let us get you to your new home,' Metcalfe said, astutely judging the situation. 'There's a cart for the trunks, your servants can clamber on that, and I've hired a coach for you and your family.'

'Thank you,' I said to him gratefully even while wondering how much the coach had cost. I put my hand on Ursula's shoulder and pushed her forward to follow after Metcalfe.

Frances stumbled over her skirts and Ursula picked her up with a laboured grunt. Frances put her face against Ursula's neck and soon her crying ceased. Metcalfe held Ursula's hand as she climbed into the coach and I climbed in after. The coach lurched to one side as Metcalfe climbed up onto the driver's seat and with a cry to the horses, we were on our way.

Our way was to Saint Marceau, a district south of the city's walls with the Seine right outside our windows. Ursula had had some notion that our accommodation would be in Faubourg Saint Germain, a far better part of Paris, but one that was, of course, much more expensive, and I told her it was far outside of our pocket. It was where those above our station lived, nobles who wanted to be away from the hustle and bustle, and the stench, of the working city.

Stench. That is one of the things I remember most of our stay in Paris. Saint Marceau could not have been called in any way salubrious. It was a hive of industry, literally, for it was where the cloth-dyers and tanners were situated. If you have never smelt recently butchered hides and the quantity of urine needed to process them, then it is impossible for me to adequately express the acrid, tear-streaking smell of this trade. It is the kind of smell that catches at the back of your throat and stays with you. The cloth-dying was not nearly so bad, but the dyes would often run down the muddy streets so that you would walk them unknowingly and then find that your shoes were irretrievably dyed red, blue or green.

'Why did you choose this shit heap?' Ursula yelled at me as we unpacked our trunk in our new bedroom. Ursula could swear like a soldier when she was annoyed, but she usually reserved such words for my ears only and Evelyn, her maid, raised her eyebrows. 'And don't you dare tell me to be quiet.'

'My dear,' I said as pacifically as I knew how, gesturing to Evelyn that she was to leave the room, 'we have to be careful with our money.'

'That's all I ever hear from you,' she said sulkily, shaking out a petticoat. 'Money, money, money. Richard was never so frugal.'

Ursula did not often mention her dead husband but whenever she did, it was ever to berate me. 'Richard never served the Queen as I do,' I pointed out, closing the shutters in an attempt to block some of the noise and smell of the tannery. 'And this area is Protestant, Ursula. We can worship without fear of retribution from the Catholics. Is that not good? I thought you were pleased for me, for us.'

Ursula rubbed her forehead and sank down onto the bed. 'Oh, I am, Francis. It is simply that my head hurts and that smell out there is not making it any easier. Frances was tiresome all the way here and I am weary.' I moved to sit beside her and put my arm around her waist. She leant her head against me. 'How long will we have to stay here?'

'I don't know, my dear. At least a year, I should think. Time to prove myself. Time to do some good work.'

'I read that letter from Sir Henry Norris,' she reminded me ruefully. 'If he struggled, what makes you think you will do any better?'

'I have to hope I can,' I said sincerely. 'I must at least try. Will you help me, Ursula? I will struggle without you.'

She lifted her head and kissed the side of my mouth. 'Of course, I will help, Francis. You're my husband. We will have to make the best of it. I just hope the Queen and Cecil will appreciate your efforts.'

As the weeks passed, I found every aspect of Sir Henry's letter confirmed. My money was spent before I even realised I had it and I was soon petitioning Cecil to supply me with funds, petitions which he ignored. I told Ursula we had to make economies, so no longer could she take trips to goldsmiths and order earrings or rings on a whim. She did not complain, she understood, although she did comment that our servants were robbing us blind, taking food from our pantry that was intended for our table and selling it on. She said we only dined well when we dined at others' houses, and there was some truth in this.

Fortunately, we dined at others quite often for, as I have said, we were lodged in a Protestant enclave. Despite this, Ursula proclaimed to never feel quite safe and was reluctant to take Frances out of the house with her unless she was accompanied by at least two of our English servants. She did not tell me so for some time for she had been unwilling to add to my worries but then she discovered she was pregnant and her condition heightened her fears. I increased her guard to three English servants.

The news of her pregnancy made me long for England more than ever before.

I realise I sound ungrateful, having wanted an official position for so long then complaining of what such a position involved. Perhaps I was ungrateful, it is difficult to tell now. But I do remember that the work did not satisfy me. Much of it was routine: negotiating the terms of trade deals, assisting English merchants who had fallen foul of the French dockyard stewards, helping those who required passports to travel onto Switzerland or Italy, or aiding those who had simply got into trouble with the French authorities. I found the work not difficult just time-consuming. What did interest me and took up more and more of my time as the weeks turned into months were the contacts I was making within the French court and with men who could prove of use to me, supplying information about what was happening abroad, who was talking to whom, what deals were being struck. This all cost, too, of course, but I felt it was money well spent. I felt it was an investment in the future and in safety.

The most important, not to say the most trying, of my work as ambassador was when marriage was proposed between Elizabeth and the Duke of Anjou. Ever since Elizabeth acceded the throne, there had been one foreign prince or duke petitioning for her hand, but Elizabeth had always maintained she wanted to remain a virgin until her death. I had believed this when I heard it, but now it seemed she was seriously considering marrying the Duke to cement an alliance with France. I could not discount the logic of such an intention, although I did question the wisdom of it.

The Duke of Anjou was a young man of only nineteen. Elizabeth was in her thirty-seventh year, in my opinion and in the opinion of many, too old to consider matrimony and its inevitable consequences. Childbirth is a dangerous time for even young women; for a woman in her middle age who had never borne a babe, it was all too likely to prove fatal, leaving England with a French king as its head, no doubt. I corresponded at length with Cecil about this matter. He did not seem duly concerned, convinced it was merely a stratagem of the Queen's to soothe her vanity and prolong the possibility of marriage for as long as it could be prolonged to keep trading matters cordial between our two countries.

What worried me most was that Anjou was a fervent Catholic. Indeed, he had taken up arms against the Huguenots and had more than once declared Elizabeth to be both bastard and heretic. Elizabeth had heard of this and yet was not discouraged. But what perhaps she had not heard of was the Duke's degenerate practice of eschewing the clothes belonging to a man and donning dresses and bodices and parading around his private rooms at court with other like-minded minions. But then, what can you expect of the French? Cecil wrote to me, requesting a physical description of the Duke, saying that the Queen had asked whether he was handsome. I could with candour state that he was well but small proportioned, though his legs were good. His complexion was nothing to speak of, being rather more sallow than myself, which is to say very sallow indeed for my complexion is dark. But I did not dare commit to paper his strange antics lest my letter was intercepted and read by Catherine de Medici who though, she herself was aware of her son's faults, was not prepared to admit them to anyone else, he being her favourite child. She herself was in favour of the marriage, for in truth, Anjou put the royal family in a difficult position at times. He was unnaturally close to the Guise family, the enemies of Catherine, and was more popular than the King with the French people, who of course, knew nothing of his preference for women's clothing and pretty young men. For England, the marriage would have several benefits. The getting of an heir, possibly, but more importantly, the acquiring of an ally against the might of Spain and a disentangling of those who were sympathetic to Mary Stuart. I could see the sense of it and with Cecil, now ennobled to become Lord Burghley, urging me on, I pursued the match with all the vigour of which I was capable.

In the end, it was Elizabeth herself who proved the stumbling block to the marriage. My favourable description of Anjou was a spur to her interest, it was true, but in fact, she was more concerned with the politics of the whole affair than the personal, for which I admired her. The marriage terms were drawn up. Anjou was not to be given a coronation, making him unable to rule except through Elizabeth as his wife. If she were to die, then he would have no power in England at all. His own servants, serving men and women, would not be permitted to hold any office of state, thereby preventing them from having any influence in the country's internal and foreign affairs. But perhaps most importantly of all, Elizabeth refused to allow Anjou to practice his Catholicism once he was her husband, and he was to attend Protestant services as if he was happy to do so. These were all terms that I wholeheartedly agreed with and I mentally applauded Elizabeth for having the courage to put them forward. But I was caught in a cleft stick. As ambassador, it was my duty to negotiate the marriage treaty, to couch it in terms that would not offend the French royal family, nor yet give them the idea that they had room to manoeuvre on any of the matters under discussion. I thought I would play my hand carefully and not mention the term that likely offended most, the matter of religion. I kept it out of the marriage negotiations. When I had to address the matter, I was careful. I pointed out that the Duke had been interested, not to say attracted, by Protestantism in his youth and that it would be no dishonour to him should he come to change his faith from Catholic to Protestant, the seeds of doubt having already been sown. Catherine and King Charles listened but made no comment.

The negotiations dragged on, neither side willing to budge. One morning I was instructed to attend the court to have an audience with Catherine and the Duke. I prepared well for the audience, confirming what my limits were regarding any concession I was able to give and keeping Elizabeth's chief objective, that of an alliance against the Spanish, firmly at the forefront of my mind.

Catherine stared at me as I entered. The Duke stood by her side and gave me a disdainful look before stuffing a small posy beneath his nose and sniffing loudly. I bowed low.

'Master Walsingham,' Catherine's croaky voice greeted me, 'what is your queen thinking of?'

I was unsure of what exactly she was speaking. 'If you could elaborate, madam.'

'The marriage terms your queen sets down are unacceptable.'

'They are preposterous,' the Duke interjected.

'Quiet, my son,' Catherine said, squeezing his wrist.

'But Maman—'

'Quiet, I say. I will deal with this.'

Anjou lapsed into a sulky silence.

'My son must be allowed to practise the true faith,' she began. I winced at her use of the term. 'It is a nonsense to say he cannot worship as his conscience dictates, even in private.'

'England is a Protestant nation, madam,' I pointed out.

'That is England's misfortune,' Catherine sneered at me. 'If my son is to marry your queen, he must do so publicly acknowledged as a Catholic.'

I opened my mouth to answer, but Catherine continued. 'And he must be crowned king. What kind of unnatural state would we be in if a woman were to have authority over a man and that man her husband?' The question was rhetorical, I knew, so I kept silent. 'And he must have authority and power. To have no role in the government of the country would be to make him less than a man.'

She watched me closely at this, no doubt expecting me to say that because of his prancing antics, he was already less than a man.

Anjou shrugged his wrist free from his mother's grasp. 'I know your queen is a woman of rare accomplishments, the rarest creature that was in Europe these five hundred years,' he said. A practiced statement, I felt sure. 'She is intelligent and has great wit, and she has, I am reliably informed, the body of a woman half her age and so meet to bear me children, but these terms she is proposing are completely unacceptable, to me as a man and as a Catholic, you must see that.'

I did see, that was my problem.

'So, is there a way out of this impasse, Master Walsingham?' Catherine asked, seemingly not displeased at her son's interjection.

'I am sure we can find some compromise, madam,' I said, knowing that on the marriage terms, Elizabeth was immovable.

'You must try your hardest, Master Walsingham,' she said and dismissed me.

I went straight home and wrote to the Earl of Leicester, Elizabeth's favourite, the man she listened to, and to whom I had become introduced following my appointment. I had had my doubts about the Earl, thinking him to be out for what he could get from the Queen, but I had been wrong. We had become friends.

I expressed to him how important it was that this marriage

proposal be pursued for the sake of fortifying England against the threat of Spain and asking him if he could help moderate the terms that were so objectionable. I knew his relationship with Elizabeth made him the person most likely of being able to achieve such an alteration, but as I wrote, I had my doubts that even he could sway her. This was borne out within a few months. Leicester wrote to me that he had tried to change Elizabeth's mind on the matter of the Duke being allowed to practise his religion in private, but that Elizabeth had been adamant. To allow the Duke this liberty would be to encourage others in her realm to openly celebrate the mass, and that was something she was not prepared to do. *'There is no easy way of conveying this state of affairs, Francis,'* he wrote, *'but the Anjou marriage is now not even being considered by the Queen.'*

I had failed in my most important task as ambassador and the weight of my failure brought on a severe illness in the lower half of my body, one that would return to plague me at frequent intervals for the rest of my life. I, along with every other ambassador in France, was required to attend the King in the Loire in August of that year, but my illness delayed me and I fear much ground was lost at a time when I could have introduced myself to the leader of the French Protestants, Admiral Coligny, who was also a guest. I returned to Paris afterwards in great pain, it keeping me to my bed for several months, so that I was forced to conduct business from my bedchamber. And then I developed an affliction in my eyes, which wept with gummy fluid and caused them to swell and become sore. Ursula fussed around me, ordering soothing ointments from a trusted apothecary, which I do believe gave me some ease, and helping me to write my letters to reduce the strain on my sight. My doctors also forbade me certain foods and recommended others. Very slowly, my health began to improve.

My account now brings me to perhaps the most unpleasant, certainly the most horribly vivid event of my life, the St Bartholomew Eve massacre. Everyone, young and old alike, knows of this dark history. It is an event destined to live in common memory forever, so heinous a crime it was, but not everyone can speak of the massacre as one who witnessed it. I was there in Paris when this horror took place. It lives in my memory as fresh as if it happened yesterday. I wish I could forget it. I cannot.

France is, and has been ever since I've known her, an unpleasant land. There is a great gulf between the King and the lowest of his subjects, and though such distinctions of hierarchy are prescribed by God and therefore indisputable, the disparity is far greater than in other, more enlightened, countries such as ours. To be brief, the King and his nobles have all the money and the rest of the people are forced to live on what they can get through whatever means, criminal or otherwise, they choose to employ. Such disparities do not make for a contented populace, and consequently, the French people are surly, their minds full of rebellious, petty thoughts and actions. Such a people are easy to manipulate. The contented Englishman who knows his place and has a judicious, fair monarch on his country's throne does not continually think he is hard done by and does not believe that others, wholly innocent others, are the cause of any misfortune that happens to befall him. The Frenchman does think this and so looks for ways to be revenged. Combine this way of thinking with the misfortune of being Catholic and ... well, I need not elaborate further, need I? In such a country was born the hearts that allowed such an evil as the massacre at Paris to be perpetrated.

I had heard rumours that something was going to happen weeks before it actually did. There was much religious discord in the air, Catholic against Protestant, Protestant against Catholic. It was palpable. I felt the animosity every time I left my house, even from behind the doors of my coach as we rumbled along the filthy, rutted and potholed Paris streets.

It was a marriage that sparked off the massacre. King Charles IX's sister, Margaret, was to marry Henry, the King of Navarre. Margaret, like her family, was Catholic, Henry, a Huguenot Protestant. A marriage that involves two faiths is never an easy event to manage, as my own deliberations in the marriage negotiations between my queen and the Duke had proved, but they are sometimes an unfortunately necessary pursuit if they enable better trade relations and facilitate peace treaties and such like. It was for these reasons that I was reluctantly in favour of a marriage between Elizabeth and Anjou, for none other. Those not involved in marriage negotiations, by which I mean the lower sections of society, neither see nor understand the intricacies or necessities of such alliances and so sometimes protest against them without good reason. Such was the case with this marriage. All that the people of Paris saw and understood was that a large assembly of Huguenots was gathering in the city to celebrate a marriage they, the Catholics, thought was an abomination. They were, frankly, outraged. And they were encouraged in their despicable feelings by the vile Catherine de Medici. She resented the influence that the Admiral Coligny, one of the Huguenots, came to have on her son the King as the wedding festivities — the unending masques and dances — were played out, but in truth, I suspect the idea of assassinating Coligny had long been in her mind. In this, I have no doubt she was perversely aided and abetted by the Guise family, who were ever ready to pour poison in her ear about all Protestants, and the Huguenot Protestants, in particular.

I heard some of this from my contacts in the French court but had no power to do anything about it, save make my records of conversations and pass on such information to Cecil and Elizabeth. And I was busy. As ambassador and Elizabeth's representative, I was expected to attend many of the wedding festivities. I remember one of these very clearly. There was to be a staging of a mock battle between Turks and Amazons at the palace and Ursula and myself were invited to attend. Ursula was by this time heavy with child and did not want to go. I had the devil of a job persuading her she must, else we would risk causing offence and end up undoing all my hard work of the previous months. She gave me a surly look, pressed her hand to the small of her back and stuck out her belly, but agreed. She complained later though because these revels went on well into the night, wearying her much. In truth, I too grew weary of all the jollity and I had not the weight of a baby to tire me. Ursula had my deepest sympathy. At last, certain we had done our duty, I made our goodnights to the King and his mother, and we departed for the relative comfort of our house.

As we rode through the streets, Ursula grunting with discomfort at every jolt, there was a feeling, indescribable, in the air. This is not mere hindsight talking. I felt... something. I noticed that some of the houses had boarded up their windows, not an uncommon sight in Paris, admittedly, but the great number of boarded windows was odd. It felt as if the city was barricading itself against an acknowledged enemy. I did not mention my unease to Ursula for fear of frightening her, but I was very glad to reach our house and I ordered the gates to be shut and locked immediately. I lingered at the gates as Ursula went into the house and told the guards to remain alert and careful. They asked me why, but I could not answer them.

I went into the house, looking over my shoulder and my eyes scanning the dark corners of the building, looking beneath the wheels of the carts and barrows that littered the small courtyard. What was I looking for? I don't know. The devil, perhaps? Tired as I was, I did not go upstairs and join Ursula in our chamber. I went to my office, ostensibly to see if any messages had arrived while I was out, but really because I did not know what else to do but work, or pretend to.

Philip Sidney, who was visiting France and had asked to be put up at my house, had waited up for my return. Have I mentioned Philip already? I cannot remember, perhaps not. What can I say of Philip Sidney that has not already been said and to which my small voice would be but a whisper on the wind? But maybe there is something I can say that has not been said before. To the world, Philip was what every man should be. He was cultured, well-mannered, intelligent, a very gentleman, in fact. He was the son of Henry and Mary Sidney, and consequently, nephew to the Earl of Leicester. Leicester adored Philip, I think because Leicester had no son of his own to love, and Philip returned that love in equal measure. As the son of a knight and nephew of an earl, and Leicester the Queen's favourite at that, it was natural that Philip should enter the Queen's service, and his intelligence and natural tact made him a perfect choice for diplomatic missions abroad, even at his young age, for he was but in his early twenties when he became known to me in Paris.

Philip had surprised me then, for I had thought he would be like his uncle, besotted with Elizabeth and eager to serve, but no. He spoke frankly of what he considered to be Elizabeth's many faults and I was shocked by his outspokenness. I suggested to him that he might want to moderate his language lest the Queen should come to hear of his words. He laughed, holding a hand against his belly.

'Forgive me, sir,' he said, 'but I have said much of this to the Queen already. Why do you think she sends me abroad?'

I had frowned. 'It is a punishment?'

'Of sorts,' he nodded smilingly. 'I have no taste for the fawning and flattery that a man must practice if he is to be successful at court. I have seen how my dear uncle is expected to behave and I soon discovered that it is not for me.'

'You do not care for the Queen?'

'As my queen, of course, and I will always do my best to serve her, but as a woman? Not a great deal, I confess. So, here I am, slogging around the Continent.'

'You do not mind being cast out in this way?' I wondered.

'Not a bit,' he assured me. 'This is freedom. I meet with whom I want to meet, I talk with those I wish to talk with… what else could I desire?'

'The favour of the Queen?' I suggested.

He looked at me disparagingly. 'Indeed, some may desire that. I just want to do what I am good at and make England a better place.'

'Admirable sentiments, Sir Philip,' I said and meant it.

From that moment on, Philip and I had become friends. We thought a great deal alike, understood the nuances of politics and always attempted to see both sides of arguments. Soon, I felt like Philip was a son to me, or at least, a much younger brother. He cared for me and mine in a way no other man has ever done, not even his Uncle Leicester.

But to return to that dreadful night. As I said, Philip had waited up for me to return. He had not been invited to the revelry as he had no official post in Paris. He put down his book and stood as I entered my office. 'How was it?' he asked with a wry smile.

'Oh,' I said, trying to be nonchalant, 'they put on a good show. But it was overlong and Ursula, well…'

'Yes, I saw her as she came in,' Philip said, his eyes gesturing to the ceiling. 'It is to be expected, in her condition.'

I nodded and moved to the window, my face close to the glass.

'Is something the matter, sir?' Philip asked, joining me there.

'Yes, something,' I muttered. I looked at him sharply. 'Have you heard anything?'

'What sort of thing?'

'I don't know. I just feel that something may happen, that the Catholics are preparing something for the Huguenots.'

'Such as?'

I shrugged, annoyed with myself for not knowing. 'There were looks and whispers tonight at the masque. Between the King and his mother, and others. I am sure of it. They are up to something, but I know not what.'

'Nothing would surprise me,' Philip said, returning to his chair by the fire and picking up his book. I wished I was able to dismiss my unease as easily as he dismissed it. 'In any case, it is no cause for you to be concerned. Whatever happens, *if* something happens, it is a French matter, is it not? If a row blows up between the King's family and Navarre, well, what of it?'

'I hope that is all it is, a row,' I said grimly.

'What else?'

'I don't know,' I snarled at him, my hold on my temper finally loosed.

'Forgive me,' he said, contrite in an instant. 'I have forgotten how weary you must be after your long day. I should not prattle on so.'

I should have waved his apology aside, apologised to him for my rudeness, I know, but I did not for I had heard a noise from outside. 'What was that?' I hissed, my breath fogging the windowpane.

I felt Philip at my side as he too peered out into the darkness. But there was nothing to see.

'Perhaps it was nothing? A fox, maybe,' he suggested.

'Perhaps,' I said. We lingered there for a few minutes more, but we heard nothing and saw nothing. 'You should go to bed, Philip.'

'Will you be retiring, sir?' he asked.

I shook my head. Even if I went to bed, I knew I would not sleep and only disturb Ursula who needed her rest.

'Then I will not,' Philip said emphatically. 'I am not tired.'

'I would be glad of your company,' I admitted.

'Come, sir,' he gestured towards the fire, 'come and sit. There is a full jug of wine and some cakes here.'

I did as he bid and sat by the fire, sipped wine and nibbled at cakes. I tasted nothing.

Philip and I sat up for most of the rest of that night but as the sky began to lighten and we felt our eyes closing, we agreed to go to bed. My sleep was not at all restful. I dreamt of blood.

I was woken later that morning by Philip bursting into my chamber. 'Sir, sir, wake up.'

I raised myself onto my elbows and immediately looked to my left to see if his sudden entrance had disturbed Ursula, but her side of the bed was empty. She had taken to rising early of late, her aching back and heavy belly making it too uncomfortable for her to remain horizontal for any great length of time.

'What is it?'

'You were right,' he said, hitching himself up on the bed so I had to move my legs over to avoid being sat on. 'Something did happen last night.'

My sleep-befuddled brain cleared immediately. Philip had my full attention. 'What? What happened?'

'There was an attempt to assassinate Admiral Coligny.'

'What?' I gasped.

Philip nodded. 'He escaped, but only by the grace of God. He was shot at as he walked home after the masque you were at.'

'He walked home?' I repeated incredulously. What had the fool been thinking? Even I, who was not hated nearly as much as he, never went anywhere in Paris by foot.

'I know, I know, but he did. The shot was fired from an empty property owned by...wait for it,' he paused for effect, 'the Duke of Guise's mother.'

'I knew it,' I thumped the bedspread, 'I knew they were up to something. But is Coligny all right? You said they *tried* to kill him. So, he is unharmed?'

'No, not quite. He's alive, but he was hit in both of his arms. He had been handed a petition, to make him stop, I suppose, and Coligny was reading it when the shots were fired. He was rushed to his lodgings and the King sent his own surgeon to attend him.'

'All for show,' I said, immediately dismissing that seeming act of concern for the fraud it was.

'The surgeon apparently was able to remove the gunshot

from the Admiral's left arm but he had to amputate the little finger of his right hand, it was so badly damaged.'

I threw back my bed covers and Philip moved out of my way. I poured water from the jug into the basin and began to wash, knowing that I had a very busy day ahead of me, even more so than usual. Meanwhile, as I dressed, Philip talked on, telling me more of the incident and the gossip that was going around town. He had heard it from one of the pages, who had heard it from one of the kitchen maids, who had heard it from the man who fetched the meat from the butchers. How much of it was true was impossible to tell, but I knew that it did not need to be true. Already, it seemed, the finger of suspicion was pointing at Catherine de Medici as the originator of the plot to murder Coligny. How long would it be before the Huguenots and their supporters would be seeking revenge?

Things got worse. Coligny escaped one assassination attempt only to have another made on him and this one was successful. No attempt to conceal the attackers was made. Men sent by the King forced entry into Coligny's house and stuck a pike in his belly as he lay in bed. The Duke of Guise was in the street below and he shouted up to the murderers to throw Coligny's body out of the window. This they did and the mob that was gathering hacked his bloody body to pieces. Church bells began to ring across the city, not for any Christian purpose, but to alert the Catholics that the time had come for Protestants to be killed.

The slaughter had begun.

Catherine de Medici had it put about the city that the Huguenots had, in fact, been preparing to depose the King and put a Protestant king of their own choosing in his place. I know that there never was any such plan; the King and his mother merely bruited this abroad to provide them with a good excuse for the carnage they had unleashed.

My God, the screams! I had given instructions that none of my household was to leave the environs of the embassy and that the gates were to be kept locked and guarded. Anyone presenting themselves at my gates had to prove who they were and if they could not and their errand was not of importance to me, they would be turned away. You may think this cruel of me but I could not risk strangers entering my home. What if they were agents of the Guises and the Medici woman and ready to slaughter all of us? I had Ursula and my daughter to think of, not to mention my servants who depended on me to protect them.

News kept coming through to me of what was happening in the city as my fellow Englishmen who lived in Paris, and those Protestants who were allied to England, turned up at my gates, begging to be allowed inside for their own protection. They believed that as an ambassador I would be safe, that the King would never allow a foreign representative to be harmed or killed in his own country. Word would be sent to me in my office that so-and-so was at the gates. Were the guards allowed to admit him or her? I knew most of the names that came through to me and I would give the order for the gates to be opened. Some, very few, I turned away, though my conscience pained me to do so. I could not give shelter to anyone whom the Guises felt they had a right to pursue and I no right to protect. To do so might mean my gates would be broken down and my home invaded, and I and my family put to the sword. I would not take that risk. The embassy, my home, became so crowded with people seeking shelter that all the rooms were full and people found places to rest in the halls and on the stairs. So many people, you would think that the noise would be overwhelming, but they were too scared to talk. They huddled together, their chins sunk upon their chests and winced with every scream and shout that came through the walls.

The screams and shouts came nearer. Fires were burning, making the sky first orange, then red, as the sun went down and night came upon us. My house overlooked the Seine and I saw there something I hope never to see again. Instead of brown, the water was red, bright red. And there were bodies, so many bodies, floating, their skins ripped open, their insides falling out, their eyes wide and staring, until the birds that were circling pecked them out. And these were not just the bodies of men, but of women and children too, babes even. I ordered the shutters in our bedroom where Ursula and Frances sat locked. I did not want either of them to look out of the window and see such a sight.

I was frightened, I'll admit. I did not know if the mob would preserve the sanctity of a diplomat and leave us alone. What would happen if they broke through the gates and entered the house? What would they do to my wife and child? Visions invaded my mind, of Ursula and Frances being raped by faceless villains, of daggers being thrust into my wife's belly and seeing my unborn child spill out onto the floor, of my Frances, my lovely little Frances, being tossed into the Seine. I buckled on a breastplate, a rusty thing barely worthy of the name, and armed myself with my sword and dagger and loaded a firearm. I bid Philip do the same and I ordered the servants to keep watch at all the entrances and exits with pikes and spears in their hands. Meanwhile, I sent out my most trusted messenger, he all white-faced and trembling to be thrust out onto the dangerous Paris streets but I had no choice, to the King to demand that he give me and my household protection against the mob. The King saw sense, thankfully, and did indeed send an armed guard to my house. They gave me a sense of some little safety but still, the screams bled through our embassy walls. Those screams haunt me still.

The mob's thirst for blood lasted a few days, by which time, so the reports I received went, they had killed at least three thousand people in Paris. The blood-lust had spread beyond Paris too so that as many as ten thousand more Protestants and foreigners were hacked to death by the Catholics. I have often been accused of being a Catholic hater. Is it any wonder I hate them so? The Pope, that so-called most holy of men, celebrated the massacre with a *Te Deum* and had a medal created that bore an angel holding a sword aloft and an inscription that triumphantly read '*Huguenots slaughtered*'. The man was a monster.

I wrote to Cecil to give a report of the slaughter. I had trouble finding the words to describe what had taken place. How could words faithfully represent what I had seen and heard? He wrote back to me to say he believed God was punishing us Protestants for our sins by allowing the Devil to wreak his work on Earth. I had to agree with him and those sins, I believed, were in being too lenient with Catholics, allowing them to thrive and spread their false faith.

Paris, I decided, was no place for my wife and child. I might have to stay but they did not and I booked them on the first passage back to England. I had to pay far more than normal because so many of my fellow Englishmen were trying to do the same; demand was high, space low and so the price went up and up. I accompanied Ursula and Frances to Calais, unwilling to trust them to the care of a servant, even though it meant I would be away from the embassy for a few days. Up to the very point of our separation, Ursula begged me to go with her. Even as we stood by the ship's gangplank, the wind whipping her skirts about her ankles, she gripped my arm.

'Francis, please,' she begged. 'I cannot leave you here. You cannot know what will happen.'

'I cannot leave my post, Ursula,' I told her for about the twelfth time.

'But the danger—'

'Is mostly past,' I assured her. 'The King has given me this armed guard,' I gestured at the twelve soldiers standing a few feet off, their halberds glinting dully in the low sunlight, 'and I will be safe. But I cannot rest easy if I am away from home and you are left in the house with only the servants to guard you. It will be easier for me if I know you are safe in England. Think of Frances, my dear, and our unborn child.'

Frances was hanging off her mother's hand, her little eyes wide at the sight of the soldiers and intrigued by the ship. She knew something terrible had happened but we had kept her from the horror. Children do not need to know such things; such things will only give them nightmares.

Ursula looked down at Frances and nodded. 'Yes, I know you are right, though I do not like it.'

Someone on the ship called out for all going to England to board, though there seemed little need because most were so eager to get away that they had hurried aboard and quickly sought sanctuary below. Ursula leant towards me and kissed me. I smiled bravely at her, then bent and kissed Frances, placing my hand upon her head and bestowing upon her a blessing that I hoped would protect her. She took my hand from her head and planted a very wet kiss on my palm, laughing as she pushed my hand back towards me. I almost wept to see her do this, so innocent, so loving.

'Go,' I said, my voice hoarse and Ursula tugged my little girl up the gangplank. They stayed on deck until the ship left the harbour, waving to me and I waved back. Then I returned to the safety of my armed guard and made my way back to Paris and my unwelcoming home.

Upon my return, I found a letter from the King's principal secretary requesting I attend upon his master at my earliest convenience. The letter had already been sitting in my office for a day and a half, but I felt no hurry to pen a response. I did not want to stand in front of the King or his mother ever again.

But I knew it could not be ignored, nor could I refuse to do my duty as ambassador. I donned my most sober of outfits — black doublet, black hose, white shirt and black cap, finished off with my black embroidered cloak — and climbed into my carriage. When I arrived at the palace, I was greeted with most obsequious courtesy by the courtiers and the King's ministers. I did my best to show my disdain for their manners, for I knew it to be of the most false kind, and asked for my audience with the King to be arranged as soon as possible. I was surprised to find myself taken straight through to the Privy Chamber, not the Presence Chamber where most of my audiences had been, in full view and hearing of the court. The King was seated beneath his canopy of estate and his mother at his side.

'Ah, Master Walsingham,' Charles greeted me, actually stepping down off the dais and coming towards me with outstretched arms. He put his hands on my shoulders and I felt their weight pressing down on me, the sickly smell of his perfume tickling my nose. 'I cannot tell you how glad I am to see you so well.'

'Unlike so many others, Your Highness,' I said.

The smile on his face faltered a little, but he recovered quickly. 'Indeed, indeed.' His hands fell away from me and he returned to his chair. 'A tragedy.'

'I believe what has happened in your country over the last week has been more than a tragedy. It has been a travesty, a diabolical calamity, a—'

'We need not quibble over words, Master Walsingham,' the Medici woman cut me off, forcing me to turn my gaze to hers.

'We are all agreed that the purging should not have been allowed to go so far—'

'It should not have been allowed to happen at all,' I said, disgusted by her choice of words. A purging? Is that what they dared to call the massacre?

She sighed, her slack bosom rising and falling heavily. 'You must know, Master Walsingham, and I entrust you to tell your queen, that we,' she gestured between herself and her son, 'had nothing to do with this... this incident.'

'Nothing, madam?'

'Nothing,' she said, looking horrified that I would suspect otherwise. 'How could we? *Why* would we? This was to be a happy time, the marriage of our dear daughter. We would not want to spoil it with all this death.'

'But the mob, Master Walsingham,', Charles interjected, 'once their blood has been roused, it is impossible to control them. The acts they committed—'

'Have the blessing of the Pope,' I finished for him, although I know those would not have been his words.

Charles smiled smugly and shrugged. 'I cannot answer for the Pope.'

I knew there was little point in pursuing a policy of blame. Catherine and Charles, who I knew to be the most deep of dissemblers, would never admit to being party to, let alone the originators, of the massacre. And this audience I was enduring was their attempt to extricate themselves from blame. They were still thinking of the marriage between my queen and Anjou. Despite everything, they were still anticipating the negotiations to continue. The thought now revolted me.

'What can we do to convince your gracious queen that we are as disgusted as she at what has happened here?' Charles appealed.

'I am not at all sure my queen can be convinced of anything at this moment. She and the whole of England are in mourning for the loss of so many fellow Protestants, so many innocents. It is a stain France will never be able to wash off.'

The Medici woman's eyes narrowed at me. 'That would indeed be a shame, Master Walsingham, if there were to be no possibility of accord and understanding between our two great countries. Perhaps a different intermediary would be able to explain our situation and desires better to Elizabeth?'

So, she was threatening that I would be replaced, I thought with some pleasure. Well, I had got there before her. In my report sent to Cecil in the immediate aftermath of the massacre, I had enclosed a request that I be relieved of my post as ambassador to the French court. I had made the request because I felt I needed to, to show him my mind, but fully expecting it to be refused. To my surprise and very great pleasure, Elizabeth approved my request for recall and Cecil told me that a suitable replacement would be sought. All I had to do was wait until one was found and get permission from Charles to quit his court and his country.

I asked for his permission.

'No, you will not leave,' Charles said with a vehement shake of his head and my heart felt leaden in my chest. His mother shot him a look that seemed to question his wisdom in refusing, but she said nothing. 'Though my lady mother has her doubts, I think you are a very good ambassador, Master Walsingham, and I believe you have the interests of both our countries at heart. You will continue to assure your queen of my deep friendship and regard for her, and that I one day hope to be able to call her sister in fact as well as in my heart.'

I have said that Charles was a dissembler. He meant none of this. I had been deceived, I realised, in his professions of friendship from the moment I took up my post as ambassador. He and his mother had lied and manipulated me, persuaded me that a marriage with Anjou was in the best interest of my queen and my country, that they were prepared to tolerate the Protestant faith... all untrue. And even after the savagery of the massacre, they were pretending to my face that they had been as innocent as me.

I had to wait six months for my release from Paris. During that time, I had to endure much, pursue policies I had no belief in, listen to so very many lies, and live in a city that bore the scars of her recent bloody history. My only hope had come from Cecil and from Leicester, who was proving to be a very good friend to me. They both wrote to me, telling me that the search for my replacement was still going on but that it would happen, I just had to be patient. It was hard to be patient and I did not even have my family with me to make my 'imprisonment' more bearable. Ursula, I knew, was being looked after by my sisters, and indeed, I did not wish her back with me, she did not deserve that, but our separation made me feel so very lonely. Only Philip made my situation bearable for he visited and stayed with me on several occasions during those six months.

At last, I received a communication from Cecil that a replacement had been found and that I could relinquish my post. In just a few weeks, the new ambassador would arrive in France and I could go home. I sought an audience with the King on the nineteenth of April to take my leave of him and his wretched country. I told him the new ambassador would be just as assiduous as I had been to keep relations between England and France amicable, and this time, he did not refuse me permission to depart.

I travelled to Calais, without the King's guard this time and the more thankful for it, and boarded a ship bound for the English coast. The last letter I had had from Leicester gave me good reason to look forward with great optimism to my return, for he had hinted that he and Cecil had a post all lined up that would suit me very well.

CHAPTER 12

It was good to be back in England.

On the journey back, crossing the tempestuous Channel, my health failed me once again. Like my daughter Frances had done on the journey out, I spent most of the voyage leaning over the ship's rail, my stomach spewing forth the little I had managed to consume earlier. But it was not just sickness in my belly that ailed me. My head hurt continually, at times an intense sharp pain behind my eyes, at others, a dull throbbing all over. And I also had occasional sharp pains in my stomach and my back. I had had such pain before, from time to time, and never paid much attention, too busy, I suppose. But I think my quitting of Paris acted on me like something breaking, like the bung bursting out of a too-full barrel of beer. Whatever the cause, by the time I reached English shores, I was in dire need of rest.

'Oh, dear God,' was how Ursula greeted me as I climbed, rather unsteadily, out of the coach I had hired to bring me home to The Papey, having decided that I was too ill to ride and would not be able to manage a horse. She picked up her skirts and hurried to my side to clutch my arm and hold me up.

'Do I look that ill?' I asked, not altogether in jest.

'You look terrible, Francis,' she said, leading me into the house.

'This was not the homecoming I intended. There are presents in my trunk—'

'Never mind the presents. You are for bed. I knew you had been neglecting yourself all this time in that wretched country.'

Her nagging words as I climbed the stairs to our chamber, its walls and furniture so welcome to me, and undressed were like balm on burnt skin. I had longed for that kind of attention all the time I was alone in Paris, though so many men would be glad not to have to endure such badgering. I had discovered that the married state is far preferable to being a bachelor. A man yearns for the comfort only a woman can bring.

I was fortunate in that I was left alone to recuperate. Ursula, I discovered later, wrote to Cecil to inform him that I had returned safely from France but that my health was too precarious for me to take up any duties at present. However, she added, she knew the good service I had done the Queen in France would not go unremembered and that I would be at the foremost of his and Elizabeth's thoughts for a post in England as soon as I was well again. She did not tell me of this letter at the time because she knew I would have instructed her not to send it. A man must not go begging to his master, or in this case, mistress. But it seemed that a wife could. Such is the way of women, we know. They can beguile and manipulate to their heart's content and everyone simply nods their head and says such is the way of women. All the same, when I learnt of her mild blackmail, I thanked her. Her sentiments were indeed the same as mine.

Ursula ensured I stayed in bed for at least a month and I made no protest for I felt truly weary. Towards the end of the month, when I had begun to feel better, I longed for activity, to rise from my bed and at least dress and use my legs again. Ursula allowed me to move to her parlour, where she stuffed cushions behind my back as I sat in the most comfortable chair, laid a blanket over my legs and never let the fire die down. She also reluctantly allowed me to peruse my correspondence which had accumulated to become a very high pile. She only relented because she could no longer stand my complaining that my mind was stagnating.

The correspondence was mostly from well-wishers who had heard of my return to England, but amongst these were letters I welcomed more than all the rest. These letters were from Cecil and Leicester. These were the men upon whom I was relying, and Leicester delivered the news that was surely the best remedy for my ill health. I was to serve the Queen in the capacity of Principal Secretary to the Privy Council.

By December 1573, my health had been fully restored or as fully restored as it was ever likely to be. For a month or more, Ursula had been making arrangements with her seamstresses and the goldsmith, ensuring that I would not be embarrassed by her appearance when she accompanied me to court for my swearing-in as Principal Secretary. She would show me the bills for their services and I would frown and shake my head at the expense but she told me to be quiet, she must needs have new dresses and jewels. She insisted that I too had new clothes, but she could not persuade me to wear anything other than black, though she tried extremely hard, showing me bolts of red velvet and grey watered silk and exclaiming how well they would look. As if such things could tempt me! My silver buttons, I did allow, and I told her they would have to satisfy.

'But the Queen likes her courtiers to be well dressed,' she protested. 'You do not see the Earl of Leicester dressed in such dreary colours, do you?'

'My dear, I am not the Earl of Leicester,' I pointed out. 'I think the Queen would think the worst of me if I were to dress like a popinjay.' I do not mean to suggest that the Earl was a popinjay. No, he always dressed with taste, even if that taste were a little too gaudy for me, just that as a noble, he had a right and an expectation to uphold. The same could not be said of me. 'I am to be her secretary and secretaries dress like this.' I gestured at my black doublet and hose.

Ursula tutted and shook her head but said no more. I did not bother to say that once the ceremony was over even the silver buttons would be taken off my doublet and put back in their drawer.

We reached the Palace of Whitehall where the ceremony was to be held in good time. Ursula enjoyed sweeping past all the others who waited in the corridors and Presence Chamber, hoping to be admitted in to see Her Majesty or even catch the eye of an earl or knight who could help them with their petition or offer them a position in their household.

A page bearing Leicester's badge of the bear and ragged staff came over to us and made a bow. Ursula and I looked at one another, wondering what he wanted, but then he told us that the Earl said he was to take us through to the Privy Council chamber. I turned to Ursula, thinking that she would have to remain behind in the Presence Chamber, but the page said no, my wife was to accompany me. I thought this could only have been Leicester's doing, knowing as he did how much Ursula wanted to see and hear everything.

The Privy Council chamber was a room just a short walk from the Presence Chamber. The page opened the Council door and I could see inside a long table covered with a Turkey carpet and littered with papers, inkpots and quills, as well as a few cups and plates of sweet mouthfuls. There were chairs all along the table and in two of them sat Cecil and Leicester, talking earnestly. They ceased as soon as the door opened. Leicester saw me and, his face breaking into the grin the Queen found so fascinating, rose from his seat and held out both his hands. He was ever courteous and he bowed elegantly to Ursula and kissed her hand before he acknowledged me.

'Francis, come in,' he said, 'and your lovely wife.'

Cecil was getting to his feet as we both edged our way hesitatingly into the Council chamber. It was smaller than I had imagined. 'Francis, good morning,' Cecil said, extending his hand. 'And good day to you, Mistress Walsingham. An important day for your husband.'

'For us both, Lord Burghley,' she corrected, and I remember thinking that she should hold her tongue, but Cecil didn't seem to mind or even notice.

'Indeed,' he agreed. 'Well, the Earl and I thought we would have you in here before the ceremony, show you where the business of governing the country happens—'

'Oh, don't be so pompous, Cecil,' Leicester said with a laugh. 'Here is where the dirty business happens,' he gestured with his hands at the room and laughed. 'Do not be fooled, Francis. Here is where Her Majesty's ministers argue all day about the best way to govern her kingdom and maintain good relations with her allies and even better relations with her enemies.'

'Really, my lord,' Cecil said with a sigh, though he did not say any more. I knew that though both men were friends to me, they had been fierce rivals for many years, and though they had become so used to one another as to have established a mutually agreeable working relationship, they would never admit to having a liking for one another.

'You will be sitting here,' Leicester said, placing his hands on the chair to the left of the table. 'On your right is where Cecil sits, preeminent.' Cecil rolled his eyes at Leicester's teasing. 'The Queen does not often attend Council meetings, but when she does, she sits there,' Leicester pointed to the far end of the table, 'and if anyone is already sitting there, then we all have to move down a place.'

Cecil took over. 'You will be required to be present at every Council meeting, wherever it may be held, and you will have rooms in each palace alloted to you. I should warn you that you will be expected to be available whatever the hour of the day or night. The Queen does not always keep sensible hours.'

I threw a look at Ursula, wondering if she had anything to say about this, but she looked back at me without query. She knew that the life of a servant to the sovereign was anything but predictable and she would go with the ebb and flow of royal service as was necessary. As I say, I have had many reasons to be grateful for such a wife.

There was a bustle out in the corridor, the sound of many skirts swishing, of heels tapping on bare floorboards and then softer taps as they passed over rush matting.

'Here she is,' Leicester said, hurrying out, and we heard him greet Elizabeth.

'Where have you been?' we heard her say and Leicester answer that he had been looking over Her Majesty's horses and welcoming her new secretary.

'Well, let us get on with it, then,' Elizabeth said.

'Shall we go?' Cecil asked, out of courtesy rather than suggestion for he made his way immediately out into the corridor, following after the Queen and her entourage.

Ursula's eyes widened at me as she picked up her skirts and we hurried after him. In the distance, I could see the head and shoulders of the Queen, Leicester at her side, and then they disappeared into a room on the left.

'Where are we going?' Ursula whispered, though loudly enough for Cecil to hear.

'The Privy Chamber,' he said, not slowing his stride, 'for your husband's swearing-in.'

The Privy Chamber is reserved for only those who have the privilege of a private audience with the Queen and an audience there demonstrates their status. There were a number of courtiers present, mostly those, I discovered later, who were to be my colleagues on the Privy Council.

I was manoeuvred into position by one of Cecil's clerks before the small dais upon which Queen Elizabeth now stood. I could smell her perfume and it was a fragrance I was to become very familiar with. Elizabeth held a parchment up to her eyes, so close that from where I was now kneeling, I could not see any part of her top half save her ruff sticking out either side. She read out the oath of a privy counsellor and at the end of all the promises I was to make — not to reveal anything said at meetings, that I was to openly speak my mind in Her Majesty's best interests and that I was at all times to serve her to the utmost — she declared, 'So help you God', to which I sincerely replied 'Amen.'

And it was done. I was sworn in as a member of the Privy Council.

CHAPTER 13

Looking back, it feels to me as if the years after the massacre were peaceful ones for England, if not for myself. Relations between our God-favoured country and those in Europe were settled for the most part. It was almost as if the massacre at Paris had exhausted the papists' desire for blood.

This is not to say that I had little to do, quite the contrary. I was extremely busy with the Queen's business and my own. Perhaps the most notable difference was that as Secretary, I was now in the presence of the Queen daily. Some might ask if she is truly as magnificent as she appears. I can answer truthfully she is not. I do not say so to insult her. None of us can be magnificent to those with whom we consort each day. We see each other in our foulest of moods, and yes, in our best, at our strangest and at our most vulnerable. We cannot always disguise our pettiness or our idiosyncrasies. We are all made of clay, even princes. Elizabeth is no exception. She is brilliant in mind for a woman, indeed she is, but she has also all the vanities of woman and is capricious and revengeful. I cannot claim to be a connoisseur of beauty, but she is no more beautiful than the next woman, and in some cases, far less. I am conscious I sound as if I dislike her. I do not. *She* dislikes *me*, though, I know this. I do not let it trouble me. Elizabeth knows well the good service I have done her and knows too that none other would have performed it more faithfully than I. The truth is, I do not need Elizabeth to like me.

Indeed, favour is a disadvantage. I saw how Leicester was entrapped by her favour, kept a bachelor for decades by the Queen's jealousy, not permitted to marry openly nor enjoy the fruits of marriage, but forced to hide his secret wife until his trespass was exposed. Often, I would listen to him bemoan his situation and he had my every sympathy.

But Francis, you chide me, what were you doing all these years? My answer is that I was busy discovering the men and women who would keep Elizabeth and England safe. This was, of course, in addition to the work I performed daily as Principal Secretary. It is quite astonishing how much correspondence, how much paperwork, there was, there is, and it all must be sifted through, evaluated, dealt with. When I took over the position of Principal Secretary, I had three clerks to assist me, but this left so much correspondence unread that I increased this number to five, at my own expense for the Queen refused for their salaries to come out of the privy purse. I considered it to be money well spent, for who knew what in the unread letters and reports might be of the greatest import to the security of the nation? Fortunately, my share in the Muscovy Company, formed through my first wife's contacts, meant that I had a steady if unremarkable income from trading ventures, and whilst I was inevitably in debt, I ask you, what gentleman is not? I was not so deeply in debt as others who must keep up appearances, maintain retinues and strive to impress the Queen. Leicester was one such and I often commiserated with him over the expense he had to go to in order to maintain his estate and influence.

It is appropriate that I now write in greater detail of my relationship with the Earl of Leicester. Indeed, it was to him that I owed much of my success in my new role. He was, like me, fiercely Protestant. Many think it odd that such a man, one so full of show and extravagance, should be so strong in a faith that advocates simplicity and humility, but the two are not incompatible, I have found. His own show of finery, his fondness for the pleasures of food and drink did not mitigate his faith one jot. Indeed, his faith was often the one point of contention between himself and the Queen. In Council, the Earl would speak up for fellow Protestants, propose action against Catholics, necessary action, and the Queen would tell him to be quiet, that she would not listen to him. And yet he would persist, which is far more than many of my fellow counsellors felt compelled or indeed powerful enough to do. Leicester was often deputed by the Council to do our dirty work, to tell the Queen what we all knew she would not want to hear, simply because we knew that she would not be angry for long at her dear sweet Robin as she would with the rest of us. Often, Leicester would come out of her chamber after delivering some unwelcome news with a deep frown on his brow, his cheeks flushed red from where he had had to endure some fresh insult Elizabeth had hurled at him, and yet he would do it all without rancour or resentment, without disliking us more cowardly counsellors who dared not face the Queen in all her wrath. It has often pained me that the Earl was so hated during his lifetime. If ever a man did not deserve such ill feeling, it was he.

The situation that troubled me most in the years immediately after my appointment as secretary was the man William Allen and his 'disciples'.

William Allen was an Englishman who had had all the promise of a good church career. He had been a canon at York Minster during Queen Mary's reign but had refused to take the Oath of Supremacy when Elizabeth had acceded to the throne. The Oath of Supremacy had become law during King Henry VIII's reign and was taken to acknowledge that the monarch was the Supreme Head of the Church in England. Mary Tudor, loyal to the Pope, had repealed this law. Elizabeth had had it reinstated and every person who occupied a public office, as well as churchmen and those at universities, had to swear the oath.

As I say, Allen refused to take the oath. Despite this, he had, unwisely, in my opinion, been allowed to stay at his university in Oxford. Allen was allowed to remain at liberty despite his refusal to take the oath and then even made very public proclamations and announcements against the English church. It never ceases to amaze me how ungrateful Catholics are.

At last, my predecessors on the Council decided enough was enough and began making it uncomfortable for him to remain in England so that he had to resign all the offices he held in the English church. He decided to run away to the Continent. He went first to Louvain, there joining many other Englishmen and women who too had refused to take the oath. He took to his self-appointed mission of destroying the English Protestant church with alacrity. He had the audacity to return to England a year after leaving to try to convince faithful Englishmen and women of the so-called error of their ways and that they should return to the Catholic church. He tried to persuade people that they should not attend Protestant services and should endure the fines and seizures of properties that would follow as a consequence. It seems that it was during this time that Allen decided in his addled mind that we were forced to act as Protestants, not that we did so willingly, and that we were only waiting for the Pope and his Catholic allies to free us from the tyranny of Elizabeth's rule and we would happily become Catholic. As I say, he was a deluded ingrate.

Allen went back to the Continent, happily freeing us from his pestilential Catholic breath, and set up a seminary in Douai, which was under Spanish rule, and which he called the English College. Its aims, according to Allen, was to accord dispossessed English Catholics the opportunity to continue their studies and worship how they wished. This seems laudable enough, I grant you, but what Allen was actually doing was assembling a veritable army of Englishmen who could one day return to their native land and attempt a wholesale conversion of the people back to Catholicism. According to the reports we received, English Catholic exiles flocked to him, including Edmund Campion, of whom I will write later. This English College was nothing more than a nest of sedition where young men were inculcated with the popish heresy and then sent over to England to spread disaffection, discontent and rebellion. This was aided by the Bull the Pope made in 1571, announcing it was no crime nor sin to murder Elizabeth as she was a heretic and usurper of the rightful monarch, Mary Stuart. This gave English Catholics all the incentive they needed to attempt to commit regicide. Fortunately, very few took up the task.

No, it was the Jesuit priests who began infesting our island that occupied much of my time during these years. Regrettably, there were still many prominent families, especially in the middle and north of England, who adhered to the Catholic faith and they provided a sanctuary for these priests. The Council as a whole were very worried about this development and employed men to seek these priests out, wherever they were, and deal with them. This was no easy task for very quickly the families who provided shelter for these men took steps to hide the priests and fashioned spaces within the walls of their homes and beneath their floors. These holes the priests would squeeze into when they heard the knock on the door of the Council's priest-takers and if they were very fortunate, or the Council's men not very thorough, they could escape their clutches.

This was a murky business and one I had little stomach for. I knew that torture was common practice in both France and Spain. There, warrants were not even needed for the apprehension of malefactors. The capturers of their heretics and prisoners were free to do whatever they wanted to the poor souls without having to gain permission from the sovereign. In England, things are different. We do not torture willy-nilly nor without recourse to law. If torture is required, the Council must issue a warrant for it and then only in matters of security of the country.

But often, the Council did give their permission. The priests who were found were then imprisoned and put to torture to extract information about any plots that were being planned. I do not say that these priests should not have been discovered and imprisoned, far from it. They were and are a cancer that needs to be cut out of our kingdom. No, my distaste for their treatment was that such a methodology yielded so few results. Torture is a strange beast. It can be effective in getting a prisoner to talk, but I question whether the information got out of them is true. Men will swear to anything under threat of the rack or the thumb-screws; they will swear that their mothers coupled with the devil when a hot iron is pressed against their naked flesh. Often, the threat of torture is far more effective. Show a man the rack and his horror of the device will be enough to open his mouth. And, of course, there is less risk of the man dying from his racking. A dead man is of no use to anyone. A live man to whom one shows mercy is far more valuable. He can be turned, persuaded that he is working for the wrong party, that he would do better, live longer, have a more comfortable life if he were to work for you. So many men do turn against their masters and begin to work for their former enemies.

I helped to turn many of these men. And then we sent them back to Douai or whatever hellhole they had come from to breed discontent amongst their own kind. And this was so very easy to do. The English College had as many factions as it had relics, it seemed. My contacts abroad kept me very well informed about what was happening on the Continent. The English College held Catholics of several nationalities, not just the English, and this would often cause conflicts that had nothing to do with religion but everything to do with country. Thus, we could not only spread disaffection amongst Catholics by infiltrating their ranks but also cause problems of political natures. This has always been my solution: do not torture unless absolutely necessary, do not execute for fear of creating martyrs and send back a troublesome man to cause trouble for your enemies rather than for you.

During my early years as Principal Secretary to the Council, my biggest problem was Mary Stuart and it was what the English Catholics would do to put her on the throne instead of Elizabeth that was my chief concern.

By this time, Mary Stuart had been in England for several years, kept in various houses that belonged to the nobility, under house arrest ever since she had foolishly crossed the border from her own country when her throne was taken from her and believing that Elizabeth would aid her with shelter, money and men to take it back.

When it happened, Mary Stuart delivering herself into Elizabeth's hands must have seemed a boon to the Council, but it soon became clear that having Mary in England created far more problems than it solved. Much of the Mary Stuart problem stemmed from Elizabeth, who simply would not make up her mind what to do with her troublesome cousin. At one time, Elizabeth was minded to help Mary go back to Scotland, at another she realised it was better to keep Mary's half-brother, the Earl of Moray, acting as regent, for he was a Protestant and someone we could do business with. But there was one point Elizabeth was steadfast upon. Despite the urging by many of her counsellors, including Leicester, that she have the damned woman's head off and thereby be done with her altogether, Elizabeth simply would not countenance it. I am not entirely clear about her reasons for not wishing to take this step. I believe she was worried about retribution from the other Catholic heads of state, and from God himself. I suppose these were not wholly unjustified fears. But I still think she dallied too long and should have had Mary's head much earlier. Doing so would have removed Mary as a potential rival claimant for the English throne.

I have checked my records and note that Mary Stuart emerged as a serious problem for Cecil and myself in May of 1574. Cecil called me to his office, which was next door to mine, and after gesturing at a chair for me to sit upon, slid a paper across to me.

'Read that,' he said peremptorily.

I did so, noting that it had been written by the Earl of Moray's principal secretary, my counterpart in Scotland. He was informing Cecil that an arrest had been made of a young man named Steward who claimed to be in the employ of Mary Stuart as a courier, delivering messages to her from her friends in the north of England. After questioning, this Steward gave up the name of his English contact.

'Alexander Hamilton,' I read aloud.

'You know who he is?' Cecil asked.

I thought for a moment. I had taken the trouble to memorise the names of the most prominent men in the north of England and I now searched my memory. The name did nudge a small memory but it was proving elusive. Cecil, growing impatient, provided the answer.

'Tutor to the Earl of Shrewsbury's children.'

It should have been obvious to me, of course. Since 1569, the Earl of Shrewsbury had had the misfortune to have the custody of Mary Stuart. He was wealthy enough and had many houses but it was no honour to have to keep the woman under house arrest. Mary insisted, and Elizabeth allowed, on having a court and courtiers to attend on her, just as if she still had a country to rule over. All this came at no small cost. Cecil, I knew, was a good friend to Shrewsbury's wife, Bess Talbot, and had often received letters from her bemoaning how much was being spent on Mary's welfare and how Elizabeth made little or no contribution to her upkeep. Cecil would sympathise but there was nothing he could do. Elizabeth was ever wont to keep her purse strings tied, as all of her servants knew.

'The Shrewsburys are loyal to the Queen,' I said.

'I agree,' Cecil nodded, 'but there have been rumours. I daresay you know of them?'

Cecil knew that, like him, I had my own people feeding me

information and he was correct. I had heard the rumours that the Earl was more than merely solicitous towards Mary Stuart, that he was lenient, even friendly, with her, and that he was incurring the wrath of his wife who suspected him of slipping between Mary Stuart's sheets, even under her own roof. Knowing of Mary Stuart's reputed charms, I thought it possible that the Earl had so far forgot himself to be swiving the woman, but there was no real evidence, only Bess's suspicions.

'The rumours are unfounded, as far as I can tell.'

'Perhaps, but that it is being spoken of at all is worrying, do you not think?'

He wanted me to agree with him. 'People will always talk,' I said instead.

'And we are thankful for it else how would we know what is happening in the country?'

'Is there any suggestion that the Earl of Shrewsbury is communicating with the Stuart woman's friends on her behalf or is this Alexander Hamilton acting alone?'

'That is what I want you to find out,' Cecil said. 'This Steward lad's claims must be investigated. I can leave the matter in your hands?'

'You can,' I assured him.

I left him to return to my office and bade one of my clerks take up his pen. I had him write to the Earl of Shrewsbury to tell him he must arrange for Alexander Hamilton to be conveyed to London so he could be questioned. I pondered where the questioning should take place, then decided as the matter had so little evidence save for the word of a frightened boy, it should be as informal as could be. I instructed that Hamilton was to present himself to me at the Palace of Whitehall at no later than a week's time.

The interrogation was to prove a disappointment. Hamilton arrived at the palace within five days, having evidently hurried hither, and stated his position as a loyal servant to Queen Elizabeth and that he had no knowledge of the Steward boy. He was vehement in his denials and demanded evidence from me that he was involved. I could produce none, of course, save for the boy's claim. Without anything to corroborate the accusation, I was thwarted. Hamilton maintained his innocence and I was forced to let him go and deliver a negative report to Cecil.

'I am glad there appears to be nothing in it,' Cecil said. 'I would not like to have to take action against the Earl. His wife would never let me hear the end of it.'

'I believe we should not be complacent, my lord,' I said carefully. 'We know that Mary Stuart communicates with her supporters freely—'

'You intercept everything she writes and receives, do you not?'

'Of course, those letters that I know about, but her friends open up new channels of communication and it takes time to discover them. She may be receiving letters we do not yet know of. I believe it would be wise not to dismiss Hamilton altogether and to keep an ever-vigilant eye on the management of the Earl's safekeeping of the Stuart woman.'

'Perhaps you are right,' Cecil conceded grudgingly. 'I'll leave it to you, but be discreet, Master Secretary.'

I told him I knew no other way to be.

Meanwhile, I was making efforts to ensure that the Reformation which Elizabeth's great father had brought to England continued to journey towards its natural conclusion. This was not always the easiest of tasks, mostly because of Elizabeth. Although never a Catholic, Elizabeth has a fondness for some of their ways. She likes to have candles lit in her chapel, for instance, and have a large gold cross mounted on her altar, quite contrary to the teaching she had been brought up in. These fancies of hers are but small things, I grant you, but her tendencies also had larger consequences, which often threatened to thwart the Council's attempts to root out Catholicism in England wherever it was skulking.

Those of us on Elizabeth's Council who were particularly keen on the Reformation pushing forward, and by this I mean not only myself but the Earl of Leicester, and yes, Cecil to a certain extent, that extent being only when his personal convictions did not put him at odds with the Queen, made our convictions tangible by patronising those men who were minded like ourselves and who would have the most influence in the country at large. Leicester, for his part, acted as patron for theologians and artists alike and put money into ventures that would expand

England's interests and influence abroad. I was not in a position financially to do as much as Leicester, nor was I ever asked to being only a gentleman and not a noble, but I did what I could. I acted as patron to preachers and writers of theology, indeed any writer who would ably promote Protestantism and denounce Catholicism, and I also arranged appointments in the universities and in the church that would be valuable. One such appointment was extremely difficult to arrange and this was because of Elizabeth. It is strange, is it not, that Elizabeth, who is, shall I say, flexible when it comes to matters of religion, should have men about her whose beliefs are steadfast and often contrary to her own? This has caused many problems over the years that I have served her.

In May of 1575, Matthew Parker, the Archbishop of Canterbury, who was disappointingly moderate in his beliefs, died and so presented myself and Cecil with the opportunity to put a more radical man in his place. We wanted Edmund Grindal to be appointed. He was then the Archbishop of York and had been, like myself, self-exiled during Mary Tudor's reign. Like me, he had promptly returned when Elizabeth became queen. Yet, despite this loyalty to her, Elizabeth prevaricated over ratifying the appointment. Grindal was too extreme, she said, always wanting to act rather than simply doing his duty as archbishop. Cecil and I protested greatly that his loyalty to her demanded that he be given Canterbury, but Elizabeth waved us away, saying we only wanted Grindal to serve our own ends. Cecil and I both agreed that we would not let the matter drop. 'Grindal is our man,' Cecil said, 'and we will have him where we want him.'

So, we kept on at Elizabeth, refusing to suggest any other man for the post and always putting Grindal's name forward. It took months, almost seven in fact, before Elizabeth relented and appointed Grindal Archbishop of Canterbury. Elizabeth may be queen but even a monarch has to listen to advisers and act on their advice. A monarch never rules alone.

Grindal acted as we hoped and quickly. Some Catholic practices still lingered in the Protestant church services and Grindal set to work removing them. He put his weight behind the recusancy laws, the laws which imposed penalties on those who refused to abide by the workings of the Anglican faith, insisting that they needed to be tightened up so Catholics were unable to wriggle out of legal loopholes. And it was to Grindal that we owe the publication of the Geneva Bible, a book that had been close to my heart for some time. This Bible was pure, far more pure than the version then favoured by most of the English clergy, and it was my hope that it would become the only Bible in the land. I recommended a printer I knew, one Christopher Barker, to be the man who would print the new editions of the Geneva Bible. His printing press was in St Paul's Churchyard and he was proud enough of my patronage to use my heraldic device as his shop sign. I was not a little proud of this myself. The books Barker produced were exceptional. No trace of Catholic practices was to be found in any of their pages. It was certainly an endeavour to be proud of.

If only Elizabeth had thought so. For some odd reason, she disliked anything that came out of Geneva, saying that Genevan teachings led to discontent amongst the populace, which would only lead to rebellion. She would then go on to cite examples of religious rebellion that her predecessors had to deal with, the Pilgrimage of Grace during her father's reign, for example, and she was wary of such an event happening to threaten her. I would agree that such an eventuality was possible but believed the risk was worth taking.

Elizabeth did not agree. And she struck out at me through my own brother-in-law. Peter Wentworth had married my sister Elizabeth. He shared my beliefs and opinions and I knew him to be one of the best of men. He was a member of Parliament and made a speech in February of 1576 that made me immensely proud to be associated with him. Peter attacked the Queen for inhibiting Parliament in its ability for members to speak their mind without fear of the monarch's retribution. Often, he said, the Queen would send a message to the House telling a speaker to stop talking about a particular subject or to propose something that the Queen favoured. This, he protested, was directly against the freedom of Parliament. I was there, in the House, the day he delivered this speech, and I can tell you, he was talking to an unnaturally quiet audience. I think they could not believe that someone would dare to say such things, to dare to tell the truth, in fact. That shows just how much influence the monarch has over Parliament, something that they should not. Peter went even further, saying that, 'Her Majesty hath committed great faults,' and even I wondered if he should leave it at that. But on he went. Peter never did know when to leave well enough alone.

Elizabeth, when she heard of his words, was enraged. She ordered me into her presence.

'Cannot you control that damned brother-in-law of yours?' she demanded before I had even finished my bow.

I had just come from the House and was feeling proud of Peter, so I confess, did not take too kindly to having this remark hurled at me.

'I am not my brother-in-law's keeper,' I replied. 'A Member of Parliament is at liberty to speak his mind.'

'Speak his mind?' Elizabeth spat. 'Speak his mind, you black-eyed toad? I will not have men speaking their minds when their minds are against me.'

'If you will forgive me, madam, Peter Wentworth is not against you, far from it, but he is *for* Parliament.'

'Do not wordplay with me, Master Walsingham,' she sneered. 'He spoke against me, against my rights as a sovereign, denounced me in my own damn Parliament.'

I started to protest, to put forward the tenet that an MP in the House has the right to free speech, but she cut me off.

'You put him up to it, didn't you, you and Cecil? Told him what to say, didn't you? Well, I won't have it, you hear me? You keep your Puritan thoughts to yourself and do not presume to tell me what I should do. And as for Wentworth, have him arrested.'

My mouth fell open. 'Madam, you cannot!'

'Cannot! Cannot!' Her eyes blazed. 'I can do whatever the hell I like, little man. I say have Wentworth arrested and despatch him to the Tower at once. And as for your friend Archbishop Grindal. You can tell him that I will have no more of his Puritan sermons. They make my people discontented. They will cease. You will write to him and tell him so.'

She dismissed me with a savage wave of her arm towards the door. One of her ladies held it open for me. I wandered out into the corridor feeling mentally bruised. I knew Elizabeth could be fierce in her anger, but up to now, her anger had never been directed at me. I had witnessed Leicester feel its full force, even Cecil on one occasion. Now, I knew how it felt.

I had no choice, of course, but to order Peter's arrest and the poor man, for his outspokenness, languished a whole month in the Tower of London. I had his wife, my sister, at The Papey during his confinement, and every day had to endure her weeping and her accusations that I was doing nothing to persuade Elizabeth to set him free. I did try, whenever I had the chance, but my sister saw none of my efforts. I was confident, however, that Peter would be released eventually. Elizabeth had no law supporting her decision to arrest him and she would not risk arousing the wrath of Parliament, so he was freed. I had him conveyed to my house to recover from his ordeal and to be reunited with his wife. In truth, Peter had not fared too badly during his imprisonment, I had seen to that. He had not been placed in a dungeon but in a well-lit and well-aired chamber where the damp did not penetrate and he had not lacked for comfort. But imprisonment is counter to man's very breath of life and no matter how comfortable he is made, prison would suit no man well. He ate heartily at my table and stayed for three nights, but he was as eager as I for him and his wife to return home. I asked him if he intended speaking out so fiercely again, half in jest but half in truth, and Peter said he did not know. For his sake, I bid him be more temperate in his language, but he gave me a look that I knew only too well and said he would do so only if his conscience allowed it.

Grindal proved more difficult to censure than Peter. He received Elizabeth's command that he cease making radical sermons and supporting other radical preachers with voluble anger. He wrote a letter to Elizabeth in which he did not show due deference nor flatter her vanity. So many of the letters that crossed my desk were full of flattery, to Elizabeth the woman as much as to Elizabeth the Queen, simply because her courtiers and other subjects knew flattery was the best way to her heart. But Grindal was not one of her courtiers or her sycophants and he spoke his mind or rather wrote his mind. He warned her that if she did not support the continuance of the Reformation, that if she turned away from God, that God would turn away from her and she would face a miserable Judgement Day.

Elizabeth was beside herself with rage. She could not believe that a man could be so impudent as to write to her in such language. He was a wretch, a cur, a miscreant, an insolent beast to have done so. She wanted him to be sent to the Tower but

Grindal was more fortunate than Peter had been. Grindal had the church on his side and Elizabeth found she could not do as she wanted with him. Grindal was not a nobody. He occupied one of the greatest church offices in England. By opposing Grindal, Elizabeth was in danger of opposing Protestantism altogether. And as Cecil said to me one evening after a particularly stormy Council meeting at which Elizabeth had presided to vent her fury, such opposition would give heart to every Catholic monarch in Europe, who would take the opportunity to persuade Elizabeth of the error of her ways and convert her to popery, not to mention the English Catholics who would also take advantage.

No, Elizabeth simply could not be allowed to confer harsh punishment on Grindal. Cecil was with me on this and Leicester, too, though he wanted to stay very much in the background of this particular matter as he had other, personal matters on his mind at this point. Elizabeth wanted to take away Grindal's archbishopric, but that would have met with staunch opposition from his colleagues in the church. In the end, as is often the way with Elizabeth, a compromise of sorts was reached. Grindal was forbidden from carrying out his duties as archbishop but he retained his office. Most unsatisfactory as far as myself and Cecil were concerned, but we could hope for no more from Elizabeth. Perhaps I should have been stronger and stood up for Grindal. Perhaps. But what is done is done.

At the start of the year 1575, the matter of Alexander Hamilton reared its head again. I had been keeping a close watch on that particular man's activities since I had questioned him the previous year.

One of the Scottish regent's men had managed to get his hands on a letter written by the Bishop of Ross and had sent it on to me, believing quite rightly that its contents would be of interest. The contents were fearful to me. Hamilton, it turned out, had been just one man in a much bigger network of communication that served Mary Stuart and the heart of the network was operating right under my nose in London. A bookseller, one Henry Cockyn, was its centre. It was at his shop that letters were collected and sent on to their intended recipients. One of those recipients was Lord Henry Howard, brother to the

Duke of Norfolk. I ordered the arrest of Henry Cockyn and had him taken to the Tower. When I informed Cecil what I was about, he suggested a particularly unpleasant cell at the Tower and was surprised when I said I intended him for the Baynard Tower.

'Is that not too good a place for this man?' he said, raising a bushy white eyebrow at me.

'I do not see the advantage of placing him in discomfort.'

'Discomfort makes men talk.'

'If you'll forgive me, my lord, discomfort often makes men say anything, not all of it the truth. And Cockyn, from what I hear, is one of such a nature that any kind of physical pressure will make him even more obstinate and reluctant to talk.'

Cecil eyed me curiously. 'Well, I suppose you know what you're doing. But if you don't get anything out of him, then I shall expect you to reconsider your methods.'

It took a few weeks, but my method proved correct. I believed that Cockyn did not act for the Queen of Scots out of any deep affection or loyalty but because he was paid to do so by the Bishop of Ross, and that a promise of payment from us would be all that was needed to turn him to our cause. I was proved right. He readily admitted he was paid to receive and send on letters between Mary Stuart and her supporters and that one of his contacts was Alexander Hamilton. Hamilton had lied to me. But that was not all, there was more to come. Hamilton did not work alone in the Earl of Shrewsbury's household. He had accomplices amongst the other servants. I immediately sent out warrants for the arrest of these men so named and they were delivered up to the Tower. But my efforts were to be all in vain. Elizabeth refused to take the matter seriously.

'What does it matter if Lord Henry Howard corresponds with Mary?' she said, shrugging her bony shoulder at me. 'The two of them can do no harm.'

'But it is not just Lord Henry, madam,' I protested. 'There is an entire network of men working with Mary Stuart. Who knows what they are saying to one another?'

'Quite, Master Secretary, who knows?' she said. 'They may be discussing the price of wool, for all you know, or the best cure for a bad back.'

'They are not discussing such things,' I almost snarled and

she raised both her eyebrows at me. I reined in my anger. 'With the greatest of respect, madam, any communication between Mary Stuart and her supporters has the potential to do harm to you. Mary Stuart is a great plotter—'

'Of course, she is,' Elizabeth snapped. 'What else has she to do but plot and conspire my death? She has nothing else to occupy her.'

'Then—'

'Oh, stop pestering me, Master Secretary. I will not be made to think on matters that are not important.'

'Not important,' I spluttered, incredulous.

'Not now,' she said. 'You will leave.'

I was ushered quickly out of the room.

So, I was powerless to do anything useful. I was forbidden to act. And meanwhile, Mary's agents went about their business unhindered, and about their devilish business they certainly did go. Another of Shrewsbury's servants, one Thomas Morgan, realised the Council was on his tail and took advantage of Elizabeth's dithering to escape to Paris. There, he openly became useful to the Archbishop of Glasgow, being made responsible for Mary Stuart's finances and other affairs, and acting as a conduit for any supporter of Mary to get in touch with her.

This put me at my wit's end. Because of Elizabeth's decision, or rather lack of decision to act against the infestation in Shrewsbury's household, the most important people in the Stuart network had managed to elude our clutches and become even more dangerous to us. I got no sympathy from Cecil, who so often favoured a wait-and-see policy like Elizabeth, and so voiced my anger to Ursula.

'*She* is responsible for Morgan getting away, Elizabeth. No one else. Now, he is at liberty to make trouble in whatever European court he decides to visit.'

A pain knifed me in my stomach and my hand went reflexively to clutch at my side. I saw Ursula's eyes narrow, but she did not bother to ask me what ailed me. She knew I suffered such pain ever since my return from France.

'Why did she do nothing? You told her of the dangers, did you not?'

'I told her, Leicester told her...' I threw up my hands, 'she just would not listen.' The pain receded a little and I sank down into my chair, which Ursula had stuffed with cushions. 'I don't know if I can go on, Ursula.'

'What does that mean?' she asked, her voice hard, all trace of sympathy and softness gone.

I sighed. 'It means I'm thinking of leaving the Queen's service.'

'Because of this?' Her tone was incredulous.

'You think I'm being ridiculous, but you do not see what I have to put up with, you don't experience it as I do.'

'I hear your complaints,' she reminded me as if it was the same, 'and I have heard this from you before, my dear.'

'This is different.'

'Is it? Sounds the same to me.'

'You have no sympathy for me?'

She smoothed her skirts. 'Francis, I understand the Queen is difficult. I understand that you have to deal with her moods and demands every day. But,' and she leant forward to ensure she had my full attention, 'what else would you do?'

She was right, of course. What else would I do? I had wanted to be in the Queen's service for so long. Now I was and it was failing to live up to my expectations.

'And just think,' Ursula continued, 'as a member of the Council, you have influence. Out of it, what would you have?'

'Nothing,' I admitted, resting my head on the back of the chair and rubbing at the spot where the pain lingered in my belly. 'Ignore me, Ursula, I am just having a moment of discontent with my lot.'

'I know,' and I heard the smile in her voice, 'and I am glad for your sake you have me to hear it.'

'I thank God for you every day.'

Her chair creaked familiarly as she leant back and resumed her stitching. I knew that Ursula was not only concerned I would be bored or find life outside the Council unsatisfactory; she was also worried about our finances if I had no good employment. There was the law, I supposed, although I had never practised it. Become a country squire? No, even I could not picture myself so. The Queen's service was what I had wanted and I had worked hard to achieve it. It gave me some power, influence and knowledge of the wider world. I might toy with the idea of giving it up, but I knew in my heart that I would never commit such a folly. England, and Elizabeth, needed me as much as I needed them.

A few years later, I was rewarded by Elizabeth for my services. I suspect Cecil's hand behind the matter, though; I doubt if Elizabeth would have thought to bestow an honour upon me without being persuaded to it first. From comments Cecil made at the time, I suspect my knighthood was as much to do with me being raised to a suitable rank to interact more ably with my peers than any recognition of my services, but I must not quibble over details. Yes, Elizabeth knighted me in December 1577 at Windsor Castle to my pleasure and Ursula's great joy. She had been the wife of a knight once and she was overjoyed to be one again.

'You see,' she said to me as she laid my black doublet away in the trunk, 'all that talk about the Queen not recognising what you do for her was all nonsense.'

'If you say so, my dear,' I replied, resting my head upon the pillow of our bed and closing my eyes. It had been a long day, and an exciting one, and I was tired.

'If I say so? How can you doubt it? The Queen does not give out knighthoods every day.' She sighed. 'Sir Francis Walsingham. It has a nice ring to it, do you not think?'

'Yes, it does,' I agreed and raised my head to look at her. I smiled. 'And now, will you come to bed, my lady?'

CHAPTER 14

In May 1574, King Charles of France died leaving his brother Henri, the Duke of Anjou, he of the predilection to wear women's clothing and mince with minions, to step into his shoes and accede to the throne. I would be ashamed to call such a man king, but then, that is the French for you.

The Anjou title consequently passed to the youngest of Catherine de Medici's sons, Francis. Francis was perhaps the oddest of the Medici's sons. He was small in stature and ugly, his skin having been scarred by smallpox suffered during his childhood. Perhaps it was his physical appearance that was the cause but his mother disliked him intensely and Francis knew it. He, for his part, disliked her and hated his brother, Henri, even more. Francis often found he was unwelcome at home in France and sought to find a home elsewhere. The one thing he wanted more than anything was to have a crown to put on his ugly head and he did not care which people that crown belonged to. In search of such a crown perhaps, he had allied himself to the Netherlanders, helping them to fight against the Spanish, although I suspect the French king saw an opportunity to be rid of his troublesome brother, maybe hoping that Francis would be killed in the fighting.

The unfortunate result of this peculiar alliance was that Francis was now considered by Elizabeth and Cecil to be a prime candidate for Elizabeth's hand. When I heard this news in Council, I was rendered speechless. I looked around the table at my fellow counsellors. Some faces registered shock; most registered resignation.

'A French marriage?' I queried, finding my voice at last.

'Indeed, Master Secretary,' Cecil said, steadily meeting my eye.

'Despite everything?'

'Of what do you speak?'

'Of what—? My lord, I speak of the massacre at Paris not three years hence.'

'That is, as you say, in the past. And the new holder of the Anjou dukedom played no part in that event.'

'Even so—,' I pleaded, appealing to the others around the table who merely looked between Cecil and myself. I found myself wishing that Leicester was present, for he would have been my ally in this, but he was away, visiting his country estate of Kenilworth. Did he know of this proposed marriage, I wondered?

'The Queen wishes us to open negotiations, Master Secretary,' Cecil said firmly, 'and we are here to serve Her Majesty in all things.'

None other around that table voiced their displeasure to Cecil, though afterwards, they said so privately to me. I wrote to Leicester immediately and waited impatiently for his reply. When it came, it soothed my troubled mind only a little. He was against the marriage but doubted that anything would come of it. '*We have been here so many times before, my friend,*' he wrote. '*Let Elizabeth play her game. She told me when she was eight years old that she would never marry and it has taken me this long to believe her.*' I was not as convinced as Leicester that the marriage negotiations were merely bargaining tools in a Protestant struggle against the Spanish, but I did not want to press him on the matter. Although I did not know the exact details at the time, I was aware that Leicester's journey away from court had been for a personal reason, not merely respite or business. Later, I was to learn that he had left court so he could marry his mistress, Lettice Knollys, in secret, which was why, I supposed, the Queen's marital intentions held little interest for him.

And so, we had a marriage to negotiate. It was ridiculous. Elizabeth was into her fourth decade by this time and her proposed bridegroom a young man in his early twenties. And what could he bring to the marriage? He had nothing but his dukedom and the support of the French king and his mother. What a boon for them if they could bring this marriage to a happy conclusion. They would be rid of Francis and have gained England as an ally.

Fortunately, I was not required to play a major role in the marriage negotiations, other foreign affairs taking up much of my time. With Elizabeth immovable on the question of the marriage negotiations, I confined my audiences with her to pursuing a policy of providing aid to the Netherlanders in their struggle against the Spanish. Leicester, back at court, added his voice to mine and together, we so contrived to be always putting this matter to the Queen, so that she had no peace. When she complained, we merely pressed the matter further. Cecil, on one occasion, took me aside into a window embrasure outside the Privy Council chamber and exhorted me to cease what he called my haranguing of the Queen on the matter of aid. 'Do you not see how it angers the Queen, Master Secretary?' he asked.

'Indeed I do, my lord,' I said, 'but I will not be silenced. Nor will the Earl of Leicester, I can assure you. If you will have your way with the Duke of Anjou, then I insist on having my way with the Netherlanders.'

I bowed my head and extricated myself from his presence. A few days later, Elizabeth summoned me.

I entered her privy chamber, my papers relating to the Netherlanders — letters from contacts there requesting aid to both myself and Leicester, how the finances could be managed, that sort of thing — beneath my arm, ready to endure another battle of words.

'Ah, my Moor, you look as sour as always.'

Elizabeth had started calling me Moor a few months earlier. She was wont to give people nicknames. Leicester was her Eyes, Cecil her Spirit, Sir Christopher Hatton, the Lord Chancellor, her Mutton, and I was her Moor. I was told it was because of the dark colour of my skin, although I also heard that it was a joke at my humour, or rather lack of it. Hatton, I knew, did not like his nickname; he said it made him sound common, but Leicester told him he had joined the ranks of a privileged few, those nicknamed by the Queen. Me? I did not care what Elizabeth called me as long as she listened to me.

'And yet I have good news.'

'Good news, madam?' I asked, annoyed by her remark and wondering what good news she could have for me.

'Will you not smile, sir?' she said, coming towards me, her thin lips twisting in a sardonic smile.

'Perhaps when I know what the good news is, madam,' I said.

She sighed and shook her head. 'I should make you promise me that smile, Walsingham.' She flopped down as much as her skirts would allow into her chair by the desk. Her long fingers spread papers over her desk until her eyes found the one she sought. She slid it out from the others and held it out to me.

I stepped forward and took it and yes, I smiled.

'And there it is. Ladies, look,' Elizabeth said, waving her hands at her ladies who were dotted around the room, 'my Moor can smile.'

'When there is good reason, madam,' I said over their titters, 'and I have good reason here.'

'I have done right, have I?' she asked, still amused by me. 'A bond for ten thousand pounds to be given to the Netherlanders to aid them in their struggle against Spain.'

'It is very well done, madam,' I said, folding up the paper and placing it inside my leather folder. 'I thank you for your wisdom in this matter.'

She rolled her eyes. 'Ah, yes, my wisdom, I thank you for your thanks. Now, you and Leicester can stop your incessant nagging.'

I did not argue with her on that for we had indeed nagged her.

'How soon will you give it to them?' she asked.

'I will have it despatched by the end of this day—,' I began.

'Did you not hear me, my Moor?' Elizabeth interrupted me. 'I asked when *you* will give it to them, not your messenger.'

'You mean—?'

'I mean for you to go to the Netherlands, my Moor, yes, indeed I do. Messengers are all very well and good, but that is a bond for rather a lot of my money. Dare you entrust it to a mere messenger? And will the Netherlanders know what to do with it when they have it? They must have instruction, Master Secretary, indeed they must. And what better man than you? You, who know what they need so well.'

So, this was to be my punishment for pursuing the giving of aid policy. I was to be sent abroad, out of court, out of her sight. My first thought was that it would indeed be a punishment to travel and my second that I should protest against the necessity. My third thought, however, was quite different. I would go and I would enjoy the chance to be away from court. I would see first-hand the situation in the Low Countries, I would talk to people directly rather than rely on second- or even third-hand accounts of conversations. And I was determined not to give Elizabeth the satisfaction of seeing me discomfited.

'Very well, madam, I shall take the bond myself, as you instruct. If you will give me leave, I shall return home and make the arrangements.'

The smile on Elizabeth's lead-painted face faltered a little, I think, but she recovered it well.

'See you do, my Moor. Safe journey.'

I enjoyed my travel to the Low Countries. The crossing was rough but I endured it well enough and recovered quickly once on land. The Netherlanders were enthusiastic about my coming and treated me, dare I say, royally. When I showed them the bond of ten thousand pounds, they were overjoyed and could not thank me enough. I enjoyed the Netherlanders' company and was convinced more than ever that it was God's will we were helping them rid their country of the Spanish menace. I left them in very good humour but also looking forward to coming home.

My joy was to be short-lived, however. I returned to England and the court only to be told by Cecil that Elizabeth had reconsidered her support for the Netherlanders and would now not be sending the money the bond promised. She had gone back on her word. I am sure you can imagine how I felt. Not sixty hours earlier, I had been assuring the Dutch rebels that they could count on my queen and England's assistance and now Elizabeth had made me a liar. What would the Netherlanders think of me?

I received an invitation from Leicester when I got back to court to dine with him in his rooms. I had entertained hopes of taking work back to The Papey and seeing my family, but I felt it was more important that I discuss matters with the Earl. As soon as I entered Leicester's rooms, I could see that all was not well with him.

'How was your journey?' he asked from his chair at the table, determined to be solicitous despite his mood.

'Well enough,' I said, 'the sea was rough, but then it always is.'

He grunted and gestured at the chair opposite his. 'I wish I had been with you. To get away from all...' he waved his cup, gesturing around the room, 'this.'

I sat. 'What is this?'

Leicester, who I think may already have quaffed a great quantity of wine, frowned at me. 'The Duke of Anjou. He's coming here.'

'To what end?'

'Elizabeth wanted to see him, so she sent an invitation. He accepted, damn him.'

Leicester's servants began setting out the dishes on the table. Leicester always dined well when he dined in his rooms, away from the Queen's eagle eye and her censorious comments about his excessive consumption. I cast my eye over the dishes. The food was a little rich for my taste — there were too many sauces — and I resolved not to indulge too greatly lest I suffer for it on the morrow.

'Start,' he commanded, his fingers delicately taking slivers of meat and putting them on his plate.

'You have heard about the bond?' I asked as I did the same.

'I should have expected it of her,' he said sourly. 'It's all been a waste of time.'

'Indeed,' I agreed, 'and it will do nothing for our relations with the Netherlanders. Does this invitation to the Duke have any real meaning or is it just a gesture to prove that the marriage is being taken seriously?'

'It's to do with the bond not being paid. Because of the proposed marriage, Elizabeth thinks it is no longer necessary to pay out. Elizabeth and Cecil have put their heads together and come up with a new strategy. Elizabeth likes it because it is a cheap option. Cecil likes it because it means that no real move against either the Spanish or the French is ever made and we can keep the status quo. What is so wonderful about the status quo, Francis? Tell me.'

'Is it merely a stratagem or does the Queen really mean to marry the Duke?'

'I cannot find that out,' Leicester threw up his hands, knocking his cup so that it nearly fell over. He reached out and steadied it. 'Damn my clumsiness. I've asked Elizabeth and she says, of course, she is serious about marrying him, but then she insists on certain terms and monies so that I can only think she is once again merely playing a game, stringing it out to get as much as she can out of the French.'

'But if she really does mean to marry... what good would it do her or us? She's too old–'

'Careful, Francis,' Leicester laughed and waggled his right index finger, 'dare you say so?'

'I dare say so to you, my lord,' I said vehemently, 'and I may say so to the Queen if she asks me.'

'She won't ask you, you fool. Elizabeth is a woman who will not admit the creep of time. In her heart and mind, she is still the young woman of twenty-five who defied all the odds and became queen. And back then, Francis, you won't believe me, but she had all the bachelors of Europe clamouring for her hand. And Elizabeth loved it. She loved it. She misses it, that's the problem.'

'Vanity, thy name is woman.'

'Quite.'

'When the Netherlanders find out they aren't getting any money,' I shook my head, 'they will blame me.'

Leicester belched and shook his head. 'They will blame the Council, all of us. You must get used to it, Francis. We've all had to take the blame for the Queen's decisions.'

He was right, I knew. Over the years, Leicester and I had had many intimate conversations and I knew how many times he had had to become an apologist for the Queen, saying he had been to blame for some incident, for some action done or not done, when the Queen had been wholly responsible. Even Cecil had sometimes had to do this duty, only less often, for two reasons. Firstly, Leicester was the Queen's choice as a representative, the man she trusted to act as her unofficial consort, and secondly, Cecil's opinions mostly coincided with Elizabeth's own, so he rarely put forward any argument that he would later have to contradict.

But I was not Cecil or Leicester. I had done a great deal of thinking since the Thomas Morgan affair, when she had refused to take my advice and we had allowed a channel of communication between Mary Stuart and her supporters to stay open to our great peril, and I had resolved to always speak my mind to the Queen, whether she wanted to hear what I was thinking or not. Speaking my mind was the only way I could ease my conscience, to continue my mission to make England a wholly Protestant country, a place where Catholics would have no home. Marriage to the Duke of Anjou was a political matter on which I needed to tell the Queen exactly what I thought.

I picked my moment to tell her my opinion, I thought, well.

I waited at the door to the Queen's privy apartments. One of her ladies, Katherine Thorne, came out and I stopped her with a tap on the arm.

'Yes?' she asked in surprise.

'What kind of temper is the Queen in, Mistress Thorne?' I kept my voice low so as not to be overheard.

'Well enough, Master Secretary.'

'Then I shall see her,' I said.

Mistress Thorne gestured for me to follow her back into the privy apartments. 'Master Secretary to speak with you, Your Majesty.'

I quickly read the expression on Elizabeth's face as she glared at me: irked, already bored.

'What now, my Moor?' she asked, returning her eyes to her book.

I noted she did not ask me how my trip to the Low Countries had gone. Doubtless, Cecil had given her a report.

'I understand that an invitation has been extended to the Duke of Anjou to visit court, madam?'

She sighed and looked up at me, a smile playing at the corner of her lips. 'You understand correctly, Master Secretary. I have invited the Duke to come to England.'

'Indeed, madam?'

'Indeed, sir,' she mimicked. 'So, now you have had that confirmed... is that all?'

'No, madam,' I said, digging my toe into the rush matting,

determined to say what I had come to say. 'I wish to tell you of my thoughts on the matter of your marriage, if you would be so good as to listen to them.'

She studied me for a moment, then closed her book and rested it in her lap. 'Very well, then. Speak.'

I straightened my back and looked directly into her dark amber eyes. 'This marriage is ill-advised for the following political reasons. There is only small advantage to be gained by an alliance with France and much to be lost. It will put us in an alliance with a Catholic power and set us against another, Spain. A Catholic alliance is not desirable for a Protestant nation such as ours. Putting us in opposition with Spain will only increase their intent to attack us, the so-called Enterprise of England that King Philip has been planning for some time now. And lastly, the country will, I have no doubt, voice their opposition to such a marriage.'

'Well, let me tell you—,' Elizabeth began, leaning forward and pointing at me.

'Forgive me, madam, I have not yet finished. Personally, the marriage is even less desirable for yourself.' I took a step forward so that I could lower my voice and yet still be heard by Elizabeth. 'I feel I must alert you to one obvious fact. You are not as young as you once were, madam. Marriage with the Duke would put you in unconscionable physical danger were you to become pregnant. Younger women than you have not survived childbirth.'

There, I had done. I stepped back and waited for the inevitable: anger, fury, a tirade of verbal abuse.

Elizabeth rose from her stool and stood, swaying for a moment, glaring at me. Then I saw her arm rise and I blinked. Something flew through the air and struck me on the forehead. I staggered backwards, my hand automatically rising to touch my brow. I saw black spots before my eyes. I looked down at the floor by my feet. Elizabeth's book lay there, open, its pages bent back beneath the cover.

'How dare you!' Elizabeth screamed as her ladies scrambled to retreat to the corners of the room. 'How dare you come in here and speak so to me! Too old to bear children?'

She started spluttering, too angry, I suspect, to find words adequate to describe how much she hated me at that moment.

'Have I not been entreated to have a child of my own body

by my counsellors time and time again? And now, I choose to take the step towards this and you say I must not do it.'

'Madam, I—'

'And not good for my country? Do you dare to tell me you know what is best for my country, I who know and love my people?'

She carried on like this for a few minutes more, striding up and down the small room, filling it with her violence, waving her arms, her voice rising as she worked herself up into even greater fury. My head where it had been struck was beginning to sting and throb. At last, she ordered me from her sight and I bowed and exited.

I found Leicester and Cecil standing outside in the corridor. The door closed behind me. Cecil looked thunderous, Leicester sympathetic.

'You told her, then,' Leicester said. 'My God, you are a brave man, Francis.'

'What exactly did you say to Her Majesty, Master Secretary?' Cecil queried, glaring at me.

I put my fingers to my forehead again. The skin had not been broken but I felt a lump certainly. Leicester peered at it.

'You'll survive,' he assured me.

'What did you say to her?' Cecil asked again.

'I told her that the marriage was politically ill-advised and dangerous for her personally.'

'Did you tell her she was too old?' Leicester wondered.

'I did, my lord.'

He said nothing, but his eyes widened and he blew out a puff of air.

'It was not your place to say anything to Her Majesty, Master Secretary,' Cecil said, his face reddening with anger of his own. 'The Queen did not ask for your personal opinion.'

'I gave it to her none the less, my lord. As Secretary and as one of her Majesty's counsellors, I felt I had the right, not to mention the duty, to speak.'

Cecil's lips pursed and his shoulders heaved, but he had nothing to counter my words. He hobbled away, muttering, not prepared to listen to me any longer. Leicester and I watched him go.

'I applaud you,' he said, looking at the door from behind

which Elizabeth could still be heard, no doubt extending her fury to her innocent ladies. 'I doubt that any of the rest of us would have had the courage to tell her what you did.'

'Not even you, my lord?' I asked with a wry smile.

'Maybe, eventually, perhaps,' he shrugged. 'If the marriage negotiations ever got that far. She needed to be told the truth, whatever Cecil says. I heard what she said to you—'

'Shouted at me,' I corrected bitterly.

Leicester gave a little laugh. 'Yes, but that is just bluster. Do you think she will actually consider what you said?'

'I hope so, my lord, though you know her better than I.'

'That's the problem, Francis. She seems dead set on marrying the Duke. We are to expect his representative in the next week or so. A Jean de Simier. Well, I won't be here to greet him, so that's something, at least. I'm off to the country at the end of this week.'

'Your presence will be greatly missed,' I said heartfelt, thinking how the Queen's mood always deteriorated in Leicester's absence. Something banged against the door, making us both jump.

'Another book?' I suggested to Leicester.

'Or one of her ladies' heads,' he joked.

I smiled. 'Well, I must get on, my lord. I have much to do.'

'Indeed.' Leicester cast a long look at the door. 'I think I will take my horse out for some exercise for a few hours.'

'A wise idea.'

He patted me on the shoulder. 'Yes. See you at dinner, Francis.'

I cast one more look at the door and then returned to my office.

I was proved right in what I had said to Elizabeth in that fearsome interview before long. Pamphlets began circulating in London that were wholly against the French marriage, saying that our virgin queen should have no truck with a prince of France, and that prince so imperfectly formed as to mock her very purity. There were ballads being sung too in the taverns and on the London streets, warning Duke Francis to stay away lest he court danger in England. Elizabeth accused me of having a hand in such publications, but I could swear to my innocence truly. I had had nothing to do with them. The people, I pointed out to her, did not need rousing to such feelings; they had aroused these feelings in themselves.

Elizabeth was undeterred. She had convinced herself that she would marry the Duke and welcomed his envoy, the Jean de Simier of whom Leicester had spoken, with what seemed to her court wild abandon. Indeed, it was wondered whether Simier was courting for himself rather than for his master, for Elizabeth seemed highly enamoured of Simier and favoured him greatly. Her behaviour with him excited the gossips at court and I remember one conversation I had with Leicester, admittedly when he was in his cups, when he speculated as to whether Elizabeth had forgotten herself entirely and had had Simier in her bed. I was astonished at this remark, especially coming from him, but Leicester admitted to feeling snubbed by the Queen of late. I had witnessed her cooling towards him and I asked him if he knew the cause.

'She knows of my marriage,' he said and downed another cup of wine.

'You told her?'

'Had to. She would have found out sooner or later and it was best it come from me.'

'She was angry, I assume.'

'She was…' he looked at me sideways, 'none of your damn business.'

'Of course not,' I said hurriedly. 'Forgive me for prying.'

'Monkey, she calls this Simier. Her Monkey,' he said, pouring out another cup of wine. 'It makes me sick.'

'And the Duke? When is he arriving?'

'On the next tide. But have you heard, Francis? He is not going to be here officially. There is to be no public announcement, no fanfares. He will be here, but not here.'

The news leaked out, of course. His arrival could not stay secret, and the Duke's presence in England, wooing the Queen and no doubt, so the people suspected, inducing her to forget herself and her country and make unreasonable concessions that would benefit France, led to the publications against the marriage becoming more offensive to Elizabeth. She judged that the punishment for printing and circulating these pamphlets should be swift and harsh.

So it was that John Stubbs, a London lawyer, came to lose his hand. As a lawyer and a gentleman, Stubbs was not uneducated and ignorant of the state of the nation's affairs. He was an erudite, well-intentioned man who sought to warn the Queen of the danger she was seemingly willingly entering into with his pamphlet entitled *The discovery of a gaping gulf wherein England is like to be swallowed by another French marriage, if the Lord forbid not the banns by letting Her Majesty see the sin and punishment thereof.*

Stubbs was of the Protestant faith and ardent in it, so much so that Cecil and Elizabeth derided him as a Puritan. I had informants working in all the London printing works and knew of the production of Stubbs's pamphlet before it was circulated. Indeed, unlike the other pamphlets that had come before, I could have been said to have a hand in its conception, for I had allowed certain information that only the Council knew to be conveyed to Stubbs for inclusion. Such information, known to be correct by the Queen herself, could not be denied as the scribblings of a churl or a loudmouth who got his information from rumour. Stubb's pamphlet would be taken notice of.

I had known the pamphlet might result in punishment for Stubbs and those who had aided him in its preparation. I could have warned him not to publish but I did not. I know that there is never any gain without risk. If Stubbs felt strongly enough to pen the pamphlet, then I reasoned he should not be hampered in seeing his creation flourish. If he suffered for it, then he had my sympathy and my pity, but not my protection.

And suffer he did. His hand was struck off as being the instrument that had written such a wickedness against Elizabeth. Elizabeth ordered the punishment, urged to it by Cecil and persuaded to it by the Duke's entreaties that justice be meted out to show her good intentions. But Anjou was to be disappointed if he expected to see the English applaud the dismemberment of Stubb's hand and greet it with enthusiasm. The cutting off of Stubb's hand was watched in virtual silence, apart from those who dared to boo and shout 'shame'.

To save face with the Duke and to mitigate the ill feeling from her people towards her, Elizabeth needed someone close to take the blame for the punishment. Elizabeth is not unintelligent and she knew that Stubbs had been fed information that he could not have got from anywhere other than from her Council. She looked around at her counsellors and landed her vengeful gaze upon me. She knew my feelings, knew my faith. As far as she was concerned, who else could it have been?

'You,' she declared, pointing her bejewelled finger at me. 'This is your handiwork, is it not, Master Secretary? I can see your scheming in this, you protector of heretics, you cur, you viper in my bosom.'

'Madam—'

'Do not interrupt me, you sly devil, you dissembler, you churl. I know it was you. And I know you did not act alone.' This she said to the rest of the counsellors who were standing around the table, forced to stand because Elizabeth was standing. Cecil turned purple.

'Your Majesty, I had no part in this,' he professed indignantly.

But Elizabeth was in no mood to hear of innocence, not even from Cecil. She ignored him and kept her glare on me.

'You have insulted the Duke. You have insulted me. I do not want to see your miserable face. Get you gone, sir. Do not return to court until, or if, I give you permission.'

She grabbed hold of her skirts, lifting them to above her ankles, and strode out of the chamber. I did not bother to protest against my banishment. I knew to do so would be pointless. And the truth was I could work just as easily at home as at the palace, with the added bonus of not having to endure Elizabeth's wrath on a daily basis. I often wished I could work from home more often.

I retired not to The Papey but to my new house, Barn Elms. This house had been presented to me by the Queen earlier in the year when I had given her no reason to be displeased with me. Surrounded by full-grown elms, it was situated by the Thames and so had a very lovely aspect over the water. Ursula had moved here when it was gifted to us and she had spent a great deal of effort and money into furnishing it in the manner she wished. I find it an extremely comfortable home, conforming to all I could wish for. The stables are large enough to house sixty-eight horses, essential for sending messages, and the park is well stocked should I wish to go hunting.

But there is no denying that although I was initially grateful for banishment from the palace, being out of favour and out of sight of the Queen began to lose its appeal. I was kept well informed, not a thing happened at court that I did not know about, but it was not enough. My old affliction came upon me so that I could not urinate without great pain, and some days I was unable to urinate at all. And then, a great tragedy came upon my family. Our youngest daughter, our Mary, the child that had been in Ursula's belly at the time of the massacre, was taken from us at the tender age of seven.

Ursula's grief was terrible. This was the third child she had lost at such an age, and the memory of her boys' deaths was merely healed over, only skin deep. The loss made her take to her bed and not even Frances's sympathetic embraces and kisses could make the pain any less. I could bury myself in my papers and distract myself with my agents, my clerks and my acquaintances far easier than she. The pain was great with me, too, of course, but I know that women feel loss far more keenly than men.

The loss of our daughter strangely highlighted that I was out of favour with the Queen and the situation gave Ursula something that she could vent her spleen upon. She railed at me when her tears had ceased and anger had taken their place, telling me that I had been a fool to become involved in sedition, and when was I going to write to the Queen and apologise for my actions?

In ordinary times, Ursula would not have asked me to abase myself in such a manner and I told her in no uncertain terms that I would make no apology. But the weeks of exile dragged on and I would sometimes find myself wondering whether I should ask Leicester to speak on my behalf (if he were not doing so already) and even whether I should write the apology Ursula wanted. I was spared the indignity of this, as it turned out. To my great relief, the Anjou marriage came to nothing. Leicester wrote to me and told me how it had happened.

Simier had found out that Leicester had married Lettice Knollys without permission from the Queen and had exposed the Earl's secret at a meeting of himself, the Duke and the French ambassador, Fenelon. Simier had believed that this revelation would act as a spur to Elizabeth's sides, who had, with characteristic procrastination, dithered over the terms of the marriage agreement and was frustrating the French as much as she was frustrating her own Council. Simier's ploy backfired, for he did not know that Leicester had told Elizabeth all, that the Queen knew very well Leicester was a married man. Elizabeth merely refused to publicly recognise the fact, causing people to believe she had no knowledge of it.

If Simier had hoped that Elizabeth would become determined to marry his master, he was disappointed. In fact, it seemed to have the opposite effect. Suddenly, Elizabeth was extremely keen to be rid of her little French suitor. Simier and the Duke were despatched back to France, with all possibility of marriage with the Queen dashed. Elizabeth, glad to be rid of her French prince and her mood substantially improved, conceded that I could return to court with no concession, no apology, needed on my part.

CHAPTER 15

Whether or not the secret Catholics of this world were inactive while I was banished to the country or whether my informants were not as well informed as they thought they were, I do not know, but as soon as I returned to court at the beginning of 1580, the relative silence surrounding their movements broke and I began to hear whispers that they were up to no good once again.

This chain of events concerned me somewhat, set me to thinking that perhaps my absence had meant both the Council and my agents had been allowed to become complacent. But to whom could I ask this question and not be rebuked for my impertinence? Cecil had been the original brains behind the spy network we on the Council utilised. It was his work I had built upon and taken over. He would be affronted and offended by such a suggestion that I was the one who headed the network. But if nothing else, it proved to me that if I was away from court, matters might be left to play out as they willed with no one willing or prepared to stop them.

But to return to what was happening. You may recall my mentioning the Bishop of Ross, he who served Mary Stuart and openly acted against us? Well, I had been keeping a firm watch on him and one of my agents in Paris managed to intercept a letter written by him addressed to the Pope in Rome. It seemed there was a new faction in the Scottish court, one that was pro-Catholic and which had the potential, through the workings of a new favourite, Esme Stuart, the seigneur d'Aubigny, who I knew had been planted by the Guise family to spread their foul pestilence, to influence the young King James against the faith of his upbringing and convert him to Catholicism. Mary Stuart had managed to involve herself with this faction through her supporters and she herself had written to the Pope to petition him to supply them with men and money, and if he wasn't prepared to do this, to ask the kings of Spain and France if they would be willing to do so. Really, Mary Stuart was going around the Catholic courts of Europe like a whore selling her wares.

In April I received a letter from one of my agents. In his letter, he enclosed another, written by William Allen, who I had been waiting for some time now to make a move. You will remember, Allen had founded the English College in Douai, training young men to become Catholic 'soldiers' to return to England and begin converting all those who would listen to their cause with the ultimate aim of deposing Elizabeth and placing Mary on the English throne.

To say I was worried by this intelligence would be to tell less than the truth. I will not be so foolish as to pretend there were none in England willing to listen to these Jesuit priests, nor that there were people who would far rather have preferred Mary Stuart as their queen. The north of England had always been a nest of papist vipers. Elizabeth's father, Henry VIII himself, had had to undertake a progress to the north following the rebellion that came to be known as the Pilgrimage of Grace to remind the inhabitants of who their king was and that it was to him they owed allegiance, not the Bishop of Rome. The rebels detested what King Henry was doing to England, having Thomas Cromwell examine the monasteries and root out their corruptions, breaking with Rome and becoming Supreme Head of the Church in England. They had risen up against King Henry, their numbers swelling with every northern churl who believed he knew better than the King about matters of religion. It had taken a great deal to put the rebellion down and King Henry had been ruthless in his treatment of the rebels. Not only that but the people of England needed to be taught that what the sovereign decreed, they must follow. Parliament acted swiftly and passed laws that penalised anyone openly practising their Catholic faith.

I knew that such penalties would not be enough, however, to stop Allen and his ilk from trying their damnedest to have their way in England and indeed, in December of that year, across the water came Edmund Campion, a man who had made a name for himself amongst his fellow Jesuits. Campion was important to Catholics because he was a prime example of a convert. He had been a deacon in the Anglican church but had allegedly expressed doubts about his faith which led to his leaving Oxford and going to Ireland, ostensibly to continue his studies and undertake research. However, his activities in that country led to him coming to the attention of the Council, who suspected him of having Catholic sympathies. These suspicions were soon borne out when Campion secretly left Ireland and headed for Douai. He was welcomed into the fold of the Catholic church. After a few years, he began moving around Europe, teaching Catholic doctrine and preaching, but it was always his intention, and Allen's, that he return to England to embark on the Jesuit mission of converting the English Protestants.

Campion managed to sneak into England, eluding our agents who had been told to keep watch for him. He was aided in his secret mission by Catholics who housed him and hid him before moving him on to another friendly family, another place to hide. At this time, he was just one of a few priests who had landed in England and had been noticed by the Council, and it was only when one of his Latin pamphlets, *Decem Rationes*, an argument giving ten examples of why the Anglican church was a heresy, began to be circulated and talked about that the Council agreed with me that we needed to find Campion and stop his mouth. It was one of Leicester's agents who caught up with Campion in Berkshire in July of 1581, and who took him as he was preaching to an eager crowd. This agent was George Eliot, one of the unsavoury characters I wrote of earlier, a good example of the type of men we were forced to make use of. Eliot was a murderer and rapist, entirely unrepentant for his crimes, but unwilling to be put in prison or hanged and so had accepted Leicester's offer to work for him as an intelligencer.

It was agreed that such a famous, I would say infamous, man should be made an example of and put to death. I was in Paris at the time of Campion's capture, trying to extricate ourselves from the failed marriage treaty without incurring ignominy or having to pay too much to be rid of the Duke, as well as other minor matters, and so played no part in his trial nor in the torture that led to his confession. Had I been in England at the time, I would have protested against his torture. My colleagues on the Council had thought it would be a good idea if Campion was made to publicly dispute theology with those of the Protestant faith, believing that his arguments for Catholicism would be exposed as the sham they were. But his torture had been extreme — I understand he was so greatly racked that his limbs had been pulled out of their sockets, his arms hanging awkward and useless and his legs unable to support him — and Campion's shallow arguments were given substance and meaning by the pity he evoked in his listeners.

I have said it before and will maintain that torture does little for the consciences of those who perform it and much for those who suffer it. Men who act on faith alone are more than willing to suffer and become a martyr for their cause. This is counter-productive. I wish more of my colleagues would pay me heed on this matter. Many is the time I have had to counsel against extreme methods. Too often have I been ignored or shouted down.

Campion was merely the most prominent of many Jesuit priests who came to England in these years. They knew where they would be welcome and so took up with noble families who would shelter and protect them against our agents, our priest-takers. Elizabeth, much to my annoyance, refused to take too strong a stance against her Catholic subjects, but fortunately, her Parliament took a rather different view. By steady gradations, Parliament passed laws that made it increasingly irksome to be a Catholic in this Protestant land. My hope is that Parliament will not cease to do so, but will soon make England too hot for even the most determined Jesuit to venture a mission of conversion here.

These Jesuits were dealt with, imprisoned or, when necessary, executed. They were flies, attracted to the dung of the Catholic faith. Several of my fellow counsellors believed these priests to be more important than they were but I managed to convince them they were of little consequence and that we should focus our attention on more important matters. When they asked what could possibly be more important than Catholic priests infiltrating our island, I could answer them with two words: Mary Stuart.

CHAPTER 16

My reputation as a collector of information grew very quickly, I do not think I flatter myself to say so. As well as my handpicked agents, there were men and women who would approach me, either by letter or in person, through an intermediary or directly if they could gain access to me, and offer to supply me with information, for a price, of course. I soon discovered this was one of the dangers of information gathering. Once it is known that you will pay well for information, every kind of worm comes out of the woodwork to say they have something to sell. The skill comes in recognising the valuable information from the dross.

And then there are the men and women who seem like they would make good agents but turn out to be more trouble than they are worth. Spies need to have certain characteristics. They need to be good liars, it should go without saying, and not suffer any qualms about dissembling. They need to be flexible, able to adapt quickly to any situation they find themselves in. They need to be many people in one, assume different identities when the need arises and be utterly believable in each guise. They need to have few loyalties so that they do not feel conflicted about their duty or responsibilities to their kin or friends. This last throws up problems of its own. Any man who will lie and pretend to be other than he is for money will often have no loyalty to the person who is paying him. If the man on the other side offers more money, the spy will turn and work for them instead. I know.

I have employed this technique too often myself to doubt the truth of it.

And then there are those agents who threaten to expose themselves as spies by the failings of their own characters. Men such as Christopher Marlowe. You will have heard of him, I am sure, the scribe who penned such great works for the stage, but did you know he was an agent of mine? A poor agent, admittedly, for he was a man who could not keep his mouth shut. More than once I had to get him out of trouble, pay a man or woman to look the other way or not call in the authorities to lay a lawsuit against him. I had thought him worth the trouble to begin with, but I came to doubt how valuable he actually was to me. In the end, the matter was taken out of my hands and Marlowe died in a tavern brawl. So typical of the man to die in such an ignominious way, and so conveniently.

My duties as Secretary did not confine me to London, nor yet even England. Wherever there was trouble, it began to seem to me, I was compelled to leave court and sort it out. My taste for travel had declined with my advancing years. I suppose it is always the way. The old man is loathe to leave his fireside. But in August of 1583, I was forced to depart north of the border.

The Scots had made more trouble for us. An internal court revolt, led by the Earl of Arran and aided by the Captain of the Guard, had resulted in the anti-English faction that had been building up its strength coming into power. This shifting of power was nothing new. The Scottish changed their loyalties as some men change their hose. What made it different and infinitely more troublesome to us was that the young King was going along with this new faction and playing a double hand, professing to still being in league with us while secretly seeking alliances with France. This latter was to be achieved through his marriage with a French princess. All of this I found out through my network of agents.

Well, of course, such a state of affairs could not be allowed to continue. The King of Scotland was our creature. He took our money to be loyal to us and in return, made no fuss about his mother being imprisoned. But it seemed he needed reminding of this. It was decided by the Council that someone of sufficient standing had to be sent to Scotland to represent Elizabeth and sort the matter out. Cecil protested he was too old and infirm to go (he had been to Scotland during the early years of Elizabeth's reign and that visit had been enough for him to swear he would never set foot in the country again) and Leicester was too dear to Elizabeth to risk leaving her side to travel to such a savage country. That left me.

I did not want to go. Not because the travelling would be irksome to me, though it would be, not because my own health was fragile because if I allowed my health to dictate my actions I would never rise from my bed, but because I knew it would all be a thorough waste of time.

I was also rather more ill than usual at the time. My stomach was causing me grievous, continual pain, so much so that I was forced to undertake the journey in a closed coach rather than ride alongside the eighty horsemen sent to accompany me. The bad roads to Scotland, however, meant that the journey in the coach was only slightly less painful than if I had been riding. The constant jolting, the threat of falling into potholes and the rain that poured out of the sky relentlessly meant that, on several occasions, I had to insist we stop to allow myself to rest. As a result, the journey took more than twenty days to complete.

Matters did not improve when we reached the Scottish border. There, we were subjected to the most intrusive and intolerable harassments and treatment. The King had despatched no more than sixty men to escort our party into Scotland, so small a number being a decided snub. To add injury to this insult, our entry into Scotland was made conditional upon us behaving ourselves. Behaving ourselves! The outrage I felt at such a threat… well, I cannot convey it in words. Had I had the strength, I would have made a much more vehement protest. As it was, I had to make my position clear by informing the King's representatives that I would not accept the conditions they had tried to impose on me and my party and that the proper etiquette had best be observed or else I would go back to England. As a threat, it worked, and we were eventually escorted into Scotland, but still, the damned Scots tried to outmanoeuvre me by putting obstacle after obstacle in my way in trying to meet with the King himself.

I knew England's worth. However hard the Scots tried to

convince me that Scotland was vital to England's interests, I did not buckle. I told the King, when I was finally allowed to meet with him, plainly that England could manage very well without Scotland, but that Scotland would struggle without England.

The King, a young man of seventeen then, looked down at me coolly from his throne.

'I doubt, Master Secretary, that your queen would be willing to bring blood and destruction to Scotland.'

I raised my eyebrow. 'I assure you, Your Majesty, that though my queen is no warmonger and does not court war, she will not hesitate to unsheathe her country's sword should she be convinced that it is the only course of action open to her.'

'I am a king, sir,' he said, 'and may choose my own course of action.'

'You are indeed a king, Your Majesty, but one of few years and as such, you lack the maturity to be able to know and understand all matters of state. Worse still, I believe you are ill-advised. You have chosen poor men to be your counsellors and they tell you what they ought not.'

'You would have me believe that your queen chooses those who serve her better than I?'

'To protest this would be an act of self-aggrandisement, Your Majesty, so I will not say so.'

James's lip curled in an ugly smile, loose, misshapen. 'You make no effort to flatter me, Master Secretary. So many men do, yet you do not. Why is this?'

'I am no flatterer, Your Majesty. I speak as I see.'

'And yet it would profit you to flatter me, would it not? After all, unless your queen lays down and spreads her legs soon, if it is not too late already, it is entirely possible that I will be your king one day.'

Is this how a king should talk? Is this the bearing of a king? I was disgusted at his vulgar language and disgusted with his person. James is an unattractive creature, bearing none of the beauty of either of his parents, and his manners leave much that can be improved upon. Nevertheless, I forced myself to swallow down my disgust and gave the only response I could.

'It is possible that you may one day be King of England, Your Majesty, I am no prognosticator, I cannot tell the future. But I would hope that a King of England would wish to have wise men about him, men who tell the truth and do not flatter. I do not seek to be my mistress's friend, nor would I seek to be yours were you my master. I do my job and I do it well. No man should ask more of me.'

That was how I left him, to think on my words and acknowledge their wisdom. He called me to his presence two days later and was all affability, conformable to anything I was ready to propose. I thanked him, wondering at this change in him, and told him our conditions. These were not unreasonable, simply that the anti-English faction be thrown out of court and that order be restored, that the Scottish lords respect the law as laid down by Parliament, and most importantly, that the King was not to believe too greatly in the absolute power of sovereigns, that he was to listen to his subjects and command them with all justice. James assured me that his acquiescence in this matter would be set down in writing and so I waited while this was done.

I need not have bothered. I could have left Scotland then and there and nothing would have changed. When the new proclamation was drafted, it was so full of holes and ambiguous language that it meant nothing. It was not worth the paper it was written on. But there was nothing more I could do and so I made arrangements to leave Scotland. I was never so pleased to do so.

The whole mission had been a dismal failure, as I had known it would be. Worse, I and my fellow men had had to put up with the most insolent of tricks perpetrated by the Earl of Arran, the head of the anti-English faction, whom I had refused to meet because of his personal vileness. He would rescind permission for members of my party to enter the palace where the King was in residence, he paid a shrewish old woman to sit outside our lodgings and hurl abuse at any Englishman who came in and went out, and later, I learnt that Arran had replaced the diamond on a ring the King had presented me with as a gesture of friendship with a worthless, low-grade crystal.

What irked me more than these childish annoyances, however, was that I had had to forgo the pleasure of seeing my darling Frances married to the young man whom I admired perhaps more than any other, Sir Philip Sidney, simply to endure this ill-mannered, puerile treatment.

When the suggestion that Philip marry my Frances had first

been made, I had been astonished. I had heard that other marriages were being discussed by his father, Henry Sidney, marriages with girls from far better families than mine. Indeed, one name that had been put forward as a possible bride was Penelope Devereux, the daughter of Leicester's wife, Lettice Knollys and Walter Devereux, the late Earl of Essex. Not only would the marriage mean that the Dudley and Devereux families would be drawn closer together, but apparently, it had been the dying wish of Walter that Philip marry Penelope. That had been years before, of course, and with no betrothal made the idea had fallen through. Philip had been travelling a great deal in the intervening years and had therefore not been around to consider marriage to any great degree. I had even joked with him on one of his visits to me that he should find himself a wife. He had smiled and shrugged and said he was leaving that to his family to sort out for him. I had not realised how truthful he was being until Leicester approached me after dinner one day at court.

'Francis,' he said, 'what say you to a marriage between my nephew and your daughter?'

He had caught me off guard and I could only stare at him.

'What say you?' he asked again.

'Philip?'

'Aye, Philip.'

'And my daughter?'

'Yes, good God, what ails you, man? Are you turned simple that you must repeat everything I say?'

I shook my head. 'Forgive me, my lord, but I was not expecting this. As your nephew, is not a grander alliance being considered for him?'

Leicester snorted. 'Grander, be damned. There's nothing wrong with your daughter. You are a knight, so is Philip. And they like one another, do they not?'

'My daughter is indeed very fond of Philip. We all are.'

'Well then,' he said, smacking my shoulder as if the matter were all arranged. 'I'll talk to Philip's father and we will make a start. I think we can have them married within a month. All to the good, do you not think?'

And that is how it happened. Ursula was so very pleased when I told her what Leicester had said. 'We could not hope for a better man for our daughter,' she said, throwing her arms around me and kissing me full on the lips.

'Will Frances be pleased, do you think?' I wondered. It was the one question that vexed me.

'Pleased?' Ursula laughed. 'Oh, Francis, have you not seen? The girl has been in love with Philip since she was fourteen.'

'In love?' I said, shocked.

'Men,' Ursula sighed and shook her head. 'You have your eyes wide open and yet you never see.'

I had not seen, it was true. I had been so fond of Philip myself, I never stopped to consider whether others were so. I was glad. I wanted my daughter to be happy and I knew Philip would make her so.

When I was told of the need to go to Scotland by the Council, the marriage between Frances and Philip had already been announced and the ceremony planned, so the short notice of the Scottish trip had meant that nothing could be postponed without great inconvenience to all parties. It all went ahead without me and I had to rely on accounts of the day written in letters. Ursula wrote that everything had gone without a hitch, although Frances had exhibited some nerves in the morning which Ursula had had to calm, and Philip wrote to me to say that he was very disappointed that my enforced journey meant I had not been present to witness the union but that he found Frances to be in every way the perfect wife, as he knew a daughter of mine and Ursula's would be. I was glad and so very proud to have such a son-in-law. The only sour note was that Elizabeth refused to give her royal blessing to Philip and Frances, and I have no idea why she should do so. Philip had been openly critical of Elizabeth in the past, it was true, but my dear daughter had done nothing to offend the Queen, and it pained me and her that her marriage was not blessed or even acknowledged with congratulations by Elizabeth.

CHAPTER 17

Back in England and the civilising presence of London once again, I could return my attention to where it was most needed. To Mary Stuart. It was well I returned when I did because by the end of my first day back in my office that woman had caused events to be set in motion once again.

Part of my duty, my self-imposed duty, I should say, as Secretary, is ensuring I know what is going on in every corner of the country and in every corner of the Continent that affects England's welfare. This means having to intercept and read letters that are never intended for mine or the Council's eyes. Not a gentlemanly pursuit, I grant you, but then I am not dealing with gentlemen.

A letter from the French ambassador, Michel de Castelnau, Sieur de la Mauvissière, intended for Mary Stuart's eyes was intercepted by my agents and the contents of this letter suggested to us that we had the chance of getting our hands on the courier who was being used by them both. Moreover, that courier was returning from Paris and would undoubtedly be carrying information of vital interest to me and of great importance to Mary. This courier was called by a code name in the letter — Sieur de la Tour — but I knew full well who this gentleman was. He was an Englishman by the name of Francis Throckmorton.

I had been aware of Francis Throckmorton for some time.

He was known to me as a fierce papist, yet another of those who had had an excellent education at Oxford and gone on to study the law. For the past few years, he had been travelling with his brother on the Continent, which was where he had made his undesirable connections with Mary's supporters.

On the fifth of November 1583, I sent my men to arrest Throckmorton and search both of his houses. He had houses in London and Kent. We were extremely fortunate that night, for when my men gained entry to his London house, they discovered Throckmorton in the very act of using a cypher to write to Mary Stuart. He was promptly arrested and removed while my men carried out a search of the property. They found much evidence of his involvement in Catholic circles, most of which admittedly could be considered circumstantial, but they did find one piece of evidence that was conclusive of his part in a plot. They found a list of Catholic men, both noble and those more lowly, who were sympathetic to Mary's cause. In addition to being in regular correspondence with the Scottish queen, Throckmorton had been keeping and updating this list and creating a record of English harbours and ports where landings could be made safely due to their proximity to the homes of Catholic-friendly families. Lastly, as if I needed more proof of his treachery, my men found copies of the pamphlet that the Bishop of Ross had published propounding Mary Stuart's right to the English crown.

Throckmorton played the coward at first. He denied any knowledge of the papers found in his house, saying they had been foisted there by my men. Nonsense, of course, and he soon realised it, a few days later admitting the papers had been in his house but that he had not written them. They had, he claimed, been written by an Edward Nuttebie, who had, very conveniently, left England. This went unbelieved by the Council, not least because Throckmorton was discovered trying to pass a message to his brother through his Tower window, telling him to confirm what he had told us if he too was questioned.

Reluctant though I have ever been to use torture, after much discussion in the Council, it was agreed that Throckmorton would be put to the rack. He surprised me the first time he was tied to the contraption by refusing to speak. I had not thought him so brave. After all, he had spoken readily enough, by stages, without any force being used upon him. He was removed from the rack and returned to his cell.

I gave instructions that he was to be racked again a few days later. I believed that the pain he had suffered from his first racking would be enough to persuade him to talk, that he would not want to endure more, and I was right. This time he confessed.

Mary's supporters had approached him and his brother in Paris to find out about good landing sites in England. The Duke of Guise intended to invade our country, landing at Arundel in Sussex, with five thousand men at his back.

Throckmorton had more to tell. This was no recent endeavour. He had acted as a courier for Mary many times and had secret meetings with the Spanish ambassador, Bernadino de Mendoza, who intended to join with the Duke of Guise to lead a second invasion force in the north of England. And his last admission had been that when my men had arrived at his house to arrest him, he had quickly managed to give a servant a pile of letters he kept under his bed that he was supposed to pass on to Mary Stuart.

It was remarkable, this plot of theirs, not least because they had thought they would be able to get away with it. When I told the Council the results of Throckmorton's racking, his confession and the scope of the plot, the news stunned them, and yes, frightened them a little too.

'We must have Mendoza here to answer this,' Leicester said, thumping the table angrily. 'That he should conspire in our own country.'

'Would you have us question him?' Cecil asked. 'The Spanish ambassador?'

'Why not, pray?' Leicester demanded. 'Is he not to be touched? Is he too special?'

'My lord, we must exercise caution—'

'Tell me why we must. We are being plotted against and you say we have to exercise caution.'

'Caution is always the best approach—'

'Damn your caution, Cecil,' Leicester spat. He turned to me. 'Master Secretary?'

All heads around the Council table looked my way. I expect they all knew what I was going to say before I spoke.

'There should be no question of us not interrogating Senor Mendoza,' I said. 'He is complicit in a plot against our queen. Her safety is our paramount concern. We need to know what he knows.'

Leicester asked for a show of hands, all those who agreed that Mendoza should be questioned should raise their hands. Every hand but Cecil's was raised.

'Very well, as you are all in agreement,' Cecil said grumpily, gesturing to the clerk at the side of the room who recorded all that was said in the Council chamber. 'Have it set down that the Council agrees that the Spanish ambassador be called in for questioning.' To the guard on the door, he said, 'Send men to the Spanish ambassador's residence and have him brought here. If he refuses, he is to be brought by force.'

Mendoza did not refuse. He was arrogant enough to think that whatever we knew, whatever we said, he was safe from our retribution. And, of course, he was. We had no power to act with any physical force against an official representative of Spain. All we could do was tell him what we knew and dismiss him. We could not throw him in the Tower or have him executed. We agreed that Cecil, Leicester and myself would have a private meeting with Mendoza rather than he stand before the whole Council.

'What is all this about?' Mendoza asked nonchalantly as he watched me close the inner chamber door.

'It is about your involvement in a plot to land French and Spanish troops in England and overthrow the Queen,' Cecil said, limping to a chair because his gout was playing him up again.

Mendoza laughed, then cut it short as he looked between the three of us. 'Please, gentlemen, you are not serious?'

'Perfectly,' Leicester said. 'We have had a confession from your contact, Francis Throckmorton.'

I saw Mendoza flinch at the name. He knew him, all right.

'Francis Throckmorton? No, that name is not familiar to me,' he lied.

'We have his confession that you were to arrange a landing of Spanish troops in Lincolnshire,' Leicester said.

'A confession? No doubt obtained under torture, no?' He looked around at us for confirmation. 'Your silence tells me that yes, I am correct. Well, sirs, as you know, men may say anything under torture.'

'How would he know of you?' Leicester demanded.

'I am the Spanish ambassador,' Mendoza laughed. 'I am, as you seem to have forgotten, an emissary of Spain. I make no secret of who I am.'

'He named you,' Leicester said. 'Master Secretary, is that not so?'

'It is, my lord,' I said, 'and despite what you may choose to believe, Senor Mendoza, we are not without power to act. To that end, Her Majesty has been informed of your intrigues with Francis Throckmorton and your complicity in a plot against her. Accordingly, she has instructed us, her Council, to advise you that you have fifteen days to quit England. You are no longer welcome at Queen Elizabeth's court and King Philip will be informed of your dismissal.'

'How dare you!' Mendoza hissed, his eyes narrowing. 'You cannot dismiss me. I am Senor Mendoza, ambassador appointed by His Excellency King Philip.'

'You are dismissed, sir,' I said, keeping my voice low.

He began to splutter, trying to find something, some abuse, to hurl at us three. Finding nothing, he chose another approach.

'Your queen should stick to ruling her own small island and not stick her nose into other monarch's countries, stirring up trouble and accusing innocent men,' he jabbed a finger at his chest, 'of being spies.'

With that, he spun on his heel and yanked open the door, letting it bang against the panelling. As he left, we heard him declare, 'Don Bernardino de Mendoza was born not to serve kingdoms but to conquer them!'

The man was an idiot.

Once we had dealt with Mendoza, it was time to deal with the French ambassador, Mauvissière. This was not going to be as easy. For one thing, we had little evidence that Mauvissière was active in the plot. I speak of evidence. I *knew* he was involved, every fibre of my being told me so, but he had been clever and left no trail of his involvement. But more importantly, I had an agent in the French embassy, a servant to Mauvissière. This agent of mine was invaluable in this position. If we were to remove Mauvissière as we had removed Mendoza, we would lose a valuable source of information regarding what the French were up to, and not just in the matter of the Queen of Scots.

'Well, what can we do?' Leicester asked one night as the dark was coming on and it was just him, Cecil and myself left in the Council chamber. 'We cannot do nothing and let Mauvissière continue.'

'I agree,' I said, looking to Cecil.

'How good is this man of yours in the French embassy?' Cecil asked.

'Very good,' I replied truthfully. 'He is Mauvissière's secretary. He has access to everything Mauvissière does. He sees every despatch, every letter, every instruction. And he has risked much to bring us the information he has. He deserves to be looked after.'

'I am surprised you harbour such a sentiment, Master Secretary,' Cecil said sniffily. 'I would have thought you were ruthless with your intelligencers.'

'I understand how people like to be treated,' I said, resenting the insinuation that I was just a user of people, discarding them when their value had expired. 'Treat them badly and they will do the same to you. That is bad business practice. Surely you can see that, my lord?'

Leicester, who sensed that relations were becoming tense between Cecil and me, straightened in his chair and held out his hands. 'Come, now, you two, this will get us nowhere. I agree with you, Francis. If we can keep your intelligencer in the French embassy and still deal with Mauvissière, then that is what we should do. The question is, how?'

'We should have a meeting with Mauvissière,' I said, 'and suggest we know of his involvement in the intrigue.'

'But won't that expose his secretary?' Leicester wondered.

'I do not see why it should. Mauvissière will not know where we have got our information from and I believe he will be too concerned with keeping himself out of the matter to wonder whether he has been betrayed.'

'He's an ambassador, Francis,' Leicester persisted. 'He will claim that he knows nothing, we can prove nothing and there is nothing we can do against him. Am I not right, Cecil?'

Cecil nodded, looking at me.

'I disagree, my lord, if you will forgive me,' I said. 'We are not impotent in this matter. We can draw up charges against Mauvissière that are unbecoming to the duties of an ambassador, such as secret correspondence with Mary Stuart, plotting against his host sovereign, and accuse him of those. We need not provide evidence, just express our suspicions. It will be enough. He will realise that his position as ambassador will be in danger that way. Mauvissière has many debts and he will not relish the prospect of losing his job. That will only expose him to his creditors. He will be malleable, I am certain.'

Both Leicester and Cecil continued to express their doubts to me over the next hour of talk, but in the end, were willing to let me play my hand. I did not doubt that I was right and so it proved. We summoned Mauvissière to the Council chamber and there had him stand while I recounted what he could be charged with if we decided to proceed. He trembled as I spoke and I could see Cecil and Leicester relaxing as they realised I had been right. With each statement I made regarding his offences, Mauvissière would hold out his hands and shake them, professing no, no, he had not had secret correspondence with the Scottish queen, he had not conspired with Englishmen to dethrone Elizabeth. On and on it went. I let him continue his bluster, waiting for my moment to say the words that would silence him.

'We have proof of your complicity,' I said, telling a little untruth but gesturing at the charge list to suggest we did. 'Unequivocal proof. And we shall send this to your king and you shall be removed from your position. What your king will do with you, I cannot say.'

Without being invited, Mauvissière dragged out a chair from beneath the table and fell into it. He snatched off his cap and threw it onto the table. 'Yes, very well,' he said, rubbing his forehead. 'It is true, all true, what you say. But all I did was write the occasional letter to Mary and pass others on. I did not conspire against your queen.'

I looked at Cecil, who leant towards me and together we talked quietly. It was all for show; Cecil was leaving this matter up to me.

'Monsieur Ambassador, we have no wish to disgrace you,' I

said, forcing a smile onto my lips. 'But we cannot let you carry on as you have been. If you will give us your assurance that you will cease all further activity, that you will not aid the Scottish queen in any future endeavour, of any kind, even the most seeming innocent venture, then we need not go any further in this affair.'

'Yes, yes,' he said, holding his arms out towards me and grabbing at the air as if he would grab at me, 'yes, I will do that.'

I had not finished. 'And reveal to us any letters that are forwarded to you that are from or concern Mary Stuart.'

He dropped his arms to the table and frowned at me. 'Show you my private correspondence?'

'Indeed,' I said.

'I am the French ambassador,' he said, rather pompously.

'An ambassador who has acted against our queen,' I reminded him. 'Of course, if you feel you cannot comply with our very reasonable request…'

He considered for only the briefest of moments. 'No, wait, let me think… yes, very well, all relevant correspondence.'

Cecil nodded at me, satisfied.

'Good,' I said, putting my papers away in my leather folio, thinking that I really should get it replaced for it was looking very worn. 'That's understood.'

I went briefly into the details of how he could pass on such information and hinted that we would know, without giving him any clues as to how, if he kept anything back. Mauvissière left, bowing and thanking us for being so good to him. The door closed behind him.

'And that,' Leicester said, smirking, 'is a lesson in how you deal with people who can be of some use to you. Do you not think so, Cecil?'

Cecil, who did not like being proved wrong, merely grunted.

Leicester rose and straightened his doublet. He patted me on the shoulder. 'Well, now all that is left is to hang Throckmorton. I suppose he is headed for the scaffold?'

'He must,' Cecil answered. 'He is not one that can be kept locked up. An example must be made. If for no other reason than it will reinforce to Mauvissière what we do to traitors.' He got up, using the table to help him to his feet and hobbled out of the room.

'Do not look for thanks from that quarter, Francis,' Leicester said.

'I do not look for thanks, my lord,' I said rising and pushing my chair beneath the table. 'If I did, I would often go wanting.'

He knew by this I meant the Queen, who never thanked me or congratulated me for my work in keeping her safe.

'Well, you have mine,' Leicester said, 'for what it's worth. Elizabeth would be in very great danger were it not for you, I know. Now, speaking of Elizabeth, it is time for me to ride out with her. See you this evening.'

I returned to my office, grateful that my efforts were noticed and appreciated by at least one man.

As it turned out, Mauvissière did not last much longer in his office. Rumours got back to the French king that he had been less than satisfactory as ambassador and within a year of our meeting, Mauvissière had been replaced by the Baron de Chateauneuf, Guillaume de l'Aubepine. My agent in the French embassy warned me that the baron was a much tougher character than his predecessor.

The Stuart woman continued her intrigues, as I expected her to, but she was always very careful about committing too much of her involvement, or her intent, to paper. It was so frustrating. I knew Elizabeth well by this time and I knew I would need solid, unquestionable evidence to convince her to act against her cousin. But Mary Stuart, through cunning or just through plain luck, was continually denying me that evidence.

Fortunately, for me at least, foreign events played into my hands a little. On the tenth of July 1584, William of Orange, also known as William the Silent, was assassinated. I had met with William when I was in the Low Countries and had been greatly impressed. He had originally been a servant of the Spanish, but his conscience dictated that he turn against his Imperial masters and become a fiercely Protestant leader of the Dutch rebels. The Spanish found this situation intolerable and King Philip had declared him to be an outlaw back in 1580, putting a reward of twenty-five thousand crowns on his head. Of course, such a man as this creates enemies and when a feeling of treachery is combined with the chance to make money, I suppose

William's death was an inevitability. A Catholic from Burgundy, Balthasar Gerard, decided he was the man to kill the traitor and he travelled to Delft where William lived. One evening after William had dined, Gerard strolled into the Prinsenhof and fired two shots into William's chest as he descended the stairs. William died within minutes.

I was upset at William's death. He had been a good man, a good Protestant, but I must confess, his assassination helped my cause. It needed only a little persuading to convince Elizabeth that she was just as great a target for Catholics as her fellow Protestant prince had been. Upon her order, the Council immediately enacted a new legislation, the Bond of Association, which we, all of us counsellors, signed. We put our names to a bond that meant should the Queen be killed, then we would persecute to the utmost not only her killer but anyone who had put them to the killing or who could then claim title to her crown. Such a person was Mary Stuart. Within days of the bond being passed in Parliament, thousands of my fellow Englishmen had signed it. I saw to it that Mary Stuart was shown a copy of the Bond of Association, so that she knew how close to danger she personally would be should she incite the murder of Elizabeth.

Meanwhile, Cecil thought it a good idea to remove Mary Stuart from the Earl of Shrewsbury's care. The Earl's wife, Bess, I knew, had been continually writing to both Cecil and Leicester, begging them to take Mary away for the sake of her purse. Maintaining Mary's court was draining Bess's substantial resources so that in her words she was close to being penniless.

But I knew there was more to her pleas than just money. Bess was convinced her husband had been Mary Stuart's lover and I read a letter, full of vitriol, addressed to Elizabeth that gave graphic accounts of what she believed had gone on between Mary and her husband. I thought it wise not to pass the letter on to Elizabeth. I knew such an explicit account of lechery would deeply wound her vanity, whether the accusations were proven or not, that her cousin Mary was so attractive that she had seduced one of Elizabeth's own nobles into so far forgetting himself as to be unfaithful to his good and loyal wife. I filed away the letter from Bess Talbot and mentioned it to no one.

So, Mary Stuart was taken away from the Shrewsburys and placed in the care of Sir Amyas Paulet, a man who I knew was not capable of being seduced by the alleged charms of the Stuart woman. Paulet could not be charmed. He was a hard, unbending man and a good Protestant, a Puritan even. I was satisfied that these qualities would result in him making a very strong prison for Mary Stuart.

CHAPTER 18

The Catholics were getting more cunning. More and more of the letters intercepted by my agents were being written in code.

These had begun as fairly simple codes, such as nicknames being given to certain people in an attempt to hide their identities, but often, these names were highly descriptive of the subject or bore a name that was associated with a particular family, so that it was child's play to work out who was meant. I have always found it surprising how unoriginal people can be. We often reveal more of ourselves in our deceptions than we realise. But either the writers of the letters realised how transparent such cyphers were or they knew we were deciphering them, so that they quickly became more sophisticated. Numbers were substituted for people's names in some of the easiest letters to decrypt but in others, the entire text was enciphered. My chief secretary, John Somers, did his best with such encoded missives, but as they became more sophisticated, he began to struggle with the work.

So, it became clear to me that we needed someone adept at deciphering. It takes a certain type of intellect to decrypt codes. You need to be able to discern patterns in the text. You also need to have a good grasp of several languages because the writers of these cyphers were of various nationalities. But as important as these skills is the possession of a fierce concentration, as well as perseverance. Decoding cannot be achieved within minutes. It can take many hours, sometimes even days and weeks, to work a cypher system out. Besides lacking the brains, to be blunt, and a willingness to keep on at the work, John Somers simply did not have the time to commit to such work. No, what was needed was someone whose sole job it was to decrypt the incredible amount of correspondence that was passing my desk concerning Mary Stuart.

My colleagues on the Council, however, needed much persuading that this was so and were sceptical of creating a salaried post for such an obscure job. Elizabeth's consent would have to be sought and my heart sank at this, for she would not be willing, I suspected, to pay for it. I anticipated a refusal and was wondering if my finances would permit me to put up the salary, when, to my astonishment, Elizabeth said yes.

Before she could change her mind, I set about finding a man suitable for the task and was delighted to find one already very close to home. Thomas Phelippes had been working for me for some years. He was neither a gentleman nor a university man but what I knew Phelippes to be was very able. He had a good grasp of languages, being proficient in French, Latin and Italian, and he even had a smattering of Spanish. He had travelled a great deal and I had used him as a courier on such journeys, where he had proved himself very adept. During 1578, whilst stationed at the English embassy in Paris, my old residence, Phelippes had deciphered many encrypted letters, forwarding on the decoded texts as soon as he had them and thereby keeping me informed. When he returned to England, he continued to do this.

Unfortunately, for others, not for him, he was not very personable. My colleagues and those nobles he came into contact with found him unbearably distasteful. He was short and thin, had yellow hair and a bristly yellow beard that always made him look unwashed and not even his beard could hide the deep smallpox scars that peppered his face. It is perhaps unfortunate that we frame our feelings around how people look and never bother to peer beneath the skin. As a result of this unbecoming appearance, as I say, Phelippes was not well liked, though the knowledge never seemed to trouble him. I did not find him unpleasant to be around — indeed, I valued him greatly for his ability — although I must confess that I never once asked him to dine with me and my family. I feared Ursula would not take kindly to him.

When Mary Stuart began enciphering her correspondence, Phelippes was on hand to reveal her very innermost thoughts to me.

I had many agents working for me by this time, but there were a few that stand out in my memory and which I hope will provide the reader of this account with an insight into the kind of men with whom I had to deal in my capacity as Secretary.

One such agent was Robert Poley. Poley was a Catholic who had spent time in the Marshalsea Prison on my orders. I despised him for not only was he a Catholic, not a fervent believer but one more out of habit than anything else, but he was far from being a gentleman. No, I will be honest, Poley was not even what you could call a decent man.

He spent a whole year in the Marshalsea and during that time befriended other Catholics similarly incarcerated, not I must tell you because he had any fellow-feeling with them but because he thought he could use them in such a manner that he would be of use to me. This is how such men's minds work, always wondering what others can do for them, for the right price, of course. In May 1584, with a character reference penned by a fellow prisoner, a seminary priest who he conned into believing he was a man of sobriety and integrity, Poley wrote to one of Mary Stuart's agents, Thomas Morgan of whom I wrote earlier, in Paris to offer his services. Morgan jumped at the chance to employ Poley on his secret business.

I was never sure of Poley, never sure whether he was truly my man or Mary's. So unsure was I that I even had him arrested again and questioned him myself. I suspected him of having had a hand in the distribution of Catholic propaganda, specifically a scurrilous piece of work entitled *Leicester's Commonwealth*. This pamphlet, so typical of the kind of trash the Catholics printed, was a disgusting attack on the Earl of Leicester in regard to his sexual proclivities. This pamphlet claimed the Earl had worked his lecherous way through all of the Queen's ladies-in-waiting, and now that he had exhausted them, was paying three hundred pounds a night to have the gentlewomen of the Queen's chamber. As I say, this pamphlet was disgusting and completely untrue. I felt keenly for the Earl, not only because of its obvious untruthfulness but because it followed hard on the heels of the death of his son. Leicester was distraught at the loss and the circulation of this piece of filth was almost enough to send him into a fit of melancholy which I was worried he would not come out of.

I could not prove that *Leicester's Commonwealth* was the handiwork of Poley, but a search of his lodgings found other banned books, as well as a letter from Thomas Morgan, which proved that my suspicions about Poley had not been wholly unfounded.

'Can you explain this, Master Poley?' I held up the letter written to Thomas Morgan.

Poley squinted at the letter, his eyes widening as he realised what it was. 'Er, yes, yes, I can,' he assured me. I waited. 'I know what you do, Master Secretary. You find men who can let you know about matters, matters of interest to you.' Still, I waited. 'Catholic matters, Master Secretary. That letter there,' he pointed to it in my hand, 'is from a Thomas Morgan and he, sir, is an agent of the Scottish queen. I have earned his trust as someone who is willing to help her in whatever matter she has in mind.'

'Indeed?' I remarked.

He held out his hands. 'To gain her trust, sir, in the hope that she will reveal the details of some plot to me, by which you can…' he shrugged, 'do whatever it is you do.'

I set the letter down, folding my hands over it, and looked at him. He squirmed under my gaze. 'You were going to pass this letter on to me?' I said at last, putting him out of his misery.

'I was, Master Secretary,' he said, nodding vehemently. 'That was my intention.'

'Because…?'

He frowned. 'Because… forgive me, I do not understand.'

'Then let me put it another way, Master Poley. Why would you act against Mary Stuart? You are a Catholic, are you not?'

He laughed hollowly. 'I am a realist, Master Secretary. Elizabeth has the crown. She is English, I am English. She has a right to her crown. If I can be of help to her, to you, in enabling her to keep it—'

'And if there is some profit in it for you?'

'Well, why else do we do what we do?' he said, winking at me.

I threw him out. I was unconvinced of his usefulness. It did not bother me that he had no religious conviction; indeed, that was a mark in his favour as far as I was concerned. Men who have no principles and are available for money are much easier to deal with. But Poley seemed to me too slapdash, lacking in potential contacts, and I had other men who appeared to me far more valuable agents than he would ever prove to be.

Poley, however, was undeterred by my dismissal; he was determined to become an intelligencer. And so, he approached Leicester, offering his services to him. As I say, all of us — myself, Cecil and Leicester — had our own people to keep us informed. Leicester's people had different objectives from myself; they were less concerned with Mary Stuart and more interested in affairs in the Low Countries, but sometimes the two worlds overlapped. Leicester had fewer reservations than me and took Poley on, and Poley continued his correspondence with Thomas Morgan. Morgan, by this time, was imprisoned in the Bastille, but it was a sign of how the French authorities felt about his Catholic enterprises that visitors were allowed freely to his cell, and his letters did not need to be smuggled in or out because the guards were either too lazy or had not been given orders to check his visitors.

I can say now that I was wrong about Poley. I should have employed him. In Paris, Poley worked hard to build up his network of Catholic informants and he was rather more adept at blending in with their company than I had given him credit for. Morgan and his cronies took to him completely and began confiding in him. After only a few months, Morgan was convinced that Poley could be trusted and handed over a copy of the cypher key that Mary Stuart was using to write her letters. Had I known this would be the way matters fell, I would have employed Poley. Fortunately, all was not lost.

Poley came back to England and requested a meeting with Leicester. Leicester was kind enough to invite me to accompany him in the meeting. Poley could not help himself and was visibly smug about my presence when he was ushered into Leicester's parlour in Leicester House. To his credit, he was not vulgar enough to say so, but I knew he believed I was thinking that I wished I had taken him on. In fact, it made little difference in the long term, whether Poley was mine or Leicester's. We both had the same ends, we both served the same queen.

'So, sir,' Leicester said, 'what do you have to tell us?'

Poley helped himself to a chair. I saw that he felt he could take it easy and not bother to have to impress us. 'I have gained Thomas Morgan's confidence. He has given me gold coin to cover my expenses.' He pulled out of his jerkin a brown leather bag. He shook it and it made a telltale jangle of metal.

'And?' Leicester pressed.

Poley smiled and put his hand once again into his jerkin. 'And this.'

'What is that?' Leicester asked, peering at what Poley was holding.

Poley rose and placed it on the desk before Leicester. 'Please, take a look, my lord.'

Leicester picked it up and unfolded the paper. I watched him frown as he read. He looked up sharply. 'Explain this, Poley,' he demanded.

Poley grinned. 'That, my lord, is the cypher used by the Queen of Scots to write her secret letters.'

'Francis,' Leicester appealed, holding out the paper to me.

I rose and examined it. It looked genuine. My heart was beating faster. In my hands, I held the key to unlocking Mary's letters. Poley had indeed triumphed. We sent Poley out of the room while we discussed what to do next.

'I was wrong,' I said, as Leicester poured us some wine.

'About Poley?'

'He has proved of value.'

'I'll say.' He tapped the paper. 'This is gold he has brought us.'

'Indeed, it is.'

'Oh, come now, Francis, show a bit of enthusiasm,' Leicester chided me. 'We haven't had something this good for, well, I cannot remember how long.'

'We must make things easier for Poley,' I said, my mind already ahead of his. 'To keep us informed. It will be too obvious to our enemies, who may have him under surveillance, if he visits court or either of our houses on a regular basis.'

'Any ideas about that?'

I nodded. 'If Poley was employed in my own household (we had moved from The Papey to a bigger house in Seething Lane near the Tower) he would appear to be of use to his Catholic contacts, informing on what my family and I are getting up to while actually working for us.'

'The story would be that he had managed to get employment with you?'

'No, not with me, I think, that would raise too much suspicion. With my daughter, perhaps? What think you of that?'

'How about with Philip?' he wondered, referring to my son-in-law. Philip was unable to afford a home of his own and he and Frances had been forced to live with me and Ursula.

'Yes, my lord, an even better idea.'

'Will you tell Philip of Poley's true purpose?'

'Of course, I could not leave him ignorant of that. Philip deserves to know and besides, we do not want him telling Poley anything we would rather Poley did not know.'

So, Leicester transferred all responsibility for Poley to me and Poley became my agent and I kept him close. Thomas Morgan loved the fact that Poley had wormed himself into working in my household. He thought it would give him all the access he and his associates would need to know what the Council were thinking and acting. We did have to feed Poley false information from time to time to keep up the pretence of him still being Morgan's man, information that could be verified and have consequences but nothing of any import, nothing that we could not afford to tell.

Another agent that proved to be of the most vital importance was Gilbert Gifford. He was yet another Catholic who had come to love his life more than his faith. Gifford came from a Catholic family. He had even trained at one of William Allen's seminaries, so he had at one time, at least, been ardent in his faith. The problem with Gifford was that he was a man unable to moderate his behaviour and conform to the strictures of the seminary. As a consequence, he had been expelled from the school. Never one to know when he was not wanted, Gifford travelled to Rheims to try and gain access to another seminary. Given a second chance, you would think that Gifford would have behaved better, but no, he caused trouble again and William Allen himself argued with him so that when it came to making Gifford a deacon, that job was left to the Cardinal of Lorraine. Frankly, I do not know how Gifford managed to convince the cardinal that he would make a good deacon, but I suppose Gifford could be charming when he wanted to be, and perhaps he managed to convince the cardinal that his past bad behaviour had been the indiscretion of youth. By 1585 Gifford was on the move again and this time he turned up in Paris. Like Poley, he made approaches to Thomas Morgan in the Bastille, who was more than ready to take Gifford at his word and believe he was ready and willing to be a courier for Mary's correspondence.

Morgan wrote a letter of introduction to Mary, naming Gifford as a man she could entrust with all of her correspondence. Morgan wrote that he had hopes of Gifford gaining a position with Sir Amyas Paulet in the very house in which Mary was held, and if not there, then Gifford would try to buy the loyalty of Thomas Phelippes. Phelippes laughed mightily when he read of this last, for the news had been communicated in a packet of letters that Poley had forwarded from Paris. He showed it to me with some pride.

'This just shows you how corruptible they believe us to be. Oh, the irony, do you not think, Master Secretary?'

'You cannot be bought, Thomas?' I asked, amused, taking the letter and reading it.

Phelippes put a hand on his chest dramatically. 'I am shocked you could even ask, sir. Even base-born men have their principles, you know.'

'I do know, Thomas. I come from lowly stock myself.'

'Not so lowly as me, Master Secretary, I'll warrant,' he said, chuckling.

But to return to Gilbert Gifford. When he arrived in England in the middle of December 1585, my men were ready and waiting for him. He was arrested at the port of Rye and brought to London. Rather than the palace, the Tower or my own home, I had him taken to a tavern owned by a Mistress Bull, a place I sometimes used for meetings between my agents due to the fact that so many people came and went in the area. I wanted to keep his arrest secret because I had a feeling Gifford was going to be very important to me.

I turned Gifford into my man rather than Morgan's quite easily.

He held out for a few days, more out of pride, I think than anything else. But then he realised that he would spend the rest of his days in prison if he persisted and he quickly accepted the position I was offering him.

On my instructions, Gifford sent a letter to Morgan in the Bastille that he had been arrested by me but that during interrogation, he had convinced me his objective had been to advance the interests of the Welsh faction amongst the seminary priests in the English College and that I was happy for him to do so because it would save me the trouble of having to do it myself. You will remember that the school Allen had founded was riddled with discord, the Welsh always pitting themselves against the English Jesuits and vice versa. I had even given him twenty pounds to fund the mission, Gifford wrote to Morgan gleefully.

Morgan believed Gifford wholeheartedly.

Given permission to proceed by Morgan, Gifford began to cultivate the acquaintances of the London Catholic noblemen and visiting the French embassy to meet with the ambassador. I left him alone for a few weeks, just in case anyone was suspicious of this most conveniently placed young man. But Gifford was nothing if not adept at charming his way into places and with people, and he convinced his new associates that he was a devoted Catholic and Mary Stuart supporter through and through.

Once this had been accomplished, I told Gifford he should show the French ambassador the letter of introduction from Morgan. He said he already knew how letters to Mary were being carried in the French diplomatic bag and conveyed into England. Now he, Gifford, was offering to convey them directly to Mary Stuart herself, something Morgan had not yet been able to achieve from behind his fortress's walls.

Ambassador Chateauneuf was no fool and he was careful about believing young Gifford purely on his say-so. The ambassador thought he would conduct a trial and gave Gifford just one relatively harmless letter to deliver to Mary. It was written in code using a cypher that was at least two years old. It was child's play for Phelippes to decipher it and he discovered a letter that merely enquired after Mary's health, which the sender had heard was not good, and to encourage her not to give up hope that her confinement would soon end. In what manner or how it would end, the sender did not elaborate.

Gifford promised Chateauneuf a swift delivery and off he

went to Chartley Hall where Mary was now being held. His journey, he assured the ambassador, would raise no eyebrows because his family home was nearby and he had been out of England for so long it was unlikely he would be recognised by anyone on the way. As I say, Gifford always had all the answers ready.

Gifford was very successful and Mary was delighted at receiving the letter, for she had been deprived of unapproved correspondence for such a long time, Paulet's security being so tight. As a result, Mary wrote a letter to Chateauneuf for Gifford to convey, congratulating him on his messenger, and now that a new method of communication had been opened up, enclosing a new cypher which she would begin to use as soon as she received more news from the French ambassador.

Mary was falling into my trap.

I wasn't about to repeat my first mistake with Mary Stuart.

When I had first discovered her secret correspondence, I had acted too quickly and had lacked the evidence needed to persuade Elizabeth to take action. I was determined not to be so precipitous again.

Back then, my discovery of Mary's courier had exposed him and he was quickly terminated as her agent. This was a mistake, cutting off Mary's primary means of communication with the outside world. It had meant that a new avenue was opened up, one that I did not then have knowledge of and it took time to discover how Mary was getting her letters out. I learnt that it would have been much better to keep quiet, watch and wait. That way, I could have read her letters, found out what she was up to and been ahead of the game. As it was, I had had to use up valuable resources trying to catch up with her.

I cannot take all the credit for the success Gifford enjoyed. In truth, the enterprise had been created by Phelippes and Paulet, they creating a situation that had no trace of government interference about it. A local brewer who delivered to Chartley once a week was the courier. He delivered barrels of beer and took away the empty ones. Gifford bribed this man to secrete letters in a hollowed-out bunghole that could then be passed to Mary and vice versa. Gifford told Paulet about how he had managed this and Paulet had the bright idea of bribing the same man to let him see the letters before he passed them on. The brewer was delighted; he was, after all, being paid twice for the same service. Paulet was careful, though, to keep him in the dark about who was whose man, so the brewer genuinely believed that Gifford was on Mary's side and never told Paulet who had set up the messenger service.

This scenario also enabled Paulet to keep a check on Gifford and ensure that he was indeed our man, that he was not double-crossing us and actually working for Mary. Once Paulet had removed the letters from the bunghole, he would pass them to Phelippes, who would use his considerable skill to quickly decode them. Thus, we were able to know the very workings of the Scottish queen's mind.

In the meantime, we had been keeping a very close eye on an English missionary priest by the name of Father John Ballard. He had left England when Elizabeth came to the throne but returned to cause trouble. Wherever he went, he always travelled under an assumed name, but his real name was once foolishly mentioned in a letter to Mary. In this letter, Ballard was recommended to her as being a man who could rally the Catholic forces in England to rebel against Elizabeth if only foreign troops could be promised.

It is a small world, this one of courts and courtiers, and Bernadino de Mendoza, the ambassador we had exposed and dismissed for plotting, had been appointed Spanish ambassador to the French. We soon discovered Mendoza had hopes of reinitiating the plot he had been hatching with Francis Throckmorton back in 1584 in collusion with Charles Paget.

Charles Paget was another of those Catholic exiles who had fled to the Continent. He spent most of his time in Paris and Rouen and became a particular acquaintance of Thomas Morgan. Together, Morgan and Paget handled almost all of Mary Stuart's correspondence as well as her financial affairs.

Mendoza wrote to Charles Paget to say that he had already broached the idea of deposing Elizabeth and replacing her with Mary with King Philip of Spain, with whom the project found favour. Mendoza asked Paget to say nothing to anyone about this, but he grossly misjudged his man and Paget, school boyishly eager to impart good news, wrote to Mary to tell her the plot was once again on.

When my agents discovered Father Ballard in London, he was calling himself Captain Fortescue. He was making a habit of frequenting the London taverns, identifying the idle and rich young Catholic men who could be roused to deeds of daring by providing service for the unfortunate, imprisoned Scottish queen. Ballard found such a man in Sir Anthony Babington.

CHAPTER 19

Sir Anthony Babington was a young man of twenty-five. He was handsome, so some women thought, though I thought him a weak-looking kind of man with pouchy, dark-ringed eyes and a nose too long for his face. He was also rich and a Catholic. In him, Ballard had discovered a young man who was not only vain and impressionable but one who had served as a page in Shrewsbury's household when he had custody of Mary Stuart. As such, in his mind, Babington had created an image of a damsel in distress, a beautiful queen wrongly imprisoned by the Whore of Babylon that was Elizabeth Tudor. Babington had been in France and become involved, in only a minor capacity, with the missionary priests there. He had once been mentioned in the letters sent to me by my agent resident in Paris, Henry Fagot, as a boy who had been helping to distribute Catholic propaganda. So, he already had experience in Catholic deception and was ripe for Ballard's plucking.

When it became clear that Babington and Ballard were meeting, I instructed Robert Poley to get to know them both. Since I had released him from acting as courier between the French and Mary, Poley had taken up residence in London and soon developed a reputation amongst the capital's Catholics as someone who gave a good dinner and who was very obliging if someone needed lodgings for a relative or friend for a few nights without the authorities knowing.

Before long, the talk between the three turned to conspiracy as it was inevitably to do, and Poley stoked Ballard's and Babington's fire in this regard. Babington, he told me, was easy to rouse. Being rich and idle, the young man had little to think of but brave deeds and having songs of glory written about him. I noted a tinge of derision in Poley's voice when he spoke of Babington and it amused me to know that even amongst Catholics there were those who were found contemptible.

And then this little group of conspirators was joined by another, a John Savage. Savage had also studied at the Rheims seminary — as I say, Allen's 'schools' churned out English Catholic traitors — where he had, as witnessed by Gifford, sworn an oath that he would, if he could, murder Elizabeth. Never was a man so full of style and so lacking in substance as John Savage. He cut an impressive figure, being tall and broad across the chest, and with a rugged head framed by thick brown hair offsetting a face that had all the appearance of integrity and reliability. But he was a fake. All his words came out of the mouth of a braggart. He would swear this and that, promise to do things that only Hercules could rival, and in the end, meant none of them. Ballard made a poor choice when he took Savage into his circle.

As will often happen with such groups, they looked about them for others who felt and thought the same as they and they managed to swell their rotten number to thirteen. They would meet, secretly, undetected, or so they thought, at various locations in London, including Babington's house in Hern's Rents and at a tavern called the Plough Inn, where the landlord was an informant of mine. The group also arranged meetings around St Paul's and in the centre of Saint Giles Fields, night after night.

These were men full of fantasies; they were men who should have known better. Ballard was the most fanciful of them all, for it was he who claimed Mendoza had made a promise that there were sixty-thousand Spanish troops just waiting to sail to England on his say-so and that it was their job to ensure they would have the English support so necessary to the invasion's success. It was also Ballard who insisted that central to their plot's success was the assassination of Elizabeth, that no good would come of it were she to be left alive to cause the same kind of trouble that Mary Stuart had done ever since her imprisonment in England. And this from a man of God! And it was Ballard who reminded John Savage that he had taken an oath to kill Elizabeth. My informant reported that Savage, so keen to swear brave oaths, actually blanched when he was singled out by Ballard to be Elizabeth's assassin.

For his part, and I suppose I must do him some justice, Babington voiced his uncertainty about whether it was necessary to kill Elizabeth. He queried the legality of the matter and refuted the Pope's Bull which stated that all Catholics had a duty to seek her death if they possibly could, for after all, he pointed out, the Bull had no bearing in English law.

But what of Mary in all this, you ask? Well, Paget was keen to keep her informed of what was being planned on her behalf and my heart began to beat faster when we received her first response. Mary wrote directly to Babington, full of gratitude for his declaration of service and support, but frustratingly, did not go into details of how such service and support would be manifested. If only she would commit herself on paper!

Fortunately, Babington was not so careful. I suppose he had not had the years of experience to be so, that he really had no idea that there were men such as I tasked with protecting the Queen, nor that there were men such as Gifford who were living double lives, who were dissemblers. Babington wrote to Mary in the vaguest of terms to tell her a plot was being devised to free her and place her on the English throne, the old story. I did wonder if Mary ever became tired of hearing of such plots. They were more frequent than rain during an English summer and none so far had amounted to anything. I caught my breath as I read the lines where he asked for her approval in the matter. Knowing what I knew of him, I could almost hear his desperation. Was he hoping that Mary would reply saying that the plan was not to go ahead, that the men must not, under any circumstances, countenance the killing of her cousin?

If that was what Babington was hoping for, he was bitterly disappointed. Mary seemed to approve of the idea, though she was circumspect in the way she dressed her approval. She did not mention the assassination of Elizabeth. She did not mention her freedom. She merely said she was grateful that she had such men as Babington willing to serve her.

Babington conveyed the details of the plot to her. He would

be the leader of ten men and hundreds of followers who would undertake her delivery from the usurper's hands, by which he meant Elizabeth. Of the assassination itself, six of the ten, with John Savage at their head, would undertake the 'tragical execution', as he phrased this terrible deed. It was the first time that it had been put in such stark words.

Mary replied to say she had received Babington's letter and that she would send on a fuller reply in a few days time. Why the delay, Phelippes and I wondered? We knew that to be at liberty and to be Queen of England was what Mary desperately wanted. Did she suspect a trap, a trick? Was she wondering if she could trust Babington? We had to wait another tense three days before her next letter could be smuggled out of Chartley.

When that reply came and Phelippes had passed on to me a decrypted copy of it, I saw that a gallows had been drawn upon the exterior. This could not have been Mary's handiwork, so I knew it must have been Phelippes. I realised as I looked at the black ink lines of the gallows that inside the letter must be the confirmation of Mary's guilt that I had been waiting so long for and this was his idea of a little joke. My hands actually trembled as I broke the red wax seal and unfolded the letter.

Mary wanted details: how many men were expected to rise on her behalf, how much money would be needed, who the captains of each troop would be and at which ports they would be landing. And then she moved on to the matter that hit closest to Elizabeth. I believe Elizabeth had always held some notion that Mary would never actively seek to do her harm, in some sort of reciprocal fellow cousinly feeling. After all, Elizabeth had always refused to harm Mary even though her counsellors had urged her to it. But Mary, it seemed, had no such qualms about causing harm to her cousin.

I shall give you Mary Stuart's words in full regarding Elizabeth's assassination, so you can read for yourself the sheer extent of her viciousness. '*The affairs being thus prepared and forces in readiness both within and without the realm, then shall it be time to set the six gentlemen to work, taking order, upon the accomplishing of their design, I may be suddenly transported out of this place.*'

There, her guilt made manifest in black and white. She also said that Elizabeth should not be assassinated before she herself was free because she feared that should the escape attempt fail, then Elizabeth would deal harshly with her and put her in some deeper, less comfortable prison from which all hope of freedom would be removed. Even then, she did not believe that Elizabeth would have her life. She never afforded Elizabeth the same respect. She was intent on having Elizabeth dead. Mary insisted that Babington burn her letter to remove all trace of her consent to Elizabeth's death and the plot.

And it is at this point that the matter became complicated. Up to then, it had all seemed so very easy. But Poley had been having regular meetings with Babington and had reported back to me that Babington was becoming less and less eager to partake in the plot the longer time went on. Mary's last letter had made him break out in a cold sweat, Poley reported. Babington really did not want to kill Elizabeth, not I think because of any moral qualms, but simply because he was terrified of being caught. He wanted a way out of the mess and he looked to Poley to help him.

Knowing that Poley had connections with myself, Babington offered him three hundred pounds if Poley could use his relationship with me to be provided with a passport whereby he could travel to France, or indeed anywhere on the Continent. There, Babington said by way of explanation, he could use his contacts to be of service to... Elizabeth! How these Catholics could change their loyalties!

Babington wanted to meet with me. I was intrigued, I'll admit. Up until that point, I had only known Babington through his letters and reports. I had also caught an occasional glimpse of him on the infrequent occasions he attended court. I wanted to meet this young man who thought he was a brave lion but was turning out to be a mouse. Although I had no intention of providing him with a passport or using him as an agent, I told Poley he could tell Babington he had managed to persuade me to meet with him.

Babington put on a good show when we met. He was full of a young man's seeming confidence, smiling too widely when he thought I made a joke or when he wasn't sure what I was making, explaining how useful he could be to me abroad. Perhaps I thought it amusing to string him along, but I said neither yes nor no to his request for a passport. Rather, I suggested that a passport might be possible but that it would take some time to arrange. He questioned why that should be. I merely shrugged and said that it was so. I did not need to make excuses, at least, not to one such as he.

Through Poley, a few weeks later I offered Babington a chance to meet with myself and Elizabeth to discuss his helping our interests abroad. Any courtier worth his breeding would jump at the chance to have a personal meeting with the Queen, but Babington seemed to shrink into himself and confessed to Poley that he wasn't sure of where he stood with me, whether he was being played like a cat's paw by both Mary and me, and whether he should just walk away from the enterprise altogether.

'We should have him arrested at once,' Phelippes said with vehemence one morning as another missive from Poley arrived to report on his latest, uneventful dealings with Babington.

'Not yet,' I told him, tapping my quill against my chin thoughtfully. 'There is one more service Sir Anthony can do for us that may just give us the evidence the Queen demands.'

'And what is that, Master Secretary?'

I put my quill down and leant back in my chair, folding my hands over my stomach. 'What if Babington received a letter from Mary in which she asked to know the names of the six gentlemen who are to assassinate the Queen? Would he oblige and write back with the names?'

Phelippes raised his eyebrows behind his spectacles and blew out a puff of air. 'If you want my opinion, Master Secretary…'

'I do.'

'Then I think Babington has already grown too suspicious. He may become very alarmed if he is asked to commit names to paper.'

'You think he would not do it?'

'I do not know the man well enough to predict his every move, if you will forgive me for saying so, but I think any man might hesitate before such an act. And then, I think it might make him move in other ways.'

'You think he may flee?'

Phelippes nodded. 'With or without a passport.'

I considered a moment. 'I am grateful to you for your opinion, Thomas, but I think it may be worth the risk. Have that clerk, the one who can write in the hand that is so very like Mary Stuart's, add a postscript to the next letter that comes from Mary that asks for the names of the assassins. Have it despatched to Babington with all haste.'

Phelippes arranged for the false postscript to be written. It read thus: *I would be glad to know the names and qualities of the six gentlemen which are to accomplish the design, for that it may be, I shall be able upon knowledge of the parties to give you some further advice necessary to be followed therein: and even so do I wish to be made acquainted with the names of all such principal persons etc., as also from time to time particularly how you proceed and as soon as you may for the same purpose who be already and how far every one privy hereunto.*

Phelippes showed me the addition. It was good. The handwriting matched well, indeed if I had not known it to be a forgery, I would have taken it for Mary's own hand. And the manner of the words matched the way Mary composed her lines. But was it too much? Was I being foolhardy? I convinced myself that I was not and I waited anxiously to see if I had been right. I was inclined to think I had been wrong when three days passed and still Babington failed to answer 'Mary's' request for names.

Phelippes appealed to me. 'What do you want us to do, sir?'

I took a deep breath before answering. 'Wait one more day and if he hasn't written, send our men to arrest him. And in the meantime, write out a warrant for the arrest of Father Ballard.'

Phelippes waited that one extra day but no letter came from Babington. Phelippes sent the men to his lodgings to take his person into custody but when they arrived, they discovered Babington had gone. I was at Richmond Palace when I received the news from Phelippes and I began to panic. The postscript that I had had added to Mary's letter, coupled with the lack of news from me about a passport, had made Babington certain he was undone and he had fled. I had lost him.

Or so I thought.

It soon transpired that Babington had left his lodgings but had only done so in order to find Poley, the one man he thought was entirely loyal to Queen Mary and could help him out of his difficulty. He told Poley everything, everything about the plot to kill Elizabeth, the freeing of Mary Stuart, Mendoza's assurances of Spanish backing and how it had all come to be through the machinations of Father Ballard.

Poley came to visit me at Richmond with this information,

adding that Babington was urgently requesting a meeting with me. Part of me remembered how close I had come to losing Babington by playing a wait-and-see game, but I had the notion that in making Babington wait to see me and so remain visible, accessible in London, he may be approached by Ballard, at which point that awful man could be apprehended. I had come this far. I reasoned that I may as well play the game out to its end.

And I got lucky. Poley seemed to have made himself the man for the conspirators to go to, and Ballard visited Poley at his London house. Poley managed to keep him there until my men could arrive to arrest him.

I had the chief conspirator. I could afford to lay my hands on Babington and the others now.

I took the news to Elizabeth.

I had been keeping her apprised of the plot, though she had not bothered to show much interest in it. I believe she thought that it was like so many of the plots that I had kept her informed of over the years, all talk and no action. She was, I knew, also weary with what she liked to call my obsession with her cousin.

But when I laid down my evidence upon her desk — the letter from Mary with the paragraph about the assassination, Babington and the other conspirators' confessions and the truth extracted from Father Ballard — her anger burst forth.

I had never seen her so angry, even in her fiercest moments with me. As well as the book she had once hurled at me, she had also once taken off her slipper and thrown that at my face, the heel causing a purple, green bruise to come out across my cheekbone. My face sometimes bore the marks of her wrath.

'How dare she!' she screamed in her chamber, her ladies scattering to the corners. 'How dare she contrive my death when I have done nothing but care for her! And these men, oh these men, that have sworn to do her service. Who is she that she can command men's hearts so, men she has not even met?'

I opened my mouth to answer her but she began again before I could utter a sound.

'Men claim they are willing to do service for her, do they?' She nodded so vigorously that her red wig wobbled upon her head and caused a pearl to drop from it. She did not seem to notice. 'Willing to suffer torment to free her, eh? Well, if that is what they want, they can damn well have it.'

'Your Majesty?' I queried, wondering where her mind was heading.

'I want them to suffer for this,' she snarled. Saliva dribbled from her lips.

'Their trial will deliver a guilty verdict and they will be sentenced to execution, madam,' I assured her.

'Oh yes, to be hung and then have their accursed bodies cut open, eh? No. What kind of punishment is that? They will be dead quickly, they will not suffer long, they will not suffer enough for this. No, I want them to suffer an exquisite agony.'

I could not believe what I was hearing. 'Madam, have you witnessed an execution? A great deal of pain is inflicted by the hangman—'

'Not enough, not nearly enough, sir,' she yelled. 'You will instruct the executioner to let them hang only for a moment or so and then cut them down while they are still conscious. And then,' she held up a finger to stop me interrupting, 'he is to disembowel them while they watch. I want them to see their insides pulled out.' She made wrenching gestures to indicate what she meant.

My stomach turned over at the hatred on Elizabeth's face and the images her actions were conjuring, though I do not believe myself to be made of womanly stuff. I had met, come face to face with some of these men, as she had not. It is much easier to imagine pain happening to someone with whom one has not exchanged words.

'Madam, are you sure?'

She came right up to me and stuck her face into mine. Her breath, sickly sweet from her decaying teeth, slid over my skin. 'Do not dare to question me in this, Master Secretary. You *will* instruct the executioner. They are to suffer greatly for their treachery. You understand?'

'I understand,' I said and took a step back. Her eyes were still blazing and I suddenly wanted nothing more than to be gone, to be out of her presence. I bowed and backed out of the door, dreading that she would call me back.

I thought what she wanted was a mistake. I told Leicester so,

I told Cecil so, but neither of them was willing to argue with Elizabeth. They too had seen her anger.

I witnessed the executions of the plotters. It was beyond horrible, the worse thing I have ever seen, well, almost the worse. I still think of the massacre in Paris as the most vile thing I have ever witnessed. Babington was the first to climb the scaffold and his suffering... I can hardly bear to put it into words. No execution is ever pleasant viewing, but with the usual kind of execution, the viewer knows what to expect: butchery, pain, punishment. But this was punishment beyond all reason, beyond all humanity. And the crowd thought so too. They made their displeasure known. Before the second group of conspirators could be brought to the scaffold to endure their punishments, the crowd threatened the executioner. 'Leave them to hang,' they cried, 'or we'll put you on your own block.'

Without instructions to the contrary, the executioner, who ensured the guards surrounded him more closely to protect him from the onlookers, continued with the hangings and disembowelling as the Queen had demanded. But I hurried back to the court and burst into her privy chamber without waiting to be announced. Elizabeth was playing on the virginals and she broke off her tune abruptly.

'What is this, Master Secretary?' she demanded, ready to rebuke me for interrupting.

'You must forgive me, madam, but what I have to say cannot wait. The conspirators are being executed according to your instructions, but...' I had to pause to catch my breath, my throat was so dry. 'The extreme nature of the executions does not meet with the approval of the crowd. They are restless and angry. They are blaming you for the agony the men are being put through and are calling you cruel.'

I knew this last would have the most effect upon Elizabeth, for she was ever eager to maintain the goodwill of her people. She stared at me for a long moment, her mouth puckering as she considered my words. She drew herself up.

'Very well, Master Secretary, you are to instruct the hangman that the rest are to be left to hang until they are dead before he cuts them up. What of Babington? Is he still to be executed?'

'No, madam, he was the first to go to the block.'

'He suffered?'

'Greatly,' I assured her.

'Very well, that will have to be enough. You may go.'

I hurried back to Tower Hill. The executioner was given his new instructions and I could see the relief on his face, for he had been genuinely concerned that the crowd would do him harm for following the Queen's orders.

So ended the Babington plotters.

And so began the beginning of Mary's end.

It was a good time to tidy up loose ends.

Once Babington and his fellow conspirators were caught, Mary and her supporters would work out how they had been caught and any of my agents involved would be suspected and no longer of any use to them.

Both Gifford and Poley anticipated this state of affairs, although Gifford was much quicker off the mark than Poley. Gifford fled to Paris, where he reckoned I could not get hold of him but took the precaution to write to my office to assure us that there was no sinister reason for his flight, save that he feared for his life from the Catholics he had so successfully deceived. It was a plausible excuse and we, Phelippes and I, came to the conclusion that it was a good idea to choose to believe Gifford and keep him as an agent in reserve. His name was carefully expunged from all of the trial transcripts, so that had anyone wanted to point the finger of blame at him, they would have had a great deal of trouble to provide evidence.

Personally, I felt that Gifford had done a very good job and decided to reward his services. I gave him a pension of one hundred pounds per annum out of my own finances, as I knew it was pointless to ask the Council or Elizabeth to pay for it. The pension was enough to give him a comfortable life, whatever he chose to do, and besides, it meant he was in my debt and always within reach.

As for Poley... well, I never took to the man and as I say, he was slow to react to the exposure of the Babington plot. Perhaps he thought he had a privileged position with me and did not need to make haste, but he was wrong. I had never been sure of his loyalty and there had been incidents, too small at the time to worry me greatly, but which nevertheless led me to conclude that it would be politic to have him locked up for a while. So, I sent him to the Tower and had the news of his imprisonment broadcast abroad, so that any Catholics who suspected him of double-dealing with them would think again. They would not believe that I would have my own agent incarcerated, would they? Feel no pity for him. I arranged for him to be released eventually and he willingly returned to my service.

CHAPTER 20

Now was the time to deal once and for all with Mary Stuart. I had the evidence that she had committed treason, had plotted with Elizabeth's subjects and even been complicit in the planned assassination. Elizabeth could no longer pretend Mary was no threat to her safety.

I ordered Mary's rooms at Chartley to be searched. Any papers found there were seized and sent on to me. We knew what papers she had, of course, for we had already seen and copied them, but I needed the original papers to be found in Mary's possession if Elizabeth was going to believe that Mary had been actively plotting against her. When I had assembled all my evidence, I took it to Elizabeth.

'You mean to put her on trial?' she asked as she picked at the debris on her plate, for she was still eating her breakfast. I had not waited for her to finish, so impatient was I to proceed with the matter.

'There are grounds for a trial, madam.'

'To put her treason on show for all to see.'

I sighed silently. 'And why not, madam? Does she not deserve it?'

Elizabeth looked up at me, her jaw moving up and down as she chewed. 'You have been wanting this for a long time, my Moor. How pleased you must be.'

'I am pleased to have uncovered her and her supporters'

treachery, indeed I am, madam. I am not at all pleased that it has been necessary.'

'Oh, very nicely said,' she sneered a smile at me. 'Very well, Master Secretary. Arrange the trial. But I want to see justice done. This is to be no show trial, you hear me? The evidence shall be judged, my cousin's involvement proved, or else I will take no action. Not against her, anyway.'

'I want no more than justice, madam, and for justice to have been seen to be done.'

It was true what I said. I did not want anyone to be able to say that Mary Stuart had been tried and convicted illegally. Her guilt had to be plain for all to see, for none to disprove.

The Council met to discuss how best to proceed. It was decided to bring Mary to Fotheringay Castle because it was well fortified. A moat surrounded the castle on three sides and the River Nene was on the fourth. It would not be easy for Mary's supporters to attempt a rescue.

At first, Mary refused to attend her own trial. As an anointed queen, she said, she had no peers who were able to judge her and she would submit to none of lower degree. But this was no stumbling block. We on the Council merely informed her that if she refused to attend, we would simply go ahead without her. That threat soon changed her mind and she agreed to appear before us.

The trial began on the fifteenth of October 1586. The charges were read against Mary. They were lengthy and there were astonished, horrified gasps from those attending who had had no knowledge of just what Mary Stuart was guilty of.

Mary Stuart was such a liar. On the first day of the trial, when questioned, she claimed not to have had any knowledge of Sir Anthony Babington nor of any plot. The confessions of the plotters were read out in which they stated they had received letters from her, applauding their intended deed. Her own secretaries were examined, and they reluctantly admitted that they had written the letters on Mary's instructions and sent them off to Babington and the others. Mary tried to fob us off, saying she was not responsible for what her secretaries chose to write and that they should bear any punishment for their unauthorised scribblings that was due. How loyal she was to her servants! How mindful of their care!

When a copy of Babington's letter was produced, Mary declared that it was simplicity itself to copy the cyphers used by others and pointed her finger at me. 'He did it, that man there, conspired with false fire to bring me to this pass.'

I was not having this woman with blood on her hands condemn me for the exposure of her treachery. I stood and appealed to my fellow judges.

'I call God to witness, that as a private person I have done nothing unbeseeming an honest man, neither in my public condition and quality have I done anything unworthy of my place. I confess that, out of my great care for the safety of the Queen and realm, I have curiously endeavoured to search and sift out all plots and designs against the same. I have done no underhand endeavour to root out the source and cause of this conspiracy.'

The many heads around me nodded, acknowledging the truth of my words. Mary was red-faced by the time I sat back down. She had tried to blacken my honour and she had not succeeded. Instead, she had shown herself to be vicious, spiteful, a damned liar. She realised her error, too, for she swiftly withdrew the accusation that I had forged her letters.

I did not doubt that we would all find against her. The evidence was too strong, too convincing and many of my judges, which included Cecil and Leicester, had long been of the opinion that it would be best for England if Mary were dead. On the twenty-fifth of October, just ten days after the trial commenced, we delivered a verdict of Guilty.

Now, Elizabeth had to be told.

Elizabeth listened with a stony face throughout my report of Mary's treason. She read with heavy breaths the evidence I laid before her. She looked at me wide-eyed when I said we judges had weighed the evidence against Mary and agreed that it all pointed to treason and that she was guilty. A guilty verdict having been reached and justice needing to be done, what came next must needs be Mary Stuart's death.

'You mean to have her head?' she said, a tremble in her voice.

'It is the punishment for treason, madam. Her co-conspirators have paid the price for their treason. It is only right that Mary Stuart suffer the same.'

'She is an anointed queen, Master Secretary.'

I had heard this argument from her lips so many times before. It carried no weight with me. 'An anointed queen without a kingdom to reign over, madam. An anointed queen who has enjoyed your protection for many years and has continually repaid your kindness with deceit and treachery. An anointed queen who corrupts all who come into contact with her.'

'How you do hate my cousin, my Moor,' Elizabeth shook her head. 'Why do you so?'

I straightened, ready with my response. 'Madam, if you had been witness to the savagery I saw on St Bartholomew's Eve, you would not ask that question.'

'She was not responsible for that slaughterhouse.'

'If you will forgive me, madam, but all Catholics of noble or royal birth are responsible. With their very words, their lack of condemnation for such atrocities, their very approval of such actions, they give heart to every Catholic rebel in the world.'

Elizabeth buried her face in her hands and her body began to shake with sobs. 'I cannot kill my cousin, I cannot do it.'

She carried on in this vein for some weeks. In the end, Cecil and I decided that only Leicester could convince her of the necessity for Mary's death. We wrote to him in the Netherlands where he was on campaign aiding the Dutch rebels in fighting against the Spanish invaders and urged him to return to England to persuade the Queen to execute her cousin.

Leicester did return, looking I thought very ill and much older than his years, and had an audience with Elizabeth. She was very glad to see him, not so glad to hear what he had returned to say to her. Leicester convinced Elizabeth that Mary Stuart must die and she, hearing the words from his lips, at last believed the truth of this.

But she was not done with being duplicitous. She signed the warrant for Mary's execution that the Council's secretary, William Davison, presented her with and told him to present it to me at my house in Seething Lane, she sarcastically joking that I would die with sorrow at the sight of it. But then, as Davison was about to leave, she called after him and said to tell me that I should write to Paulet and have him administer poison to Mary, such a death being so much more convenient than an execution. What Elizabeth really meant was that it would be so much better for her conscience if someone else killed Mary Stuart. Her hands, then, would be clean.

Davison passed on Elizabeth's words. I was appalled at the suggestion of a secret murder, however justified, but I did as I was bid and wrote to Paulet to tell him what the Queen had said. Paulet, I have to say, made me feel immensely proud of a man I called friend and who was my fellow in faith. Not for him, unlike the Catholic wretch he guarded, was the dishonourable murder. He refused to countenance such an idea, saying he would not make such a foul shipwreck of his soul or leave such an ignoble stain on his honour as to cause a death in such a manner that was not sanctioned by English law.

I called Paulet an upright, honest and faithful Protestant. Elizabeth called him a precise and dainty fellow, a sneer in her voice.

There was more trouble to come. Elizabeth had signed the warrant, but she refused for it to be despatched and thereby acted upon. Davison was forced to remain in possession of it. Upon reflection, I realise I should have helped him more. Davison did not know Elizabeth so well as I, he did not know how to interpret her moods, her actions, her damned indecision. He did not understand the game she was playing.

Davison appealed to Cecil, asking what was to be done. He said that the warrant was signed, Elizabeth wanted Mary dead. Now what was he to do? Had Elizabeth changed her mind? Had she forgotten that the warrant needed to be despatched?

We discussed the matter in Council at a time when we knew Elizabeth was otherwise engaged — she was out riding with the Italian ambassador. We decided we needed to act, with or without her consent. Some of my fellow counsellors baulked at taking such an audacious step.

'But Her Majesty has not ordered us to despatch the warrant,' they protested.

'She has signed the warrant, need I remind you,' I ventured, appealing to Leicester to step in. As her closest friend, he knew Elizabeth best. I looked to him to know how to act.

'The Queen wants Mary dead,' he confirmed, breaking the silence that followed my words. 'But she has so much womanly feeling that she does not want to condemn her own cousin to such a death.'

This was a little hard to swallow, I confess, especially with the brutal executions of Babington and the others still fresh in our minds. For my part, their deaths were seared into my brain.

'I say we take this burden from off her shoulders,' Leicester continued. 'Elizabeth has done her part, she has signed the warrant. It is up to us to despatch it and have the whole damned business done with.'

To signal his intent, he pulled the letter I had had drafted that bore the instructions for Mary's execution. Leicester signed his name at the bottom: R. Leicester. He held out the quill to Cecil. They looked at one another, then Cecil took the quill and signed his name. He passed it to me. The nib was dry and I did not hesitate to dip it in the inkpot and sign my name too. I looked at it: Sir F. Walsingham. My name was on Mary's death warrant. I passed the quill and paper to my neighbour and so around the table it went until we had all put our names to the instructions.

'Send it,' Cecil instructed.

And so, at last, on the eighth of February 1586, Mary Stuart went to her maker.

She made a drama out of it, of course. At around ten o'clock, the appointed time, she climbed the two steps up to the scaffold that had been specially built in the Presence Chamber at Fotheringay Castle. This scaffold had been well prepared for a queen, being covered in black cotton, from the railings around the edges to the boards she stood upon, as well as the block upon which she would lay her neck. She was even given a soft pillow to kneel on. It could not be said that we treated her like any common criminal meeting his end.

The warrant for her death issued by Elizabeth was read out for the record-takers to note down. Then the Dean of Peterborough stepped forward and began to speak to Mary, attempting to prepare her soul by asking her to die in the true faith of Christ, the Protestant faith. Mary held out her hand and turned her head away.

'I will listen not to you,' she said. 'I will have nothing to do with you, neither will you have aught to do with me. Your faith is a lie. I will die in the True Faith, the Roman Catholic faith. I recognise no other.'

Mary held a crucifix in her hands and she began to pray in Latin, so loudly that even those at the back of the hall could hear her. When done, she knelt on the pillow and began another prayer, praying that heretics should realise the error of their ways and return to the true church, for her son who even now occupied her throne and gave not a thought to his mother, and lastly, incredibly, to preserve the person of Elizabeth to prosper and serve God.

She got to her feet again and her servants stepped forward to remove her cloak after Mary had waved away the two executioners who had stepped forward to relieve her of it. When her ladies took away her cloak, they revealed a skirt and bodice of deepest red. Mary had gone through her life portraying herself as one kind of victim or another: the young virgin wife of King Francis, exiled from her home by her wicked mother-in-law, the cheated wife of the rake, Henry Darnley, the reluctant mistress and wife of a Scottish rebel and the prisoner of a heretic queen. Her last role was to be that of Catholic martyr, hence the dress of red. She would have history remember her as such and conveniently ignore all the misery she had caused.

Mary knelt once more and laid her neck on the block, her face to the side. She almost shouted, *In manus tuas Domine*, which means 'Into thy hands, oh Lord, I commend my spirit'. It took three blows of the axe to chop off her head. The first hit the back of her head, causing a spray of blood. The second found its mark on her neck but was not heavy enough to cut through the bone. The third swing of the axe severed Mary's head from her body.

When the executioner held up her head to declare the death of a traitor, the blood-dripping head fell out of his grasp and bounced on the wooden planks to roll to a rest at the edge of the platform. All he was left holding was a red wig.

The crowd of watchers as one cried out, 'God save the Queen, and so perish all papists and her Majesty's enemies' as they had been instructed to do.

And so ended Mary, Queen of Scots.

CHAPTER 21

If we had thought that the world would suddenly come aright after the bosom serpent, Mary Stuart, was dead, then we were miserably wrong.

Elizabeth went to pieces. She acted as if the death of her cousin had come as the greatest of surprises and she went about the court openly mourning Mary's end. Fortunately, I was at home when this so-called mourning took place. I had had another attack of my stomach illness and pain in my privates and was unable to attend court. Poor Davison bore almost the entire brunt of the Queen's anger, despite the Council's best efforts to assure Elizabeth that the decision to despatch the death warrant had been taken by all of her counsellors. No, as far as she was concerned, it was all Davison's fault. The poor man was arrested and taken to the Tower. Elizabeth was even threatening to have him executed.

At first, I thought all this wailing and finger-pointing was just for show, something for the ambassadors to witness so they would stop looking at her askance and whispering behind their hands and make excuses for her when they wrote their letters to the masters. But then I received word from Robert Beale that Elizabeth had even consulted lawyers as to whether she had the legal right to execute Davison.

Forgive this digression for a moment, but I must say a word about Robert Beale. Robert had been a clerk at the French embassy when I took over as ambassador and I had kept him on in that capacity. It was one of the wisest decisions I ever made. Robert proved himself more than a servant to me. He became not only my friend but kin to me when he married Ursula's sister, Edith. He has been alongside me in every position I have occupied. He has always made himself available when I have needed him, whether for his clerical abilities or just as someone to talk and unburden myself to. In short, he has been the brother I never had. I owe him so much.

To return to the matter. Elizabeth was told she did have the right to execute him and I truly worried for Davison's life. Cecil was also greatly concerned. He wrote a letter to the lawyers and told them that it was a sad day and a hard decree if a man could be killed for doing his duty and for the Queen to be erroneously told that, to all intents and purposes, she is above the law of the land.

We all tried our hardest to absolve Davison of any crime at all, each of us begging an audience with the Queen to ask her to show mercy and pardon his faults, but in the end, the best we could do was reduce his alleged crime to one of 'contempt and misprision'. Elizabeth would countenance nothing less. He was fined ten thousand marks and sentenced to remain in the Tower until she saw fit to release him. It was a poor reward for his service, but it was better by far than losing his head. By 1588, after many months spent in that grim fortress, we managed to have Davison freed and the fine cancelled. The poor man would never have been able to pay it anyway. Though Davison could not continue visibly in his post, nor did he wish to for the very sight of the Queen caused him to tremble and sweat, I saw to it that he continued to receive his salary and due allowances.

Can I tell truth? Can I say, without fear of retribution, that I detested Elizabeth for what she did to Davison? The way she treated that honest man was not the act of a just sovereign. It was the act of a bitter, vindictive woman. I will not absolutely say that a king would have acted any more kindly, but I believe a man would have acknowledged the dishonour he committed had he acted so. Again and again, I found and still find myself believing that a king is infinitely preferable to a queen. There, I have said it and I am glad to have done so. And indeed, now I think about it, what harm can be done me? I am too close to the grave to fear the Queen and her wrath.

When Mary Stuart was protesting her innocence and undergoing the trial that would lead to her death, a personal tragedy struck my family.

After Leicester had signed his name to Mary's death warrant, his work in England done, he reluctantly returned to the Netherlands to continue fighting against the Spanish. He rejoined my son-in-law, Philip, who had been managing things in his absence. Poor Philip. Not only did he have to bear this great responsibility, a responsibility for which there was no financial recompense or even thanks from the Queen in whose service he performed it, but he had to endure the loss of first his father then his mother, both in the space of a few months of each other. The Sidneys and the Dudleys were not like other noble families. They loved one another greatly. When the news reached Philip of the death of his father, he petitioned Elizabeth to be allowed home to be with his mother in her time of grief and help put the family affairs in order. Elizabeth refused. He petitioned again when his mother died; again, Elizabeth refused. Philip wrote to me and his sorrow and his anger was suffused into every word. I felt so sorry for this young man who was doing his duty and more than his duty for a woman who never appreciated him and had no mercy in her heart.

Elizabeth's unfeeling heart pained Frances greatly. Although heavily pregnant, she asked Leicester if she could travel with him when he returned to the Netherlands to be with her husband. Ursula and I were very much against this, fearing for her health and general safety, but Frances was adamant. She would go if Leicester would take her.

I asked Leicester not to agree, but he knew how badly Philip was feeling and was more concerned with him than he was with my daughter. So, off they went to Flushing in the Netherlands and I hoped that the presence of Frances would help Philip get through this mournful time.

She and Leicester arrived safely and Philip wrote to me, thanking us for allowing Frances to go to him, for she had indeed revived his spirits. We were glad, Ursula and I, but still worried about our daughter, of course. And then word reached us that Philip was ill, having received a wound in his thigh during an assault on the town of Zutphen that had turned gangrenous. When I read that word — gangrenous — I knew there was little chance that Philip would survive. Indeed, he hung onto life for three weeks, three weeks when Frances had to perform the duties of a nurse, but despite her ministrations and the assiduous treatment of the camp surgeon, Philip died.

The death of Philip not only left my family in great mental and emotional anguish, it also caused financial problems. Like Leicester, Philip had been forced to spend a great deal of his own money in maintaining the Queen's army and in acting as an intermediary between the Queen and the Dutch rebels, money he simply did not have. His death meant that his creditors called in his debts which rang to the tune of more than six thousand pounds. With no son to inherit, for Frances lost the child she had been carrying in her grief, Philip's estate went to his brother, Robert, leaving my daughter with only an annual allowance and a small sum held in trust for her daughter. I was a named executor of Philip's will, and with both his parents gone, it fell to me to try and sort out the Sidney family finances, which were greatly confused. It pains me to say it but Leicester, whom I turned to in desperation to help me, refused to help pay off any of Philip's debts. I was greatly hurt by this at the time, but I later discovered that Leicester had huge debts of his own and simply did not have the finances to help me.

To my shame, it was Cecil who helped me. Cecil and I had, by this time, often been at odds with one another, constantly arguing, and on my part, constantly suspecting him of double-dealing with me. I wish I could take my suspicions back for he was there in my time of need. I had long exhausted any personal credit I had with Elizabeth. She had grown weary of my pleas for intercession, to provide more money, more men for the Dutch, and I admit I did myself no favours by so often speaking my mind, knowing my opinions to be invariably contrary to hers. But Cecil played my part with her, pointing out how much she owed to me in terms of her personal security alone, which was entirely true. The estates of Sir Anthony Babington, Cecil reminded her, had been seized by the crown. She could gift them to me to ease my financial burdens. It would have been a small gesture on Elizabeth's part (she would not have missed the revenue) but one that would have been of immense value to me, but no. Elizabeth would not do as Cecil asked and give me the estates. Instead, she gave them to Sir Walter Ralegh, one of her handsome young men who did not criticise her but instead told her how beautiful she was. There was nothing I could do. I had to put off the creditors for the time being and they would just have to wait for their money.

Elizabeth mourned for her treacherous cousin yet shed not a tear for the young man who had been hailed as an ornament to her court, a man of which a monarch should be proud and of whom other monarchs were jealous.

Despite the debts, despite everything, I refused to let Philip's passing go unnoticed. I wrote to Leicester, who was beside himself with grief, and asked if I could have the honour of arranging Philip's funeral. He wrote back with an affirmative. I could almost hear the relief in his words.

Philip was no common man and no ordinary funeral could be good enough. I arranged for his body to be brought back to England where he would have a state funeral, where the streets of London would be lined with people mourning the loss of such a son of England. I heard later from Robert Beale that Elizabeth had only agreed to the state funeral because she believed it would serve as a good distraction from the death of her cousin. I am glad I did not hear that from her lips. I may not have been able to control myself in my anger.

CHAPTER 22

If there was one significant result of the death of Mary Stuart it was the fact that it acted as the catalyst for King Philip of Spain to finally decide to embark on his Enterprise of England.

Have you heard of this? You must have done. Over the past decade or so, there had been skirmishes between our two countries, nothing too alarming, nothing to provoke war. But then Spain invaded Portugal, overthrew the Portuguese monarch and with this shift in power, suddenly, Continental Europe presented a very menacing face indeed to England.

We had to be ready for Spain.

We made some efforts to be ready, or at least, make some pre-emptive strikes.

Francis Drake was causing the Spanish some problems. Drake was a Devonian, short, sturdy, with none of the gloss of a courtier, yet he came to court often at this time. Officially, he was a sailor, exploring the known world and expanding English possessions. Unofficially, and this is what bothered the Spanish, he was a pirate, raiding Spanish ports, attacking Spanish ships and plundering them.

Personally, I was in favour of this means of disrupting Spanish activities. As a long-term investor in the Muscovy Company and holding various other investments in voyages, it was in my interest for sailors such as Drake to open up new trade routes and take over those already in operation by our competitors. Leicester too as an investor approved, as did the Queen, but she mostly approved of Drake's piracy because it meant she got her hands on hundreds of thousands of pounds of Spanish gold and silver without ever having to pay out for it. The only one who did not like the practice was Cecil, who always wanted to be on the best of terms with Spain. Whatever booty Drake acquired, Cecil would insist on giving back. Fortunately, his insistence went unheard and he even had to suffer the Queen knighting Drake on board the Golden Hind, the very ship that had raided Cadiz.

Our successful trade ventures aside, the situation in the Low Countries was very grim. The people there were suffering greatly under the Spanish rule. Leicester's campaign was going extremely badly, not entirely through his own ineptitude, but because Elizabeth made things very difficult for him, as the Dutch even started to do. From the letters he wrote me, I knew that he desperately wanted to be allowed to return home. He was ill and depressed, having lost Philip, his right hand out there. Unfortunately, there was nothing I could do for him. I drew up a list of matters regarding the Dutch that needed to be discussed in Council, matters that could not be left to drag along on their own devices, which was how they had been left until then. I thought we were actually, finally, getting somewhere because agreement to act was made on some of my points, if not all of them. I took those terms agreed upon to the Queen, who I feared would do her usual and agree one moment only to retract her agreement the next.

I was not disappointed in this. Elizabeth acted exactly as I expected and was supported by Cecil. He argued for diplomacy in the matter of the Netherlanders and the Spanish, but on this, I could not compromise. Diplomacy would not work, I felt sure. I told Cecil it wasn't possible, and I thought I had persuaded him to come round to my way of thinking.

Unfortunately, I fell badly ill again at this time and had to retire to my bed. Robert, tripping between my house and the court, ensured I saw most of the despatches that were being sent to the various ambassadors while I was indisposed. As I read them, I became incredulous.

In Council, Cecil had eventually come round to supporting me in my pronouncements that we should take a more active role in the fight against the Spanish. He had even planned out ways in which we could do this. But it became clear in the letters I saw, which Cecil presumably had not intended me to see, that he and the Queen were actually pursuing a very different agenda, one of negotiation, and were doing so behind the Council's back. Ill as I was, I roused myself from my bed and travelled back to the Palace of Whitehall.

I had to clutch at my side as I strode through the corridors towards Cecil's office. I did not bother to knock but went straight in. One of Cecil's clerks, Johnson, I think his name was, jumped up from behind his desk.

'Master Secretary,' he declared, 'were we expecting you?'

'I very much doubt it,' I growled. I gestured towards the door at the back of the room, the door that led into Cecil's inner office. 'Is he in?'

Johnson glanced at the door. 'I... er...'

'I'll take that as a yes,' I said and forestalled any protestation by making my way to the door.

Cecil looked up through milky eyes at my abrupt entrance. The creases on his forehead deepened and he slowly put down his quill and the eyeglass he held before him. 'Master Secretary, did we have an appointment today?'

'No, my lord, we did not.' I shut the door behind me. The pain in my stomach jabbed at me. I pressed my fingers deep into my side, trying to ease it. 'I thought we had agreed in Council a policy regarding Spain.'

I could tell from the look in his eyes that he knew I knew what he and Elizabeth were up to. 'We had,' he said.

'So, why do I discover that you and the Queen are talking with the Spanish about a different kind of policy altogether?'

'Discover... how?'

'It is true, then?'

'Take a seat, Francis,' he said, gesturing me towards the chair before his desk and waiting before I complied to continue. 'I think, and so does the Queen, that it is well to consider all our options in regard to the Spanish. We are a little island, Francis. Ask yourself. Can we really go up against the might of Spain and win?'

'We should try,' I persisted through gritted teeth.

'Why should we so?' he asked. 'Really, why? When there is so much to lose?' I made to answer, but Cecil held up a finger. 'You advocate harassing the Spanish on the seas and fighting them both in the Low Countries and in their own country, at their ports. All that costs money, money we do not have. I believe, and the Queen believes, that we would do far better to fortify our own ports so that they could withstand an attack by the Spanish and train and equip our own men here.'

'The militia could never hope to fight against a trained army such as the Spanish possess.'

'They would do their best.'

'Their best would not be good enough. You know that as well as I.' I sighed deeply and shook my head. 'This policy of yours, Cecil, is one of defence only. Hunker down on this tiny island and hope that the Spanish do not come knocking.'

'Is that such a poor policy?'

'It is a damned shortsighted one, my lord. Do you think the Spanish will not try to invade us?'

'I cannot tell. No one can tell.'

'*I* can tell and I tell you, my lord, they will. King Philip will use Mary's execution as an excuse to invade. Till now, we have been like bees, stinging him here and there. We have done no great harm so far, but all our stings mount up to create one great irritation. Philip wants to be rid of us and he will come.'

'Oh, you exaggerate, Francis.'

'Indeed, no, I do not. You have agents abroad, as I do. You know what preparations are being made in Spain. Great fleets are being constructed for one purpose, King Philip's Enterprise of England. The Spanish are coming, my lord, and we will be woefully unprepared to meet them if we do not stop these bootless negotiations and take action to prevent them.'

Cecil picked up his quill and eyeglass. 'I am grateful for your honesty in this matter, Francis. I will certainly inform the Queen of your feelings. Good day.'

I had no option but to leave. At least I had voiced my concerns. Over the next few months, I voiced them as often as I was able, in Council and in my private conferences with the Queen. Eventually, I managed to persuade Elizabeth of the rightness of our cause, helped in no small part by the fact that

King Philip had ordered that any English ships docked in Spanish harbours were to be seized and refused permission to leave.

I had thought we were finally making progress on our alliance with the Dutch too, but then they started making difficulties over the terms of the treaty we had proposed. Elizabeth had decreed that the English were to have several Dutch towns turned over to us and put under our control to act as surety for the debts the Dutch were incurring. The Dutch were outraged by the proposal and refused to ratify the treaty. I did my best, through agents and by letter, to show them how unreasonable they were being by expecting Elizabeth to provide so much aid without asking for recompense. Finally, an accord of sorts was reached. It looked like we finally had a chance against the Spanish.

CHAPTER 23

Portents and omens had been observed. We all knew something was coming.

The previous century, an astrologer had predicted that the year 1588 would bring '*either an universal consummation and final dissolution of the world, or at least a general subversion and alteration of principalities, kingdoms, monarchies and empires*'. There were other signs too: thirty porpoises had swum up the Thames and gathered at the palace's watergate while at another time, a servant discovered a huge pile of flies littering the sill of a window in the Queen's privy chamber.

From all of Europe, it seemed, my agents were sending in reports of the preparations the Spanish navy were making. Ships were being victualled, gunpowder ordered, timber cut down. It was obvious King Philip was constructing a massive fleet of ships, but for what purpose, I could not confirm. The reports we received were contradictory. All confirmed that a fleet was being prepared for sail, but where it was to sail, no one seemed to know. Some reports claimed that King Philip was intending to send the fleet at once and attack England at Dover, some said the fleet would head for Scotland and enter England from there, while others said the fleet would come across the Channel with the intention of seizing the Isle of Wight.

Elizabeth could not deny the reports that were coming in, she could not refuse to believe them. She realised that the Enterprise of England was all but poised to attack. Yet still, incredibly, she held back. Even Cecil pleaded with her to mobilise our own fleet, while Drake begged to be allowed to attack more Spanish ports. The expense was too great, Elizabeth said, and how did she know this time was any different from all the other times we had told her the Spanish were coming?

I could do nothing but make plans should Elizabeth ever agree that they were needed. By April, even Elizabeth could not pretend the Spanish were not coming and my and the Council's plans were finally set into motion. Leicester, back in England after being released from his martial duty in the Netherlands, was made Lieutenant and Captain-General of the Queen's Armies and Companies and despatched into Essex to gather troops and make preparations to defend the Thames against a Spanish invading fleet hoping to make their way to London. Across the country, bonfires were made ready to be lit as beacons should the Spanish be sighted off the coasts.

And nothing happened. No ships were sighted. No reports came through that the Spanish ships had left their ports. I was worried. Had Elizabeth been right after all? Days passed and still nothing. Then finally, twelve days later, we received news that the Spanish Armada had sailed. Thanks to Drake and others like him, we beat off the Spanish attack. The big galleons were no match for the small ships that we set against them and his armada was dispersed, powerless to do us any harm.

Too much has been written, told and sung about England's victory over the Spanish Armada that I shall not recount the events here. But this account has been written to tell the truth and I will be honest and say here that the victory was not as great as the ballads would have us believe, but that is only because the people who pen such scribblings did not see what we in the Council or at the court saw. They did not see the Earl of Leicester struggling to keep his army together as men deserted and officers lined their own purses with funds intended for the army. They did not see how Elizabeth stumbled over her speech to the troops at Tilbury, nor the work that went into perfecting the lines of the printed copy intended for distribution amongst her people. And when the threat was over, no one but the Council witnessed the way Elizabeth mistreated the men who had rallied to England's defence by refusing to pay the salaries already owed and ordering their disbandment so she could avoid paying any more.

Still, England was safe. King Philip's armada was either burning on the water or sunk at the bottom of the Channel and he had neither the finances nor the inclination to launch another Enterprise of England.

But Leicester died soon after. He had been ill himself for a while with a fever that plagued him from time to time, and he too suffered from pains in his stomach akin to mine. After the armada was defeated, Leicester declared his intention of visiting Buxton to take the waters in an attempt to feel better but he only made it as far as Cornbury in Oxford. He died in the house of friends with his wife at his side. Not an ignominious or unpleasant end, I grant you, but a death that came too early. Leicester had so much more to give.

I was at home in Barn Elms when I heard the news. I remember thinking I was fortunate that I was not at court and it was not I who had to deliver the news to Elizabeth. Cecil had the misfortune of performing that particular duty. When told, Elizabeth locked herself in her rooms for days, so stricken with grief was she. For my part, I had lost a friend, one who, I regret, I felt had not been much of a friend in the most recent of years, but one that had been a close companion for twenty years or more, and such as he cannot be forgotten.

The failure of the Spanish Armada and no longer having to deal with Mary Stuart and her supporters meant that England finally began to feel safe to me. Secret correspondence had diminished and my workload no longer seemed as heavy, though there was still much to do. However, I felt able to delegate much more of it by late 1589.

It was fortunate that this was the state of affairs for, in truth, I was not at all well and also had to suffer an extreme disappointment at this time. My daughter, Frances, who I had thought to possess excellent judgement, became associated with Robert Devereux, the Earl of Essex.

Frances knew him from when she had been with Philip in the Netherlands. Essex was Leicester's stepson, being son to his wife Lettice, and a handsome young lad but not one, I fear, to compare with Philip. Philip was not handsome, admittedly, his face having been scarred by smallpox in his youth, but he had a dignity of bearing and intellect that I found to be entirely lacking in Essex. Yet, an affinity had sprung up between Essex and my son-in-law whilst in the Netherlands and it was to Essex Philip foolishly entrusted the care of his wife.

Essex took the responsibility seriously and after Philip died, he took the trouble to visit my daughter to see how she fared. I wish he had never done so. My daughter, no doubt still grieving for her husband and desiring the friendship of one who had known him well, agreed to meet with Essex in London. I do not know the details, nor did I wish to know of their subsequent assignations, but the result of their various meetings was that my daughter discovered she carried the Earl's child. Once this was made known to Ursula and myself, it was obvious that Essex and Frances must marry. I was troubled, not least because such a marriage was far above Frances's station as she was only the widow and daughter of a knight. The Earl could expect to make a much better match. But there was another reason why I wished Frances had not fallen in with his company. Essex had taken over after Leicester's untimely death as the Queen's favourite.

Elizabeth viewed Essex as her property. As she had done with Leicester, she kept a jealous watch on Essex and believed him to be faithful to her. Of course, in this, she was deceived. I knew, even before Frances told us of her own indiscretion with him, that Essex was a rake, one who had bedded all the women he could get his hands on at court. And I knew that very many women were very willing to leap into his bed. All this licentiousness carried out beneath Elizabeth's nose but without Elizabeth ever realising it.

Secrets will out, I knew this better than anybody, but Ursula and Frances pleaded with me to let the marriage with Essex be conducted clandestinely. I agreed, mostly because I feared Essex would refuse to marry my daughter if it were not on the terms he stipulated. The marriage took place secretly. Essex was desperate that the Queen not find out he had become a husband and was soon to be a father.

But it did not take long for the marriage to become known to Elizabeth. I was ready for her to vent her wrath upon me, blame me for the marriage and for the secrecy, but instead, she threw all her anger at Essex and my daughter.

She banished them from court. For Frances, this was a welcome turn of events. She wanted nothing more than to be away from court with her husband at her side. She was already complaining that Essex did not pay her enough attention, that the Queen took all and left nothing for her. Essex, though, was not happy at his banishment. He was ever changeable; one moment he was angry and railing at anyone who would listen how about badly treated he was by the Queen, the next he was fallen into a melancholy and crying that she must be missing him. This was hard for my daughter to listen to.

Eventually, Elizabeth relented. She was indeed missing Essex and she allowed him and my daughter to return to court. Essex was back in favour. At least I no longer have to worry about them.

EPILOGUE

In fact, I do not think I have much energy left me to worry about anything.

In December of last year, I had my will drawn up, thinking it long past due. I made what I have, which amounts to very little on account of my copious debts, over to my daughter, my wife having money of her own from her previous husband that will at least leave her able to live comfortably. In my will, I have stipulated that my funeral should be inexpensive and quiet. My wife and daughter will have little enough means to bury me decently without having to put on a show.

I hope this account of mine will shed some light on what my life has been and what I have achieved which, I think I do not flatter myself, is not insubstantial. As I said at the very beginning, I have not written this to justify what I have done, merely to explain.

The evenings are growing lighter now that spring is here but I feel the dark approaching. I find I am more tired than I have ever been and I am in pain almost all of the time. It will be a relief to feel nothing anymore.

But enough. I have done. My story told.

There is nothing more to say.

Written by my hand,

*Sir Francis Walsingham,
in the year 1590
at Barn Elms,
Richmond, Surrey*

PLEASE LEAVE A REVIEW

If you have enjoyed this book, it would be wonderful if you could spare the time to post an honest review on Amazon.

Reviews are incredibly important to independent authors like myself. Your review will help me to get noticed and also help to bring my books to the attention of other readers who may enjoy them.

Thank you so much.

JOIN MY MAILING LIST

Join my mailing list to receive your FREE and EXCLUSIVE eBook, ***The Poet Knight and His Muse***, a short story about Sir Philip Sidney and Penelope Devereux and one of the greatest love poems of Queen Elizabeth I's reign.

It is completely free to join and I promise I will never spam you – I'll only be in touch when I have something I think will be of interest to you. You can easily unsubscribe at any time.

Visit my website and click the link to sign up.

www.lauradowers.com

ALSO BY LAURA DOWERS

The Queen's Favourite
The Queen's Rebel
The Queen's Spymaster
When the Siren Sings
The Queen's Rival: A Short Story

Coming Soon

The Last King of Rome (Book I in The Rise of Rome series)

FROM LAURA

I'd love to hear from you. If would like to comment or ask a question about one of my books, then get in touch. You can find me at:

www.lauradowers.com

laura@lauradowers.com

Facebook.com/lauradowersauthor

Printed in Great Britain
by Amazon